Refraction Series

Rebellion in Ulster
Rendezvous in the Himalaya
Requiem for Vukovar

Angela Koenig

Refraction Series

Rebellion in Ulster
Rendezvous in the Himalaya
Requiem for Vukovar

Angela Koenig

Affinity
Rainbow Publications

2017

Refraction Series
© 2017 by Angela Koenig

ISBN: 978-0-947528-55-3

Rebellion in Ulster
The Refractions Series Book One
© 2012 by Angela Koenig
Editor: Day Petersen
Proof Editor: Alexis Smith
Cover Design: Irish Dragon Designs

Rendezvous in the Himalaya
The Refractions Series Book Two
© 2014 by Angela Koenig
Editors: Day Petersen, Nann Dunne
Proof Editor: Alexis Smith
Cover Design: Irish Dragon Designs

Requiem for Vukovar
The Refractions Series Book Three
© 2015 by Angela Koenig
Editor: Nat Burns
Proof Editor: Alexis Smith
Cover Design: Irish Dragon Designs

Table of Contents

Rebellion in Ulster

Angela Koenig

Rebellion in Ulster
Book 1
Refraction Series

Angela Koenig

Affinity
Rainbow Publications

2017

Acknowledgments

I am very grateful to Affinity eBooks for bringing this first novel of mine back into publication. Heartfelt thanks to Julie, Mel, and Nancy—the awesome Affinity team.

Dedication

This is for Beth, who remembered me as an author when I forgot.

Chapter One

"Would you look at the new one, Rosie."

Rosie looked across the prison dining room. The "new one," as easy to find as a black sheep in a flock of white woolies, had placed her tray on an empty table.

"Setting herself off like that, Liz, I'm betting she'll not last long."

"She won't have much choice, will she? I heard a rumor says she's here for running guns. An American gunrunner."

"A Yank. Oh well, then." Rosie's tone carried a world of attitude. "We don't get much of that in Armagh."

The gray-haired woman sitting near Rosie and Liz permitted herself a brief smile. In the perpetual murk of prison boredom, these two could occasionally amuse Arkadia O'Malley; she, however, was almost invisible to the younger women. Far from young but not yet old, O'Malley had been at Armagh Prison when they arrived and she was likely to be there when they left.

Arkadia O'Malley looked past the empty table between to the new arrival. She saw a very young woman who might be pretty behind the dark hair that partially obscured her down-turned face. A tray with a plate and a drink sat in front of her but she only stared at her food, apparently disinclined to eat. O'Malley had the impression that the newcomer was actually absent, as if she had somehow managed to leave her body behind and escape. Drugs, probably, and that would be the reason she was here. A gunrunner would be IRA, and the Rah prisoners kept to themselves. Since the newcomer was in with the general population, her offense was more likely drug smuggling. She certainly appeared downed out on something. Then again, just the reality of arriving in prison could send a woman into shock. The body searches were the worst, but the whole process of becoming incarcerated was designed to make the new prisoner aware that she was being severed from her previous life.

As if on cue to clear up the mystery, Jill Leary entered the dining room. Leary was in her late twenties, a woman of pleasant appearance with ash blond hair and the delicate, doll-like features that were pretty enough but long since gone out of fashion. All the women in the dining room watched as Leary, walking with as much authority as if she herself was a prison official, threaded her way among the tables and sat down across the table from the American. Anything unusual was a fascinating distraction to the women watching, but the presence of the IRA Section Commander, second only to Mairead Farrell herself, talking to a newly inducted prisoner in the general population dining room, that was well out of the ordinary.

"Tiocfaidh ar lá."

The new prisoner continued to stare at her food.

"That means 'our day will come' in Irish."

O'Malley was close enough to hear Leary translate her own greeting. She wasn't close enough to hear the reply, but she thought the words were all Irish.

"At least there's nothing wrong with your hearing, Geraldine O'Donnell," Leary said. "I'll tell the screws that you belong with us."

The newcomer raised her head and fixed Leary with a gaze that was full of agony. "I'm not one of you."

That was the first full view that Arkadia O'Malley had of Geraldine O'Donnell, and the sight elicited a startled shock of recognition despite the fact that she had never seen the young woman before. Shock lasted only an instant and then vanished, leaving O'Malley dizzy. Just as quickly, any liveliness in O'Donnell's expression also disappeared, leaving behind empty blue eyes in a blank face.

Jill Leary also seemed disturbed. She waited, as if hoping for more, but the newcomer had returned to staring at the table. "As you wish, O'Donnell, for now at any rate."

†

Arkadia O'Malley had learned to float on prison routine as a ship might float on a rhythmic sea. She worked in the library, such as it was with its motley assortment of donated books, and it was not a location that was very often frequented. A variety of bizarre rumors had once been whispered about her, like the one that said she was a Russian spy who had assassinated a bishop. Some of the older officers remembered when the mystery of the woman had been a challenge, but all attempts to solve her had been in vain, and after a while Arkadia O'Malley simply became a prison oddity. A fixture. A cipher. The rumors still made their rounds, but they now excited no more interest than would an odd keepsake acquired by a seafaring uncle in his youth. Arkadia O'Malley had taken Hamlet's boast to heart for close to two decades: she was bounded by a nutshell, but she had made herself ruler of infinite space. She was as anonymous as someone could be in a prison. Unfailingly polite, answering whenever spoken to, O'Malley rarely initiated or extended contact outside the library.

That was before Geraldine O'Donnell arrived at Armagh.

In the days that followed O'Donnell's arrival and Leary's surprise visit to the general population, O'Malley kept her usual distance, watching and listening. Rumors accompanied every new arrival, but the story, when sorted out, was simple on the surface. O'Donnell was on remand, with no trial scheduled. The American had been a tourist, it seemed, driving through the countryside with two companions. When they were stopped at a British roadblock, their rented car was searched and contraband was discovered, and it had not been drugs. Liz had been right; the car had carried guns or explosives, and during a scuffle with the soldiers, gunfire killed O'Donnell's two companions.

There would be more to it than that. Something more was needed to account for the despair that enveloped the young American. O'Malley had not made peace with her imprisonment by entangling herself in the lives of Armagh's inmates, and over the years she had tended her distance like another might tend a garden. Only during the clashes of the no-wash and hunger strikes that turned the entire prison into a battleground, drawing stark lines between prisoners as well as between the officials and the IRA, only then had O'Malley found it difficult to remain aloof.

In what became known as the Dirty Protest, the IRA men held at Long Kesh demanded status as prisoners of war and refused to wear uniforms that would mark them as common criminals. Led by Jill Leary and Mairead Farrell, the IRA women at Armagh supported the men, and soon the Rah inmates at both prisons were engaged in a fierce conflict with British authorities. When guards refused to let the women empty their chamber pots, they smeared the contents over the cell walls.

Armagh was an old prison and stink was everywhere even at the best of times. Whether or not they could actually smell the cells of the Dirty Protest, the other prisoners were united in their disgust. Arkadia O'Malley knew it was more than the smell; the protesters were offending against the very basic notion that women were supposed to uphold standards, especially those of decency. With a word here and a comment there, Arkadia O'Malley inserted her own position into the general chatter.

"It might smell bad," she would say, "but wasn't it clever to find a way to continue to fight even after they'd been counted out?" Farrell and her group had found a way to turn the prison itself into a battleground, and they fought with their bodies, as soldiers always did.

Their struggle was not O'Malley's, but her heart had ached for the conditions the IRA women endured. Mairead Farrell and Jill Leary had started on the hunger strike along with Bobby Sands and the men at the Maze until they were ordered to stop. When the government of Iron Maggie gave way to the IRA demands, O'Malley felt as if she, too, had won a victory, a feeling shared across Ulster and beyond. The hunger strike had done more for The Cause than any pitched battle, showing the entire world the courage of the rebels pitted against the intransigence of Maggie Thatcher and her gang.

Geraldine O'Donnell was a different matter, and O'Malley didn't understand why she was drawn to the new prisoner. The American would not be the first or last to arrive in the clutch of depression; in fact, this was a perfectly sensible response to finding oneself in prison. Depression could be the mind's way of fitting a personality to her new circumstances. Speculating about just what had brought O'Donnell to Armagh, O'Malley remembered Oscar Wilde's *The Ballad of Reading Gaol* with its plaintive refrain: "Each man kills the thing he loves." O'Malley could not forget the flash of recognition that had shaken her when she first saw the new prisoner's face.

†

Days passed. Weeks. A month. Geraldine O'Donnell went through the motions of adjustment, a heavy sluggishness signifying her continued depression. She ate little, spoke less. Some prisoners tried to make contact, but they might as well not have bothered. Jill Leary returned, but got no more joy of it than she had on her first visit. The prison rumor mill now reported that Geraldine had been in Ulster on vacation when she had fallen out with the law, that she had been studying in England, at Oxford.

"They say she was studying motorways," Liz told Rosie.

"Not motorways, you silly git. She was a Rhodes Scholar. That's different."

"And what makes motorways different from roads?" But Liz was taking the piss, and Rosie knew it.

The day that Mattie Malloy went for O'Donnell, Arkadia O'Malley was present. Mattie Malloy was a prison type that came and went at Armagh with unfortunate regularity. She was a bully who claimed status by terrorizing the meek and the weak, especially loners. She worked at her reputation for brutality, and picked up minions who admired her bluff and swagger. Even women who weren't particularly afraid of her didn't challenge her either; prison was not known for generating altruism.

It was only a matter of time until Mattie decided that Geraldine was an outsider whom the herd would allow to be culled. On the way to evening meal, when the guards weren't near, Malloy chose her moment.

"Wha'cher do that for?" Malloy snarled as she deliberately bumped into the American.

O'Donnell had her on height, but Mattie was a solid bull of a woman. She pushed Geraldine out of line. The chosen victim stared blankly and then tried to step around. Mattie blocked her. O'Donnell simply stopped, becoming the equivalent of a rag doll, an empty space. This way of disappearing was not an altogether absurd defense, but only if the aggressor was not determined to push the issue.

Arkadia O'Malley was watching, and she wondered if, in her depression, Geraldine might even wish for the pain that Mattie was threatening.

The guards were preoccupied elsewhere, but the dining room was watching.

Mattie Malloy struck, a ham-fisted blow aimed for the midriff that could have stunned an ox. Malloy's anger was always on a hair trigger, and something about O'Donnell had roused her to the point that she meant to do real harm. But the blow never connected. Geraldine caught the hand aimed at her and held it, just held it, as if Malloy's strength were nothing. Blank eyes lost their habitual emptiness and focused on Mattie.

Arkadia O'Malley was close enough to see the look that Mattie saw, a look that bespoke murder. Anger at last animated O'Donnell's features, an anger that, now awakened, clearly hoped for more action. Mattie Malloy, the bully, realized that she had seriously miscalculated and backed away. The encounter began and ended so quickly that very few watchers even realized that anything had happened. Arkadia O'Malley had been watching, and in that moment believed that it might just be possible that Geraldine had been sent to Armagh for good and righteous reasons.

"Did you see that?" Liz asked Rosie.

"I'm not blind. I thought my sister was getting it wrong, what she was telling me last visit. She read in the papers that O'Donnell's from this part of Boston in Americay where the Irish go. They make them tough there, she says."

That night, Arkadia O'Malley was reminded that Hamlet had said he could be content in a nutshell were it not for bad dreams.

The dream wasn't exactly bad, in the sense of nightmarish, and in fact it began quite pleasantly. O'Malley had lately been re-reading Spenser's *The Faerie Queene*. The lengthy poem had a certain repetitive beat that slipped easily into prison life, but O'Malley read it primarily for the vivid images that often stayed to populate her dreams. She had trained herself to hold a level of consciousness during dreaming, and she immediately recognized Britomart when Spenser's lady knight came riding out of the mists. She herself, an old woman leaning on a staff, seemed to be located in a forest glade when the lady knight appeared. Britomart rode a gray horse, her bright helm dazzling, one hand resting on her sheathed sword. Her long dark hair flowed over silver armor with a collar that was studded with red, yellow, and green gems. A blue gem gleamed from the pommel of the sword encased in a silver sheath inlaid with gold.

"Have you seen my garland?" Britomart asked.

The old crone looked across the glade to a tree on which the flowery garland hung: marigold and chamomile, poppy and periwinkle, lilac, rose and jasmine.

"There is your garland." Even as she spoke, she saw the garland grow a dainty hoof in each quarter and when the feet had formed, the garland leapt from the tree and left faster than mortal horse could gallop.

The crone looked again to Britomart, and the sight was like to break her heart. The dazzling figure had lost all beauty. Her armor was dented and streaked with tarnish. The gems had disappeared from their settings. The horse was gone. The woman's hair was wild and tangled and she had no helm, only a broken sword, but her face was worst of all. There was no doubt to whom the features, so downcast and lost, belonged.

"Where is my garland? Help me find and keep her," pleaded Geraldine.

Arkadia O'Malley woke into the prison darkness of stone walls, and the colors of her imagination fled back to the harbor of her soul. She lay awake, committing the dream's images to her waking memory. Such dreams came in their own time, and she considered it part of her work to prepare herself for such visitations. She recognized the importance of this one by the intensity of the emotions it evoked. Still full of feeling, she wanted to weep and, at the same time, to sing and bless her life.

When the feelings subsided, and when she was sure she had remembered every detail so that it wouldn't disappear with daylight, O'Malley began to wonder at the meaning of the dream's imagery. Obviously, Geraldine O'Donnell was Britomart, and she had lost something precious. There were many things that might signify: her freedom, her identity, her life's purpose. Arkadia O'Malley was supposed to help her find her four-footed "garland". O'Malley might have thought the garland was a woman, except that having four legs implied something other than human. Still, Geraldine had wanted to keep "her". The absurdity of the notion of a four-footed garland kept nagging O'Malley until suddenly, in the darkness, she smiled and nearly laughed aloud.

She gave Freud his due for demystifying many secrets of the dream, but she also knew that one should never underestimate the mind's love of punning. The garland was "forfeited". That came from *The Faerie Queene*, a reasonable setting considering O'Malley's daytime reading. Britomart was one of the heroes who still pursued the "goodly usage of those antique tymes, In which the sword was servaunt unto right." The lady knight's terrible sorrow was for a lost life that might already be forfeited.

†

"Well, would you look at that!" Rosie jabbed Liz with her elbow, a large gesture, as unusual as a shout would have been.

"Jesus, Mary, and Joseph!"

Liz and Rosie had grown so used to the quiet presence of Arkadia O'Malley sitting near them at meals that any change in her behavior might have roused them to comment, but their surprise was because the prison's resident mysterious inmate had just taken a seat at the table with the prison's most recent focus of gossip. Liz and Rosie weren't the only two in the dining room who were watching.

Nothing happened. Neither the American nor the Irish woman was given to talking, so even if it was disappointing to the rest of the population, it was not surprising that the two ate in silence. In fact, it wasn't until several meals had passed in silence and no one was giving any notice to the odd pairing that one of them spoke.

"I have a book for you," Arkadia O'Malley said in a tone that had, once upon a time, made her listeners determined to read quickly and attentively.

Chapter Two

Jeri O'Donnell stared at the book in front of her as if she'd never seen one before. "I don't read novels." The book was thick, pale green, clothbound; the title was impressed on a worn cover: *The Mill on the Floss*.

"I work in the library. You can always come there to choose something else."

Jeri looked up from the book to the woman sitting across from her. Not quite as old as her gray hair and wire-rimmed spectacles suggested. She had brown eyes, a direct and steady gaze that put Jeri in mind of a hawk, and an air of self-possession that contradicted her status as an inmate. Jeri would not have been surprised to find this woman seated in the warden's chair.

She made an effort to be polite. "Why this book?"

Arkadia O'Malley gave the question some thought. "I prefer it to *Middlemarch*. *Mill* has always seemed to me peculiarly Irish in its passions and complications, and I think it has a tighter and truer focus. And, *Middlemarch* is missing." O'Malley suspected that it had been taken by someone who decided to transform the thick book into a conveyer of contraband, but at the moment that was neither here nor there.

Jeri looked again at the book in her hand. She had read Eliot before, but didn't remember just what or when. The older woman's short description had roused some slight curiosity that was now followed by a wave of profound disinterest. Simply to end the need to talk, Jeri mumbled, "Yes, thank you."

Jeri carried the book with her after that. She carried it more than she read it. The weight of it felt good, like a balance, or ballast. She tried to read it but more often than not, her mind would drift away. Before Armagh, she always read quickly and her memory stored whatever she gave it. Before Armagh. She needed something active, some sport. She was good at sports, especially track. And rowing. She had just discovered rowing at Oxford. Before Armagh, she always found time to run. Good at sprinting, Jeri had been even better at distance. Now the distance she had to negotiate was time, but she had no clear sense of it. She had been studying languages. At Armagh, she was learning to parse time: I pass; you pass; it passes. It was passing. Like a river. She was passing in a river at flood tide, being swept further and further away from what had so recently promised to be an exceptional life.

Not that anyone who had known her would be much surprised to hear she was in prison. She was from Southie, South Boston, and kids from Southie were always ending up in prison. Her brother Mickey—who got shot dead by other hoodlums, or her brother Kenny, who overdosed but survived with brain damage—they wouldn't be surprised. Her sister, Kathleen the nun, wouldn't be at all surprised. Kathleen had always known Jeri was heading for sin and chaos. The joke was on Jeri for ever thinking that she'd end up anywhere else. The joke was that she was alive.

Her last sight of Fiona hung in the air before her, rendering the prison invisible. Fiona, with her midnight hair and her moon-white skin; Fiona's anguished eyes pleading for forgiveness. Fiona's eyes, suddenly startled and then wide with knowledge that this was the instant of her death.

Jeri shut the memory down. For a long, long time she saw nothing, felt nothing, was nothing. Then the misery that was stalking her grew bored and moved on, leaving her be for the moment. Jeri opened the book and began once more to read.

†

Jeri stared at the food on her tray. She was uncomfortably aware of Arkadia O'Malley sitting across from her. "I started the book. I don't seem to be reading as fast as I used to, but I suppose jail is a good place for long stories." The comment contained no self-pity, only surprise at something unexpected. "Maggie's in for trouble."

"What makes you say that?"

"She makes too much of herself. She can't see that she doesn't belong." Jeri picked up her sandwich and tried a bite.

"Why do you suppose?"

Jeri set her sandwich down. She didn't have the energy to chew. "I don't know. I don't care that much about her."

"Give her more of a chance. I find her one of fiction's most

14

honorable characters."

†

Jill Leary located Jeri at association outside in the prison yard and deliberately sat near her. A pointed look aimed at another prisoner sitting nearby caused the woman to leave. As OC, Officer Commanding of a section, Leary was rarely argued with. Armagh Prison maintained its official dominion over the prisoners, but it had learned not to interfere with the IRA women as long as certain rules were followed.

"So, old Arky's got you reading a book."

"Arky?" Jeri was surprised to hear someone refer to the dignified woman in such a familiar manner.

"Arkadia O'Malley. The old lady." Jill waited until it was clear that Jeri wasn't going to respond. "There's better ways to use your time. You're too good to go to waste, you know. We can help you when you're ready."

"Ready to what?"

"To throw in for Ireland." Jill Leary had received orders through her own commander, Mairead Farrell, that she was to recruit O'Donnell. Jill didn't understand why the attempt was being requested, unless the American had some unlikely access to money or contacts. To Leary, the woman seemed somewhat dense. She understood that new prisoners often experienced periods of depression, but she'd seen nothing about O'Donnell to make her worth the attention she was getting.

"Like you threw in Fiona and Devlin?"

Leary had been watching the prison yard, but Jeri's tone made Jill turn to look at her. Blue eyes could be cold, like ice, but Jeri's were dark sapphire and fixing Leary with a burning fury. It wasn't for lack of courage or nerve that Jill Leary was a chief in the IRA so she managed to hold her ground, but she was relieved when the fire dimmed in the American's eyes and they looked away. *Not so dense after all.*

†

Jeri dreamed that Fiona found her. She had found her way into the prison, and she was happy to see Jeri. "It was just a mistake," she said. "I'm not dead. Don't send me away." As if Jeri would ever send Fiona away.

Jeri wondered where Devlin had got to, because Fiona had never kissed her before."Don't worry," Fiona murmured fondly, and her lips were soft. Jeri returned the kiss she had imagined so often during their drive through the Ulster countryside. Then she felt Fiona's hand touch her breast, and a bright burst of feeling blossomed inside her. As she began to wake, she understood that she would soon discover she was alone, that she was about to lose Fiona again, as she did on every morning that she awoke.

Jeri wasn't alone, someone was with her. There really was a hand was on her breast and a soft mouth against her own.

"Don't worry, you'll like this." The lips were warm and a tongue began to explore Jeri's lips, slipping inside her mouth. There wasn't much room on the narrow bed, but the woman lay beside her, moving her hand to caress Jeri's face, her shoulder, the length of her. It had been too long since Jeri had been with anyone, too long since she'd made love. She needed little reminding of just how good it felt to be kissed, touched, held, how good to feel another woman next to her in the night.

"Don't worry, you'll like this." The whispered words were repeated, as feather light as the kisses tracing her eyes, her hair, her ear. The moving hand found its way beneath her nightshirt and onto skin.

Jeri recognized the woman now. She didn't know her name, but they worked together in the laundry. A solid, red-headed girl, with freckles of course, who had been throwing looks Jeri's way for a while. Jeri didn't think she had responded. She might have done, but it took too much effort to figure out all the emotions involved. There was nothing to figure out now, in bed, in the night. The hand moving beneath Jeri's shirt found its way back to her breast, and she could feel its strength. A farmer's hand. Jeri had overheard the woman say to someone, "We washed clothes by hand on my father's farm."

Now she was saying, "You feel so good," over and over, a murmured mantra.

Jeri was waking up. Perversely, the more she woke, the more her arousal diminished. Christ, she wanted this. She really did. She moved in response, trying to recapture the pleasure that had been there. She felt the pressure of the hand kneading her breast. *Like some damn cow*, she thought, and knew it was over.

"No," Jeri said. "I can't." She stiffened and moved away.

"It's all right. It can be good with a woman."

"I don't need telling," Jeri muttered.

"Please. You don't have to do nothing," the woman said, and her hand left Jeri's breast in a determined move toward her crotch.

"No." Jeri took hold of the hand and moved it away. "I can't. I really can't."

The other woman tensed, and then went slack, her persistence gone. She lay beside Jeri, not moving. "Can I stay?" The request was so quiet that not much more than the need was audible. "Can I stay a while?"

Why not? "What's your name?"

"Kathleen."

Of course. Same as the name of her only living sister, the nun. When Jeri woke next, she was again alone in bed.

†

"What's wrong?" Arkadia O'Malley asked. Jeri was usually distant, but today she was fidgety, cranky.

Jeri started to say, "Nothing," but changed her mind. "Someone tried to fuck me last night."

"Tried?"

"I wouldn't let her."

"You don't make love with women?"

"Oh, I wanted it." The few words held a depth of longing, a desire for all that desire might bring. "Then I didn't." Suddenly Jeri asked a question that took her companion by surprise. "Why are you here?"

Arkadia O'Malley sidestepped the question. "Why are you?" She really didn't expect an answer.

"I killed my cousin."

O'Malley was startled. Several things began to fall into place, and she waited for Jeri to say more, but that appeared to be the end of the day's revelations.

†

Kathleen Healy did not go back to Jeri's bed, but a certain bond had been established. Kathleen worried that Jeri would avoid her, but instead, the next time they met at the laundry, Jeri greeted her by name and managed something that might pass for a smile, as if now they were friends. Kathleen wasn't the only woman to let Jeri know that she had only to agree and pleasure could be in arm's reach, but whether the offers were subtle or bold, Jeri turned away. Speculation decided she was too straight by half if she wouldn't accept what scant comfort there might be in prison.

17

†

When the weather grew too cold for sitting outside, Jeri had taken to coming to the library to read, especially on days when new donations arrived. More than once she had interrupted reading Eliot's novel to scan through some new book, but she always returned to the story of Maggie Tulliver.

"Poor Maggie. She's compulsively independent, but then she loses her nerve. That's a bad combination." Jeri eyed the closed book as if she could read it by staring at it.

Arkadia O'Malley thought a minute and then answered neutrally, "She may grow into it. Her independence."

"Does she? I don't see how, unless she learns not to want to be loved so much. That's a weakness." It was winter, a time that always made Jeri restless for activity, and even more so now that prison circumscribed her world.

"A common one."

"You, you probably think you're a Saint Theresa type, 'foundress of nothing,' right?"

"That isn't in this novel," Arkadia observed.

Jeri shrugged. "I wanted to know what the book was really about, so I read the essays at the end. One talked about how Eliot speculated that for every person who succeeds in realizing what they're meant to do, like Saint Theresa, the world has so many more who attempt a destiny but fail."

Arkadia O'Malley remained silent for some minutes. "I've made my peace with fate, one that I find suitable. You have not. Unless you find a way to make this place useful, it may destroy you, and that would be a waste."

"One more lost Irishman would be missed? You sound like Leary, both of you so worried I might be wasted."

"If you don't discover your own use, someone else is bound to use you." O'Malley permitted herself this oblique criticism of the IRA. She didn't so much disapprove of them in principle as she was sure that Jeri's future lay elsewhere.

Jeri had intended her comment about Saint Theresa to sting O'Malley, but she regretted her bad humor. She couldn't apologize, though, since O'Malley's response had effectively shut down any further talk along that line. Prison had its rules of conduct as strict as any convent. Not that it was Jeri's habit or nature to apologize. What was it to O'Malley anyway if Jeri wasted away in prison? The only problem was that it was taking so long. She wasn't being charged with anything; she was just "detained" while inquiries were made. She might be here for years, or be released tomorrow.

†

"Your cousin understood the cost that she might need to pay."

Jesus, it was Leary. Would none of these people ever just leave her be? Jeri had found a corner to read where she thought she'd be alone.

"We're proud of Fiona O'Donnell. She did good work, and she's sore missed."

What was Jeri supposed to say? That if Fiona hadn't lied, she might still be doing good work?

"We hear the Brits tried to make a scholar out of you until it didn't suit them. Now Arky's at it, but something tells me you're more for the fighting than the schooling, right, Jeri O'Donnell? Remember, you were kings once, you O'Donnells. You knew how to fight for the people then."

"Last I heard, Red Hugh O'Donnell ran away from Ireland."

Jeri knew she was being hustled, but the whole conversation gnawed at her. She had, in truth, taken Fiona from the struggle for Ulster's freedom. Devlin, too, for that matter. And now she'd galled Arkadia, the only person who seemed to care about her, though why the old woman bothered was beyond Jeri's understanding. Maybe O'Donnells once were kings in Ireland, but in Southie they were just cop fodder. Round and round the thoughts churned. Jeri's intelligence, keen and fine as it was, had never before needed to turn inward, and for the moment, George Eliot was the only escape she had from the weight of imprisonment.

†

Time, it was said, heals all wounds, and it sometimes does this by blurring recall of reality's sharpest edges. Mattie Malloy found that time blurred her memory of why she had been afraid of the Americunt. Mattie wasn't particularly bright, but she made up for it through a combination of cunning and meanness, and as time passed, she felt more and more that she had to get her own back from the Americunt. She liked that word. She'd made it up. Mattie Malloy had plans for her life, big plans,

19

and those plans didn't include being bested by some fucking foreigner. She was going to run a gang when she got out, like one of those drug gangs in Dublin. When she left Armagh, she intended to have a reputation that no one ever got the best of her, particularly not some fucking Americunt. An accident would do, any accident.

†

"May I have a word, Jill?"

"Arky! Now isn't this a grand surprise."

Arkadia O'Malley ignored the familiarity. Truth be told, she rather liked Leary. "I think we both would prefer not seeing Geraldine in trouble with the authorities."

"And who would that be, Arky? Who is the authority here? You talk like a posh Brit aristocrat, not a proper Irishwoman."

"I've not come to discuss politics. Have you seen how Mattie Malloy is stalking Geraldine?"

Leary hadn't. The information took her by surprise, and she was supposed to attend to such things. And, Arky was right. She didn't want Jeri in trouble with the Brits. She had instructions to recruit the American, not let her come to useless harm.

†

It wouldn't do for Jill Leary to talk to the likes of Malloy, so she sent one of her people. "Leave O'Donnell alone, Mattie. She's our business."

Mattie sneered at the idea. "What if I don't? You plan to shoot my kneecaps?"

"You don't need a gun to break a knee, Mattie. Mind yourself now."

Like hell she would. She was more determined than ever to get the Americunt. Back down now and she'd never get up again. That was the way of it when everyone was against you and you needed to fight for whatever you got. She just needed to be more careful; she was pretty sure it was the old aristocunt who had grassed her to the Rah.

She'd seen how those who were so inclined followed O'Donnell with appreciative eyes, Mattie wasn't immune herself, but if she couldn't own it, by God, she could destroy it. Mattie had a plan. One of her people already worked in the laundry.

†

20

Lill was working at getting Mattie to climax; it was hard going. Her own fellow had never taken this much work, and he'd even knocked her around less. You never could fault Mattie in the knock-around department, like now—she had a grip on Lill's shaggy blond hair that was like to push her ears into her skull. The thing was that the closer Mattie was to coming, the harder she gripped and the more she pushed against Lill's face. Still, you couldn't always count on that being the end of it. Sometimes Lill could swear she'd got Mattie off, but the woman was that greedy, she'd keep Lill at it for more. At last she heard a particularly deep groan and hoped that meant she was in for a rest at last. Abruptly, the hands let loose of her head.

"Is it ready for tomorrow?"

So that's what took Mattie over the edge, thinking about what was going to happen to O'Donnell. "It's all set."

"You're a good lass, Lill." She handed over a small chunk of hash. "This is good stuff, sweetheart. Should do for you about as good as you did for me, eh?" Mattie Malloy mellow was not much of an improvement.

†

Kathleen Healy reckoned that Lill and Ellen were up to something. This particular laundry shift was a good one for someone who was willing to pull her weight, and Kathleen liked hard work. It felt less like prison and more like home, and it helped her sleep at night. Jeri was a good work mate, too. She wasn't given to talking, but she kept up her side of things and she was quick. Kathleen was still attracted to Jeri, but she had been able to let that be. Living with an unrequited attraction wasn't that much of a novelty for a Catholic Ulster farm girl, especially considering that was how she ended up in Armagh in the first place. So Kathleen just took what pleasure she could from working with Jeri and ignored Lill, who slacked off whenever she could. Kathleen let the laziness go because she wanted no trouble from one of Mattie Malloy's girls. Jeri never seemed to notice.

But for a week, now, Ellen had joined their shift, and she and Lill were thick as thieves. Kathleen did her best to avoid them, and they ignored her. To the city slicks from Belfast, she was just a farm girl, and she didn't try to correct any notions that she was also a bit dim. Only she'd seen the looks they'd been giving each other all morning, and she was pretty sure that it meant trouble.

When the guard left the room, Kathleen's heart sank. Whatever was going to happen would happen now, and this appeared to be one of the days when Jeri was particularly withdrawn, going about her work as if she were miles away. Jeri was wheeling a cart of laundry down the narrow aisle between rinsing tubs toward a wash machine where Lill was fiddling with something. Ellen had disappeared. No, Ellen was back, and she had a metal bar from one of the rinsers. Ellen was behind Jeri. Kathleen looked back toward Lill and saw that she had loosened the hose that drained the large washer. She shouldn't be doing that yet; the water would be scalding hot.

Kathleen suddenly saw the whole meaning of the situation laid out clearly: Lill was going to burn Jeri, and Ellen was going to follow up with the iron bar.

"Jeri!" Kathleen called out in warning, and moved forward to put herself between Jeri and Ellen.

Most of the Armagh women, if asked, would have described Jeri as brainy. They'd heard about Oxford, seen her with Arkadia O'Malley, and noted the large book she constantly carried around. In a way, they would have been right, but in another way Jeri had much more in common with Mattie Malloy. In Southie, they might have noticed that Jeri O'Donnell did all right in school, but first they would have said that she was a first-rate scrapper from a family of brawlers. No one from Jeri's old neighborhood in Southie would have come at her from the front like Lill did now.

Depression might have diminished Jeri's attentiveness, but instinct and adrenaline took over when she heard Kathleen's warning and the tone woke her. She saw Lill advancing toward her. The shaggy-haired blonde gripped the washing machine hose in one hand while her other hand fumbled with the water release mechanism. The release knob seemed to be hotter than she had expected, and she was unable to get enough of a hold to turn it. The hose, meant to reach from the washer to the concrete trough that carried the dirty water away, was long enough for Lill to keep advancing.

Jeri looked behind and noted Ellen's stance, a sturdy woman holding a heavy metal rod and barring any escape from the aisle that was bounded by the large machines. She couldn't see Kathleen. Jeri grabbed towels from her cart and spun them around one arm which she held up to deflect the initial stream of scalding water that Lill sent spurting in her direction. Lill had expected to be in control of the situation, had expected Jeri to try to get away. Instead, Jeri ducked aside from the direct spray and pushed her cart toward Lill, causing her to swing the hose wildly. Jeri heard a cry from behind just as the cart struck Lill a body blow that pushed the woman back against a hot washer. Lill screamed and dropped the hose.

Jeri looked back and saw that Kathleen was wrestling with Ellen for the iron bar. Then both women screamed and dropped the bar. Like a stricken snake, the hose was thrashing wildly, sending sprays of scalding hot water everywhere. Jeri still had the towels, and they helped her recapture the hose itself, but she needed her hands to wrestle the hose into a lock on one of the troughs. The pain was intense, but she managed to snap it in place.

The whole episode had lasted scant minutes. Machines still sloshed and thumped rhythmically, but the screams had brought several guards. Jeri was the only one left standing.

"O'Donnell! What happened?"

The question was far more alarmed than suspicious, and another instinct from the old neighborhood prompted Jeri's answer. "I don't know. The hose got loose somehow."

†

Mattie Malloy was waiting for word that her plan had succeeded. She was even practicing how to express her regret that such a pretty face had been ruined for life. Maybe O'Donnell was even blinded.

"Did you hear about the accident in the laundry?" It was Jill Leary's lieutenant.

"No. I been here all morning." Mattie was pretty sure her innocence sounded right.

"Oh, aye? Seems two of your girls got hurt."

Mattie didn't need to pretend. "Fuck, no!"

"Aye. They got burned. The real surprise, though, is how you fell down, you were in that much of a hurry to see to them."

†

"It's not your fault, Geraldine."

"No?" Jeri had just been released from the infirmary where

23

Kathleen, Lill, and Ellen were still being treated for burns. Jeri's burns had been painful, but not as bad as those of the other women. "Kathleen got hurt helping me."

"She chose that. You'd not rob her of her courage?"

"You don't understand." Jeri was even trying on a bit of regret for Mattie Malloy who was also in the infirmary with some cracked ribs, a leg cast, and a story about having fallen.

Arkadia O'Malley assessed Jeri with a skeptical eye. The younger woman sounded more petulant than depressed. Perhaps the laundry incident had broken through the cocoon of misery in which she'd been wrapped. Perhaps the opportunity for action had awakened her like the kiss of a prince in a fairy tale. The idea of violence as redemptive momentarily distracted her, but O'Malley had made a decision not to be deterred this time. She'd been willing enough to leave Jeri in the healing safety of her cocoon, but it was past time to bring her out, to turn her mind and heart back to the world.

"You didn't kill your cousin. The military at the roadblock did that. I suspect that you didn't even know the car was carrying explosives."

Jeri could only stare at the older woman in outrage. Without fair warning, Arkadia O'Malley had crossed a line. As if she were a telescope being refocused from the wrong end, Jeri felt herself retreating to a far, cold distance. Her words were precise, contemptuous. "Yet I would have thought that you, of all people, would realize that responsibility isn't about what is or isn't legal. I pulled those triggers as surely as any Brit did."

Her anger, her damned anger. She had been furious that Fiona and Devlin would use her, furious that they had hidden C-4 explosive in the car that she had rented for their holiday.

†

It began in second grade, when Sister Brendan suggested that since most of the class had relatives in Ireland, the children should write letters. Jeri's father was himself from the Bogside in Derry, and one of his brothers had a daughter near Jeri's age named Fiona. Eamon told her that no matter what anyone said, she was never to call the city anything but Derry. When the first letter came back in response, the thrill sent Jeri to the back of the classroom to an atlas. She found Ireland, and she found Ulster, but it took her a while to work out that to some people, Derry was called "Londonderry". She wrote back to her newfound cousin to find out why, as her father was not given to long explanations. Fiona wrote back and said there had been a terrible time with fires, but that the British soldiers had come and stopped the riots. Later, in other letters, she wrote that people weren't so happy about that anymore.

Jeri and Fiona exchanged pictures and odd bits that could fit in a letter, like bubble gum wrappers with good jokes. Jeri preferred George but Fiona liked John, and she even liked Yoko before Jeri did. Fiona thought changing the spelling from "Gerry" to "Jeri" was a brilliant idea, no matter what Jeri's pious, rule-bound, older sister Kathleen thought. Their letters grew less frequent as they grew older, but the contents became more serious. Jeri wrote about everything except her discovery that she preferred girls to boys, a preference it was clear that Fiona did not share.

What Jeri didn't realize at the time was how much writing to Fiona gave her a life separate from the streets of Southie. She saw things with an eye to turning them into words, and that also made it necessary to determine a point of view and to take a stand, to make judgments. In her letters, Jeri exercised her mind past the cunning required for survival on the streets of Southie. The letters that came back from Fiona in Derry were full of heart and principle. Fiona told Jeri to read the poems of Seamus Heaney and Bernadette Devlin's book *The Price of My Soul*. Fiona's respect for the genius of Dr. King, and her thoughts about the differences between the civil rights struggles in America and in Northern Ireland forced Jeri to review and reject the racism of her own family in Boston's bussing crises.

Years passed. Jeri and Fiona clung to the correspondence that served both of them. Jeri often felt like someone else was with her wherever she went. Only when Jeri won the Rhodes scholarship did she hesitate to write to Fiona. The scholarship would take her to Oxford in England, and England was the enemy of the republicans of Derry. She needn't have worried. Fiona's response was generous with congratulations and praise for her cousin, and full of anticipation that now, being so close, they would at last get to see each other in person.

Jeri wrote and told Fiona she was gay. Fiona wrote back and said that must make her even more committed to all the struggles for liberation.

Jeri had only been in England a few short months before she took the anticipated holiday. She rented a car, drove to Scotland and took a ferry to Belfast, then drove to Derry. The cousins met as if they'd always been in each other's company. Physically, they were much alike, tall women with the family's dark hair and deep blue eyes. Jeri's hair was full of red highlights, but Fiona's brought midnight into any day. Fiona's skin was milky smooth and moon pale, while Jeri tanned easily in the sun. Jeri's features were a matter of angles and planes that suggested a stage where dramas of deep import might be found. Fiona's face was softer, sadder, connected always to her heart, communicating a range of passions and sympathies. Fiona's open affection eliminated any distance that Jeri's more hesitant reserve might have created between them.

They had planned a driving trip through Derry and Galway. Accompanied by Devlin, Fiona's fiancé, they drove the scenic bays and hills of the north. Jeri was never happier than on that holiday. She was in love with Fiona in a way that envied but never begrudged Devlin his place in her cousin's bed during their stays in the little country inns.

Then they came to a roadblock in Armagh.

†

Jeri had no idea how long she had been staring at Arkadia O'Malley. The cascade of memories had shaved some of the sharpness from the edges of her anger, but not all. Along with memory had come the realization that she was being ejected from the swaddling safety of her grief. Depression and shock were disappearing like fog being burned off by sunlight. No peace took their place, only the harsh knowledge that she would have to live in full awareness that she was in prison. The relentless misery that had been stalking her could at last attack, and she would need to fight it with weapons other than hiding. More than anything, she wanted some kind of physical exertion. Had she been anywhere else, she would have found a boat and rowed herself to exhaustion. Abruptly, Jeri turned away and went to find Jill Leary.

†

The Section OC was with her own chief, Mairead Farrell. Jeri hesitated to approach the woman whose standing was legendary in Armagh, but despite her reluctance, something about Farrell made Jeri glad she was with Leary at this moment. Farrell's eyes were shadowed and sad, not unlike Fiona's had been, but her smile was warm and welcoming, as if she and Leary had only just this moment been waiting for Jeri.

"How are your hands, O'Donnell?" Farrell spoke first. "Healing, I hope."

Jeri frowned to hide a sudden shyness. "Nothing to worry about. Thanks for asking."

"Have you come to join us?" Leary lifted an eyebrow to give her question humor.

"No. Sorry. Maybe in a way. I thought maybe you could put me to work. I'm qualified to teach any number of things, history for instance."

Leary was disappointed but Mairead Farrell nodded, pleased. "Did you speak with the Governor?" Farrell asked.

"No. I thought I should go through channels first." Jeri ventured a smile.

Chapter Three

"Come on, Arky, put in a good word for us. O'Donnell belongs to the struggle." Leary's wheedling betrayed the difficulty she was encountering in her attempts to recruit the American.

"I have never said a word against you."

"Aye, but you've said nothing for us, either." Jill took a cigarette and offered one to O'Malley, who declined. The OC lit the tip, inhaled deeply, and leaned back against the stone wall that enclosed the courtyard. "Do you not support the struggle?"

"I don't believe that Geraldine should be involved. She's American. An accident put her here, but if she stays on this path it will inevitably destroy her."

"How many fathers who can't get work to feed their own children are being destroyed? How many families who have to send their children off to far countries forever are being destroyed? Lives are being destroyed every day. She's Irish, her family's Irish. She'd not be the first one from Americay to fight for the Auld Sod. And you may have been in here too long to have heard, Arky, but it's a war we're fighting out there."

Despite the harshness of her words, Jill Leary's tone was mild. Left on her own, she would have given up the campaign to recruit O'Donnell, but she persisted because she had orders to succeed. Jeri was willing to acknowledge the Provisional IRA's authority, but she still refused to join them. Leary had no idea why; it could be due to some philosophical reason, or just plain Yank cussedness. Jeri clearly knew about political theory and history, and, more to the point, she enjoyed sharing what she knew. Jeri was proving to be an able teacher, encouraging the inmates who came to her class, bringing the past to life like a storyteller bard of old. Jeri also joined the Provo women in their daily exercise, and the physical exertion worked like a tonic on both her mind and body. The depression that had once dulled her eyes was gone; her walk had a spring to it; she even began occasional conversations. But she still balked at joining the republican struggle. At times Jill thought of herself as a jockey, urging a reluctant horse 'round and 'round to the hurdle. Jeri would go the whole course in fine form, only to refuse the final leap.

A more difficult task had been getting Jeri to take part in the political classes based on the Green Book, the manual that was part strategy and part a manifesto of basic IRA beliefs. Leary ran this class herself, and she could see that O'Donnell often restrained herself from arguing. Not that Leary minded; she recognized that an argument with O'Donnell would likely be a contest that she'd lose. Jeri was brilliant, no doubt about that. But Leary still didn't understand why Jeri never flat out turned her down instead of skirting around the edges like a canny fox. Jill was hoping Arkadia O'Malley might drop some piece of information that would explain what kept O'Donnell from simply turning away if she wasn't at all interested.

From another corner of the prison yard, simply enjoying the brief period allowed for absorbing sun and fresh air, Jeri could see that O'Malley and Leary were talking, and she suspected that she might be the topic. Jeri liked the IRA women well enough; she respected them for their focus, their sense of purpose. Other prisoners at Armagh had stories that ranged from venal to tragic: one woman was a prostitute who had been sent up for stealing from a John; another had performed abortions for free until one of her young women, most of whom came from across the border, died of infection. As a group, these women were simply crossing off days until their release. The Provos, on the other hand, never appeared defeated; instead they viewed prison as another field on which to fight the republican battle.

The Cause was familiar enough. Eamon O'Donnell, Jeri's father, had been born in the Bogside, the Catholic ghetto in Derry, eighteen years before he emigrated and married a pretty Boston Irish girl. Family rumors said that Eamon had been one step ahead of the law when he left Ireland, but since that implied something criminal in Southie, Jeri had never connected it with the politics he carried on about whenever he got a drink or two in him. Now she wondered whether his brush with the law might not have been political. She had absorbed the vocabulary of the struggle as a child. She knew the difference between a black-hearted, British-loving Ulster unionist and a good working-class nationalist who lived and breathed the republican cause; she knew that the Provos were the old IRA transformed into the new Provisional Irish Republican Army; she knew the difference between Bloody Sunday and Bloody Friday. The letters from Fiona had always been about politics rather than sectarian loyalty, using the terms of class struggle rather than religious division. Jeri had the vocabulary, but for her it had been the language of myth rather than of experience. Besides, Jeri had liked the English people she met in Oxford.

"Some of us started out just asking to have the same rights as an ordinary Englishman. We're not after hating a people, O'Donnell," Leary had responded to such a comment from Jeri. "We're after winning a war, and good people always die in a war."

Which was exactly the point on which Jeri balanced, unable to move either toward the struggle or away.

†

Jeri had only spent overnight under observation, but Kathleen had been gone much longer. Jeri was waiting for Kathleen when she was released from the infirmary. "You're looking better."

"I'm fine, but you should see the other lass." Kathleen smiled shyly.

To Jeri's eye, Kathleen still looked pale, her freckles standing out more than usual. "Are you okay? You could have been hurt, or even worse."

"Aw shucks, Tex, it was nothing," Kathleen drawled in imitation of every American western movie. Then she returned to her normal way of speaking. "See, I practiced talking American for you."

Jeri smiled. "At last, something I can understand." She held out her arms.

What was meant for a hug started that way, but then Kathleen's arms tightened and she tucked her head beneath Jeri's chin. Quickly, Kathleen pulled back, unable to look at Jeri. "I'm sorry," she murmured.

"Don't be. It's okay." Jeri still had her arms around Kathleen. "Could you . . . could you come to my bed tonight?"

Kathleen looked up, her eyes wide with disbelief. "Aye." A bit of humor asserted itself. "Maybe first I should stop by and thank Malloy?"

As the hours passed, Jeri felt more and more anxious. Holding Kathleen had stirred a response, and that brief feeling had been followed by an emotional longing whose force surprised her. At the same time, she knew she was not in love, that her feelings in no way matched Kathleen's, and she was angry with herself for taking advantage of the

30

woman. By lights out, anticipation and dread had raised Jeri's senses to such a pitch that she heard Kathleen's approach long before the woman fiddled the lock and then slipped quietly into the narrow bed. Jeri could feel need flowing like waves of heat from the tense body that lay alongside her.

"Where were you hurt?" Jeri whispered. "I don't want to make it worse."

For answer, Kathleen took hold of Jeri's hand and led it, not quite touching, to the skin of her neck between her right ear and shoulder. "Don't worry. It's better already."

They lay quietly kissing for a while, both tentative in their initial contact. Kathleen's lips were soft and yielding despite the apparent need that had brought her to Jeri's bed. She lay on her left side and Jeri was careful to avoid the burn while she caressed Kathleen's head, ruffling the soft, curly hair. When Kathleen's lips parted and Jeri's tongue slipped between, a suppressed moan and a tightened grip on her arm informed Jeri that the intensity was increasing, but when Kathleen attempted to shift positions and move her free arm, she soon found herself lying on her back with Jeri raised above. If Kathleen wanted to protest, she soon forgot why. Jeri made love to her with a concentrated attention that played off Kathleen's need, using it to bring her to a gasping climax that she muffled against Jeri's breast.

While Kathleen lay limp, catching her breath, Jeri caressed the length of her body, enjoying the feel of smooth skin and easy curves. Kathleen's body was solid and round, putting Jeri in mind of art books that suggested one ought to sketch figures by first drawing circles. Kathleen's breasts were full and her belly curved into round thighs. The muscles of her arms and butt were strong, testament to the hard work of her life outside prison. When it seemed that Kathleen was ready to exchange positions, Jeri intensified her stroking until, after a while, she once again got Kathleen to come.

"Will you not let me touch you, too?" Kathleen whispered in Jeri's ear.

"I can't."

"Why?" Jeri was quiet for so long that Kathleen regretted asking.

"I don't know. But it's okay, really. I like this."

†

"Today I'm going to talk about the Brehon Laws. Some say that the

Brehon Laws of Ireland go back to Saint Patrick; others claim that they're older still."

Jeri surveyed the small group who sat listening. At the moment they were attentive; she could tell from their eyes. They were polite women, so their eyes would provide the first indication that she was losing them. Without textbooks, she had to rely on her own memory for a series of lectures on Irish history, and she knew that not everyone would find the topic innately interesting. At the back of the room, she saw Jill Leary and Mairead Farrell. Farrell gave her an encouraging smile. Kathleen was sitting closer. Jeri knew she could recite the contents of the corner grocery in Southie and Kathleen would listen with the same rapt attention.

"Those experts who want to stake an ancient claim compare the laws with other Indo-European customs." It was interesting to watch how little movement it took a face to shift meaning. Jeri was going to have to improvise before she'd even really started. "Indo-European, that's the name the experts give to a whole group of people stretching from here in Ireland all the way to India. Mostly it means languages, related languages. Usually they use a tree to illustrate the idea. Closely related languages, like Irish and Welsh and Scots, are on the Celtic branch, but the trunk is Indo-European, and even if no one has spoken Indo-European for several thousand years, you can work back to it through related words."

That's all very nice, a face or two seemed to say, but the point is?

"Same thing with customs," Jeri continued. "Take fasting. A hunger strike as a response to injustice is a custom common to both Indian and Irish history. To sit outside the lord's doorway and shame him by starving indicates that you're among people for whom hospitality is very strong value."

†

"I finished." Jeri held *The Mill on the Floss* in both hands in front of her, a curiously defensive posture that was unlike her.

Arkadia O'Malley waited to hear more. This was the first time that Jeri had sought her out since O'Malley had confronted her about the tragedy at the roadblock. O'Malley had waited, biding her time with the patience that was a useful talent in prison. She'd watched with approval while the young American gained strength under the Provo's fitness regimen, and gained confidence as she set up classes of her own.

"Do you want to talk about it?" Jeri shook her head. "I put some new books aside for you. An odd assortment arrived last week. Perhaps you'll skip the one on bee keeping, but there's another on Russia in the Thirties you might consider."

"I'd rather… I'd like to read this again." Once more there was that uncharacteristic hesitation. "When I started, I just read words, but by the end I did admire Maggie, although…" Jeri paused and made a face, "falling for Stephen Guest seems more heaving bosom romance than classic novel." She took a deep breath. "I don't usually take this long to read a book, but I needed to prepare for my classes."

If O'Malley was amused by the defensive comment, she didn't smile. She approved of taking pride in one's intellect. "I meant to applaud your work. I hear the women speak of your class. One even said, 'For someone bright as a penny, she's not that full of herself.' I believe that's a very high compliment."

The two women shared a smile. "Don't think I don't appreciate the time you've taken with me, particularly since I've done nothing to deserve it."

"'Deserve.' There's a concept we must discuss one day. I have to go now, Geraldine. We'll talk again soon."

Jeri watched Arkadia O'Malley cross the prison yard, but her grip on the book didn't loosen until the woman was out of sight. She hadn't expected that it would be so difficult to talk, but she had felt transparent, exposed. Arkadia—there, she had used the name—Arkadia always fixed her with that gaze that had a hawk's hard brilliance, softened by something like affection. At first, Jeri had thought of her as old, but she wasn't that old. Her thick hair was streaked in shades of gray, a tarnished silver mingling with gun-metal gray, cut short with no regard for style. She was only slightly shorter than Jeri, with the spare frame of someone indifferent to food. Arkadia O'Malley even resembled a hawk in her sharp features and the observant set of her head that never ceased scanning her surroundings, but what impressed Jeri the most was her presence, the constant dignity that was in no way diminished by her being a prisoner.

During the night, before Kathleen had gone back to her own bed, while Jeri was still making love to her, Jeri had not been surprised when the face of Fiona had intruded. Jeri's eyes had been closed, she had been listening to the Kathleen's breathing, and then she had seen Fiona, just before the soldier fired. Her cousin's eyes had been pleading with her for forgiveness, for understanding, and it nearly broke Jeri's heart to remember that her own face must have been cold and angry. Determined to make up for that cruelty in some small way, Jeri had concentrated on Kathleen, working her way past the obstructing memory. But when at last Kathleen gripped her hard at the height of arousal, Jeri was astonished to find that the face in her mind belonged to Arkadia O'Malley.

†

"I don't need a mercy fuck, O'Donnell." Kathleen was whispering, but the bitterness was palpable. "Nor do I need a 'thank you kindly for all your help' fuck either."

Once again, Jeri had made love to Kathleen, and when the woman would have made love to her, Jeri had attempted to get Kathleen to come again. Kathleen had stopped her.

"Kathleen, it's not like that."

"Oh? What is it like then? You don't care that much for me?"

"But I do. That's the point."

It was true. Jeri did care for Kathleen. She liked the woman's pluck, her vulnerability that she couldn't quite hide in spite of her dogged determination to soldier on. Jeri suspected that prison for Kathleen was more than punishment, it was a shame gnawing deeply into her spirit.

"Then why won't you ever let me touch you?" A need that all of Jeri's expertise couldn't abolish was in those words; Kathleen needed to love as well as be loved. "Don't you fancy me at all?"

"Oh, I fancy you. Here." Jeri took Kathleen's hand and guided it to where her own wetness backed up her words.

"Then why?"

"I can't." Despite her reluctance to ever explain herself, Jeri let some of her own anguish show. "It hurts."

They lay a long time in a fugue of mutual misery. Jeri stirred first. "Tell me why you're here." Kathleen was silent and Jeri thought she might just leave, but then she responded.

"We Healys, we're quiet folk. Some of our neighbors are Catholic and some aren't, but we mostly keep to our own and there's never been any Troubles where I'm from. I always knew I fancied girls but I thought I'd just live with it, until I met Audrey Barnes. Not that she'd give me the time of day that way, but her brother did. Aubrey Barnes. Aubrey and Audrey. Twins. It all seems so foolish now, them being Prods particularly, but I took up with him so I could be with her. They were both fast, and I'd sneak out at night so I could run around with them. One night we lifted a car parked by the hotel. It was shiny and new and Aubrey fancied driving something that powerful. We figured no one would miss it and we'd have it back in a couple hours. I could make a longer story of it, but there's no point. Me and Aubrey Barnes and Audrey and her fellow, we all went riding and we had a bottle with us. Aubrey dropped off Audrey and Tom and he was taking me home. He took a corner too fast and we wrecked the car. We both were knocked out cold. When we came to, there were sirens and cops, and neither one of us hurt bad enough to make them feel any pity." Kathleen paused. "I'm the shame of my family. They'll be paying for that car for years. That's what made the judge give us prison. The car was new. The Barneses don't feel the need to pay anything back, but my da does."

Jeri couldn't think of anything to say. She kept her arm around Kathleen until they fell asleep. In the middle of the night, Kathleen left, and never again came to Jeri's bed.

†

"Good work, O'Donnell. Keep that up and you'll be taking your cousin's place in no time. No time at all." Jill Leary was watching as the exercise group performed a particularly strenuous series of moves. She spoke mainly out of habit, these days her probing more of a ritual than because she actually expected Jeri to change her mind.

Someone with an eye less sharp would likely have missed Jeri's reaction: a tensing of muscles that was almost immediately masked by being turned into a stretch. Someone else might have interpreted the tension as mere annoyance. Jill Leary, however, saw the reaction and experienced a flash of comprehension, the excitement of an answer finally falling into place: O'Donnell felt she ought to become Fiona! Since she was the reason her cousin was no longer in the world to pursue her destiny, then, by rights, the responsibility that had been Fiona's now fell to Jeri. It was a complicated motivation, based primarily on guilt, and Jill Leary by no means understood it completely, but then she had no need to know more.

Gotcha, Leary thought. *Gotcha young Yank*. Like an angler who knows her fish is hooked, Jill began to lay cautious plans to reel O'Donnell in.

†

"Do you have anything that's not English?"

Jeri's question took Arkadia O'Malley by surprise. This was the first indication of sectarianism she had ever heard Jeri voice.

"No," Jeri said quickly, seeing O'Malley's face, "no, not political, linguistic!" She grinned, and then laughed. "I'd like a book in another language, if you have one. I was studying languages at Oxford."

This was the first time O'Malley remembered seeing Jeri truly smile, and the effect was startling. No one who ever looked at Geraldine O'Donnell would be unaffected, and responses to the strong character shaping her appearance would vary: some would be attracted; some repelled; and some astonished for reasons they might never understand. But to see her smile was to see her beautiful, to see her dark blue eyes grow warm, and to become aware of her great reservoir of generosity.

Arkadia O'Malley was not unaffected. She had already identified the reasons for Jeri's odd reactions recently; she had encountered them often enough in the days when young women came to her for guidance and approval. Schoolgirl crush was the generic diagnosis, and to someone familiar with the symptoms, the condition was usually benign and charming. One was simply careful not to encourage the situation. When she recognized that attraction had wakened in Jeri, Arkadia O'Malley ignored it. Until this instant, when the sunlight of a smile wakened a response in herself.

"I believe I have one or two books that might be suitable," O'Malley said to end the moment. "Is there a particular language or a particular level you prefer?"

Jeri's quick mind had registered something happening, but it went by too fast to identify. Her smile faded, but she was still in a lighter than usual mood. "Anything, actually, although if the alphabet is different, I need something to get me started. I've picked up Greek. I can usually pick up anything Indo-European, but other language families need a kick-start. It's a gift."

"A gift indeed."

After Jeri left, Arkadia O'Malley drew a deep breath. She had never been tempted before, not in all her years in Armagh. Her considerable presence, her self-containment, had been armor enough to ward off intimacy, and the armor had worked so well that she had forgotten what it protected. Now, in an instant, the armor had been breached, and O'Malley realized she might still be vulnerable to the need to be loved. It was a thoroughly unpleasant consideration.

But what could it hurt?

There it was—the whispering serpent, bent on seduction. Never mind that Saint Patrick had driven all the snakes out of Ireland, or that Armagh prison was a far cry from Eden, the metaphor was appropriate. O'Malley shook her head to clear it. To even consider a relationship with the young American was silly. Absurd. Unseemly.

Why? She's not that young, and you're not that old.

Unseemly, and beside the point. Just as she was sure that Jill Leary's aim to recruit Jeri could put her on a path that would end in disaster, so she knew beyond question that, although they might love, she was not the one that Jeri's soul longed for. And knowing that, she dared not obstruct the search of one heart for another.

Arkadia O'Malley dreamed again that night. Odd and restless dreams, beginning like images in a kaleidoscope that were seeking to shift into focus, but the center of clarity was immeasurably far away.

†

Remembering the ritual of the Old Ones that she had been taught, but had never used, required concentration of mind and heart. The rites for joining two companions who had not merely survived but had won through all the testing had never been seen in living memory. Not one member of all the gathered tribes had witnessed such a celebration. There was silence except for the hissing of more than a hundred torches lighting the night before the rising of the new moon, and the breathing of several hundred folks come to witness this awesome moment. Children yet unborn would hear the tale of this night and tell their own children. A slow drum whispered into the silence, at first no louder than a heartbeat. Another joined it, and another, until the beat grew strong and steady but never loud.

They came then, the two who had won through the trials. She knew them, of course, had known them since they were children, but she saw them now as though through a mist that might have been tears, might have been time. She did not feel as if she were entirely present, but more as if she stood somewhere between, somewhere both close and far away.

"You have won with courage, counsel, and strength," she would tell them, "but you have also cast your souls upon the hazard of time, and so what you have won becomes the greatest trial of all." She would say this to them, but for the moment, she let them stand before her, rightfully proud in this moment, where all who gathered could see their triumph

37

and savor it with them. Bruises marked them, and wounds that would turn to scars, yet they carried these as badges of honor willingly earned.

She was so proud of them; she loved them to the limits of her soul and beyond. She pitied them, too. They would hear the words that she had rehearsed as if they were but confirmation of their efforts, as if answering the questions she would put to them was mere form. How could they now refuse what they had fought so hard to win? But her words were not form, they were a deep and dire warning. Would they still yoke their souls, knowing that this life would be short, and that in those lives to come they would not always meet? Would they pledge their hearts knowing that even if they met, they might not recognize one another, or perhaps would come to that knowledge too late? Would they still claim the right, the gift, to be keeper and companion to one another, knowing that their souls might diminish rather than grow from one age to the next? Would they dare proceed despite having no assurance at all but that fragile pride that exalted them in this moment?

Ah, the pride might be fragile but the love was not; that was strong as the night and as enduring as the stars.

She might as well not ask. Flush with their victory, their astonishing trust in one another now tested and proven, they would dare without hesitation. And she would complete the ritual, placing on each the necklet of black feathers from the crest of the night heron woven around with bright butterfly wings; but she would not tell them that she, too, was being bound. That she must follow their yoked fortunes through age upon age, and that, for her soul along with theirs, there was no assurance of winning through.

†

Arkadia O'Malley lay awake in the darkness. The prison was never truly silent; there was always an undercurrent of furtive mutterings, the whimpering of bad dreams, the thudding beat of despair that added to the creaking adjustments of a building grown cranky with age. O'Malley heard it all and found it reassuringly familiar, but only with a small part of her awareness. The dream still held her. Dreams had long become the stage on which her real drama played, but now they seemed like the circling of a raptor who has hunted from the higher air, waiting, searching. Soon a motion below would cast a line to the sky and, inevitably, she must dive along its length, hurl herself from the heights, risking all.

†

"Russian." Jeri shook her head in wonder. "A Russian grammar. Who would have thought to donate that to Armagh?"

"I doubt anyone thinks much about the books they send. More likely they're cleaning out after the uncle has died and they don't look close at one volume in a dozen. It's a rare book I get that was published less than ten years ago."

Jeri smiled. "More luck for me, then."

Jeri's smiles were becoming less rare, but they still affected O'Malley. She realized that she was beginning to attempt winning one during their conversations. She was not pleased with the realization.

"Are you thinking it was luck brought you to Armagh?"

O'Malley meant only to cool the exchange, but Jeri looked as if ice water had been thrown on her.

"I know exactly what brought me to Armagh," she said, her eyes gone hard almost quick enough to hide the hurt.

"Perhaps I was too hasty in my phrasing. I meant to consider the nature of luck as a concept, not your situation."

Jeri took no notice. Her voice was tight and harsh. "I killed my cousin." She stood up and walked away, the Russian grammar clutched tightly in a white knuckled hand.

The wound that was Fiona's death wasn't healing. The spirit of the Irish cousin had projected her invisible presence into Jeri's life for far too long for death to make her disappear. Neither Jill Leary's discipline nor Arkadia O'Malley's steady pressure to continue learning was enough to keep Fiona's ghost at bay. The letters Jeri had written over the years had been a form of courtship, aiming to gain respect, approval. She had been in awe of her cousin's passion for justice, sometimes perceiving it as a rebuke to her own less serious nature, sometimes finding it a spark setting alight her receptive young mind. Jeri was open to her cousin in a way that she could never be with the people around her. With people nearby, she was wary and distrustful despite appearing to be one of them. If it had not been for Fiona, the streets of Southie might have claimed Jeri, made her one more statistic, careening from chemical excitement to adrenaline danger. Fiona had caused her to lift her head, to test for keener air, to aim for more than what was easy or close. Jeri had never put it into words, but at some point what Fiona might think had become her own standard of judgment.

†

"Want to learn to make a bomb?" Leary's bland face and light hazel eyes were at odds with the outrageous suggestion, but the challenge was clear.

"Don't be absurd."

"Absurd? What do you think your cousin planned to do with that plastic? Make toy trucks?"

Leary scored a hit but Jeri didn't realize that the OC had been aiming. "I don't know what she meant to do. I was never asked, was I?"

"And if you had been?"

Christ! There it was. The most obvious question and Jeri had managed to avoid seeing it. Would she have agreed to smuggle the explosive if Fiona had asked? Why hadn't Fiona asked? Had she thought Jeri would refuse? Had she not trusted her to keep a secret? Had she thought Jeri would agree and she only meant to protect her from such an act? Would Jeri have turned her conscience entirely over to her cousin?

Leary could see that her presence had been forgotten. "Let me know when you get the answer," she muttered.

†

Liam O'Donnell reminded Jeri of her brother, Mickey. Something about the eyes, blue-gray nestled in creases made by smiling. Jeri had noticed it in their brief first meeting seven months earlier. Liam wasn't smiling now, but Jeri could see that the tendency of a lifetime wasn't necessarily erased by tragedy.

"How are you?" her uncle asked. "Getting along?"

"I'm okay."

"I talked to your ma and da before I left. Told them I was coming. They both send their love. Said to tell you they're not much for writing. I said you'd probably noticed by now. Don't think I've ever heard from Eamon but when it was his name signed by your ma."

"Uncle Liam, I–"

"Doesn't need saying. Not in this place. I'm working with a solicitor for you." He smiled, and if it didn't quite match anything she remembered, the attempt was still warm. "You're not forgot. They haven't let us in before, but we're working for you. I hear you know someone named Leary."

Jeri nodded. Liam's smile was still in place, but his eyes had lost their mirth.

"Her aunt says to keep up her prayers. You'll tell her that?"

Jeri nodded again, but she didn't think the message was from any aunt, or about religion, for that matter. Still, she almost forgot to pass it on. In any case, it was Leary who sought *her* out after the visit.

"What's wrong, O'Donnell?" Leary had never seen Jeri looking as if she might lose the battle to contain the anger banked inside.

Jeri took a long, deep breath. "Nothing. My uncle was here. He brought me a message for you. Your aunt says to keep up your prayers."

"Looks like it's you could use some praying." Leary felt real concern for the younger woman. Then she got it. "Ah. Was that your first visitor?" Jeri looked away. "Sorry, young Yank. Wish I could say it got easier, but the body searches are meant to humiliate us and this is one job where the screws don't shirk."

"They had a male guard in the room. Isn't that against the rules?" That was as close as Jeri could get to talking about the body search.

"Sure and I'd advise you not to take that to the warden."

"You have visitors a lot."

This time it was Leary who looked away. "And I said it doesn't get easier."

Jeri wrote and asked her uncle not to visit again.

†

Jeri almost shut the memory down from force of habit. She was trying to read, but today concentration eluded her. "The sea." That was all, just those words and memory erupted like a geyser out of the depths. She gave up and lay back on her bed, letting the memory play out. At least it wasn't the roadblock.

All day the three sightseers had driven through Donegal, with low scudding clouds off the sea making a particularly bold drama of the light. Colors were so vibrant and richly hued that they might have been on another planet altogether. Devlin slowed the car for a particularly sharp turn as they crested a hill and then they were overlooking a sea of churning blue, darker than any blue Jeri had ever seen this side of black. Jeri felt a clutch at her chest and tears came to her eyes. Devlin found a place to park and Jeri got out, incapable of speech. She was unused to

41

such strong feelings coming from something so apparently impersonal as a landscape, and though she tried to free herself, the emotions were irresistible. She took a path, steep and rocky, down closer to the water. Above the spray of the incoming waves, she found a place to sit.

At the edge where land and sea struggled to hold what each claimed, Jeri felt as if something inside her was pushing for awareness, for birth, as if something she knew but had forgotten wanted to return. The frustration of being so close to understanding made her want to cry out and weep, and she almost did, knowing that the crashing waves boiling so close below would mask any sound she might make. Almost. Then she gave up the struggle and, instead of weeping, let the rhythms surround her. The sea swelled toward the land over and over, breaking against the rocky coast in pulsing sprays of sound and saltwater, fierce and impersonal, creating rainbows in the slanting sunlight. Gray-white clouds passed overhead like a rushing flock of mythical birds. When Jeri returned to the car, Fiona and Desmond smiled but left the mood unbroken by words.

Not until they were having sandwiches and ale that night in a battered old pub was there conversation.

"I can count on one hand the times I was fifty miles from the Bay," Jeri said to Fiona. Devlin had disappeared somewhere. "And here I am, across the Atlantic, and already I've been to Scotland and Wales, and now here."

"The old gods touched you today. I saw."

"The old gods…" Jeri murmured, embarrassed.

"They still live here, in the land."

"I don't believe in gods and things. That's for Kathleen." The thought of her religious sister was annoying. "If God was really around, why would the world be like it is?"

"Ah, Jeri love, don't make the mistake of thinking of gods as such grand and distant beings. They're just another folk we share the world with."

Jeri laughed, happy with the day and surprised by the curious concept that Fiona had just voiced. She'd need to consider the notion of gods as a kind of seldom-seen species. She'd need to find out more about the Irish gods.

"I didn't know you were a romantic, Fiona. I always think of you as solid and centered."

Fiona smiled. "Did you forget I was Irish?" Then she frowned. "Jeri, love, there's something I… Dev, you're back."

42

Remembering, from the prison in Armagh, Jeri was sure that if Devlin had returned a few moments later, Fiona would have told her about the explosives. In fact, that's probably where Devlin had been, hiding Semtex, the C4, in a door frame before they crossed the border back into the North the next morning. There had always been the trip *she* had been taking and the trip *they* had been taking, and if she could bring herself to remember, how much more might she add to the whole of what she knew? At the time, she had just been annoyed that Devlin had interrupted, thinking that Fiona might say another odd and lovely thing about gods or the like.

The next morning, both Fiona and Devlin had been out of sorts, short with each other. Jeri, assuming it was some private lovers' argument, had been uncomfortable. At first she just retreated into silence, hoping that the Ulster countryside would be enough to distract her, but the tension in the small car only seemed to thicken as the day went on.

"We should stop for a bite soon," Fiona said. It was well past noon.

"Not yet." Devlin was curt. "Time enough when we get to Omagh."

If he was so determined to get to Omagh, he should have gone a more direct way than this tree-lined country road. Not only was the countryside not distracting, Jeri was getting angry. Bad enough they couldn't keep their problems to themselves, but they didn't have to wreck her vacation, especially on the last day of touring.

"Shite!"

Devlin slid the car to a stop before Jeri realized why. A roadblock. But there was only one car ahead of them so they shouldn't be held up too long.

Jeri was curious about the process at first, but more than that, she was hungry. When the British officer politely asked the three to get out of the car, she didn't argue, but Southie habits soon took over; police were police, whether in Boston or Ireland.

"Gets boring out here, does it? Have to stop the natives for a little fun?" she said to the soldier standing nearest. He was a boy, really, with the uniform and gear nearly drowning his weedy thin frame.

The soldier's lips compressed but he refused to make eye contact. Fiona, however, was bothered. "Don't be going on, Jeri. They're just after doing their job."

Which made Jeri even madder. Fiona sounded so meek. She never imagined her cousin would get so deferential to a mere boy.

"Some job. They want to be mechanics, they should stay in England. If they hurt this car, I don't want to have to pay for it. Damn.

What are they doing now?"

"Stay where you are and shut your mouth."

The soldier was plainly getting nervous. Since when did they give such dangerous toys to children?

The soldiers at the car were fiddling about with the doors. If they didn't know how to do whatever they were doing, the car company would keep the deposit and Jeri was counting on getting it back.

"Well, well, what do we have here?" One of soldiers held up a brick-sized package.

"What the fuck!" In that instant, Jeri was furious. She knew what the soldier was holding, and she knew who had put it there. Devlin and Fiona had used her. Everything fell into place: why they were on this road; why they had to get to Omagh. She swung toward her cousin.

"Jeri, love, don't–" Fiona raised her hands, imploring forgiveness, and for just less than a second, it was only the two of them standing there in the tree-lined lane. Then the instant was broken by a burst of gunfire. In effect, the soldier was standing almost alongside Jeri while Devlin and Fiona were directly in front of him. Jeri saw them both fall, saw the blood blossom on Fiona's blouse like a horrid flower. Saw the life leave her eyes.

†

Arkadia O'Malley was wise enough to recognize the rarity of second chances, and then she became too caught up in Jeri's story to be concerned with anything else. She listened without comment until Jeri was finished.

"Does it matter if I remember?" Jeri had brought the question to Arkadia O'Malley reluctantly. She was reluctant to share it, and she was reluctant to give O'Malley another chance to hurt her. She had kept the memory to herself until the weight of it grew too heavy. Then, as if she brought something crusted with salt and sand from a distant shore, Jeri told the story to the one person who might see it without a bias of guilt or politics.

"Of course it matters. The part of you that says 'I' misses more than it catches all the time. If you keep something, there's always a reason for it. This day you speak of seems full of things important to sort out, important to remember, and what Fiona meant to tell you is only one of them. What do you think she might have said?"

"I think she would have told me about smuggling the Semtex."

"How long have you thought that?"

"Since Leary... Since I began wondering why she hadn't just told me what she and Devlin were up to."

"Go on."

"She was going to say something important before Devlin came back, I'm sure of it. I've been trying to think if he said where he'd been, but all I remember is he was gone for over an hour. When he sat down, he had grease on his face. Fiona said something about it. He took the cloth napkin from the table to wipe it off, and she stopped him and used paper from her bag instead. She said for him not to be ruining good linen."

O'Malley nodded for Jeri to go on.

"That's all. I can't remember much else important from the evening."

"And the next day?"

"I thought we were all just tired, with not much to say. Devlin drove, and I watched the sights. Fiona was in the front seat with him and they only said a word or two now and then. I wondered if they'd had some sort of fight, they were so quiet, it seemed that kind of quiet, plus I put it down to being near to the end of the vacation."

"And?"

Jeri wondered what O'Malley had heard to alert her to something left unsaid. "I wasn't a great fan of Devlin Mulroney. I know I was jealous of him and I'd have liked for him not to be with us, so I ignored him when I could and was just a bit too nice when I couldn't. That's what you're hearing."

"Did Fiona care for him?"

"The sun rose from his nether parts." Jeri avoided a more crude version out of deference to O'Malley. "She was so smart about everything else. I didn't even try to slide an objection between them, not after seeing how it was the first day or so, after seeing how important he was to her."

"Would he have put the Semtex in the car without telling Fiona?"

It was a lifeline. Reluctantly, Jeri refused it. "No. He'd have told her. It probably would never have occurred to him she might object to anything he decided."

"Would she have objected?"

This thought took longer to examine. "No. I've been thinking about her letters. I always knew she was a nationalist, for her that was just being Irish, but there were subtler thoughts tending toward theories of

45

armed struggle that I didn't recognize. I didn't realize the new Provisional IRA was bending toward Marxist ideas, so I missed the early implications. Or I just pretended they weren't there."

O'Malley permitted herself the ghost of a smile. "I doubt that you've ever deliberately attempted to hide anything from yourself, Geraldine."

"Don't be so sure. I try to pretend I'm not in love with you."

The shift in topic was breathtakingly abrupt for both of them. The declaration of affection was singularly lacking in that emotion; instead it was tossed between them like an angry challenge. Jeri lifted her dark blue eyes to face directly whatever would be found in O'Malley's hawk brown gaze.

Arkadia O'Malley was not entirely unprepared; still, she took her time to find an answer. She wanted to give herself time to understand, intuitively if not entirely rationally, what had made Jeri speak at this moment when they had both been so focused on her cousin. If it was an attempt to avoid reliving the feelings of that day, it was a stunning deflection. Or it might have been that the unspoken emotions had simply reached a pitch where they couldn't be ignored, and Jeri had simply lunged desperately for the opening to say anything. O'Malley gazed into a pair of darkly intense eyes that reminded her of midnight. For an instant more she hesitated. It would not be difficult to allow herself to accept what was being offered. Her own life was not so happy without the affection she knew would follow a simple nod of acceptance. Then she remembered that all deep emotions are born in a single source, and her own path was not one of resignation.

"You're not in love with me." She ignored the flash of anger this elicited. "That does not mean that there are not many things between us: respect, admiration, obligation, and yes, love, but not the kind you hunger for. I would betray all of these if I let you think that I am the one your soul craves."

"You can't know this."

"But I can, my dear. I can."

"How?"

Arkadia O'Malley leaned forward to make her words stronger. "The same way you know that Fiona was going to tell you about the hidden explosive. The same way she knew that she was living the last day she would ever be Fiona. The same way you know that everything I'm saying is true." O'Malley retreated to a less intimidating distance, but she reached out to put a hand on Jeri's arm. "It was well done of you to say this. All of it. You have wonderful courage."

†

For all the confidence that Arkadia O'Malley had expressed in the actuality of just *knowing* something, it was not a concept that Jeri entirely accepted or was able to hold on to as time passed. But pass it did, with aching slowness by the minute and with terrible swiftness as weeks, then months, then most heartbreaking of all, years slid by. Very little changed in the prison to mark the passing of time, seasons and holidays were only thin echoes from outside. A guard changed. An inmate left, a new one processed in. When Kathleen was released, Jeri missed her more than she would have thought possible considering that they rarely spoke, but when they had, the affection was real and the words honest.

The guilt that had, perversely, eased the initial weeks in Armagh by making Jeri's imprisonment feel deserved did not disappear, but as time passed, guilt lost ground to the animal need for freedom. Jeri was young and she longed for freedom, and there was no discernible end to her captivity. The injustice of her imprisonment began to fuel a rage that grew stronger simply by needing to be repressed.

Arkadia O'Malley blessed people's tendency to accumulate more than they ever needed and then to pass the overflow on to charity. Many of the books that she gave to Jeri had never been opened; nevertheless, they held solid facts and thoughtful opinions, even when they were woefully out of date. It didn't matter that Jeri learned Conrad's Polish or Dostoyevsky's Russian, those languages could always be updated later. Sometimes O'Malley would look over the shelves of now-dusty volumes that Jeri had returned, and she would marvel at the sheer amount of information that had passed through the young woman's hands. If she remembered one-hundredth of it, that would be more than what was contained in many encyclopedias.

O'Malley might be able to use the physical presence of the books as a kind of talismanic measure, but for Jeri there was only the sense of time slipping away. The pain of her cousin's death never disappeared, but the inevitable boredom of a meaningless treadmill dulled the sharp edges of memory. On bad days, her life felt like a draining sieve, a waste. Liam honored her request not to visit, but a bored US embassy liaison came once simply to make sure she was not being mistreated. The official left with a completed list of rote inquiries answered and the vague assurance of doing something soon. Jeri read, she exercised, she taught, she discussed with O'Malley, she argued with Leary. Every several months she allowed herself to be drawn into a brief liaison, but each time the emotional consequences caused more discomfort than they resolved and so, each time, Jeri resolved not to get involved again. It was usually after one of these entanglements that Jeri felt her life most wasted and O'Malley found her most difficult.

†

"Looks like another storm brewing from the Americays."

"Well didn't that turn to heavy weather in a hurry."

Arkadia O'Malley didn't bother to wonder which inmate Liz and Rosie were discussing. She had seen Jeri take her tray to a solitary place. Just the day before, Jeri had been with a woman who was now absent.

"Thank Jesus and Mary she doesn't go in for the hysterical types."

"That's not Paula's way at all. By tomorrow, it'll be all over that the American lass has some disgusting disease."

"She'd better make it a good one. There's plenty that would line up in hopes of catching any disease of hers."

†

"Christ! Is that another book?"

Arkadia O'Malley might have been amused by the absurd comment if she hadn't understood its source lay in a turmoil of rage. Jeri's pride would not allow her the easy venting of emotion that fueled much of the prison violence, the many fights that flared like flames suddenly leaping from smoldering coals. Instead, she burned hotter and in silence. Only in rare moments like this did O'Malley see the color and potential of the pent feelings, and in these moments she feared that all of her careful tending might come to nothing in the end.

"How do you do it, Arkadia?"

O'Malley chose to answer the words rather than the despair that prompted them. "This is not my life. I live here mostly among shadows; there are very few that I see with color and substance."

"That's crazy."

"Yes. If I spoke to anyone else about this I would be thought crazy."

"You can walk through shadows. These walls are real."

"I suppose. To me it doesn't matter. You, however, do live here and

48

not among shadows."

Jeri considered. It had been a long time since she had treated a conversation with Arkadia O'Malley the same way she might enter a fencing match. The older woman was pointing out a difference, not criticizing. Jeri had been looking into a middle distance, but now she raised her gaze to her mentor's. "Should I try to make my world more like yours?"

She suddenly found herself transfixed by a hawk's fierce stare, held in motionless thrall to eyes to whom her own hopes and wishes were but feeble and doomed stirrings. She felt her heart race and her breath disappear as the hawk stooped, diving, striking with merciless talons. Armagh prison was freedom itself compared to the grip of those claws. A voice filled her head: *You pledged yourself to this.*

That much, Jeri would remember. What she could not recall was what followed. She returned to time with only the impression of suddenly comprehending something utterly familiar, as if she had viewed it whole, not merely like a landscape spread out below, but a vista seen intimately as one who knew the entire history and thus the circumstances that led to the moment of sight. Then it was gone, in an instant, and not one shred of it was left to cling to, not even a thread to lead her back. She searched desperately for the thing, the name, the action that might become a clue, but all was gone except the feeling that once there had been clarity.

Jeri found herself looking into the gentle amber gaze of Arkadia O'Malley, who was again her friend, and more, her teacher, and more. "I think," Jeri heard her say, "I think that you are back in the world where you now belong."

It wouldn't have been in keeping with who Jeri was if she had accepted that. She was still searching for tatters of the ebbing vision as she stood and walked away, careful not to stumble, which wasn't all that easy. She had no idea that these were the last words that Arkadia O'Malley would say to Geraldine O'Donnell in Armagh prison. She fell asleep that night while vainly attempting to retrieve the vision. The next morning, she was awakened by the sound of an officer calling her name.

Chapter Four

"Come along, O'Donnell. I've more to do than babysit you."

Jeri followed the officer to the warden's outer office. She was told to sit and then was kept waiting for a long hour. A secretary aimed curious glances her way, but avoided any direct eye contact. Indifference vied with boredom as Jeri waited. She supposed the summons had something to do with her uncle, but a tiny hope, which she refused to entertain seriously, wondered if there might have been some change in her situation.

The phone on the secretary's desk rang. She answered it, then looked directly at Jeri. "You can go in now."

The warden was a gray man, carefully nondescript, a civil servant of high enough rank that he could afford to be invisible. He made her wait moments longer in his silent presence before he looked up from his papers. She was to think that she was a minor irritation for a very busy man, but Jeri also understood that the man actively disliked her.

"You may retrieve your belongings from the officer at the gate." He refused to address her by any name. "Please do not loiter. Your uncle is waiting for you. He will take you to the airport. The condition of your release is that you return immediately to America."

For several seconds, the words made no sense. Disoriented, Jeri had difficulty finding her voice. "Please, may I say good-bye, or write a short note?"

"Surely by now you know our rules. That would be disruptive to good order and discipline, and my officers have more important work to do than acting as postal employees. I would suggest that you refrain from attempting any form of communication even after you leave the country."

†

In its way, the release was as abruptly cruel as the incarceration had been and, just as she had at her arrival in Armagh, Jeri retreated into silence as the means of maintaining her dignity. Even when she was turned over to Liam and he ushered her to a waiting car, she nodded rather than spoke. A quiet man himself, perhaps he thought her silence as they drove away from the prison was due to the sight of so much she had been deprived of for so long: houses, trees, hedges, children, dogs, cows, hills. The simple view of a horizon line in the distance. She did see all these things, registered them, even found them vaguely threatening, but the sudden shock of their appearance drained them of meaning. The freedom she had longed for through countless hours arrived like a new form of punishment.

Liam's attention was on the road as he drove, and Jeri assumed they were on their way to an airport. Even when her uncle turned off the road and into a farm with decrepit buildings that appeared to have been unused for years, maybe decades, she found it difficult to focus.

"Come in, lass," Liam said as he stopped. "Her Majesty wants you on a plane by tonight, but I think you'll be needing a strong whisky first."

The offer of a drink was appealing.

All things being relative, the sight of a grim-faced stranger waiting just inside the door had to take its place in the queue of recent shocks. The room itself was bare of any furniture, and a dim light struggled through cracked and cobwebbed windows. Standing with his hands in the pockets of a belted raincoat, the man looked as if he might pull out a gun and shoot her. It occurred to Jeri that she might be about to be put on some kind of IRA trial for killing Fiona and Devlin. The man in the overcoat looked her over for a long time, measuring her from behind glasses so thick they hid his eyes as effectively as a mask. Suddenly he smiled broadly and stepped forward, holding a bottle that might be the drink Liam had promised.

"Hello, Geraldine O'Donnell. I'm Sean. Mairead and Jill have told us all about you." He took the cap off the bottle before offering it. "Here. We're short of good crystal, but the flavor won't suffer." A professional, never mind at what, Sean exuded a kindness that was not at all personal.

Jeri sipped, felt the warmth of the strong liquor flowing down her throat, and then she took another drink before handing the bottle back.

Sean, and there was only the remotest possibility that was his real name, passed the bottle to Liam. He turned back to Jeri. "You have to decide now. You can go back to Boston, or you can join us."

51

Jeri glanced around the room. Her uncle's face was hidden in shadow as he stared toward a grimy window. Sean waited. Jeri registered several impressions. She was still angry over the warden's abrupt dismissal, she was uncomfortable in Liam's presence, and she was relieved to be back in a confined space where she could account for everything.

More than that. At this last hour, when there still seemed a choice, Jeri realized there never truly had been one. Ever since Jill Leary had asked what she would have done had Fiona told her there was Semtex hidden in the car, Jeri had known what her answer would have been. Fiona's fight would have been hers, by way of family, of belief, of blood. She could remember the terrible days in her home when she was ten, old enough to understand such things, when her father wept and raged with grief at the massacre of Bloody Sunday.

"I'll join."

Liam turned away from the window but shadow still hid his expression. He stood silent for a long minute and then nodded. "God keep you." He raised the whisky one more time before giving it back to Sean. "Mind how you go, lass."

The sound of a motor starting and then fading underscored the finality of Jeri's decision.

Jeri's period of legal freedom was short-lived. It expired when she failed to board the plane to take her to the United States within the allotted time. Near dusk, two men arrived at the farm, and Sean informed Jeri that they would drive her across the border to a Provo training camp in the Republic. As soon as darkness arrived, Sean bade farewell and Jeri went to the waiting car.

She was having second thoughts. Or rather her mind was a whirl of conflicting thoughts.

You'd let the arrogance of one little man decide your life?

The question was posed in the unmistakable voice of Arkadia O'Malley. It was the first time that Jeri's conscience would take on the familiar voice, but far from the last. Jeri stared through the car window into the moving darkness and felt the full, heart-rending loss of Arkadia O'Malley.

Of course it wasn't the warden who had tipped the balance, it was everything that had put that man in a position to determine anything about her life.

Three years had been stolen from her, and she had not lived so long that three years were inconsequential. Still, with O'Malley's help, Jeri had made use of that time. What Jeri hadn't considered was how much she had believed that she might still continue as she had been. Not on the same path but one not too dissimilar. Just because she was no longer at Oxford did not mean that she would stop learning, and Arkadia O'Malley's steady tutelage had created the illusion of programmatic, guided instruction. She was still a student, still progressing toward a future that held use and purpose.

Jeri had never consciously thought of her life as still being on a forward track during the three years at Armagh, but not until she had stood in the warden's office had she seen her future disappear like a mirage. He had diminished her. He and his like could still order her about, even outside of prison, with no regard for her hopes or her talents. She was just like any other Catholic in Ulster. No matter how she might cling to an image of herself as beyond his reach, he had diminished her. With no apologies, not even the least hint of remorse or acknowledgement that a mistake had been made, he had made it clear that she was simply a piece of debris that needed tidying.

The people who allowed such things to happen needed to be made to see, and if they would not see their responsibility, then they needed to pay for the lives they so uselessly wrecked. Jeri felt a hot fury at the injustice, and a need for redress that went beyond her own injuries.

Not the arrogance of one man, Arkadia, but the arrogance of all those who give power to such men and think that what happens to people like me are simply regrettable accidents on the way to the larger achievement of order. Their order.

Jeri needed to mend the tattered cloak of dignity that O'Malley had helped her weave and the warden had shredded. In every generation for seven hundred years, England had diminished Ireland, and in every generation, some refused to be made less than they were. Somewhere in the darkness ahead was the way to her own personal destiny, and to reach that destiny she would bind her own life to the land of her cousin, her kin, her ancestors.

Through the night, the car bumped over local roads until, at some point long after midnight, it turned into a lane and the headlights revealed a whitewashed cottage. An older man with a shock of thick white hair appeared. He came close to the car, bent to recognize and nod to the driver, and then turned to look at Jeri.

"He'll take you from here," said the driver's companion.

Jeri hoisted the duffel bag that held the items that she'd brought from Armagh: some clothing; a Christmas card; a letter from her sister Kathleen the nun; a Timex watch; and a guidebook to inns of rural Ireland. The watch and the guidebook had been hers when she entered; the letter and the Christmas card had been the only communication from her family. Not much for starting a new life, but then this was a land where the homesick songs of loss recounted the sorrow of countless Irishmen who had left home and country with less.

Jeri had barely closed the car door behind her before the engine started and the vehicle began to move. She watched it disappear into the darkness. She turned to where the elderly man had been standing and was just able to make out his shock of white hair. He said something, and for a few seconds Jeri was as mystified as if she'd been delivered into the care of a resident of another planet, and she was closer to panic than she ever remembered being. Then she realized that she'd just been spoken to in Irish.

"Talk you to death, those two. You must be worn out from all the conversation."

"Exhausted," Jeri answered in the same language.

"Well, then, follow me. There's a bed waiting for you."

†

Jeri woke when dawn was still more idea than reality. She had slept only a few hours, but once awake, the need for sleep vanished. This day, this dawn, she felt herself alone; it was a novel feeling. She slipped into loose slacks, a t-shirt, and a pair of gym shoes. She had no idea who else, if anyone, was staying at the cottage. She thought she'd heard the sound of a door closing and footsteps leaving before she fell asleep, and she had assumed that the old man had left. Not surprising, since his clothing had looked better than what a rural cottage owner might be expected to wear. She closed her door quietly, eased her way down a flight of steep stairs, and then found her way outside.

Outside.

Overhead, stars crowded the moonless sky, but a thin gray line indicated the general direction of east. The path on which Jeri was standing led the other way, into darkness. She followed it through a wooden gate and then up a steep grade. Nothing stopped her—no wall, no fence. Occasionally the dark shape of a tree or a larger bush gave some indication of its presence, but for the most part, Jeri walked with her attention on the sky. Stars arranged themselves into patterns, and Jeri began to recognize constellations that she knew. Orion for one. Even a city child might learn to see Orion overhead.

The ambient light increased with each step she took, and by the time Jeri reached the crest of the hill and turned to look behind her to the east, dawn had changed from gray to rosy pink. She felt a momentary clenching of her heart as she wished she might share some comment about "rosy fingered dawn" with Arkadia O'Malley, but then she drew a deep breath and set aside the thought. Instead, she became an observer of the age-old drama of night-becoming-day that was playing out before her. Colors appeared and shifted in the sky, dimming the reign of stars, and the massive dark shape of the land began to take on detail and distance.

Her land. Home wasn't a feeling, yet there was no other word for the feeling growing in her. And freedom, maybe. Since leaving Armagh, she had felt no corresponding change within until that moment, as she watched dawn break over her land. Jeri turned and began walking west again and then broke into a loping run. Freedom was real at last. It was part of the uninterrupted sights that filled her eyes, it was every deep breath and the tangy air of sharp scents that she could distinguish even if she didn't have a name for them. It was the sense that she could run forever and no one might stop her. It was the exultant feeling that filled her so full, she might happily burst apart to disperse among the other atoms of the universe.

The sun was well above the horizon when Jeri returned to the cottage. She hadn't reached the door before the aroma of fried ham woke up her appetite. She opened the door to find someone cooking in the kitchen, a room that which was not much more than a sink and stove in a corner of the one-room cottage.

"Oh! You startled me. I thought you were upstairs sleeping. Did you have a nice walk, then? Come in, come in, here's breakfast waiting. I may have overdone it, but I added everything that might go in a fry-up. Except pancakes. I tried to remember what it is that Yanks like, but pancakes are just a little beyond me."

The words were English. The speaker worked a pan of scrambling eggs with a spatula. She wore a faded apron that covered most of her clothes. The table, covered by a brightly colored oil cloth, held only a single plate, but that was surrounded by what seemed an enormous amount of food: a serving plate with slices of ham; a small but uncut loaf of bread; a saucer of jam and a small plate of butter, real butter. Fried potatoes, coffee, a bowl of blackberries.

"Sit. Eat." The woman filled a plate from the frying pan and then handed the plate to Jeri.

Cautiously, Jeri took a seat at the table and tasted the scrambled eggs. The taste of the fresh-cooked food startled her prison-dulled appetite. "Do all new recruits get a four-star breakfast?"

"Only the ones just out of prison. We find it imprints them like a new-hatched chick. Also, they don't realize I'm really no great shakes as a cook."

Jeri gave the woman closer attention—medium height, with curves that were pronounced without appearing soft. She was wearing slacks and a white blouse with long sleeves rolled to her elbows, clothing which looked much more expensive than the faded apron. She had poured herself a cup of coffee and was standing by the sink. Light from the window behind her highlighted coppery blond curls that had escaped from hair tied back from her face by a pale blue scarf. Eyes were a darker blue. The face was pleasant enough, friendly, apparently not discomfited by Jeri's appraisal.

Jeri took another bite. "I thought I'd already gone as happy as possible," Jeri said, "but you've raised the bar even more. Thank you for breakfast. You're an angel."

"Always pleased to find someone with an appetite."

The smiling face of the cook appeared to mean no more than what she'd said.

"You don't speak Gaelic?"

The woman's accent added a slight Irish lilt to BBC standard. "No. I never got much of the Irish. I leave that to Thomas and the others. Thomas is the man who met you here last night. He says you speak the language well."

"Others? Where and who are the others?"

"I'm not to know much about all that, and I don't. You're the only one here for the moment, but Thomas will be along soon to tell you the drill. For now, Geraldine O'Donnell, you're to relax and get used to not being in prison."

Jeri suspected there wasn't much the speaker didn't know; she had the look of a woman who paid attention. "Please, call me Jeri. Won't you sit down?"

"You can call me Millie. I like it much better than Millicent. Thank you for the invitation, Jeri, but I really must run now. I'm sure I'll see you again." She smiled and removed the faded cotton apron, hanging it on a wall hook near the sink. Then she was gone.

Jeri heard the front door open and close, and shortly after, she heard the engine of a car. She thoughtfully gave herself a failing grade for her first lessons as an unincarcerated Provo. She had not noticed any vehicles when she returned to the cottage, and it did not take a great deal of imagination to realize that soon any such lapse might be dangerous. She had let the apparent isolation of the cottage lull her. She had assumed that there were people in charge who would take care of her business. Nor had she known that a simple cotton apron could so completely disguise such a lovely body. She doubted she would ever call the woman "Millie."

†

Jeri gave herself better marks for observation and caution in the days that followed. Thomas came by occasionally, and although his authority was unclear—he might as easily be either a commandant or a caretaker—he cultivated the casually paternalistic attitude of their first meeting. Thomas gave her the IRA manual, the *Green Book*, to study, and discouraged too many questions from her. After years of prison discipline, Jeri had grown accustomed to gathering information indirectly, so she let Thomas tell her what he would and used her own intuition for more.

The other visitors had more circumscribed roles. A bulky man in his late twenties came every third day to take Jeri for long, grueling hikes into the hills, carrying heavier and heavier gear each time. Jeri had thought she kept herself in good shape, but the terrain taxed her prison-diminished endurance. When her trainer wasn't present, he set a regimen that he expected her to maintain on her own. He never gave his name, but Jeri thought of him as Rocky. She felt certain that he disapproved of her for some reason known only to himself, but it certainly wasn't because she slacked off, not when her growing strength was sheer pleasure.

Danny, on the other hand, was a chatty wee man who never used one word when six would do. He taught her weapons. For the initial visits, he never had a firearm in evidence, only pictures of everything imaginable used by every army that marched. "Now here's a darling piece of work," he'd begin. "Look at the sweet curve to that stock and how easy you might fit your hand to the trigger. But looks are, as ever, deceiving, and that lovely form is naught but a piece of shite, one that will work every time in practice and betray you the very first time ever it counts. Ah, now here's our best friend, the Armalite, or the AR-18 to give her real name, though sometimes she's called the 'Widowmaker'."

The curious thing was that Danny's poetic method of speaking stuck in Jeri's memory like an infallible mnemonic device, attached to a variety of armaments she would probably never encounter but which she grew to feel she knew intimately.

Millicent did not return, but although Jeri had to prepare her own meals, the cupboards were often restocked while she was out with Rocky, and occasionally there would be a surprise that reminded her of Millicent saying, "I try to remember what it is that Yanks like."

"I think it's better if you're not seen in the village, my dear," Thomas said when Jeri asked about going to town. "You're not exactly a fugitive, but the Brits have put out a bulletin that one Geraldine O'Donnell, who was supposed to leave Northern Ireland, disappeared before doing so. The local Garda might not arrest you, but they just might let Belfast know where you are. You know how curious people in small towns can be."

"I don't, actually. I've never lived in a small town. At least get me something to read. I've memorized every last regulation in the Green Book, and I don't want anything by Freire or Mao or Marx either. I'd rather read a cereal box than any more political education."

"I'll do my best, my dear. By evening, most of our recruits are too tired to read."

†

"A grand afternoon, wouldn't you say, Arky?"

Arkadia O'Malley had intended to use association time for a meditation on smell. Even in Armagh jail, the scents of early summer seeped in, bringing unexpected memories to mind. She wanted to walk the small patch of outdoors and consider how little humans used smell for information, at least consciously. Most registered what smelled good or what smelled bad, smell as a sense for judgment, and relied on sight and sound for conveying information. She couldn't be sure, but she assumed that if Jill Leary's reason for hailing her had a scent, it wasn't going to be one she liked.

"Say it and be done, Jill. I haven't time for foolery."

"That can't be true, Arky. We've nothing but time here. And a little foolery now and then can be pleasant."

O'Malley gave the matter a moment's consideration. "You're right, of course. So tell me what word you've had of Geraldine.

"Now you've added mind-reading to all your other talents?"

"You talk to me very little unless it's about Geraldine."

"And I'm sure that's my loss. It's true. It's the young Yank I've had word of. Not gone back to Amerikay, so I've heard."

Arkadia O'Malley nodded slowly. She was not surprised. Saddened, but not surprised.

The humor was gone when Leary continued. "We can use her, Arky. She has courage as well as intelligence, and her heart is with us. Maybe our time is the time when we get Ireland back, and if not, we'll join all the brave folk who've struggled against England's tyranny for the last eight hundred years. That's not bad company for our Yank to be in."

"*Tiocfaidh ar lá*," O'Malley said, barely above a whisper, and then repeated in English, "Our day will come. Perhaps you're right, Jill Leary. I was here to teach her, not to keep her. I want Ireland free, too, perhaps more than you and your genuflecting folk can know."

What friendliness had been there disappeared. "I thought you were Catholic, Arky."

"Did you? There are older gods sleeping in our poor land."

"Ach, you're an old romantic. For a moment I thought you were one of *them*." The emphasis on "them" indicated she did not mean romantics.

"Neither am I one of you. I do thank you, though, for the kindness of telling me about Geraldine. That was well done. I wondered. But I suspect that you'll not keep her either."

Arkadia O'Malley watched the Provo woman walk away, leaving behind a chaotic welter of emotions. Gone was the prospect of the exercise she had intended; she was having trouble keeping control of her own breathing. Geraldine's departure had left an ache and an emptiness in Arkadia's heart that she had not anticipated. That was probably why they called it prison. It had been a good many years since she had felt the loss of another so deeply. She knew that Geraldine had not been allowed to say good-bye, nor would a letter from her be allowed into the prison. She would bear it.

Echoes of the conversation with Jill came back to her. "Keep, keeper." Why did variations of that word cling to thoughts of Geraldine, teasing with almost-meaning? She'd tried the word out in other languages, but they were just as elusive with their suggestions of maintaining and sustaining. She let it go. It did no good to clutch for a meaning that would come in its own time.

"How are you this fine day?"

It was Liz. Arkadia had almost walked by Liz and Rosie without a nod. They'd been noticeably companionable of late, careful not to be familiar but letting her know they were there. O'Malley found a smile to add to her nod.

†

After an arms lesson in the late afternoon with Danny, mostly about the Armalite and its history, Jeri was jogging when she heard a car approaching from behind. She considered leaving the road and sprinting across country, but the meadowland, cropped short just here, looked to give scant cover, might even make her a better target. On one side, the road was bordered by a dip, not even a real ditch, but that actually might provide better protection if she waited until the last minute to dive. It was a gamble, one that might give her an edge if she needed one. "Always look for an edge" was a lesson she was taking to heart.

Jeri heard the car slow and gathered herself in preparation for whatever happened next, then she slowly turned her head.

The driver was Millicent, the woman who had greeted her the first morning, the woman who had fixed perhaps the best breakfast she had ever eaten. The woman whose coppery blond curls were even more chaotic from driving with the car window down than they had been on that first morning. Millicent, who was smiling. Jeri smiled back and kept running.

Millicent matched the speed of the car to Jeri's pace. "How are you getting on?"

"Grand," Jeri answered. "Someone keeps my pantry from going empty, though there's not been much in the way of home-cooked meals."

"I've just come from shopping now. There's a place up ahead where I could pull over and we could have tea and biscuits if you like."

"Grand."

Jeri watched the car pull ahead and climb a slight incline before parking at the edge of the roadway. It looked to be a pricey vehicle, but Jeri had only a small acquaintance with the cars of Northern Ireland. She decided that the odd sensation she was feeling was just relief from not having to dive into a ditch.

The cropped field ended at a stone fence at the crest of the hill. An uncut meadow on the far side was being grazed by a flock of sheep. The tall grass nearly hid the animals, despite their white backs against the green. Had Jeri been running by this field as the car approached, she might have left the road to dive into the tall grass, and then she would have missed Millicent.

"I hope a wee bit to eat won't interfere with your run." Millicent set out a thermos and a package of Oreo cookies.

"A wee bit never hurts." Jeri accepted the cup of tea from Millicent and looked out over the field where the wind was making waves ripple through the tall grass.

"You're looking much better."

Jeri looked away from the field to find Millicent staring at her.

"Not that you didn't look well before, but you have a healthy color now. You look, oh," the woman paused and then smiled, deliberately echoing Jeri's expression, "you look grand. More confident."

Jeri didn't feel confident. Millicent's words might be complimentary, but her scrutiny was unsettling.

"You don't look so bad yourself."

Millicent laughed. "Sorry. I suppose I am being rude. How are you?"

"Healthy." They both smiled. "But a bit cut off. America and Russia might have called off the Cold War for all the news I get."

"Not much chance of that. They say Yuri Andropov is ill, but Ronald Reagan is healthy as a horse and still the best of friends with our Iron Maggie. There's a film that's all the rage, called *Indiana Jones and the Temple of Doom*. I fear it will make a mess of real archaeology."

"I thought it was mostly rubble anyway."

"Oh, well done, Jeri. Yes, I suppose so. If you call lovely heaps like Stonehenge and Newgrange 'just rubble'."

"You sound proprietary."

"I am a bit. I do work in the field. There's a site in Clare that we're studying at the moment. Goes back to the Bronze Age. There are even some hints it may be Neolithic."

"What makes a 'hint' of the Neolithic?"

Millicent hesitated, then answered in detail, describing the site and its particular grave style. "We think we've found a wedge tomb. That's usually late Neolithic."

"Or early Bronze Age? I always forget the specific dates." Jeri's comment established actual interest and some knowledge of basics, and won a smile from Millicent.

With some encouragement, and the occasional artful question on Jeri's part, Millicent explained more about the site where she was working. Jeri tried hard to pay attention, tried to ignore how much she wanted to touch the coppery curls, to kiss Millicent. It was almost

61

enough just to savor the company of another woman, particularly one who was speaking with such intensity. Armagh may have been a prison, but it never lacked for the company of women. Besides, Jeri really was interested in Ireland's past. Late afternoon turned to early evening before Millicent regretfully said she had to be getting on.

"Can I give you a lift back? Some of these are for you."

Jeri accepted, and soon found they were far too close to the cottage. She hoped Millicent might come in, she even offered to cook something, but along with a rueful smile she was given her groceries and told to mind how she went.

A few days later, Jeri returned from a hike with Rocky to find a book about Ireland's archaeological past on the kitchen table.

†

Four men and one woman greeted each other briefly in a room where the ornate woodwork matched the heavy frames around a series of paintings whose unifying theme was hunting on horseback. On the wall above a cupboard that held a decanter of very expensive scotch, one man on a placid black horse gazed out from a Seventeenth Century portrait with a look that suggested both pride and ownership, a man well aware of noblesse oblige. He bore a distinct resemblance to Thomas Ormond, who was pouring liberal glasses of scotch for his guests.

"Well, gentlemen, how is our newest recruit progressing?" The question was aimed at Danny and the man Jeri had nicknamed Rocky, but it was asked for the benefit of the fourth man, the one who had called himself Sean at his meeting with Jeri and her uncle.

"She's a whiz, that she is," Danny answered with enthusiasm. "Tell her something once and it's hers. Now I can't say for sure that if she was holding the real thing she might not turn out to be gun shy, but somehow I doubt it."

Thomas nodded. "She's doing much better psychologically than I anticipated. I didn't expect her to accept these isolated conditions so willingly. I would have thought that after years of being incarcerated, the solitude would be weighing heavily, but she seems to be very attuned to the countryside."

"She does outdoors well enough, I'll allow that, but what will that matter if she's to be an ambassador like?" Rocky aimed his question at Sean.

"Not an ambassador, a liaison. We think that with her education and her language skills, she'll be good to send abroad. And she should have no trouble carrying American passports. I know Jill told us she had nerve and could fight, but from what you tell me, she appears to have a talent for more physically challenging assignments. I believe we can send her east for more training."

"Just don't be forgetting she's a queer," Rocky muttered.

"That's neither here nor there," Sean said.

"They're unreliable, everyone knows that. Besides, it's just wrong."

"Let be, Dominic. You're her trainer, not her confessor." Thomas turned to the woman in the room. "Millicent, dear, what are your impressions?"

"Intense. With courage and integrity. Not as damaged by her experience as one might expect, but certainly not untouched. And very intelligent. I'd say that Jill's assessments are accurate. I think we'll find her very useful."

†

Rocky was having to work himself harder in order to push Jeri to her limits. He began training her on rock climbing, and then scaling cliffs while carrying weight, which did indeed work different muscles. For Jeri, the exhilaration of freedom for its own sake was wearing off, but exercise was the surest way of keeping her mind sharp. Daylight was clinging to the landscape far into an evening, so Jeri took to running until the first stars appeared. Though she was not entirely certain, she had decided that the cottage was located near the Slieve Bloom Mountains of County Laois. Irish guidebooks had been plentiful in the prison library. Occasionally she would see other folk about, hiking the trails, but she avoided contact and she varied her routes for her own interest as well as not to establish any pattern.

Whenever her groceries ran low, Jeri jogged along the roadway, but she missed any sightings of Millicent.

One evening, going east rather than west, Jeri paused to examine a wooded area that nested in a valley. She had seen it before from above as she ran a series of hills, and noted that a road disappeared into the trees from the farther side. This evening, curiosity drew her closer, and as she entered a stand of ancient oaks, she realized that she was at the edge of a landscaped estate. She could make out a large house that had been invisible from above, and beyond the house were outbuildings; one even appeared to be a stable. With panes of glass which age had bent from their original shapes, mullioned windows on the house caught and reflected the evening sun like fiery facets on a gemstone. Jeri stopped beneath an oak tree and gazed at the house and grounds, fascinated by a feeling that history had happened there. It was a feeling she'd had before, the sense that some twist of path, some rock, some tree possessed a story that it ached to tell.

"I wondered if you'd ever find this place."

Recognizing the voice but schooling herself not to appear too surprised or delighted, Jeri turned to see Millicent standing several yards away, by the gray trunk of an oak. She must have been watching as Jeri approached. Millicent seemed appropriate to the house and grounds, like them, illuminated by the setting sun. Her unruly curls caught the sun to give her a halo of red gold, and her olive blouse was of some soft material that shimmered in the hazy light, reminding Jeri of Pre-Raphaelite paintings.

"I thought you might be off chasing hints of the Neolithic."

Millicent smiled. "I have been. And more than hints now. We're almost sure it's a Neolithic tomb, but I had to come home for a change of clothes and a reference book."

Jeri gestured broadly. "This is yours." A statement, not a question.

Millicent looked at the house. "Yes. I like to come up here in the evening when the windows catch the light. It seems outside of time now, or perhaps more a part of any time." She paused and appeared to be considering something. "Do you like it?"

"It looks rich, a lovely camouflage for the new socialist Ireland."

Millicent walked over to Jeri's side until she was quite close. "Yes, it is rich. But that wasn't my question."

At the suggestion of a challenge, the cheeky streets of South Boston stirred and Jeri stared boldly at the woman. She wondered if Millicent ever looked anything but beautiful. "Oh, I like what I see. Do you?"

Millicent nodded slowly, then closed her eyes in anticipation as Jeri bent toward her. Only their lips touched. Millicent smelled of smoke tinged with cloves, like an orchid ought to smell. Jeri pulled back. She was afraid her own scent must surely be less inviting.

"I'm sorry. I've been running."

Millicent leaned forward to re-establish contact. "I like that," she murmured.

A deep purple orchid with veins of crimson highlights were the colors coursing through Jeri's mind as the kiss was rejoined. Millicent was a curious experience of yielding energy—initiating nothing but not exactly passive, either, in accepting what Jeri offered. And Jeri was discovering that she wanted Millicent more with each passing second. She moved her tongue to touch the other woman's lips and found herself falling into a mouth ready to accommodate her hunger. Such yielding was an ardent invitation, and Jeri pulled Millicent into an embrace that left no space between them. She buried her face in the soft golden curls that smelled like flowers, intoxicating flowers, and Millicent nuzzled along Jeri's neck, murmuring soft sounds that sent shivers of delight through Jeri. She leaned back against the trunk of the oak and pulled Millicent even closer, searching again for the mouth that was once more there, eager now, telling of a hunger of its own.

"Wait."

Jeri stopped, breathless, and found herself mirrored in eyes that were dark with roused passion.

"Wait ... I ... not here." Millicent was breathless. She gave a small laugh. "I'm not the kind of woman who does this outdoors. I prefer sheets and a large bed. If you can come the day after tomorrow, the same time, I can arrange that."

"I can come right now."

"Yes, I'm rather close myself." Millicent was still leaning against Jeri and one hand was on her shoulder while the other traced idle circles on the bare skin above Jeri's breasts. "But I don't want to be rushed. You need to be savored." She turned her face up for a kiss meant to explain what she meant by savoring, but it quickly turned into the kind that threatened to sabotage any notion of waiting.

"We're saving ourselves, remember, Lady Millicent?"

"Millie, please."

"I'll be back the day after tomorrow, Lady Millie."

Jeri thought she would simply leave and not look back, hoping mostly that she wouldn't stumble and ruin her exit, but as she passed a low hanging bough of the oak tree, she saw that it was full of young, green acorns. The urge to touch something made her reach out and pluck a pair attached to a single stem. When she realized that they resembled two round breasts, she did look back. Millicent was still by the tree's large trunk, in shadow now as the sun sank behind the hills, watching Jeri leave. Jeri tucked the acorns in her pocket.

Loping back to the cottage, she began singing *Whisky in the Jar* and discovered that she remembered all the words.

†

65

The next night, at a room in the country house where Jeri was to meet Millicent the following evening, another meeting took place. Thomas Ormond again poured generous glasses of scotch for his guests.

"I don't know why you're in such a hurry." Rocky stared glumly at the boots on his outstretched feet. He knew the scuffed leather was out of place against the carpeting and that's why he left them where they were. "She's got some talent, but she's nowhere near ready."

"It's not like we're sending her on a mission," Thomas Ormond answered.

"Well and I'm sure I don't know what that would be, but she's an odd one, I'll say that," said Danny. "Today I'm telling her about shoulder-fired rocket launchers and fuck me if she doesn't start clowning about how lovely sweet it would be to hold one so close and lay your cheek on the smooth barrel. I know she was just taking the piss, I do get a bit lyrical about my armaments, but most days you can't get hardly a word from her that's not business, and then today you'd have thought she was soon to meet her sweetheart for dancing at the crossroads. Giddy as a colt, and that's a rare sight with her."

If anyone in the room noticed Millicent's small smile, they likely attributed it to Danny's amusing manner.

Sean sipped from his glass. "I'm sure this plan solves a number of problems. From what Thomas says, she appears to be getting restless. If we send her east, she'll get more extensive training and we'll get high marks from them for being cooperative. She's sure to come back to us a much better asset."

Thomas nodded. "Quite so. She's a bit too independent for my taste, but sending her to make allies is a good move. Don't take me wrong, I like and admire her, but I could wish for a stronger commitment. Sometimes I think it's the challenge that drives her more than the Cause does."

"You'll make the arrangements, Thomas?"

"Of course. I'll start tomorrow, and when I come back, I'll tell her. This will be fine exercise for her languages, if nothing else."

†

Jeri realized that the prospect of meeting Millicent was filling her with an uncharacteristic giddiness, but she allowed it. She had no intention of questioning her excitement. It was the well-being that was so much a part of her days, of her freedom, of food that had flavor, of muscles that relished being used to exhaustion. Millicent was almost inevitable, a lover to go with a landscape without walls, more fantasy than real, but she was also lovely and willing, intoxicating and bewitching.

After restless hours of anticipation, during which she gamely resisted the temptation to sing *Tonight*, Jeri was seized by shyness when she at last saw Millicent. The woman was standing by the same oak, as if she had never moved since Jeri left her. Thoughts of Millicent had been impossible to banish, thoughts that made her breath catch and took her into dazed reveries, but seeing her in reality, Jeri was suddenly unsure of her welcome, especially as she drew near and found the expression on the other woman's face completely unreadable. She stopped a few feet away.

"*Oiche maith,*" she greeted in Gaelic. "Good evening."

Millicent drew a very deep breath. "Hello, Jeri. I don't have the Irish, remember?"

Jeri nodded. She was remembering everything, but something about the land wanted to hear its own language. Something in Jeri had wanted to acknowledge the old gods.

"Come with me, I'll show you my house."

Jeri walked toward the house where windows again glittered in the setting sun. She drew on her irony to cover the vulnerability she now felt. She had the sense that something was bothering Millicent, and, in Jeri's experience from long before Armagh, such bother often preceded a woman expressing second thoughts. Self-protection flared up and Jeri decided that no matter how disappointed she might be, she would let none of it show. Lady Millie could have all the second thoughts she wanted, and be damned to her.

As if she were entertaining an acquaintance come to tea, Millicent showed Jeri a number of rooms on the ground floor of the house, and despite her determination not to give any of herself away, Jeri was impressed with the grandness. She followed Millicent up a stairway lined with large portraits to a room with a piano, a wall of bookshelves full of old and new volumes, and a thick carpet of rich colors in Oriental patterns. Millicent stopped before a cabinet.

"Would you like a drink?"

"I might. Before Armagh, beer was my usual."

"We have ale, of course. Thomas usually pours scotch for me."

"Thomas?" Jeri repeated, using Millicent's intonation.

"Yes, he's my husband. Does that matter?"

Jeri considered. Of course it mattered, but *how* it mattered was another question. She didn't feel any great loyalty to Thomas, but she didn't particularly relish the thought of being a married woman's adventure. Of course, the married woman might no longer be feeling adventurous.

"I'll try a scotch. Does Thomas know about this, Lady Millie?"

"Don't be absurd. Of course he doesn't know." She brought a drink to her guest. Jeri had managed to put a distance between them that had nothing to do with space. "Does it matter?" Millicent asked again.

Jeri frowned, a fierce look that made her appear dangerous. The scotch was thick with overtones, rich with subtleties, and a warm glow spread immediately after she swallowed. It did matter, but so did the fact that Millicent was so close.

Jeri reached out and took the glass from Millicent's hand and set both drinks carefully on a nearby table. Then she turned back and placed her hands on Millicent's shoulders and pulled her close. "This matters," she murmured, and bent toward Millicent. She was angry, unclear as to the exact reason, but the emotion had removed any sense of shyness and it generated an unexpected intensity in the kiss she initiated. Millicent's surprise gave way to an answering intensity of her own.

"My god," Millicent whispered, breathing hard, keeping hold of Jeri's hand. "Come with me."

Focused as she was on the woman, Jeri hardly noticed where they went. When they reached a room with a bed and Millicent turned to her, Jeri gathered the woman into her arms and began another kiss that was triumphant in its anticipation, its confidence, that now the course they were on would indeed be run. Jeri slowly unbuttoned the top two buttons and then slid the silk blouse over Millicent's head. She smiled at the sight of the lacy bra, but she was more interested in what it held, and soon bra joined blouse on the floor. Touching the smooth skin of Millicent's back, sliding her hands down over the curve of her waist, Jeri bent to kiss her breasts and was rewarded as the nipples hardened in arousal. Caressing the woman with her mouth and tongue as well as her hands, Jeri let herself be drawn toward the large bed that Millicent had promised. The small part of Jeri's awareness that was not engaged was astonished. She was sure she was discovering the missing piece to her freedom, and Millicent's response was a miracle of passion—eager and hungry, urgent and demanding.

Thinking continued in only a very small part of Jeri's mind while the rest was intent on responding to Millicent's pleas for more of whatever Jeri was doing. At first, Millicent whispered her excitement, but as Jeri grew bolder, Millicent gave voice to her pleasure, urging Jeri on. Then the words gave way to incoherent moans that were even more encouraging. When Jeri at last slid her fingers deep inside the velvety softness, Millicent gasped and stared at Jeri in amazement, her lips parted, her eyes dark with desire. Jeri moved in her, slowly, deliberately, increasing pressure and rhythm until she was so aroused that the sight and sounds of the other woman's pleasure became her own. Despite Millicent's pleading, Jeri was in no hurry, sure that she knew the way, confident that she could take Millicent far past any expectations. At last, poised on the summit, Jeri took her over and into the darkness, and then it was to be hoped, given Millicent's voicing of her release, that they were truly alone in the big house. Exhausted, they lay in a tangle of limbs, breathing heavily like runners at the end of a race.

Full of pride and yearning for more, Jeri slowly began kissing Millicent, aware that the woman thought herself finished. Jeri savored Millicent's breasts and then moved slowly down, pausing to kiss circles on her belly before moving lower. If this position denied Jeri a view of her lover's pleasure, that was the only one of her five senses that was denied. Fingers, tongue, and teeth once again took Millicent to a far peak, and then propelled her over.

"I've never ... never like this before." Once again they lay tangled, skin glistening and damp, and Millicent moved to kiss Jeri's shoulder. It was the portion of her new lover's body that was closest to her mouth.

Jeri thought to comment about Thomas, but then decided her triumph was enough. "Your pleasure is my own, Lady Millie," she said with mock gallantry.

In a surfeit of sensuality, Millicent had been stroking Jeri randomly, running her hand along Jeri's face in a gesture that spoke of gratitude and wonder. Her hand wandered lower, tracing a shoulder, shyly over a breast, the soft curve of waist to hip, and over the thigh to the inner leg. Jeri was anticipating the hand's move upward when Millicent withdrew it.

"That's nice, don't stop."

Lovemaking had closed the gap between thought and speech, and Millicent was not quick enough to stop herself. "But I thought Jill...."

Later, during one of the many times Jeri recalled this moment in the coming months, she wondered why she had been so surprised. Of course Jill Leary had sent reports to her superiors, and there was no reason that she wouldn't have included prison gossip about Jeri's sexual habits. It was unpleasant to think that strangers knew such things, but the unpleasant could be survived. And she had never really believed that Millicent knew as little about IRA matters as she had claimed at their first meeting. So, where lay the betrayal? Because it was betrayal that had clamped its cold hand around Jeri's heart and spurred her to anger. Later she would remember that what she felt at that moment had happened before, in Boston, when some woman or another who had been attracted by Jeri's Southie background let slip that it was risky sex she wanted and not some low-class lover. Jeri began to gather her clothes.

"Don't go."

"Do you make a habit of shagging all Thomas's new recruits? Or was I just an easy experiment and you wouldn't have to get your hands dirty?" She was almost frightened by the bitterness she felt.

"I'm not sure enough about what you're thinking to give you a real answer. Yes, I knew you liked women, and that made me interested. Please, don't go, I want you to stay."

"You want, I don't want. Maybe another time."

"There won't be another time. Wait, please, I need to tell you something."

†

The next day, when Thomas Ormond told Jeri she was going to Eastern Europe—Prague first, and from there to a place she would find more intense training than she could find in Ireland—she was less surprised than he had expected. He wondered what on earth had made Danny describe her as giddy. Jeri seemed indifferent, as if neither pleasure nor pain might animate her flinty features. He had thought she might react to a change with a bit more enthusiasm.

Jeri had stayed to hear Millicent out. When she learned she was leaving Ireland, the surprise had cooled her hot anger but did little to diminish her feeling of betrayal. Perhaps she had been betrayed by herself, by presuming to dream that her life belonged to her and that joy could be a part of it. She and Millicent tried to make love again, but neither of them could recapture any true ardor, and when Fiona appeared to Jeri, she was expecting the visitation. She had not expected her cousin's look of pity.

Chapter Five

The rushing mountain stream was so cold that Jeri almost released the branch she was clinging to and let the current sweep her back through the narrow rapids. The frigid water only came to slightly above her knees, but her legs were numb, putting her threatened balance in even more jeopardy. Remembering how much effort it had taken to get this far and knowing for certain that the Sadist would order her to stand at attention all night was what kept her in the water. Her name for the instructor wasn't just a private joke; the man might not take any sexual pleasure from the recruits' pain, but he did very publicly relish their failures.

Summoning the resolution for one more step, she used the branch to pull herself forward. Once again in the rugged Carpathian uplands of Romania, she had reason to be thankful for Rocky's rigorous training, but she still had a long way to go before reaching the marker that signaled the end of the exercise. Jeri wasn't sure she could make it. She had already passed two others who had pulled themselves out of the stream only to collapse on the bank. At least they would have some time in the sun before the Sadist got to them.

"Irish!"

Jeri could see no one on either rock-strewn bank.

"Irish!"

A bush to one side seemed to be shaking from more than the wind. Jeri set her teeth, pushed toward the outstretched branches and managed to grasp a twig, a larger twig, then a branch, until she could pull herself toward the bank. A position just a few inches forward revealed the trainee who had called to her, the Yugoslavian boy. He beckoned for her to come closer, and as she did so Jeri saw that he had found a sort of cave within the rocks that lined the stream. As he slipped back inside, she pulled herself out of the water and followed.

The space wasn't particularly deep, more of an indentation than an actual cave, but it provided enough protection to keep them from being seen by either of the Sadist's two minions when they came looking for anyone who had left the water. For just an instant Jeri felt a twinge of regret at failing the course, but then she remembered that she was training for survival, not to win an Olympic medal. Improvisation was part of survival.

"Here." The boy resting against the opposite wall was holding out a piece of chocolate. He'd spoken to her in English.

Jeri took the square, about the size of a cigarette pack and half as thick. It was as good as medicine for countering hypothermia. She ate in small bites, watching the other trainee as she chewed. He wasn't so young, maybe close to her own age, but he would look disarmingly boyish for most of his life. He had thick dark hair and a ready smile that she had already noticed because it was so unusual in the group she had joined. Most of the other trainees were as grim and reserved as Jeri felt herself to be, although she couldn't say whether or not they all carried the same core of banked anger. She knew that anger was her fuel, so she made no effort to lessen it. There were about twenty others, most of them men. The three other women were from the same somewhere and made no effort to include Jeri in their group. Jeri didn't mind. She respected their need to sustain each other. The training camp fostered hostile competition more than comradeship; it was meant to turn out individuals who could survive, often for long periods of solitude.

She eyed the Yugoslav warily. Rafi, that was his name. He'd smiled at her more than once; she'd done nothing yet to encourage him.

"I'm not going to fuck you." Jeri scowled to reinforce her statement.

"Thanks be to God," Rafi said in a passable Scarlett O'Hara accent. "I was afraid you would force me against my will."

Southern belle English and Yugoslavian combined to make a most improbable accent.

"Amazing! You can smile! But not too often, Irish. Please. Even without it, you are almost better looking than I am."

Among the grim and humorless trainees, Rafi's irrepressible sense of fun made him stand out. Jeri had been sure he would wash out early, but instead he had managed to withstand the grueling workouts and trials devised to produce urban guerrillas. He had a wiry strength and fearlessness that his attitude belied. Only during the dreaded nightly study lecture, conducted in German, did he fade into the private silence common to his comrades.

Jeri finished the chocolate and then rubbed her legs. She was beginning to have feeling in them again.

"We must be friends." Rafi broke the silence. "This place is not good for the soul. To succeed here, one must either be willing to serve without question, or so arrogant as to believe that other humans are a lesser species."

"Why would a Yugoslav Marxist care about souls?"

"Everyone should worry about the soul. Besides, I'm half Roma, and you're Irish, so we both understand about souls."

Roma. That was Gypsy. "I'm Irish American. Our souls drowned crossing the Atlantic. So which way will I be corrupted?"

"I don't think you are one who can serve a master without question, Irish."

"That leaves arrogance. And you? How will you survive here?"

"Me? I will be clever, and I will take what they teach and I will put my little soul where they will never touch it." He mimed catching something from the air and furtively hiding it in his pocket, a Yugoslav Charlie Chaplin in the mountains of Romania.

"Shouldn't we be moving on?" The prospect of getting back in the icy stream was daunting but at least now, after resting, Jeri was sure she could finish the course. "The Sadist will soon be sending out his minions to look for us."

"The Sadist? I call him Darth Vader, but I like your name better. All right. Last one in is a donkey's tail."

Rafi pushed himself away from the rock wall and began wading against the current. Jeri followed. It seemed she had a friend, whether or not she wanted one.

†

"Ready, Irish?" Rafi's dark hair resting in Jeri's lap might have made them appear to be brother and sister, except for their apparent romantic interest in one another. He lifted a blue cornflower to tickle her chin. "You be Rosalind and I'll be Orlando."

Annoyed, Jeri brushed the flower away. "Whatever you like, Rafi," she answered distractedly. She had seen someone emerge from the alley behind the building across from the park where they were dallying on the late summer grass. The old building, three stories of gray stone, had probably been built before the second World War.

"'Whatever you like' is not a good translation. You should just use the English title."

"That's as good as you get in Serbo-Croatian, and I'm not about to speak any English in a Belgrade park. Besides, I never liked that play. Quit clowning around, Rafi, I thought I saw something."

Rafi might also be anxious, but if so, he showed it by becoming even more his casual, dilettante persona. "Oh my sweet, fair Rosalind, how can I refuse you anything? I only picked this flower from yon gardens because I hoped it might match your eyes, but I see now that it is but a drab, earthly shade compared to your heavenly hue."

"Jesus, Rafi, do you ever stop?"

"Never, and that was not the man we are waiting for."

Jeri thought he was probably right. So far Rafi's clowning had never interfered with his ability to focus, but this was their first real mission and Jeri's nerves were stretched thin. They had been given their assignments in recognition of their talents, but also for less worthy reasons. They looked like young people who might dally in a park, and while Jeri was adequate in the language, Rafi was a native speaker.

The fiercely intense Irish colleen and the studiedly whimsical Yugoslavian youth were still an unlikely pair of comrades. Jeri's constant anger welcomed the camp's climate of hostile competition while it fueled the energy required for training in the mountain terrain of Romania. Jeri recognized, as the Sadist never hesitated to repeat, that her future survival could depend on the ability to make it as a loner, ready to cut and run at any instant. Her only problem was the dark-haired, Yugoslavian youth with the intelligent, warm brown eyes who insisted on treating her as a friend.

Rafi usually found some way to make Jeri smile, but it hadn't taken long for her to discover that behind his frivolity was an alert intelligence that fitted him for clandestine work. As well as admiring his considerable skill, she began to like him in spite of herself. There were times when her commitment to Fiona's cause did waver, when her vision of Ulster's freedom blurred, and at those times she leaned on the camaraderie offered by Rafi.

A block away a car horn blared, and Jeri was pleased to note that even though she was startled, she held steady; her nerves were under control. Showing no sign of looking away from her, Rafi said, "Ah, here comes our contact. How could you ever mistake him for anything but a dealer? Can these people never play against type? Or do you wake up one morning and decide that with your looks and style, you can only be a criminal?" He had been using her dark glasses as mirrors to keep watch behind him. Slowly, nonchalance manifested in his catlike stretch, Rafi rose to a sitting position.

Jeri's pulse shifted into a higher gear. The world about her took on a bright shimmer as surfaces grew hard and shiny. Everything slowed down so that the background sound of traffic separated into a truck motor, the downshift of a Yugo, the squeal of tires on a small sports car pulling away from a curb. Sparrows chittered nearby as they scratched in the dry grass.

Jeri schooled her face to vapid disinterest in the approaching stranger. Rafi was the connection; she was no more than his complementary accessory. Pretty background. Her hair had grown since her release from Armagh, and she wore a skirt and blouse; she was simply the girlfriend. The stranger gave her no more than a cursory glance and this allowed her to study him more thoroughly.

Rafi was right; the man was clearly a stock villain. He wore a cheap leather jacket that hung over loose pants that might have once been khaki. His unshaven face was thin to the point of appearing rat-like, suggesting he used the drugs he sold. He walked with a slouch, head forward like a near-sighted turtle, and Jeri caught a glimpse of a slight bulge beneath the jacket that suggested he had a gun. So did she and Rafi, but she hoped theirs were better concealed.

"You're a long way from Zagreb, schoolboy." The man pushed a grimy hand through the dark hair falling in greasy strands over his forehead.

"Hey, my mother's from Belgrade," Rafi answered. The statement was a lie, but it gave him the status of being at least part Serbian. As well as being capital of all Yugoslavia, Belgrade was also the capital of the federal state of Serbia, while Zagreb was only the capital of Croatia. Serbia and Croatia were not simply different areas, they had once been separate countries. Official Yugoslavia attempted to ignore ethnic backgrounds, but old prejudices persisted.

"I am a most fervent supporter of Peace and Brotherhood," Rafi said, referring to the official government program for ethnic unity, "particularly if it can make me rich." He gave the man one of his disarming grins. "My uncle says there is money in Belgrade."

"Maybe." With a faint nod of his head the rat-faced man turned and walked away, leaving them to scramble after him. He had not given the code response to the mention of the uncle, but Jeri never doubted he was their contact. It was probable that, as a runner of errands, his place in the pecking order didn't often give him an opportunity to be rude.

Holding hands, Rafi and Jeri followed as he walked the short distance across the park to the street. He waited for a break in the traffic and then all three crossed to the gray stone building where it was expected they would meet the people who actually had the drugs. Then, surprisingly, their guide veered from the main door and led them to a different entrance in the alley. The door slammed shut behind him before they reached it so that they had to re-open it in order to follow. Rafi shrugged, masking any concern he might feel.

They expected their guide to take the stairs up to the second floor. The apartment that their plans had prepared for was on the second floor of this building. Instead, the man was walking swiftly along a corridor that led toward a back entrance. He came to a rear stairway and when he took the stairs there, he took them down. One level lower, he entered a corridor that took them even farther from the park. They were no longer in the building they had entered. More importantly, they were going farther away from their backup protection.

Jeri stumbled and, as she regained her balance, she activated a tracking device in one of her shoes. It had been grudgingly included in their requisitioned materials because their superiors hated using official material for official purposes. According to Rafi, they preferred to sell it. There was even a small chance the little device might work.

Just why they were in Belgrade, the capital of Yugoslavia, hunting drug runners was something their masters in Romania thought unnecessary to share with green recruits to the clandestine world. Jeri and Rafi, along with their backup group, had been instructed to slip into the country on their own and then follow a scenario laid out in the training camp. The exercise had been portrayed as simple and straightforward, excellent for gaining field experience. Rafi had been selected as the contact because Yugoslavia was his home country; Jeri was the only other recruit who could speak Serbo-Croatian.

The rat-faced man paused momentarily at another door and then once again they were in a stairwell. They climbed until they arrived at the third floor. Jeri and Rafi weren't even breathing hard, but the man they were with suffered a sudden fit of coughing and then paused to light a cigarette. The smoke actually smelled fresher than the dank corridor. After several seconds, their guide recovered enough to lead them a short way to a door that he knocked on before opening.

Rafi gave Jeri's hand a squeeze before releasing it, and she hoped this meant that he was as bothered by the change in the original plan as she was.

The room they entered was filthy. A murky haze of smoke further hampered light filtering through grimy windows. An overhead bulb stuttered in a feeble attempt to add visibility but was more annoying than useful. Litter covered the floor, and most horizontal surfaces had become ashtrays. The burn-scarred furniture was a lumpy couch, a couple of chairs, and a table near the window, a table only slightly less cluttered than the windowsills or the arms of the couch. Training had taken Jeri through some rough living, but she found herself hoping that under no circumstances would she be required to sit anywhere.

She counted three more men; this was another departure from what they had been told to expect. They were to be guided to a room and there they would meet another man, maybe two. Certainly not three, and not so far from where they could expect help. Despite their obvious differences, there was something clonelike about the three men in the room—an attitude, a presumable meanness. One was bulky and solid, while the other was taller with a shaved head. These two immediately moved lazily but definitely between Rafi and Jeri and the door.

The man nearest the table, probably the group's leader, was studying them more thoughtfully than his comrades, who simply stared as if Jeri and Rafi were the latest relief from boredom. The leader wasn't much taller than their guide, but he was sturdier and his clothes fit better. He, too, wore the hip-length, loose leather donkey jacket that must be some sort of gangster chic here in Belgrade.

"Were you expecting someone else?" he asked with apparent amusement. His question was addressed to Rafi, who was looking around.

The question was unsettling because they had, in fact, been shown a picture of their main quarry. One Zeljko Raznatovic, who preferred to be called Arkan after a comic strip character, a petty criminal in the Yugoslavian underworld who, of late, had been gaining notoriety as a possible assassin outside the country. Jeri was displeased that somehow they had communicated their expectation of another presence. That was not good spy work.

"I am expecting only the person that my Uncle Dragan said can make me rich. You know my Uncle Dragan?"

This was a fictional name for Rafi's fictional backer who would supposedly profit from selling drugs in Zagreb. In the scenario that was to be acted out, Rafi was a university student who would distribute to all his acquaintances. Uncle Dragan existed, after a fashion, at least enough to make the cover story hold up under light scrutiny, the cover story that should have put them in contact with Arkan.

"Your rich Uncle Dragan?"

"Yes," Rafi replied happily. "He is the one who says I am to meet with Orkin and I will get the goods."

Rafi was a sponge when it came to absorbing markers of the world's pop culture. He didn't expect anyone to recognize the humor behind calling a man who aspired to arch-criminal status after an American bug killer; he did it for his own amusement. Jeri was not amused. Their situation was extremely perilous. Belgrade was known for producing particularly vicious gangsters.

"Arkan." The speaker couldn't resist correcting Rafi. "He doesn't leave home for the likes of you, schoolboy. Just let me know if you have the money. Maybe I can manage a discount if I can get some time with your girlfriend." He leered openly at Jeri.

Rafi shrugged. "She's not much of a girlfriend, but I want to see the goods."

Jeri felt a tingling along her spine. The leer had contained more menace than idle talk; the man intended to act on it. He expected to be in a position to act on it.

"Ivo, hurry up." Jeri used Rafi's cover name with a bored whine. "You said this wouldn't take long."

As she spoke, she turned toward him, using the move to cover her reach through an opening in her skirt for a hip-holstered gun. The bulky fellow behind her caught her eye and smiled the same menacing leer that his boss had. He would not have been out of place in an American biker gang. The third man, bald, with a Serbian eagle tattooed above one ear, kept his unsmiling eyes on Rafi. Ratman the Errand Boy was by the door, staring at some distraction by the couch that probably existed only in his mind. For a few seconds, there was a motionless tableau in the room.

"Is there money in your backpack, schoolboy?"

Rafi shrugged the pack off his shoulders and tossed it on the table.

"I have to go to the bathroom," Jeri whined. Nothing could have induced her to actually use a bathroom in this place, but she wanted to try and get behind the men. Something had gone wrong with the plan, she could feel it, but just how wrong was still unclear.

"Not just yet, pretty thing." The leader took another opportunity to leer. He nodded toward the tattooed head. "Bosko, get the kid."

Jeri's focus reached an even higher pitch as she felt the prickling release of more adrenaline.

The man with the tattoo reached for Rafi and, foolishly, the bulky man by Jeri moved to help his comrade. Jeri shot from the hip. She saw the look of surprise as the bulky man registered that the whole scenario had just changed, particularly for him, before he lurched to the side and fell.

Bosko had a hand on Rafi's shoulder. Expecting resistance, he was easily put off balance as Rafi shoved toward him while taking out his own gun. Quicker than his bulky comrade, Bosko threw himself to the right and avoided the first shot aimed at him, but not the second. Rafi's reflexes were proving as quick here as at the training range.

Jeri was having more trouble. Concealing the gun in her skirt worked fine in theory, but in reality, the material had tangled and she was wasting precious seconds getting the weapon free. Apparently the skirt had also deflected her aim, because the bulky man was only wounded and now he struggled back into the fray. The sight of him getting up, holding a knife, and heaving himself at her enraged Jeri. He should have been down, he should have been out of it, now he should just be dead. She quit trying to free the gun and simply fired, over and over, so that this time when the bulky man fell, he was bloodily, obviously dead.

In the planning phase, the rest of the team should already have burst into the room, but Jeri and Rafi were still alone with two lifeless bodies. The leader of the thugs was gone, along with the backpack and the skinny addict, the open door testifying to their retreat. The backpack had contained real money.

"Irish, come on."

"But— " Jeri didn't want to stay, but the scene had gone so wrong that she felt she had to right it, fix it somehow.

"Now."

Rafi's command moved her out of the room and once in the corridor, it was as if she were released; she followed her comrade without reservation. They descended a wide staircase, not the one they had ascended, and in minutes found themselves back out on the street on a sunny afternoon, as if everything since they had gone indoors was only some trick of a deranged imagination.

"This way."

Rafi took her hand like any ordinary boyfriend might, but he waited until she agreed with his choice of direction before starting to walk. It might appear that he was leading, but he would never have presumed to do so. That was one of the things that drew Jeri to him in spite of herself. They were on the way back toward the building they had first entered, strolling, seeing no sign that the action behind them had been noticed by anyone. Jeri found Rafi's touch more welcome than she would have expected. She had just killed someone, and she was finding it difficult to stay in the present. She hoped she appeared reasonably normal because, internally, she was careening through an array of conflicting emotions. Uppermost was simply the relief of being alive and free, but nausea and fear followed close behind.

Jeri didn't even see the delivery van until it stopped right beside them. A side door opened and she clambered in without help, scowling at the group inside, three men whose names were entirely lost to her for the moment. Two were students like herself and Rafi, the third, an instructor. This was the group that should have followed them into the apartment building, backing them up at the first sign of trouble.

And they had lost the money. That was going to be a problem.

†

The next few hours were a bore and a blur. Jeri and Rafi were taken to a safe house where they were separated and the story had to be told over and over, and each time the narrative was probed by questions that tested for truth, for covering up, for assumptions, for faulty memory. Total strangers kept arriving to ask more questions. Any feelings that Jeri had about killing another human being were sucked dry by the debriefing process. Primarily the questions were about the backpack and its contents. Why had it been on the table? Did they see who took it? Did they see which way the man they assumed had taken it had gone?

Near midnight, they were finally told that would be all for the time being, and the last questioner left the safe house. Jeri leaned back in an overstuffed chair, eyes closed, mentally and physically drained. The hardest part of the last several hours had been keeping her temper in check. Anyone would find it hard to face hostile interrogators attempting to connect them to a theft, but even a thorough understanding of the method used on her had done little to keep Jeri from wanting to either retreat into silence or smash their irksome faces.

"They had some compassion, Irish. Look what I found." Rafi had been prowling and now he stood in front of her, holding a bottle of slivovitz.

"They had great tactics," Jeri grumbled. "They fuck up and we get the blame."

"Fucked up?" Rafi repeated the phrase like someone trying on a new hat. "I don't think so. I think it went just like they planned, like someone planned. Or maybe we're supposed to be dead. I think it was a pay-off, or that someone on our end is going to get a split."

Jeri stared at Rafi, feeling offended that she had not even considered such an obvious possibility. "But what would they tell the people who sent me here? I don't think my homeland would appreciate that I was dead instead of trained."

"Dead is dead, fair Rosalind, and they would be so very regretful. Things always go more wrong than right."

Jeri turned the theory this way and that, weighing it against her memory of the events. It made more sense than accepting that so many things had simply gone wrong. The trouble with thinking was that it brought back the bulky man's presence.

The plum brandy, dry and clear and strong, was welcome, but after a glass, Jeri found herself still agitated. Rafi was saying something, but she couldn't concentrate on the words and his voice was becoming annoying. Without any real forethought, she stood up and walked over to his chair. She bent and kissed him. It was not a tentative, questioning, first kiss.

Rafi was surprised but Jeri gave him no time for thinking, only the option of surrendering to her mounting urgency. More than once, he tried to slow her, tried to make the encounter more personal, but Jeri's need to lose herself overpowered his need to find her. They made it to a bedroom. Jeri's previous encounters that had involved men had never been particularly interesting or stimulating, but the hunger that drove her now required very little from a partner. What she wanted, what she needed, seemed possible if only she tried harder, and part of her was furious that Rafi seemed to be keeping her from her goal. When he did at last understand his role, it was as if he also shed who he was, and then he began to meet her raw ferocity with an unleashed appetite of his own.

The problem was that the bulky man's face kept intruding. Jeri would have sworn she remembered little about him, had found it difficult to describe him during the debriefing, but now she saw his face with terrible clarity, even to noting that his eyes were an icy blue and a small, sickle-shaped scar was located just to the right of his nose. It was when she became aware of Fiona's presence behind the bulky man that Jeri screamed in despair, and drove harder for what Rafi could give her at that moment. At last, after an eternity that was more battle than lovemaking, she reached a space where there was no one else, and then Jeri found release. Exhausted, she lay still until her breathing was steady again, and then she slid from the bed's disarray and went about retrieving her clothes. At the door, she looked back to find that Rafi wasn't dozing as she had expected. Instead, he was staring at her, and not like a lover.

"We will never, never do that again," he said, more serious than she had ever seen him.

"Why? I don't remember you asking to quit." Still angry, the sneer hid the fact that she also felt relieved.

"That was not you. For that matter, that was not me. I do know I must not lose you, so we will never do it again."

A number of things came to mind, cutting, sarcastic, clever things, including an argument that Jeri thought that this indeed had been her, but she resisted saying them. In spite of herself, Jeri was moved by his speech, and almost embarrassed.

"As you like it," she said in English, and strode out of the room. A few seconds later, after he worked his way past her tone to the words, Rafi's laughter followed her.

†

They worked at forgetting, but a certain awkwardness remained between them. Rafi's jokes were often forced, and Jeri laughed where before she might simply have ignored him. Still, they now had the will to maintain and keep a friendship along with the belief that they could trust each other. Then they were given a new assignment, one that made the trip to Belgrade appear like a picnic.

"So you get to be Yugoslav again, while I'm to be a Cuban student who is really an American CIA agent."

"I envy you, Rosalind. Such a role to test all your talent."

"That's bullshit, Rafi. I'll be an *agent provocateur*. I'll be pushing students to cross a line into real criminal activity."

"I do not think you will have to push these Chechens too hard."

"They want their country to be free. What makes Grozny different from Belfast?"

"Don't think Ireland, think about the American Indian Movement in the U.S."

"Yeah, well, they have my support, too, Rafi."

"Enough! I'll have to report you for anarchist thoughts if you say another word."

"And you don't?"

"I am a good socialist. I want the best for the most. Seriously, Irish, I am sick of the kind of empty corruption I grew up in. My government pretends to socialism, but it just bribes the people with shopping trips to

Italy."

"And you think that the people who run our school are different?"

It was his silence that made Jeri give him a sharper look. She had always discerned a streak of idealism in Rafi, but it appeared to go deeper than she'd thought. For a few seconds, they stared at each other in mutual unhappiness. They would go where they were sent, good soldiers and young, more willing to follow the directions of people who took command than they cared to admit. If this particular stretch of their chosen road made little sense, the way must surely eventually lead to the better world that wiser minds than theirs had envisioned.

†

By the time they began the long rail journey to the Soviet republic of Chechnya by the Caspian Sea, Rafi was once more his usual irrepressible and exasperating self.

"So, Elena—I like Elena for a name. It suits you. Tell me again why a beautiful young woman from Cuba is going to Grozny in the middle of Russia."

"It appears that my mother could not resist the charms of the handsome Russian adviser who was helping Castro maintain his—"

"No, nyet, no. No politics. Just family."

Jeri, working at adding a Cuban accent to her Russian, nodded. "My father's mother is still there. I am going to visit my *abuela* and stay with her while I finish my degree in oil engineering."

"Ah, *abuela,* your grandmother."

"Over the rivers and through the woods to grandmother's house we go."

"What is this, what, what?" His questions matched the clackety rhythm of the train.

"A song, Rafi. One of those kid things you learn. For Thanksgiving or Christmas."

"Yes? Teach it to me."

Jeri obliged, the noisy progress of the old train masking their voices. Not that any potential eavesdroppers were likely at this point. They made a joke of translating the song into Russian, and then Rafi taught Jeri some songs from his own youth.

Still, there were days of traveling left as the train skirted the Black Sea. At some point in the journey, the last of their awkwardness drained away. They talked about a thousand topics, finding areas of disagreement as stimulating as those of agreement. Sleeping on the worn seats was uncomfortable and cold, and more than once they woke to find themselves huddling together for warmth, a situation that produced only good-natured insults as to who was taking room from whom. Only about their pasts were they reticent, and not because they distrusted one another but because neither one of them wanted to add that particular burden to the other. Jeri did learn that Rafi had a younger sister, and he learned her family was somewhat larger. Beyond that, they kept their own secrets.

†

All journeys end. A day before reaching Grozny, they moved to separate cars and became strangers. For the duration of the assignment, they would have no apparent contact. Rafi would be Jeri's link to their handlers, but they would communicate with each other only through signals.

As planned, Jeri arrived at her purported grandmother's small apartment only to find that the woman had been unexpectedly called away to Moscow, leaving behind a message that her student granddaughter should make herself at home. From that base, much was left to Jeri to improvise how to make the mission work.

Her first order of business was to make contact with the students suspected of anti-Soviet activity. It was easy enough for Jeri to identify the woman she had been instructed to cultivate. Mirynia Kadynova was studying for a degree in Petrochemical Engineering, the field that Jeri was also supposedly pursuing. For a while, Jeri simply stalked Kadynova, discovering her habits and rhythms, the people she talked with, ate with, studied with. Jeri made no attempt to hide her presence, only her interest. She wanted the Chechen woman to become used to seeing her around.

Jeri also walked about Grozny. The city, a major center for oil refining for close to a hundred years, was a hub for oil engineers. It had started life centuries before as a fort, and its name meant "terrible" or "fearsome", but whatever had given rise to that name was far in its past because now the city was often called the "Pearl of the Caucasus". Wide boulevards rewarded a walker with lovely parks and beautiful plazas, pleasantly surprising to a walker who had expected to find only drab Stalinist grays. As Elena the student, the city's several theaters would be beyond Jeri's means, but she took advantage of the museums. Learning wasn't simply part of her cover, it fed her heart.

Almost as if time had folded upon itself, Jeri felt as if she had returned to Oxford. Physical similarities between the two universities were nonexistent, but the sense of the two places was easily merged. Jeri hadn't been in England that long before she had gone on holiday to Ireland. Now, once again she was in an unfamiliar setting dedicated to scholarly pursuits. The most unsettling personal response was that Jeri found herself longing for a sexual encounter. She found herself staring after women she found attractive, no particular thoughts in mind other than a kind of dozing reverie, which held her until something actual roused her back to the present. It was as if, completely anonymous and alone, some part of herself clamored to be known and acknowledged.

A forgotten memory from Oxford emerged, a memory of a tall woman with gray eyes and light brown hair, and that long English face that can project a range of intelligent emotions. Just as now in Grozny, Jeri had been beset by heightened sexual longings, dreaming of encounters by night and gazing after strange women by day. The English woman had met her eyes one particular day, and Jeri had felt her wooly longing begin to focus, to take aim. Surely there had been a similar speculation in the other woman's eyes when she looked at Jeri. Thoughts of how to meet the woman had intruded when she ought to have been studying, and when Jeri left Oxford for her vacation to Ireland, she was sure that she would approach the woman when she returned.

"You look homesick."

England had been so strong in her mind that the comment in a language other than English startled Jeri. For a few seconds, she just stared at the young, round face looking at her with such sympathy. At Mirynia Kadynova. Then she realized this was a great stroke of luck and, careful to add a Spanish accent to her Russian, she answered, "I am. I am not used to cold weather."

"This? This is only autumn."

"I know, but I am from Cuba," Jeri responded wistfully. "I am Elena Ramona Sanchez. My father was Russian and even though he and my mother never married, my grandmother is most attached to me. I was supposed to be staying with my grandmother, but she has gone and now I am staying by myself." Jeri dumped the information with the gush of someone who had been long deprived of someone to talk to.

"You have a place to yourself?" Mirynia was clearly impressed. "But no one our age ever has a place of their own."

"Perhaps that sounds good to you but I'm a terrible cook and, besides, all your food is so strange. I haven't had a decent meal since I got here."

"Then we must change that! I am a good cook; I will make you the best meal ever."

Jeri felt Mirynia's excited hand on her arm and was sure that the woman was straight. In Jeri's experience, only straight women were so thoughtlessly flirtatious with other women. But she hadn't been lying about missing a decent meal.

So began Mirynia and Elena. Jeri decided that the old-fashioned term "chums" best described the pair of them. They went for walks together, went to the university together, where they separated for classes only to meet afterwards. Mirynia's enthusiasm for the apartment was boundless. She praised the view which overlooked the Sunzha River and the wooded hills beyond, she loved the small refrigerator and stove that actually worked, and this meant that she found various excuses to stay over. Jeri readily agreed. As part of her cover and assignment, this was all working better than had been expected, but the downside was that Jeri always had to be on guard against contradictions in her story. She used a certain clumsiness with the language to give her time to consider replies to questions about a past that she had originally thought only needed to be imagined in outline. Mirynia was relentless in her questions and they concerned areas that Jeri knew little of in the United States, much less Cuba.

She was forced to use Rafi as the prototype for the boyfriend back in Cuba whom Mirynia found endlessly fascinating. Jeri had thought that the weakest point in her cover would be her scant knowledge of chemistry, but weaker still turned out to be her lack of familiarity with girl-talk. Mirynia wanted to know about Western hair styles and skin cream, and theories of how best to apply make-up. She wanted to talk about boys, and she assumed that her new Cuban friend had loads of experience. Jeri longed for some question on the Periodic Table of Elements, something, say, about the noble gases, rather than having to field one more query about how to have good sex.

Mirynia's major concern was her own background and its intersection with Soviet history. Her grandparents had been deported to Central Asia after Stalin decided that Chechens had collaborated with the Nazis. When the deported Chechens were allowed back in their homeland in the mid-Fifties, Mirynia's parents had been rather more than less assimilated into Soviet culture, although this was not true of all their countrymen.

"I heard Shamil say that he would never marry a woman who had

86

gone to University, but I cannot get him out of my heart. You have seen him, Elena. He is so handsome, isn't he?"

Jeri had met Shamil and had no argument. He was handsome, but she didn't like him. When Mirynia introduced the two of them, he had nodded coldly and then subjected her to a silent scowl.

"I like Ramzan better," Jeri answered. "At least he has good manners."

"Do you? I will tell him, if you like."

"No, no. That's not what I meant. I am engaged, remember? I just meant that I think Ramzan would be a better choice for you."

At their first meeting, Jeri had thought that perhaps Shamil suspected her of being what she was, spy or lesbian or American, but then she realized it was her cover persona that he disliked. He, too, had decided that a single Cuban woman almost certainly had looser morals than a good Islamic Chechen woman. She was also an obviously educated woman, which added to the marks against her. Jeri had attempted to give her new best friend a basic course in feminist theory, and Mirynia agreed with everything Jeri said and then promptly contradicted it.

"You can do better, Mirynia. You do solid work, you are so smart, and you can make a future of your own choosing."

"But I can't be in the same lectures as Shamil. If he sees me as a competitor, he will never see me as a possible wife. It is easier for you. Your men must be so much more accepting of smart women."

Jeri was discovering that she didn't like being a spy. A brief camouflage, a moment's lie, the forged documents to get you through a checkpoint, those were all simply moments in a battle. This business of being someone else for a sustained period, of being an alien someone else, felt like having to bear up under a slow, corrosive, acid drip. She longed to be a strong sword flashing in sunlight, not a stealthy dagger striking in the night. Even when she decided there was no more to be gained by pretending and that it was time to take the next step by appearing to reveal herself to Mirynia, she was only replacing one lie with another.

At least it was gratifying to experience Mirynia's surprise. The young Chechen had never doubted a word of Jeri's cover.

"But what about your grandmother? Is she American also?"

"I have no grandmother. It's just a story to make it okay to have this apartment."

"You look Cuban."

"Oh, I am. That part of the story is true. Many Cubans who went to America have been recruited by the CIA."

"And Rogelio? Is he real?"

Jeri decided that it was best not to completely deflate Mirynia's image of her. "Oh, yes. Rogelio is truly *mi esposo*."

Mirynia nodded slowly, more silent than usual. Jeri could see the machinery of her mind in motion, and when she suddenly remembered something that meant she had to return to her own dormitory, Jeri was not surprised. Mirynia at last had a piece of information that would get Shamil's attention, and she could not wait to take it to him.

Jeri watched from the window as Mirynia left. When the young woman was out of sight, Jeri went out herself. She walked briskly for about a kilometer. As she approached a corner kiosk, she suddenly seemed to notice a stone in her shoe. Leaning against a building, she bent, took off her shoe, and shook it out. Before she stood up again, she drew a quick short line on the building near the pavement with a piece of chalk concealed in one hand. She stood and proceeded briskly to the kiosk. The line she had drawn was short, likely to be overlooked by most passersby, but it told Rafi that she had crossed into a new phase in the assignment. She bought a paper in Russian and went back to the apartment overlooking the river.

†

Jeri slept fitfully, waking now and again to go over the story, but she could find no good basis for her worry. The worst that could happen was that Shamil and his friends, with no intention of committing treason, would turn her in to the authorities. Since Jeri's assignment had originated with the authorities, that would be the end of it. Jeri had never, in the times she'd been in their company, gained anything more than a feeling that they preferred being Chechen to being Russian. If Shamil had always been overtly hostile, Ramzan and the others had always been simply polite, students more prone to being carefree than rebellious.

But Jeri could not shake the feeling of dread that accompanied her to the university the next day. As usual, she met Mirynia for classes. This was ordinarily a late day, and they often spent part of the afternoon studying before the last lecture. Jeri had prepared herself to meet the boys, assumed that they would be curious about the American agent, but instead she found only Mirynia in the study room. The boys were nowhere in sight.

"What happened to Shamil?" she asked. "I thought he and Ramzan would be here."

Mirynia shrugged but could not quite manage to sound offhand. "Oh, they were here, but then they decided to skip."

Jeri almost felt sorry for Mirynia, sorry she was such a poor liar. After the lecture, she and Mirynia began walking back to the apartment through the sunny but chill late afternoon. They even stopped to buy something Mirynia said she needed for the meal she intended to cook.

Leaving the store, Jeri saw Shamil across the boulevard; he was trying not to be seen. Though she ignored him, she had noted the look on his face. Even in the scant seconds available, his hatred was clear. All the way back to the apartment, the skin on Jeri's back twitched as she expected some kind of attack, and yet the two young women strolled on without an apparent care in the world.

Just as they reached the doorway, Mirynia's hand flew to her mouth.

"Elena, I forgot. This is the night we have the dorm group meeting. I must attend. Oh, I am so sorry. Tomorrow I will come and cook."

It was a fairly good performance, better than the earlier lie. Jeri might have been convinced if she hadn't known this was not the regular night for a dorm meeting. She watched Mirynia walk away, using the opportunity to scan the neighborhood. Mirynia wasn't so good an actress that she could avoid looking to her left as she passed a corner, and whoever was there wasn't so good at being clandestine that they knew to stand far enough back. The setting sun had lengthened shadows. Two shadows.

Jeri went upstairs. She checked the door, but the apartment had not been entered in her absence. She hesitated for a few seconds and then decided to trust her instincts. She would break silence. She crossed to the telephone.

"I've been blown," she began. The line went dead.

This was worse than she had imagined. Mirynia had been sent to make sure she returned home, and now, deprived of a phone, she had effectively been isolated. There was no mistaking the look she had seen on Shamil's face, the hatred mixed with anticipated pleasure, and the severed phone line provided confirmation. Jeri could only assume they intended to kill her.

Her mind began racing on several levels. She had no idea of the size or makeup of the Chechen group. Learning that would have been the next step. Becoming friends with Mirynia had only been the beginning of finding a way into the resistance group, if such a group actually existed.

It wouldn't do at all to assume that the few boys she had met through Mirynia were the only ones involved, not if she meant to escape.

And how was she going to do that? It was dark out now. Clearly they had wanted her back in this building, in the apartment. They would come for her here. She had no idea how soon. The front and side entrances would be watched, and the river cut off escape to the rear.

How had they found her out so quickly? It didn't matter. Not much mattered now. Now she needed to work out where to stage the last battle. With the lights out, she chanced a look through the front window. There was still a lot of foot traffic, people from the neighborhood. She guessed that nothing would happen until later in the evening. As she watched, she saw several figures that she guessed were there for her. More than she expected. She was being taken more seriously than she had expected, and she could only assume that whoever was out there meant to make some sort of example of her, send some sort of message. That was when she knew she was going to die.

A world away from anyone she knew or cared about, she was going to die during a senseless mission that meant essentially nothing. The absurdity of it struck Jeri with the force of a blow and made her furious. She peered again through the window. Traffic was sparser now. An elderly woman burdened by two bags approached the front door; a drunk staggered by on the far street causing a mother herding two small children to cross to avoid him. And the watchers. Jeri thought of Arkadia O'Malley, and the knowledge that she would never see the woman again filled her with sadness.

Arkadia O'Malley would not approve of this death. Most likely, she would not approve any of the choices Jeri had made since leaving prison, but this in particular she would find useless. At least Rafi was safely away. Jeri had accomplished that much by the telephone call. Rafi was a good man and Jeri hoped the world held what he was searching for.

A scuffle outside on the street sent her senses into higher gear. She would go down fighting, that was for sure, and at least it was good to be quit of the need for pretense. Then Jeri realized it was the drunken man carrying on and, for a second, she was angry at the notion that as she lived her last moments, something so dismally ordinary was also occurring. Then, momentarily, she was amused. This was a Southie moment for sure. Nothing important ever happened without somebody nearby being drunk.

"Stell-la!" The slurred name was called out so loudly that Jeri heard it clearly. In a heartbeat, she knew it was Rafi. He was the drunk. He was calling to another building, but no one else would have the gall, the humor, to scream out the signature name from *A Streetcar Named Desire* on a Russian street corner.

"You know you love me! Stella!" The words were Russian; the name was for her. In that instant, Jeri loved Rafi unconditionally. The fool. He had to leave. He couldn't help her; he needed to save himself. Their superiors would kill him for this if the Chechens didn't.

"Do not throw away our love! Remember?" He started singing a song distorted by shouting and badly out of tune and Jeri had trouble making out the words. It must be some Russian folk song.

Someone in a building near Rafi called out for him to go away. He only sang the louder.

"Above cold river," he sang as if accompanied by a balalaika, "through dark forest …"

Now Jeri did laugh out loud as she understood. She didn't even need the rest of the song.

"… to house of grandmothers we go …"

Again, someone called out for Rafi to leave. This time he seemed to take the instruction to heart, but Jeri was already making preparations.

Of course. She should have thought of it. The watchers must surely assume, as she had, that the Sunzha River was a barrier. Even though they would be watching the back of the building, they wouldn't expect her to go to the water. A slim chance perhaps, but any chance was worth taking. The biggest danger would be the river itself. The Sunzha was deep here, and the current was strong, but Jeri was a good swimmer. On a normal day, she could cross. On a normal, summer day. She had no idea what the water temperature would be, but it was undoubtedly cold enough to bring on hypothermia and that could kill her as surely as any Chechen.

Among the things she had brought to Grozny was a duffel bag that was supposedly waterproof. She quickly stowed her warmest change of clothing and hoped the bag worked as well as purported. Now she began to wonder just how much time she had. Jeri went into the kitchen and stripped down to bare skin. On the stove was a container of lard that Mirynia used for cooking, and Jeri slathered it over every inch of herself that she could reach. With a wooden spoon, she managed to get most of her back, but in particular, she coated her face and hair. Then she dressed again in loose clothing.

She thought about taking the stairs to the ground floor, but decided not to risk it. Undoubtedly there were now people hunting her inside the building. Action and the possibility of escape had focused her so that only scant moments passed between her making the decision to leave the building by a second floor window and actually doing it. She dropped her bag first and the sound of the muffled thump as it landed gave her a sense of how far the ground was. She slipped out and gripped the ledge with her hands, ready to drop if necessary, but her feet found enough unevenness in the brick to allow her to work her way down several feet to another level. It took precious seconds to keep a grip because of the grease on her hands, but still she thought she might be able to make it all the way to the ground until she heard someone call out from the corner of the building.

Jeri dropped the rest of the way, and it was still far enough down that she felt pain in her legs, but nothing broke, and she scrambled quickly to regain her footing. She grabbed the duffel bag and headed for the river. The voices behind her were angry as well as alarmed. She stumbled and fell as she ran, bare feet unprotected from the sharp rocks, but fear was a useful antidote to pain. Then she was close enough to leap into the dark water.

The icy, shocking cold took her breath away. The mountain training camp had not neglected cold water swimming, so Jeri was somewhat prepared. Clothing was only a hindrance now. She had dressed knowing this moment was ahead. It didn't take long to slip out of what she was wearing while keeping a grip on the duffel bag. Then she launched herself into the deep.

Jeri tried to remember how far it was across, but she had spent very little time looking out at the river. If she got out of this situation alive, she would remember never to ignore any part of her surroundings. The river was wide, that she remembered well enough, and she had noticed that the current seemed to be slower on the far side, swifter by the near. That was an advantage, if true, because the cold was going to leach her strength.

She angled downstream, letting the current help her progress. The dark water was cold, and not a cold that the body could get used to. This had to be endured and fought. Anything was better than staying in the apartment and waiting for some kids with skimpy beards to come shoot her. Arkadia O'Malley might even approve of going out like this. The training camp had been in the mountains and there had been sessions in water this cold, but it had never been necessary to endure immersion of this duration.

Jeri was competent enough at swimming, but it wasn't something that she had ever really enjoyed. Not like her sister, Kathleen. Kathleen had taken to water like a fish; she even did well in swimming meets organized by the city for poor kids in the summer. St. Mike's didn't have the money for frivolous things like swimming pools. Too bad Kathleen, now known as Sister Mary Brendan, wasn't attempting to swim the Sunzha River; she'd be a lot closer to the other side by now, but then she'd be swimming in her nun's habit and that would drag her down. Maybe not. That would make it a bad habit, and Kathleen O'Donnell had never allowed herself any bad habits.

Jeri recognized the pun as a sign that her mind was drifting. The cold would do that, would defocus and confuse her. The current was stronger now, and she wanted to just drift, to pull in her arms and legs for warmth. She struggled to swim, she couldn't just let the river carry her, but exertion was also working against her survival. Swimming made one lose body heat faster. The less she did, the longer she could stay alive in cold water. Her body would try to keep the core warm, protect vital organs like the heart and brain, but cold blood moving in from arms and legs would diminish her chances.

Her hands were numb. Jeri consciously checked to make sure she still had the duffel bag. That bag would save her life if she made it to the other side. To grandmother's house. Rafi had been a genius to remember the song. And how to tell her where to go. She didn't feel so cold now. Maybe she could just drift, just let the river carry her until she bumped against a shore. Surely the Chechens had given up following her by now. They wouldn't expect her to survive.

But she would survive, damn it. And not by thinking of just drifting with the current. Jeri moved her arms, her legs. It was easier now. Really. She had at least made it through the strongest part of the current. She could see nothing but darkness ahead of her. At least that meant she was going in the right direction and the city was behind her.

She felt something against her knee. Christ, she was in shallow water and her feet were too numb to know it. Jeri stood with difficulty. Fell. Stood again. She stumbled through the water on feet that had no feeling. She was naked. She should put some clothes on. But not until she was out of the river. Not smart to open the bag, not when she might fall and get everything wet. She wasn't walking, she was teetering on what felt like far away stumps.

Then her heart sank. She had not escaped. Someone was coming toward her. Well, death would be warm. She could rest.

"Stella! I hate to do this, you are so very naked and beautiful, but you must have clothing. Put my coat on. Come on, keep going, I've got you now, my poor, brave Stella. My smelly, greasy, grand Stella."

"Think I liked Rosalind better."

"What? Hush now. I can't understand what you're saying, anyway."

Jeri decided not to argue. Stella wasn't that bad.

†

"I still don't get it, Rafi." Jeri was staring moodily into a glass of ruby wine. The two of them were seated at a restaurant table beside a plate-glass window overlooking a snow-covered slope. Visible in the valley below was the city of Sarajevo, in Yugoslavia, but Jeri was oblivious to the charm of the view.

"I keep going over everything and I don't remember a minute when Mirynia seemed suspicious. How did they know I wasn't who I said I was?"

"Give it up, Stella. You'll never know. You're wasting our leave, and I didn't bring you to Yugoslavia to have you be miserable. Don't you find this view familiar?"

Jeri thought the view fine enough, but she didn't remember seeing it before.

"Every tv reporter in the world used it for background in last winter's Olympics. How could you miss it?"

Because I was in prison, Jeri thought, but didn't say. For Rafi's sake. For herself, she would have trusted him with anything.

The city was still full of reminders of the games. Everywhere they went, they saw the clever logo of the stylized snowflake or the games' official mascot, Vuchko, the little wolf with the happy grin. Jeri, however, still thought of Sarajevo as the place where WWI began rather than as the site of the most recent Olympics.

"Let it go, Stella." In Serbo-Croatian the name sounded exotic. "There are things a good spy will never know."

"I'll never be a good spy, Rafi. I hate it."

"Ah, now I understand. If you had succeeded, you could just quit, but you think you failed, so now that competitive heart of yours needs to stay and win. Listen, here's what I think happened. I think those students, their group, already had a CIA contact. Don't look so surprised. Do you think there are no American agents in Russia eager to exploit a place like Chechnya? I think that's why the Russian major who debriefed us seemed so pleased, because we proved that such a possibility was no possibility but a fact. We have flushed the squirrel."

Rafi paused to give Jeri time to examine the idea. When he started speaking again, he looked as happy as the various representations of little Vuchko. "Now I am going to distract you. I am taking you to a bar where, impossible as this may seem, the women will find me much less interesting than you."

Perhaps time's reputation for healing was not all that overrated. A few days later, as Jeri woke full of memories of the pleasure she and the woman nestled against her had found during the night, it occurred to her that she might just stay in Sarajevo. Or go back to the United States. It wasn't too late to put her life back on the track it had been following before she went to Ireland. She could find a life like other people, pursue her own interests and make her own goals. She could even, like other people, pursue her own happiness.

That was the day that the order to return to Ireland arrived. The vision of a different life disappeared as if it had never been. Jeri took only soft memories away from Sarajevo, along with a gift from Rafi of a T-shirt with a brightly colored, smiling Vuchko.

Chapter Six

The luxury suite of the Rotterdam hotel made Jeri uncomfortable. Cream-colored curtains, bouquets of blossoms tastefully placed on shiny accent tables with scroll-carved wooden legs and marble tops, a thick carpet of beige with flecks of gold and rust, and none of it related in any way to the room where she had last slept in Belfast. In the crowded Catholic Ardoyne section, that room — with its cracked ceiling, lumpy mattress, and the nearest toilet two floors down — was at least appropriate for someone fighting to free an oppressed people. It occurred to Jeri that Rafi would laugh at such thinking, warning her that the danger of becoming a puritan meant losing the ability to recognize rare moments for rest and renewal. If he were here, he would probably already be sprawled on the large sofa.

Jeri prowled through the several rooms, took an apple from a fruit basket, and then, turning off the lights so she would be less visible, went out onto the balcony. At least she could savor the crisp sweetness of the apple along with the irony of her circumstances. Several days earlier, her unit had been planning a bank robbery, a job that ought to go like clockwork with a minimum of drama or fuss, when her OC told her that she had been picked for something special. Soon after, just about every automated mode of travel except a ski lift had been used to disguise her transit from Belfast to Rotterdam. A handler had met her to explain the mission and give her all the necessary documents, funds and suitable clothing. Once Jeri had understood the identity she was to assume, the handler had disappeared from the private train car where they met.

Through the smother of fog and drizzle, few lights were visible to show that Europe's busiest seaport lay below the balcony. Finishing her apple, Jeri imagined tossing the core into the mist as if into a river. The notion betrayed how tired she was. Since leaving Belfast, she had only slept in short naps. She would never give in to an impulse as dangerous

96

as it was senseless. That tossing the apple entered her mind at all was an indication of her discomfort with the role she was playing.

Just the fashionable outfit worn by Condesa Maria Isabella Josefina Pilar O'Donnell y Monterio, such a far cry from what Jeri O'Donnell would wear, made her uncomfortable. That the two women shared a name was purely accidental. Those who were interested in such things knew that the O'Donnell, chief of the clan, was also the equivalent of a prince among Spanish royalty. There really was a Doña Maria Isabella among his titled relatives, but she was an elderly woman who hadn't left her villa in the lower Austrian Alps in over a decade. She would most likely never learn that Jeri had borrowed her identity. Dona Maria Isabella's name was also on the board of directors of a linen factory in the Irish Republic.

Jeri changed from a Condesa's clothing into her own and immediately felt better. Remembering the lessons of Grozny, where what seemed a secure refuge had suddenly become a trap, she decided to leave the hotel and put real details on the maps she had studied on the way to Rotterdam. She might be tired, but she would sleep better after gaining a fuller image of the city's reality. The addition of a knit cap would turn her dark wool slacks and a pea jacket into an effective disguise. She could pass for a dock worker in the port city. She'd been forced to leave her favored Sig P226 behind in Belfast, despite her protests, but it was unlikely that Dona Maria Isabella would have such a gun. Her handler had agreed that at least a Condesa might have a small pocketknife. Still, the absence of any other weapon made her uneasy.

Checking that the hall was empty, Jeri took a back stairway without meeting anyone. Before leaving the hotel, she assured herself that the lock on the exit door would cause her no problem when she returned. Outside, the chill mist from the North Sea obscured any view beyond a few feet. Jeri had memorized most of Rotterdam's streets and byways from the maps, but it took some luck to find her way through the drizzle to the particular dock she was looking for. Situated on a delta where three major rivers entered the North Sea, Rotterdam had been a port for at least a thousand years. More than once Jeri had to retrace her steps, but the walk worked wonders for calming her nerves and restoring her focus. In the end, she located the dock with the warehouse holding bales of flax labeled for shipment to Cork in the Irish Republic.

The cargo was real. Everyone in the business knew that Dutch flax made the best linen. The factory to which the bales would be trucked from Cork was real, too, and it manufactured a high quality linen for the world market. The factory was part of the economic boom which was making the south of Ireland a beacon of prosperity while the six counties of the north bled and suffered. It was only fitting and proper that the bales would soon contain arms that were destined for Ulster's rebels.

Nothing of any note marked the warehouse. Head down against the weather, Jeri walked past it until she was several blocks away, merely someone in transit. Then she took an alternate way back to a doorway not too distant from the building and stepped into its dark shelter, where she became only a shadow. She wasn't looking for anything in particular; she wanted to absorb the feel of the wharf, let its reality become part of her: dark square shapes from bins to buildings, an occasional hesitant movement that might be a cat or rat, the not unpleasant odor and sound of the nearby lapping water. After about an hour, Jeri walked about the perimeter, three sides only since the fourth was a narrow dock. The warehouse itself was an older structure, and she noted two or three possible points of entry. She considered attempting to enter the building, but decided that might result in more trouble than anything she might learn would be worth.

As she left the wharf, Jeri felt she was being followed. She tried a couple of simple methods to check for a tail — pausing to tie a shoelace, peering into a dimly lighted shop window — but she saw no one. Spotting the neon sign of a dockside bar, Jeri went in. She found that it hosted a mixed crowd of dockworkers and sailors, a few tourists whose bright plumage identified them immediately, and several women who were working the group. Jeri took a place at the bar where she could watch the door and ordered ale in Serb-accented Dutch.

She was surprised that he entered so soon after she had. He didn't look like a seaman, but neither did he stand out in the working class crowd. Something made Jeri think he was English, but it was just a feeling. His hair was short-cropped, a military buzz cut. Not a tall man but solid and stocky, he made his way to the bar, ordered a beer in English, and then drank about a third of it before looking around. He stood only a few people away from Jeri.

"Buy me a drink, sailor?"

Jeri almost laughed. The invitation was in Dutch, but too preciously clichéd not to be enjoyed. Even so, she managed a scowl and slight shake of her head. Undaunted, the woman looked around for more promising drinkers.

If the stocky man had taken note of the interaction, it wasn't obvious. Jeri suspected that he hadn't actually seen her outside, except as a dark shape. The fog would have blurred any details. She was sure she hadn't been seen leaving the hotel, so if she was being followed now, it was because she had been seen near the warehouse. And if he had picked her out at the dock, he was very good at his work.

The same woman who had approached Jeri sidled up to the stocky man just as the door opened and two more dock workers entered. Before the door closed, Jeri slipped out and quickly made her way up the street. She waited in the shadows for nearly half an hour before being satisfied that no one else was on the street, nor had the stocky man emerged from the bar.

†

Doña Maria Isabella appeared at the appropriate offices the next morning and presented all the necessary papers and signed them as required in order to insure that a shipment of flax would embark for Cork in two days. Then, all bills properly certified, she went shopping. It might seem short work for such elaborate preparation, but the certified papers were worth far more than gold.

Among the many shops along Rotterdam's famed Weena was one which sold very fine linen. The Condesa was looking for nothing in particular. She bought an olive-hued kerchief and then was attracted by the celadon color of a simple summer dress.

"There's nothing like the luster of fine linen," commented a nearby shopper.

Two replies were possible, one a comment on how soon it would be summer, the other on how easily the fabric wrinkled. Jeri had difficulty remembering either because the voice of the speaker was so unexpected. She lifted her gaze slowly, not daring to believe she would see the shop lighting making a halo of red-gold curls. Millicent Ormond recognized Jeri at the same moment, and her wide-eyed surprise transformed into a broad smile.

"A pity it wrinkles so horribly." Jeri spoke coldly, assuming the distance of someone who preferred not to be spoken to by strangers.

Millicent, too, was fumbling her assigned role. She ought to have just nodded and turned away, but instead she blushed and stammered an apology. Jeri started to put the dress back on the rack, but it slid off the hanger. As she bent to pick it up, Jeri muttered the name of her hotel and room number and could only hope that Millicent had heard. By the time Jeri stood up, the other woman had turned and was exiting the shop.

Jeri watched. In the doorway, it was daylight that illuminated the unruly curls that made Jeri want to rush after and run her hand through them. Instead, she watched as a stocky man with a buzz cut who looked vaguely English also left the shop.

At the hotel, Jeri found it impossible to relax. She changed out of the Condesa's clothing, but then couldn't decide what to put on. She suddenly realized she was attempting to dress for Millicent. At that, she angrily grabbed her outfit from the night before, and thereafter avoided looking into any mirrors. Just as she had the night before, Jeri began prowling about the suite. She wanted to go out onto the balcony and watch the street for Millicent's arrival, but that would have been as absurd as it was dangerous. Presumably the stocky man had no idea that she was acquainted with the woman he was following, but the game would be up if he happened to see Jeri as he followed Millicent into the hotel.

It was stunningly unbelievable that Millicent Ormond was Jeri's Rotterdam contact. The first few months back in Ulster, Jeri had thought about attempting to arrange a meeting, but decided the idea was foolish and dangerous, and then let thoughts of the woman fade. And they had. Not altogether, but enough. Survival in Belfast meant attending to the moment, not daydreaming about a married woman in the Republic. And yet, though the thoughts of Millicent had faded, they had not disappeared.

Jeri was momentarily glad that Millicent would find her in such an expensive setting, but that only ratcheted her anger higher. No matter how royally she dressed up, she was a poor kid from Southie and she always would be. Lady Millie was the one with a pedigree. Would she even have known if Jeri had died in a gunfight in Belgrade? Or drowned in a freezing Chechen river? Did she even remember their time together?

The memory impeded Jeri's struggle to keep a professional grip on her feelings. The mission was important. Millicent had been followed. Her part of the operation had been to shepherd the arms to the same warehouse where the linen bales waited. If the arms had been compromised, the whole mission was in jeopardy. That was what was important. Getting guns to Ulster was all that was important.

There was a light knock on the door and Jeri opened it, and Millicent was standing there, and nothing else was important. Jeri moved away. Millicent closed the door and entered the room.

They stared at each other, looking for changes, looking for the familiar, the distance between them growing much larger than a few feet.

Curiously, it wasn't the woman whose scent had put Jeri in mind of orchids and who had been so willing to be bedded that Jeri remembered at that moment; instead she remembered the woman who had appeared in the kitchen of the country cottage that first free morning out of Armagh, wearing a faded apron and offering a feast of a breakfast, part of the promise of life beginning again. Jeri willed away the memory.

"Lady Millie. What a surprise."

"I had no idea you would be my contact."

"Well, what do foot soldiers ever know?"

"These are awfully nice digs for a foot soldier." Millicent tried for a smile but got nothing from Jeri. "How have you been?"

"Well enough. Hasn't Thomas kept you informed?"

"He said you were back in Ulster. I thought it best to not ask further."

"Why?"

"I suppose I would have been unwise and tried to see you."

Dangerous ground. Distracting. Jeri turned the conversation. "You were being followed. Did you speak to anyone downstairs?"

Millicent appeared surprised, but she thought back. "I've done nothing since we met in the shop but wander through shops on the Weena. You gave me the room number, so there was no need to stop at the desk. And I came up alone on the lift." Statements, yet behind every word seemed to be a question.

"Are the guns in Rotterdam?" Jeri hated the coldness she heard in her own voice, but she couldn't seem to speak otherwise.

"Yes, a shipment of Armalite AR-18s, broken down into parts. I have a crew to transfer them from their current containers tonight."

"Good. But what about the man following you."

"It should be all right. We expected there might be some problems, so I've arranged for clues that suggest these guns are going to ETA."

We. Millicent had said. In Ireland, she had always acted as if the politics had little to do with her. Even when she told Jeri she would soon be on her way to Eastern Europe, she had made it seem a fact she had overheard, something a wife couldn't avoid knowing. Now she said *we,* and that felt much more true.

"Then I imagine everything is in order." Jeri searched for something else to say. "Are you still mucking about in the Stone Age?"

"Bronze. The dating for the wedge tomb verified early Bronze Age. Jeri… "

"Would you like a drink? The suite comes with everything. Scotch, right?"

Millicent nodded. Jeri went to the small bar and took out an ale for herself and the bottle of scotch provided by the hotel. The scotch looked as expensive as the rest of the suite.

"Jeri."

She felt Millicent behind her, placing a hand on her shoulder. She turned, and now there was too little distance between them.

"Jeri, please. I've thought of you so often."

Her hair smelled like candlelight and rain, like parchment and cloves. It wasn't orchids that came to mind as Jeri buried her face in the thick curls, breathing in as if she would take all of Millicent inside her; it was firelight indoors on a stormy night. She held Millicent as if she meant never to let go, but Jeri's arms were no tighter than those holding her. Millicent's face was pressed into the curve of Jeri's neck, and Jeri heard her name murmured like a mantra of warmth and soft sound that pulsed against her skin. Then Millicent raised her head, seeking Jeri's face, her lips.

Jeri remembered their last encounter. Last and first. Millicent had responded then, to be sure she had been eager enough to follow Jeri's lead, but there had also been the unmistakable hesitancy of someone who had never been with a woman before, someone willing to be led. Now Millicent was compelling Jeri with a confidence aroused by knowing what she wanted and determined to have it. Her hands were inside Jeri's sweater, tugging it up and off, and then her own blouse was gone and there was a pause just to relish the thrill of skin meeting skin. Barely a pause as Millicent, her mouth wide and hungry and her hands stronger than Jeri remembered, pressed herself against Jeri with an urgency that blasted away the last barriers separating them. Jeri struggled to maintain some distance, but Millicent's need defeated her and she surrendered to the fierce rush of her own desire.

"Where on earth have you been since I left?" Jeri finally was able to ask. She was holding Millicent close as the lingering tremors of climax subsided. Any remnants of Lady Millie had disappeared in the general dishevelment of bed sheets and clothing. Her skin still glistened with perspiration, and Jeri was surprised to notice the suggestion of freckles sprinkled over the woman's nose and cheeks. Jeri had not enjoyed simply looking the last time they had been together.

Millicent opened blue eyes, the color nearly lost in pupils still full dark with pleasure, and grinned. "I've been reading."

"Reading? Are you sure that's all?"

"And remembering. I think I've remembered every second with you at least a hundred times."

"You truly are a very clever scholar."

"I always have been," Millicent said. There was a breast near her mouth and she kissed its nipple. Her hand moved along Jeri's inner thigh, sliding upward. "Let me show you what I've learned."

For a moment Jeri let Millicent explore, but then she felt the old pain beginning. "That's okay." She shifted position slightly.

"Please, let me do for you."

"You've done enough. It's all right, really."

They lay quietly for a few moments before Millicent ventured cautiously, "Is it because of your cousin? Because of Fiona?"

Jeri remembered how betrayed she had felt when, their last time together, she had learned how much of her life had been a topic for discussion. She felt none of that now. Instead, she was rather relieved not to have to explain. "I suppose," she said. "I don't really know. It just is what it is."

"I'm sorry," Millicent said. "I still can't believe you're here. I never expected to see you in Holland of all places."

"Where else would you expect to find a dyke?"

It took a moment before she got the reference. "What! Surely I misheard. Surely you didn't just make a joke?"

"Yeah, well, don't get used to it."

"What can I get used to?"

So it was necessary to begin kissing again, and then to explore various areas of interest — like the effect of a tongue inside an ear, of being pulled atop a long body, of discovering how the rounded curve of hip and haunch was as delicious for a hand as for an eye, of fingering the knobs of a spine like an improvising musician, of feeling desire reawakened when groin pressed against groin and a leg slid between thighs.

This time, when they again lay quietly together, Jeri felt the creeping onset of sadness. What they had, after all, was only this brief, even stolen, interlude, no matter how much memory and longing had combined to make the moments rich and deep. Already the room was growing dimmer as the day diminished. She wanted to hold on to the moment, postpone the need to resume the roles they had been sent to Rotterdam to play.

"Why ever did you take up archaeology?"

Millicent nestled herself deeper in Jeri's arms and smiled fondly as she reached to brush a strand of dark hair away from Jeri's forehead.

"Ireland. Always Ireland. I was raised in Devon, but the family is Irish and I fell in love with the stories early, those fierce, tragic stories. I thought I was going to study mythology and legends, but it turned out that I wanted to find what's behind them. So I came to our wee island to dig up our past, and then the past led to the present and politics. I met Thomas at a fundraising, and he said something about how easy it was to sing rebel songs and give a penny or two to salve the southern conscience for abandoning the north. So I had to show him I was deeper than that, and then one thing led to another."

"Were you happy?"

"Happy?" Millicent considered the word. "I didn't think much about it. It was enough to discover a purpose. Mucking about in the past like I do, all those tombs, all those graves holding people who once walked where I walk, dreamed and sang and loved, same as you and me, what I want is for them to be proud of me, to have a right to call them my ancestors."

"I should have guessed you're a romantic."

"I don't know how you mean that. Our people are a grand nation, Jeri. We need to be free, to use the power that can come to us through so long a struggle. Centuries we've fought and died. Centuries we've been under someone's yoke. We know something important for more than just ourselves. Listen to the songs. You can hear the understanding of what the world's truly about that's yearning to burst from night into daylight."

Jeri heard then the rest of the passion that Millicent embodied, part of that same passion that made her lovemaking so deep and elemental. At that moment she reminded Jeri very much of Fiona.

"I do go on, don't I?" Millicent sighed. "I blame you, Jeri. Usually I just know these things; I don't try to turn them into words. Now you tell me, where have *you* gone since I sent you for to be a soldier? What far realms, mine own true love, have you traveled ere you came back to me?"

It would take more than one charming afternoon to bring Jeri to a place where she could lower her guard, to attempt being truly open. She did want to. Wanted to try. She gave Millicent a brief account of her time out of Ireland, saying nothing of Rafi but then making a fine and hilarious tale of Mirynia.

"You must let me tell Thomas," Millicent said. "Who would have thought that not knowing much about engineering would be no problem while not being able to talk boys and make-up almost ruined your cover.

No. No-no-no. Not that look, not again. You know I'm married. Jeri, no."

Jeri was leaving the bed, turning her back to Millicent.

"I know you're married. I don't like it, but I know it. I can't ... I don't know. When you talk of the past, it's one thing, but when you talk of tomorrow, you and him, I can't. You have to get back now anyway."

"Yes, yes. I'll go soon, but Buzz-cut can wait a while longer. Come back here and talk to me. I won't lose you again, I won't. Jeri, we can make this work somehow."

Jeri returned to the bed and sat, and whatever she was thinking retreated as she felt Millicent kneel alongside, felt Millicent's naked skin against her own, felt the full force of the ardor and affection she was being given.

"I will make this work, Jeri, I promise," Millicent whispered.

"Somehow." Jeri repeated Millicent's word, testing it, hoping it might be true. "We can make it work somehow. But we should go now."

"Not 'we', Jeri. You have to stay. The Condesa can't be associated with me. There's a shipment of tractor motor parts for Bilbao in that warehouse, too, and that's where Buzz-cut needs to think the guns are going. I'll lose him after we move the parts to the flax bales, and then I'll come back here. Wait for me; we'll work it all out then."

Jeri waited until Millicent was on the elevator and then she took the back stairs as she had the night before. She exited the hotel with caution, but no one had any interest in a sailor out for the evening. In the early winter twilight, neon took on a rich vibrancy that belied its commonness. So near the Weena, people roamed this part of the city at every hour. Jeri turned to a store display window, her cap pulled down and her collar up, and watched the reflection of a woman followed by a stocky man crossing the street. She was surprised by the pleasure she felt at the mere sight of Millicent. They were easy to follow because Buzz-cut — Jeri took up the name — Buzz-cut didn't check behind him. Jeri gave Millicent high grades for the careless manner in which she moved, giving no indication at all that she knew she was being tailed. Millicent led the way to her own hotel, and when she went in, Buzz-cut and Jeri remained outside. The hotel was a much less classy establishment than Jeri's.

It was full dark when Millicent reemerged and the three proceeded to the warehouse. Millicent entered through a narrow door by the loading dock, and Jeri waited to see what Buzz-cut would do. He prowled around for some time and then took up a station not far from the entry. Jeri left him and went to a place she had seen the night before and thought might be a way in past locks. It wasn't a direct route, but by climbing a ladder fastened outside an adjacent warehouse and then working her way back, she was able to scramble to the corrugated roof of the building she wanted. Faint light shone through the window that was one in a row of skylights. She thought at least one might give her access. The first one she tried was stuck. Cautiously she made her way to the next window. It too was stuck, but there seemed to be some give to it. Jeri took out her pocketknife and worked quietly.

The window opened grudgingly, but without a screech or squeal, and Jeri eased herself through and onto a metal ledge that ran around the interior perimeter of the building. Two metal ladders sloped to opposite sidewalls and then down to the concrete floor. Below, stacks of varying sizes of crates, divided by narrow walkways, took up most of the interior. The flax bales in rolls nearly five feet in diameter were near the wall closest to the water. The boxes with machine parts had been placed not too far distant.

Jeri eased herself along the perimeter ledge until, still in shadows, she could look down at Millicent and her crew as if watching a play from the furthest balcony. The crew was small, five men and Millicent, but they appeared to be quite efficient. They worked with a minimum of talk, opening crates, taking out parts and placing them carefully on plastic sheets, then resealing the original crates. Millicent had changed into jeans and a thick wool sweater and was working alongside the others, placing the gun parts, twisting the sheets so they appeared like so many large sausages. These were then slipped into the large rolls of flax. Certain bits of machinery were left in the crates, and although Jeri was unfamiliar with them, she assumed they were meant to fool any officials into thinking that the crates were still the same as originally shipped. Even so, anyone investigating closely would recognize the boxes were half empty.

Jeri thought about leaving her hiding place and lending a hand, but decided against it; the crew would likely only be disrupted by such a gesture. It was odd and curiously exciting to be watching Millicent while the woman was unaware of her presence. This must be how she was at one of her archaeological sites, working down in the dirt with everyone else. Jeri wondered if perhaps she had misjudged the whole Lady Millie thing; the woman certainly looked more and more like Millie the factory maid as the night wore on.

Thoughts of Millicent had more than once resisted Jeri's attempts to forget her, but they had always kept Millicent among the aristocratic settings of the Ormond estate. In Jeri's mind, Millicent had been at home in the luxury, the lady of the manor. The woman at work below demanded a complete revision of that impression. This woman was competent and focused, energetic, obviously a trusted comrade among her crew. She was walking out of Jeri's fantasies, revealing her own substance and worth. She was becoming a person whom Jeri very much wanted to know.

At one point, Millicent stood and wearily brushed her hair off her forehead, and then paused in mid gesture. For a moment it was as if she and Jeri shared a single mind, caught suddenly and taken away by the same memories of the long afternoon.

Jeri hoped Millicent had some idea how they were going to make this work, because she couldn't figure it out. There was no way Jeri could make a habit of leaving Belfast. As long as she stayed with her unit or in the Ardoyne, she was fairly safe, but crossing the border south was a sure way to get caught. And Millicent probably shouldn't be making many trips north. Maybe Scotland. Maybe Jeri could take the Belfast ferry to Glasgow, and they could meet there. Right. Dream on. Maybe Millicent knew someone with a boat and they could find some wee island where Jeri could chop wood and draw water while Millicent cooked amazing breakfasts and there they would live happily ever after.

It was near midnight, or soon after, when the work was done. The crew left the warehouse, but Millicent stayed for a final check to be sure everything appeared in order before following them. Jeri was about to leave when she heard a slight noise from the far side of the warehouse, from somewhere in the shadows. It wasn't long before a figure to emerge. Jeri cursed herself for a fool for thinking Buzz-cut had intended to wait outside. She should have remembered from the night before that he was good at his work.

Jeri watched him approach the area where the crates bound for Bilbao were stacked. Slowly, quiet and cautious, she backed down the ladder that stretched from the floor to near the window where she had entered. Buzz-cut was placing one of the resealed crates on the floor now. Jeri had had a balcony view of the work; he had probably not been able to see exactly what had been done. Even so, he couldn't be allowed to find the guns or their destination. The half-empty crates would be a sure tip-off that something was afoot. He might even know that the crates had once held guns.

Jeri scrambled quietly to the floor and stopped.

She needed a weapon, something more than a pocket knife. She should have planned for that before leaving her hotel. She ought to have thought about looking for one earlier when she was perched above. Then she remembered a trash area she had seen. The Dutch were notoriously neat, but there was a heap of broken crates near a bin and Jeri made for it. She could hear the squeal of protest as Buzz-cut pried apart boards. He might possibly have a gun, but for sure he did have whatever he was using to open the crate.

The scrap heap held all sorts of junk, but the only thing that looked to Jeri as if it might be useful was a piece of broken wood about two feet long. It looked too thin to be very sturdy, but the break had given it a point and it would have to do. It was like a game of pick-up sticks to remove the board from the pile while keeping everything else in place.

The sound at first made Jeri think she had dislodged something in the scrap heap, but immediately after she realized it was the door to the warehouse. Opening, then closing. The scrap heap was situated where she could see neither door nor Buzz-cut. Holding her makeshift weapon, Jeri moved as quickly as she could to the corner of a stack of crates and then peered round. Buzz-cut was standing with his back to her, facing the newcomer, the open crate at his feet.

And walking toward him, a smile on her face, was Millicent.

The bottom dropped from Jeri's world so abruptly it was dizzying. Snitch. Grass. Judas. Traitor. None of the words even began to touch what Jeri was feeling — an anger so violent as it struck, that it nearly blinded her. For long seconds she could hear nothing but her own blood pounding in her ears. Christ, she should have known, should have seen something. Distracted by her own needs, deluded by her own longing, she had left herself wide open for betrayal once again. Millicent had seemed so real, so possible. Surely that alone should have warned her. Slowly Jeri was able to see and hear again.

"Your boys did a right fine job."

"Thank you. We aim to please." Millicent was still smiling, as if they had been friends for a long time.

"Where have you moved them?"

"I'd think you'd be able to figure that out easily enough." Millicent was still moving forward, her arms at her sides, palms forward as if about to lift them.

"Stay where you are, you bloody cunt; stay right where you are. Just tell me where the guns are." Buzz-cut stepped over the open crate toward her.

Now Jeri could see that he had a gun pointed at Millicent. In an instant she realized she had made a mistake, that her hair-trigger anger had fired too soon, but she had no time for relief. The adrenaline that always made such moments so enthralling slowed time as she emerged from behind the boxes. Everything had a shine and a fine edge. She knew just how many steps she needed to take, just where she would strike.

Millicent saw Jeri, but kept her eyes fixed on Buzz-cut.

Instinct must have made him start to turn.

"This way," Millicent called out to distract him, and then louder, "the guns are this way."

Buzz-cut pulled the trigger.

Jeri hit him with the board; with all the considerable force she was capable of, hit him above the cheekbone and felt the wood shatter and heard his skull crack even as the noise of the gunshot echoed through the warehouse. She didn't even wonder whether he was dead.

Millicent was leaning against the stack of crates that had once held parts of AR-18s, then she was sliding to sit on the concrete floor. She looked as if she were considering a very complex set of problems.

"Were you hit?" Jeri knelt beside her but could see no wound.

Millicent nodded.

"Is it bad? Can you move?"

Millicent shook her head.

"I'll get you to a hospital."

Millicent grasped Jeri's arm in a grip that was extraordinarily strong, but her voice came in short segments. "No. There's no time. You have to fix this. Take anything that can identify us, put us both in the water. The guns will be gone before they find any bodies."

"No. You can't know this."

Millicent looked up at Jeri and smiled. "I'm so sorry."

And then Jeri knew, too. She felt the grip on her arm weaken.

"Tell Thomas."

"I'll tell him."

"I'm glad you're here. I love you."

Jeri took Millicent's hand and lifted it to her face. She had to bend to hear Millicent's whisper.

"I'll give Fiona your love."

Jeri couldn't speak. At last she managed, "As long as you keep some for yourself." She was afraid she had taken too long to reply.

Chapter Seven

Jeri wasn't asleep when she heard the light tapping on the door to her room. She'd been lying awake in the dark, bedeviled by sleeplessness, but she waited until she heard the knock again and understood from the code that the person outside was no enemy. Even so, she reached for her pistol, a SIG P226.

"Who is it?"

"Paulie." The voice was too young to be anyone but the wee messenger lad. She set the gun on the bed and slipped into jeans and a sweatshirt, then picked up the gun again. You could never be sure who might be outside when you opened a door in Belfast, but this time it was only Paulie, looking eager and anxious. "Martin's wanting you."

"Wait. I'll just be a minute."

Jeri put on her dark wool pea coat, made sure the SIG was secure in the waistband of her jeans, and then followed the boy down the stairs and out into the night. It was dark and quiet along the street, not a neighborhood for much traffic day or night. Paulie took the first possible opportunity to turn off the street, a narrow way between two buildings, and then into an alley. The way was lit by whatever light seeped out of a few windows from the crowded buildings in the Ardoyne section of Belfast, but Jeri had no trouble following the boy as he alternately trotted and walked through the twisting back ways. After about ten minutes, they arrived at a door where Paulie knocked. Jeri knew where they were, but stepped back into the shadows until she recognized the person who opened the door, and then she followed Paulie into the room.

Four men waited inside, sitting in the room's only chairs around a worn table, playing cards as usual. They nodded to her. She knew them all — Kevin, Donnie, Patsy, and Tim. They were her unit. Martin, the OC, and Lawrence, his second, were missing. Jeri nodded to the men stepped over to a wall and leaned against it. She knew these men as well as you'd know anyone you planted bombs and robbed banks with but didn't much care for. During close to three years in Belfast, Jeri felt she'd rather lost the knack for friendships. Kevin was okay. Kevin wasn't as tall as Jeri, somewhere in his thirties though thinning gray hair suggested he was older. He'd been in prison in the Maze, and he had recognized right off that he and Jeri saw the world in a way the others didn't. He could disappear into himself the same as she could, just as they were both practiced at patience during times like now. He and Jeri usually got paired together during jobs, and so far that had worked well enough.

Patsy was older than Kevin, a burly man who felt it necessary to prove he could keep up with Donnie and Tim, who were both barely out of their teens. Donnie was thin, with brown hair long enough that he often tossed his head to keep it off his face. Tim played soccer every chance he got, and that was keeping him from the weight that would overtake him when he got older. *If* he got older. Patsy, Donnie, and Tim all thought of themselves as hard men, and no doubt they could be, but Jeri found them callous and too often careless. They thought themselves up to any foe, and she was sure that they'd discover sooner rather than later they were wrong. She just wanted to be somewhere else when that happened. They didn't care much for her, either. She was usually the Yank to them, or Jer, at least to her face. She figured they used other names behind her back. Patsy just didn't care much for women past their usefulness at baking and mopping, but Donnie and Tim were too adolescent to be able to ignore any woman not their mother or sister, and they resented her for their own interest.

Jeri wondered what Martin had called them out for. Any action was preferable to another night of trying to sleep followed by a day of nothing much to do. There was a bomb placement in the works, but at this stage it was mostly a matter for her and Kevin to be establishing their fictional identities.

The door opened, and Paulie leaned in. "Hurry up. Rides are outside."

That was how it went. One minute you're leaning against a wall watching a glacially paced card game, and the next you're piled in a car rushing into the dark. Martin was in the lead car, Jeri in the one behind, so she was going to have to wait a while longer before learning where they were going.

After an hour of bumpy roads and a climb through a weedy field, the unit found itself on a high hill overlooking a farm house, a couple of sheds, and a barn. The buildings were just dark shapes in the night with no lights or movement.

"We got a tip there's going to be some sort of handover to the UDA," Martin told the group gathered about him. "When we got the word, there wasn't time to get any but us out here, so we'll be on our own."

"Guns you think?" Patsy asked.

"I'm not thinking. We're just doing what we were told."

The unit settled in along the hilltop. Jeri squinted to see if she could make out anything below, but the darkness was too thick. A low snorting to her right startled her for an instant before she recognized it.

"Jesus, that'll bring any Prods in the neighborhood," she heard Donnie say.

"Yeah, but if we tell Patsy he fell asleep, he'll deny he ever did," Tim answered. "Think I could get a smoke?"

"You do and it'll be your last," Jeri said. "I'll make sure of that. You could see the light for miles."

"You ever lighten up, Yank?"

She didn't answer. The only sound after that was Patsy snoring.

†

There were only the night sounds and memories. Almost a year had passed since Millicent had died. Two weeks after Jeri returned from Rotterdam, Thomas Ormond had come to Belfast looking for her. Jeri couldn't understand what he wanted, she'd told Martin everything he needed to know. Waiting in the pub for Thomas, Jeri had been afraid that he'd come to accuse her of something, and she'd steeled herself against the meeting. Then he arrived, and she understood immediately why he had come. His eyes begged her for some shred of hope.

Jeri had shaken her head. To make sure he knew, she said, "I put her in the water myself."

Thomas turned away. When he turned back, he had a hold on his grief. "I've given the authorities some story about a shopping trip and then no word from her. If—when they find her, I'll let you know."

"You got her ring and the other things?"

"Yes."

"I— She was wearing a silver triskelion. I couldn't take it. She needed something to take with her."

Thomas nodded. "That's good. It will help later." His voice cracked. "When they find her." He started to leave, turned back. "She always

112

asked how you were getting on."

He meant to be generous. Jeri had no intention of revealing how little he had to give her.

As far as Jeri knew, Millicent was yet to be found. After all those graves she'd worked in, she ended with none of her own.

It wasn't regret, exactly, that kept Millicent so alive in Jeri's mind, although there was enough of that. She would often find herself returning to the warehouse and wishing she had been seconds sooner in rushing the Brit. And she understood that once again her anger had caused her harm, the anger that came so quick, especially when she was distracted by happiness. But she could deal with all of that. There had been no accusation in Millicent's eyes as she let go of life. What went deeper, what made her want to find some high meadow on a dark night and howl in anguish was remembering how she had misjudged the quality of Millicent, not known when it was there, and had not offered to her the love deserved by a bright, brave, generous heart. She wanted to have a moment back in which to give something in return.

†

When dawn arrived, Martin decided it was safe enough for Donnie to have his smoke. The farm looked deserted in the daylight, no animals, weeds around the weathered house and dilapidated barn. The road to the barn, though, looked like it got occasional use. After another hour of waiting, the growl of engines announced something might soon happen. The noise was followed by the arrival of two mid-sized trucks with canvas-covered backs that churned into the yard between the house and barn and then stopped. No one got out.

Jeri looked over to Martin, but he was staring worriedly at the trucks. They were British army, and if by some chance they carried troops out on maneuvers, it would behoove Martin's unit to disappear as quickly as possible. For another quarter hour, no one got out of the trucks, and then a black taxi pulled into the farmyard and parked behind the trucks. Five men got out, men wearing jackets and pants. Not uniforms. Now two men emerged from the cab of each truck, and none of them were in uniform either.

"UDA?" Jeri heard Kevin ask. UDA. That would be the Ulster Defense Association, a Loyalist Protestant paramilitary group with ties to the British army. If the rumors were true, and they often were, it was the UDA that had broken into their home and shot Bernadette Devlin and her husband in front of their children.

Martin nodded. "Yeah. I recognize the bastard in the brown coat. But I'll wager anything the truck drivers are Brits." The group of men below went to the first truck and began unloading wooden crates that they took to the barn.

"We'll take 'em now," Martin said.

"Could just wait and get the goods after they leave," Kevin suggested. He was the only one of the group who could question the OC. Sometimes Jeri thought this was because Kevin's tone was always more curious than critical. And he had a past that Martin respected.

"Can't, Kev. What if the boxes are full of tea bags? We don't often get a chance to put the fear into this many Prods at once."

The plan was spur of the moment, and simple, but seemed like a good one. They'd spread out in a semicircle and then go in shooting.

"Yank, you and Lawrence go to the road in. They'll probably try to use the taxi to escape, and you'll be there to stop them."

Lawrence looked less than happy but kept silent. He and the OC were both veterans in their forties. Martin had a commanding officer's solid appreciation of Jeri's abilities, but Lawrence wouldn't have cared if she was Wonder Woman. To him, she was Lucifer's own, a damned soul who ought to at least be shunned, since burning at the stake was no longer possible. Jeri had long ago decided that Lawrence and her sister, Kathleen the nun, would get along just fine if they ever met.

Jeri paid no attention to Lawrence as she retreated to a place behind the brow of the hill, out of sight of the farm, and then started running toward the road. After days confined to her Belfast room, after a night hunkered on the hilltop, any action was welcome. She had put the daylight to good use and studied the layout of the land and the farm, so she was able to move quickly. The adrenaline rush began and the day took on a shine; the blue sky deepened in color, and the cool air had a pleasant tangy smell.

Jeri had already picked the place where she wanted to take up her position. Patches of dried weeds lined the lane from the farm; she could hide there until the action started. She waited for Lawrence until he was near, made sure he saw her, and then slipped into the weeds. Wouldn't do for him to have any excuse to shoot her. For a few minutes it was quiet enough to hear the early morning birds. The abandoned farm supported enough that their chirruping sounded more like the cacophony of fans at a soccer game than a pleasant woodland chorus. The men unloading the trucks were around a curve in the lane and out of sight, but she could hear them as they worked. She could hear Lawrence still breathing hard, too. She checked her AR-18, the iconic Armalite of the IRA, inspecting it visually as well as by touch, as much as possible. She would have liked to do a quick takedown, but she couldn't be sure when Martin would start the action. If she'd had her way, she'd have claimed a particular weapon for herself and kept it in order, but she'd had to just take what came to hand from the car boot.

Gunfire broke the morning quiet, gunfire and yelling. For a few moments, the only shots came from the direction of the attackers, and the quality of the screaming suggested that one or more of the shots might have scored a hit. Then the quality of the shooting changed. Some of the men in the farmyard had begun to return fire. This went on for some time until Jeri was tempted to leave her position and join the battle, but she knew Martin would skin her for that so she stayed where she was.

Then she saw Lawrence start moving up the lane. He'd made the opposite choice. At the same time, over the shooting, she heard the car engine suddenly roar into life. Jeri stepped from the weeds and faced toward the sound. It must have been longer, but it seemed like immediately that the car came into sight. With Lawrence standing right in the middle of the road.

Jeri screamed for him to move. It looked for sure like he was about to be run over, and Jeri couldn't shoot and take a chance of hitting him. Then he dived, the front bumper missing him by inches. With Lawrence out of the way, Jeri began firing. Several rounds hit the front of the taxi, and Jeri raised the barrel toward the windshield.

The gun stopped. Jammed. Jeri jumped to the side of the road, and as the car rushed past she could see faces inside. Most had the angry fear that faces wear in battle, and she was sure they were screaming though she heard nothing. One was twisted in pain. The driver was concentrating on getting out fast. But one knew what had happened with her, and she saw him laugh. In sheer frustration, she swung the AR-18 in the air and threw it. Then the car was past.

The next thing she knew, Kevin and Martin were there. They'd been running after the car. Usually among the least talkative of the unit, Kevin had a huge grin.

"You're to shoot them, lass, not play catch with them."

Even Martin smiled at that, although he had no smiles for Lawrence. But he said nothing. He'd not berate the second in command in front of the others.

Back at the trucks, some of the crates had been opened to reveal that the boxes did indeed have arms and ammunition. One contained grenade launchers.

"So, it's true the Brits have been arming the UDA." Donnie almost sounded betrayed.

"Did you ever doubt it, lad? Here, bring anything back from the barn."

"Are we taking the guns, boss?" Jeri asked.

"No. There's no way they won't have people in real uniforms out before we could know where to take the trucks. We need to leave soon, but first we'll burn all of this. The grenades will fix the rest."

"We won't have to burn this." Kevin had been searching the cabs of the trucks, and he tossed a leather satchel to Martin. It opened as it fell to the ground, and Jeri and the others all saw that it was full of bills. "Seems the Brits have been supporting the Prods in more ways than one."

Something in the way Martin looked first at the money and then around to see who else had seen reminded Jeri of rumors that not all the funds from bank robberies had gone to the cause. Not that she thought Martin himself was crooked, but she was long past any surprise that where there was power, there was probably corruption. That wasn't Irish thinking; it was what you knew from birth in Southie. But she was not about to let any hint of such thinking show. You learned that early in Southie too.

They made it back to Belfast without any mishap and with the memory of a very satisfactory explosion. They'd decommissioned a fair amount of Loyalist arms that day. But when they entered the room where they'd begun hours before, they found Paulie waiting, and something about the way he looked boded ill. Paulie came up and whispered something to Martin. The OC's face went pale with shock, and Jeri felt a nub of fear in the pit of her stomach. When Martin turned to address them all, she wished she could leave before hearing whatever had caused that look.

"The British have killed three of us. An ambush on Gibraltar. Some of you will know them: Sean Savage, Daniel McCann, and Mairead Farrell."

†

"Do not stand at my grave and cry, when Ireland lives, I do not die...."

Roisin O'Hara held the last note, letting her voice soften and fade into the keening lament of Liam's tin whistle, her voice yearning for the day of Ulster's freedom for which Mairead Farrell had died. The song was new, and when it was finished, the pub room was spellbound in a silence more appreciative than any amount of applause. Roisin lifted her bodhram above her bowed head and took a step back, and immediately the band began a reel that, starting softly, was meant to shift grieving past the recent deaths of the three IRA volunteers in Gibraltar. Roisin lowered her bodhran and joined the music, looking around now at the audience, finding several rapt faces still gazing at her.

Sure enough, she'd be getting offers of a pint at break. Free drinks were nice, but they were also a sign that she'd be asked back to play this Ardoyne pub again. Work was what was important, preferably a nice long gig. They were a nice crowd here in this section of Belfast, perhaps a bit too ready for the rebel songs, but generous as could be with coin and cup. Roisin smiled at a couple sitting close to the band; they were holding each other's hands, misty eyed, and not just from pub smoke. Alone at a corner table, a likely looking lad caught her eye. He seemed quite relaxed, lounging with his long legs stretched out, his dark pea jacket open with the collar turned up so that it framed his strong, regular features. He was staring at her, and Roisin saw the unmistakable trace of tears catching the light. He nodded his appreciation and lifted a glass. He seemed young, sure to be too young for her.

Roisin was beginning an answering smile when she realized that the lad was a lass. A very handsome lass. Confused enough to miss her rhythm, Roisin hastily averted her gaze.

She knew she hadn't misunderstood the kind of interest directed at her; no, that had been clear enough. What dismayed her was the interest she had felt in response, and her as straight as a Midsummer's Day is long. With considerable effort, she kept her eyes away from the corner until the reel was finished; then, during the applause, she let her eyes drift back. The handsome lass was gone.

That was how Roisin thought of her, "the handsome lass." She found herself looking toward the corner table during subsequent nights at the pub, and being oddly disappointed to find it empty or with someone else sitting there. Roisin was enough her mother's daughter to understand that such a strong effect from so brief a cause meant that they would most surely meet again, but she had no notion why or for what. Her mother would have nodded knowingly and said "unfinished business", and not been too particular in reference to which lifetime.

†

Ever so slowly, ever so carefully, the last wire needed to connect timer and C5 explosive slid into place. Jeri held her breath, not wanting to disturb so much as a molecule of air in the dank Belfast basement. This bomb was destined for the docks, not to sink a ship but to shake the moorings of the good captains of industry in Ulster, to give them more cause for worry. The happy news was that if this bomb did prematurely explode here in the basement, likely no one in the building would die a lingering death. Only when Wee Will looked away from his work and favored her with a wink from beneath one shaggy eyebrow did Jeri draw a regular breath.

"Safe as a kitten," Wee Will pronounced. A large man of burly build and thick limbs, Wee Will had the doughty look of a fisherman, which he wasn't, and the manners of butler, which he was. Tufts of gray hair defied careful combing and, along with large, thick glasses, gave his round features the appearance of an old owl. A mean old owl.

"Why don't you stay with your comrades?" Wee Will looked toward the door through which the sounds of a card game in progress could be heard.

"What difference would a few more feet make?"

"None at all."

Will placed his hands on either side of the bomb, flat on the scarred wood table, and stretched like a cat, moving shoulder muscles that must be wound tighter than the wires he had just connected. He leaned back in his chair and favored Jeri with the odd stare she had come to recognize, intense and calculating. At first she hadn't understood the dislike that radiated from him, but after a while she worked out that he found her both attractive and repulsive. Lust took some people that way. They resented the object of their attraction, feeling as if the other had taken their power. One of the reasons Jeri watched Will at work was because she thought part of him wanted a bomb to go off while she carried it. He didn't know the extent of her training, and she wasn't about to tell him how little she actually knew about such things.

"You'll be placing it?"

Jeri nodded. "Along with Kevin."

"That lad's in no hurry to get back to prison." Will liked Kevin. Kevin had been among those who were never recaptured after thirty-eight men escaped from the Maze, a state-of-the-art prison that the

British had believed was escape-proof. When Jeri didn't reply, Will took a different tack toward antagonizing her. "That dress doesn't suit you at all."

She was wearing a worn house dress with faded flowers that had once been cabbage-size roses of red, blue, and yellow, but now the colors were barely distinguishable.

"It suits good Presbyterian Myra Murray. After a long week of scrubbing floors, Myra just wants to get home to her kids at her mother's house in Glasgow."

Along with other weekend travelers, Jeri and Kevin would soon queue up at the docks carrying identity papers for Myra and Ronald Murray. They had tickets on the ferry to Stranraer near Glasgow in Scotland, a trip they'd taken several times to establish their cover identities. What ought to have become routine still raised Jeri's heart rate, but with an uncomfortable, thudding anxiety rather than the sharp-edged adrenaline rush that accompanied more immediate danger. She didn't like placing bombs, although her steadiness made her good at it. Of the bombs she'd placed, only two had actually exploded; the others had been disarmed after phoned warnings to authorities. None had harmed anyone. Jeri preferred robbing banks.

Wee Will decided to be chummy. "I brought you some magazines. His Lordship is through with them." Will always referred to his employer as His Lordship, but the man was an economic rather than blood aristocrat.

"Anything interesting?"

"There's one grand piece on Iron Maggie and how she's teaching Ronnie Reagan the ways of the world. And the usual rants against the Agreement."

IRA Provos and Ulster Unionists both were united in their dislike for the Anglo-Irish Agreement, a piece of legislation that said the Republic in the South had an interest in Northern Irish affairs. The Provos thought it legitimized Ulster as a separate state, and the Unionists considered it a betrayal of their status as part of Great Britain. "Ulster is as British as Finchley," Margaret Thatcher had said soon after becoming Prime Minister, referring to her own district. The Agreement signaled the end of that strategy, and bitter Unionists, feeling utterly betrayed and abandoned, had burned Iron Maggie Thatcher in effigy.

"Does His Lordship still side with Britain?" Jeri asked.

"Of course. But for all he sings the old 'a Protestant state for a Protestant people', what he really wants is a state he and his kind can run. They're smuggling more drugs and porno than guns these days."

"Drugs? Are you joking?"

"Sure but they're sending them south. Who cares about Dublin junkies? One of these days our own hard lads and the brethren are going to wake to the fact that there's more money to be made from smuggling than from fighting."

"Jesus!" Memories of Kenny fueled Jeri's revulsion. Her brother had od'd but had not died, only suffered irreversible brain damage. Kenny would never leave his wheelchair by himself, or wipe away his own drool. She wondered if Millicent had known how much corruption and cynicism was making its home on both sides of Ulster's war.

Wee Will had no idea what had prompted Jeri's reaction, but he was perversely pleased that somehow he had caused her pain. "Mark my words, when peace comes, it won't be God's doing, it'll be because the devil showed both sides they could make more money working together."

Jeri favored him with a look that combined rejection with pain. "You're wrong, Will. Too many good people have given all they have to make this a better land."

He started to pat her knee, a gesture looking like comfort that would give him a chance to touch her, but thought better of it. She had a reputation for dealing with anyone who tried to take liberties, so he took another direction.

"His Lordship and the boyos are beginning to worry about some Yank girlie. Seems she's getting a reputation with the Prods. I heard them saying they've got to make an example of her before long."

Jeri matched his bland expression with one of her own. He was searching her face carefully to find some twitch of fear. "That's not really news, Will. They've known about me for quite a while now."

"But now they have you in their sights, the way they got our people in Gibraltar."

Jeri thought of the valiant woman she had known at Armagh and wondered how Mairead would like the sad, haunting song that was her tribute: "Do not stand at my grave and weep", it began. The singer Jeri had seen at the pub she sometimes went to had sung the ballad the first time Jeri had heard it, and music and memory had brought Jeri to tears. The song had even reminded her why she had chosen to remain in Ulster.

Will began to gather his tools. "Are all bean flickers as cool as yourself?"

Jeri was tempted to tell him she preferred to be called a dyke, but since that would only encourage him, she kept her silence and started to leaf through the magazines. She was not about to let the explosive device out of her sight. She didn't really think that Will would use one of his bombs to kill her, but you didn't stay alive by believing your own assumptions. She watched until she was sure he had left the building.

†

An hour later, Jeri and Kevin were at the docks. Her faded flowered frock hung slightly lower than her thin, gray wool coat, and she had a paisley scarf tied round her head to ward off the harsh November wind. Heavy dark shoes with a bit of extra heel made it easy to maintain a slow, weary walk. She carried a medium-sized suitcase and a large shoulder purse. Kevin kept pace slightly in front of her. He was wearing gray pants with a padded workman's jacket and cap, and he carried his own suitcase. He was meant to look as if he worked at a Belfast construction site. Contractors routinely gave day labor to Protestant Scots rather than local Ulster Catholics.

Their queue moved slowly. Previous trips had revealed that a particular clerk made a virtue of methodical ticket checking, a virtue which had probably first given occasion to the impatient feet that kicked against the counter boards near the floor below the clerk's grille. Once the loose boards had been discovered, more focused footwork went to work over several months. Back in the basement, Kevin and Jeri had practiced slipping a package between the boards, using moves that might also work well on a soccer field. The trick they most needed to master was to maintain bland, bored expressions while they performed moves as intricate as any dance step.

The slow line, so much a part of the plan, was desperately hard on the nerves. Kevin's knuckles were white from his tight grip on his case. Like Jeri, he was better suited to action than to the kind of long-term stress this kind of job required. He claimed that all his nerve had been used up in escaping the Maze. During their several ferry trips to Scotland and back, he had broken his normal reticence and told Jeri a little about the Great Escape that had made the best propaganda for the IRA since the Hunger Strikes. The Brits had thought the Maze absolutely secure, until prisoners commandeered a food van and almost waltzed out to freedom. Unfortunately, a guard at the main gate realized what was going on and, when gunfire erupted, the prisoners were forced to scatter on foot. It was the biggest prison break in British history. The authorities, egg all over any number of official faces, called in thousands of police and military to search.

"I wasn't going back," Kevin had told her, gazing out over the boiling wake left by their ferry as it churned through the North Channel. "You've got to know that I won't let them put me back in cells again. I didn't know how much I needed to be free until I was out."

Jeri understood. She had thought she was surviving in Armagh until, once out, she too realized how deep was her dread of ever being imprisoned again. Staying free meant controlling that fear now as they shuffled along in the slow line. She laid a hand on Kevin's arm and murmured something soothing about the children waiting for them when they reached home. While the story was false, the touching of hands was real enough. Kevin nodded. His knuckles stayed white on the case handle but he drew a deep breath and a little of the tightness around his mouth relaxed. Just for an instant, Jeri wished it was Rafi with her. But then the whole scenario would be different. Rafi could never pass for a worn-down laborer, and he would certainly never let Jeri wear a faded cotton dress.

The uniformed guards stationed around the office appeared attentive, alert but not on edge. Jeri recognized them from previous visits. She also recognized several people in the nearby queues. This ferry often carried people who worked in Belfast through the week and returned to Glasgow on weekends. Protestant people. The authorities claimed that the Belfast Catholics would rather stay on the dole than work outside their own neighborhoods, but then it could be worth life and limb for a Catholic to try and work outside. Jeri and Kevin had maintained their cover by returning to Northern Ireland on Sunday evenings. Another regular caught her eye and gave her a vague smile. Jeri nodded slightly and looked away, glancing at Kevin as she did so. She was a woman whose husband would be displeased by any attention given her by another man.

Two people separated them from the desk. Jeri shifted her shoulder bag and focused on the clerk. He was an elderly man with a little gray hair low on his head, not unlike a monk's tonsure. He studied the ticket that had been handed to him, leafed carefully through the tissue thin copies, and pursed his lips as he came to the end. Maddeningly, he looked about for the stamp which he always set in the same place between tickets, found it, studied the paper for a few seconds more, and then carefully placed the stamp. He slowly tore off his section, looked up, and then slid the ticket beneath the grille to the waiting traveler.

One night, someone ahead of Kevin and Jeri in line had muttered loudly enough to be heard, "Have youse never done this before?" The speaker had not been the traveler whose ticket was being processed, and to the dismay of everyone in line, the clerk had paused, peering up and down the queue. When he satisfied himself that he had discovered the culprit, he waited until he had that particular person in front of him and then subjected the man to several minutes of lecture on why it was important that proper procedures and cautions be maintained. Aware that he had gained the ire of his fellow travelers, the man had kept his peace, but he unwittingly did several hours worth of IRA work as he stood and kicked at the board beneath the grille during his reprimand.

They were next. Kevin stepped back to let Jeri go first. She fumbled in her purse and couldn't find the ticket. Impatiently, Kevin took her place. Jeri set down her case to better hold her purse and search through it. There was the ticket, slightly crumpled. The clerk did not like crumpled tickets. Jeri set her purse on the floor beside her case and moved beside Kevin so she could smooth the rumpled paper on the counter. Kevin's left foot had opened the loose board and Jeri used her own left foot to slide her purse through the opening. It caught, the opening too narrow. Jeri coughed, the signal if this happened, and Kevin moved the board farther. Just enough. Jeri pushed the purse all the way through.

The clerk had also heard the cough and he paused, frowning at Jeri. "Move back, please," and he watched until she was again in her proper place.

But it was done. The bomb had been slipped through the opening and was now beneath the clerk's desk. As soon as he stamped Jeri's ticket, she and Kevin hurried from the office and out into the night, unimpeded by authority. No one appeared to have noticed the placement, nor that Jeri was leaving carrying only her suitcase. She and Kevin walked to the ferry, each carrying their case with their left hands. This too was a signal, and it meant that as soon as the ferry embarked, a call would be placed for a warning. If everything worked properly, no harm would be done to persons, but another blow would have been struck to diminish the fiction that Britain was able to govern the rebellious North.

Once aboard, Jeri nodded to Kevin and made her way to the ladies loo. She waited until the ferry was well under way before emerging, dressed now in black wool trousers and a thick knit black sweater. In one hand she carried the case, in the other, a coat very different from the one she had been wearing. She took one of the seats, bolted to the floor same as those in a movie theater, the accommodation provided for those who bought the cheapest tickets. She caught no sight of Kevin. He might be somewhere about, but she didn't look too carefully; they had never shared information about what they meant to do after the bomb was in place. Jeri stayed put for about an hour, making sure that no one had noticed her change in appearance, and then stood and went toward the door, putting on a dark wool pea coat. Outside, where the headwind whipped past full of spray, she took a black knit cap from an inside pocket. Myra Murray had completely disappeared now, replaced by someone who would be taken, at first glance, for an off-duty mariner. Few hardy souls would be interested in fresh air on such a chill November night. Near the back of the ferry, Jeri leaned on the railing, kicked off the suitcase with the flowered frock and thin gray coat inside, and stared at nothing, letting the tensions of the previous hours wash away in the dark boiling water of the wake. Then, as usual, her thoughts returned to Rotterdam.

Chapter Eight

Roisin looked around the pub room and found the corner table again occupied by the handsome lass. She sang through her set and then walked directly to the stranger's table.

"I wondered if you'd come back," she said as she sat down.

"I meant to come sooner. My name's Jeri. For Geraldine."

"Roisin." She pronounced it out: Roe-sheen.

"Would you like a pint?"

"I thought you'd never ask. Is that an American accent I hear?"

Jeri nodded. "I like the songs you choose. They fit your voice."

The conversation slipped easily into a discussion of Irish music, and Roisin was surprised at how much the American knew. She took her admirer for a scholar, a student come to do some post-post degree, but before they had done little more than skim the surface of the topic, it was time for the next set. Without planning it, Roisin heard herself asking if Jeri could stay until after the band was through. Not until she was singing again did it occur to her that the American might take the invitation the wrong way.

"I'm not one of you." The words just erupted from Roisin, the first thing she said as she rejoined Jeri.

The American seemed taken aback. Her eyes narrowed and, for an angry instant, it seemed she just might get up and leave. Then her face cleared, as if she had first misunderstood, and she smiled. "I never thought you were. Do you know where we can get some coffee?"

Roisin was from Antrim, not Belfast, but she knew a place only a short stroll away that served food. Despite their walking in the Ardoyne, the working class area where a Catholic could feel relatively safe, Roisin noted that her companion kept a wary eye as they walked, confirming her idea that the American was new to the North. Sure and she probably thought everyone not a Prod in Belfast belonged to the Rah.

"How long have you been here?" Roisin asked as soon as they were settled.

"Not long. I have family in Derry."

"Ah, Derry. Sure they're all mad in Derry."

Jeri laughed. "Why do you say that?"

"No reason. I'm from Antrim near Cushendall, but one of my uncles lived in Derry, and when he'd come to visit, my ma always said that: 'Sure you're all mad in Derry.' He'd laugh and tease her the more. They were the youngest in their family and had a special bond. He could always get her to laugh, and I can tell you that laughing was rare in my home. My da thought if there was life enough left for a laugh, then he wasn't working us hard enough." The memory that had begun with a smile turned sour by the end.

"Does your uncle still live in Derry?" A question meant to guide Roisin back to happier thoughts tripped yet another regret.

"No. He was caught in an ambush by a bunch from the UDA. That's the Ulster Defense Association. He was just home from a visit with us, and they came right to his door. Like they'd been waiting. He should have known they'd be on to him since he was a barrister. Ach, Jeri, you'll be thinking we're all mad terrorists."

"I'm sorry."

"No, don't be. I like remembering him. When I was not old enough to talk, he'd pick me up and call me his Roisin Dubh, his Black Rose, and me with the reddest hair in a red-haired family. He'd sing the song, the whole song, in this wonderful sweet voice. I think that's when I first wanted to be a singer myself. And when he was killed, that's when I decided this whole mess needs to end. He was just one more mad Irishman ready to die for a hopeless cause. That would be waste enough, if good people who only want to live their lives weren't dying too." Roisin glanced around, but there were few others in the room and no one near. "I have to be careful where I say that; this isn't an area where peace thoughts are welcome. I'm not saying that I'd lose a kneecap, but sure there's people wouldn't like such talk and would let me know. At least I'm safe saying it to you, you being from Americay."

"You're not a nationalist?"

"Ach, I don't know what I am. I'm not one of those Peace People, but I don't want any more dying. I have two of the loveliest nephews, and I want them to have a happy life. Still, I can't imagine ever being a Brit, ever feeling like one. But then they never let Catholics feel part of it, do they? And sometimes, when the band is in the middle of a wild rebel song, I want to just march off the stage and throw myself at a barricade, I feel that deep down Irish. Not that feeling Irish has to be about murdering oppressors, but I like feeling part of this ancient land and in the long line of such brave and gallant folk. If you're born Catholic here in Ulster, you get all these constant messages from the day you're born that you're one of a bunch of lazy, savage, drunken eejits, and you're always made to know that. It just seeps in that Catholics are second class. You're lucky, Jeri, being out of it, you know."

They talked for hours. Roisin's mistaken belief that Jeri had no direct connection to the Troubles allowed her to speak her confusion in a way that she never could with another Northerner. That same mistaken belief gave Jeri room to voice questions of her own, hear her own thoughts. They talked about identity and whether it was something internal and constant, or external and given meaning by consent. Was Jeri American or Irish, and where did being a lesbian fit in? Was an Ulster Catholic an Irishman the same as someone from the Republic in the south? As politics inevitably commanded their attention, they argued from left to right and back again. They remembered the time only when they saw a vendor bring in the new day's papers.

As they stepped into the street and the surprise of daylight, Roisin noticed that Jeri became wary once again. "You're still for driving to Cushendall with me Thursday next?"

Jeri carefully folded the newspaper she had bought and gave Roisin a fully attentive smile. "God willing and the creek don't rise," she said, using a broad American accent guaranteed to amuse her new friend.

Later, when the giddiness of the night wore off, Roisin remembered that Jeri had spoken very little of her own life apart from using her attraction to women as a further example for talking about identity. Thinking back, she realized that not once had Jeri explained directly why she was in Belfast. She knew so much about so many things, and where else but in a university would someone get all that reading done? *You'd have a lot of time in prison, of course*, came the humorous mental reply.

Suddenly Roisin remembered a rumor that the British were hunting for an American woman who had spent time in Armagh. Roisin recalled the look she had received when telling Jeri she wasn't "one of you", and she was seized with a cold dread, knowing that any number of things she'd said to Jeri could be taken for close to treason in the Ardoyne section of Belfast. She cursed herself for a fool because the image she had associated with the rumor of "an American woman" had been from some old Hollywood movie, a woman who looked like Ingrid Bergman or Deborah Kerr.

Sleep. A little sleep should calm her nerves. Since Roisin could not undo what was done, she could only wait for any consequences. Surely the things they'd both said had been sincere, and how likely was it that Jeri did belong to the Rah? *Too likely*, said her inner voice.

†

For Jeri, the night of talking had been an unanticipated pleasure. She liked listening to Roisin sing and had no illusion the woman was anything other than straight, but when they began talking, she found that she could say just about anything, as if they had been acquainted for years. It was when the night ended and they had emerged into the morning that Jeri had seen the headline in the paper: "Casualties in Ferry Office Bombing".

By the time she reached her rooming house and climbed to her third floor room, Jeri was giving no thought at all to the night's conversation. Reading through the story, she learned that the ticket agent's name was Arthur Clarke, that he had held his job for eighteen years, that he had refused to leave the room while still technically on duty, that the full extent of his wounds was still to be determined but it was sure that he would never see again. The British bomb expert who had been engaged in disarming the device when it exploded was dead. He was a veteran of the Falklands War and left behind a young son and daughter.

Jeri lay still on her bed, staring at branching cracks that made a map of the ceiling, the map of a fabled land of many rivers.

†

Thursday next, there was a chill in the air, but the sky was a brilliant blue without a cloud visible. At the designated corner where Jeri waited, Roisin pulled up in a dented and rusty Fiat she had borrowed from Liam, one of the boys in the band. The two women greeted each other with more than a little awkwardness. For both, the intervening days had contained a multitude of second thoughts, and more like wary strangers than friends, they tried out cautious words with one another.

"I wasn't sure you'd still be coming. I thought maybe I'd drive up to the corner and there'd be no one there."

"I've been looking forward to it. Seems a fine day for a drive in the country."

"Did you do that much in Americay? Go driving about the country?"

"No. Never, really. I think I was ten the first time I ever left Boston. I didn't even know that I'd like a landscape without houses until I saw Ireland."

By halting fits and starts, they attempted to regain the closeness that had come so easily during their first meeting, but it remained out of reach, just beyond the next sentence or around the next turn. They stumbled along with attempts at talking, but the silences grew longer as they left Belfast behind. To fill such a silence, Roisin began singing *Whisky in the Jar.* Hesitantly, Jeri joined in the first chorus, and Roisin discovered that her companion had a rich contralto voice, a voice that gained confidence as they went along.

"Ach, Jeri, you're a fine singer. Do you know this one?" Roisin sang the opening words to *Carrickfergus,* and Jeri joined in immediately. Roisin cautiously attempted harmony and, to her delight, Jeri held the melody.

They sang their way inland to Ballymena. If the music did not entirely mend the raveled friendship, at least it brought them closer. Roisin had considered taking the coast road through Carrickfergus and then up, but that road was as slow going as it was beautiful and she wanted to get to her mother's before nightfall. Besides, the A14 from Ballymena would take them through Glenariff Forest and that way, too, was beautiful.

Past Ballymena, in the middle of a song, Roisin suddenly turned the car into a lay-by and stopped. For a long moment, she stared at Jeri.

Jeri was surprised at the intensity with which she was being scrutinized, and for a moment was sure she was about to be kissed. The sunlight was making a red halo of Roisin's curls.

"Who are you, Jeri? I want to know before I take you to my mother's house." The tone was carefully neutral but adamant.

Jeri was torn. Instinct told her to lie, but a deeper longing told her to tell Roisin everything. Since returning from the continent, her life had held scant emotional comfort. Had she been a nun like her sister Kathleen, she could not have been more engaged in selfless service to a cause. She'd felt herself shutting down slowly, as if each day another small connection was being turned off like lights going out for the night in a house. All of her energies were being channeled into making her a weapon, a smart reliable war machine. And that had been enough for a while, had needed to be enough.

The ferry office bomb had damaged that weapon. Perhaps Jeri felt the impact more because she learned of it after the night spent talking with Roisin. She had been absorbing something her soul was starved for, an affirmation of who she was, from the company of another woman. Her mind and heart were like shriveled roots too long deprived of water and at last allowed to drink. Then she learned that she had killed one man and maimed another.

Knowing that Roisin was less than sympathetic was not the reason that Jeri hesitated in telling the truth. The real reason was a deep sense that to speak would be like asking forgiveness, absolution to which she had no right.

"If you're asking, then you probably know. And you ought to take care how much more you want to know." Jeri looked away and out the window, using tone to make her words more a caution than a challenge.

"Did you tell anyone what I said to you?"

"What? Did you think I'd run straight to my OC with a story about a folksinger who doesn't care for Provo methods and tactics? Who thinks the Irish cause might be better served through politics than blood."

Roisin noted that the simplest level of her question had now been answered. "Ach, Jeri, why? Why are you here? This isn't your fight."

"Maybe once it wasn't. But aren't I as Irish as if I'd been born here?"

"That's not the point. And to be honest with you, I'd say you're not, but if that were all that mattered, then all those happy blind folk in Dublin and Cork and Waterford would be up here fighting for us instead of making money hand over fist and pretending that up here we're all just savages. They're the ones who threw us off the freedom boat and sailed blissfully into the future while we stayed slaves to the Brits and Unionists."

Roisin took a deep breath, shaking her head. "Don't get me started. Look, I asked, and you answered and this is much too long a talk to be held in a lay-by. We'll sort this out later."

"Do you still want me with you? You could put me off at a station, and I'll get back to Belfast."

Roisin started the Fiat's engine. "Well, I told my ma you were coming with me, so I suppose she's already gone to too much trouble. She'll be that disappointed if I don't bring you." Roisin was grinning.

"Well, I wouldn't want to disappoint your mother."

The atmosphere in the little car shifted and the camaraderie of the first meeting came seeping back. Jeri doubted that any later "sorting out" would be possible, but at least she had managed honesty while sidestepping telling Roisin too much. The tension had somehow been dissolved. They drove on to the coast in a comfortable and easy accord.

"Are you sure your da was from Derry?"

They were passing through a lovely stretch of forest, and Jeri had lost herself in looking at the landscape. "Yes, why?"

"Just thinking that if you were McDonnell instead of O'Donnell, you might be from around here."

"But then I'd be Scottish instead of Irish."

"So you don't think that being the McDonnells of Antrim since 1400 makes them true Irish? Aren't you an American just for being born there?" The question was a sly return to the unfinished question of identity.

"Leave me be, woman!" Jeri said with mock ferocity, and then broke out laughing. "It's too fine a day outside to argue about such things."

From the Glenariff Forest, they soon came to the coast road and turned north. Roisin gave names to places as they passed, and despite an attempt to maintain a note of mockery at herself for sounding like a tour guide, Jeri could hear the pride in her voice. Pride and love. Soon they passed through Cushendall, and Roisin announced that it wouldn't be long now, but the twisting lanes they took away from the coast slowed them considerably. It was close to an hour before they turned from a lane into a short drive leading to a farmyard.

"This is it, the O'Hara dairy. Our milk is rich and our cream is thick, but wait till you taste the cheese Ma makes."

Jeri couldn't keep from murmur with pleasure at the sight of the old stone, two-story house. It stood sheltered by several trees whose thick trunks testified to a venerable age. A few small outbuildings, none in the best of condition, were almost hidden by growth around the rutted dirt yard, but the barn, with its whitewashed wood and stone foundation, was perhaps in better shape than the house. Jeri considered that she'd just been driven onto a page of a scenic calendar.

Roisin, however, was seeing it all through different eyes. "Ach, wouldn't Da be complaining to see the bushes growing so wild if he were alive? Then it's his own fault if he's not resting easy. He made living here that hard that everyone left as soon as they could. Dennis went off to Oz when he was sixteen, and Rita married her Scotsman just before she started showing. Michael's teaching in the Republic, and Sean's a clerk in Derry. Peggy's the oldest; she married a shopkeeper right here in

Cushendall. It's her boys, Danny and Rory, come help Ma, so the cows are all likely fine, but somebody needs to be clearing those sheds. Listen to me. Not like I want to be living out here either."

For the briefest of seconds, Jeri indulged a fantasy of having a room in the stone house and getting up every day to chop brush in the early morning dew. Then she took the box that Roisin handed her, gifts for the family, and followed her friend to the house. Jeri thought they would use the front door, but instead Roisin followed a well-worn path around the side to a back door, stepping on carefully laid stones to avoid any mud. An elderly black and white collie rose from beside the door and barked, but a wagging tail indicated this was a greeting and not a warning.

Roisin took the dog's head between her hands in a fond gesture. "Tara," she said to Jeri by way of introduction.

A faded and wrinkled woman, Margaret O'Hara looked like the mother of six children and the widow of a hard husband, yet her smile was broad and her eyes bright as she greeted her youngest daughter. Two red-headed teen-age boys with shy smiles, introduced as Rory and Danny, stomped their feet outside the open door, kicked off the galoshes they wore for barn work, and then came to hug their Auntie Rosie. Not long after that a woman came in who looked a little like Roisin but very much like the two boys. Peggy had brought supper with her, and the food was heated on an iron range that still burned wood for fuel. Sometimes a question was directed toward Jeri, but that seemed mostly for courtesy. Roisin was the true center of attention as she told stories about the band and the pubs where they played. There was enough warmth in the kitchen by then that Jeri simply leaned back in her chair and absorbed it like sunlight. Peggy was deep into a discussion of what the dairy would be needing soon by way of equipment if it was to continue supporting itself when Roisin interrupted.

"Ma, I think we're losing our guest. Should I give her the boys' room?"

Mrs. O'Hara nodded assent, and Roisin led Jeri up a steep and narrow stairway to a second floor room. "Take your pick," she said, gesturing toward two large beds, one to either side of a gabled window. "I'll be across in the girls' room. It's me back downstairs to be discussing the features of different milking machines."

"So how many milk cows do you have here?"

Roisin laughed. "As if you cared. I know you're a bright one, but leave farming to farmers." She paused, bit her lower lip. "Jeri, I'm glad you came along. You're grand company." She closed the door and left.

132

Decoration was spare — a crucifix on one wall, a chair, an oval rug of braided material. Still the room was luxury itself compared to the one where Jeri slept in Belfast. That was windowless, and small enough to have been a closet in any situation other than a place where housing for Catholics was, by definition, a slum. As she slipped between sheets that smelled as if they'd just been brought in from airing outside, Jeri wondered briefly if it was too much to expect Roisin to join her. Nothing, however, that had passed between them suggested such a visit might happen. Then she fell asleep, and it was the first sound night she had managed since reading of the death of the man who had attempted to defuse her bomb.

†

Jeri thought herself an early riser, but when she came down for breakfast, she found Roisin and her mother already at the table. Roisin opened the oven door to the range that was heating the kitchen and handed her a plate of eggs and sausage, potatoes, and thick-cut bread.

"I thought I'd go for a hike. I saw some hills toward the sea that looked gorgeous," Jeri said.

"That's a grand idea," Roisin answered. "Ma and I have some errands to run, but we'll be back before supper. The whole clan is coming."

"Do you need me to go with you? I could go walking tomorrow."

"No. Go. It's a lovely day. Don't worry, the clan isn't all that big. There'll be a cousin or two, and Peggy and Mike will probably bring someone they think might tempt me to settle down. Now, Ma, you know they always do, except this time they're probably all in a dither because they never planned on bringing anyone for Jeri." Roisin looked at Jeri and winked broadly. "I can't wait to see who they decide to try on you."

Jeri went upstairs to get her coat and when she came back down, Mrs. O'Hara stopped her. "I'm making you a lunch," she said. "Go wander around our little place for a wee bit and then come back."

A ragged mist lingered outside, and the air held a chill along with a faint smell of the sea. Jeri wandered near the house, peering into the outbuildings. One was so dilapidated that it was roofless, with weeds growing inside. Another had an old motorbike that might have worked during the World War, the first one, and rusting tools lay about on a gray wood workbench. Outside in the weeds, Jeri came upon a round stone the size of a bicycle wheel leaning against a tree. She considered it with thoughts of stone-age bicycles until she realized that it was probably a whetstone, once used for sharpening things like scythes. Chickens scratched about inside a fenced area by the shed nearest the barn, a building kept in good repair. Jeri watched the chickens for a while, bemused by their ceaseless clucking as they pecked about for scattered grain. This was where the breakfast eggs had come from. She felt like she had stepped into a Seamus Heaney poem and wished she knew the old local words for things she was seeing.

The barn door was slightly ajar so Jeri peered inside.

"Hi. I thought I might see cows." One of the boys, Rory if she remembered rightly, was pitchforking hay into a line of feeder troughs. Tara, the collie, glanced at Jeri long enough to give her a welcoming wag.

"I turned them out first light," he said. Curiosity got the better of his shyness. "Where are you from in America?"

"Boston. In Massachusetts."

"What's it like there? The whole country, I mean."

"The whole United States?" The boy nodded. "It's a big country. Some of the states are bigger, more than twice as big as Ireland, than the whole UK, for that matter."

Rory frowned. Apparently he didn't like thinking about the United Kingdom. "What about mountains?"

"Oh, plenty of those. The Appalachians, the Rockies, the Sierra."

"Have you ever been to them?"

Jeri shook her head. She had seen more of Europe than the United States.

"I like climbing mountains. I took a holiday last year in Switzerland."

Jeri listened as Rory told about his trip. He wasn't trying to impress her, but he had clearly taken to her.

"Would you like to go hiking with me?" Jeri inclined her head in the direction of the hills.

"There's chores got to be done." His regret was genuine. "But I can tell you the way toward an old well if you want. Some say it's from St. Patrick's time, and some say it's a holy place, older than that."

Rory gave directions with admirable clarity and then waved her off with a "Mind how you go." The same wish was echoed by Mrs. O'Hara as she handed Jeri a small, much-used canvas haversack. Jeri doubted that she'd ever be hungry again after the huge breakfast, but thanked Roisin's mother and slipped into the pack.

The O'Hara farm was situated at the narrow end of a valley that widened as it meandered toward the sea. Thin rags of a November fog drifted over the grass, and clumps of gorse showed yellow flowers here and there in the haze. Jeri hadn't gone far before she came upon the grazing cows she'd missed in the barn. The animals barely glanced at her as she passed.

Arthur Clarke had seemed nothing but a fool when he'd only been a cog in the mechanism of the plan to target the ferry office with a bomb threat, just an officious fool to be used because his silly habits would make it easier to place a bomb. Jeri and Kevin had shared a laugh at his expense often enough, but Arthur Clarke didn't seem at all funny now. Now he seemed tragic, a methodical man whose sense of duty lent him dignity and then led him into harm. He'd given equal treatment to everyone in his queue, with never a hint of favor as he sent travelers past his station. The British soldier, for whatever reason, had chosen the military path that brought him into harm's way, but Arthur Clarke had only chosen to lead a life of honest labor.

But was justice truly unbalanced by what happened to Arthur Clarke? Ordinary people always suffered in war. In anything for that matter. What if the ferry had capsized? Would the passengers be more innocent than the crew? Everyone on a boat had a piece of its reason for being at sea. Arthur Clarke had his job because, however indirectly, he supported the injustice of Northern Ireland, particularly if his job started eighteen years earlier when Catholics were allowed little or no work at all. If you ate while someone starved, how could you complain when they came for your bread?

What of Fiona and Mairead? Were they innocent? Millicent had been born elsewhere, too, though not as far away as Jeri, and she had taken up the fight. Jeri thought Millicent would likely not be concerned with innocence, not in the large sweep of history. And, as always, thinking of Millicent was accompanied by a deep ache.

So you were only a small measure of weight in restoring the balance of justice? Jeri asked herself. Too easy an answer by half, at the least, this sidestepping of responsibility by blaming Clarke himself. If people formed a network of connections, of obligations and responsibilities, with one person never truly isolated from another, then looking for where to lay blame was not the way to discover justice.

Jeri had the oddest sense that Arkadia O'Malley had asked her a question, a question that, if she could just hear it right, would be halfway to getting an answer.

She had reached the far side of the valley. The ground was beginning to rise, and Jeri could see the path that Rory had described. The worn trail wound round the rocky hillside, but Jeri paused to consider. If she tried to go straight up, the cliff that looked just barely possible from here might prove too difficult, and she'd have to come down and take another way. Jeri exercised routinely to maintain her strength, but a good climb was inviting with its promise of stretching muscles that rarely found use in city living. Rory's story of his trip to Switzerland gave the notion of climbing an even more favorable place in her mind.

Climbing required an attention that emptied her mind of other considerations. At first there was just the steep grade and loose scree to negotiate, but soon large outcroppings of rock needed decisions whether to climb them or find a way around. Whichever way she chose, small pebbles made each step precarious. She was over three quarters of the way up when the grade ended in a cliff. Now she needed to do real climbing. The sun was almost overhead, warm despite the small clouds that scudded past on the west wind. She took off her jacket and fastened it to the canvas pack.

Jeri carefully chose each handhold, each foot placement. Maybe climbing's pleasure came from the sense that it was all on you, win or lose, to discover your own balance of risk and safety, to make a sure step out of the merest of cracks, the thinnest of ledges. She'd have to ask Rory if he had ever come this way.

One has to add, to any list of climbing pleasures, the view as well as the sense of success when one gains the top. Jeri rolled over the last ledge and lay on thin grass and pebbles, watching the clouds sail overhead. When she sat up, she could see bright blue water in the distance, the waters of the North Channel between Ireland and Scotland.

The soldier's name hadn't been in the paper; maybe it had been in some other edition. He was just the "British soldier," a man trying to hazard his own way between risk and danger. And his luck had run out. Would his children see it that way? Or would they take as their legacy a need to go to battle, to avenge their father and finish his work, the same way she'd accepted the need to take up where Fiona left off? Roisin claimed Jeri wasn't really Irish, not in the sense that it was her place to take up the fight, but then Roisin didn't want anyone to be fighting.

Jeri opened the pack and found water and a thick sandwich of cheese and homemade bread. The cheese was likely homemade too. Outdoors, and after the climb, the meal tasted like a feast. Jeri crumbled the last bite for an impatient sparrow, then she lay back and closed her eyes for a moment, savoring the smells and the sounds, the sheer peace of where she was.

She must have fallen asleep. She stood, stretched, and went searching for the well.

The well was more of a spring. She found it a distance from the cliff's edge, in a slight depression, almost surrounded by a thicket of wind-stunted trees. The water rose out of the rock, pooled, flowed a short way, and then disappeared back into the ground. A rubble of stones set in a nearly quarter turn of a circle suggested that at one time there had been an enclosure about the pool. Those rocks that were still in place had the look of age, but Jeri saw no clue whether they had been there for centuries or longer. An expert would know. An expert like Millicent. Jeri suspected the place had been sacred for as long as it had been known. Springs were always sacred to the ancient Celts.

The Brits didn't have the right to rule in Ireland. You took your side. Jeri wanted to be in the company of Fiona and Mairead. And Millicent.

This place still was sacred, if the raggedy cloths tied to a nearby twisted ash tree were any indication. Such places were called Clootie Wells, and more often found in Scotland than Ireland, but then the people of Antrim had a solid Scots strain. Some of the knotted rags were faded and weather-worn to shreds, but a few appeared to be recent additions. Jeri remembered that Samhain, otherwise known as Halloween, had taken place a short time earlier. Samhain was one of the cross-quarter holy days of the old Celts, Irish or Scots, the night when the dead might return.

Jeri took from her jacket pocket a square of olive-hued Irish linen that she had found in a shop one day, the only thing that she had brought back from Rotterdam. That is, the only thing if she didn't count the hurt that was like the constant background beat of a bodhran. She hesitated for a moment and then tore it in two. One piece she put back in her pocket, then she knelt by the pool and dipped the other half into the water. Sitting back on her heels, clearing her mind as much as possible, Jeri wiped the cloth over her forehead and closed eyes. The water was quite cold. She sat until thoughts began to seep back, then she stood and walked to the tree and tied the cloth to a branch above her head.

Chapter Nine

November days were short, and the climb to the well had taken longer than Jeri expected, but there was at least an hour of daylight left as she began the walk back to the O'Hara farm. The path homeward wound around large, lichen-covered boulders. By keeping to easy slopes, Jeri was able to set a quick, comfortable pace for herself. She stopped at a point where the trail came out of the rocks and gave a wide view toward the inland end of the valley where the roadway entered it. She could see the farm nestled in its verdant setting, impossibly romantic in a rustic way. Even a car on the distant lane, taking the way she and Roisin had taken the day before, looked like part of the bucolic scene.

As Jeri watched, the car slowed and pulled off the road just short of the drive into the farm. Maybe this was one of the cousins Roisin had mentioned, arriving early for the evening get-together, someone who knew another way into the farm. The car passed into a copse where the trees hid it from view. When it emerged, it was from the same side as it had entered.

Jeri could think of several reasonable explanations for the maneuver, but she didn't survive by making reasonable assumptions. She stepped back over the lip of the hill so that she could watch without being seen from a distance in any direction. She watched the car regain the road and then drive on. The dark green coupe was just the kind of nondescript vehicle used by the 14, the British surveillance unit known by either side of the conflict as being efficient and effective. The unit's usual targets were weapons caches and highly placed IRA officers. Jeri didn't rate a 14 team after her, even if they knew where she was, and she was unaware of any weapons kept in this part of Antrim. Before leaving the ridge, she gathered several fist-sized stones and put them into the empty haversack. It didn't make for much of a weapon, but she had left the Sig behind in Belfast. Bringing a weapon along had seemed a breach of hospitality. She began working her way down toward the stand of trees.

When Jeri had informed her CO of where she intended to be for these few days, Martin had said nothing beyond wishing her a good rest. Roisin had given her no reason to believe any members of the local O'Hara family might be Provos, but keeping cells separate from one another did cut down on the possibility of betrayal. Running low to the ground, using gorse for cover whenever possible, Jeri let the gravity of moving downhill augment her speed. Twilight had sapped much of the light by the time she slid silently past the outer trees of the copse and gained the narrow lane near where the car had entered. She lay on the ground and cautiously looked about for some sign that a person or persons had been dropped off.

Slim trunked trees, tall grass but not that tall — nothing immediately presented itself as a probable hiding place, but 14's reputation was not exaggerated. The members were experts at camouflage and ambush. Jeri looked toward the farmhouse. Almost invisible from here, surrounded as it was by sheds and brush, only one potential line of sight offered a view of the house. Jeri followed the sightline back and found what she was looking for. On the far side of the road, there looked to be a dark hummock, low but just where it would need to be to for someone to keep watch on the farmyard.

Jeri was still considering her options when she heard an approaching motor. She used its arrival to mask the sound of her own quick move to get even closer to where she had identified the surveillance point. A car, not the one she had seen earlier, stopped only a few feet from where she lay on the ground.

"Edgars!" The driver got out of the car and called out in a voice not much louder than a normal speaking tone, "Edgars, where are you?" The accent was Irish.

Jeri chanced a look in the deepening twilight and thought that there might be at least three passengers in the car. Two for sure.

"Right here, you stupid arse. Why don't you just announce to everyone where I am." This time the accent was definitely British.

"Doesn't matter if Gerry bloody Adams knows you're here. I'm to let you know that plans have changed. We'll be going in soon as it's good and dark. You're to wait here until you get picked up."

"Yeah? I haven't heard anything about that."

"Because your commander has been told to keep radio silence, got that? That means you, too. Just wait until you get picked up."

"What I'm picking up is a smell I don't like."

"Yeah? Then stick your fucking nose back in the dirt if you like that better. We're in charge here, Edgars, not your lot. We can handle these wee taigs on our own."

"'Wee taigs'? We were told to watch for a high level meeting." Though the Englishman hadn't bothered to conceal his disgust before, he communicated even more now.

The only answer was the slam of a car door, and then the idling motor shifted into gear. As the car moved off, Jeri listened as the deserted Brit continued to swear aloud, describing all Irish, north or south and of any religion or none, as women's reproductive organs with excrement for brains. Despite being included in this description, Jeri found herself in sympathy with the speaker. Still, she was sure he had guns, at least one, and she needed one. She was beginning to work out the answer to her puzzle about what was going on that made the farm a target, and it was a dark answer indeed.

A number of recent killings of Catholics had been judged to be strictly sectarian, of no tactical use but that of revenge and terror. The O'Hara farm was isolated by the shape of the valley, insuring that the nearest neighbors were out of sight and sound. Gunfire and yelling would not be heard, except by the cows. Jeri wondered who was at the farm. Roisin and Mrs. O'Hara were probably back, particularly if there was cooking to be done for the night's guests. Maybe Peggy and the boys to take care of the cows. Maybe the other people who were invited for the evening. Jeri wondered if the people targeting the O'Hara farm knew there would be a large family gathering.

Edgars had not gone back to his hiding place; instead he had lit a cigarette and was leaning against a tree, shielding any glow, staring across the field toward his former target.

Knowing that she would be close to invisible against the trees behind her, Jeri started across the road, testing each footstep before committing herself to it. The road was dirt, not gravel, and this helped make her movement silent. Meaning to be more quiet than a shadow, and keeping low, she placed one foot and then another. Something, perhaps instinct, made the man start to turn before Jeri was as close as she would have liked. She was ready. Running the last few steps, she swung the haversack in a short arc. Taken totally by surprise, the man had no chance. The rock-filled bag slammed against his head, and he dropped where he stood.

He carried nice gear. Jeri especially liked his G3 rifle. A body search turned up extra clips, as well as a small Walther PPK in an ankle holster. Jeri strapped the handgun to her own leg. She tied the soldier's hands with cord she found in his pack, then lashed him firmly to a tree in a sitting position. She didn't want him more damaged than necessary. A small moan suggested he wouldn't be unconscious much longer. She wondered if she should gag him, but thought better of it. He'd have to yell very loud to be heard at the farm.

She stepped back into the shadows and went to examine the hummock where the soldier had been hiding. She examined the cleverly arranged branches, but there was nothing there. Edgars had already removed everything he'd brought.

"Edgars!"

"Over here." The words were slurred but still clearly expressed relief.

Someone had come back. Holding the canvas pack with the stones and the G3, Jeri slid back into deeper shadows. She hadn't heard anyone approaching, certainly not a car. The newcomer was making no attempt at silence, so Jeri guessed she must have been too preoccupied to notice.

"Well, well. What's happened to you? Good news and bad news, I'd say." An Irish accent, but not the same voice as earlier. "What? Hurt? Who did it?"

"Didn't see, did I. Just get me out of here." The English voice was weak but angry.

"But that's the good news. Saves me the bother of setting you up." A single pistol shot broke the quiet. "The bad news is there's someone else around."

A long period of silence followed. The newcomer had the choice of either going back where he'd come from or trying to find the someone else he suspected was near. After a long while, the sound of rustling grass indicated he was going back. Jeri listened to the footsteps diminishing in the distance before she moved. Cautiously, she went to where the British soldier was still tied to the tree. She could see how his head lolled to the side. She moved close and checked for a pulse. There was none. He was dead. He'd come over the water looking for god knows what adventure or advantage, and now he'd not be going home alive. Jeri was sorry for that.

If she had needed the lesson, the cold-blooded murder of the soldier would have told her that the men out in the darkness were dangerous, but now speed was essential if she was going to keep the O'Hara family from learning the same harsh lesson. Using her memories from the morning to guide her, Jeri hurried across the pasture, hoping that only the cows might notice. Then she remembered that the cows should now be back at the barn for milking.

A dark puzzle, growing darker. Jeri could think of no obvious reason for people who called Catholics "taigs" to be killing British soldiers in cold blood. The most likely explanation was that they'd shot Edgars so there would be no witness to whatever was going to happen at the farm. Jeri knew from Wee Will that there was often little love to be found between Brits and Northern Irish Loyalists. Looked at from a distance, the Troubles appeared straightforward, but get closer and there were factions swirling within factions, and the enemy was often the person right beside you. Some English soldiers actually thought they were in Ulster to protect people, Catholic or Protestant, not to back up one side against the other in cold-blooded sectarian murders.

Jeri was close to the barn now. She had slipped on the haversack, still full of stones, and was holding the G3 with both hands. Dim light glowed from small grime-smudged windows. Even if she reached one, Jeri doubted she would be able to see through. Instead, she headed toward a door she remembered seeing in the morning. Since it was a door for people and not for cows, it hadn't seemed to matter that it was slightly ajar. Jeri changed her direction of approach until she could see the door and was rewarded by seeing a line of light. It was still ajar.

She crept toward it, wondering how much time she had. The killer of the British soldier had likely taken a more direct route back than hers had been across the meadow, and he was probably alerting his comrades that there was an unexpected change to their plans. There always was, in every plan. Jeri hoped that the attackers' need to improvise would work to her advantage, but then she heard a shot inside the barn. Immediately the single pistol shot was followed by a melee of noise: Tara barking furiously, several more shots, and shouting, all of it nearly lost in the distressed bawling of startled cows.

"Get that fucking dog!"

"Danny! No! Don't."

Jeri was about to enter the barn when the back door of the house opened and a woman emerged.

"Danny! Rory!"

It was Roisin's sister, Peggy. The boys' mother. Someone pulled her back inside.

Jeri pushed the door and entered the barn firing the G3. She aimed high, not intending to do more at this point than to let whoever was inside know that they had more to worry about than two unarmed boys and an old dog. It must have worked, because the strangers who turned to face her were caught absurdly off guard. The yellowish light in the barn gave a lurid cast to the tableau that presented itself to Jeri. Two men stood above the boys, one of whom lay on his back while the other knelt beside him. The cows had become even more agitated by Jeri's shooting, making a din that drowned out any other sound, so it was a movement that alerted Jeri that there was someone to her right, someone who had been looking out a window toward the farmhouse. A burst from her G3 knocked him sideways, and Jeri turned back to where the two men were regaining the presence of mind to understand that they faced only one person.

The world had taken on the adrenaline shine that lifted Jeri outside of normal time to where she felt her every move a marvel of efficiency. She was a fire blazing with varicolored flames. Joy was the brightest, her sense of purpose pitched so sharp that action was sheer pleasure. Her certainty was absolute; she would emerge from this encounter alive. She even had room for pity, because her adversaries were stupidly standing so close together, not even realizing that because the boy was kneeling, she didn't have to worry about hitting him. The pity disappeared in anger because she knew it would turn to despair, and she needed to burn that away. Now. The fools didn't even have cows behind them. She would have hated to hurt a cow.

She almost laughed as the men crumpled like puppets whose strings had been cut. One short burst, that was all it took. She would have laughed if the boy hadn't looked up from the body of his brother and on his face she could see that she was adding to his fear, not reducing it. She realized she was smiling.

"Rory!" She said his name to bring him back from whatever dark place he was sliding toward. It was questionable if he could hear her over the moaning of the cows. She moved quickly to his side. From only inches away, she repeated his name. "Rory."

"They killed Danny. They said they were going to cripple us and shot me in the leg. But then Tara tried to help and they shot her, and Danny was trying to protect Tara. They killed Danny." He was sobbing, and it was difficult to understand what he was saying.

Jeri glanced to where the black and white dog lay in the straw not far away, then turned her attention back to the boy. "Is this all of them?"

"No." The word stopped his tears, as if he had forgotten that the horror wasn't over. "No. When we come to milk, there was a whole mob

143

of them in here. Ten, at least. Oh, Jesus, it hurts."

Somewhat quieter, the cows were still unsettled. They had crowded themselves into a far corner, unwilling to come to the hay-filled feeding trough that separated their side of the barn from the side with the distressing noise and sights.

"Let me see." Rory's pant leg was soaked in blood. He was sitting now, holding his brother in his lap.

"They were knocking us about and laughing until that one came in." Rory nodded to the first man Jeri had shot. "He said there was someone else around, and for them to quit fooling about and just get on with it."

Jeri looked for something to cut with, but then gave it up and ripped the material from the hole that the bullet had left in Rory's pants leg. The wound wasn't as bad as it might have been. The bullet might have nicked some bone, but it was too low to have hit Rory's knee. The boy was trying hard to control himself, but sobs kept escaping.

She could hear him. That meant that the cows were growing quieter. A new sound could be heard, a thumping from the direction of the house.

"Rory. Who is in the house?"

"Ma, Gran, Auntie Rosie."

"Rory, I have to go."

"But the cows. Who's going to milk them now?"

"We'll sort that out later. Tear off a piece of your shirt and wrap it round your leg. Can you make a tourniquet? Good. I'll be back. Is there another door out of here?" She did not want be visible from the direction of the house as she left the shelter of the barn.

Rory nodded, pointing as he did so.

The thumping noise continued, methodical and rhythmic, as Jeri exited the barn and then ran crouching in an angle that would take her away from the barn but closer to the house. She gained the shelter of one of the outbuildings she had explored earlier in the day, and then paused, attempting to ascertain whether anyone was near, letting her ears do the reconnaissance while her eyes adjusted to the dark. It wouldn't do to run into someone.

Jeri could hear little aside from the mysterious thumps and the lowing of the cows. Carefully, she peered around the corner. Someone in the farmhouse had had the presence of mind to turn off the lights. She still couldn't identify the noise, but it was coming from the house and it was changing in nature — less of hollow thump and more of something breaking. Then Jeri understood. Someone was trying to break down the back door with a heavy tool, an axe, maybe, or a sledgehammer. She could see now and made out two figures near the door, perhaps others standing farther back.

†

Roisin heard the gunshots from the barn with a sinking sense of inevitability, as if all her life she had known this moment would come. She had heard gunfire in Belfast, but always from a distance and always involving strangers. Now the horror had come for her and hers. For long seconds, the three women in the kitchen stared at one another, wordlessly confirming that what each was thinking was true. Then Peggy uttered a strangled moan and flung herself toward the door. Roisin ran after, reaching her sister as she threw open the door and called her sons' names into the darkness.

"Danny! Rory!"

"Peg, no." Roisin pulled her back in. "What's done out there is done. Lock the door." She turned back in and saw that her mother had gone to the phone. Roisin turned out the lights and then ran through the parlor and locked the other door into the house.

"Did you get through, Ma?"

"It's dead," Mrs. O'Hara said. "There's no tone."

They were speaking barely above a whisper. Outside they could hear the cows bawling from the barn.

"Peg, when was Mike to come?"

They had gathered at the end of the room farthest from the door, yet they all heard when someone tried the latch, then cursed and pounded it with a fist.

"When the store closed. Oh, Jesus, he'll drive right into them."

"Girls. Help me." Margaret's command carried a lifetime of authority, and her daughters responded immediately.

The three women lifted the kitchen table and pushed it against the door. The table was old and heavy, and there was comfort in any action.

When the pounding began, Roisin stared at the door, hearing her death knell in the blows. She fought back nausea and forced herself to move to the cabinet where her mother kept the kitchen knives. Taking three, she returned to her mother and sister. Each thud on the door felt like a direct blow to her body.

"Upstairs," she said. "We can push something down when the first ones try coming up."

†

Impossible as it seemed, the events in the barn must have gone unnoticed by the attackers outside. Or not unnoticed so much as misinterpreted. They must be so sure of their surprise, so confident in their numbers, that they assumed any gunfire had been their own. Nor had she done that much shooting, Jeri remembered. The noise and confusion of the distressed cows probably muddled any other sounds.

If the thudding attack of the farmhouse door was surely terrifying to those inside, it was also mesmerizing, rhythmic. Those outside waiting for the door to break were like leashed hounds, straining to be loosed. And it wouldn't be long now, from the cracking sounds that accompanied each new blow. Jeri needed to do something quickly or the door would go. Once the attackers were inside, she would lose her chance to deal with them as a group.

Despite the need for haste, Jeri suddenly saw the whole scene as if in another time. The same coast, the same farmstead, with those who lived there taking a last refuge in their sturdy home while outside the Norsemen hammered the door, anxious to be loosed among their prey. In that time, flames from burning buildings lit the night, and the bawling of cattle added confusion then as now.

The wood of the door gave way in a ripping crash. "We've got them now, boys," someone yelled.

Jeri shook her head for focus. Maybe things didn't change a lot over time, but weapons did. She might have rushed in then with a sword or spear, but that was then. Now she had an assault rifle. She fired the G3 at random, separating the shots for more effect, screaming as she claimed the attention of those poised to enter. She didn't worry about aiming as she dove from where she'd been standing and rolled to the right. She heard a yelp of pain that was satisfying, even if it didn't sound serious. She continued firing, even as she rolled and scrambled to not stay in one place.

The clip ran out of bullets. Jeri reached for the extra she'd put in her jacket pocket. There were two more in the rucksack if she needed them. She knew about the G3 assault rifle, but she had never worked with one before, and it took extra seconds to reload.

She could make out a gash in the door to the house, but it wasn't large enough for anyone to have entered. The pack of attackers had scattered and gone to ground. Jeri waited. There was a movement, a shifting in the darkness. She fired. Heard nothing. Moved quickly to another position.

Noises. Rustling. Jeri fired in that direction and moved again. The attackers would have no idea she was alone.

"I never signed on for this," someone yelled. "I'm out of here."

That seemed all the urging needed to begin a rush away from the farmhouse. Jeri had the new clip in place, but she waited. She might hurt one or two more before they left, and she dearly wanted to, but that might also change their minds about leaving. She listened to retreating footsteps and then the ignition of two car engines. One sped away, while another idled. Jeri guessed that vehicle was waiting for missing comrades from the barn. She fired into the air and, in the end, the dead men were left to their own devices as the second car followed the first.

The house was still locked, but Jeri was able to call through the broken door, "They've gone. Rory needs you in the barn." She reached inside and undid the lock. She was moving aside the overturned table when the women emerged from the stairway.

"My boys, where are my boys?"

"In the barn. Rory needs you." Peggy and her mother hurried outside, and Jeri was left facing Roisin. The lights were still off and there was only a glow from the cooking range, not enough for Jeri to read the expression of the woman facing her.

"You should take something for Rory," Jeri said. "He was shot in the leg, I don't think it's bad. But Danny's been killed. I'm sorry."

Jeri left the farmhouse and went to where the little Fiat had been parked. All four tires were flat, and Rory needed a doctor.

Jeri was on her way back toward the house to try and fix the phone wire when she heard an approaching motor. She stepped quickly into the protection afforded by trees, and waited, the G3 ready. Something about the way the car drove into the parking area, as if the driver had done it more than once, and with its lights on, gave her hope that this might not be a new threat. The car stopped, but the occupants hesitated to get out. Perhaps the lack of lights in the house, perhaps something else held them back.

Jeri waited. Finally two men emerged. "Who are you?" she asked from the shadows.

"Mike. Who are you?"

Mike. Peggy's husband and the boys' father. Jeri stepped away from the trees. She held the rifle out of sight, but the Walther was in her pocket and pointed. "I came with Roisin. There's been trouble. Everyone's down at the barn."

Jeri watched as the two men hurried away, and then she went into the house and upstairs to the room that had briefly been hers. She put the few things she had brought with her into the rucksack that she had used during her day in the hills. When she came back outside, the men were carrying Rory to the car.

"Roisin."

The face that swung toward her was tear-stained and drawn. In that instant, Jeri understood that she was being seen not as the savior, but as part of what had attacked the family.

"When the constabulary get here, tell them everything you can, whatever you know. I'd skip our talk in the lay-by, that you knew anything about me before tonight, but don't hide anything else. Don't volunteer anything either."

"Where are you going?" The voice was tight.

"That you don't need to know. I'll give you a shout when I get back to Belfast."

As she walked away, Jeri thought she heard the words, "I never want to see you again," but she chose to ignore them.

†

Before she had left Belfast, Jeri had informed her OC where she meant to go, and in turn she had been given a contact "just in case". It was over a week before she could make her way back to the city. She meant to find Roisin as soon as possible, but when she went to the pub, she learned that the band had taken time off for personal reasons. Indefinitely.

Martin was troubled when he debriefed her. "They got your name from the O'Hara family. They knew who you were before, of course, but now they're adding the cold-blooded murder of the SAS soldier to your docket. Along with the cowardly ambush of three 'innocent volunteers' in a barn. The lad is being portrayed as a civilian who just happened to get caught in the crossfire."

"I didn't kill the Brit."

"We'll put that out, O'Donnell, but this is going to stick to you, and there will be those that want to hang you for it. Those SAS lads have long memories. Still, I don't suppose it will hurt for you to have a fearsome reputation."

Wee Will, on the other hand, was quite cheerful.

"I hear you've been a busy lass."

"Nice to see you again, too, Will. Maybe you should make this one easier to take apart."

"Not losing sleep over a Brit, are you? You think I should enclose disarming instructions? Or do you only like doing them yourself? Up close like."

"Half of what you say always sounds like gibberish. What are you on about now?"

"Three Prods and a Brit. Not bad work."

"I wouldn't believe half of what you hear, Will."

"They'll be after you now, lass. Kill all the Irishmen you want, but this time you got one of them. Wait. Two of them."

"Good of you to worry, Wee Will." She knew he disliked the nickname. It was probably a bad idea to annoy the person working on the bomb you were supposed to place, but Jeri had been out of sorts since returning to the city.

"I'm sure I don't know why they've given you and Kevin this job, as it's only a park and go. None of that fancy footwork the two of you are known for."

†

The target was an RUC police post in one of Belfast's outer precincts. Most constabulary stations had come to resemble fortresses surrounded by barbed wire, some even having watch towers. This one, however, was quite small and located in an outlying suburb with well-to-do residents. A strange car would stand out. Still, the very things which made the location difficult as a target also made it extremely attractive.

The cars usually parked along the street had been noted, as well as the times they were to be found there. A gray Cortina that matched a local vehicle had been lifted, and fitted with counterfeit plates as well. Jeri would drive to the post, park the car where the local driver usually parked, set the timer, and walk to a corner where Kevin would be waiting in another car. The only complication was that the warning would be called in regardless of however long it took Jeri to reach the destination. If she were late, she might just find a contingent of the Royal Ulster Constabulary waiting for her. If anything threw off the timing, she would have to find somewhere to ditch the car and its bomb. Still, the plan gave enough lead time for Jeri to get to Kevin and for them both to be well away.

Jeri was usually able to clear her mind of extraneous thoughts or

149

worry, but ever since she had walked away from the dairy farm, she had found herself trying to explain things to Roisin. A useless enterprise on so many levels, and one so very unlike her, but the need was too strong for her to resist. In the conversation in her mind, Jeri would raise the certainty that if she hadn't been there, then Rory as well as Danny would be dead, and likely the three women. But Roisin knew that. Jeri had seen her face as she emerged from the farmhouse, the fear and horror marking her features so strongly she looked like something drawn on a wall with charred ash. From every vantage point she could imagine, Jeri had weighed the possibility that she herself had been the cause of the attack, but in the end she could only believe that it was the farm that had been the target all along. It was the O'Hara's good luck that Jeri had been Roisin's guest.

And still Jeri could hear Roisin saying, "I never want to see you again."

Jeri recognized that her need to believe that she was not to blame was rooted in the need to have Roisin acknowledge that she was guiltless, that her presence at the farm, and in the country, was a good thing. Those thoughts had gone round and round for days until it came to Jeri how solitary she had become. It wasn't knowledge of guilt or innocence that Jeri was reaching for, she was desperately longing for the affection that had been hers for so very short a time. And reaching this understanding, seeing the shape of her loneliness, she would know a few moments of peace before some new thought strayed in and precipitated the whole long mental trail again.

†

Traffic was light in the area where Jeri's target was situated. She would probably be early rather than late.

Jeri thought about how best to get in touch with Roisin. Returning to the farm was out of the question. A stranger in the rural coastal area would stick out, particularly after what had happened. She might call, but the thought of attempting a phone conversation held very little appeal. She wanted to see Roisin. Perhaps she could get the pub to give her the name of one of the other band members, and she could contact Roisin that way. She thought the lad who had played the uilleann pipes for the band had been fond of a Belfast girl, and if Jeri asked the right questions, she might be able to find him.

She was thinking of a way to get the name of the girl from the bartender that night and almost missed the turn that would take her to the spot where she would leave the Cortina. Jeri summoned up the focus that was usually so easy to maintain and she demanded it of herself now. She had work that needed every last bit of her attention. As she approached the constabulary post, she checked the time. She had arrived sooner than she expected, so she drove two blocks past the target and noted that Kevin was already in place. Now there was a partner to count on. He saw her, although he did nothing to acknowledge her as she drove by. Still early, Jeri drove back to the RUC post.

Elsewhere in the city, the owner of a dark gray Cortina fretted over the slow arrival of a good tire. He had intended to be home by now and being held up by both a flat and flat spare was making him very cross.

Meanwhile, his parking spot was being taken by another dark gray Cortina.

Jeri was still several minutes early, but that should make little difference. The bomb should go off at precisely five o'clock, in forty minutes. Jeri got out, taking with her the rucksack she had been carrying since she'd left the O'Hara farm, and began walking back toward Kevin. She didn't hurry, but she did use a purposeful pace intended to show that she was someone with a reason to be where she was. The area was residential, well-to-do but not wealthy, and there were few people about. A car passed, its driver not looking her way; a bus went by, but Jeri turned her head slightly so that it was unlikely anyone on board would see her face, would have any reason to remember her. She had almost reached the corner where Kevin waited with his car's engine idling when something made her turn back.

She saw the gray Cortina explode in a ball of flame. Forty minutes early, just as the bus was passing, the car exploded. For what felt a long time, her mind and heart stood still, willing the noise and the fire to go back, to disappear. Jeri looked over her shoulder toward Kevin, his face a mirror of her own shock. Then he pulled himself together; he waited only steps away. He mouthed her name.

Jeri turned back. The street was still empty, but the bus was burning and she could hear screams. She started running. She heard Kevin call after her, and she knew he wouldn't wait.

The bus had been thrown across the street toward the RUC post, one side nearly crushed all the way to the other, turning the bus into two sections. Jeri reached the rear door and found it closed fast. Stuck. Someone was pushing from the other side, and she could hear voices from inside. Terrified, panicked voices. She had turned her face away as the bus passed and not taken note of how many passengers were aboard, but this was the time of day that many people would be heading home. Looking about desperately, she saw something resembling a handle, a piece of a tire jack or some such thing. It was metal, and it would do. It was so hot that she nearly dropped it, but she shucked off her jacket and ripped the sleeve off her sweater. Wrapping it round one end of the metal, she wedged the other end into the door and pushed. Then pulled. There was a slight give. From inside she could hear voices shrill with panic. She pushed again. She felt the door begin to give way, and she pulled with every ounce of will. The door snapped. A rush of heat fell on her, followed by several people clambering out as she attempted to move aside.

"Help me with this one."

Jeri looked up to see a man holding up a middle-aged woman who seemed to be in shock. He handed her down, and Jeri held her until he was able to follow her out. Jeri thought she recognized the scent of the woman's shampoo, but she couldn't recall the name. She waited until no one else emerged, and then she stepped inside.

The heat was intense and swirling smoke made her cough. Even as she looked about, she knew this scene would be with her until she died, and in that moment, she hoped that her death wouldn't be too long in coming. She always knew that human flesh was no different from other meat, but the aftermath of an explosion revealed how true that actually was. In the gray, smoky interior, the red of blood and white of bone were shocking colors. Through the smoke, the heat, among the motionless, Jeri saw movement. A woman was crushed where the side of the bus had pushed in. She was very dead, but beside her, on the floor, sat an elderly man, tugging on her arm.

"Get out of there. Now!" The authoritative voice came from behind her.

Jeri moved as fast as possible among the broken seats and buckled floor to reach the old man. He didn't respond to her urging him to leave, so she lifted him bodily.

"No! No! I can't leave her. Help me get her out." He struggled, but Jeri was able to lift him. He began sobbing. "She's my daughter. Please, she's my daughter."

He flailed awkwardly and uselessly, like someone drowning who fights the lifeguard. She held tight and breathed shallowly, trying to inhale as little smoke as possible. The old man was difficult, but surprisingly light. She pulled as much as carried him toward the doorway. Then she felt someone take him from her and someone else grab her arm and help her down and out of the bus. She recognized the uniform.

"Are you all right, miss?" The constable pushed her hurriedly across the street and they had barely reached the sidewalk when, behind them, the crumpled bus mushroomed into flames.

She must have said the right thing because he left her. There were others hurt worse who needed his attention. She walked back to where she had left her jacket and the rucksack, picked them up, and walked away.

†

Jeri walked west. The sky lowered and winter's cold rains began to fall during the night, and Jeri walked on. Daylight came and the rain turned to drizzle. Now and then a car stopped, and she would take the offered ride. Often she walked across roadless terrain. She did not try to avoid police or roadblocks, she simply walked. Something about her discouraged those drivers who did stop for her from asking questions. She slept rough, walking until fatigue forced her to find somewhere to sleep. Vaguely, she knew where she was. She skirted Lough Neagh to the north, and then continued west. On a day when she felt her hunger, she stopped and bought bread and cheese and filled the water bottle she couldn't remember acquiring. Somewhere she lost the SIG. She might have thrown it into the lake. She could remember very little of the time. It wasn't until she reached the Sperrin Mountains of Tyrone that real awareness began seeping back in. It was not a happy event.

A thought would begin, a phrase, a few words, and Jeri would immediately see all the way to the thought's conclusion, and she would shut it down. *But Will must . . . In any war . . . An accident . . .* These were the opening words to some justification, the beginnings of argument for an attempt toward claiming innocence. She was not innocent. Explanation there might be, but all that mattered was that if she had not brought the bomb, people who were now dead would be alive. She needed to open to that entire truth, to stay with all of it, to not shut out any least part, to accept the terrible truth with her whole soul.

She was in some rock-strewn shelter, and she could hear rain outside. Rain, and wind that sighed and moaned. She remembered kneeling by the Clootie well on the cliff above the O'Hara farm and dipping the linen cloth in the water. She had held the wet cloth to her eyes, thinking, with little or no deep belief, to clear her sight, her mind, and most assuredly the life she had chosen for herself in Ulster had been revealed to her from root to leaf. *But any soldier . . .* By choosing the path, she had chosen each and every consequence, and there was no averting a gaze that had asked to see. Each and every consequence.

More time passed. If few words marked her thoughts, they were full of images. Not clear at first, rather rising out of murky water or pushing out of restraining rock or descending from a starry darkness. A vision of a net pulsing with currents of light seemed to grow, as complicated as Borges' map that matched the world point for point. Everyone lived at a knotting that fixed one in time and place, yet one place was connected to all other places and nothing was separate.

The rain abated. Jeri rose and walked the few paces that took her outside the rocky shelter. She discovered she was on a round hilltop. Swirling fog cut off any but the closest view. Turning back, she saw that her shelter was an ancient tomb of huge stones that had been brought to this place thousands of years before. One stone, twice as tall as herself, stood at a slight distance, standing like a sentinel in the mist. She went back inside and slept, dreaming troubled dreams.

She woke thinking of Arkadia O'Malley. O'Malley had warned her that if she stayed in Ireland, she might lose her soul. Thus it had happened. *What do you do after you lose your soul?*

Find it, came the answer, so imperative and sharp that Jeri looked around to see who had spoken. She went outside, but no one was there. The gray sky still hung low, but from her own hilltop, Jeri could see others. The Sperrins, she knew, were bleak and windswept, rounded heights rising like the undulating waves of a time-frozen sea.

She went to the sentinel stone and sat at its base, and watched all day as the fog came in swirling and heaving around her. Then she went into the tomb and slept.

In the morning, she took her place at the foot of the tall standing stone. The mist seemed to hide a storm of shapes that swept past, becoming almost visible, only to disappear again into the grayness. A stag with branching antlers took shape some ways away. Stepping with regal dignity, the grand beast posed against the skyline, only to be claimed by the thickening gray. Then, with no particular strangeness, a woman walked out of the fog directing a goat with a wooden staff. The goat stopped to graze a tuft of brown grass, and the woman waited. Neither of them seemed aware of Jeri. After a while, the goat shook its horned head and walked on, followed by the woman. The tuft of grass was unchanged.

Sometime later, a group of men, maybe a dozen, maybe less, passed by. Two were supported by comrades, but none were without bruise or bloody bindings. While she watched, a chariot made of wicker came rushing from the fog, trailing wisps of mist like flags. Drawn by a pair of wild-eyed horses, the driver raised high a spear. The wounded men scattered, though the chariot's driver seemed not to see them and passed noiselessly back into the gray.

Three shapes flew out of the gloom and settled on a stone that time had tumbled lengthwise. Ravens. Or dark-cloaked old women, who regarded Jeri with bright eyes lacking kindness. Ravens who came to feast on the dead. It seemed that Arkadia O'Malley was standing before the old women who ranged above her. "This is unbecoming," one of them said in a croaking voice, and then they all flew away.

What ought she to do now?

She could go down to one of the few villages that hugged the river valleys and turn herself over to the RUC. If she were lucky, or unlucky, depending on the point of view, she might be delivered alive to the court and from there, to prison. Few along that road would have any question regarding her guilt. Not exactly because of who was dead, though plenty would want to take the price of the dead from her living flesh, but because in their view she had no right to kill. Only the state had the right to violence. And the state belonged to those who ran it.

Jeri fought waves of nausea. The arguments came flooding back and she was tired of them, sick to death of them. She would have a fifty-fifty chance of getting to prison alive, because the people to whom she would deliver herself were the same as those who had killed Danny O'Hara. Did she owe the so-called authorities her life? Or did she now belong to those who had taken on the work of opposing the regime that existed because it was propped up and held in place by the power and prestige of Britain?

These were people who took their right to wage war, to use violence, from the claim that they were the latest in the line of people who fought for Ireland's freedom. Jeri was one of their weapons. They had claimed her, trained her, forged her like a sword and aimed her like a gun, and if some god of justice ever asked, they would say that on them should fall any responsibility for what she had done in their name. But which court would judge this argument? No such court existed.

Worn and exhausted, Jeri fell asleep in the shelter of the ancient tomb. She woke in the dark. She was hungry and took some of the bread, moldy now, and cheese from her haversack, but after a few bites she put it back. The act of chewing took too much energy. It would be nice to sleep here and never wake, to slip from one world to the next. Maybe she would find other O'Donnells there, ancestors for whom this land had been a true home. Surely Millicent would find her here among old tombs. Maybe Fiona would say that she had done enough. She felt at home here among these stones that had witnessed the passing of ages.

The fanciful thought came to her that maybe she could draw her life from the watchful rocks, like Arthur had pulled the sword Excalibur out from the stone. It was the first thought she had had in days that came without a burden. The image grew until she saw herself in Arthur's place, laying her hand on the hilt of a scarred and dented, strong bronze sword and pulling it free from the confining rock. That was her life; it could belong to her if she had the courage to take hold. That was the soul she had lost. Maybe a life couldn't be lived without betrayal. She could let others use her, or she could lay claim to her own life.

†

In her dream, Jeri found herself walking into the dining room at Armagh, between long rows of tables where all the prisoners were standing, and even the guards were looking toward Arkadia O'Malley. Jeri hesitated. Arkadia waited, her aspect stern and grim. Jeri moved forward along a stony path. Overhead, the tall pines meshed into a shadowed canopy.

This is a true dreaming, said the woman who was almost Arkadia.

May I keep it? Jeri asked.

A sigh ran through the people assembled beneath the tall pines, a sigh that shook Jeri like a wind.

Did we win?

You have not failed. When you remember who you are you will know what to keep.

†

Jeri woke. She would go to mainland Europe and disappear among the motley troupes of young drifters roaming through Brussels and Budapest, Amsterdam and Rome. When it was safe, she would send a message asking, since she had lost her own, where she might get another Little Vuchko t-shirt. That was the code they had chosen. Rafi would find

156

her.

At dawn, she began walking west. In the end, Jeri simply walked away from Northern Ireland, across a field in Tyrone, and out of Ulster.

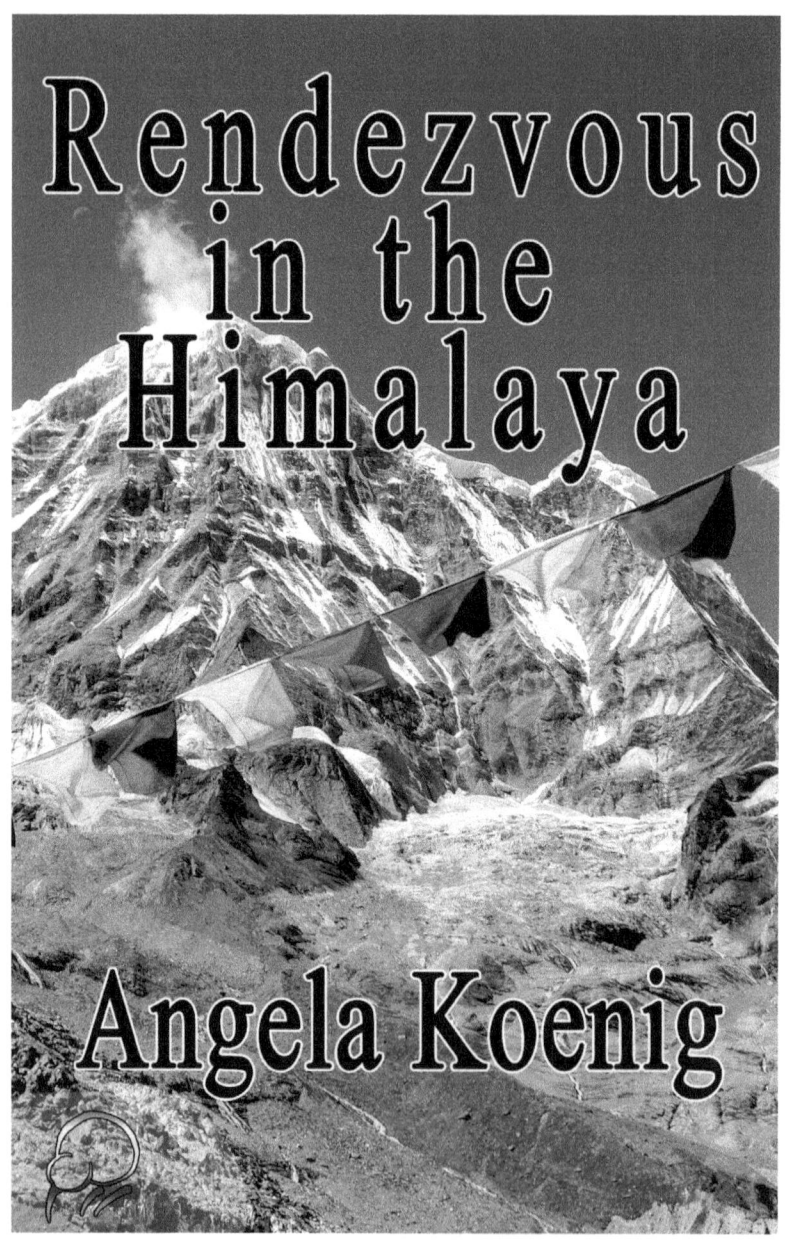

Rendezvous in the Himalaya
Book 2
Refraction Series

Angela Koenig

Affinity
Rainbow Publications

2017

Angela Koenig

Acknowledgments

I am very grateful to Affinity eBooks for bringing this story of mine back into publication. My heartfelt thanks to Julie, Mel, and Nancy—the awesome Affinity team.

Dedication

For Sharon and Nicole, who brought me home

Chapter One

"Have you been asked to a meeting in Nepal?"

The carefully neutral voice of the man from the embassy was contradicted by his aggressive posture and narrowed eyes.

UN Secretary Louise Bolingbrook had known many military men from dozens of armies, and she recognized their breed in the man who had driven into the refugee camp and demanded an interview with her. Although he called himself "Davies from the embassy," she guessed he held the rank of major, maybe colonel.

"We're in Afghanistan, Mr. Davies. The UN has no current writ in Nepal."

Bolingbrook was not antimilitary; her family roots were generations deep in all forms of soldiering. Even so, a UN career devoted to easing the plight of refugees had brought her into contact with a wide variety of belligerent personalities, and the man calling himself Davies was an arrogant, dismissive type that she particularly disliked.

"We aren't concerned with the *where* of this meeting, but with *whom* you're to meet."

"And who is this concerned *we*, Mr. Davies?"

Davies let the silence build before continuing with what seemed an irrelevant statement. "I believe you are related to Paul Bolingbrook?"

"I'm sure you know that Paul was my nephew."

"Do you also know that the person I think you are to meet is the woman who placed the Belfast bomb that killed him?"

Louise Bolingbrook's visits home to England were infrequent, but the last time she'd gone had been to attend her nephew's funeral. Paul was her younger brother's son. A wide gap in years separated her from the brother and sister who had been born following the war that she had spent in a Japanese internment camp. She didn't really know them, let alone any of their children. She did remember the bewildered eyes of

162

Paul's two small children.

Another memory was of her adult relatives discussing, with similar bewilderment, the baffling behavior of Northern Ireland's rebels. In particular, they spoke of the woman who had killed Paul and was said to be an American, an American who had been in an Ulster prison. Released with the understanding that she leave the country, the American had gone to ground instead and emerged not long after as a very effective terrorist.

Commissioner Bolingbrook looked past Davies, through the open tent flap to the bare and dusty plain outside. There, the wretchedly hungry refugees fleeing from Afghanistan waited for the future to alleviate their condition. They, too, had children with bewildered eyes.

"I have made no plans to meet such a person. Now, I do have work, Mr. Davies."

The statement was, technically, true enough.

†

A baby started to cry and the sound was quickly hushed. Despite the narrow and twisting mountain road, Jeri O'Donnell chanced a quick glance into the rear of the canvas-covered military truck she was driving. The eyes of the small group of women and children met hers. Ezma, the woman nearest the open window, shook her head to indicate there was no real problem. Jeri turned her full attention back to the curving road. Pine trees hid any long view, but according to the map she had memorized, they should be reaching the border crossing in a very few minutes.

Jeri resisted the urge to pull her Turkish army cap lower. If she was stopped and questioned, the mission was already in too much trouble for her simple disguise to remedy. Rafi had assured her the border guards had been adequately bribed. All they needed to do to earn their money was let a single truck pass through, even if it was arriving from the wrong direction.

The grade grew steeper, and Jeri shifted down a gear and gave the laboring engine more gas. Ezma reached through the open window and put a hand on Jeri's shoulder, either to reassure Jeri or herself. Once they passed the checkpoint, the road should be free of problems until they reached the meeting point where members of the Kurdish resistance could take over. The U.S. and its allies were still building up troop strength for what Saddam Hussein was insisting would be the Mother of all Battles, and the Kurds of Northern Iraq were trying to prepare for the fallout that was bound to come their way. Memories of villages where

Saddam had killed all the inhabitants were still fresh in Kurdistan, and Jeri was conducting one extended family to a safer haven.

"We need a country of our own," Ezma said, more to herself than to Jeri.

"Doesn't everyone?" Jeri muttered, but she patted the hand that rested on her shoulder. She was saved from making any useless assurances when the road suddenly leveled and revealed a guard station. Situated among pine trees and large boulders, it was nothing more than a hut with a flag. Ezma eased back among the other refugees, and Jeri noted that she kept her AK47 close to hand. Jeri checked the green canvas pack beside her on the seat to make sure of her own SIG P225.

Not until the truck had stopped with the engine idling did a guard emerge from the small post and hesitate. Jeri considered just driving through. She hated checkpoints. The soldier who finally stepped into the clearing and came toward the truck looked far more nervous than Jeri. He was a stout man, not too far from middle age.

"Have you any contraband?" he asked in French.

"Just cigarettes," Jeri answered in the same language.

Jeri reached for another pack, nylon, and twice as large as her canvas bag, and handed it through the window. Along with the money Rafi had already paid, the cartons of high-quality cigarettes made for a tidy bribe. The guard tried to smile as he took it and thanked her, but he still seemed very nervous. Something was wrong, but Jeri couldn't see anything but the guard and his post. Still, her spine itched as she shifted into gear and drove forward.

†

A slight breeze ruffled the leaves on the bush the sniper had set up to camouflage his rifle barrel. After a few seconds, the air became still. Hornet checked his scope again. There had been these occasional stirrings all morning, tiny puffs of wind in otherwise calm air, and they were making what ought to be an easy shot rather chancy. He had already compensated for distance and the downhill trajectory, and he was as certain as it was possible to be that a vehicle arriving in the compound would park where his rifle was aimed. But the wind was erratic, and there was nothing he could do about that but wait.

Waiting was a sniper's specialty. He imagined a newspaper ad: *Sniper wanted. Applicant must have patience, caution, and attention to detail.* A call had told him the truck had arrived at the checkpoint, so he knew his waiting wouldn't be in vain.

Some buzzing bug was taking an interest in the foliage he had tied together and placed on his head like a leafy crown, like part of a summer fest's Green Man costume. He heard the insect first and then felt it crawl through the leaves to examine his shaved head. His hair had been thinning anyway. There was a world of difference between the projected manliness of a shaved head and one with thinning hair. The fly didn't bother him. He was aware of it, but where he was living right now was in the trajectory between the end of his rifle and the place where the truck would stop. The target would get out there, and he would shoot. He wanted this kill. Edgars had been a buddy. They'd had drinks together. The target had done Edgars in cold blood. She had tied him to a tree and executed him.

He cleared his mind. She was the target. Just the target. Assign anything more emotional to her, and it would interfere with the precision he needed to make this kill. He wanted a slow heart rate when he pulled the trigger between one beat and the next.

†

As Jeri O'Donnell swung down from the cab of the truck, she realized how tense and tired her muscles had become from driving the mountain road. She leaned against the cab to stretch each calf and bent to touch her toes. Her passengers were exiting with a minimum of fuss; this was only one leg of their journey. Turkey might be safer than Saddam's Iraq, but it was still not friendly to Kurds, who thought themselves separate from other Turks. That wasn't Jeri's concern. Rafi had only asked her to get them safely across the border. Jeri suspected it was a personal matter with Rafi, not one of his contract jobs. Loyalty was important to him, and as a former KGB agent, it was likely that he had contacts in the Kurdish Resistance.

Thinking of Rafi made Jeri smile. Who would have ever suspected that a young Yugoslavian—so inspired by socialist principles that he volunteered to join the Soviet system that he believed was the hope of the world—would discover he had a talent for being a capitalist entrepreneur as the Soviet system disintegrated?

Rafi Gregoric was now the head of an enterprise that contracted for information, goods, and services. Want a detailed resource map of the Irkutsk region, or a dozen slightly used tanks, or a few mercenaries to truck some oil? Here's a phone number for someone who knows someone. Or maybe you want to retire from the Provisional IRA and need work that will use your considerable talents without causing any more harm to innocent people.

Jeri's smile vanished. Remembering was an enemy to her peace. One thought always led to another. She lifted her eyes to the pine-covered mountainside. It was a dramatic landscape, very beautiful. Suddenly Ezma was standing in front of her, blocking her view. Ezma was rather dramatically beautiful herself—strong features, dark eyes, and a wide smile.

"We are ready to leave. Rafi wants you to get in touch as soon as possible. And I wanted to thank you."

Jeri was going to miss her. Ezma had been attentive and friendly throughout the trip, and while Jeri had enjoyed it, she hadn't felt she knew enough about the woman's culture to interpret exactly what that attention might mean. Eyes that held hers maybe a little too long, a very ready smile, a hand that seemed to find its way to her shoulder or arm quite often—one could get in serious trouble if they made the wrong call about that.

"I didn't do anything but drive."

Ezma favored Jeri with a smile that was only slightly mocking. "But you drove so very well."

Since she was leaving anyway, Jeri decided to chance it. "Are you flirting with me?"

"Yes." Ezma's smile widened. "Seriously, you should come drive for us again." She held out a hand, and when Jeri took it, Ezma surprised Jeri by pulling her forward into a hug.

Something slammed into the truck.

Jeri pushed forward, throwing Ezma to the ground along with herself. They were both familiar with gunfire and, scrambling, reached the boulders at the edge of the drive at the same time. There was silence now as the entire compound held its breath. One shot, that had been all. Jeri looked back at the truck and saw where a bullet had torn a hole in the metal door. She looked at the angle revealed by the ragged metal.

"Sniper," Ezma said.

†

"He was a professional, Rafi. If it hadn't been for your Ezma, that would have been a kill shot. Me."

The hotel in Tajikistan was reputed to be top notch, but the furniture in the room was worn and none too stable. When Jeri had laid out the map on the table, she had felt one of the legs sway. Even so, Rafi had found decent ale for both of them.

"Not my Ezma. I just thought the two of you might have common interests."

Rafi managed a look of such profound innocence that Jeri almost laughed. "I can take care of my own private life, if you don't mind. And don't change the subject. I climbed the hill and checked out the nest, but of course he was gone. I could tell he'd been there awhile, and from that position, I was the only probable target."

"It was not your time, Stella."

Stella had been Rafi's name for Jeri ever since Chechnya.

"I'd bet good money he was SAS. Is there a price out on me?"

"Of course there is. Quite a lot of money. And nowhere near what you're worth, if you're worried about me."

Jeri gave him a sharp look. "Christ, Rafi, I owe you so much that if you ever want to sell me out, I'll sign the receipt. No, I want to know how they knew where I'd be. Any ideas?"

Rafi sighed and shook his head.

Now that she was looking at him, Jeri saw signs of deep fatigue that she had missed when she arrived. He was adept at maintaining the mask of carefree cleverness that he had worn since she first met him, and his dark, boyish good looks would last until time transformed him into a handsome, white-haired elder. Even so, he had changed since those early days. His eyes had secrets now. She supposed her own eyes looked the same. Initially, each had refrained from sharing their pasts out of concern that such knowledge might one day compromise the other. Now, however, they kept their own secrets out of an even deeper kindness. Jeri hoped that Rafi slept more peacefully than she did, but she doubted it.

"You still think we should go ahead with this new project?"

"Yes. It's just the kind of work you asked for when you came to me, Stella. Even though I would rather you were my partner than an employee."

Jeri ignored the veiled offer. She knew he was sincere, and Rafi was closer to her than her own brothers, but she wanted no part of a business or a partnership. "Just think of me as one of your private contractors. Is this a favor, like the last job?"

"A favor? It's true I owed Ezma's brother for some risks he took when we were both in Iran. That was his family you drove, but now I still owe him. I promised him I would also find a way to take his sister off his hands, and you failed me there."

"Sorry. She wasn't my type," Jeri lied.

Rafi lifted an eyebrow in exaggerated disbelief. "You have a type?"

"Forget it, Rafi." If she said anything specific, she knew she could expect to find someone outside her door fitting the precise description, probably wearing a red bowtie and holding a Christmas tree over her head. "Let's just get down to planning how I'm going to get an old Englishwoman to go hiking across the Himalaya with me."

"Whatever you want, but you need someone in your life."

To get them killed? She gestured impatiently toward the open map spread on the table. "What I need is a Tibetan grammar and vocabulary."

"Work, work. Of course I brought you a book. I also have a special present for this job."

"Not somebody's sister again?"

Rafi laughed happily. "No, no. For this work there is only a tough old Sherpa and his nephew."

"What makes you think the Bolingbrook woman will want to go to Tibet?"

"The monk told me he thinks she will."

"You've met him?"

"Yes. I told him I could bring him out, but he won't leave. Still, he wants to see, in his words, 'Darling Louise.' He didn't say more than that."

"Let's hope Darling Louise wants to see him." Jeri's tone was dry, but in fact the prospect of a trek through the mountains was appealing. With luck, the SAS would lose her trail.

Jeri was sure Rafi knew her well enough to recognize that she was actually pleased with the chance to see a new part of the world.

"I have something for you." He walked over to where his unopened bags were stacked and picked one that was long and narrow. With the drama of a magician revealing a rabbit, he undid the zipper and held up what appeared to be a very old, single-shot rifle.

"Jesus, Rafi, that looks like something Daniel Boone might have used."

"Just the thing for a poor Sherpa, but let me show you what I've done."

Cheerful that he had engaged her interest and humming the unmistakable *Ballad of Davy Crockett*, Rafi showed her how he had upgraded the rifle that only appeared old.

Chapter Two

I guess it's just one of those lives.

Kelly Corcoran found the sentiment curiously appropriate as she watched the bus disappear into the mountain fog. She had just been abruptly abandoned on a roadside in Nepal, a country where reincarnation was a common belief. She would be the first to admit she probably looked ridiculous, but she wasn't that far off the main tourist trail in the mountain kingdom, so the people on the bus surely must have seen their share of peculiar tourists.

At home in Cleveland, she usually blended into the background with her medium height, sandy brown hair, and rather ordinary features, but on the bus she had stood out like neon. Kelly had agreed to most of what the clerks at Treks & Tours had suggested she bring on a trip to the far Himalaya. Consequently, she was standing on a mountain road dressed like a mannequin in a camping goods store: wrinkle-free khaki cargo pants with a matching vest that had enough pockets to transport a small general store, a green and teal backpack, and a purple nylon hat. If they hadn't seen her coming, they certainly couldn't miss her going.

Was just appearing laughable reason enough for the driver to stop, come back to her seat, and demand that she leave the bus? She had been doing nothing more objectionable than reading her guidebook. Kelly had protested, rather vigorously, perhaps the only vigorous action she could remember taking recently. But the driver had insisted in his limited English and with many gestures, and in the end, he simply shooed her out like she remembered her mother shooing away chickens who wandered too close to the flower garden. The other bus passengers had added to Kelly's confusion by trying to explain the situation in Nepali, and since they all kept pointing toward the door, she doubted that knowing the language would have helped her keep her seat.

Kelly looked around, but the fog was so thick she could see no more

169

than a few feet in any direction.

Two weeks earlier she had been wandering through her apartment in search of something on which to focus her skittish attention. The administration of the community college where she and George had both worked thought she could ease back into teaching with a summer course, but that was still several months away. Kelly had pulled Dante's *Inferno* from the stack of books she was considering for the course, but even scanning the first few lines proved too much. As she stood with her eyes closed tight against tears that were never far from the surface, she had been seized by a notion to go to Nepal. The urge wasn't entirely without context. Billy had talked a great deal about his visit to Nepal, about a village past Pokhara called Umahthi, and according to Billy, the mountains there rose like prayers toward heaven. Her sudden impulse to visit Nepal had come a week after Billy's funeral.

So here she was, alone on the side of a steep mountain road in Nepal, with no idea what to do next. In fog this thick, a four-star hotel might be just a hundred yards away and she would never know it.

The gravel crunch of approaching footsteps caused her to turn toward the sound. The gray thickened into a dark shape, and the shape became a figure. Wearing a long, loose coat and a scarf that revealed little more of his face than his eyes, the figure's most ominous feature was a rifle slung over one shoulder. Clearly the stranger resembled a bandit more than a bellhop, and Kelly decided this probably ruled out the proximity of a four-star hotel.

Kelly looked away. If she avoided eye contact, perhaps the bandit would just continue past her. In Cleveland, even if you were the only two people on the street, you didn't have to speak if you didn't look at the other person.

The stranger apparently wasn't from Cleveland, because he stopped a few feet away and spoke. "What are you doing here?"

The bandit had a woman's voice. Speaking English. American English. And eyes that were a dark sapphire blue. A strong sense of déjà vu gripped Kelly. She reminded herself that fog could do funny things to perception, because she hadn't just come home, she was lost halfway around the world from home.

"What am I doing here? Good question. How much time do you have?"

"Not much. Can I get the short version?" The speaker didn't sound amused.

Kelly had to look up. At five-six, she never thought of herself as

170

short, but this woman was taller. Her scarf had slipped to reveal features that might be thought attractive if not for a severity that banished such inconsequential concerns.

"Too bad," Kelly said. "I was so counting on finding philosophy in Nepal. Maybe I'm not far enough up a mountain. The bus driver dumped me."

"You're not Louise Bolingbrook."

Not a question, though not a particularly astute assumption.

"You mean the UN person?"

The "UN person" under discussion regularly had her picture in the world's papers alongside stories about human rights and refugees. Once upon a time, Kelly had even gone to hear Louise Bolingbrook speak as part of a university lecture series, and she been duly impressed by the woman who had put her intelligence and energy into service to humanity.

"Right. Louise Bolingbrook, from UNHCR."

UNHCR, Office of the High Commissioner on Refugees. Kelly didn't want any bandit thinking she was a total dunce. "I knew that. Really. I even heard her speak once." Long ago. Before AIDS changed the world.

Memory caused Kelly's mind to stumble. She heard her own words with a profound disinterest. The grief that had been ebbing during the bus ride now turned and began to rise. A counselor had explained that grief feels like depression, but damned if Kelly could understand what difference the difference made.

The stranger was staring speculatively at Kelly. "I imagine the bus driver thought you were Bolingbrook. She was supposed to arrive on that bus."

That almost explained the driver's insistence that Kelly disembark. He had probably never heard the Englishwoman give a lecture. The stranger with the rifle slung over her shoulder was studying Kelly intently.

"Who are you?" Kelly asked. "Not that I'm not glad of the company, but you look like some relative of Che Guevara."

"I do? I was trying for Lawrence of the Himalaya. There won't be another bus along until tomorrow, so we can talk later. Right now, you'd better come with me."

Kelly picked up her backpack from the road and slipped it on. "I'm only halfway through the guidebook, but there must be a rule about following a complete stranger into the fog. Tell me your name so at least you won't be a complete stranger."

"Jeri."

Was there finally a hint of amusement in the dark blue eyes?

"Kelly."

The woman named Jeri nodded and strode off into the mist. Kelly followed. The woman spoke English, American English, but the rifle wasn't part of any standard tourist gear that Kelly had seen at Treks & Tours. Maybe there were safaris in Nepal that she hadn't heard of. The country did have jungles as well as mountains. Oddly, Kelly was more content than worried. Maybe being thoroughly lost in a foreign country and following a tall, dark, armed stranger into the fog was so far out of control that she could just let go and relax.

She hadn't been in control of anything for so very long. She began to drift back into the inner haze that had become her familiar companion.

Soft and calm, the muffling cocoon had become her default position ever since George, older brother and dearest friend, called and asked for her help nearly two years earlier. In a way, the cocoon was like being on a time delay; she heard words, but it would take a second or two before they made sense. She continued her work well enough, teaching English at the same city college where George had been an administrator. She had a knack for presenting the basics of composition. The students liked her even if she did seem to forget their names or returned their papers a day or two late. Most just thought she was a younger airhead version of someone who would age into a true absent-minded professor. On her occasional steps outside the cocoon, Kelly found everything thin and jarring, with colors too bright and noises too loud.

The stranger walking ahead of her turned to see if she was following. Not a stranger now. Jeri. Jeri gave Kelly a nod of approval for keeping up. Good. Kelly didn't want any mysterious American bandit to disapprove of her ability to keep up. Kelly had jogged for years. Jogging and the gym were the only relief she allowed herself while she cared for George's lover, Russell, then for George, then for Billy.

The outer fog of Nepal shimmered with light and then abruptly disappeared. Kelly turned around and saw that they had simply walked out of it. The bank lay behind, like a wall, and below, like a sea of gray. After a few more steps, Jeri left the road to take a faint path that led slightly downhill. Trees and steep hillside limited the view, but the terrain was easy enough to hike. They emerged from the rocks and the view opened out, and Kelly gasped at the sudden beauty. She was looking into a valley terraced by stone retaining walls, green steps for giants to take up and down the mountain. Jeri paused to let her take in the view and then led the way along a path that eventually took them to one of the stone retaining walls. Apparently they were going to use it as a path to the far side of the valley.

Jeri gestured toward the stones. "Be careful along here. Most of the rocks are okay, but the fog makes them slippery and some are loose."

Kelly nodded and followed Jeri onto the retaining wall. She concentrated on her footing. The terraced field to her left was full of plants she didn't recognize, rice maybe. Her farmer father would shake his head in annoyance at such ignorance on her part, but then he hadn't done much more than shake his head at her ever since he learned that both his eldest children were gay, especially after one of them had the bad sense to die of AIDS. Not recognizing the local crop was just the sort of thing one could expect from such children. The drop-off to Kelly's right was considerable, maybe twenty feet, and although she wasn't afraid of heights, the fall was far enough to be dangerous.

Kelly's new hiking boots were finally getting a workout, and they had as good a grip as they were comfortable. Just as advertised. Perhaps she still knew how to shop. When she had decided to fly halfway around the world, the first step had been to the library for background, and the second had been to travel stores for all the things a hip tourist should have. The library reminded her of school, and the school reminded her of George; shopping was much more distracting. She should send Treks & Tours a fan letter.

A rock slipped sideways, and Kelly's balance wavered. Her arms flew out as she fought for footing. She leaned forward, began to fall that way, toward the field, and then righted herself. She almost got back into balance, but she wasn't accustomed to the weight of her pack and she overcompensated.

In a rush of adrenaline clarity, Kelly knew she was going to fall toward the right, and it would be very bad.

"Gotcha! You're okay. Hold on."

Quick hands caught her and then gripped her, pulling her into strong arms and back to safety. Steadied her. Kelly felt a shiver from head to foot. Fear, yes, and adrenaline shock, but something more—a crazy feeling of familiarity, too strong to be ignored, deeper than déjà vu. This could not be the first time that this voice had assured her of safety and these arms had gathered her in to comfort. She should step back, get herself together, but she wanted only to lean into the harbor of this embrace.

"I feel it, too." Jeri's deep blue eyes demanded Kelly's attention, her voice pulling Kelly's mind back from shock. "I don't know what it is, but it's real. We'll sort it out later, I promise, but we can't stop here. Can you keep going?"

"Yeah. Sure. I'm okay."

Kelly pushed back the memory of the instant before being rescued by Jeri's arms. In that moment she had wanted nothing more than to give herself up to falling; in that moment, the lure of surrender had been even stronger than fear.

Jeri O'Donnell had been annoyed when she reached the bus stop and discovered it wasn't Louise Bolingbrook standing in the haze. This was where she had told the bus driver from Pokhara to leave the English lady, and he probably thought he had. The last thing Jeri needed on her hands was a silly American who was dressed like she had been given five minutes to grab everything that caught her eye in some up-scale store for the modern tourist.

And where was Bolingbrook?

To be fair, this tourist looked sillier than she was acting, perhaps was even sturdier than she first appeared, walking with a strong country stride despite the backpack. The odd purple hat contrasted nicely with the walnut shell hair that speckled ginger in the sunlight. Her eyes, somewhere between green and hazel, had assessed Jeri directly, and back at the road, she had been quick to gauge the situation, quick to make up her mind. Something about her tugged at Jeri's memory. Maybe it was the way she tried to appear tough when anyone with an ounce of sensitivity could see that she was just a touch away from shattering. Kelly reminded Jeri of some new prisoners in Armagh women's prison, women who had been both galvanized and nearly petrified by the shock of incarceration. Acting tough and smart was often one of the responses, but Kelly's toughness was more than an act. Stretched and strained though it might be, the strength holding her together was real.

Strong or weak, something was broken. Jeri didn't have time for someone who needed mending.

She chided herself for inattention. She always needed to size up anyone around her, but in the case of the woman following her along the mountain path, she was merely woolgathering. She had no need to speculate about this stranger. She'd make sure Kelly got another bus tomorrow, and that would be the end of it. Walnut hair with ginger highlights, indeed. A more important problem was to understand why Louise Bolingbrook had not been on the bus. Engineering a meeting with

174

the English aristocrat who was also the UN's regional commissioner on refugees had been complicated and tricky, and now just might have become impossible. Jeri would bet money the SAS had some hand in it.

Jeri had never met the woman in person—Rafi had set up this whole arrangement—but she would hold no favor in Bolingbrook's estimation. Jeri might be acting for a Tibetan who could not leave his own country, but to an Englishwoman, Jeri was first and foremost the Ulster rebel on Britain's Most Wanted Terrorist list. The SAS still believed that Jeri had killed one of their own in cold blood at the O'Hara farm in Antrim, and the SAS had very long memories. The irony was that while Jeri had sins to answer for, she was not guilty of that particular death.

It would be useful to find out if the UN commission was leaking any information.

Jeri felt the stones shift beneath her feet and turned to warn Kelly, just in time to see the tourist begin to fall.

One stride, two, and Jeri had a hand on the backpack and pulled. She dug her feet solidly into the rocks she hoped would remain stable, shifted her grip to Kelly's arm, and pulled. She had her. Eyes wide with fear turned toward her, and suddenly Jeri herself was in danger of falling as pale fire ripped through her like lightning.

She kept her grip and pulled Kelly back to level ground. Steadied her. They were both going to be okay. Sudden as a clap of thunder, Jeri felt seared by an understanding deeper than language, but immediately behind it came words: *Too late. You're too late.*

Jeri muttered something and turned her back to Kelly, needing to arrange her face and control her breathing. It was as if someone was running sandpaper over her back, that's how strongly she felt Kelly's presence behind her. One step, two. Away from this feeling that something had just changed profoundly. She had no time for this, no place. No right.

The sun dried the fog-slick rocks of the retaining wall before the two women finished crossing. On the far side of the fields, the path took them higher up the mountain. After about an hour, they reached a narrow defile that opened into a sudden blaze of color. A number of trees, heavy with large red blossoms, surprised Kelly into a laugh of delight. Jeri turned to look at her, and Kelly raised an eyebrow in question.

"Rhododendrons. They're the national flower," Jeri said. "Come on. We're almost there."

They walked through the grove of rhododendrons, and on the other side, another valley appeared. Like the valley they had crossed, this one was also terraced and a twisting road meandered alongside the fields. Just below them, a small cluster of sheds or huts surrounded a relatively flat, open space. A narrow track led away from it in the direction of the distant road.

"I imagine you're hungry," Jeri said.

"Hungry? I'm starved. I could eat a horse." Kelly surprised herself by the admission, but quickly said. "Unless horse is actually a dish here. Please say it's not."

Jeri laughed. "Don't worry. If something tastes like chicken, it probably is."

The path down to the huts was steep but short, and Kelly followed Jeri to a structure that was half stone and half wood. The two men who were waiting followed them into the hut. Only an opening near the roof and a small fire lit the dim space, and it took Kelly's eyes some time to adjust. A barrel and some crates suggested the hut was used for storage. The younger man used a match to light a lamp that brightened the interior.

Jeri greeted both men and spoke at length to the older of the two. Kelly recognized the rhythms of the language as similar to what she'd been hearing since she arrived at the airport in Katmandu.

Jeri slipped out of her long coat and hung it on a wall peg. In a pair of blue Levis and a green sweatshirt over a flannel shirt, she looked much less like an exotic bandit. She left the scarf, although it now hung loosely around her neck. Her hair was held back from her face in a thick braid. Kelly found her strikingly attractive, although her strong features might be too much for some. Dark hair and eyebrows, a wide mouth and thin straight nose, pronounced cheekbones and deep-set eyes, all animated by a fierce intelligence, a determined integrity.

"Suruwah."

Kelly was startled from her study by the younger man, who was holding out a steaming bowl of something that smelled delicious.

Jeri responded to Kelly's apparent confusion. "That means soup. Boiled eggs and rice. His name is Kaju. He's the best cook I've ever met."

"*Dahn ya bahd*, Kaju ji." Kelly thanked him with her guidebook's suggested phrase.

The young man, a boy really, beamed brightly at Kelly's attempt at the language and then ducked his head shyly.

"You are wel-come, Kel-ly la," he replied, pronouncing each

syllable. "You say 'Kaju ji' in Nepal way. I say 'Kelly la' in Tibet way."

For an instant, Kelly was reminded of Billy. He, too, had smiled quite broadly, but he had also tilted his head in such a way that it seemed he was inviting you to be his accomplice in some wicked matter. In a roomful of people, Billy's smile could draw a magic circle around the two of you. It had been Billy's smile that protected Kelly when they took George home for burial.

"What?" Kelly became aware that Jeri had asked a question. She had to quit drifting away from the present.

"Kaju wonders if you'd like some tea."

"My English not good?" Kaju asked.

"No. No. I mean yes, I would like some tea. Your English is very good. Sorry. My head was not here." Kaju laughed, and Kelly smiled with him as she considered the literal meaning of her last sentence.

The soup was as good as Jeri had promised. Jeri and the older man had gone outside. When Kelly was finished with the soup, she took her tea outside into the late afternoon sun. She wandered around the area, intrigued by everything from the stones in the gravel of the drive to the weathered wood of the sheds. Even the familiar seemed exotic by virtue of being in Nepal. She'd never been outside of the United States before, other than to Canada, and although she had expected that her wide reading would substitute for experience, she'd been continually surprised by reality. Books could get the big things right, but they conveyed little of the smells and sounds and colors. Besides, if you read everything from cookbooks to mysteries to travelogues, part of your mind believed it was all fiction.

Some distance from the buildings, Kelly found another retaining wall that overlooked the slope down to the valley. It rose a few feet off the ground, and Kelly sat on the sun-warmed stones. A rushing stream ran alongside the twisting road she had seen earlier and bordered the terraces that stepped down in ledges of emerald green, dotted here and there by more bright groves of rhododendrons.

The extraordinary feeling of recognition that she had experienced with Jeri had receded. Culture was doing that. Rationality didn't recognize what she'd felt, so it was looping the experience out of the normal lines of connection. If she lived in a culture that didn't believe in sunrise, she would wake up to a daily surprise: "By heavens, Frankie Lee, look how that old sun that was gone has come back again." How many times had she been thinking of someone just before the phone rang and it was that person, and still she thought each time, *What an amazing coincidence,* unable to fit the event into a pattern linking belief and evidence.

Billy had always spoken of Nepal as a place where the unfamiliar could emerge from the familiar to take you by surprise. She hadn't even liked Billy when she first met him. He'd been George's friend, George's assistant at the college. George and Russell would arrange for the four of them to do things like go to movies and restaurants, and Kelly learned to not mind what she thought of as Billy's cultivated superficiality. Then Russell died, and as George grew weaker, Billy was just there, seeming to appear by magic whenever he was needed, and Kelly began to find in his lightness a reliable form of courage.

"What brings you to Nepal?"

The question was asked quietly. Kelly wondered how long Jeri had been sitting beside her. When she answered, she felt as if she were speaking to another part of her own mind.

"'I woke and found myself in a dark woods,'" Kelly answered, quoting the opening lines from the *Purgatorio* that had been the spark for the trip.

"'Mi ritrovai per una selva oscura.' What woods were so dark?"

"Death, funerals."

"An accident?"

"Maybe. Most call it AIDS."

"'And youth grows pale, spectre thin, and dies.'"

"Yes. I used to think of that line from Keats a lot. I teach English— at least I used to—so it's a natural. George was my brother. His lover, Russell, died first. Then George. Their friend Billy, my friend, too, helped me take care of them. I think he was in love with George. Billy died last. A couple of weeks ago."

Kelly felt a hand rest lightly on her shoulder, steadying her as surely as when she had almost fallen crossing the rice field. She drew a deep breath. "I'm sorry. I shouldn't just drop this on you."

"Is there someone else you have to talk to here in Nepal? Where are you from?"

"Ohio." Kelly drew another deep breath. "George and I, we both worked at the same college in Cleveland, but we grew up on a farm in southern Ohio."

"A farm. A big farm?"

"Not for the area. We grew corn and some cows. Chickens, too."

"Are they planting there yet?"

"No. Too early. Soon though."

178

Soon it would be spring on the farm near Stone Creek. This was the time of year that she and George had hunted for baby squirrels in the trees by the creek. It was easy to see the nests in trees not yet in leaf, although not many were situated so that they could be reached by climbing. Kelly and George had raised one squirrel all the way to adulthood, and it used to come when they called. Then one spring, it was just gone. Rusty, they had called it.

"Is your farm near a city?"

"Oh my, no!" The thought made Kelly laugh. "The nearest town— we felt lucky when we finally got a Dairy Queen."

Kelly was aware that Jeri was guiding her memory with easy questions, but even so it was pleasant to talk about the town where gravel streets led past white houses and large yards full of tall elm trees. It would be nice to be there now, the two of them, walking along and eating a regular chocolate sundae or even a banana split from the Dairy Queen. Floating on the surface of life, like a cloud, like foam on a creek. Like that large bird rising up from the valley.

"What's that?"

"A griffon," Jeri answered. "A vulture. They have two kinds of vulture here in the mountains."

Kelly turned to face Jeri without moving away. "Who are you?"

"Jeri O'Donnell. From Boston. I know a bit about people dying, too."

Kelly had heard of a shadow crossing someone's face, but she'd never before seen it happen. She watched as memory closed Jeri's eyes and a dark pain moved through her. For the briefest instant, Kelly felt she knew exactly the shape of Jeri's sorrow.

"How do I know you?" Kelly whispered.

Jeri opened her eyes, and they filled the whole of Kelly's world. She felt herself tumbling toward understanding.

The grating growl of an engine shifting gears broke the moment. Jeri leapt to her feet, crouching and facing toward it. The sound of the motor drew closer.

"Stay here," Jeri said, in a voice used to giving orders. She sprinted back toward the hut.

No! Kelly wanted that instant back when she had been sure she was on the verge of understanding.

Who was this woman who roamed through foreign countries carrying guns and getting important officials thrown off buses? Of course, if the important official had been on the bus, she might have gotten off on her own, but that was beside the point. Jeri O'Donnell must be government herself, maybe CIA. Kelly only knew CIA from movies, but she couldn't think of any other explanation that would account for the confidence and the weapon. Clandestine. Kelly had stumbled into some international—what? Clan-des-tin-ery?

Curiosity got the better of Kelly, and she walked back the way Jeri had taken. She reached the edge of the grove just in time to see the truck as it cut its engine. More rust than metal, the truck looked as unreliable as its motor sounded. The front hood had one R and the outline of other letters that might once have read ROVER. Metal protested against metal as the doors opened and two people emerged. The driver was from somewhere in South Asia, and the passenger was Louise Bolingbrook.

The UN official was tall, though not as tall as Jeri, and whip thin, and could have been any age between fifty and seventy. She wore rumpled slacks and a khaki jacket, but Kelly would have wagered money that her outfit never came from a tourist shop. Unsure of her exact title, Kelly knew that Bolingbrook was from UNHCR, Office of the High Commissioner on Refugees. She probably had her choice of titles, considering that she was someone who had kings and queens in her bloodline, but her presence came from her own sovereignty of spirit. Ever since hearing her speak those many years ago, Kelly had followed related news stories with admiration, and Bolingbrook was always in some news story, photogenic and good for a quote. The woman had taken her wealth and privilege and forged them into a tool in service to those who had neither. And not from a safe distance. She worked at the bedsides of people who were sick, ate rice tainted by beetles with people who were hungry, came under fire to aid people near battlefields. She gave her voice to the voiceless in refugee camps and prisons.

Bolingbrook and her companion stood beside their truck and waited until Jeri emerged from the hut. Jeri once again wore the long coat, and the scarf concealed most of her face, but her ancient blunderbuss was absent.

"Did you miss the bus?"

Bolingbrook ignored the question. "Are you Geraldine O'Donnell?"

Jeri nodded.

"Before we go any further, I want you to know that my brother's son was killed disarming a bomb placed in the Belfast ferry office."

"I'm sorry to hear that."

"It is my belief, Miss O'Donnell, that you may quite possibly have killed him."

"You can believe anything you want."

"Do you deny involvement in that or other murders?"

The atmosphere in the yard was so charged that it nearly sparked. Kelly held her breath. A cloud shifted, and the sun, shining between mountains, cast a long ray of light that illuminated the two women as they faced each other like severe angels of opposing gods.

Kelly thought she could see hesitation, but Jeri's voice when she answered was strong and calm. "I have no intention of discussing any matter other than the one we came here for."

Kelly breathed again, but the tension remained. The question of who Jeri was had just been answered; at the same time, it had grown much more complicated. The Troubles of Northern Ireland were something Kelly knew very little about. Her family was Irish, at least on her father's side at some "great-great" relationship, and her mother had liked giving the girls Irish sounding names. Kelly's sister was named Megan. Her father had named the boys and settled for common Christian names: George, Robert, and Edward. Irish to Kelly meant plastic shamrocks on St. Patrick's Day and little Disney leprechauns cavorting around a pot of gold. Also there were romantic legends, sad songs, and dramatic dancers. If she were pushed, Kelly would admit to sympathizing more with the Irish than the British, but it was a distant, meaningless sympathy, like favoring one sports team over another.

"Who is that over in the shadows?"

Kelly realized that Bolingbrook meant her. She stepped forward eagerly. "Kelly Corcoran, ma'am. I'm so pleased to meet you."

"Corcoran. Do you also believe in killing your way to a better world?"

Jesus God. It had never occurred to her. She was just one more ignorant, white American adrift in history, and this stranger had suddenly fixed an identity to her on no more than her name. Kelly stopped, as stunned as if she had been struck. If she hadn't been in the midst of admiring the woman so much, she might have felt the blow less, and despite the remark's lack of accuracy, Kelly had no defense against the withering sarcasm and bitterness that had been flung at her. She felt guilty. She was guilty. When someone dear has died, it can feel like murder. All the things you should have done and should have said weigh into the dreadful secret of your culpability. *Not fair*, wailed her heart, as if the world were a grade-school playground and such small words might bring a teacher who could soothe away death like a scraped knee.

"Miss Corcoran is a tourist whom the bus driver thought was you and dropped off where you were supposed to be. This is the first time we've met, and she has no idea what's happening here."

"Is that so?" Bolingbrook sighed, and Kelly's existence was dismissed. "Then let's get on with our business."

The two women entered the hut, leaving Kelly and the Rover driver outside.

Kelly turned and stumbled back toward the stone wall. She didn't want anyone to see the tears that were so much a part of her life these days. Anything could make her cry—a missed bus or a misguided insult. What a useless nuisance she was turning out to be. Jeri O'Donnell and Louise Bolingbrook were alike in that they both saw big needs and plunged in with their sleeves rolled up, willing to get bloody if necessary. Maybe neither would like the comparison, but they both had guts and nerve. Kelly was feeling sorry for herself just because she had been asked to be a part-time caretaker for people she knew and liked. Loved and then lost.

The tears turned into shaking sobs.

Jeri watched from a distance. She ached to go to Kelly and offer comfort, but she had been called a killer by Bolingbrook. She had no idea what this curiously familiar stranger would make of that, she only knew that she dared not take advantage of Kelly Corcoran's vulnerability. The evening shadows lengthened until Kelly cried herself to some balance, and then Jeri stepped forward.

"Here. I brought you some tea."

"Thanks. I'm sorry for losing it."

"Drink. You have to keep up your fluids at this altitude." Jeri watched as Kelly sipped, and then added. "I'm sorry she mistook you for one of us."

"Why is she here?"

Jeri considered. There seemed no reason for Kelly not to know. "We have some documented information from Tibet. She's our conduit to the Refugee and Human Rights Commissions. They have to know how bad conditions have become for Tibetans."

Kelly nodded. Jeri could see how she was struggling to reach the present and understand what was happening around her.

"Come on, it's getting cold. Tashi, he's Kaju's uncle, built a fire for Bolingbrook's driver."

The driver and Jeri's companions stood around a fire contained in a rusty barrel. The fire radiated warmth, but the evening was still growing cold. Jeri took off her coat and slipped out of the green sweatshirt.

"Here." She handed the sweatshirt to Kelly and slipped back into her long coat. "I'm guessing you don't want to go into your pack for a jacket." Jeri nodded toward the hut.

Kelly managed a tiny smile. "Thanks. I'd rather not incur any other misinterpretations she might have."

"I don't think she has many. Kelly, don't think she's wrong about me."

Jeri was looking up into the distance, but Kelly could see the pain etched on her face. She was trying to find words to ask Jeri to say more when the door opened and a line of light shot across the yard. Louise Bolingbrook walked over to the fire.

"This is extremely impressive. Where did you get it? How?"

"I'm really not at liberty to answer that."

Bolingbrook looked as if she had expected such an answer. She indicated the batch of papers she was holding. "Can you put me in contact with the author?"

"It's too dangerous. He's still inside Tibet."

"It would make a great deal of difference if I could speak to the person directly involved in this report."

Tashi had left the fire, but he suddenly reappeared and gestured urgently to Jeri. They spoke intently in Nepali.

"Lady Bolingbrook, I believe some of your countrymen are on the way. You gave me your word you would come alone."

The UN official was used to reacting quickly to circumstances, and she saw that Jeri was preparing to leave. "I did not break my promise. If you're correct, I've been followed without my knowledge. I must talk to you further about your source."

"We'll see. I have to go. Take Kelly to a bus."

Kelly watched as Jeri walked toward the hut and then started up the trail beside it, following Tashi and Kaju. She suddenly understood that Jeri O'Donnell was about to disappear from her life as abruptly as she'd entered it. The idea was unbearable.

Kelly sprinted after her. Hearing the footsteps, Jeri spun around holding a handgun. More than anything that had happened previously, the presence of this weapon in Jeri's hand impressed Kelly with how serious the situation was. She stopped and backed a step away. Jeri

183

nodded a farewell and began to turn.

"Take me with you." The words seemed to spring of their own accord, and yet Kelly had no inclination to retract them. She was not, in her own experience, an impulsive person, but this felt deeper than impulse, and Kelly understood what she was asking.

Jeri stared intently.

They would both replay this instant many times over, wondering which of them had been braver, wondering how they had known so decisively that they had to meet again.

"I can't now, but go on to Umahthi. I'll find you there, and soon."

"Your word?"

"My word." A few seconds longer, they looked at each other. "Thank you, Kelly Corcoran."

For what? Kelly wanted to ask, but Jeri was gone.

Chapter Three

Kelly stared into the darkness after Jeri O'Donnell, only partially reassured by Jeri's promise to find her again. Slowly Kelly returned to where the UN commissioner and her driver waited beside their vehicle. The fire still burned in the barrel, emitting a small glow. Kelly was accustomed to urban nights where there was always some streetlamp or neon sign or lighted window. The small fire did little against the mountain night, either in terms of light or heat. A large, dark SUV entered the yard and stopped beside the battered old Rover. Kelly's courage faltered as she saw four men emerge. Four large men, each of whom might have auditioned to be a professional football lineman, loomed like shadows in the dwindling light from the barrel's embers. She stepped back toward the hut, an instinctive move away from trouble.

"Stay where you are."

Kelly stopped, fixed in the headlights.

The man who had ordered Kelly to stay turned to Louise Bolingbrook, but she cut him off, and although Kelly was unable to hear the words, the UN official was clearly angry. Remembering how scathing the woman could be, Kelly almost felt sorry for the man as she saw him lean back defensively. Then he turned his attention back to Kelly. He gestured toward her, but Bolingbrook barely glanced in her direction. The UN official's comment was short, accompanied by dismissive gestures. The man shook his head, denying whatever he heard.

"Get in," he barked at Kelly, pointing toward his utility vehicle, his English crisp and British.

Kelly looked to Bolingbrook and for the first time saw indecision there, perhaps even sympathy. "Go with them, Miss Corcoran, although I doubt you have any information they want. I shall inquire about your circumstances tomorrow." The last was a promise to her and a warning to her countrymen.

"I have to get my backpack," Kelly said.

One of the silent men moved toward her.

"Do you have any weapons?" the leader asked. When Kelly shook her head, he added, "Then you won't mind if Nigel checks."

She did mind, but the pat down was quick and impersonal.

"I do have a Swiss Army knife. With a really tiny blade." No one smiled.

Nigel accompanied her into the hut. Kelly took her time removing a down jacket from the pack, carefully keeping her eyes away from the burly Brit lest he think she was asking permission of some sort. She felt oddly unafraid. Perhaps the totality of the outlandish events of the entire day served to buffer her from the reality that she was about to be taken to an unknown somewhere by an unknown group of men. As she put her jacket on, Kelly let her hand linger on Jeri's sweatshirt, taking comfort in this proof that the woman she had met was actually real.

Comfort was harder to come by as the utility vehicle swerved and jolted down the road in a silence colder than the mountain air. Kelly was in the backseat, wedged between Nigel and another man.

"I can't believe we missed the bitch." The driver suddenly broke the silence. "We should have—"

"Shut it," the man sitting beside him commanded, and once more the only sound came from the engine.

For half an hour or perhaps more, Kelly endured the silence, and then the long and complicated day finally took its toll. She fell asleep. When the vehicle stopped suddenly, she woke with no sense of how much time had passed. It might have been minutes or hours. At first she thought they had stopped at another grove of rhododendrons, but through flower-laden branches, the headlights revealed the doorway of a single-story building. Directed by a hard hand on her elbow, Kelly was escorted inside. She was nervous but not afraid that they might harm her physically. Perhaps she should have been.

Announced by the whirr of a motor, a sudden, very bright light revealed the room to contain a battered table, a chair, and a bench. The floor and walls were stained cement, patched and painted repeatedly in pale shades of green, pearl, and gray.

"Sit there." The light revealed the group leader to be a sandy-haired man who now moved the chair to the middle of the room and pointed to it. "You may fool a posh old do-gooder, but we've met your kind before."

Kelly sat, while Nigel and his companion took places at the rear of the room. They felt much more threatening now they were out of sight. The fourth man, the driver, brought in her backpack and unceremoniously upturned it, spilling its contents over the dirty floor. Kelly started to protest and then stopped as she recognized the futility. Obviously they could do anything they wanted, and any comment of hers would merely sound like a whine. She hated whining, especially when she was doing it, but to see her carefully folded and packed clothing dumped onto the floor was unnerving. After tossing her pack aside, the man moved to stand by the door, as if Kelly might suddenly jump up and run into the foreign night, leaving all her belongings strewn about behind her.

The sandy-haired man began the questioning. Over the next exhausting hours, Kelly was amazed at how many times the same thing could be asked in slightly different ways. More disturbing was the constant urge to get up and take her things off the floor. The sight of her underclothes offended her in a way that the questions didn't.

"Do you make a habit of consorting with terrorists, Miss Corcoran?" It was the leader, the sandy-haired man.

Kelly drew a deep breath and began again to describe the day's events.

"Where did you first meet O'Donnell?"

Nigel's companion, a bald man with glasses, interrupted her narrative. He was behind her, and she had to twist to answer him.

"I told you, on the side of the road. The driver insisted that I get off the bus."

"He 'insisted'? Do you speak Nepali?"

"No. He stopped the bus, came back to where I sat, and shooed me off."

"He kicked you?" The sandy-haired man was skeptical in the extreme.

"Not 'shoed' but 'shooed.' It's an American word. It means—"

"Why were you on that bus?" The bald man again.

"I was going to Umahthi." She needed to keep the answers short and simple.

"Meeting your contacts there?"

"Contacts?"

"Drugs, Miss Corcoran, drugs."

Drug dealer. Terrorist. And they said travel wasn't what it used to be.

The questions went on, repeated and expanded, her answers

scorned, dismissed. Kelly found her tendency to drift off useful. There was a stain on the wall that looked like Hudson Bay. She started looking for some passable version of the Great Lakes to make the wall more geographically accurate. Maybe these guys would turn her into a version of the Little Drummer Girl, someone to infiltrate and spy for them. Who was it had that part in the movie? Diane Keaton? Kelly had liked the book better.

"What did O'Donnell look like when you first met her?" A reasonable question, if it hadn't already been asked a dozen times.

"Tall. Black coat. Long black coat. A scarf around her head. A rifle on a strap over her shoulder."

"You make a habit of going off with strange women carrying rifles?"

Bald man's way of saying that she was straining the credulity of any reasonable person.

"Why not?" The questions were growing extremely tiresome. "There wasn't anything else to do, and she had a nice voice."

Damn. She should just answer what they asked.

"Nice? Nice?" The bald man leaned forward until he was only inches from her face. He needed a shave soon, especially since his stubble looked somewhat gray, belying the youthful impression of his shiny head. "You think someone who kills innocent people is nice? I've got photos of people, of pieces of people, that show just how nice your girlfriend is." The emotion in his voice sounded almost sincere. "And if you think it's all humanitarian on my part, get this. She did a buddy of mine. Cold blood. Tied him up and shot him."

Jesus, it could be true. Kelly had no way of knowing. And it did matter. "I'm sorry," she said wearily, "but I can't help you."

The sandy-haired man asked something in a language she didn't understand. When he repeated it, Kelly thought she recognized some cadence that reminded her of an Irish accent.

"You a lesbian, Miss Corcoran?"

The bald man's question took her by surprise. Was she a lesbian? Good question. She had been one before George called and asked if she would help him with Russell. "I'm sorry, sis, I can't do it by myself anymore." The renewal period on her practicing lesbian card had probably lapsed. These days, she was more of a companion. A driver. Runner of errands. Taxi to the doctor. Pill counter. Nudger of reluctant insurance companies. Caller of surviving relatives. Funeral mourner.

"Did you think you'd just follow your IRA bulldyke into the hills

188

and get your nuts off?" Sandy-haired creep guy. Sandy-haired creep dickhead guy.

The curious part was that Kelly hadn't thought about Jeri O'Donnell in such terms, not at first, not as she followed the woman into the mountains; probably because it had just been too long since she'd had any emotional energy left over for such concerns. Nor had butch ever been a particular attraction in her former life. Something else drew her to Jeri, but she doubted that sandy-haired dickhead would be interested in lesbian erotic nuances.

Kelly forced herself to fix on her interrogator's eyes. "I get from your accents that you're not American, but we have a legal saying: if you're not going to charge me, then let me go." Odd how they weren't getting to her the way Louise Bolingbrook had.

Abruptly, the sandy-haired dickhead gestured sharply to the others in the room. "Thank you for your cooperation, Miss Corcoran. We'll be in touch." His tone, thick with sarcasm, suggested that she had been nothing but a waste of time.

And they were gone. Just like that. They even took their light. Kelly had been abandoned once again in Nepal, this time left somewhere in the middle of the night. She found her reading flashlight, and it gave enough light for her to shake out and repack everything. Then she pushed the rickety bench against the wall, lay down on it, and closed her eyes. She'd think about what to do in the morning.

†

Bolingbrook gestured toward the man who had driven her the night before. "This is Yusef Jamali. I want Yusef to come with us." Her tone made it clear that there could be no argument.

Jeri remembered encountering Jamali's name when reading background information on Bolingbrook. The man was also an official from the UN, and although he worked more closely with Human Rights than Refugees, he and Bolingbrook often worked in the same locations.

Jamali nodded to Jeri politely. He had not spoken much during the meeting, deferring to the two women, but concern had marked his attention to their discussion. From his appearance, he might be South Asian. More than likely, considering his accent, he was from London.

Jeri had been expecting something of the sort, so she merely nodded to Jamali in return. "The American. Kelly Corcoran. Did she leave with you last night?"

Louise Bolingbrook and Jeri had met at a crossroads, which gave Tashi a vantage point from which to keep watch. Bolingbrook's companion had remained in the old truck. The negotiations had been constrained by the same mutual hostility of the night before, and neither wanted to linger a moment longer than necessary.

"No." Bolingbrook hesitated, then went on. "The military men took her. They assured me they would let her go after they asked a few questions, and I was able to put a call through to them this morning. Their commander told me she had already been released. I'm sorry, that's all I know. Does asking mean you're more acquainted with her than you indicated?"

"What I said yesterday was true, but I'm responsible for her being with us when your soldiers arrived. She's an innocent."

For an instant Bolingbrook's features softened. "Innocent," she repeated softly, as if the word was some strange but valuable artifact. In the end she simply said, "They're not my soldiers."

Jeri watched the old truck grind away as it left.

"Did she decide the way we wanted?" Tashi asked.

"She did just what Rafi said she'd do—she wants to go to Tibet. She'll meet us on the mountain, day after tomorrow."

"Alone?"

"No. She insists on bringing someone she says is a colleague. The same man who drove her yesterday and again today. It makes sense. Otherwise it will be a long walk for her without a companion. The SAS is obviously getting information from someone in her group. I don't think it's from her, but we'll be able to tell if she's being followed when she joins us."

Tashi nodded. "Better than here. We should go."

"Tashi la." Jeri added the honorific *la* that was the equivalent of "Mister" in Tibetan. Generally she spoke Nepali with the man, but she knew that he had been born in Tibet. "Something Rafi didn't know—Bolingbrook and I are enemies back in her England. No matter how much she wants our information, she won't forget who I am."

"Did you do what she says? Kill her nephew?"

Jeri had been deeply shaken by learning of the relationship of the UN commissioner to the English soldier. She had never known the name of the young man who had attempted to disarm the bomb in the ferry office.

Jeri squinted into the distance, choosing words for honesty but not for excuse. "Yes. My group put a bomb in a travel office. We called to let the authorities know, and her nephew was in the squad that came to disarm it. It went off. It wasn't supposed to harm anyone, but it did."

The two stood in silence. In the time Tashi and Jeri had been planning for the meeting with Bolingbrook, they had learned to respect each other's abilities, particularly the ability to balance caution with necessity. Jeri wanted the man's trust—they had a long way to go together—but she had no idea how he would feel about what she had just told him.

Tashi nodded again. "I know Rafi la, and he says you are his friend. The world changes. We should leave here now."

"Right. But, Tashi la, you go back to camp. I have to go to Umahthi."

Tashi frowned but didn't object.

"I'll walk. I need all the altitude exercise I can get."

Tashi got into the battered Nissan pickup they were using. When it was out of sight, Jeri climbed to a trail beside the road. She wanted to avoid being anywhere that the SAS might be watching.

She let her mind settle on Kelly Corcoran, an indulgence she had avoided until matters with the UN commissioner were settled. Their time together had been short, and yet it was as if every second with Kelly had been etched into Jeri's memory. She recalled walking through the fog and then a dark shape had appeared, acquiring form and detail until, startled, Jeri had found herself looking at a stranger who nevertheless was unaccountably familiar. Jeri had discounted her feelings as interesting but not meaningful, until Kelly had almost fallen from the retaining wall. In that instant, she had been overwhelmed with a sense that Kelly's life was more precious to her than her own.

Reality asserted itself. She had work to do, and Kelly Corcoran, no matter who she was or could be, was not part of that work. If getting Bolingbrook to accept the report out of Tibet didn't carry enough weight on its own merits, the Englishwoman's relationship to a young soldier who had once disarmed bombs was a sharp reminder to Jeri that she had old debts to repay. And yet, a familiarity in the timbre of Kelly's voice, a certain way she cocked her head when listening intently, a determination to ignore her own vulnerability in favor of honesty—these tugged deeply at Jeri's memory.

Memories were not friends to Jeri. She knew them more as the source of nightmares. Just the night before, she had dreamed of a body sliding into dark water, then rolling over as the eyes opened, accusing, longing, hands lifting and reaching, and Jeri had wakened gasping for breath. Millicent had been undeniably dead when Jeri put her into the water, but she was always alive in any dreams. The dead in Jeri's dreams were always still alive.

She forcefully cleared her mind and concentrated on walking. She had promised to find Kelly again, but that was all. Nothing but a brief meeting would be possible. Perhaps, just perhaps, they might meet again somewhere after the matter of Tibet was settled, but for now, Jeri would keep her promise and then send Kelly Corcoran on her way.

†

Kelly woke at dawn, surprisingly refreshed considering that she had slept only a few hours, and fitfully at that, on the bench. Dawn was welcome, bringing the relief of knowing that now there was light, she could get up. She went outside and discovered that her shelter was simply the one room she had been in, probably a hiker's shelter, set a few paces back from a road that was little more than a rutted trail. Behind the rhododendron grove that surrounded the shelter was a shallow stream flowing through a wide valley. A thin mist drifted above the stream, tinged slightly green in the morning light. Bounded by steep slopes with tall but thin trees, the valley itself was contrastingly sparse in vegetation. What trees there were held a waking world full of chitters, chirps, hoots, and screeches. Kelly found the raucous familiarity of the dawn cacophony actually soothing, not unlike the sounds she had once wakened to on the family farm. Only a rooster was needed to complete the chorus.

She hunted through her pack and found a collapsible plastic cup and some tea bags she had squirreled away at some point during her flight from the States. It wasn't coffee, but water from the stream slowly took on the faint taste of tea. Since she had no way to make a fire, this improvised version of sun tea would have to do.

She was unwilling to think about the events of the day before. Rather, she was just content to be enjoying where she was, aimlessly bemused by the colors and sounds surrounding her. The mood held while she shouldered her pack, fastened the waist strap, and picked a direction based on the flow of the stream. She would go upstream. Umahthi was the last stop for the bus that she'd been on, and so her logical direction was up. Whether this was the right road was another matter. Kelly remembered Billy saying that he'd found Umahthi by chance, because a tourist shouldn't be too concerned about destinations. She accepted the memory, noting that this time it came unaccompanied by any emotional intrusions.

Kelly walked for about an hour before she was overtaken by a rusting red pickup. She stepped aside to give it plenty of room to pass, but instead of going on, it stopped. A smiling Nepali man leaned out the window. Kelly assumed the woman and three small children in the cab were all part of his family, and she smiled back at the group. The driver asked a question, which Kelly assumed was about her destination.

"Umahthi?"

His smile grew larger, and he gestured toward the rear where crates of cackling chickens were stowed. Kelly climbed aboard, and soon the little vehicle was protesting its way up a series of switchbacks. In what seemed no time at all, they rounded a curve to reveal a town spread out over the mountainside, a town of white buildings and blue roofs. The driver took her to what appeared to be the town center, stopped, and leaned out the window.

"Umahthi," he said with a broad smile, gesturing about him. When Kelly offered him money, he waved it away and drove off.

They had been this close to the town and knew where she was going, and the British jerks had left her out in the country. Kelly didn't doubt for a minute that they were somehow keeping an eye on her. She was so sure of it that she was extremely tempted to raise her hand in a one-fingered salute.

She considered her next problem, finding accommodations. She solved it by stopping a young couple in matching backpacks, obvious Westerners, striding purposefully down the street. The tall, thin boy looked disdainfully over her head, but his girlfriend spoke enough heavily accented English to direct Kelly to a hotel called Namaste. Just a short walk up a narrow side street, the Namaste was as welcoming as its name. Kelly was given a simple room on the second floor and, once inside, thought she had never seen a more inviting lumpy mattress. She merely meant to lie down and rest a few moments, but she promptly fell asleep. She slept through the day, woke to note it was dark again, and went right back to sleep.

This time when she woke, her previous mood had become decidedly less tranquil. The contradictions had become decidedly starker. She had met a woman who purportedly killed people, and despite this, she wanted more than anything to meet that woman again. Not that Jeri's history didn't matter, it was just inconceivable. Things like IRA ambushes happened in movies and news reports of faraway lands. Even ordinary killings—how was that for a phrase—happened far enough away from her world that they could be successfully ignored. Just like others could successfully ignore thousands and thousands of young men wasting away in an array of hideous diseases. It wasn't distance that made different worlds, it was experience and expectation and the web of drama you spun yourself into. She and George had grown up in a town where everyone lived in each other's pockets, and they'd ended up in a city where an ambulance could come for you and the people in the next door apartment didn't even know you were gone.

If she had an ounce of her Midwest American brain left, she would get on a plane and let yesterday become no more than an interesting episode to tell while dining out with friends. She was in over her head, way over. But she couldn't leave. She didn't want to leave. She picked up the green sweatshirt from where it hung over a chair by the bed and held it up, spread out. She wouldn't leave. Some kind of connection had been made that went beyond words, beyond reason, beyond blood and bone even, something that roused a knowing so deep that if she didn't trust that knowledge, then trust had never and would never make sense. She put the sweatshirt on. Jeri O'Donnell had promised to find her.

†

It was early morning, but Kelly found a restaurant advertising American-style breakfasts. There was something odd about the way the scrambled eggs tasted, as if they were imitating rather than actually being eggs, but the coffee was right. Kelly drank a large cup of it, and she could swear she felt it moving through all her nerve endings with the first sip, bringing with it a sense of well-being. By mid-morning, the hilltop market town of Umahthi was crowded with local people as well as tourists. A stupa carved from living rock dominated the town. Kelly's guidebook described stupas as being constructed in the shape of mandalas, balanced geometric patterns meant to create and inscribe sacred space. Seasons of wind, rain, and ice had smoothed the surface of Umahthi's shrine, but new paint and colorful prayer flags still drew mind and eye to this reminder of Nepal's vibrant religious heritage.

A labyrinth of stalls covered the flagstones below the stupa, and Kelly plunged into the market and immediately became surrounded by exotic sights, sounds, and smells. She bought a thick chapati, a small round of flat bread, and munched as she wandered among languages that sounded much like the chirpings and chitterings of the early morning outside the hiker's shelter. Along with Nepali, she thought she heard Swedish and Greek. Anything not European was beyond her recognition. She was so bemused by a sense of the exotic that, at first, when she overheard two tourists speaking English, she didn't even recognize it.

The colors were as entrancing as the sounds. Kelly paused at a stall to examine a particularly bright and complexly patterned piece of cloth that was spread over the counter, and then she realized it wasn't the cloth that was being offered for sale, but the array of crystals displayed on top of it. They ranged in size from some that were like small candles to one that was as thick and large as her fist. Kelly had seen quartz crystals before, but these were astonishingly clear, as if light had been refined and folded and refined again, forged the way master smiths forged iron. The woman behind the counter smiled encouragingly at Kelly's obvious delight.

With so many to choose from, Kelly's hand moved uncertainly over the array, until she noticed one the shape and size of a pointed plum. She lifted it to a ray of sunlight falling between the market stalls and immediately discovered the interior of the stone held an enchanted vision, a starscape in a faraway galaxy that disappeared with a slight shift of her hand to be replaced by a cascade of rainbows.

"Gemmy things, aren't they?" The speaker sounded as satisfied as if she'd made them herself. "That's how they grow quartz here." Her English was American, and she was a decade or so older than Kelly, braids wound round her head, dressed in a blend of comfortable styles, some local and all colorful.

"Do you know about crystals?"

"I sure do. I'm here to buy some and take them back to Berkeley. California. I'm Tracy, by the way."

"Kelly." Something made Kelly hand the crystal she had picked up to Tracy.

Tracy from Berkeley nodded and took it as if she were used to such gestures, closed her hand around the stone and shut her eyes. When she opened them, she looked closely at Kelly, as if scanning her the way she had the crystal.

"It's lovely," she said quietly, returning the crystal to Kelly. "You have a guide. They come to you when you're ready." She started to say something more but then stopped.

Kelly suddenly felt as if this particular stone must be much more than she could afford. "Do you think it's expensive?"

Tracy smiled reassuringly. "Probably not, but I find it a good idea not to haggle over a stone. Other things maybe, for the game of it, but a crystal needs a different kind of respect."

Kelly turned to the woman behind the counter and discovered that the price was absurdly low.

"It was waiting for you," Tracy said. "I'd say it's a keeper."

Tracy and the Nepali woman seemed to know each other, and they began talking about someone who was absent. Kelly nodded to both and continued wandering the market.

She had put the crystal in her pants pocket but found she really wanted to hold it. Nor did she want to shop; she wanted to be away from the crowds. She made her way to the edge of the stalls and followed a dry streambed that took her to the outskirts of the mountain town. Near a steep slope that rose to jagged heights, she found a boulder to sit on that gave her a view across a rock-strewn flatland. The sun was quite warm. The mountains made it easy to forget that this was a tropical latitude, that Nepal also contained jungles.

Kelly understood she was making herself available in case Jeri was anywhere near.

"What do you think, George?" she whispered aloud. "Do you think I'm crazy to want to be with someone I've only just met? Do you think I've crossed a line to be attracted to her in the first place?"

Clutching her new crystal, she discovered she liked the feel of it, the odd comfort of it safe in her palm. She opened her fist and turned the stone this way and that, enchanted by the shifting interior vistas, watching the facets catch and transform sunlight into rainbows. Toward the base, she saw a sprinkling of black flecks, like five or six grains of pepper. "A keeper," Tracy from Berkeley had called it. Keeper. Like a name.

"I can't take care of myself and Russell anymore, Kell. I hate to ask, but could you help?" Her brother's voice had been full of shame for his need, and his struggle to ignore the shame had broken Kelly's heart. George was her big brother, the guy who took care of her, and it was costing him dearly to lose his capacity to cope. Smart, handsome, effortlessly kind, he had always made everything appear easy.

"I think I like girls," Kelly had said on a visit from college.

"Oh, my dear. I was so hoping, and you just wouldn't decide. Russ, break out the champagne! Kelly's one of us!"

George was so big—big hearted, big minded—that Kelly had grown up in the shade of his protection without encountering much of the world's harsher aspects. He ran interference with their parents,

196

supporting her choices, encouraging her independence. Then he got her a job teaching composition at the city college where he was part of the administration, but he never overstepped a line. He had an acrobat's skill at negotiating between holding on and letting go.

After they became too sick to work, Russell and George stayed home. They were endlessly gentle with each other. Through the waning days of their lives, Kelly felt she had been given more a gift than a burden through the opportunity to share this time with her brother and his lover. Everything was taken away from them but their tremendous hearts, and their love grew visibly stronger as their bodies diminished. Only once did she see despair intrude.

She was living in the condo's spare room, and she had just come home from teaching. She knew something was wrong as soon as she saw George in his robe, sitting at the kitchenette table, silently weeping. George made a point of dressing every day, as if it were a monk's litany of prayers or a warrior's exercise drill. When Kelly tried to hug him, he waved her toward the room he shared with Russell, although the big double bed had been replaced by two smaller ones. Kelly entered the room reluctantly, unsure what she would find. Although death was the silent other presence always in attendance, Kelly was unfamiliar with the actual end stage. As of yet. By the time Billy died, she had learned to recognize to the hour when death would arrive.

Russell wasn't dead. He was sitting propped against pillows, the room full of the paraphernalia of the very sick. A commode sat covered in a nearby corner, and the bedside table was full of pill bottles. A stand held a plastic bag attached by tube and tape to the arm that Russell was staring at, a terribly thin arm, so shrunken that the bones were visible beneath the skin marred by dark Kaposi's marks. Russell looked up with eyes that were large in his gaunt face.

"My grandfather and two uncles died looking like me." Russell's voice was weak but astonished. "They had tattoos, and I have these marks. But even if there's no barbed wire, I'm in a camp, too. What does it mean, Kelly? A holocaust is a sacrifice. Who wants this sacrifice?"

What does it mean, Kelly? she heard him asking long afterward. She could still hear him.

Russell died first. George lingered. From thin, he went to impossibly thinner. All the strength of young manhood that was in him fought to live when he himself would have been content to leave. His body's capacity for health, once a joy, now bound him to longer suffering. Still George managed to live with grace and humor. He and

197

Kelly would sit in the lounge chairs on the balcony overlooking Cleveland and talk about the small town in southern Ohio where they had been children. Billy, George's assistant, came to stay and help with caring for George.

At first it might have been her own internalized homophobia in the presence of Billy's advertised and exaggerated gayness that kept her from liking him, but then she realized he used quips and cleverness to keep people at a distance. In the beginning Billy was like a rich dessert, nice in small amounts, but when AIDS arrived with all its desolating reality, Billy's humor became more like rain in a parched and arid land.

Kelly thought Billy was tired, like she was; George's last days had been so dreadfully wearing. George was ready, but his body had struggled for one more hour, one more minute. She and Billy were getting ready to take George home for the funeral, when she walked in while Billy was changing his shirt. Kelly saw the spot on his back, near his shoulder, large as the lid of a peanut butter jar. He must have known for quite a while it was there. She could do nothing but stare, say nothing, incapable of pretending she hadn't seen.

Billy turned and saw her, started to pull together the ragged tatters of his attitude, and then sagged. Kelly held out her arms and he came to them and they wept together.

What does it mean, Kelly?

It was after Russell's death. She and George were sitting on lounge chairs on the balcony. A late autumn evening with stars faint in the dusk lingered over Lake Erie. She had something she wanted to ask and was searching for words.

"George, later, when things get worse, do you want me—"

George interrupted her. "No, Kell, I want to go through this. The whole thing." He spoke slowly. It wasn't easy for him to breathe. "It seems to me that what we know about anything is so little. Does anybody read RD Laing anymore? Let me get this quote right: 'What we think is so much less than what we know, and what we know is so much less than what there is, and what there is is so much less than what we love, and to that extent we are so much less than what we could be.' Something like that. I want to believe there's meaning in this, and I want to be as true to that as I can, Kell. So I am where I am, and I won't try to put my tiny knowing to deciding what part is worthwhile and what part isn't."

It had been a very long speech for someone so desperately ill. He was quiet for a long time, and Kelly thought he had nothing more to say.

"It's about love, Kell. I'm sure it is."

The sun slid behind a ridge, and the Himalayan air immediately grew chill. Kelly stood. This didn't seem to be the day that she would see Jeri O'Donnell again. Kelly walked slowly back toward the town. The haze that was so much part of her internal landscape was gone, for the moment at least.

It's about love, Kell. I'm sure it is.

†

"Kelly!"

Kelly turned, startled to hear her name, thinking for an instant that it would be Jeri, only to find she was being hailed by Tracy from the market. It occurred to her that the woman might be working for the British, but she discarded the thought. The Californian was just too unrepentantly old hippie with her braids, her open smile, her happy mix of colorful styles.

"Where are you going?"

"Back to my hotel. I'm staying at the Namaste," Kelly answered.

"So am I! Great price for what you get. I found it years ago when I first came here."

"I just found it this morning. How's the restaurant there?"

"Fine for breakfast, but I know a little place not far from here that has great *dahl bhaht*. That's a curry with lentils, rice, and whatever other vegetables they have fresh. Come with me. I was just on my way."

In the way of travelers on their own, they were fast friends before they reached the restaurant that was a single room with heavy wooden tables and chairs painted turquoise and coral. Kelly let Tracy order for them both and was pleasantly surprised with a sweet milky tea, warm, that reminded her of the drink that Kaju had given her the night before.

"Did you find any crystals for your business?"

"Some. There's a Newari man that I'm waiting for. He usually has great stones, but he's late to market. He should be here in a day or two."

"So tell me about crystals. I noticed some black flecks in mine. Is that a flaw?"

"I'd call it a feature. Every crystal has something that makes it different, like people. I'm not sure about the chemistry of the flecks, but the color means that they help ground the stone. Black in a stone links it to the first chakra, the root, and the clear crystal is the crown, so this helps you balance all seven chakras. You'd be surprised how many features there are on a crystal quartz. May I see your stone again?"

"Sure." Kelly patted her vest pockets, searching for the one with the stone.

"Not 'sure,' my dear. You'll bond with your crystal, and you don't want just anyone handling it. People who know will always ask your permission to touch it."

Kelly hesitated only a second. It was a bit late to distrust Tracy. "How do you bond with a stone?"

Tracy smiled. "Just like you're doing. Look at it, hold it, carry it." She examined the plum-shaped stone in the restaurant's low light. Squinting, she tilted it slightly, and then gave a sharp laugh of discovery. "I thought so! Here, on this plane by the point, tilt it 'til you have a focus on the surface. Tell me if you see anything."

Kelly's eyes kept seeking the interior until she found an angle that revealed the flat plane of the surface. No, not quite flat. There was a triangle, actually there were several triangles. She ran a finger over them, but felt nothing. "I see triangles."

"Yes. I wondered if you would. You have a Record Keeper stone. Some say the revelations can be about past lives, your own or humanity's history. Some say that these are from Atlantis, and some say they're not even from Earth."

Kelly stared at her stone, suspended between skepticism and belief, unable to quite move in either direction.

"And at the base, you can see that it hasn't been broken, or that the surface has grown over a break. We call that self-healing. It's a property it will share with you."

For the rest of the meal, Tracy told Kelly about stones. Kelly learned that a crystal was the structure certain molecules made. She had a quartz crystal, but table salt was also a crystal. Gemstones in the rough, like rubies or topaz, all had distinctly shaped crystals. Tracy's sense of humor kept her information from becoming a lecture.

"There are a number of ways to clear crystals, get rid of any undue influences they might have picked up. I like to bury mine for a few days, but some people put them in water overnight. I had this one batch from Arkansas that I buried, and then I couldn't sleep. You know how it is when you just keep tossing around, well, I had to get up in the middle of the night, go out and dig up this burlap bag and take out this big crystal. The big ones really let you know what they need. I took that one out, reburied the rest, and put the big one in the bathtub covered with water. Next day, I had to go to the ocean and bring back seawater for it. Sure is lucky I live in California. Would have been a lot longer drive from

Arizona."

"But how did you know?"

"It was just there in my mind. Why would I have thought of it on my own?"

After the meal, they strolled back toward the hotel in a comfortable camaraderie. Before they parted company, they made plans to meet and go sightseeing in the morning. Kelly drifted off to sleep, clutching the plum crystal, secure that they were undergoing a proper bonding. This day had been so different from the one preceding it. The life of a tourist was truly unpredictable.

Chapter Four

Kelly woke to the feel of a gentle hand on her forehead. She didn't even need to open her eyes.

"Jeri." She put the crystal she was still clutching on the bedstand and took hold of Jeri's hand. It was a strong hand, a hard-working hand, a competent hand. "I've been waiting for you."

"Yes. I promised."

Kelly felt a soft kiss brush her forehead. Everything was so familiar, as if pieces of a puzzle were sliding into place to make a whole picture. She was still somewhere between waking and sleeping, and she felt happy, such an unusual feeling she almost didn't recognize it. Afraid she might fall back to sleep, Kelly opened her eyes. The room's ambient light revealed the shape of the already familiar woman sitting beside her.

"You need to be careful. I think the bad guys are watching me."

"Kelly, they're not the bad guys, I'm the—"

Kelly reached through the darkness and placed her fingers on Jeri's lips to stop the words. "Your enemies, then."

"Yes, all right. That will do. Did they give you a hard time?"

"Only thumbscrews, no rack. They don't believe we just met."

"I'm not sure I believe that." Jeri's quiet laugh was shaky.

"They told me things about you. They said you killed people."

"They probably exaggerated, but essentially it's true. There are people dead because of me."

Kelly was thinking how to answer when Jeri spoke again.

"I came to say goodbye."

"No you didn't."

"Yes. You don't know how much it means to me that we met, but we can't be together."

"Why? Is there someone else?"

"No." The response was short and sharp, but then repeated more sadly. "No. There's no one else."

"You're not going to tell me you're straight." Kelly spoke with exaggerated disbelief.

Even in the dark, Kelly could see the gleam of a challenge in Jeri's eyes. She could see this because the eyes came steadily toward her until she closed her own and lifted her head to meet the kiss. Jeri's lips were soft and gentle, almost comradely, and then, without warning, the world changed. In an instant they were swept into a need that took them like a riptide and still felt as familiar as a homecoming. Everything that might be asked was known in that instant, everything that might be taken was freely given.

Jeri drew back, breathing raggedly, holding tight to Kelly's hand. "I can't. God, I can't, I'm sorry."

"Why?" Kelly struggled to find her voice. "Don't tell me you've taken a vow of celibacy!"

"No, you idiot. You dear, sweet idiot. You can't get involved with me. You can't know what that would mean, but I do, and I want you safe.
"

"Jeri, listen, please listen. Carefully. We're already involved." Kelly had no idea where the words were coming from, but she believed every syllable. "That's why you're here. That's why I'm here. I trust this more than life itself. If this isn't true, then true isn't possible. If we betray this, then the rest of our lives we'll be nothing."

Kelly gripped Jeri's hand, willing her to understand what she was feeling. Meeting Jeri was like regaining a limb that she hadn't even known had been amputated but that she had still longed for in its absence. Kelly wouldn't argue that the recent events of her life might have swayed her balance, cast her adrift, but she was also certain that Jeri was the only line that could guide her back to wholeness.

The voice that answered out of the darkness was broken with pain. "You don't know... I can't. Don't you see? I've already betrayed us."

Kelly understood. Dimly. Perceiving how violence could be an act of despair and betrayal, she was almost tempted to give in. Yet despite the crimes that the men had been so eager to describe while they hinted at even worse, Kelly was sure she wasn't about to play Bonnie to Jeri's Clyde. She didn't want to join Jeri so they could be outlaws together; she just wanted to be home.

She shifted gears and asked in a normal tone of voice, "Where are you going now?"

"I can't," Jeri started to refuse out of habit, then realized Kelly had asked something entirely different. Since the destination wasn't the route, there was no reason not to tell Kelly. "Tibet."

"Why?"

"Bolingbrook wants proof of what's in the report I gave her."

"How will you get that for her?"

Jeri hesitated briefly. "I'm taking her to Tibet. To meet the author of the report."

"That settles it. I thought maybe I'd slow you down or put you in danger, but even if I haven't been shepherding refugees, I can go anywhere she can go." Kelly slid out of bed. In less than a minute, she was dressed. "What can I take with me?"

"Kelly—"

"No, Jeri. I'm going. You didn't come to leave me. You came to get me. You know you did." She waited for a denial, but there was none. She could see Jeri sitting with her head bowed. As surely as she knew her own mind, she felt Jeri's shame as she accepted the truth of what Kelly had said and took it for weakness.

Kelly returned to the bed and knelt beside Jeri, taking hold of the hand she had just released. "And I'm glad to go. You're a dear, brave woman, and we'll work through this. If you hadn't come for me, my heart would have withered. From now on, your eyes are my home, your arms are my shelter, and your heart is my safety."

The words came easily, as if they had been waiting a lifetime to be spoken, a pledge waiting to be renewed.

Jeri already knew that Kelly was stronger than she looked. Kelly might be vulnerable and used to conditions that were softer than the mountains where they would be going, but she had a core of adamant strength that had yet to fail. She would always face life squarely, without turning away or denying what was true. It wasn't Kelly's ability to survive wherever Jeri survived that she doubted, only her own right to bring Kelly into that life. She listened to Kelly's pledge, heard the words and felt the truth of them deep in her own heart, but she knew just as surely that she had forfeited all right to such trust.

But, apparently, the decision was no longer hers to make, not at this moment. Jeri lifted Kelly's hand to her lips. "Bring your papers, money, a change of clothes. Anything warm. Sleeping bag. But only what you can fit into the small pack."

Kelly moved quickly, shifting things out of the large backpack and into the smaller daypack. It had taken long hours back home in Ohio to list and rethink and pack for the trip to Nepal. It took her less than fifteen minutes to leave most of it. The one thing she hesitated over was leaving her books. In the end, she decided to take the *History of the Himalayas*, but she left the guidebook and Dante's *Inferno*.

"Jeri, there's a woman I met. I had dinner with her."

"I know. Tracy. From California." Jeri's voice carried just a touch of satisfaction in admitting to this piece of cleverness.

"We were to have breakfast together. I want to leave a note so someone knows that I didn't just disappear."

"All right. But you can be sure the SAS will read it at some point."

"Who?"

"Sorry. The Brits, they're SAS, Special Air Service. Like the U.S. Delta Force."

"Wow. I can't wait for you to teach me all this stuff." Kelly's reply was dry and distracted. She was trying to think what to write in the note to Tracy. *Sorry to skip out on breakfast. Apparently these Record Keepers work fast. I seem to have found my new path. Please take anything you want from the stuff I'm leaving. Kelly.*

Kelly read the note to Jeri and briefly explained the crystal reference. "That way, she'll know the whole thing is from me and leaving is my own choice. Where are you going?" Jeri was standing by the door. Kelly couldn't imagine that they would just walk out the front door. "Won't the Sassy boys be watching the hotel?"

"Our first adventure. We're going out the window at the end of the hall and then over a couple of roofs. Ready?"

"Ready."

Jeri began to open the door then stopped. She placed a hand on Kelly's shoulder, drew her close, and leaned down until their foreheads were touching. "I'm glad you're with me. But please, Kelly, remember you can leave anytime you want, and I won't try to hold you back." Then she turned and opened the door.

†

Maybe it was the high Himalayan air or maybe it was just her own giddiness that kept threatening to make Kelly burst into laughter, as if her heart were singing. Jeri set a moderately quick pace toward peaks that loomed dark against the starry sky, but Kelly would have preferred to jog. Or run. Or skip. Instead, she followed Jeri quietly, matching her steady steps. They walked for the next two hours as dawn dimmed the stars and paled the sky to reveal that they were on a wide, dry plain that burst into relief as the sun swiftly lit the far snowy peaks like so many candles suddenly topped by flame.

"I need food," Kelly said. Her giddiness had diminished considerably. "Can you make me any promises?"

Jeri turned around. "I can do better than that. Let's stop over there."

The plain that had at first appeared almost flat was proving to be broken by numerous crevices and gullies that required cautious crossing. Jeri indicated a scattering of boulders that would shelter them from the wind and anyone looking for them. Once there, in the lee of the wind, they sat facing each other, using the rocks for backrests. Jeri took a thermos and a cloth wrap containing thick chapatis from a worn canvas rucksack. Patched and carefully mended, the pack looked like a survivor from another era.

"Café Himalaya," Jeri said with a sweeping gesture.

Kelly chewed the cold, barley chapati with relish and sipped from the thermos. She would have preferred coffee, but the warm, strong tea was almost as welcome. "You do know the way to a girl's heart. If only you had coffee. Are there any Starbucks in this country?" She enjoyed making Jeri smile. Jeri's features seemed to settle so easily into a dark, harsh intensity, but a smile changed her into a different person. "What's next after the picnic?"

"Aren't you the cheap date? We should reach our mountain late this afternoon and get to our campsite in a couple more hours. I don't expect Bolingbrook to meet us there until tomorrow. How are you holding out?"

"Fine. At home I usually jog every day. And I like hiking. I'm in pretty good shape."

"Fishing for compliments already? You'll get no argument from me." Jeri cocked an eyebrow in an appreciative leer, a hint that she might be experiencing some giddiness of her own. She continued in a more informative tone. "Even lowlanders in good shape find mountains a challenge. We won't be going too much higher today, but it's the thin oxygen of the heights that will do you in up here."

"How dangerous is it where we're going?"

Jeri chewed thoughtfully for a moment. "It's a crapshoot, Kell. Where we're going isn't where the Chinese usually patrol, but they've been unpredictable since Tiananmen. We'll have to be careful."

Kell. George had called her that. Most people called her Kelly. It felt as if Jeri knew her true name, her secret name. She might be tired, but Kelly's heart had the energy for another burst of melody. "How did you get involved with Tibetans?"

Jeri wrapped her half-eaten chapati and replaced it in her pack. A finger traced wear patterns on the canvas as she stared at it. Kelly waited. When at last Jeri answered, she spoke in a flat tone, as if choosing her words was part of a penance. She was responding to the question behind the one that Kelly had asked.

"I placed a bomb in Belfast. It wasn't the first one, and it wasn't the first one that killed someone, but this one blew up a bus by mistake. Before that, I explained these things to myself by saying that's how you had to fight in the Twentieth Century. I said that bombers in planes kill more, that war always has unintended casualties, and I told myself that the Unionists and the Brits did worse. But this time, I knew better. I killed those people, me, and I owe a debt that can never be paid. I owe my life to the dead. I wanted to get myself killed after that, but that would have been too easy. Besides, I can be hard to kill. But I won't give any government that has more rules than honor the right to judge me. So, I choose my own work."

"They told me that last night. The Brits. About the bus, not about that being when you quit. Is that what Bolingbrook meant? About her nephew, I mean. Is that when he died?"

Jeri was silent so long that Kelly thought she wasn't going to answer. She wanted to apologize for asking, but if she did, she would be letting Jeri stay hidden. Kelly had the feeling that their future depended on coaxing Jeri out of hiding.

"That was a different time. We, another Provo volunteer and I, we put a bomb in the Belfast ferry office. To let them know that no place was safe, nowhere could count on business as usual. After we left, the usual warning was phoned to the police so that the office could be evacuated. I read in the paper later that a soldier was killed trying to disarm the bomb. I think that was Bolingbrook's relative."

Jeri looked up. Kelly was still waiting for more.

"He was a soldier for the other side, but I was never happy he was dead. This isn't a confession, Kelly. I don't want absolution. If you're coming with me, you should know these things—where I've been, what I've done. There are some bank robberies back there, too. That's how we raised funds. Gunrunning. But it's ironic that the main thing the SAS won't let go of, the death of one of their own, that wasn't me. But that's a long story, and we should be moving."

Jeri stared into the distance where a large vulture sailed in lazy circles, looking for carrion. Kelly thought her face looked as harsh and sculpted as the gray rock behind it. Kelly let the silence settle. She could think of nothing to say. It occurred to her that she just might have made a mistake by going off with someone who was essentially a stranger. She waited until once again she felt reassurance from her own heart that she had made the only choice possible. There was one more question.

"One of them, the bald one, he said you shot a friend of his. He said you tied him up and shot him."

"Jesus." Jeri drew a deep breath. "No. It doesn't really matter, but that's the one I didn't do."

"Why doesn't it matter?"

"Because they think I did. And in the long run, it's not about scorekeeping."

"But now you do things like this? Like helping the Tibetans if you can?"

"Sort of, but not as a quid pro quo. This sort of thing, I'm just good at it. And it's not all that dramatic. I'm more like a bus driver. Actually, Tashi is the driver. I'm just the tour director." She stood. "More questions?"

"Heaps." Kelly smiled up at the waiting woman. "You left out the part about how you got from Boston to Belfast, but I do want the long answer. I can get it later, right?"

Kelly took the hand that Jeri extended. As she was easily lifted to her feet, Kelly was again surprised by Jeri's astonishing strength. "What do you do to keep in shape?"

"Why, ma'am," Jeri drawled, "I run from the law. Keeps a gal on her toes, it does." She pointed across the plain. "See that formation that looks like a ragged Z or a piece of lightning? Just to the left of the closest mountain? That's where we're headed."

"Is Bolingbrook walking, too?"

"No. She'll drive by the road."

"The road? There's a road?" Kelly's gape-mouthed surprise was real.

Jeri laughed. "I'm not making us walk for the fun of it. The road is being watched. Besides, I think someone near Bolingbrook is grassing to the SAS."

They set out again. Kelly had thought Jeri was overestimating the time that it would take them to reach the mountain, but after an hour or so she changed her mind. The deceptively level appearance of the plain became even more broken by gullies. Some took considerable negotiating to cross, while others were relatively shallow. The terrain made it difficult to maintain an even stride, but Kelly found that concentrating on her footing cleared her mind of its usual slide toward anxiety and sorrow. And when she looked up, the sight of Jeri was still a source of wonder, a marvel. Every so often, she would realize with surprise that she hadn't been thinking of the past at all, at least not her own.

Jeri was having less difficulty than Kelly with her footing, but her mind was more troubled. To say she was having second thoughts about Kelly's presence would be a massive undercount. She truly had planned to find the American tourist as promised, have a rational conversation about their situation, and bid a fond farewell. Hadn't she? All right, maybe she had acted under a less conscious compulsion, maybe she had even hoped she might spend an hour or two in Kelly's bed. But she had never for a moment imagined she would be returning to the mountains accompanied by anyone. Had she? She hadn't been that surprised by Kelly's request to go along to Tibet, and in the darkness of Kelly's room, everything had seemed so clear, so possible. So inevitable. And now what she felt was suspiciously like panic. She should never have just dumped her whole history out like that, without any real explanation or softening. She had meant to shock. Did she mean to drive this woman away?

Jeri glanced back. Kelly was concentrating on her footing, but she was keeping up. This woman, who had sworn to be her companion, was making her way with considerable confidence, at ease in the outdoors. Jeri turned her attention back to her own footing. It felt oddly right, as if there were nothing in the world better to do, nowhere better to be, than crossing a cracked plain in Nepal accompanied by Kelly Corcoran. They came to a particularly steep gully, and Jeri had to concentrate on assessing and choosing the next step. Loosened pebbles bounced ahead of her, and then the ground leveled and she began to climb the far side. Jeri kept her eyes ahead, but she listened to Kelly's progress behind her. When she reached the top, she turned, gave her hand to Kelly, and pulled her up the final few feet.

Then they were standing together, only inches apart. Kelly was smiling a happy, open smile, nothing held back, her cheeks flushed with exertion, her eyes a forest green with flecks of dark amber. Her hat had slipped behind her head, held by the chinstrap, framing hair that reminded Jeri of a sandbank in a river—tan with bits of cinnamon and ochre highlighted in the slanting morning sun. Without thinking, Jeri lifted her hand and began returning loose strands to a more kempt array. Grooming. Primates were immemorially pleased to groom and be groomed. A wave of desire swept through Jeri, so intense that she would not have been able to stand if Kelly had not, at that moment, stepped forward into an embrace that Jeri was able to use for balance.

Kelly lifted her face for the kiss, and Jeri was unable to deny either one of them the pleasure. Kelly's lips were soft, inviting, and she smelled somewhat of cinnamon and citrus as she leaned into Jeri and sighed.

"Do we have time to stop here?"

Jeri felt the question, felt the breath of each soft word against her neck. Time came back. Memory came back. She covered her fear by tightening her arms and brushing a new kiss on Kelly's forehead. "No. Not now."

Kelly must have sensed the shift of feeling, because she stepped back. "All right, then, we'd better get on with it." Her smile was as open and clear as before.

Now and then since leaving Ireland, Jeri had found women for company, for affection, but the encounters had always been brief, always more about need than satisfaction. What began in hunger and hope would become an episode of frustration for her, if not for her companion, and Jeri would emerge angry and empty. Tucked away in a very rarely visited corner of Jeri's mind was a belief that love might just make loving work again. Might. Since love was notably impossible in her life, this was a belief Jeri had been able to maintain without testing. Love was something she had neither expected nor sought, at least not until she had walked out of the fog and into Kelly Corcoran's presence.

What would Rafi make of this? Jeri wondered. He'd laugh most likely. Laugh delightedly to discover that his Stella had been caught by something so human as love. The whole notion of love was howlingly absurd. Jeri tried to put words to what was happening, but bringing Kelly with her made no sense. Still, if she just accepted Kelly's presence, nothing seemed saner. Even so, she understood that the prospect of a closer relationship—no, be honest, the prospect of making love— terrified her. What was Kelly going to make of a lover who was so haunted by ghosts that sex only roused the pain of wanting what was impossible?

Jeri wrenched her mind back to the task at hand. After she left

Ireland behind, it hadn't been too difficult to make her way to mainland Europe and disappear among the aimless hordes of young drifters who haunted the streets of Amsterdam, Paris, and Rome, until she could contact Rafi. When she found him, he was delighted. He could use her. The deteriorating authority of the Soviet state had carried him into a maelstrom where he discovered that he was much more capable of swimming than sinking.

Even as a talented new capitalist entrepreneur, he maintained the same happy-go-lucky insouciance he'd had when they met, but the years had marked Rafi as they had her, and shadows had gathered in his eyes, too. Curiously, this brought them even closer.

Kelly was a stranger to what Jeri and Rafi shared, and Jeri very much wanted her to stay that way. Innocence as well as desire had been in Kelly's kiss, a kiss wholly open and generous. Need had been aroused with such sudden urgency that Jeri had wanted to continue pursuing her own desire, but a stronger knowing demanded that she must not take what was being offered. And not solely because she feared the treachery of her own body that would first hunger and then refuse, but because she could not, would not, bind Kelly to her in the way that making love would connect them. It was more than just foolish to bring Kelly into her life; it was wrong. Kelly was standing at the edge of something she couldn't possibly imagine—a life that would almost certainly destroy her.

Once again the two women found themselves wending their way through a narrow ravine. There weren't many paths across this plain that hadn't been used before, for centuries most likely. Jeri trusted to following what she could see, even though the trail did seem to be taking them lower instead of higher. She relaxed when the path began an upward slant, but part of her automatically registered what a good place it would make for an ambush.

As if on cue, a scattering of falling pebbles prompted her to look up in time to see a figure step out of the shadows not far ahead, blocking the narrow way between embankments.

Jeri stopped.

He was wearing a motley array of worn-out sneakers and jeans, a sweater, and a nylon jacket. A hand rested lightly on the curved blade attached to his belt. The blade was worn, too, rusty, showing neglect. A kukri. Khukuri. The weapon of Gurkhas, Nepal's famed soldiers. The man, more a boy than a man, was no Gurkha, but this fact didn't diminish the danger Jeri felt from him. In the current world, there was not much that was more dangerous than an armed teenager.

"Namaste." He waited just long enough to make his greeting sound threatening. He smiled, a grimace that didn't reach his eyes, which remained narrowed and hidden.

Attuned to the danger, Jeri's being nearly vibrated. She wanted to laugh. This was something she knew, even welcomed. It was so much easier than working through the jumbled strands of her own damaged spirit.

"Namaste," she responded. She looked back to see where Kelly was. Kelly had stopped, looking somewhat alarmed. Good. Her instincts were good. Jeri caught sight of a fleeting motion from someone attempting to stay hidden above and to the right.

Jeri turned back to the boy in front of her.

"You are campers?" His English was heavily accented.

"Hikers," Jeri answered.

The boy called out something, and a few more pebbles slid down the path just before another figure came into view. He was dressed similarly to the first youth, including carrying a rusty kukri of his own. He had emerged from somewhere other than where Jeri had seen movement, so there were three bandits at least.

The one who had spoken first said something. To Jeri, it sounded like, "Need someone to carry?"

Jeri shook her head. "No. Thank you. We can manage."

The boy presented a larger smile. "Yes. Yes. We help. You let us carry," He caressed the handle of his kukri.

"Do you have friends, too?" Jeri asked.

The boy called out, and two more companions appeared in the rocks above them.

Jeri heard Kelly mutter, "A gang."

"Yes," she answered quietly. More loudly, she repeated, "No. Thank you. We carry our own things."

With a slight movement, she let her long coat fall open to reveal the Sig at her belt. As she rested a hand on it, she suspected that her own smile was as devoid of warmth as his. Then she waited, giving the young men time to think about what they were seeing.

She felt adrenaline give the scene the familiar shine that accompanied the time-out-of-time experience of danger. She would have to be careful that no shots went astray. She didn't want any bullets ricocheting among the rocks, as dangerous for her and Kelly as for the bandits. She hoped they would try something. Action would burn off all the banked feelings of the last hour. Perhaps the leader sensed something, her lack of any fear, her eagerness. He stared at her, his smile fading. For a moment he appeared angry then uncertain. It might have been the sight of Jeri's smile, which grew wider. After a moment, the boy barked a command and almost immediately the four disappeared into the rocks overhead.

"Stay close," Jeri said to Kelly. "Let's go."

"They just left?" Kelly asked.

"Yeah." Jeri turned so that Kelly could see the Sig. "Let's go."

They moved on in silence, but to Jeri it felt different from the earlier, more companionable silence. She assumed Kelly was thinking about what had happened, what it meant, what it might portend. Good. Maybe Kelly would realize that, where Jeri was taking her, such encounters might be the norm.

†

By mid-afternoon, the terrain Kelly and Jeri were crossing had developed a definite upward slope. Easy at first, the tilt became ever more pronounced until they were no longer walking, but climbing. Jeri called frequent stops for rest and tea, but they were silent for the most part. Jeri could sense a withdrawal, and she made no attempt to call Kelly back. Better to let her feel her way through whatever was troubling her.

As they drew closer to the landmark that Jeri had pointed out earlier, the lightning-shaped formation resolved itself into dark boulders that had fallen during some long ago avalanche.

"Jeri."

Kelly's voice, almost a whisper, was more alarming than a shout would have been. Jeri spun around. "What?"

"There. What's that?"

Jeri followed Kelly's pointing arm to where a speck hung in the sky. With relief, she identified it as a vulture, then she looked again. Vultures moved; this did not.

"You're right. Damn. That's a helicopter. Don't run, but pick it up a pace. Make for our landmark over there."

Jeri waited until Kelly had reached the rockfall and was hidden before joining her. Kelly had found a place to sit and was leaning back against a rock, her eyes closed. Jeri peered carefully toward the helicopter's last position. It wasn't as stationary as she had first thought,

213

rather it was moving in small circles while drifting toward their mountain, but not at an angle that would bring it across the path Jeri meant to climb.

"I think we're okay. Good thing you saw them first." Jeri's assessment was hope as much as judgment. If anyone was going to have state-of-the-art equipment, it would be the SAS, and they would be using it to scan the plain.

"Tell me again why we couldn't just drive?" Kelly's eyes were closed. "I'm just tired, Jeri. There's so much I want to say, but I'm too tired to find good words. It's been ages since I spent a whole day hiking."

"Either way, we'd have to walk now. Even Bolingbrook will have to climb from here tomorrow. There are no more roads, but at least there's a footpath."

"How will she find it?"

"I made her a map."

"Will we have to climb in the dark?"

"No. We should reach Tashi and Kaju while it's still light."

Kelly opened her eyes. "Who are they? Why are they along?"

"Tashi's from Mustang, that's where we're going." Jeri paused to make sure Kelly recognized the name was one of Nepal's states and not a variety of wild horse. "Mustang is kind of an autonomous region jutting into Tibet, and you're supposed to have special permission to go there. We don't, but Tashi will get us through. His sister married a Tibetan from Lhasa, Kaju's father. Kaju was born here. Tashi also has connections to Bolingbrook's old friend in Tibet, that's how he got involved in this project."

"Old friend?"

Jeri nodded. "We're not supposed to know this, but the writer of the report we gave the commissioner is someone she knew a long time ago. In England. We were pretty sure she'd want to see him. He's a monk now, at a gompa in Tibet."

Kelly nodded but lapsed into silence.

After a while, Jeri said, "Is something bothering you?"

Kelly looked up, fatigue marking her face. "The gun thing. I'm thinking about it."

"Having second thoughts?"

Kelly gazed quietly into the distance, then looked again at Jeri. "Not really. Once you decide to do something, the reality is always full of things you don't anticipate. I think it's the difference between abstraction and reality." After a moment, she added, "I am pretty tired. I hope I'm

214

not going too slow."

"You're doing just fine," Jeri answered, and she meant it. "If you go all the way to Tibet, you won't even notice a little hill like this." She pointed up the mountain.

Kelly had looked as if she might argue about the suggestion that she might not get to Tibet, but she let it pass. "Why do we have to go there? To Tibet. Will Bolingbrook really learn more than what's in the report?"

"It's always been part of the plan to get her to go. The person she knew at Oxford years ago, he wanted to contact her, but it was much too dangerous to do it directly. We suspected that when she realized the report was from her old friend, she'd want to see him in person if it was at all possible."

"We. You keep saying 'we.'"

Jeri thought for a minute. Kelly was clearly tired, but her questions showed her mind was still engaged. "It's complicated, Kell. The world is shifting fast since the Berlin Wall came down, and the Soviet Union itself is coming apart, for all that Gorbachev wants to stop it." She paused again. It was a relief to talk about impersonal areas. "Do you follow much news?"

"I know we just won the Mother of All Wars," Kelly answered brightly. She continued more seriously, "I keep up. The outside world seemed very far away when it was so much effort just to get across town, but George loved the news. He hoped we were on the brink of some kind of new Eden. He hated that he'd be missing it. I suppose it seems a silly thing to regret, that you'll die and miss history, but we've had the Cold War all our lives, and now it seems it will just disappear."

"It's definitely melting, but it was war enough to leave a lot of debris in its wake. I work with someone who figured out how a far-sighted entrepreneur could put some of the loose pieces together on a paying basis." Jeri kept her explanation general, aware that she was oversimplifying a great deal. "Maps, tanks, airplanes, even armies are all being traded and sold."

"Is that legal?"

"Legal?" Jeri rolled the word around. "Legal. Think of it like this. It's like when Rome called the legions home and the world left behind had to find a new order. Law became local then, too. Sometimes you got Prince Give-Me-All-Your-Stuff, and sometimes you got King Arthur."

"I'm starting to feel like Rip Van Winkle myself. Is this, the Rome example, what's really happening? Was George wrong about Eden?"

"From his mouth to God's ear, if She's listening, but Iraq and

Kuwait don't seem very close to paradise." Jeri reached for her backpack. "Enough history for this break. Ready to climb some more?"

"But you never said what this has to do with going to Tibet."

"Oh. Let's see. This monk in Tibet, sort of a monk, wants his old friend, Louise, who is now a big deal in the UN, to stop some Red Chinese outrages, so he got word to my guy who deals in information, who asked me to take Bolingbrook to visit her friend in Tibet. Ready?"

Jeri settled the old canvas pack on her back, extended her hand to Kelly, and they began to climb.

†

"Maps, tanks, oil, airplanes, uranium, it's all lying around, Stella, just waiting to be picked up." Rafi must have noted some skepticism from Jeri, because he had amended his description. "All right, not just lying around, but it's sitting on the shelves and the store owner has run away."

"So why doesn't everybody just take what they want?"

"They do. But having a warehouse full of uniforms is not much good unless you find someone to buy them. I do that—I find a person who wants uniforms. I find buyers for sellers and sellers for buyers. Usually."

"You're a broker."

"Often. But I also want to own more of the source material. I want you to be my partner, Stella."

Rafi had looked so earnest, so boyish, that Jeri had laughed. Rafi always looked innocent as a choirboy when he was working his charm.

"No. No partnerships for me."

"I thought you would say that." Rafi had sighed as he favored her with a speculative gaze, but he refrained from arguing.

†

The footpath up the mountain was winding, narrow, and steep. From the worn look of the rock beneath her feet, Kelly judged the age of the path might be measured in hundreds of years, perhaps even longer. Although Jeri stopped often to make sure they drank water, fatigue still nibbled at Kelly's will to keep going.

Ignoring her aching legs, focused on following Jeri, Kelly didn't even realize they were nearing the top of a ridge. The jagged rock tricked

216

her sense of distance, so that it wasn't until she drew alongside Jeri, who was waiting for her, that she saw a shallow valley between where she stood and where the mountain resumed its rise. She followed the path down with her eyes and saw, flickering like neon in the deepening twilight, the glow of a campfire beneath an overhang.

"Did they leave the light on for us?"

"I believe they did." Jeri put an arm around Kelly, who leaned her head against Jeri's shoulder. They stood so for several minutes, savoring the successful end of their trek, a companionship that felt as if it were rooted in years rather than hours.

As the two women approached through the juniper trees, Tashi and Kaju rose in greeting, and Kaju broke into a wide smile when he recognized Kelly. Almost as if he had been expecting her, Tashi nodded in recognition.

"What's this?" Kelly was looking at the wooden cup that Kaju had handed her. In it lay what looked like a large raw dumpling.

"Tsampa," Jeri explained. "It's a mountain staple everywhere in the Himalaya, usually made from baked barley and buttered tea, but this has some kind of berries, too. Another example of Western cultural corruption, I suppose." She aimed this last at Kaju, along with a disarming wink and a grin.

Kelly nibbled the dumpling and discovered she liked the taste. Either that, or hunger and fatigue had combined to make anything edible delicious. When she finished, she walked over to the nearby stream and rinsed out her cup, but when she tried to give it back to Kaju, he shook his head. She understood that the cup was now hers.

"Try this on." Jeri was holding out a thick bundle. Jeri shook it open to reveal a fleece-lined leather coat, a chuba, not unlike what she herself wore. Kelly slipped into it. The coat was roomy and fell to below her knees.

"It's nice, Jeri, but I brought a down jacket with me. That should be good enough."

"You may be glad of both when we get higher, but what I really want is for you not to be taken for a foreigner, at least from a distance. That's probably what got us accosted earlier." Kelly gave her a sharp look. "Not your fault, I should have gotten you something from the market when I was there. Tashi got this for his wife, but he can get another one before he goes home. We have a cap for you, too. Your shoes will be okay. Lots of folks up here have Western sneakers or hiking shoes."

"Can I keep your sweatshirt?"

"Sure. I guess we've been together long enough for that." Jeri's grin momentarily lit her face. "You can keep that vest of many pockets, too, as long as you wear the coat over it. Start wearing everything tomorrow before Bolingbrook gets here. When she arrives, stay with Kaju as much as you can."

Kelly nodded. "Wait. Are you trying to hide me from Bolingbrook?"

Jeri nodded. "If I can. For as long as I can. But also from anyone who sees us from a distance."

"I don't want to hide that I'm with you."

"Let's talk about that later. Right now, you look too tired to stand. But, Kelly, remember there are people who want to kill me, and they will include you if they learn about you." She paused. "Besides, you never give anything away for free."

"Jeri's Rule: Never give anything away for free. Got it." Kelly tried to stifle a yawn but couldn't. In another minute she might fall asleep while talking. "Okay. Where do we sleep?"

"Over there. By the tree."

Jeri helped Kelly arrange her sleeping bag by the twisted trunk of a juniper, not far from a little stream. "I'll be back in a few minutes," she said. "I have to talk to Tashi."

Kelly just nodded.

Jeri was gone for more than a few minutes. She knew she was stalling, reluctant to deal with the unsettling emotions that had been with her all day. When she did get back, she saw that Kelly had arranged her sleeping bag beside Kelly's. And she was asleep. Relieved, Jeri slipped out of her jacket and jeans and slid into the down bag. For long minutes, she listened to Kelly's breathing as it blended with the murmuring ripple of the nearby water. Bright stars overhead and the pungent smell of the juniper grove folded into the natural lyric of the night.

"You're back." Kelly moved herself close to Jeri's sleeping bag with the ease of flowing water, laid her head on Jeri's shoulder, and immediately fell back to sleep.

In that instant, Jeri fell irretrievably in love. Again. It would appear that falling in love with someone happened over and over, not just once. Kelly's total trust, the complete gift of herself, of her life, without reservation, were all in that short move to Jeri's side, and it took Jeri's breath away. It brought her to tears, and she knew that she would die for this woman who now lay nestled in her arms, her hair soft against Jeri's cheek. She would die for her and die if anything should ever happen to her. Far into the night, Jeri lay awake, learning the feel of her love, the scent, the rhythm of her sleep, and as much as possible, she accepted the truth of how this changed everything.

Chapter Five

Jeri adjusted her binoculars to focus on the path winding up from the plain. No sighting yet of Bolingbrook, not that she expected the UN official at this early hour. The nest of rocks where she perched gave her a clear view of her own camp, as well, and she shifted the binoculars to where she had left Kelly sleeping soundly. The space beneath the junipers was empty, and the sleeping bags were rolled up. She moved the glasses until she saw Kelly joining Kaju and Tashi by the fire. Jeri readjusted her range so she could watch Kelly's expression as Kaju poured a dark liquid into her cup. She wasn't disappointed. Kelly's face suddenly registered pure delight. Jeri was thankful for whatever last minute impulse had prompted her to add packets of instant coffee to the supplies, when she herself preferred tea. Tashi pointed toward her perch, and when Kelly looked up, Jeri waved.

It took several minutes for Kelly to climb, especially because she brought her cup along, careful not to spill a drop.

"Coffee. You got me coffee. I can't believe it."

"Glad to be of service." Jeri smiled. While Kelly savored her coffee, Jeri tasted the oddness of feeling close to someone.

"What are you doing up here?"

"Waiting for Her Ladyship. Want to look? Set your cup over there. You can see most of the way down to the plain from here." Jeri handed Kelly the binoculars and stepped aside to let Kelly take her place. "Careful. Angle away from the sun so it can't reflect off the glass."

Kelly lowered the binoculars and checked where the sun had cleared the horizon. "Is this a test?"

"Sure, and if you pass, you get to hike all the way to Tibet and back."

"Do we need to be so careful? Doesn't she know where we are?"

"She knows in general, but not exactly. Never give anything away

220

for free, remember? And she won't be alone. The driver from the other night will be with her. Yusef Jamali. I think they're a couple, but I'm not sure."

Kelly turned the thought over and nodded. "But won't whoever, the Sassy boys, be able to follow this trail all the way up the mountain to our camp?"

Jeri smiled, pleased at Kelly's process, at her quick grasp of a situation. "You'd think so, wouldn't you? Whoever follows Bolingbrook will assume we're on our way to that pass." Jeri pointed toward the saddleback above them that was the only obvious route between peaks. "And the trail will take them there. Our camp is just above where the trail divides. Thanks to Tashi, we're on the lesser-known way. Actually, it's thanks to his family. The Himalaya Mountains have always been a barrier to travel and trade between Tibet and the Indian subcontinent, and all the usual crossings have been used for centuries, but some families own secret trails the same way that other families own land. Just about as valuable as land, too. Smuggling is an honorable occupation wherever you have borders. We're going to take an unexpected way up and through that pass."

Kelly had been scanning the trail while Jeri talked. Jeri watched as she moved the glasses slowly. Kelly was wearing the chuba, and Jeri decided that the disguise just might hold, for a while at any rate. The dark tan coat covering most of Kelly's clothing gapped open to reveal the nylon vest of many pockets over a loose plaid shirt. And nothing underneath. Kelly was leaning forward, her elbows on a rock to steady the binoculars, and Jeri could see how the delicate skin in the hollow space of her collarbone began a slant toward her breasts.

"Jeri..." Kelly lowered the binoculars.

Taken by surprise, suddenly and uncharacteristically shy, Jeri looked away.

Kelly had already interpreted the gaze.

She set the glasses down carefully and moved through the short distance between them. She recognized anticipation in Jeri's eyes and then she was too close to see anything, and her mouth found Jeri's. Jeri's lips were soft and parted, while her strong hands pulled Kelly close. Jeri leaned back against a rock, and Kelly leaned against the full length of her. Everything disappeared except the sensation of a mouth as hungry and urgent as her own, of hands moving—her own or Jeri's, she wasn't sure. She found the edge of Jeri's shirt so she could touch skin, and then she was savoring the strength of a muscled back.

It had been so long. So very long. How had she forgotten the absolute pleasure of simply touching another woman? Unbelievable. Kelly's mind formed single words that floated like parts of a song through her awareness: *soft, hungry, warm, now.*

"Jeri?"

"Yeah?"

"I felt the earth move. Was that you, or did it really?"

"It wasn't me. Just a tremor."

Kelly pulled away. "What do you mean, 'just a tremor'? I'm from Ohio. The only thing that makes 'just a tremor' there is a big truck passing nearby."

"Happens all the time here—India pushing Asia and making the mountains grow."

"All right, you don't get the credit." Suddenly Kelly swore and moved back. "Crap!"

"Something wrong?"

"Bolingbrook. I saw her. That's what I was going to say before—before the earth moved."

Jeri picked up the binoculars and scanned the trail below.

Two figures were making their way up the trail—Louise Bolingbrook and Yusef Jamali.

"It must be instinct," Jeri muttered.

"What?"

"The Brits, always a trouble to the Irish."

"Do we have to stop?"

"Sorry."

"Yeah, me, too." Kelly smiled. "Do you hate them?"

"Who?"

"The British."

"You do go right to the heart of the matter, don't you? No, I don't hate them. That would be like hating Californians, or Canadians. We're too much alike. Besides, I admire Bolingbrook. She's put her life at the service of a better world, and she gets things done. She doesn't let not being able to do the best thing stand in the way of doing a good thing."

Jeri paused, and Kelly saw her face grow harsh. "But those guys who took you, they are my enemy. They think who they are excuses anything they do. They're all alike, whatever country they're from. Sometimes the state uses and protects them, but they always make their own laws." Another pause. "I know them because I'm one of them."

Jeri's features were no longer soft, but suddenly as stony as the rock around them. Kelly shuddered at what memories Jeri might be seeing, memories far from a mountainside in Nepal. Kelly had stepped back while Jeri scanned the trail, but now she put a hand on Jeri's arm. "I love you, Jeri. I know you're not like that."

Jeri's eyes stayed hard and distant for a long moment, but then she drew a deep breath. "God. I'm sorry. You shouldn't be here."

"I shouldn't be anywhere else."

Slowly the harshness in Jeri's eyes softened. "Just because I don't ask you to leave, doesn't mean I've lost all my good sense. Would you keep watch? I'm going to get us ready to go as soon as Bolingbrook and Jamali get here. Remember to stay with Kaju today, okay?"

"Sure. It's your world. But never question any of my grammar decisions, all right? I have extensive expertise in gerunds and participles, and *Fowler's Usage* is on my bedstand at home."

It took a few seconds for Kelly to get her reward, but it felt good to make Jeri smile. Despite any argument she could offer to the contrary, and there just might be one or two, at that moment Kelly felt like the luckiest woman in the world. The most amazing woman she could imagine loved her. Was falling more and more in love with her. The dark drama of Jeri's looks would always turn heads, but there was more. Her intelligence, her dignity, her emotional integrity, these had sculpted her appearance until beauty was the least of what made her attractive. She watched Jeri make her way down to the camp, enjoying the chance to linger over the sight of her.

Reluctantly, Kelly turned away and trained the binoculars on the two figures climbing up through the rocks. They were still quite far away, but they appeared to be making good time.

How absurd to think she and Jeri were going to attempt a life together under such conditions. But wasn't that what people had always done? Since they were hominids on the savannahs eons ago, surrounded by predators huge and hungry, people had made a life with one another and taken joy where and when it was to be found. Kelly resisted the urge to turn the glasses toward the camp and look again at Jeri. It seemed that eyes had appetites, too. People who took safety for granted could indulge themselves, but if Kelly was going to become competent and useful in this new world, she was going to have to cultivate discipline.

"Do you wish you'd known AIDS was coming?" Kelly had asked George. They were on his balcony, and it was after Russell had died.

"You mean do I wish I'd known the candy store was closing?" George used the metaphor that had come into fashion for referring to the long season when the post-Stonewall gay world spread through American cities with the energy and enthusiasm of a summer beach party.

"You must know," he said in the tone he always used to introduce some drollery, "I have come to believe that AIDS is divine punishment for disco." He allowed Kelly time to laugh, and then he continued more seriously. Speaking was an effort because he was fighting another bout of pneumocystis, the pneumonia particular to AIDS. "If you're asking whether I wish I could live my life differently, of course I would have changed some things if I'd known. But the point is that you never know. So you have to live like you have all the time in the world and love like you only have the moment."

Could she do that? Kelly wasn't a fool; she could feel Jeri's hesitation, her reluctance to make love. And more than that, there was the anger, as if all Jeri's emotions were knotted into a snarl, where one feeling set off another. In another time and place they might have time to work through whatever issues were there, but instead they were here, on a mountain in Nepal, and they might only have the next few hours. Yet even if their life together was to be measured in hours or minutes rather than months or years, Kelly would respect Jeri's reluctance. She believed the heart had its own reasons and set its own required pace. But by all the mountain gods of the Himalayas, she intended to make it clear— whenever or wherever—that she had no hesitation at all. She reached for the crystal in her pocket, already grown used to the comfort of its presence, and closed her fist tightly around it.

She focused again on what she could see through the glasses, Bolingbrook and her companion. They were making steady progress, not particularly fast, but steady. The two paused for a moment, perhaps to catch their breath, and Kelly saw Bolingbrook lean against Jamali and he put an arm around her. Clearly they were a couple. Kelly smiled and moved the glasses in an instinctive wish to not intrude on their privacy. A movement on a far slope to the right drew Kelly's attention, but when she refocused the glasses, careful to prevent any reflection from sunlight, she saw nothing. She should remember to ask Jeri what animals roamed the mountains. Goats of some sort, most likely. There it was again. Something near a boulder. Now she saw a man. Dressed in camouflage. With a sinking in the pit of her stomach, Kelly recognized the sandy-haired dickhead guy who had interrogated her.

Jeri struggled against the dark mood that threatened to take over. If Bolingbrook hadn't shown up, she would be making love to Kelly right now. And that made her remember other things. Like a woman with red-gold curls named Millicent. Millicent was dead, her bones sunk somewhere in the cold waters where the Rhine rolled into the North Sea.

"What?"

"Everything is packed," Tashi repeated in Nepali. "Should Kaju start trekking?"

Jeri waited until she was sure she had her voice under control. "Good idea, Tashi la." She deliberately added the suffix that the Nepali used to show friendship and respect. "I'll get Kelly down, and the two of them can start while you and I wait for the English lady. She has Jamali with her."

A pebble landed on the ground between them, and they looked up to see Kelly waving urgently. Jeri sprinted for the rocks, and it took only a minute or two to climb back to where Kelly waited, her face drawn, her eyes fearful.

"It's the special soldiers from the other night," she said.

Jeri aimed the binoculars according to Kelly's directions. She found a camouflage-clad SAS soldier and searched for more. In a moment, she had found three more. Then she searched the rest of the mountain and ended with Bolingbrook and her companion. At their present speed, they were still a quarter hour away.

"I see them. Good," Jeri said, for Kelly's benefit. "Now we know where they are. I suspected that Bolingbrook's UN group had some kind of leak. I was afraid we wouldn't know when to expect the SAS."

"But they can reach the top before us. They're between here and the pass."

Jeri looked up toward the saddle pass. "They'll reach the regular trail, but we won't be using that one, remember? If we're careful, they may never see us when we go by them. I've been up there, and our trail is a fair distance above the main path."

"But what about Bolingbrook or the guy with her? What if they're the ones helping the soldiers?"

"I trust Bolingbrook. She trusts her friend. Now listen, Kell. I've talked to Tashi, and we want you and Kaju to start out now. He knows the way, so just go with him. If you run into a problem, send Kaju back and he'll let me know. Just tell him, he understands more English than he can speak." She braced herself for some objection.

225

"Sure. But be careful."

Jeri began to reach out but checked the gesture. Kelly had no such hesitation. She took Jeri's hand and raised it to her lips.

"Kaju likes you," Jeri said. "Trust him. Mind how you go." She watched Kelly make her way down to the campsite and then turned her attention back to the climbers below. She had told Kelly nothing that wasn't true, but in fact she was worried. The British SAS were trained and experienced, and they were making their climb toward the saddleback pass at good if not record speed. And they were motivated. Until Kelly had reported the questions from the night the SAS had taken her, Jeri hadn't understood how determined they were to get payback.

"It's the British soldiers," Kelly said to Tashi. "Jeri says you and she will wait for Bolingbrook, but Kaju and I should start for the pass."

Tashi nodded, apparently unconcerned, but Kaju looked frightened. Tashi said something in Nepali and turned to Kelly. "Go along now, Kelly la. Take care of my nephew."

Kelly stared, but then she caught the slight grin that creased the corners of the older man's eyes. "Okay. I'll make sure he doesn't go too fast." She heard Tashi laugh as she followed after Kaju.

The boy tried to pick up all the packs until Kelly stopped him. Not only would being treated like a tourist weaken her already thin disguise, but Kelly did want to be able to pull her own weight. Well, at least carry her own pack.

That was all Kaju would let her carry.

"Tomorrow," he said, pointing to her pack and another one with some of the camp gear. Then he pointed back to hers. "Today."

It didn't take long before Kelly was glad Kaju had been so insistent. She had thought that her exhaustion the day before was due to the long hike across the plain, but as she and Kaju settled into their climb, she realized the altitude was also affecting her. She concentrated on advice from Jeri, about shorter steps being best because long strides used up more calories, and at these heights, calories were about oxygen and oxygen was scarce.

"It's not like climbing steps," Jeri had said. "That's a lowland way of thinking. Take short, sliding steps so your legs use less of your oxygen."

Kelly tried to imitate Kaju, but he was so graceful that he looked like he was water flowing uphill. Her own gait felt fitful and halting by comparison. Kelly remembered to relax her throat so that the airflow was less impeded. That was about oxygen again. Kaju had drawn ahead, but he stopped and waited and offered again to carry her pack. Kelly shook her head. She was determined to manage.

Jeri slipped into her own long coat and assessed Bolingbrook and her companion as they descended into the camp from the ridge. They each carried a relatively small pack. Clearly these were seasoned travelers who knew how to be ruthless in assessing their own needs. Both walked with a steady gait. As they drew closer, Jeri saw that Jamali didn't appear overly tired, but Bolingbrook was showing signs of fatigue. The commissioner nodded a curt greeting to Jeri when she drew close.

Jeri turned to Tashi. "This is Yusef Jamali, Ms. Bolingbrook's colleague." She turned back to Jamali. "Tashi is our guide for this trip." Tashi and Jamali nodded to each other.

"I had hoped to let you rest, but someone alerted your countrymen. They're about a half hour behind you, maybe less. Take five minutes, but then we have to be on our way."

Bolingbrook stared at Jeri then abruptly sat down. Using her pack as a backrest without taking it off, she closed her eyes. Experience had taught her how to use a rest stop when it was available.

Yusef, however, had questions. "You have seen these people?" His accent was British, with only the slightest trace of somewhere else.

"I've seen SAS," Jeri answered. "They're on their way to the pass. Give me your water bottles, and I'll refill them before we leave."

Jeri took her time, and when she returned she found Bolingbrook standing and ready to go on, a sign that the woman had merely been tired and not on the verge of altitude sickness.

"Give me your pack," Jeri said.

The other woman bristled. "I can carry my own weight."

"I'm hoping you have plenty of time to prove that," Jeri said, allowing a slight note of humor to enter her voice. "But right now, I want to make sure we get through the pass as soon as possible."

Again Bolingbrook showed herself willing to sacrifice pride to practicality. With grace. "Thank you," she said, as Jeri adjusted the extra pack to her own gear.

The group began its ascent out of the far side of the small valley. Tashi went first, followed by Bolingbrook, and then Yusef. Jeri walked last. For some distance, the steep and narrow footpath wound through junipers, but after several twists, it turned around a slope and leveled somewhat, allowing the group easier progress. Unfortunately, the sheltering trees were also left behind.

"Wait here," Jeri said, and she went ahead. The main trail aimed directly for the saddleback, but the one she and Tashi had chosen was the path through an upland valley that was home to a few families. Some structures were evident in the shallow valley below, along with fields already planted with barley and potatoes. Jeri saw nothing of the British force as she studied the scene. When she returned to the group, she overheard Yusef and Bolingbrook in conversation.

"But, Louise, who is it that we can't trust?"

"I don't know. I told two absolutely reliable people, that was all, but perhaps someone else wasn't fooled by my so-called leave of absence to go to Italy. I may have been wrong to assume that everyone is too taken up with the Kurdish situation in Iraq to pay much attention to my itinerary."

Jeri felt reassured, not so much by the words as by their tone. Yusef and Louise spoke to one another with a companionable intimacy. Yusef's presence, though unexpected, would go a long way to making the trip into Tibet smoother. Jeri almost smiled, wondering about the argument that must have preceded his joining the trek. She would wager money that Bolingbrook had tried to make him stay behind.

The small group, led by Tashi, was well past the fields and was approaching another stand of trees when suddenly a figure emerged, running toward them. With a shock of fear, Jeri recognized Kaju.

Kelly suspected that Kaju could travel much faster than he was, but Jeri or Tashi must have told him to set an easy pace for Kelly. Easy but steady, just like the guidebooks recommended for hikers at high altitude. By the time they reached the trail above the farms, Kelly had even begun to enjoy the rhythm. She drew deep, slow breaths and matched them to short steps. Several times Kaju looked back, checking her progress, and when he was assured that all was well, he gave her a thumbs up gesture along with a smile.

The valley farms looked small but appeared to be kept by people who cared. A herd of stocky animals grazed leisurely on a far slope, and at first, Kelly thought they might be sheep, but a closer look showed them to be yaks. She had seen pictures of the smaller animals in her *History of the Himalayas*, diminutive versions of the large ox-like animal that provided mountain dwellers with everything from food to fuel, butter and cheese to clothing. The small ones had the odd name of dwarf Lulus.

Several other fields were terraced and reminded Kelly of the contour maps she and George had obsessed over when they were young. A teacher had explained topography to Kelly's class, suggesting they do independent work for extra credit, and Kelly had enlisted George's help in mapping their farm. Even after the class ended, Kelly continued to look at landscapes with an eye to relative elevations, a habit that only disappeared when she moved to Cleveland. She had, once upon a time, even considered mapping as a profession but set that notion aside along with the idea of becoming a veterinarian. For George, the experience had been transformed into a collection of old maps, and not all copies, that were framed and hung about the home he shared with Russell.

Sadness washed over Kelly in a wave, the wave that always accompanied thoughts of George when a forgotten memory took her by surprise. He would have loved hearing how farming made contour maps of Nepal. Maybe Billy had told him. Now she would never know. She felt tears threaten, and for a moment, her vision blurred and she stumbled. Kaju looked back in alarm, not that there was danger in falling off the wide path, but stumbling could be a symptom of altitude sickness.

"Rest?" he asked.

Kelly shook her head and gestured for him to go on. He did, but he kept glancing back more often now. Kelly concentrated on getting her walking and breathing rhythm back. She'd think about Jeri and how it had felt to partially wake through the night and realize where she was and whom she was sleeping beside. Each time she woke, Kelly had been immediately aware of Jeri's presence, and she had moved closer before drifting back into sleep. How on earth had Jeri ever become involved in the IRA? Had the IRA come recruiting in Boston, like the missionary nuns had recruited in Kelly's home parish for girls to go to South America? Kelly had heard that urban Irish communities like Boston or Chicago collected money for the IRA, but she had never heard of any people being recruited.

Kelly gave a thumbs up as Kaju looked back again to check on her. They were past the valley farms now and entering more trees. The slope had an easy grade, but even so, they were gaining considerable height. Kelly wondered how much Jeri would tell her about her past. She seemed willing enough to answer any question. Just how much did Kelly want to know? She didn't like thinking that Jeri had probably killed people.

The path grew steeper, and the effort required to climb the grade took all of Kelly's concentration. The wind, constant as it was, also picked up steadily until it was whipping her long coat, making it necessary to fasten the belt. Kaju had stopped. As Kelly reached him, she saw that they had wound around the mountain until they were well above the main trail through the saddleback. Up here among the trees, the chill wind funneling through the pass forced Kelly to lean into it, but despite the wind, the view was breathtaking. High as they were, still higher peaks, crowned in white, towered above, and if she looked down, it was like floating just to try and to peer to the plain below. She understood why Everest was thought to be a goddess; every Himalayan peak Kelly had seen had the dignity of some splendid deity. No wonder people often went to the high places to look for their gods. Kelly had only a superficial knowledge of the region's spiritual beliefs, but she instinctively understood that the soaring Himalayas were home to gods of both earth and sky.

A vulture hung in the air below. Kelly knew from Billy that vultures were still used for what were called "sky burials," placing the dead where the birds would strip flesh from bone. Billy had liked the idea, found it fitting. At the time, not knowing that one day she would actually be in Nepal, Kelly had not paid much attention to what he said. She ought to have asked him if he'd seen such a sight or simply read about it.

Then Kelly realized that the figure was not a vulture but a helicopter, just like the day before. Instinctively, she stepped further back into the shelter of the trees. How likely was it that a helicopter would be in this area? Coincidence? Helicopters flew tourists in and out of some places; there had been ads for renting rides in the Kathmandu airport. It could be military. Nepal was between China, India, and Pakistan, one of the most chronically dangerous areas in the world, but the probability was that the machine belonged to the SAS group she and Jeri had seen earlier.

"Kaju." She had to strain to make herself heard over the wind. "Look."

He followed her pointing finger, saw the helicopter, and frowned.

"Go tell Jeri." She gestured back down the path. "Tell Tashi. I'll stay."

The youth hesitated only a moment, then hurried off.

Jeri's heart was thudding by the time Kaju reached Tashi.

"Ahshang! Ahshang! There is a helicopter. Kelly la sent me to you."

Jeri's heart slowed slightly. A helicopter, not troops. Not troops on the ground at least.

"Where is it?" Tashi asked.

Kaju described what he had seen, including the distance to the helicopter. Jeri's heart rate slowed almost to normal.

"I'll go ahead, Tash," she said. "You stay with Jamali and Bolingbrook."

She held herself to a slow lope, but Jeri was breathing hard by the time she reached Kelly. Altitude and Bolingbrook's backpack. Jeri noted that Kelly had stayed out of sight among the sheltering trees. She took her binoculars and aimed them where Kelly pointed. The copter was hovering below them. British, no doubt about that, but it was too far away and at the wrong level to have seen Kelly or Kaju.

"I think it might have picked up the SAS group," Kelly said.

Jeri nodded as she shifted the binoculars so she could examine the pass. The main trail wound through wind-scoured boulders and ice-rimmed pools of water. From her higher vantage point, Jeri could see a wall of white hovering on the other side of the pass. The peculiarities of the Himalayan microclimates made it possible for a near-jungle to thrive below the summit on the far side, while the mountains had turned the pass itself into a wind tunnel. The damp jungle and the cold heights had created a nearly constant bank of cloud that heaved and shifted like the edge of an ocean. As Jeri watched, tatters of fog tore themselves from the bank to whirl through the pass like dancers in the wind.

It wasn't far to the fog, less than a kilometer, but the path from here to there required care. From below it would look as if the rock above was a sheer wall, but if the path was invisible, someone traversing it would not be. Dangerous in bad weather and narrow all the way to the far side, it grew even narrower for a short distance, and anyone crossing would be visible from the pass below. The helicopter had continued its rise, but the closer it got to the gap, the clearer it became that the big machine was not up to fighting the fierce wind that was funneling through the cleft. Jeri and Tashi had come this far soon after they joined forces. Jeri had been counting on the wind and fog for protection. She still did.

Jeri lowered the glasses and pointed out the path ahead for Kelly. "If we bend low, we should be okay except for about thirty feet at the far side. I think we can all make it, and we don't really have much choice," she said.

Jeri was less confident than she sounded. Still, even if they were seen crossing, they should be able to reach the safety of the fog before anyone could catch up to them. She looked back and saw that Kaju was approaching, the rest of the party strung out behind him.

Jeri assessed Kaju's mental state. He appeared anxious, but not overly fearful. "*Bhai*, little brother, take Kelly and go to the fog."

To Kelly, she said, "I want you and Kaju to go ahead again. He knows where we're going, and once you reach the fog, there's practically no chance anyone will find you."

"Will you be far behind?"

"No." Jeri grinned. Her grin was almost as fierce as her frown. "I live for this."

I'd like to change that. The words sprang to Kelly's lips, but she left them unsaid.

Kelly felt as though she ought to be more frightened than she was, but Jeri's presence gave her a sense of safety, as if nothing could go wrong, as if every possibility had been anticipated and prepared for. Not even when several figures dropped off the helicopter from where it hovered below the pass did Kelly feel much more than curiosity.

After a glance back to make sure Kelly was ready, Kaju started out, keeping close to the rock face, and Kelly followed. Staying to the side and bending low kept them out of the full strength of the wind as well as shielding them from the soldiers below. With the wind howling too loud for any speech, Kaju gestured for Kelly to wait when they reached the place where the path was at its narrowest. He peered carefully over the edge in the direction of the SAS group and then scrambled quickly ahead.

The risky section was only about thirty feet long, but it also involved a climb. Kelly could see that the ease with which Kaju moved was deceptive. The trail looked solid, but there was a layer of weather-loosened stones, not enough to be called gravel but still capable of making trouble for a climber.

When he was safely on the far side, Kaju turned and gestured for Kelly. She took a deep breath. The Himalaya was worlds away from southern Ohio, but Kelly had grown up outdoors. She could handle a short, fast climb. She used the sliding foot technique, instinctively understanding that a dislodged pebble might alert the soldiers below. As she reached the far side without mishap, she took Kaju's outstretched hand and they grinned at each other.

Jeri waited for Bolingbrook and Jamali to reach her. They arrived just as Kelly and Kaju reached the relative safety of the farther side.

"Is there a problem?" Yusef shouted above the wind when he was close enough.

Jeri pointed through the trees. The helicopter had settled itself well below the pass and out of the wind. "British," she said. "SAS."

Jamali's lips thinned, but he simply nodded.

"Can we still go?" Bolingbrook asked.

"With luck." Jeri pointed out the dangerous section and explained the best method for crossing.

Tashi went first, Bolingbrook followed, then Jamali. Jeri took another look at the pass below and saw that the SAS soldiers had fanned out. As far as she could tell, they were looking down, not up.

Jeri was worried. Did they think that even if there was only one trail, she would simply walk into their waiting arms? She'd wager good money that another group was on its way up, thinking to trap her from behind. With luck, she'd never have to learn if she would win that wager; she and her party should be long gone into the fog before the two military groups met.

If they made it through this section, Jeri didn't expect the British to follow. There were just too many routes to choose from on the far side. Jeri set off after her companions.

Bolingbrook and Jamali followed Tashi's example and hugged the rocky face of the mountain. Tashi didn't even look down as he crossed the narrowed portion of the trail. The group was committed at this point, and speed was important. Bolingbrook went next, and she managed well enough until she had almost reached the farther end, where Tashi waited for her. Then she slipped. Tashi was there in an instant, reaching for her, steadying her, guiding her forward to surer footing.

It probably wasn't noise that alerted the watchers below, not with the wind howling. Maybe it was a sixth sense attuned by training to motion, or maybe someone above dislodged a pebble. Whatever it was, someone looked up and the party was seen. Jeri looked down and saw the soldiers sprinting toward the cliff face. Tashi guided Bolingbrook quickly toward the fog, and Jamali scrambled up the narrow way after them. Jeri was watching to see him across when a spray of stone stung her face. The damned fools were shooting. She ducked low, in time to see Jamali slip.

She got to him, half pushed, half took his weight, and supported him to where they couldn't be seen from below. He was leaning on her heavily, and Jeri didn't need to see a wound to know that Yusef Jamali had been shot.

They didn't make it to the fog bank, but they reached a place where they were sheltered from the wind when Jeri helped the man to sit. She could see easily enough what had happened. The bullet had gone into his arm above the elbow and exited the back of his shoulder. She couldn't tell if it had hit any bone.

"Yusef! Oh, my dear, how bad is it?" Bolingbrook had returned and was kneeling beside him.

Jamali just shook his head, not up to talking over the wind.

"Damn it, we have to go back."

Now he did speak. "No, Louise. You must go on. Leave me and get on with our work. I'll be fine, but I can't go with you like this."

"I can't just leave you."

"Of course you can, my dear. I'll just wait here. They'll take me back, is all."

"Yusef—"

"I'll stay with him until I'm sure he's safe," Jeri said. Tashi and Bolingbrook stared at her in surprise, but Jamali's look was grateful. Jeri turned her attention to Louise. "But if we're going on, you have to go now. Right away."

Indecision was not a familiar state to Louise Bolingbrook. She wavered momentarily, then leaned forward and kissed Jamali fondly. "Take care of yourself, my dear."

Jeri glanced to where Kelly and Kaju waited at the edge of the fog. "Tashi la," she spoke in Nepali, "take them to the first camp and wait for me. I'll make sure the soldiers don't follow."

There was only one place where the SAS could access the upper trail from below, and Jeri kept her eye on it as she waited for Tashi and Bolingbrook to reach the fog bank. Jamali was sitting with his eyes closed against the pain. Jeri examined his wound, and although it was bleeding, an artery had not been hit. Lucky.

"Hold this against the wound. That should stem the blood flow until the soldiers get here. They're bound to have some kind of first aid with them."

"Take care of Louise, will you? She'll try to do more than she should. And take my pack. I know it's an extra load right now, but it has the warmer coat, and I brought some of her favorite biscuits. For a

234

surprise." He grimaced as he shifted out of his pack and stared at the blood on it.

"Don't worry, Yusef. I'll watch out for her."

"This is important work. If you get this information, the world will have to take notice."

Jeri wondered just what Jamali's work was if he still thought that anything could actually catch the notice of the world. In her experience, the world was quite capable of averting its attention from any number of horrors.

She saw a head peer cautiously up over the trail. "Do you have your papers?" she asked, reaching for the extra pack.

"Oh, yes. Go ahead. And rest assured that several people besides me are going to be very upset over this incident. I am not without connections."

Jeri was remembering a soldier she had left tied to a tree in Ulster, so she waited at the edge of the fog bank until she saw the first SAS man reach Jamali. He called out to a comrade, who came running, and only when Jeri saw this man take out a first aid kit did Jeri enter the fog and set about laying a false trail into the jungle.

Chapter Six

Thick fog forced Kelly to keep her eyes fixed on Kaju's back, which was a few feet ahead of her but still only a dark blur as they trudged along on slippery mud. The way was further impeded by hundreds of tall plants with thin stalks and long flat leaves that stung her face as she passed. The air was so damp and chill that she thought actual rain might be more comfortable. Kelly wondered how Bolingbrook was doing, but the one time she looked back, she could see nothing through the gray mist. Tashi must be with the Englishwoman. Kelly remembered Bolingbrook's look of pain as the woman had turned away from her companion, leaving him behind. And Jeri had stayed. Kelly could only hope that Jeri's long experience with avoiding capture would guide her once again.

How Kaju knew where he was going was a mystery; maybe he had an internal magnet, like the ones said to guide migrating birds. It would be nice to be a bird and be flying above the soggy ground. Kelly slid sideways and grabbed at a nearby stalk as thick as her wrist to keep from falling. It was a stalk of bamboo. They were walking through a forest of bamboo. She remembered the guidebook saying something about bamboo, but her own familiarity with the plant was limited to its use as a fishing pole.

Kelly recalled an Easter when she was about seven. George got a fishing rod, while she was given a straw bonnet with a scratchy blue ribbon that tied under her chin. She envied her big brother, but she knew better than to complain to her parents. Her father would just ignore her, and her mother was always tired with the new baby. Besides, George promised to let her use his new rod and reel, and he always kept his promises. The very next Saturday after Easter, as eager as her brother to go fishing, Kelly hurried through the morning chores.

Stone Creek was a fair hike from the Corcoran farmhouse, at least to any spot where there was a chance of catching anything. The creek was wide and shallow, but there were deeper stretches, particularly under shady banks, where bass and catfish could be found. Kelly and George dug up some earthworms before they left, but as they walked, George talked about how a real fly lure would be better bait than any worm. He said he was sure that bass would immediately go after a lure. When they reached the creek, George looked around for something he could use to make a fly lure. He said he saw something in a nearby bush and sent Kelly to investigate. She didn't see anything, but he said it was red and to keep looking.

Kelly was sure George was just teasing her, but she kept looking until she saw a glint of red. At first, she thought someone had lost a plastic ball, then she recognized it as the red half of a bobbin. On a string. Wound round a brand new bamboo fishing pole. George had bought it with his own 4H money, won at the country fair the year before for having the third best calf. The pole was a golden yellow, twice Kelly's height, and it had a silvery lead sinker as well as the red and white bobbin. Kelly didn't remember whether she caught a fish that day, but she remembered being happy—happy with her fishing pole and happy with the knowledge that George was always there to take care of her.

The bamboo forest came to an abrupt end, and two or three steps farther, the fog also came to an abrupt end. Kelly felt slightly dizzy as her eyes adjusted to distance again. Then she nearly gasped at the beauty of the scene before her. She and Kaju were standing on a ledge above a landscape of heaped folds and ridges, stretching below and ahead, all in a verdant covering of dense, rich greens so dark that some areas appeared black. Fog drifted here and there like thin rivers, creating islands of emerald peaks. After the arid plain of the previous day, Kelly understood how appropriate the legend of Shangri-la was to the Himalayas. The sudden, surprising beauty before her made it easy to believe in the possibility of travelers stumbling into a hidden paradise.

Kaju was smiling as if he himself had prepared the scene just for her. He coughed a warning at the same time as Kelly heard movements behind her, and she remembered not to turn around. Kaju set off quickly, and Kelly lowered her head and walked on. For the next several hours, they took a more or less level path, although they must have descended somewhat as they passed through the fog, because breathing had become decidedly easier. Occasional twists allowed Kelly to sneak glances back along the trail. Bolingbrook appeared weary and preoccupied, understandable enough considering she had been walking since early morning. Not to mention that she had seen her companion shot. There was no sign of Jeri.

Considerable daylight was left when Tashi called to Kaju to stop. They had come to a shallow lake, almost a swamp judging from the birch trees growing in the water, although the water appeared fresh and clear. Kelly busied herself with helping Kaju set up camp, and she kept looking toward the way they had come, hoping to see Jeri. Kelly avoided Bolingbrook, but she couldn't help overhearing when an argument broke out between her and Tashi.

"I am certainly capable of setting up my own tent. I have been managing my own shelters for decades."

Bolingbrook was reaching for the green nylon bundle that Tashi held, but he shook his head and removed the covering. With a shake of his hand, the bundle blossomed into the shape of a small but proper tent that Tashi held out at arm's length, the newest thing in lightweight, shock-corded camp gear. Tashi's impassive expression gave way to a huge grin as he handed the tent to Bolingbrook.

"Yes, well, you must teach me how to do that," she said with a wry smile as she accepted the tent. "It appears to be something I might still manage to learn."

A fire was already going when Kelly brought in a last load of firewood and couldn't think of anything more to do. She walked back among the trees to keep watch for Jeri's return. Tashi didn't appear worried, but Kelly didn't know him well enough to recognize if he was.

"Kelly la." It was Kaju. "The soup is hot."

Kelly nodded in the direction of Bolingbrook and handed Kaju her cup. She watched as he crossed the clearing to the fire, poured some liquid, and started back to where she remained among the trees.

"Miss Corcoran, don't be ridiculous." The Englishwoman didn't raise her voice, but it carried quite clearly. "Come to the fire. Surely you didn't think I'd be fooled for long by that absurd coat and cap?"

A bit shamefaced but glad to be called to the fire's circle of warmth, Kelly asked, "How did you know?"

Louise Bolingbrook considered. "It's the way you move. Different cultures have subtle and not-so-subtle styles in how people walk. I've been too many places in the world not to recognize differences. I suppose you are due congratulations. I was fooled when I first met you. The British government now believes you to be just a misplaced tourist, as did I."

"But I was then," Kelly said without thinking.

"I see. What changed?"

Kelly suddenly blushed and looked away.

"I see." Bolingbrook repeated herself with a shift of emphasis and the ghost of a smile.

Suddenly Bolingbrook stood up, and Kelly turned to see Jeri approaching. She looked back at Bolingbrook, and not until that moment did she realize how well the woman had been concealing her anxiety. Fear etched deeply drawn lines in her face as she waited for Jeri to get close enough to question. Jeri spoke as soon as she could be heard.

"Mr. Jamali is fine. As well as possible. I waited until I saw the SAS help him away."

Bolingbrook abruptly sat down and closed her eyes.

Jeri said, "He assured me, before I left, that he would not be the only one to suffer from the ambush. And he insisted I bring the pack with the warmer coat."

Louise Bolingbrook opened her eyes and smiled. "That sounds like Yusef. Thank you. I'm going to sleep now." With a nod to the group, she rose and went to her tent.

Kaju handed Jeri a bowl of warm soup. She tasted it and nodded in appreciation. Somehow Kaju always managed to add something extra to flavor even the simplest fare.

"We are safe?" Tashi asked.

"I think so. For the moment. You were right in suspecting they would take the trail up out of the fog. The other direction," she added for Kelly's benefit. "I followed them for a while. But they're SAS, and they're too good to underestimate. Still, I think the bamboo will stop them. By the time they figure out which way we went, we'll be long out of this area." Jeri sipped from the bowl, holding it so it also warmed her hands.

"How badly was Mr. Jamali hurt?" Kelly asked.

"The bullet went in his arm and out his shoulder. I don't know much more than that."

†

Jeri was haunted by the memory of Jamali grimacing with pain; she kept seeing a wounded Kelly beside Bolingbrook's companion. If Kelly had been hurt, there would have been no quick helicopter ride back to medical care. Jeri wouldn't have left Kelly anyway. Couldn't have. She couldn't even be sure that the SAS would take Kelly anywhere alive, not if they decided she was attached to Geraldine O'Donnell, notorious Irish terrorist. The three IRA volunteers ambushed on Gibraltar were never far from her memory. The fear that Kelly might be hurt and at the mercy of the Brit military reminded Jeri that when you loved someone, you gave your enemies a hostage.

"Jeri?"

Jeri realized she had been staring wordlessly at Kelly. "Sorry. Long day."

Darkness had fallen and the fire had been banked. Jeri had followed Kelly to their tent among the trees where Kelly related the story of Bolingbrook's reaction as Tashi had demonstrated the usefulness of shock-cord tent poles. Then she told of how Bolingbrook called her to the fire.

Jeri struggled to dismiss images of harm to Kelly. "So, Bolingbrook figured out who you were?"

"She said it's the way I move. Not like a person from Nepal, I guess."

"It doesn't matter," Jeri said. "I don't think Jamali had time to notice or think about you, so nobody but Bolingbrook knows you're here. I don't want the SAS to know about you if I can help it."

"What about Tashi and Kaju? Do the Sassies know them?"

"Did they ask you about them the other night?"

"No. I hadn't thought of that. Everything was about you."

"Then they aren't interested."

"Do you think he'll be okay?"

"Jamali? He's probably in a warm bed right now. But I know he misses Louise."

"Louise?"

"Bolingbrook. I'm sure they're more to each other than colleagues. What are you doing?"

Kelly had knelt down at the edge of the sleeping bag, behind Jeri, and was massaging Jeri's shoulders. "You always take care of everyone. Let me take care of you for now."

It was easy to begin to let go as Kelly's hands worked her muscles. She was tired, and she could feel love flowing through the touch along with the ease. After a while she felt Kelly's breath on her hair, and she turned to accept the kiss that was waiting. Aware that the night stretched out ahead of them, they began with slow, exploratory kisses, pausing now and then to rest against each other and simply listen to the sounds of the night: splashes from the lake, skitterings among the trees, a distant cooing that might be an owl.

Jeri could feel both arousal and dread growing as she buried her face in Kelly's soft hair, hair that smelled like rain and flowers. Maybe it would be okay, or maybe she should just tell Kelly what was happening to her, but it was hard to stop and talk with Kelly moving against her and murmuring her name. She slid down so that Kelly would be more comfortable, felt the length of her as Kelly shifted to get closer.

Kelly drew back, her face only a fraction of an inch from Jeri's own. "You smell like fog," she said.

"Oh? And how does fog smell?"

"Like you. Wonderful."

Jeri smiled. "I was thinking the same thing," she whispered. She breathed in deeply again and slowly exhaled near Kelly's ear. "You like that?" she whispered. It was an unnecessary question, considering the response she was getting.

"Oh yes. Do you think they'll hear us? Me? You're so quiet."

"Prison habits, I guess."

She tried, but Kelly couldn't mask her surprise, not as close as they were at that moment, when there was no distance at all between them. She stiffened, then attempted to cover it by asking quietly, "Prison?"

But Jeri missed nothing. And something broke. She read and understood Kelly's reaction intuitively, in seconds, and she was furious. It had been that way when she used to go to one of the Boston bars. A woman would be all over Jeri until she learned she was from Southie. The woman would pretend it didn't matter, but it did. Jeri was Southie Irish trash, maybe good enough to fuck somewhere but not to consider taking home. Some women were attracted by the difference in class, while women like Kelly were scared by it, maybe afraid they'd get infected and lose their own precarious grip on respectability. Or maybe they just believed they were too good to be with someone like Jeri.

"So murder and bombings are okay, but god forbid you get close to an ex-con. Sorry. I suppose having all my own teeth fooled you."

"Jeri, please, that's not fair."

Jeri found her sleeping bag, gathered it, and stood. "Kaju's not going all the way into Tibet. You can stay with him and get a bus out when we get to the border." She moved off toward the trees. She didn't care if the exit plan she had given Kelly appeared too well formed to have just been thought of on the spur of the moment.

"I'm not right in this," Kelly said to Jeri's disappearing back, "but

241

you've been waiting for something like it."

And that was true, too.

†

Kelly woke remembering everything, woke to a misery that looped back to the grief that had filled her days before she met Jeri. Kelly couldn't believe that everything had changed so utterly between them in just an instant.

Moving with a heaviness that made doing anything difficult, she rolled up her sleeping bag and clumsily turned the tent into a small bundle. Depression, so very much like the fog of the day before, was such a familiar state that she was able to approach the fire, take coffee from Tashi, be told that "Jeri la" had gone out earlier, refuse any food, nod to Bolingbrook, and then help Kaju pack. Everything happened separately, distantly, with no resonance, no meaning, like pebbles tossed onto a bed of sand.

Over and over she heard Jeri say: *So murder and bombings are okay, but god forbid you get close to an ex-con.* It was true enough, Kelly knew, not completely true, but true enough, and even though she wanted it not to be true, she actually was more dismayed by Jeri's revelation of having been in prison than she had been by her confession of having killed people. It was irrational, but such things never were about reason.

Kelly walked through the early part of the day, paying scant attention to the others in the group, wrapped in a muffling misery that slowly gave way to words. But the words that began to penetrate her awareness were barbed words dripping with poison, words that accused herself of stupidity, recklessness, dishonesty. It occurred to Kelly, with bitter irony, that compared to her own inner self, her British interrogators had been rank amateurs in the area of malign accusation.

Jeri was dogged by demons of her own as she back-trailed her group. She had told Tashi she would stay behind to make sure they weren't being followed. There was a possibility, of course, that the SAS had discovered their whereabouts, but the truth was that she didn't want to see Kelly. She'd heard the words that followed her into the dark and knew that she had been looking for some excuse to distance herself. And as the anger drained away, she knew she had been far too quick and harsh in her judgment. Kelly had been surprised, that was all. Anyone would be. And as anger left, she began to want Kelly so much that she couldn't sleep the rest of the night, tossing and turning in a fever of desire and denial.

One moment she was sure that, no matter the excuse, she had done the right thing; the next moment, all she wanted was to go to Kelly and take what she knew would be hers simply for the asking. She could still feel Kelly's hands, still taste and smell her. Sometime near dawn, Jeri drifted into a troubled sleep, in which she went to Kelly only to find her lying in the arms of an old man on a bus who kept saying, "I can't leave her, she's my daughter." Inches ahead of approaching flames, Jeri woke into a calm Nepalese dawn.

She desperately distrusted her attachment to Kelly. If you loved someone, you wanted the best for them. To bring anyone into her life was so decidedly far from the best, that Jeri wanted to howl in despair. If Kelly had been shot the day before, she could not have left her, could not have gone on to Tibet, could not have continued the only life that made any sense of who she was, who she had become. She had no right loving anyone. She had to make Kelly want to leave, make her believe that she, Jeri, had ceased to care.

Around midday, the group stopped for a lunch of cold chapatis and then continued on. Bolingbrook seemed wrapped in her own thoughts, while Kaju and Tashi spoke only occasionally to each other in their own language. They were still at a lower altitude that didn't tax Kelly or Louise to any great extent.

In the late afternoon, Tashi called a halt for the night near a grove of flowering rhododendron. Kaju had the evening meal well in hand, so Kelly wandered off. She climbed a short way above the trail until she had a view of a distant peak shimmering white in the cleft of closer mountainsides. She stared without thought for a while, aware of little besides her misery, until slowly she became aware of the visible drift being carried from the top of the distant peak as if it were a pale flag. The wisps of bright white trailing off the jagged rock created a scene that looked as forbiddingly cold as it was brilliantly beautiful. Where Kelly sat, the sun was tropically hot and the hills were lush with bamboo. It would be difficult to imagine a starker contrast.

Kelly took the crystal from her pocket and turned it slowly, watching the sunlight catch tiny rainbows.

Despite her resistance to the thought, she allowed herself to consider that just possibly her attachment to Jeri was rooted only in fantasy. Flailing about emotionally, she had latched on to this woman who appeared so strong, so absolute in a world that had become contingent and uncertain. From the outside, her attraction to Jeri seemed as predictable as it could be rootless, a textbook case of vulnerability resulting in irrational choices. Of course she would want to be near, to absorb, the qualities that marked Jeri.

Relationships had never been Kelly's strong suit. Even before George became ill, Kelly had never been with anyone for any length of time. She called it dating, but George and Russell insisted on calling it sleeping around. There were some women with whom Kelly had thought she might try to make something work, attempt some sort of commitment, but in the long run none of them, she had told herself, were really keepers.

The word echoed in her head, and she looked at her crystal. That was the name she had given it: Keeper. It was an interesting word. It could mean to possess, but also to care for, to maintain. Keep was one of those words that expanded into wonderfully suggestive byways the more you tried to pin it down to a single meaning.

Then she realized that Kaju was there and had asked her a question.

"What?" Kelly asked Kaju.

"Soup," he repeated. "Is not good?"

Kelly looked at the cup of soup she held. Her cup. She tried to remember when she had filled it.

"Sorry," she said. "I'm sure it's fine."

"I look for you?"

"What?"

"This English is bad?"

"Your English is good, I think. I don't understand what you mean."

"You are gone. Someone need look here for you."

"Like watching a car when the driver goes?"

Kaju nodded solemnly.

Suddenly Kelly was laughing. The image of parking her body and then just wandering off was too funny. Perhaps she needed a keeper. Aware that hysteria was somewhere in the mix, she still gave herself over to the laughter. For a few seconds, Kaju stared, and then he grinned, and then he joined her.

And then something shifted, like a slightly blurred image coming into focus through binoculars, Kelly became aware that she was in a beautiful place with some very interesting people, and on an adventure that, no matter how it ended, would likely be important to the rest of her life. And what kind of malarkey had she been telling herself about bonds if, at the first sign of opposition, she lost her own belief. She and Jeri were connected, and that connection would assert itself; she had to trust that. She did trust it. She was where she belonged. In the meantime, she might as well enjoy the view, because she was amid the most amazing views in the world.

"Laughing is good," Kaju said, still smiling, "but soup is also good."

Kelly took a drink. Even cold, the broth was full of flavor. Kaju waited while she sipped at the soup. As he gazed toward the mountain, there was a calm quiet to the boy that made him seem far older than his age. When Kelly had finished, he gestured for her to follow him.

They walked back along the way Kelly had walked earlier, and she thought Kaju was taking her to the camp, but then, at a little ridge, he turned to the right. They walked for several minutes along a wind-scabbed, pebbled ridge until, topping a slight rise, they suddenly were looking down into a shallow valley that took Kelly's breath away. It was a riot of wild flowers, for the most part pastel violets and pinks, but here and there, patches of deep and vibrant yellow. The flowers looked something like a cross between daffodils and snapdragons, and they stood tall, swaying slightly in the wind.

In that moment, Kelly felt that all was as it always should be. The next moment, memory began an argument with the feeling, but the terms of the argument were so familiar, so threadbare, that she was able to ignore them like a radio with the volume turned down.

"Thank you," she said to Kaju.

They stood a bit longer and then started back. "Where did you learn English? From tourists?"

"From my uncle. He learned in Colorado."

Kelly thought she must have heard wrong. "Where?"

"Colorado. Your country. He is soldier at Camp Hale in state of Colorado. He come back here to fight Chinese."

"I didn't even know that ever happened." Kelly realized she had even less of an understanding of who Kaju and Tashi were than she had thought. No wonder Jeri found her hopelessly self-involved. "I'm feeling better now, Kaju. Thank you."

Kaju looked at her thoughtfully. "You were with Annapurna. The mountain. She gives rich harvests, but she is also Durga. I think Durga is help you."

"Durga?"

"She is fearless, but always she laugh."

Kelly filed the name away to look up in her history of Himalayan nations. "You are not going to Tibet?" she asked Kaju.

The young man's smile fell away. "No. My uncle says I cannot."

"Why?"

"My father go back to Tibet. Now he is lost and never return. My mother weeps at night. My uncle says he not make her to weep for me."

"I'm sorry. How long ago?"

"Much time. If I go, maybe I lost in terrible feelings. I want to be a monk. A monk not have anger."

The connections between the thoughts were obscure to Kelly, but she understood that they made sense to Kaju.

"We go now?" Kaju asked, looking at Kelly's empty cup.

"Yes. Thank you, Kaju la. Will you help me to learn more about Durga and the things a monk knows?"

Kaju nodded happily.

Jeri adjusted her expression to hide any emotion as she approached the evening campsite. *Prison habit*, she thought with humorless irony. Her cursory scan informed her that nothing appeared amiss. Bolingbrook was using the waning light to read over what looked like the report Jeri had given her, the report that had induced her to travel to Nepal. Kaju and Tashi were sitting near each other, discussing some matter. Kelly was a little separate, sitting with a book that Jeri recognized as the Himalayan history book she had brought with her. Kelly looked up immediately at Jeri's approach, her face drawn but otherwise unreadable. Jeri held her eyes a moment, then looked away.

"I didn't see anyone," Jeri announced to the group in general as soon as she was close enough. "Either we lost the SAS, or they quit following us."

Bolingbrook merely nodded at Jeri's mention of her countrymen. "How did you get this report?"

"From the author," Jeri said.

"Directly? Indirectly? If the latter, was it from someone who knows Detsen?"

"I really can't say," Jeri answered. "Any response might put a number of people in danger. Are you questioning whether Mr. Phurba is the author?"

Bolingbrook scowled at the paper. "No. I recognize a number of phrases that I know Detsen would use. I used to read his history essays at Oxford." Her scowl softened with memory. "I'm satisfied concerning the authorship, but I know that some of my colleagues won't be."

"That's why we brought it to you, Lady Bolingbrook."

"Don't be ridiculous, Miss O'Donnell. Call me Louise, rather than that absurd title."

"Only if you call me Jeri."

"I'll be more comfortable with Geraldine," she said and referred to the paper again. "There was a reason for Yusef to accompany us. He works in Human Rights, and that would be a more appropriate association than my area. Refugees and Human Rights do overlap, of course, and Yusef is sure that this will be important no matter who brings it to world attention."

Jeri nodded and walked over to the fire where Tashi was readying her supper.

"Could I read the report, Louise?" Kelly asked.

"Yes, of course"—there was a slight hesitation—"Kelly. I just presumed you had already seen it. The author, Detsen Phurba, and I were acquaintances at Oxford. That was well before Geraldine's time there, of course."

Bolingbrook responded to Kelly's apparent surprise. "You didn't know? Geraldine is a Rhodes Scholar, although I believe her studies were interrupted before she could finish her degree. Here. Take this portion, and I'll give you more as I finish." She handed some pages to Kelly.

Kelly stared at the pages, but the words wouldn't focus. She gave up and took them to where Jeri had gone to sit. She had no idea what kind of welcome to expect, but she hoped Jeri wouldn't simply get up and leave. Despite getting no invitation to stay, she sat on her heels a few feet away. She remembered with daunting clarity the bitterness in Jeri's accusation the night before, and then she remembered the wild flowers that Kaju had shown her.

"I want to tell you a story," Kelly said. She ignored the sharp eyes that fixed on her from under dark eyebrows. "Years ago, some friends and I went to Canada for Spring Break. We were in Quebec, at the port. There were a number of ships there, and I saw one that was from the Soviet Union. I knew that because it was painted bright white, with a huge, red Hammer and Sickle on the smokestack. I was shocked. Before

I could even think about it, I was shocked. I couldn't believe that they'd be so bold as to put that insignia right out in the open."

Kelly paused, hoping that Jeri would give some hint of what she was thinking, but Kelly was getting no cues. Earlier, before Jeri returned to the campsite, Kelly had been reading about Durga. The description of the Hindu goddess with each of her ten arms holding a weapon had made her think of Jeri. The comparison had made her smile then, but now, as she searched the familiar face for any encouraging sign, she found little reason for amusement. Jeri's inscrutable look was much like that of a pitiless deity.

Gamely, Kelly continued. "I wasn't even particularly anti-Communist or anti-Soviet or anything, but it was like seeing a skull and crossbones as the logo for some cough syrup. Until that moment, I had no idea that I'd accumulated such a load of attitude simply about the symbol. It wasn't what I actually believed, Jeri, or anywhere near what I wanted to believe. It was just something that had happened to me without my noticing."

Still Jeri said nothing.

"I don't think you believe, really, that I think any less of you today than I did yesterday, but maybe on another level, you're right. Maybe there is a distance between us that can never be closed. Or maybe we—maybe I—tried to close that distance too quickly, without finding out what else there is to know about you. Like you going to Oxford. Maybe, if we back up a bit and try, we can just get to know each other until we get to the border. Like we might if we had met under ordinary circumstances. You know—exchange coming out stories, or talk about our favorite movies, you tell me what your major was. Do you prefer football or baseball. Nothing complicated, just ordinary stranger stuff."

Jeri continued to stare, unreadable. Kelly drew a deep breath. Keeping her voice from quavering had taken enormous effort. Well, at least she'd given the moment her best shot. Kelly smoothed the papers of Detsen Phurba's report and started to stand.

"Mary Duffy," Jeri said flatly.

"What?"

"Mary Duffy. She was a senior, and we were at Donahue's Drugs after school. Mary Duffy was there and asked what I thought of the color lipstick she was holding. I was just a sophomore and couldn't believe she'd even talk to me, but I told her I thought any lipstick was dumb. She kissed me and asked if I liked the taste of it better than the color. I had to say, I sure did."

"Then what?"

"Then what? It just takes a kiss, and then you know."

"So it happened right there in the drugstore?" Kelly hardly dared breathe, afraid Jeri would remember to whom she was speaking.

"Of course not in the drugstore. I'll tell you, if you'll find a more comfortable way to settle. You look like you might topple over if I just breathe in your direction. And it's basketball I like. The Celtics, of course."

"Did you ever play basketball?"

"Sure. In high school. Did you?"

Angela Koenig

Chapter Seven

Day by day, Kelly grew stronger, restored to a vitality she hadn't felt since she'd left her home on the farm. Years of urban living had sapped the energy she had once taken for granted. Even jogging was a city pastime, a substitute for running through woods and across fields. The rhythms of backpacking amid the Himalayan peaks, of rising at dawn and falling asleep soon after nightfall, returned her to a more basic mode, requiring the kind of presence that fed her mind and heart as well as her body. Despite the distance between herself and Jeri, Kelly woke to days that began with anticipation, if not happiness. Even the distance now had a permeable nature as they negotiated a balance that allowed for an undeniable affection while they painstakingly avoided physical contact.

The mountain trails took the travelers through an ever-varying landscape, from lush tropics to windswept heights to grazing meadows near farmsteads to wild rocky highlands. One evening, they went to sleep in a grove of rhododendrons only to wake to a layer of fallen snow. The snow melted quickly enough when the sun rose, but the vision of pink and red blossoms covered by bright white snow took longer to fade.

The travelers became comfortable in one another's company. Although no one would mistake Jeri O'Donnell and Louise Bolingbrook for friends, their careful courtesy contained mutual respect. In the evenings, Jeri and Tashi would discuss the next day's terrain and travel agenda, while Bolingbrook read her monk's report and wrote notes for as long as the light permitted. Sometimes Kelly and Kaju worked on Kaju's English, and sometimes Kaju told Kelly tales from Tibetan lore, such as the legend of the Four Harmonious Animals.

†

There were times that, as the light faded, Bolingbrook set aside the report and closed her eyes, but she wasn't sleeping, she was listening to Kelly and Kaju, and remembering.

Disconnected impressions of the Japanese invasion were all that remained in Louise Bolingbrook's memory: huddling in a dark room while thundering explosions shook the earth, dragging a very large and heavy leather suitcase with brass buckles, a man in a khaki uniform who screamed at her frightened mother. Cascading images, too swift to sort into any useful narration, suddenly slowed into the full memory of standing in a group of women and absorbing the fear being transmitted through the painful grip of her mother's hand on her shoulder. They were being lectured to in Japanese. Louise couldn't see because she was too short, but she noticed a pretty blonde woman nearby, looking at her. The woman rolled her eyes and gave Louise a broad wink. In spite of herself, Louise grinned, and the woman grinned back.

Louise didn't know the blonde woman, but she did know the woman standing beside her. That woman was Miss Lucy Redfern, and she worked at the Embassy where Louise's father worked before the Japanese came. Louise's father, who got salutes from almost everyone, always seemed about to salute whenever Miss Lucy Redfern appeared. She was secretary to somebody important, and she was very tweedy, formal, stern, and serious. Louise was surprised that such a person was friends with someone who would roll her eyes and wink.

As days passed, Louise understood without being told that the women around her mother disapproved of Lucy Redfern and her friend, Rachel. It didn't take long, however, before it became known that Sister Rachel was one of the camp's most important people. Louise learned this the day she accompanied her mother to the makeshift infirmary where a number of women lay on cots or on pallets on the wood floor.

"Are you ill, Lady Bolingbrook?"

Louise's mother indicated that she wanted more privacy before she spoke. The two grownups moved a short distance away, but Louise could still hear. "Alice Harris said you helped her." Lady Bolingbrook paused and then continued in a tone that tried for condescension but slid toward pleading. "I simply can't do it. Not here. Not under these conditions. You must do something. Please."

Rachel had stood in thought while young Louise nearly trembled with anxiety over this latest in what was recently a never-ending stream of terrifying episodes. "Louise, why don't you help Lu with that screen while I go with your mother?"

Louise had always been frightened of the Embassy's Miss Redfern, so while she stayed behind, she kept her distance from the woman who was building a sunscreen of palm fronds for the dirt area in front of the small hut beside the infirmary.

"Louise, could you come here and hold this for me? I want to make some stringy sort of thingy with this leaf."

Louise held one palm frond while Miss Redfern pulled strands off another to make bindings. Later, the two of them admired the clever perfection of the screen they had made, congratulated each other, and became fast friends.

"Do you play chess?"

"A little. Father says I have a lot to learn."

"Set up those logs for chairs, and I'll get my set."

In a world where makeshift was the order of the day, the red-and-white-checked cloth that Lu used for a board was standard, but the pieces themselves were objects of wonder. Large and solid, carved from ivory and mahogany, each piece was a work of art. The rooks were elephants carrying both a mahout and an archer. The knights were armored warriors on rearing horses. Even the pawns appeared as individuals, each of them standing at attention but accoutered in a variety of arms and armor. One ivory pawn reminded Louise of Cary Grant, and sometimes she fought harder not to lose him than to protect her king.

Lu was a formidable chess player, and even that first day, she insisted that they play for stakes.

"But I don't have anything," Louise said.

"Then we shall play for a forfeit. If I win, you have to learn to decline a word in Latin."

"What if I win?"

"Then I shall tell you a fantastic tale."

They were working their way through first declension endings when Rachel returned.

"Hello, hello. If it isn't Lu and Little Lou." She looked tired and sad, but her smile was full of affection. "Your mother's resting, Little Lou, but you should probably run along now. Come back tomorrow if you want."

By the time good health might have enticed Lady Bolingbrook out of the malaise that followed the abortion of her second child, semi-starvation had set in place a listless disinterest that never truly disappeared, not even when the war was over. Louise was left to her own devices in the large camp, and most of her time she spent with Lucy and Rachel. Somehow, they always seemed to have something extra for her to eat—a banana, a scoop of rice. When Louise began to win a chess game now and then, Lucy told her the story of the Danish prince who wanted to avenge his father's death, and another about an Italian boy and girl who fell in love but whose families were enemies. Lucy even knew words from plays about these people.

One evening, Louise came back to her own hut and overheard another woman speaking with her mother.

"You really should keep the girl here with you, Peg. It's not good for her to spend so much time at that infirmary."

Louise held her breath, aware that such a comment was the kind of thing that could cause her mother to make a rule.

"What would she do around here but just fuss? Besides, whatever difference could it possibly make? None of us is ever going to leave here."

Sometimes Rachel would let Louise help with the sick, and if she was learning classics from Lucy, she was later surprised by the amount of medicine she had learned from Rachel. Louise grew used to people dying. She would see someone in a particular bed, and then one day she would arrive at the infirmary to see the bed empty or another woman there. There was a particular period when it seemed that more internees than usual were ill.

It was probably at this time when she overheard Rachel crying. Even now she could remember how inconsolable the woman had sounded.

"There's nothing I can do, Lu. It's simply impossible. I don't know enough. They're dying, and I can't even make them comfortable."

Louise couldn't abide the sound of sorrow, and she went into the room and found Rachel weeping, her head in Lucy's lap. It made Louise cry. She climbed up on the cot and laid her head against Rachel's arm and patted her hand. Maybe it worked, a little, because soon Rachel stopped crying and sat up.

"There, there, my darling," Lucy said. "You know more than enough. Even a doctor who had gone to the best medical school in London couldn't do more than you do. Right, Little Lou?"

Not long after that, Louise got sick. It was her turn to get a bed in the infirmary, and she was sure she would leave it like all the others had. She wouldn't mind, not really, because she felt so awful. Either Lucy or Rachel was always by her bed, and sometimes Lucy would sing songs. Then Rachel got some kind of medicine, and Louise started to feel better. It took a long time. But then, after a while, she even wanted to play chess again.

"I think we'll have to settle for checkers until you're better. I seem to have lost the chessmen," Lucy said, "but I have a plan. You and I will make some pieces. Look, I've already collected enough pebbles for pawns. Let me tell you a story of two cities."

Louise knew that the chess set had gone for her medicine. What she couldn't remember, no matter how she tried, was when Lucy died. She thought she remembered the grave, dry and gravelly, but there were so many graves; and she remembered that Rachel never really smiled again, although she sometimes tried. Louise worked with Rachel every day in the infirmary, every day until the war was over and groups of people began leaving for different destinations.

"Good-bye, Little Lou. Keep well." Then Rachel was gone, riding in the truck, still taking care of her sick people.

When she was old enough to know how, Louise tried to find Rachel. Records were still in a shambles, and even having a titled general for a father didn't help much. When she did at last locate the records, Louise learned that Rachel had only survived the war by a month at the most.

†

Louise had not missed the transition when Jeri and Kelly began treating each other with studied politeness. She had been on enough assignments to recognize when two people who had attempted intimacy replaced it with polite behavior. Then she overheard a comment by Tashi that suggested Kelly would leave the group along with Kaju when they reached the Tibetan border. Louise knew it would be for the best if Kelly Corcoran ended her life as a fugitive before it actually began, but she did regret the circumstances. She saw how each of the young women carefully watched the other when they thought they could do so unseen. It would have been apparent to a less discerning eye than Bolingbrook's that neither Kelly Corcoran nor Geraldine O'Donnell had stopped caring for the other. Louise, who conducted her own liaison with Yusef in a way designed to draw as little attention as possible, was familiar with the relationships that formed amid strife and chaos, relationships that brought solace and meaning into places where hazard left little room for either.

Louise had never relished the prospect of being in the company of Geraldine O'Donnell. She might sympathize with the plight of Catholics in Northern Ireland, but her work had engendered antipathy toward violence used as a political tactic, and she heartily objected to adventuring expatriate Americans who brought grief and harm to families on both sides of the Irish Sea. More personally, her brother had been devastated by his son's death. Louise had rarely met the youth, whose bent toward electronics steered him into bomb removal, but she did remember a laughing child who raced around a family lawn party in search of more cake. Then again, children grew up, and though their families remembered fair-haired and apple-cheeked children, those children quite often turned into people who killed and maimed the apple-cheeked former children of other families. Louise had more experience than most with how quickly and often people descended into bloodletting.

Yet, during the days of hiking through the highlands of the Himalayas, Louise found herself growing more and more approving of Jeri O'Donnell. In part, it was gratitude for the way Jeri had protected and helped Yusef, but even before that, Bolingbrook had begun to wish she had sought more information about the young woman. Even at their first meeting, Louise had been impressed. She was used to weighing character quickly, and she had seen a steadiness of purpose that she reported to Yusef. Louise wished he were with her; she would have welcomed his wry comments about a government that could afford to send helicopters to remote mountains after outlaws while it complained about the cost of feeding victims of famine or war. He would certainly agree that Geraldine possessed courage and competence; but she wondered if he would also recognize the banked anger that Louise feared could flare into reckless violence at the right provocation.

Chapter Eight

"How long was Tibet independent?" Kelly asked one evening, of the group in general. She had been reading her history, and now she used a finger to keep her place. This particular campsite was a rocky ledge in the lee of the wind, and the fire was yak dung that Tashi insisted they look for and gather while they climbed.

"Tibet is always free," Kaju answered. "Songzen Gampo made Tibet a great empire a thousand years ago."

"My book says that some people think Songzen Gampo was a Chinese warrior, because Tibet was always part of China."

Kaju looked hurt. "Then your book writer is very confused person. Only a Chinese person writed that."

"Wrote," Kelly said automatically. "Only a Chinese person wrote that."

"Does it matter?" Jeri asked. "I mean, does a state need a long, or even short, history to be legitimate? Look at the Kurds. I don't know if they've ever had their own state, at least not since before the Persian Empire, but the world has recognized their need to live an autonomous, protected life."

"I was just trying to understand who has authority to govern in Tibet. Doesn't it make a difference whose territory it was?" Kelly asked.

"By the ancient-times standard, the Welsh should run Britain," Jeri said.

Bolingbrook grimaced. "The English would dispute that, of course, but the Israelis find ancient title a useful standard to rally 'round. And technically, the United Nations is not claiming independence for the Kurds. It's protecting a de facto autonomy. This ought to apply to Tibet or any place where a portion of the population is oppressed, particularly if it has its own language and culture."

"The Chinese say that Tibet is no different from the southwestern

256

United States, where the Navajo and other Native Americans live," Jeri said. "It makes you wonder how long until Nuevo Aztlan makes a resurgence."

Kelly had never heard the term. "Nuevo Aztlan?"

"Aztlan is the Chicano name for a pre-Columbian territory that includes Texas and California. They claim it as the homeland for la Raza, the Race—the mestizo and native people. Almost all that land has been claimed by the United States for less than two hundred years, and that's only the blink of an eye when it comes to claiming territory on historic grounds."

"Power. Who can take and who can hold," Tashi said, staring into the fire. "Then those people who win tell any story they want about why a land must be theirs."

"But that is wrong," Kaju said to his uncle. "How can it be right for Chinese to take Tibetan land and kill Tibetan people?"

"The Chinese have the guns and the will. And they are near. The Americans gave us guns, but then they stopped. They were far away." Tashi looked up from the fire and spoke to Kelly. "When we were young, Kaju's father and I, we were taken to Camp Hale in Colorado and taught how to fight. Then they sent us back with dreams and promises of a free Tibet. We did fight. Even after the CIA quit helping us, we did not stop fighting. Nothing changed."

"They say you got particularly good intelligence about China for the CIA," Jeri said, and her tone was thick with sarcasm.

Tashi's response was a rude noise. "I wish them good fortune with it."

For a while no one spoke, and then Bolingbrook broke the silence. "According to Detsen, what the Chinese are doing in Tibet amounts to genocide. They're attempting to destroy the culture, the religion, and the ability of Tibetans to make a living in their own land, not to mention actually killing large numbers of people."

"Lots of luck getting your UN colleagues to agree to the use of the 'g' word," Jeri said.

Bolingbrook looked ready to argue then sighed. "Yes. It's almost impossible to bring a charge of genocide. Especially if it's generally accepted that the 'problem' is an internal matter for the country."

"Wouldn't you say most genocide is internal, Louise? Look at the Khmer Rouge in Cambodia or what happened to the Kurds in Iraq under Saddam Hussein."

Bolingbrook nodded. "I don't disagree, Geraldine, but the UN has a strong aversion to interfering in a country's internal affairs, and I don't see that changing."

"Expecting a union of sovereign states to limit their own authority is like expecting medieval kings to denounce divine right. At a certain point, people need to protect themselves." Jeri looked at Bolingbrook, but refrained from making the reference to Ireland more explicit.

"Aren't democracies better at protecting rights than other kinds of governments?" Kelly asked, but with a hesitancy that betrayed her own skepticism. The people around her all seemed to have personal experiences to draw from that suggested otherwise.

"For their own people," Jeri answered. "Or rather, for those it considers citizens. And there are always some citizens who are considered more bona fide citizens than others."

Kelly nodded. AIDS had certainly come as a surprising reminder to many of George's friends that their homosexuality trumped their identity as white men.

Kelly remembered that the talk she had heard Bolingbrook give had been about genocide in the Twentieth Century. Bolingbrook had spoken from the perspective of refugees, but Kelly had been shocked at the picture being presented from the Armenians to the Kurds. Nothing might compare with what Hitler had unleashed against the Jews, but that was not the sole example of an attempt to murder a nation, a culture, in the Twentieth Century.

"What's wrong with people?" The question burst from her before she even knew it was in her mind. It hung in the air, unanswerable, it seemed.

Then Jeri did answer. "It's what we are."

The words opened a vision of spinning darkness that absorbed light, eliminated hope, denied all comfort.

"No. No, that can't be all." Kelly knew her protest was feeble in the face of Jeri's desolate accusation, but still she rejected the vision.

Bolingbrook rallied. "At least your President Bush used his power to set up a safe haven for the Iraqi Kurds. I'm still not sure how, but that happened."

"Perhaps the Buddha helped him to find his own compassion," Kaju said.

Four pairs of eyes turned toward the youth with varying levels of disbelief, but no one had the heart to disagree with him.

†

258

It wasn't much of a tremor.

Plate tectonics was one more thing Kelly intended to look up when next she found a library or bookstore. By now she was familiar, on a personal level, with the understanding that the entire Himalayan Mountain Range was the result of India grinding into Asia, and that the mountains were still growing. She had almost grown used to the earth moving during the trek. One particular episode had been violent enough to be quite alarming. They were moving across a high meadow, and everyone had stopped in their tracks and stared around wide-eyed, but otherwise there had been no other visible effects from the tremor. Kelly might barely have noticed this most recent one had she not happened to be looking at Tashi.

The morning had taken them past a small village and through an upland valley. Shortly after the midday meal, they had been climbing a trail that Tashi said would take them to another valley before nightfall. The tremor caused a shaking that reminded Kelly of something fun, like skiing or skating, and she had turned to say something to Kaju when she saw Tashi. His face was registering shock and terror. Kelly couldn't understand what was causing his fear, because his eyes were rapidly shifting right and left. Then Kelly saw that Jeri and Kaju, too, were riveted on Tashi and waited, crouched and frozen.

"Jeri! Kaju! There!" Tashi flung out an arm and pointed to the mountainside.

Kaju was near Kelly. As his uncle yelled, he leapt forward and pushed or pulled or both, forcing Kelly toward the wall of the mountain. Kelly had the fleeting impression that Jeri was doing the same to Louise, but she was primarily concerned with doing exactly what Kaju wanted. She did not have to be told that her life depended on doing so; somehow the knowledge had been implicit in Tashi's yells. She tried to move faster, but stumbled over her own feet, got them sorted, and managed to keep moving.

She could hear the rumble now, feel the thunderous roar that nearly drowned out Kaju's mantra, a repeated scream to "Hurry, hurry, hurry." The words were unnecessary; the tremendous sound was physically propelling her forward. Her mind registered that she was being rushed toward a hole in the mountain wall. A very shallow hole, but an indentation nonetheless.

As the roar of the avalanche smothered all else, Kelly scrambled into the dark recess. Then, above the thunder, she heard Kaju's mantra become a scream. She turned, terrified, in time to see Kaju grimace and start to fall. A rock, or a piece of one, had ricocheted into the cave and hit him. Kelly grabbed for the boy and pulled him inward, ignoring his cries of pain.

"Cover your heads!" Kelly heard Jeri yell, only inches from her ear, and she did, pulling her chuba over herself and Kaju.

The noise of falling rock subsided into silence, a deep profound silence that was a thing itself rather than an absence.

"You may get off me now, Geraldine. I am quite all right."

"Of course, Louise."

Kelly suppressed a giggle and lifted her chuba. The air was thick with dust and she coughed; she could see nothing. She heard Kaju moan and then cough.

"Kell, are you all right?"

"I'm fine. It's Kaju who's hurt."

"Hold on. Don't move. I'm getting a light."

The darkness was utter. Unable to see anything, Kelly closed her eyes against the dust until she heard a zipper and then a click. Even with the flashlight on, there wasn't much to see. The chamber in which they were trapped was about six feet deep by twelve feet wide and perhaps twenty feet up to where the rock fall angled into the mountainside. Thick dust in the air obscured most detail.

"Hold this," Jeri said, and handed Kelly the light.

"Ahshang, ahshang," Kaju whispered, calling for his uncle.

Tashi was not in the cave. Kelly thought back, remembering that Tashi had been somewhere in the center of the group, the person who had known where they should go. Kelly looked toward the rock fall. Heavy boulders intruded into the little space. Involuntarily, she flinched at the thought of Tashi caught beneath a ton of rock.

"Tash! Tashi!" Jeri called, her voice loud in the small area. There was no answer. She said something to Kaju in Nepali.

After moving all the packs out of the way, Louise joined them. "How are you?" she asked.

"Arm. Breaked," Kaju answered.

"Broke, broken," Kelly corrected automatically.

Jeri carefully removed the clothing from Kaju's right arm. The air was slightly cleaner now, and in the light they could see that the arm, although not bleeding, was somewhat askew.

"Louise, could you get one of the tent poles for a splint? I have some tape in my canvas pack."

"*Break* is not regular?" Kaju asked.

"No. *Crack* is regular. Crack, cracked."

As if to illustrate the sound, Jeri broke one of the tent poles. "Hold him," she said to Kelly. "This is going to hurt."

Jeri took hold of Kaju's arm and, in the quiet of the chamber, they all heard the sound as the bone slipped back into place. Kaju cried out. When Jeri had the tent pole bound and holding Kaju's arm in place, the women moved the boy to the back wall of the cave. Jeri switched the flashlight off.

"We should go easy on batteries."

"Jeri, is air getting in? I can't tell."

"I think so. Hold on."

The sound of Jeri scrambling up the boulders sounded loud in the dark. Apparently she had studied the rock fall at the same time as she worked on Kaju. The sounds stopped and then resumed as Jeri returned.

"There's no light, but there is a bit of a draft. We don't have to worry about suffocating."

"What about food?" Louise asked.

"I think Kaju has some, but Tashi was carrying most of it. Water is going to be more of a problem." They never carried much water since there was usually a supply available near their campsites.

Kelly became sorely aware of the dust in her mouth. She wanted a big drink of water to wash it away. "What about Tashi?" Kelly asked.

"I don't know. I just don't know. We have to assume the avalanche got him."

"So it's up to us. Somehow."

"Somehow," Jeri echoed in the darkness.

For a long time, the only sound in the small cavern was that of four people breathing.

"I think I have a plan."

There was a quiet British laugh. "Very good, Geraldine. I knew you would."

The plan involved climbing as far up as possible and then removing rocks, by loosening, moving, chipping away, or any other means that was available. Jeri was assuming that the fall would be thinnest the further up they were, and that gravity might aid any movement they could cause in the rock fall. They had two tools for the work: a short-handled hatchet and a folding trench shovel. Jeri and Kelly would do the digging; Louise would keep the living area from being overrun by rubble.

Trial and error consumed the first few hours as a pathway was picked out over the rocks, then wobbly boulders that might cause Kelly or Jeri to slip were firmed in place by wedging in loose rocks. They decided that the best course would be to use the mountain as one wall of what would hopefully be a tunnel out, an idea that was sound as a plan but not at all easy to carry out. They had no idea how much rock lay between them and freedom.

"We might as well use the batteries when necessary," Jeri decided. "Kaju has some extra in his pack, and there will probably be enough for as long as we need them."

"You mean as long as we last?"

"We can turn them off most of the time, but I want to avoid anything slipping and falling on us."

They worked steadily for several hours until Louise called them down. She and Kaju had taken the food from his pack as well as prepared a sleeping area. Kelly noticed that Louise had set the bedding where it would be least likely to be endangered by rock falling from where she and Jeri were working.

Waking into absolute darkness was disorienting, but the quartet managed a determined grip on behaving as if it were just another ordinary day. Predictably, having only a small supply of water was the largest hardship but, despite the demands of the altitude, they limited themselves to small sips.

Kelly understood that working was the best preventative against despair, but she also felt her hope ebbing as she chipped away at a slightly movable boulder. Given enough time, it was quite possible that they could dig themselves out, of that she was sure, but she was also sure that long before that happened, they would all be too debilitated to bring about their own escape. Kelly was pushing and prodding at the mid-sized rock when she was surprised by how suddenly the rock gave way. Just as she gave one last push, Jeri pulled her off her perch and down.

"Kell, over here." Jeri pulled her into the relative safety of the sleeping area as the sounds of an avalanche put her in the grip of terror.

The noise was muffled, nowhere as overwhelming as that of the avalanche which had trapped them, but the sounds of falling rock still triggered a body memory in each of the survivors. None of them moved until the noise subsided. Kelly felt Kaju clamping her arm with his good hand and suspected that he was unaware he had had done so until he suddenly let go with an apology.

Once again, the air was full of dust, causing them to keep their noses covered and their eyes closed. Not many rocks had clattered into the small cavern, but Kelly was still afraid of what she would find when they examined the results of the newest event. Slowly, she opened her eyes. In the dusty murk, she could see Jeri a few feet away, grinning at her.

Louise, sitting farther away in the back of the chamber, coughed, then said, "Oh, my, look at that."

And they did. Look. The light was extremely dim, but it was there, welcome to eyes starved of sight. Jeri was up first, scrambling up the rocks to where they had been working. In a few moments, she returned.

"I can't see out, but whatever happened, it has to be good."

"I agree," Louise said. "I think the occasion calls for a drink. I think mine is a vintage red, possibly Burgundy."

"I believe it's a Guinness dark ale for me," Jeri said. "How about you, Kell?"

"The farm next to ours has an old tree that the neighbors say was planted by Johnny Appleseed himself. I'm having a hard cider from the Appleseed Tree in its prime. Kaju?"

Kelly wasn't sure he had followed the lighthearted chatter, but she needn't have worried.

"Yak-butter tea is for me plenty enough good," he said primly, throwing them all into a fit of laughter.

Despite the optimism that light provided, the rock pile remained as resistant to escape as before. As the cavern grew dark with night, Kelly felt her spirits begin to match. She knew she was weaker, and although Jeri showed no such signs, even she must be beginning to feel the effects of little food and less water. There was a new warmth to their interactions that, like the light, provided nourishment that had been missing. Kelly was reminded of the kindness and care that had been present in her time with George and Russell and Billy, a careful kindness that managed to focus on what was immediate and yet acknowledged the extremity of the situation.

She woke into the darkness, momentarily unsure if she were actually awake, or if she still slept, but then the breathing of those around her brought assurance that she was truly awake. Her mouth was dry and gritty. If only she could drink, or dream of a cool stream of clear water. Careful not to make noise, she stretched her cramping legs, another sign of dehydration. The guards were not bothering about the needs of prisoners who would have none in a few short hours. She heard the rhythmic breathing of her companions. Let them sleep. She envied them. They would all die tomorrow, and the manner of it would be far from pleasant. Sleep was the only real escape from their fate. If only they had been able to fight on longer, perhaps they might have made it to the sanctuary of the mountains. She should have anticipated the ambush, should have expected that this foray would indeed stir the hornets' nest and bring troops in pursuit. Too late for regrets. Now all that was left was the necessity of dying well, and that would be hardest of all. She feared pain so much more than dying.

"Kell, Kelly. Wake up. It's only a dream."

"What? Oh, Jeri. It was so real."

"Your brother? George? You were crying," Jeri whispered.

"No. You were there, too, I think. But I can't remember." Kelly shivered, still caught in the emotions stirred by the dream.

Jeri drew back in the dark cavern. She was too close to reaching out, putting her arms around Kelly and pulling her close. Maybe later, maybe if it got worse and they all started to hallucinate. She'd awakened with the strangest feeling that she was part of Kelly's dreaming, as if she didn't have enough bad dreams of prison of her own. She knew Kelly thought they were going to die. She could sense Kelly's slow withdrawal, a gradual acceptance, and the dreams were seeping in, as if finding their way into a space that ordinarily resisted them. Jeri accepted what connected her to Kelly, even accepted that it might be deeper than a single lifetime. She was far from understanding this, further still from granting it an active part in her decisions, but nevertheless she accepted it even if it made no useful sense.

A fragment from the German poet, Rilke, came to her: "*Ein mal jedes nur ein mal. Ein mal und nicht mehr.* Once for everything, just once and no more." So even if some part of you did live a hundred lifetimes, you only got this lifetime for once.

They weren't going to die here. She wouldn't let them. She wasn't ready to put her arms around Kelly and let them both slip off, becoming withered mummies in some forgotten Himalayan cave.

"Fight it, Kell. Fight it. We're getting out of here." She paused. "You're going to get back to Cleveland."

Jeri was surprised to hear a sudden fit of giggles.

"Oh, Jeri, if only you knew just how much that idea is lacking in consolation." Kelly smothered her laughter.

Jeri was surprisingly put out by Kelly's response. She had been sincere, had only wanted to encourage Kelly's hope. What was so damned funny about that?

"If Cleveland has lost its charm, dear, I'm sure we can find something for you in work with refugees."

"Really, Louise? I think I'd like that. Then you'd know where to find me, Jeri."

"I'll know where to find you," Jeri muttered.

Jeri took the trench tool and hatchet and climbed up the rock face. No sense wasting time if everyone was awake anyway. She must be getting weaker herself if she let a little laughter hurt her feelings. She found the particular bunch of stones she had been working loose the night before, and every so often she was rewarded by the sound of pebbles and chips rattling down into the debris near her feet. The boulder was next. About as big around as a car tire but considerably thicker, it was wedged into place by a protrusion on its right. It was going to fall back into the cave when it was loose enough, and there was a danger that it might bring down considerably more when it fell, but it had to be moved. Maybe if she could knock the protrusion off, it would fall toward the side of the cave they were using as a latrine.

The dim light of day had arrived in the cave. Jeri tapped at the boulder with the back of the axe, listening for some shift in tone, something to tell her where there might be a weakness. She heard movement below as Louise and Kaju arranged a breakfast of stale chapatis. She tapped again. A series of faint taps seemed to echo in response.

Jeri's stomach clenched, and she gripped the handle of the hatchet. She must have imagined it. Holding her breath, she hit the rock again, but this time she used the SOS code: three short, three long, three short. The silence that followed seemed to stretch toward eternity.

"Geraldine! Come get something to eat."

"Hush!"

Jeri thought she heard an answer, but couldn't be sure. Again she tapped out SOS. Everyone was listening now.

And heard the answer. A definite tapped answer. Jeri translated the code into alphabet.

"It's Tashi, Kaju! Tashi's out there! Tashi's going to get us out!"

It took longer than that, of course, but by the end of the day, a way had been found to lower a leather water bag to the people trapped in the chamber. It was another day and a half before Tashi and the people from a nearby village moved enough rock to free the four.

Louise went out first, a rope tied round her waist to guide her and keep her from falling. The rope was necessary because Tashi and the village people helping him had made a way through the rubble from upslope, using gravity to help them move rock. Then Kaju was taken through the opening.

Kelly and Jeri waited in the cavern for the rope to fall back in and when it did, Jeri helped Kelly fasten it about her waist. When the knot was secure, Kelly leaned forward and kissed Jeri lightly on the lips.

"I'm not going back to Cleveland," she said and then pulled hard on the rope and began climbing.

Outside, Tashi was waiting with a dozen mountain village people, maybe more if she counted the children. Everyone was grinning and laughing, creating a festival of life retrieved. Kelly looked about her and was sure that the sky had never seemed a happier blue nor the shades of purple distance more demanding of gratitude. She turned to see Jeri emerging from the rock and knew again that she was exactly where she ought to be. A hand fell on her shoulder. It was Kaju beside her, grinning with complete understanding.

Tashi had understood immediately that he couldn't run with the others to shelter from the avalanche. Even if they survived, they would be trapped. This was far from the first time he had taken this route to Tibet, so it was from experience that he had known to run at an angle away from the mountain and dive over the lip of the rock shelf that held the trail. It was experience also that took him to the village. The folk there were mountain born and bred, and everyone from children to elders accompanied Tashi to help move rock.

A curious audience of stolid but curious yak watched the straggling line of travelers and villagers that trooped into the grouping of low stone homes along the trail. The foreigners were taken to the largest, where an impromptu celebration began.

Kelly sat back in the dancing shadows of the crowded, fire-lit room and sipped her tea. Louise and someone from the village had discovered a language in common, while Jeri was talking with Tashi. Jeri was smiling, and Kelly was glad of the chance to simply look at the woman who had become her true north. While in the cave, Kelly had accepted the probability of dying. Approaching death was a familiar enough circumstance to her, but it appeared that there would be more time, more time to find her way to Jeri.

She was surer than ever of her love. There was a lost child in Jeri, the deep part of her that was starved for love and connection. Jeri had always been alone. Kelly knew this as if she had been with Jeri through all the long years until they met. While Kelly had George to rely on and teach her, Jeri had only had her own bravery, a single-minded courage that kept her focused on becoming something clear and bright. She honed her spirit and sharpened her mind and tucked the lonely child's heart away somewhere far and deep. Then something had betrayed her, betrayed that dimly glimpsed purpose. Despairing of ever becoming what she knew she must be, Jeri banished the hope that she had nurtured and passed into an even more distant exile.

Kelly reached into her pocket to feel the comforting shape of her crystal. In the firelight and shadows, amid the rich odors and lively laughter of a crowded Himalayan home, Kelly promised herself, and Jeri, that she would find that exiled heart, even if the way took her through nightmares and sorrow beyond bearing.

As if she had heard the thought, Jeri looked over to Kelly. "Did you say something?" she asked.

"I think Kaju was right," Kelly answered. "Yak butter tea is plenty enough good."

Chapter Nine

Inevitably the day arrived when the small group of travelers reached Tibet. They made camp on a ledge at the end of a narrow cleft in the mountains. Not far below, a shallow river curved sinuously in several bands, a braiding of silver ribbons. On the far side, the undulating plain stretched like a sea of brown and tan. The beauty of Tibet was striking and forlorn, an immense space that felt vast and eternal. Kelly found a vantage where she was able to gaze into the distance.

"It's not marked." She was unaware that Jeri had come up behind her. "This is the working border. PLA patrols have been seen along the edge of the mountains."

"PLA?" Kelly was less interested in an explanation than in keeping control of her expression. She didn't want their time together to end, but she was reluctant for Jeri to see the depth of her dismay.

"People's Liberation Army. The Chinese."

"Jeri, why isn't Kaju going on with you?"

"Tashi promised his sister he wouldn't take a chance on the boy being caught across the border. If the rest of us get picked up, we might just get expelled, but Kaju looks Tibetan, and he could disappear like his father did. No one's ever mentioned it, but Kaju is a cousin of Detsen Phurba."

"What about Tashi?"

"Tashi's willing to take his chances. This project has always been mostly his doing."

"What if the British pick me up after I leave?"

"They can't be watching every place in Nepal, but if they do find you, they don't really know how you left Umahthi or that you've been with me. Just say you picked up with a group of backpackers and what's it to them anyway."

"And don't give anything away for free."

"That's right, nothing for free."

For an instant, they enjoyed the pleasure of sharing a thought.

"Jeri, let me come with you."

"Kelly, look, I'm sorry it didn't work out, but this isn't the life for you. Go home."

Kelly shook her head and took a deep breath. "I am home, Jeri. I'm not going back to Cleveland. If I can't go on with you, I'm staying here with Kaju until you come back, and then I'll probably work with Louise. But I want to be with you."

"No, Kell, don't." Jeri turned her head so Kelly couldn't see her face. "It won't work. If you go now, we'll both have this time to remember." Jeri paused and then added carefully, "This time, it's been more precious to me than you can know. But believe me, please, this way is for the best."

"You can't know that."

Getting no response, sensing a conflict in Jeri and reluctant to cause more pain, longing instead for Jeri's whole-hearted acceptance of her presence, Kelly shrugged and tried a smile. "I'm sure you're wrong, but either way I'm keeping your sweatshirt."

Kelly listened as Jeri conferred with Tashi, and they decided that next day would be soon enough for Kelly, Tashi, and Kaju to go to the market town where Kelly could find transport of some kind. Kaju would keep the extra supplies they had needed when hiking, and he would stay with distant relatives of Tashi until the travelers returned. Tashi would help make the various arrangements, as well as acquire some of the tough Tibetan ponies that he, Jeri, and Bolingbrook would ride for the rest of the journey. They meant to travel as lightly and as quickly as possible from here on. Kelly listened until, suddenly afraid she would break down, she gathered her backpack and made her way down to the riverbank. If she was going back to civilization, she might as well have clean clothes.

Kelly walked along the edge of the river, searching for a place where the bank would dip toward the water. The river was wide, but it appeared to be only inches deep. The air was warm below the pass and out of the wind. Kelly checked the sky. The sun was bright and strong, except in the distance where a few dark clouds hung over a section of the mountains, indicating a storm in the upper reaches. Anything she washed should dry quickly. She could put her wet clothes on any of the branches of the scrubby trees that grew along the bank, and the sun would probably dry them in an hour. That was what the camping gear people promised: strong, quick-drying material.

Leaving Jeri was wrong. There was nowhere in the world Kelly could go and not have every day be full of wondering where Jeri was, how she was, missing her voice, the way she walked, the quirk of an eyebrow when she was keeping back a comment, her steady gaze as she thought through some problem. When Jeri came back from Tibet, Kelly would argue again. Let Jeri go to Tibet and find out that she couldn't live without Kelly.

It was a plan. And she was going to have clean clothes.

Standing barefoot on the warm rocks in the cold, shallow river, Kelly used hand soap to make a respectable lather, rinsed, and then wrung the water out. She hung her clothing on a bush with small gray-green leaves that reminded her of sage, her feet welcoming the short trips out of the icy river water that was fed by mountain streams. The more she thought about her decision, the better she felt about it. Working with Louise would give her the kind of purpose that always felt as if it were missing when she thought about going back to Ohio. She wanted a change big enough to reflect everything that had occurred since George had died. Kelly hung the last piece of her washing on a branch.

Being barefoot was a pleasure all its own, an impossible pleasure in a city of sharp and broken edges. Here the stones were smooth and river worn, easy to walk on. Kelly moved over to a flat rock that was inches above the water and sun-warmed. The peace that had settled in her throughout the trek ebbed back. The sound of the current, the sparkle of the water, the light wind rattling through the brush—everything reminded her of being a child again, before knowing the world that existed beyond her family's farm. That's what innocence was—believing in the essential goodness of wherever you were.

Kelly let herself slip into a daydream of what might be. She would turn and see Jeri walking toward the river's edge, holding out her arms, saying: *I've changed my mind, I can't live without you.* And Kelly would move into Jeri's arms, and they would kiss. The thought of kissing Jeri made Kelly's mouth water, and the hope and pain of it filled her. She stood there, eyes closed in the warm sun, waiting for the onslaught of feeling to drift away.

Eyes still closed, Kelly felt water flowing over her toes, cold water. She had been stepping from one dry area to the next, but when she opened her eyes she saw that there weren't any more such places ahead. She turned to go back and was surprised to see that there were no longer any dry rocks behind her.

The farm child in her knew immediately what had happened, although she was not alarmed. The clouds that she had noticed earlier were raining and filling some, even several, mountain streams, causing the river to rise. She wasn't afraid, merely worried that she hadn't set her boots far enough back from the water's edge. The river was rising, but not that much. She would have to wade.

The water was above her ankles, but she had rolled her pants legs up. Still, the cold water was already numbing her feet. She moved more quickly to get out of the cold. The water grew deeper, almost to her knees. The rounded stones were loose in the current and slippery beneath her numb feet. She stumbled, missed her footing. She fell on her butt, and the indignity of getting dunked made her feel silly and glad there was no one to see her. She still wasn't worried, just irritated at getting wet. She tried to stand but couldn't get up from this angle, so she rolled over in order to push herself up with her hands.

The current grabbed her, took her, lifted her as easily as if she were a mere twig or leaf.

She was worried now, scrambling by instinct as well as by thought. The water still wasn't deep. She could breathe, although she could feel the rocky bottom of the river scrape and bruise her knees, her thighs. She scrabbled against the bottom, grabbing for something to hold onto, something to stop the drag of the current. She was in trouble now, and along with that realization came a surprising clarity. She wanted Jeri, needed her help desperately. Kelly grabbed for a rock, anything heavy enough to stop her, found one, and then felt it loosen and herself slide again, and she was amazed at how out of control she had become, at how quickly she had been swept into mortal danger. The current flipped and pulled her, and suddenly her head was under water and she was bumping along the bottom. Rather than grab, Kelly pushed against the riverbed in order to get her head above water, and when she did, she cried out for help, loud and long, because now she was very afraid.

You can't know that.

The quiet words, spoken with adamant conviction, had a familiar ring, like an echo that Jeri couldn't quite recall. Then she did remember, and vertigo accompanied the feeling of coming loose in time. She had said exactly the same thing to Arkadia O'Malley when she was in the Armagh prison.

"You can't know that," she had said, angry that O'Malley dared say Jeri wasn't truly in love with her, and O'Malley had been right. Jeri's feelings of affection and attraction were strong, but O'Malley had been right to not accept them as love. Now Jeri's own words came back to taunt her, so very much the same and so very different, because she did love Kelly and knew Kelly loved her. She could admit that to herself, admit that she did not know that sending Kelly away was for the best. Yet it had to be. Kelly could still go back to her own life, the kind of life that Jeri had once thought she herself might live after Oxford, a life she had lost when she decided to visit Ireland. Kelly didn't have to be an outlaw, a fugitive, hunted, constantly in peril.

Jeri had not seen Kelly leave, but at a certain point she noticed Kelly was gone. That fact didn't bode well for the near future. How could she leave Kelly behind if she couldn't even let her out of her sight for a few minutes? She might as well get used to the absence because, by this time tomorrow, Kelly would be gone for good. To her complete surprise, Jeri was on the verge of tears. She never cried. Ever.

Cursing herself for several kinds of a fool, she went to sort through the supplies she and Tashi would need to repack for the change from backpacking to riding horseback. She looked out over the river to the plains beyond and drew a deep breath. Empty, that's how they looked. Empty.

They would leave the tents with Kaju. Sleeping bags would be enough for warmth, and it wasn't likely there would be much rain inside western Tibet. Jeri set aside the cooking pots. If she was going to miss someone, she ought to miss Kaju, the cook. Tashi had no aptitude for it, and she certainly didn't. Bolingbrook hadn't attempted to make a meal, but Jeri had a sour notion that if the woman did try, she could probably present something that went with silverware and candlelight.

Jeri picked up a looping of rope they had needed to get out of the avalanche. A rope would probably not be useful in Tibet, but it was one of those things that, when you did need it, nothing else could substitute. Jeri put it back. Food. Tashi should buy more tsampa. They could each carry their own supply of Tibet's instant breakfast, lunch, and supper. They would need to avoid villages, and there would be little chance of acquiring food once they left Nepal. Then Jeri saw the packet of mixed tea biscuits that Yusef Jamali had meant for Bolingbrook. She had forgotten all about giving them to the Englishwoman. Perhaps this

272

evening, before actually entering Tibet, would qualify as an occasion for cookies.

A cloud slid between the mountain and the sun, casting a shadow, causing a momentary chill. Something wasn't right. Jeri looked at the river and noticed that it appeared to have risen slightly, not an uncommon occurrence in waters fed by mountain streams. Uneasy, feeling somewhat foolish, she stood and took a step toward the edge of the ledge to get a better view. That was when she heard the cry for help. Jeri knew without a shred of doubt that the cry was from Kelly. And then she saw her. From this height, she saw Kelly in the water, fighting the current.

Jeri grabbed for the rope and then she was running, not bothering to find a path but leaping onto the loose scree, sliding down the gravel, hoping to keep her footing in her headlong plunge down the slope. Then she was on the rounded dry cobbles of the flat, dry riverbed. It was possible that the water might rise this high, although Jeri thought not. The presence of plants testified to the rarity of that occurrence. This was an older riverbed, higher up the slope than the current one, but the loose cobblestones were an impediment to running as they slipped about under her feet.

Jeri ran at an angle. She had an image of the river as she had seen it from above, seen where it curved back toward itself, and if she ran across that curve, and luck favored her, she might get to the water before it swept Kelly past. It was possible. Jeri reached the edge of the water and listened while she scanned the bank in both directions. She stripped off her jacket, tossed it aside, and then looped one end of the rope around a large boulder that she was confident no amount of water would budge. She knotted the other end of the rope around her own waist. With growing dread, she realized that she hadn't heard any more cries for help.

Jeri waded slowly out into the rushing water. It was shockingly cold, icy. She saw pieces of brush spinning in the current that bucked against itself, foaming, resisting its own surge. She looked downstream. Surely she couldn't have missed Kelly. *Please, no. Please, by all that's holy, no.* If she didn't see her soon, she was going to slip the knot on the rope and plunge into the current, trust the rush of it to take her to Kelly. Just then, not far upstream, she glimpsed the bright color of the plaid shirt Kelly had been wearing. Jeri edged deeper into the water, pushing through it, trusting that the rope would be there when she needed it, but first she had to reach Kelly. The water was so cold, breathtakingly cold.

Jeri didn't have time to test each step, but she was wearing boots and they were helping her keep her footing. She was terrified. It didn't look as though Kelly was fighting the current. Surely she hadn't been in the water long enough to drown. But the rocks, she could have hit rocks, and that damage might be considerable. The patch of color was close now. Jeri flung herself forward.

Jeri got hold of Kelly's shirt with one hand, but the current tried to rip the body away. Damned if she'd lose Kelly, Jeri's fingers locked around the fabric. If it came to that, she'd slip the knot and they could both go down the river. Jeri had her now, gripping Kelly with two hands, pulling her close, and then they were both dangling on the rope like two fish caught on a single line.

Jeri turned the limp body and saw Kelly's eyes were open but not at all focused.

"Help me, Kell," she said, her mouth close to Kelly's ear. Jeri struggled to find her footing. "Help me get us out of this." The water was only waist deep, but the current was wildly fierce.

Jeri got one arm around her, and with her other hand she got a grip on the rope and started pulling.

"Help me, Kell. I need you to hold on to me."

One of Kelly's arms was over her shoulder, and with a lift of her heart, Jeri felt that arm tighten. Then Kelly's other arm moved.

"That's my girl. You can do it. Hold on to me. Just hold on, just hold on."

Jeri could now use both her arms to pull on the rope, slowly getting them into shallower water. Slowly, ever so slowly, they were getting closer to the water's edge.

"Don't let go yet." Kelly had her feet under her, was taking some of her own weight. "Hold on until we're out of this."

Together they stumbled out of the river and onto the stony ground. Kelly's head lolled against Jeri's shoulder, and she would have dropped, but Jeri held her up until they reached the boulder where the rope was fastened. It was large enough to be an effective windbreak, and once there, Jeri let Kelly slump to the ground. Already the river water was lowering, the ferocious spate also brief.

"Cold, I'm so cold." Kelly's teeth were chattering like rattling dice, but that was a good sign, a sign that her body's reflexes were working.

"You'll be fine," Jeri said, mustering a confidence she didn't feel. "Remind me later to tell you about a Chechen river. Now, help me get you out of these clothes. They're too wet, they'll keep you cold."

Kelly hadn't been in the water all that long, but shock as well as icy water would be lowering her temperature. A number of bruises were visible, at first on her face, but showing elsewhere on her pale skin as Jeri got her out of her soaked clothing. Some of Kelly's fingers were bleeding from having scrabbled on the river bottom for something to stop the current from sweeping her away.

"What? You're mumbling." Jeri had actually heard, but she wanted Kelly to work against the effects of freezing by putting out more effort.

"Always—always thought—it would be more fun when you undressed me."

"Idiot. And they say a sense of humor is the first thing to go."

"Actually—one of the last."

They were out of the wind, and the sun reached them with considerable strength, but Kelly's lips still had a bluish tinge. Jeri located her jacket, got it, and helped Kelly slip into the heavy denim.

"Don't leave me, Jeri."

"I'll be right back. Don't go anywhere."

Using the path this time, Jeri ran to the camp, considering what she would need to bring back.

Everything at the campsite was just as she had left it. Bolingbrook was working on the report, making her notes as usual. Kaju and Tashi were discussing some matter over by the cook fire. Kelly might have died with no one knowing, and the world would have just continued. The most basic drama of life and death had taken place a short distance away, and no one had noticed; nothing had altered up here.

Kelly could have died. Jeri fought a surge of nausea.

Bolingbrook looked up and her eyes widened in surprise. "Have you been swimming, Geraldine?"

"No. Just wading."

Kelly was where Jeri had left her, her head resting against the rock, her eyes closed, but she was still shaking. After Jeri got her into the sleeping bag, she changed into her own dry clothes and slid into the sleeping bag behind Kelly.

"Here. I brought us both some chocolate. It's the best medicine for hypothermia." Jeri took a bite from the bar before handing it to Kelly.

"Jeri?"

"What?"

"I don't want to leave you."

"Since I can't leave you alone for even a little bit, it looks like you'll have to come along. Oh, baby, of course you'll come along." The endearment sprang easily to Jeri's lips, as if she had always used it. "I don't think I could let you go, even if you wanted me to. I can't believe I almost lost you. I guess we're stuck with each other."

They sat together in the warmth of the sun, Jeri's back against the rock, her arms enfolding Kelly.

"Jeri? You said to ask you about a chicken liver."

"What?" For an instant, Jeri thought that Kelly might have suffered brain damage, then she remembered. "Not chicken liver. A Chechen river. A river in Chechnya. That's a place in southern Russia." Jeri began the story.

Chapter Ten

Waking from a dream of mewling kittens, Kelly wondered if some sort of small Himalayan wildlife had crept close to where she and Jeri were wrapped in their separate sleeping bags. Then she realized the sounds were coming from the woman beside her. Jeri must be caught in a dream, and not a happy dream, either.

"Shh. It's okay," Kelly whispered, and slid as close to Jeri as their sleeping bags would permit.

Kelly's presence seemed to ease Jeri because the sounds of distress subsided, but Kelly was awake now. Bright stars glittered above, as if light had exploded and left itself behind in drifting pieces. The tent was gone. Kaju and Tashi had taken all the tents when they set out for the town soon after Jeri had told Tashi that Kelly would be going on with the group after all. Without the duty of accompanying Kelly, the two men had decided there was no need for them to wait for morning.

For hours Kelly had felt the lingering effects of nearly drowning in icy water, the most pronounced effect being that she could muster very little energy. Jeri had gathered Kelly's dry clothing from the brush and retrieved her hiking boots and with Jeri supporting her, they had climbed up to the camp. As Jeri helped her sit near the fire, Kelly felt as though she were observing everything from a distance. She was surprised to see that Kaju looked like he might cry as Jeri described what had happened. Tashi's lips drew into a thin, taut line, and his eyes narrowed in a look that Kelly had begun to know meant concern. Bolingbrook, unexpectedly, almost gushed.

"Tea. You must get something warm inside in addition to just that chocolate. Kaju, start the water. I have some tea I've been keeping. Are you sure you're all right, Geraldine? 'Wading,' you said you'd gone wading."

"I'm fine, Louise." Jeri sounded embarrassed.

Kelly had a momentary vision of Bolingbrook fussing over her staff in some far-flung, isolated camp near a war zone, letting her people know how much they were cared about. Kelly would have bet there were any number of people scattered around the world who would work their hearts out for Louise Bolingbrook.

Jeri walked over to Tashi. "Tash, do you think you can manage to find another horse? For Kelly?"

Tashi considered the question and then nodded. "If we do not have to find a room or a bus, Kaju and I will go now. Kaju will be staying with my friend who has the horses."

Somewhat put out that the English lady thought her tea better for Kelly than his, Kaju brought the drink to her. "My uncle and I go now," Kaju said. "Please. Do not fall into any more rivers. Or other dangerous places."

"Oh, Kaju, I'll miss you." Kelly managed a smile as she took his hand. Squeezing it was still beyond her capability, but she brought it to her lips, and Kaju, very embarrassed, looked ready to cry again.

"I forgot something, Louise." Jeri had been sorting out the supplies left behind by Tashi and Kaju. Now she held out a wrapped package. "Mr. Jamali asked me to give you this."

"Biscuits! Oh, Yusef. Thank you, Geraldine. Please take as many as you want. At least two. Tea and biscuits and Tibet. I shall one day write my autobiography, and that will be the title. Kelly, dear, you must have a biscuit with your tea."

Kelly wanted to argue that biscuits were something entirely different, that these were cookies, but talking at length was still too much trouble. After urging Jeri and Kelly to take more, Louise wrapped the remainder carefully and stowed them among her things.

The cookies, like the chocolate earlier, seemed to help Kelly recover physically but there were moments when the memory of scrabbling for a handhold and knowing she was going to drown came back with frightening immediacy. As night fell, Jeri had picked up their sleeping bags and gone away from the fire. She found a place to spread them where she and Kelly could look out over the darkening plain of Tibet while an ocean of stars emerged overhead.

"You probably noticed that I have trouble being with you." The unexpected admission was spoken slowly, barely above a whisper.

Kelly lifted the hand she was holding to her lips. "Sure. But I hoped we could work on that. Don't worry, being close to you is plenty enough good for me." Kelly didn't think Kaju would mind that she'd borrowed his phrase.

"It's just... when we get started... I can't handle it," Jeri said. Pride made the discussion difficult, but beneath pride was also the fear that by talking, she might make her failure permanent.

"Have you always been like this?"

"No!"

The answer was so adamant that Kelly would have laughed in other circumstances.

"No," Jeri repeated more quietly. "Not before Ireland."

"Do you know why it started?" Kelly's head was on Jeri's shoulder, and Jeri's arm was around her, so she felt Jeri's reaction. "Don't answer if it's too hard."

"I want to. I can't. Not right now."

"Post-traumatic stress?"

Jeri gave a bitter laugh. "Nice they've named it. I'd consider some phrase that used the word 'revenge' myself."

"Don't worry, we'll just keep trying. I don't care, as long as I'm with you. But, Jeri, promise me you'll never try to make me leave you again."

Jeri was quiet for so long Kelly thought she was refusing.

"I promise." Her voice was barely under control but grew stronger as she spoke. "I'll never ask you to leave me, Kelly Corcoran. You're free to choose to go anytime, but I'll never ask you again, and I'll do my best to keep you safe."

Kelly felt the lightest of tender kisses brush the crown of her head, as if a butterfly might have settled there.

"Jeri, something odd happened out there in the river."

"Right. You almost drowned."

"That, but something else. When I... when the water was pulling me down... I saw this old woman, or maybe I just heard her voice, but she seemed so familiar and she said, 'she knows now' and 'keep her.' That's not quite right. If the slang wasn't so out of place, I'd swear it was like 'she's a keeper.' It doesn't make sense now, but I remember feeling that it made all the sense in the world then."

"Don't worry about it, Kell. You've just been in America too long."

"Come on, Jeri, that doesn't make sense either."

"Sure it does. You're Irish, and you almost died. You should have expected a hundred leprechauns and fairies and a banshee or two to show up."

They fell asleep soon after that.

Jeri was making lost kitten sounds again, and Kelly snuggled closer. The effects of hypothermia seemed to have worn off, but the river's bruising was another matter entirely. She was sure she must look like she had been in a bar brawl, and there were twinges whenever she moved. She lifted herself on one elbow and smoothed Jeri's forehead with her other hand. Jeri seemed to be saying a name, repeating it.

"Hush," Kelly murmured. "Everything's going to be all right."

Jeri's eyes suddenly opened wide, though she didn't seem to be aware of Kelly, then she pulled Kelly to her and their mouths met in a frantic kiss that was wild, harsh, and demanding, and Kelly wanted to protest. And then she didn't. It was like being in the river again, swept into a force too strong to resist and too powerful to escape. Kelly couldn't even be sure that Jeri was awake. The need she felt engulfing her was intense, overwhelming, even impersonal. Jeri kicked out of her sleeping bag and urged Kelly out of hers. Freed from any constraints, she stripped away Kelly's clothing, as she had done by the river.

Kelly had looked forward to this moment, imagined it, anticipated it, dreamed of how it would feel to have Jeri's hands on her bare skin, have Jeri's mouth covering hers, then moving down, over her throat. She had imagined nothing like this. The hands that gripped her were hard and tight, holding her as if she might attempt to get away. The mouth that Kelly had always found soft and yielding was open wide, clumsy and feverish, and Kelly felt teeth, as if she were about to be eaten alive. Jeri was straining to pull her even closer, demanding, like the river, that she let go and surrender.

Despite surprise and an initial resistance, Kelly felt herself responding. She wanted Jeri, had wanted her for so long, had despaired of ever feeling her this close. Nothing mattered but that they were together and that Kelly was filling with the cresting spate of her own need to meet Jeri's heedless urgency. She felt as if she were rising toward the stars, into a fiery darkness, no longer in some earthly river but ascending on a swell of desire into the fury of comets hurtling through planetless space. But if emotions were fuel, then passion was fast becoming a dark furnace that threatened to propel them away from each other, separating them as they desperately struggled to come together.

"Jeri, it's me. It's Kelly," she heard herself say again and again. It wasn't an excess of passion the made Kelly want to stop, it wasn't even that Jeri was calling another woman's name, it was what Kelly felt inside the furious passion, driving them dangerously toward extinction.

Jeri stopped, just stopped, and lay limp in Kelly's arms.

"Oh, god, I'm sorry." She buried her face against Kelly's shoulder.

Kelly held her until the cold air diminished the heat that had driven them out into the night. Then, without ever completely letting go of Jeri, she got them both back into the warmth of a single sleeping bag.

"Kelly. Oh, Kell, did I hurt you?"

Kelly heard the anguish in the voice muffled against her. "Not much. I'm okay. Who's Fiona?"

"No." The grief was unmistakable. "I can't."

"Yes, you can. Now. Now, you have to."

And so Kelly learned of Fiona, whose death had derailed Jeri's life—the cousin, the mentor, the ideal, the beloved, the betrayer, the ghost. As Jeri talked in the dark, there were moments when Kelly felt she wasn't being told a story so much as being given a second life, Jeri's life twinned to her own, as if she were present during the moments Jeri recounted, present and absorbing them. Later, she hoped, later she would be able to sort through the impressions, to understand.

"I love you," Kelly said when the story was done.

Kelly made love to Jeri then. Gently, slowly, she coaxed Jeri into the sphere of desire. When they reached the point where Jeri would have stopped, Kelly persisted, gentle but insistent, weaving a harbor of love and trust to shelter them both. It wasn't the deep end of lovemaking, scaled no great heights nor plunged to profound depths, but now that Kelly was aware of the cause of Jeri's distress, they made it through. And after Kelly heard Jeri's deep sigh of release, she wasn't surprised that it was followed by wracking sobs. Kelly's arms held fast through the storm until they both fell into an exhausted sleep.

†

Tashi returned next afternoon with four horses, not much larger than ponies, but sturdy descendants of those horses that had once carried Genghis Khan and his armies across all Asia and into Europe. The rest of the day was taken up with instructions on how to mount and ride Tibetan style. Kelly's family had not owned horses, but one of their neighbors had, and Kelly had gone riding often enough to feel at ease on horseback. She quickly learned that riding in Tibet would not be like riding in Ohio. The saddle was unlike any she had encountered before. Little more than a frame meant to keep their belongings together, the contraption relied on a kind of small pillow for its small comfort. In addition, each rider could use their sleeping bag, and Tashi showed Kelly the traditional way to fold her chuba so that it, too, could provide padding.

"This one is for you, I think," Tashi said, pointing out a dun horse that had shadings of black in his stockings, mane, and tail.

Tashi showed her how to guide the horse using neck reining. Despite her horse's tendency to balk, Kelly readily picked up the basics.

"Does he have a name?" Kelly asked.

Tashi looked unhappy. "No one told me a name."

"Is it okay if I call him Lungta?"

A slow grin spread over Tashi's face, and he moved his head from side to side. Kelly hadn't yet worked out whether the gesture meant "yes" or "no" or something in between. Jeri, however, gave a definite nod. Apparently Kelly's suggestion pleased Tashi.

Lungta was the name for the prayer flags strung from temples and along mountain heights. The word meant "wind horse," and the flags carried blessings, the kind of blessing depending on the color, but in particular, a blessing for good energy. Kelly hoped her own Lungta would be pleased at being given a fortunate name.

The thoughts that came to mind as she dismounted later were much less ethereal. If she was feeling so wracked by aches after just one afternoon of practice, she couldn't imagine how she was going to feel after a full day of serious travel. Horseback riding strained unaccustomed muscles mercilessly, not to mention that she had been slammed into rocks the day before by a wild river. Then she remembered the night before, and certain other twinges registered.

"I know exactly how you feel, my dear." Louise Bolingbrook joined her, stretching gingerly. "I've been riding horses all my life, but I seem to be sadly out of shape."

Kelly knelt to adjust a bootlace so she could regain control of her face and quell an urge to giggle. She hadn't been thinking of horseback riding. "It's been years for me," she said as she stood up. "My family didn't have horses, but my brother and I used to go riding at the neighbors' farm."

"Does your brother still ride?"

"No. He... George died last fall. He had AIDS."

"Oh, my dear, I am so sorry. I've seen it, you know, particularly in Africa, and it's a terrible disease. What did he have?"

"The wasting, of course. Then in the end, it was pneumocystis. Pneumonia." God. Such short words for such long suffering, yet it was a consolation to say the words to someone who understood what they meant. Knowing AIDS was like membership in a secret society with its own language and rituals.

At the evening meal, the travelers realized they were going to miss Kaju very much. Tashi's cooking was adequate, but that was about all. He made butter tea and showed them how to add barley meal to make tsampa. Tashi managed to make a proper, finished example, a doughy dumpling, but the women weren't able to achieve the right mixture of tea and ground barley.

"I suppose we'll get the knack of it," Jeri said.

"I'm sure it's nutritious no matter how it looks." Bolingbrook eyed her bowl and seemingly weighed it alongside many former meals that were also better forgotten.

"I wonder if Kaju misses us," Kelly said wistfully.

"How long until we get to Detsen's gompa?" Louise asked Tashi.

"Three, four days. Maybe." The guide's answer was vague. "Between here and there, things could go wrong."

Before Kelly could even spread her sleeping bag, she was pulled into an embrace that told her she wasn't the only one whose mind had drifted away throughout the day. Jeri's arms held her like a homecoming, and Kelly wondered if they would ever need to speak again when gestures and touch carried so much meaning. Then she discovered a purpose for words.

"I want you so much," she murmured, and Jeri responded with unreserved fervor.

Chapter Eleven

Louise Bolingbrook was quite aware that when Kelly almost drowned, the event had precipitated a change for her two young companions. Nor, she found, was she the only one to notice. There was a moment when Jeri was explaining something to Kelly; her smile was particularly open and fond as she reached out to brush away an errant strand of hair from Kelly's forehead, a small gesture that revealed more than any quantity of words about their feelings. Tashi, who had been showing Louise how to adjust her saddle, looked at her, then at the younger women, then back at Louise, and they shared the indulgent smile that age reserves for comment when youth discovers love.

Bolingbrook had matters other than new love claiming her attention, and she turned her mind to the problem of Detsen Phurba's report. With a face-to-face meeting becoming more imminent each day, she was annoyed to find her anxiety growing. As students they had been Dets and Lou, and as for Louise, she had loved the handsome Tibetan boy. When he went home one spring, she had expected him to return in a month or two, but he never did. Her feelings bounced from anger at being dropped without a word to fear that something terrible had happened to him. Detsen had never been one to talk much about himself, and faced with his absence, Louise realized she had no way to find him. She hadn't even known the name of his home village, if indeed it had a name. She sent letters to Lhasa, inquired in all the places she could think of, and had been forced to abandon her inquiries. Months and then years passed. Then one day, a call came, and she was told that a Tibetan monk named Detsen Phurba had something for her.

Fond memories of a handsome young man, memories safely tucked away, suddenly emerged from mental mothballs with all the perplexing feelings of anger and worry that had accompanied his disappearance. She was not still in love with him, but time had provided no opportunity for

284

any other feeling to take love's place.

Louise understood that any time they would have together would be brief, and while she hoped there would be an opportunity for an explanation of their past, she also had official hopes for this encounter. If there was ever a moment when the UN just might be willing to put pressure on China regarding Tibet, it should be now, when the plight of the Iraqi Kurds presented a precedent. Every nation was reluctant to have its internal affairs put under international scrutiny, and so it was self-interest that made them all protect each other's most reprehensible actions. Still, if Bolingbrook could present undeniable evidence that China's activities were truly genocidal, there just might be a chance to get some kind of autonomy for Tibet. She was much too pragmatic to expect independence.

†

Tashi woke the women long before dawn. After only a cold chapati for breakfast, they set out across the now shallow river. A waxing moon, just past its first quarter, gave ample light for following Tashi, who set a bone-jarring pace, and by dawn, they were well away from the particular dangers of the border and into an area where low hills undulated with a rhythm like waves on a sea. They rode until the sun was a short way above the horizon, and then Tashi called a halt in the shadow of a bluff.

"I think I'll change Lungta's name to Spinecracker," Kelly announced.

"Can't," Jeri answered. "It's already taken."

"Where's Tashi going?" Bolingbrook asked. Their guide had spoken briefly to Jeri and then left.

"He has contacts somewhere around here. Herdsmen, I think." Jeri finished removing the gear from her horse.

"Herders? Of yaks?" Kelly asked.

"More probably sheep. Anyway, these people don't trust strangers at all."

"I don't imagine they should, if Detsen's report is correct," Louise said. "We're more likely to be from Beijing than from the UN."

"This far west, they've probably been able to avoid most PLA soldiers, but I doubt they ever heard of the UN. Here, Kell, give me Lungta and I'll take the horses over to graze. Did you name your horse, Louise?"

"I was thinking about it, but then I heard that Spinecracker was

285

taken."

Bolingbrook and Kelly dozed while Jeri kept watch until Tashi returned. He looked worried and tired as he slid from his horse, and he made no fuss when Jeri removed his saddle and gear and led his weary mount to where the others were tethered.

"These people"—Tashi gestured vaguely toward the distance when Jeri returned—"they say there are more patrols than ever. We must be very careful. They go by in planes, usually, but sometimes in trucks. If a plane catches us in the open, we must keep our faces hidden. We will have to stay away from roads, and that will make the trip longer."

Louise nodded. "I'm not surprised."

"But why?" Kelly asked. "The Berlin Wall is down. The whole Iron Curtain is coming down. Why won't the Chinese let up in Tibet, too?"

"China isn't the Soviet Union, Kell. It's not about to go the way of Russia."

"Geraldine is correct, my dear. Tiananmen Square gave notice that China intends to keep what it has."

Kelly had almost forgotten the events of Tiananmen, the orderly demonstrations that began as happy celebrations and then were so brutally put down by tanks. It had happened during the time she was still driving from her place to George and Russell's nearly every day. She recalled a photo she had seen in a newspaper.

"What was the name of the statue the students made?" she asked.

"The Goddess of Democracy," Bolingbrook answered.

"Like the Statue of Liberty?"

"I suppose it looked like that to Americans, but the students wanted to play down that aspect. They wanted to inspire their countrymen, not antagonize the government, so they intended her to look like one of those works of revolutionary realism."

Jeri's eyes narrowed as she listened to Bolingbrook. "Were you there?" she asked.

Louise sighed. "Yes. In early May, about the same time that Gorbachev came to visit. They were such children, so sure they had caught the crest of history and were riding it forward. They came from all over China. I was afraid for them, but they were so proud and so full of a belief in the power of goodness."

Bolingbrook's sadness was evident. Jeri thought about Ulster and about how Louise Bolingbrook must grieve for much of the world.

†

When Kelly woke, it was still daylight but well into the evening. She had fallen asleep with Jeri nearby, but now the sleeping bag next to hers was empty. She didn't have far to look; Jeri was sitting only a few feet away, her back against a boulder. Jeri smiled as soon as Kelly sat up, a smile that suggested Kelly had been the focus of her thoughts. Kelly moved to Jeri's side. The view was of the same undulating plain they had ridden across, but Kelly thought she caught the sparkle of water in the distance.

"It's a lake," Jeri said. "Quite a large one. This was all sea bed a couple of eons ago, now it's the highest plateau in the world. Did I remember to mention I love you?"

Kelly was still half asleep. "Once or twice. Tell me about Armagh," she said.

"Armagh? Why?"

"I think I was dreaming about a prison."

Jeri put an arm around Kelly and drew her close. "Armagh seems so long ago now, I don't even remember getting there. I mean the process, not the reason. I was in a fog, and nothing really mattered. About the first thing I remember is this woman who insisted I read a book."

"What book?"

"The Mill on the Floss."

"By George Eliot? I love that book."

"You'd like Arkadia, too. Arkadia O'Malley. She's a bit like Louise, about the same age, only stronger."

"Stronger than our Lady Bolingbrook? How is that even possible?"

"Different. You can get Louise's sense of purpose and how she's strong because of it. You know she'd hike through the Himalaya if she thought she could do some good for the world." Jeri smiled at how implausible the reality of their situation could be made to sound. "It's different with Arkadia. With her, it's more like she's keeping something safe against time itself. Do you know much about the ancient Irish?"

"Not really."

"When Celtic warriors would go into battle, there were bards who stood by the battlefield to sing them to victory. Arkadia is something like that—as long as she stands, then victory is possible. It's what she is, who she is. And then sometimes she would just be this harmless old prisoner who took care of the books, someone you'd hardly notice."

As she spoke, Kelly had the feeling that Jeri herself was the battlefield, and no matter where she was or what happened, she never completely lost the echo of Arkadia O'Malley singing.

"I think she must have saved you. Saved your heart anyway. Was she part of the IRA?"

But that was too long a story. Tashi had wakened and gone for the horses, and by the time everyone was saddled and mounted, the first stars of the evening were visible. Once again, Tashi led the way and Jeri rode last. There seemed to be a trail that they were following, but although the moon revealed shapes in the night, not much else was discernible until they reached the lake. There the water shimmered in the moonlight and ripples lapped against the shore rhythmically. They skirted the edges of the lake for over an hour until Tashi led them up a rise and back onto the plain. Reluctant to risk the horses, he held to a slow pace.

As they rode through the night, Kelly's thoughts drifted as if in a dream, circling first around Fiona O'Donnell. It was certain that Jeri would never stop blaming herself for her cousin's death. Kelly touched the crystal where it lay safely in her vest pocket. She thought she understood. Death was always complicated; a survivor always wondered whether enough had been said or done, wondered at just what point there had been a moment when the past might have been changed. Besides, to say Jeri wasn't to blame was to ignore the true web of connections binding one person to another. It wasn't about blame, but about acknowledging who people are. George would quote Laing: "What we know is so much less than what there is."

Kelly thought about Arkadia O'Malley. She rolled the improbable name around in her head, liking the feel of it. The syllables conjured an image that might have come from some book of illustrated legends she'd read as a child, a page with a pen-and-ink rendering of an old woman with a tangled mane of white hair standing at the edge of a wood, chanting a benediction or a warning, her arms raised above her head, one hand directing a knotty staff skyward.

†

Far to the west, on an island as steeped in ancient lore as the Tibetan plateau, a prisoner sat dozing, the spring sunlight warming her face. The chatter of the women around her had a quality similar to the chittering of the sparrows scratching the ground nearby: two separate worlds inhabiting the same space, essentially oblivious to one another. The chittering gained a certain raucous quality, perhaps due to a tussle over a particular seed or piece of nesting material. Arkadia heard several women's voices raised in argument. Without opening her eyes, she smiled, in some obscure way made content by her awareness of both worlds. Her smile intended no mockery of either; to the contrary, the intersecting of worlds made her more aware of the importance of every life in the grander drama. It was good to feel content. For far too long the colors of her mind had been hued in shades of desperation, but recently she had found a place of peace. She was reminded that she always felt so when the Keepers had joined each other. She hoped that this time she might meet them together. She was curious about why they were riding in darkness through such a far country. It seemed much too soon for them to be there. A bell rang, signaling time to go back inside, and what O'Malley had just known in fullness narrowed, faded, did not quite disappear. Her sense of contentment remained.

†

"Kell, wake up. Tashi says this is a good place to rest. That's not a half-bad trick you've managed—learning to sleep while you're riding."

Tashi led them to a rocky rise where they would have a view of the surrounding land as well as shelter. The dry land would still provide some grazing for the horses.

"And to think I used to want to be a cowboy." Kelly was stiff and every muscle felt ill-used, particularly her thighs. She limped gingerly to the place Jeri had chosen and laid out her sleeping bag.

"Didn't we all?" Jeri held out her arms for Kelly to lie down. "Do you want me to sing a verse of *Home on the Range*?"

"Not if you value your life. How did you learn to ride in Boston?"

"I didn't. I had to do it a couple years ago, and I just took to it."

"Like everything. What can't you do?" There was a silence, and Kelly realized she had been taken literally. "Jeri, I didn't mean—"

"I know. It's okay. I should tell you, Kell, I see ghosts. It used to just be Fiona. Now there are others."

"Like now? Do you see them now?"

"No. I mean when we start making love. I've read that there's a belief in Tibet that the souls of the dead, especially the recent dead, are attracted by the energy of sex, and they come hoping to be reborn. I don't think that explains my ghosts, though."

"Are they angry?"

"Sometimes. Some are. Fiona just always seems sad. But it's me. I get angry."

"And here I thought it was just the two of us in the dark. I didn't expect an audience was seeing how much I love you."

"Kell, there's one more story I need to tell you."

"Another ghost?"

"Sort of. Millicent haunts me, but not as a ghost."

†

Kelly woke to a sound so familiar that it took longer than it should have to remember the sound of an engine here in Tibet meant danger. She sat up to see Jeri already running toward the horses, wearing her long coat with the scarf wrapped around her head. Kelly gathered the sleeping bags and remembered to put on a cap as well as her chuba before joining Bolingbrook by the gear. The sound of the plane, which had been receding, began growing louder again.

"A spotter plane, I think," Bolingbrook said. "It didn't have the look of a fighter jet, but it might be more dangerous for that. And I believe they've seen us."

Tashi and Jeri arrived with the horses, and in minutes all four were ready for mounting. Kelly was surprised to see that Jeri had slung a rifle onto her shoulder, the same aged rifle that she had been wearing the day they met and carried occasionally as they traveled. It looked much more like some relative of the flintlock than a modern weapon.

"It's part of the disguise. And more modern than it looks," Jeri explained to both Kelly and Louise. "I don't actually want to shoot at the plane, but I want them to think twice about buzzing us and to go away. Hurry up now and follow Tashi."

Jeri rode away from the shelter and deliberately turned to face the approaching plane.

"What is she doing?" Fear gripped Kelly's gut. She was mounted, but unable to turn away in the direction that Tashi was urging. "Will they try to shoot her?"

"I don't think so, my dear." Bolingbrook rode up beside her and placed a hand on Kelly's arm. "It happens wherever there are military airbases and the military is some kind of occupier. Pilots just seem unable to resist harassing local people."

Kelly was far from reassured, but she forced herself to turn Lungta and start moving after Tashi's horse. She turned back to see that Jeri had the rifle in her hand and was brandishing it at the swiftly approaching plane. She hoped that the pilot was not a country person to be reminded, as she was, of adult birds fluttering haplessly in order to draw a predator away from fledglings.

The plane angled into a steep dive, heading directly at the stationary rider. Jeri turned and galloped away, making sure her direction took her away from her group. The plane swooped less than a hundred feet overhead, rose, turned, and prepared for another dive. Jeri's horse had no way to know that the exercise was not in earnest, and she could feel the animal's terror. With some difficulty, she managed to hold him steady as the plane again angled toward them. Again she brandished her ancient-looking weapon. Jeri could imagine the pilot's face, grinning with amusement at being challenged by a fool on horseback. She had set herself the task of alerting the pilot to potential danger without rousing anger or a wish for vengeance, so when she fired at the passing plane, she only intended for it to suggest she might be as risky as a bird strike, which any pilot knew could be very risky indeed.

After she fired and missed, Jeri set off at a gallop. Weaving among the dunes, she could hear the plane behind her, and after one particularly close pass overhead, she wheeled her mount to face it. Again the plane dove toward her, but this time the pilot pulled up far higher than before. Again Jeri turned and urged her horse to a gallop. The scene was repeated one more time, and then the pilot tired of the exercise, or maybe remembered it was past time for his evening meal. At any rate, he flew off. Jeri hoped he had lost track of her companions and had scant interest as to where they might be going.

The plane dwindled to a speck and disappeared. Jeri slowly rode to the top of a hillock, resting her pony and attending to its need to release the anxiety built up during the encounter with the plane. From her vantage point, despite the lateness of the hour, she could see miles in any direction. There was no sign of her companions; she would need to ride on her own through the night. No matter, she knew where they were headed and she had the map of the area in her head. For the moment it was enough to rest along with her horse, to savor the small victory before heading toward more battles.

Kelly came into her mind. Or rather she let Kelly come to the forefront, because Kelly was never truly out of Jeri's mind. With a sense of wonder, Jeri recognized how much had changed in the last few days. She had thought herself brave and responsible by keeping Kelly at arm's length, by thinking she could create a distance that would preserve

Kelly's option to leave if she wanted. Of course it had been herself she was protecting; she hadn't really been any stronger than a child afraid of the dark and what it might hold. Then Kelly had gone with her into the dark, and although it was truly a place where monsters lurked, it was also a place where she had encountered more love than she'd ever thought possible. The wonder was that she had ever been able to live at all without Kelly.

Never again would there not be Kelly. Jeri smiled. Not the most grammatical construction, but nevertheless a sound lover's construction.

Chapter Twelve

Tashi, Kelly, and Bolingbrook rode through the dark until dawn slowly began to give shape and focus to the landscape. Along with the terrain, the riders' destination became visible: Tashi was taking them toward a tall, imposing elevation of rock that jutted from the surrounding plain. Perhaps it had long ago been an island rising above a surrounding sea, or perhaps it was the once-molten core of a volcano that had long since cooled and the outer shell of stone had eroded. Whatever its geologic history, it spoke of great forces, testified to its own vast age and that of all the surrounding land. Kelly had thought the dramatic mountain views of Himalayan Nepal would overshadow any other vistas, but she was discovering that Tibet was even more awesomely impressive. She felt as if she had arrived at the high heart of the world. There was a Tibetan mountain, she recalled, the source of four great Asian rivers, and pilgrims came to walk a sacred journey around the mountain's base.

Jeri would know the name of the mountain, but Jeri still had not rejoined the group. Tashi had assured Kelly during a rest stop that there was little danger that the plane would actually have harmed her. The herdsmen he had met with had told him that planes and helicopters rarely indulged in direct damage, although terrified sheep and horses suffered as surely as their shepherds. Kelly had been grateful for the assurance, but she couldn't help imagining scenarios in which Jeri was hurt, unable to ride, thoughts she had so far managed to dismiss as absurd.

"Kelly la."

Tashi was pointing off to the right, and Kelly saw a distant rider. She stared until she recognized Jeri, and immediately the world felt back in its proper order.

Jeri reached the elevation first and waited for the others. She greeted Tashi and Louise with a nod, but the smile she gave Kelly was wide and as warm as a kiss. Then she turned her horse and led the way up a narrow, switchback path. Near the top, she stopped and dismounted.

Kelly was absorbed by the distant vistas that height made visible, and she was surprised when Tashi dismounted and immediately prostrated himself full length on the ground. Kelly looked about, at first seeing only rock, and then slowly she saw that the rocks were broken remnants of a structure that once must have covered the entire summit. The more she looked, the more she discerned that the rubble had not been shaped and strewn about by nature.

"The cultural revolution?" Bolingbrook asked.

Jeri nodded and turned to Kelly. "This used to be a gompa, a monastery. Do you know about Chairman Mao's Cultural Revolution?"

"Dimly. Not much. Tell me."

"In the late sixties, Mao's Chinese Red Guards were unleashed on anything that wasn't part of the revolution. They were mostly young and had all the faults you would expect of ideological children, especially since older people who wanted to stay in power were manipulating them. The Red Guards focused a huge amount of their energy on destroying anything religious."

"And anything historical," Bolingbrook added. "'Smash the Old World. Make a New World.' That was one of the slogans. I suppose I would have gone the way of this place."

"No doubt. You can see how Tibet would have particularly infuriated them, since religion and history are so central to Tibetan people's lives. This place was destroyed by dynamite."

Tashi had approached while they were speaking. "My father remembered coming to this place when he was young. The monastery was very large and very beautiful. It was made in memory of a demon subdued by Padmasambhava. He was the saint who brought Buddhism to Tibet, but first Padmasambhava had to fight a great many demons."

"Like St. Patrick and the snakes," Kelly said.

"They say St. Patrick drove the snakes out of Ireland when he brought Christianity," Jeri explained to Tashi.

Tashi shook his head. "Padmasambhava did not drive out the demons. He fought with them until they agreed to become protector spirits. The guardian of this place still lives here, and we must remember to be respectful. Even the Chinese cannot kill the spirit of the land." Despite his defiant words, Tashi was downcast.

Kelly looked around with more attention and gradually the shapes of what had been grew clearer. She could see the outlines of foundations, pieces of rock walls or stone fences. The others seemed to be doing the same until Tashi broke the silence.

"We should go soon if we are to reach Rinpoche's gompa by nightfall."

"Right. We should be back by tomorrow morning," Jeri said to Louise and Kelly.

Louise nodded. The plans had been discussed a number of times during the trek. Tashi and Jeri would go the last leg of the journey and bring back Detsen and the companion who reportedly had taken pictures. The ruined monastery would provide a much safer haven for a meeting than the town near the gompa, where there was a small but active military post.

"Where will you find Mr. Phurba?"

"Rinpoche," Tashi corrected Kelly, using the term of honor for a respected monk. "He will be at his gompa."

"But I thought the monasteries were all destroyed."

"Not all." Jeri looked about at the ruins. "Beijing concluded there was more profit in controlling the population than in trying to destroy it, so religion has been licensed. The monasteries are licensed now and are becoming tourist destinations."

"Come walk with me," Kelly said, and took Jeri's hand.

They walked among the ruins that had once been part of a large, beautiful structure, not speaking, simply being in each other's company. In the lee of a wall, sheltered from the wind and from the view of their companions, they stopped and kissed.

"If something happens," Jeri said, "stick with Bolingbrook. Her reputation should get you both out."

Kelly stared at Jeri, as if by looking she might absorb her. "I love you so," Kelly whispered. "Don't let anything happen. Please be very, very careful, and come back."

"Yes," Jeri said. "I think I'm getting the hang of that. I feel like my whole life has been coming back to you."

Kelly watched Jeri and Tashi ride away, her hand clenched around the crystal in her pocket. Four horses and two people. They reached the plain below the heights and rode toward the north, growing smaller and smaller until they topped a rise and disappeared. Still Kelly stared at the spot. No thoughts turned into language in her mind, instead there was something rather like a drumbeat repeating: *come back to me, come back to me*. After a very long while, Kelly sighed and returned her attention to her surroundings, to the reality of place.

Built on the largest rise in the landscape, the monastery must once have capped the heights like a castle. Clearly the builders had intentionally taken advantage of the natural grandeur. Even now, despite its destruction, the heaped rubble and damaged walls revealed the former grace and solemnity of the structure. Eternity wasn't a concept in Tibet, it was a constant presence. Kelly felt her spirit being urged to understand her connections within all the vastness of sky and earth. Maybe this was why someone left a home that had become too familiar. Maybe every tourist was a pilgrim, seeking a renewed sense of the sacred.

Kelly found Bolingbrook sitting by a heap of rubble, out of the wind and in the warmth of the sun, and engaged in her perpetual occupation—scanning the Phurba report. By now the woman ought to have memorized every word, yet she still read with a poised pen, stopping now and then to write in the margins. The volume of her notes surely had to exceed the length of the original document.

Kelly went wandering through the ruins, letting her mind rest so that the spirit of the place might speak to her. Now and then her thoughts would skitter toward worry for Jeri, but she was determined not to let anxiety dominate. She climbed a tumble of large stones and found herself atop a broken wall that was one side of what had been a large room. To either side, the former walls were nearly completely deconstructed, stones toppled and scattered, but the opposite wall was structurally intact although it appeared to have been pitted by gunfire. Faded by snow and sun, wind and storm, the remaining colors of a large mural still suggested shapes. Kelly took a seat on the stones to better contemplate the picture.

She thought she could make out a large figure with its arms extended. How many arms wasn't clear. It was like looking into her crystal—just the slightest shift of viewpoint could reveal something totally unexpected. Once the depiction had been meant to teach, to awe, to transform, and it made Kelly sorry for the loss of things humans could ill afford to lose. Tibetan beliefs emphasized how people might best journey through numerous lives. The Chinese, however, claimed that their actions were freeing living people from bondage to an oppressively religious feudal state.

Kelly wondered what her feelings would be if the broken wall belonged to a cathedral and the scene before her showed the crucifixion. The religion she had been born into held little attraction for her. Indeed, she felt that she and George had been lucky to escape the intimidation that had been aimed at them in order to quell their right to love as they must. Intimidation was another facet of awe. Kelly thought she might not have minded as much if she had been looking at a ruined cathedral wall. As she stared, she felt caught between contesting arguments: one desperate to express the depth and needs of a spiritual dimension, the other raging in fierce anger at systems that bound and burned and maimed and enslaved their terrified people. Which was she looking at?

When Kelly let her gaze drift off center, she could see a row—no, two rows—of skulls near the bottom of the wall. Death, death in life: both states of illusion, the soul moving from one to the other like the same note sounding through different instruments. Like most people she knew, Kelly had thought at least vaguely about reincarnation. Sometimes it seemed like a comforting notion, a chance to fix mistakes, to find real justice and virtue, a way to get around the absolute end that death appeared to be. If pressed, Kelly might have described her idea of one's time between death and rebirth as kind of a Greek agora, where people wandered around in pleated robes and greeted old friends and planned their next life, like deciding where to go on vacation. But Kaju had told her about the "bardo," a state where most souls wandered in terror and illusion as they sought desperately for a way back into a body. The bardo was not comforting to contemplate.

From the beginning, her connection to Jeri had seemed like renewing an acquaintance, like in the old tale of separated souls seeking their lost halves. That legend encouraged the belief that you could find your wholeness by pursuing your desire, that the yearning which haunted the silent spaces of a life had reason and purpose. In that long instant when Jeri had drawn her back from falling off the retaining wall on the day they met, Kelly had felt blown open by a wind from out of eternity. Being with Jeri felt like recognizing the intention of her spirit. Making love did more than she had ever expected. Sometimes she felt propelled along and through connecting webs of meaning. She knew things in the deep dark of arousal that she knew nowhere else.

Words were inadequate things, but some seemed to be like lodestones pulling truth toward them—darkness, meaning, desire.

"I believe this is a picture of Padmasambhava and his consort."

Startled, Kelly wondered how long Bolingbrook had been standing there, wondered if her thoughts might have been visible in her expressions. "Consort?" She squinted at the mural, but could only see the hint of a large, dark blue figure.

"She's sitting on his lap. They're making love."

And Kelly had been thinking... She felt her face grow hot with embarrassment.

"Some people think sex is a way back to our eternal nature, that it's a spiritual practice available to everyone." Bolingbrook's tone, at first amused, grew serious. "Don't you worry that you might be out of your depth?"

"You'll have to explain that."

"Geraldine O'Donnell is a very dangerous person, and she lives among dangerous people. I have come to respect her, and I don't doubt you love each other, but is it wise for you to stay together?"

"We've done all right so far." Kelly was sure she sounded like a churlish adolescent, but she was struggling with her surprise at the personal nature of the discussion. "Would you say the same thing if one of us were a man?"

"Yes, I would." Louise sighed. "Let me tell you a story about two women I knew when I was very young."

When the tale of the internment camp ended, both women sat in silence until Kelly spoke. "But that story says I should stay with Jeri. Things happen, Louise, whether you prepare for them or not. I belong with Jeri. I'll figure out what that means as we go along. How much preparation did anyone have before the Japanese came?"

Bolingbrook nodded reluctantly. "And your family? By now they must know you're missing."

"Rather tidy for them. Now they can forget there were ever any queer family members." Kelly had intended to sound amused, but she could hear the bitterness in her own voice. "I suppose they'll be unhappy, but they were horrible about George. They never acknowledged Russell's death, and George and Russell lived together for years. They never came to see George, even after they knew how sick he was. I remember George on the phone once, saying ever so patiently, 'No, Mother, I don't think I will get better soon.' It broke my heart, how they pretended nothing was wrong, even to the very end." Kelly stared into the distance, remembering a cold day in southern Ohio when the open grave was just another shade of gray.

"I'm so sorry, my dear. You were very brave to have gone through that with your brother. But was it only you your parents failed?"

Kelly found herself remembering something she had resolutely put out of her mind. At the cemetery, as the family stood around the open grave while the priest murmured the ritual Latin of grieving, Kelly happened to look at her younger sister. Megan's face had been twisted in a hopeless, tearless grief, and Kelly had been about to go to her when she suddenly heard Billy sob beside her. Her own tears had come then, and without thinking, it was Billy to whom she turned. She and Billy had left that afternoon for the long drive back to Cleveland, and Kelly never had spoken to Megan. She should have. She was older, and she should have paid more attention to her siblings.

It had been so easy to be angry with her parents that she had disregarded her sister and two brothers, lumping them all together as "the family." She and George habitually forgot the younger kids. Perhaps not forgetting, so much as overlooking, and she actually didn't much like Edward, the oldest of the little ones. He was still in grade school when Kelly went off to college, and already he was cold and emotionally careless, but he liked farming and worked hard, so her father favored him. Megan and Robert, younger and close in age to one another, were likable enough, but Kelly was well aware that she didn't know them.

The memories prompted by Bolingbrook's reminder nearly undid Kelly. For an instant she was back standing by that grave, knowing that her young sister, Megan, needed some word to ease her pain, some sign to relieve her confusion. Kelly had left without making a gesture, left the gravesite, left the farm, too caught up in her own grief to offer comfort to anyone but Billy. He had been her rock through those last days, even though they both knew that his own days were limited. Kelly understood her reasons might excuse her behavior, but they would never be enough to comfort young Megan. Her mother and father weren't the only ones who had betrayed love.

Kelly felt tears welling up, tears that would have spilled over had she not been suddenly drawn to the present in Tibet by the growl of an approaching engine.

Cautiously, both women hurried to the edge of the summit. An unmistakably military truck, with its camouflage cab and canvas covered back, had shifted to a grinding lower gear and was ascending the switchback trail.

"Hurry, Kelly, go get our packs together. I'll catch up."

Kelly ran ahead of Bolingbrook, thanking whatever spirits still remained around the monastery, that neither she nor Louise had unpacked anything or started a fire of any sort. It took only scant moments to sort everything into two bundles and then check whether anything had been overlooked. Kelly was ready to flee, but Louise had still not arrived. She dashed back around the corner of a broken building, and with a sinking heart, Kelly saw Louise approaching. Slowly. With a pronounced limp.

"No, no." Bolingbrook waved her back. "I don't think anything is broken, but it is a bad sprain. Go that way. I came by here earlier." She gestured toward the far side of the ruins where there was another, narrower path.

When Louise picked up one of the bundles, Kelly started to protest but gave it up when she remembered how stubborn the woman could be. Instead, she hurried ahead until she reached the edge where the path began to descend. She looked about. This side of the summit was strewn with boulders. Several feet down and to the side, Kelly found what she had been hoping for. The sound of the truck was much fainter on this side as Kelly reached a group of rocks and carefully moved two of them aside. When there was space enough, she put her bundle into it and went back to where Bolingbrook was struggling downhill.

Louise understood what Kelly meant to do and handed over her burden. She made her slower way down while Kelly went ahead and hid Bolingbrook's bundle with her own.

"There's no room for us, we'll have to find another place to hide." She could still hear the truck engine. "Why do you think they're here?" Kelly was whispering, though there was no need.

"Scavengers, no doubt," Louise replied. "Looters. There's a lucrative market for Tibetan artifacts." With no protest at all, the Englishwoman took the arm that Kelly offered. Her limp had become a hobble, and each step was accompanied by a sharp intake of breath.

"Let's hope that's what they want, then they won't be looking for us."

Behind and above them, the engine grew louder and then stopped. The women paused, waiting to hear what might be happening. Kelly looked around and saw a formation that suggested it might provide shelter.

"Stay here a moment," she whispered and pointed. "I'll see if that will hide us."

Louise nodded. Above them came sounds of laughter that didn't need translating. A group of young men were on an unsupervised outing.

The promising cluster of rocks that had attracted Kelly was even better than she had hoped. They formed a sort of den, and there appeared to be enough room for both women. She waved for Bolingbrook to come. Kelly glanced around. They were in luck. If the soldiers were bent on scavenging, this side of the summit looked as if it had nothing in the way of artifacts.

Louise fell again, uttering a cry of pain and dislodging several small rocks. The sudden silence above was evidence that she had been heard. Kelly gestured toward the cluster. The lair should be protection from anything but a direct search, but in that case, it would also effectively become a trap. Up above, the soldiers had started speaking, and Kelly felt their phrases didn't need much translating: *What was that? Where did it come from? Over there. I don't see anything.*

Kelly waited until she was sure Louise was safely inside the lair, and then she pulled her cap from an inside pocket and covered her hair. That and her fleece-lined chuba should make her appear Tibetan from a distance. She looked down the slope and planned as many details of her next moves as she could. From above, the voices told her how close the soldiers were.

She went laterally first, in an attempt to take them as far from Louise as possible. A shout informed her that she had been spotted. With a deep breath and a thought of Jeri for courage and comfort, Kelly began moving quickly. She jumped, slid, leaped, and slid again. The soldiers were shouting now, excited, hounds that had caught sight of their quarry. Suddenly her footing was undermined by loose rock, and she began to fall. All the fear she had managed to ignore surged through her in a sickening rush of adrenaline as she fought to keep her footing, her arms flailing like windmills. She found herself sliding on her butt; that was the best of all body parts to land on in her situation. Before she came to a full stop, she was able to regain her balance and then continue once more in the direction she had planned.

Incredibly, she had made it to the bottom of the escarpment. The voices seemed to still be at the height of the summit, but Kelly fought an urge to turn around and look. Instead, she began a zigzag run across the plain toward a dip she had seen from above that was not quite a gully. The last weeks had acclimatized her to the altitude, and adrenaline was doing the rest.

Something whined past her ear, and there was a puff of dust ahead of her. She heard laughter from the summit. Damn them! They thought shooting at her was funny. She took a dive into the dip in a move she had only used once before, in a softball game, when she was quite a bit younger. Out of their sight now, she moved a distance away from where she had disappeared and crawled to the edge of the gully where she could peer back without being spotted.

The summit rose steeply, and at the top, the soldiers appeared as distant figures in dark olive. They milled about the edge for a while and began to lose interest. One by one, they disappeared, although now and

301

then one would come and look out over the plain, presumably for her. None came close to where Louse was hiding. Slowly Kelly's adrenaline high seeped away, leaving her shaken with the knowledge of how close she had been to disaster. When that feeling also diminished, she was just bored. And hungry. There was nothing to do but wait for the soldiers to leave.

The soldiers weren't leaving. As the night came on, Kelly saw the glow of a fire on the summit, and what sounded like singing. Great. The Chinese occupation army in Tibet had decided to have camp night out. It was cold on the open plain with its ceaseless wind, and although her sheepskin chuba was warm, Kelly usually wore her down vest beneath it. That piece of clothing was now most likely providing Louise with an additional pillow in her cozy lair. Kelly considered returning to Louise now that it was dark but decided against the notion. If some watchful soldier heard one accidentally dislodged rock, both women would be in danger again. She was just cold, that was all, and she could look forward to a time when she would be warm again. Russell, George, and Billy had endured worse, with no prospect of time making anything better. And besides, she was waiting for Jeri. The sun would rise, and Jeri would come back to her.

Chapter Thirteen

Keeping the extra horses on a loose lead, Jeri and Tashi followed the switchback down from the temple ruins, and Tashi turned off the road. Jeri matched her horse's gait to her companion's steady, loping pace over the dry, weatherworn hills. Up one brown hill and over, and then up another, they rode as if coursing the swells on a vast calm sea. For several hours the riders saw only the occasional foraging antelopes that bounded away at their approach. Jeri was captured by a sense of timelessness, by a feeling she accepted without analysis. Then suddenly, with a jolt of recognition, she realized she had been feeling whole, content. Happy. She wanted no more than what she had: a task before her, and a love awaiting her return. The only other time she remembered feeling something similar, and recognizing it, had been when she started studying at Oxford.

And that had turned out so well.

Sometime around noon, the plain tilted into a definite upward slope. Tashi called a halt for rest and let the horses graze while the riders ate a cold chapati. Soon after they remounted, a distant snow-capped massif came into view. Now they were no longer simply traveling over rounded hills but following a particular ridge, a long outlier that buttressed the far mountain. They crossed what looked like recent tire tracks and began to see other signs of human presence in the form of paths and prayer cairns left by pilgrims and herdsmen. The ridge took them ever higher off the plain, growing sharper, rockier. They were riding more slowly now, the horses more cautious with their footing and following a definite trail.

Tashi raised his arm in a signal to halt. Jeri reined her horse to a stop beside him.

The distance was bounded by the peaks of a far range, but nearer, and above them, a mountain towered like a jagged pyramid held in place by buttressing ridges, its summit bright white with pink and purple shadows cast by slanting sunlight. Below, in the shaded valley, hints of green told of new growth struggling amid the tans and browns of a fading winter.

"There." Tashi pointed across the valley to the farther slope. "There is Detsen Phurba's gompa, just above that village."

Jeri looked. A cluster of small buildings built of dressed stone blended with the terrain. Two new structures at the farther end appeared gracelessly out of place, larger, hasty wooden buildings that screamed military barracks anywhere in the world. Tall wire fencing created a compound for one, while the smaller building appeared to be for housing vehicles. Jeri studied the site and then turned her gaze upward to the gompa.

The monastery overlooked the village like a shepherd sitting above a flock of sheep. Made of local stone, the large building appeared to have issued forth rather than been set upon a broad swath of tableland. Even from a distance, the grounds appeared well tended, sheltered by dark green junipers that softened all the corners.

"I wonder if Detsen will be ready for us," Jeri said.

"Detsen Rinpoche is always ready." Tashi smiled. "We can take this trail to just before it separates to go to the gompa or the village. It's longer than going through the valley, but we should reach those trees before dark."

"That ought to work fine, Tash. We can't go up there before evening anyway."

The trail took them along a path below the ridge, where the wind was less strong. Their luck in being unobserved seemed to hold as they rode. They saw only a small group of wild yak grazing on a far meadow, but Jeri had the feeling that they themselves were watched as they progressed toward the far slopes. She didn't discount the feeling, but she hoped that any watchers would be local folk and not someone who might take an official interest in two travelers. Evening was almost upon them when they arrived at the juniper grove Tashi had pointed out to her.

"I'll go," Jeri said.

"I should go," Tashi said. "Detsen knows me, and I will look like any other villager."

"Yes, but if anything happens to me, you can get Louise and Kelly out of the country better than I could. Don't worry, Tash. From a distance I'll look like just another pilgrim arriving at the gompa."

Tashi looked ready to argue, but then he and nodded.

Jeri breathed deeply. The fragrance of the junipers offered more than just a familiar smell: after the open plains, the shelter of trees was a welcome refuge. She handed Tashi her rifle, adjusted her long coat, and wound the dark scarf around her head. When Tashi nodded his approval, she left the grove. The stony path she moved along was well worn; the monastery had its beginnings in an earlier century, and countless pilgrim feet had made their way to its gates. As she walked, Jeri studied the village layout below and to her right. Most of the buildings appeared to be family dwellings, built wherever the terrain permitted, and most appeared solid but not particularly prosperous. At the far end of the collection of houses was the newer, long, single-story building, constructed of wood and out of place next to the stone houses. This closer view of the pre-fabricated government structure reinforced Jeri's original assessment that it was a barracks.

As she drew closer, she could see that the gompa was not a single structure, but several buildings of various sizes. A low stone wall, fallen in some places, surrounded the site. There were other signs of past glory, such as a faded mural with a row of statues before it. Someone had begun to restore the painting, and the short section of bright colors stood out like a promise.

Jeri didn't expect that finding Detsen Phurba would be as easy as walking up to his monastery and knocking on the door, but in the end it proved almost that simple. Just past the gate, she encountered a young monk sweeping the flagstones. As soon as he saw her, he stopped his work and hurried forward. He bowed courteously, but his eyes betrayed a wariness that might be explained by a wide scar that marked one cheek from eye to chin. The scar still had a puckered newness. As she drew close, Jeri could see that the sleeves of his robes were frayed and carefully patched.

Jeri's Tibetan was basic, and she had no faith in her accent, so she kept her question short. "Detsen Rinpoche?"

The young monk thought a moment, or perhaps didn't immediately understand her, but then he gestured for her to follow him. He took her up a short series of steps, pushed open a heavy wooden door, and stopped in the room immediately inside. When he gestured for her to wait, Jeri thought her accent must indeed be atrocious if the young monk wasn't even going to speak to her. Or maybe he was bound by a rule of silence.

Alone in the spacious room, Jeri looked about. Several yak butter lamps sputtered and flickered along the walls, the fluttering light and rich scent mingling with that of incense. The heavy combination reminded her of Sunday Mass when she was young. The smell was different, but the atmosphere of piety was quite similar. At the far end of the room hung a large cloth with a picture of the Buddha. His hands were arranged in a gesture that Jeri knew had meaning, although she was ignorant of what it was. There had been no books on Buddhism at Armagh.

Jeri recalled the day when Rafi had first explained his need for someone to go to Tibet. As he described the nature and purpose of the assignment, she had grown excited by the prospect. It was the kind of work she wanted—dangerous, but in service to something she could believe was good, work that called for a warrior and not a mercenary. And maybe there had been something more to her anticipation, maybe a hint, some prescient understanding that more than work awaited her along this particular road.

She shook her head. Lovers always thought Destiny brought them together, that Fate meant for them to meet. She didn't so much disbelieve the notion as she was suspicious of the impulse to believe in it, and besides, it still left unanswered what Kelly meant to her future. Jeri would take the monk to the UN representative as planned, and then she would leave Tibet, but what then? Go back to Rafi and, in effect, report for further duty, ask for further work, only less dangerous? She owed Kelly a real life together, if that were possible.

Why was she thinking of this now?

Maybe it would be possible. All the signs pointed to the probability that history was headed toward gentler times. Surely somewhere she could find a place for herself and Kelly to live. Odd how, in this room, prospects of the future felt comfortable, as if time were a garment already sewn and fitted.

"I hope I have not kept you waiting." A robed figure emerged from a door to the right of the statue. He stayed back in the shadows, and although he had spoken in Tibetan, Jeri understood him well enough.

"I fear it is I who may have kept you waiting," she answered in the same language.

It was a simple enough exchange, but it served as an introduction. Jeri had rehearsed her part in the greeting several times with Tashi. The monk emerged from the shadows, smiling broadly. He was almost as tall as Jeri, and although he looked roughly similar in age to Bolingbrook, his hair was black with no hint of gray. He continued their conversation in English with a decided British accent. "Have you come to tell me I missed a footnote?"

"Footnote?" Jeri laughed. "Your old friend has made such a study of your report that I doubt a misplaced comma has gone unnoticed."

"Dear Louise. Is she well?"

"Well, and doing well. I don't know how much you know of her, but her reputation for working with people in need is totally deserved."

"I am not surprised. When I knew her, she was already a person of great compassion. I am so looking forward to this meeting. We were what you might call 'an interrupted story,' and perhaps this meeting may soothe an old wound."

The monk paused, but Jeri could think of no answer. "I am not familiar with your story," she said.

"No matter. It is not unusual. We were in love when we were young."

"Did something happen?"

"Very much has happened, to both of us. But not, I hope, to what we felt for one another."

Jeri felt as if she knew Detsen Phurba. He presented himself with humor and unhurried grace. For a few moments she wondered if this was some echo from previous lives, but then she understood what she was recognizing—the signs of someone who had spent time in prison. It was nothing specific about him, perhaps it was only what someone else who had been there might notice, but it included the way he was aware of the room, the way he spoke to her so that no one else might hear, even if they were only a foot or two away. There was more that she couldn't put into words, but Jeri thought he probably recognized similar traits in her.

The monk seemed to read her mind. "I believe you may be familiar with imprisonment?" He smiled as she nodded slightly. When she did not volunteer any particulars, he did not press. "If you can wait a few moments more, I will find my companion and we can go."

"There is no problem if you just leave?"

"None at all. We have been planning this pilgrimage for some time. We have other places to go after we leave you. Is Tashi's nephew, Kaju, with you?"

Jeri shook her head. "No. For safety, he is waiting for us back at the border."

Detsen nodded. "Best that he's safe. I know he wishes to be a monk, and I have a gift for him, but I can give it to Tashi. If you will be so kind as to wait, I shall get my companion and be right back."

Detsen left but returned in only a few moments along with another monk. Each man carried a small bundle slung over his back.

"This is Nuru," Detsen said, introducing the somewhat younger monk, who smiled and inclined his head in a small bow.

Outside, twilight had deepened to almost full dark as the three left the gompa. Fortunately, stars were spread so thickly across the sky that there was light enough to make the path easy to follow. The small party hurried along the ridge to where Jeri had left Tashi with the horses. As they approached the juniper thicket, Jeri began to feel uneasy, a feeling that grew stronger with each step. Although it was full dark now, shapes were easily visible in the ambient light. She wanted to attribute her disquiet to the ease with which she had contacted the Tibetan monks, but she dared not take the chance.

"Wait," she said, barely above a whisper.

Detsen and Nuru halted.

"Tashi should be waiting where we can see him," Jeri explained. "Let me go ahead."

"No," Detsen replied with authority. "We can have a reason for being here. You wait."

Detsen and Nuru walked purposefully toward the grove, but before they reached the first trees, a small figure came running toward the monks. Jeri reached them at the same time as the child, but she understood only a few words like "horse" and "stranger."

Detsen finally nodded and turned to Jeri. "She was seeking yak droppings for fuel when she met the stranger. He spoke to her politely, and then they saw a patrol of Chinese soldiers approaching. When it was clear that the soldiers would soon find them, Tashi asked the child to stay with the horses. He told her that when the monks would come, she was to tell them what had happened. Then he walked out of the trees and started down the hill as if he hadn't seen the patrol. He pretended to suddenly see them and try to hurry away. She says he was like a bird who takes you away from her nest. They followed and caught up with him. The child says she thinks the soldiers took him because he didn't have papers. He told her if the soldiers caught him, she was to tell the monks to finish their journey and he would find his own way home."

"How long ago?" Detsen asked the child.

"Not long. Thirty minutes at most."

"Where will they take him?" Jeri asked.

Detsen didn't answer immediately. "I think I know where he is. This village has only two holding cells. Anyone not released soon after being detained is kept until they can be transported to army headquarters. They do this by truck once a week. Tashi will be held here for two more days."

†

Night has its shadows, particularly beneath a starry Tibetan sky, and Jeri kept to the deeper darkness as she worked her way past the village homes toward the headquarters that Detsen had described. He had been taken there several times, a form of harassment that many of the monks were forced to endure. Detsen had made no objection when she said she was going to get Tashi. Not that it would have mattered if he had. No way was she leaving Tash behind. He was one of the world's good men, and the world needed all its good men. She was in Tibet for a number of reasons, some better than others, but Tashi was here because this was where he lived, and because he believed that he could help his land, his people. He was loyal and steady, and Jeri had known she could rely on him from the first day they met. Even when trapped by the avalanche, she had believed that if Tashi had survived, he would save them.

No, she would not just ride away and leave him. For a moment, she thought of Kelly and understood just what this decision might cost, and then she put such thoughts aside. If worse came to worst, the monks would go to the ruins and find some way to get Louise and Kelly out of Tibet.

As she passed by the small homes of the village, Jeri began to hear shouts and laughter ahead. There was even light, enough light to let her move more quickly through the dark buildings around her. Drawing closer to the lighted area, she located the commotion as coming from inside the fenced enclosure she had seen earlier. Shadows created by the enclosure light provided cover for her to glide unseen to the wire fence.

Inside the wire, a group of four men in uniform stood in a circle, pushing a fifth man back and forth across the center, jabbing and hitting at him with wooden batons. The light was coming from a single source above the doorway, where one other man in uniform was leaning on a rifle, supposedly standing guard. He was laughing and shouting encouragement to his comrades. All the laughter sounded as if it came from alcohol as much as from the pleasure of beating an unarmed man.

Tashi, the man being pushed and pummeled, was using his arms to protect his head as much as possible. A soldier on the farther side jabbed his baton into Tashi's belly, and instinct made him bend in an attempt to protect that vulnerable area. As he turned away from more blows, Jeri could see blood seeping from a head wound. The man who had jabbed him stepped forward and roughly shoved him toward the soldiers on the other side of the circle.

Tashi's moans of pain ripped at Jeri like a serrated blade. Restraint was nearly impossible, but she forced herself to observe. Jeri wanted to plan six moves ahead before she would have to start improvising. At least four, but the first move would be the most important.

Adrenaline lit the scene like neon, and the prospect of imminent battle sparked a rush of pleasure. She pushed aside the unlocked door and entered the compound.

Even though Jeri heard one soldier alert the others, and she felt them all turn to look her way, she kept her eyes on her chosen target. Tashi raised his head. Time slowed, and Jeri saw the soldier she was focused on look first alarmed and angry, then confused as he registered her smile, and then alarmed again as he began to understand that the smile was actually a wolf's grin and it was meant for him. He was her prey, and he was terrified.

Jeri found it almost too easy to swing one foot and knock him off both of his. She was after his baton and she took it from him as he fell, her eyes already seeking her next objective even as, without needing to look, she disabled the man on the ground with a strike to his hip. They were punks, really, bullies in uniform who were brave if they thought they overmatched their victim. She knew their kind from the streets of Southie, from Armagh. Separate them somehow, isolate them as individuals, and they were nothing.

The soldier standing nearest to her was recovering his wits, and she struck a blow to his head that resounded with a devastating crack. She didn't intend to kill anyone, but neither did she have time to gauge the effect of every blow. To be honest, she didn't really care. Not now. Later she would, and that made her somewhat careful.

Now there were only three still standing. She dismissed the man by the guns because he seemed too drunk to be very dangerous, but one of the other two had backed toward the guard and was reaching for one of the stacked weapons. End of plan. The dance was over; it was time to improvise. She still had some element of surprise and momentum, so she rushed the soldier trying for the rifle. When he turned to face her, she spun aside and delivered a blow to his knees with her newly acquired baton that sent him to the ground. When she turned back, she saw that adrenaline, that promiscuous whore, had now come to the aid of the fourth soldier. He was crouching, holding his own baton like a very serviceable weapon. And from the corner of her eye, Jeri saw that the soldier guarding the rifles had managed to hoist one.

He was close. She might just let him shoot; he would probably hit nothing or, just as likely, his comrade. But the shot would bring more soldiers. She swung on him. Her baton strike broke his arm above the elbow, and the pain was enough to slice through his alcohol haze. Even if he had wanted to use his hand, it was now impossible.

That left one.

Even as she turned, she felt a sharp pain in her back. Although instinct and training moved her away quickly, she knew the soldier had landed a solid blow. She completed her spin. She should have paid more attention to deciding who was going to recover his wits the quickest and become dangerous. She could see his eyes, and they were dark and angry, wary and calculating. He bent and feinted to the left then moved sharply to the right. As Jeri moved to keep him squarely in front of her, she saw that Tashi was still staring blankly, most likely in shock. They had to get out soon. Someone was bound to hear the noise and come to investigate.

She couldn't let herself be distracted. One choice at a time. Escape came after fighting, not before or during. The soldier rushed her. A glancing blow got through her guard; if it had connected with her head, it would have killed her. As it was, the baton grazed her cheek and ear, and the pain was considerable. Not enough pain, however, to make her miss the opening that her opponent's move had left. In a now-or-never move of her own, Jeri followed him as he went past and struck a disabling jab to his collarbone.

He was hers now. She could move in and finish him off, and he knew it. He could see it. Pain inflamed her anger; she wanted him to suffer for her pain. Jeri moved toward her quarry.

"We have to go." Tashi spoke in Nepali and not very loudly.

For a scant moment, she ignored him, wanting only to take that half step forward and finish the soldier with the broken collarbone. Jeri saw Tashi stumbling away. She could take the time for one more blow. Instead, she turned and ran after Tashi.

They ran. Slowly at first, more like a fast shuffle than a run, but then motion seemed to work in Tashi's favor, and they were able to move more quickly. Jeri didn't have to tell him that any pursuit would most likely go directly to where the soldiers had first seen him, but they had to go there themselves because that's where the horses were, and that's where Detsen Phurba and his companion waited.

Jeri kept seeing the eyes of her last opponent. She had wanted to move in with the blow that would punish him for hurting her, for thinking he could go against her at all. Every instinct she possessed had told her to finish him. Truth to tell, she still wanted to turn back, and damn the consequences.

The feeling would pass. She usually managed to control the desire for battle that made these encounters more dangerous for her soul than her body. She knew that part of Tashi's shock came from seeing her pleasure as she had entered the compound yard, seeing her naked of everything but a wild will to prevail. And she knew she would pay later. She would not be swallowed by the abyss of remorse that had enveloped her after the bus bombing, but whatever came to haunt her would have eyes like a soldier in Tibet who thought he was seeing the face of his final nightmare.

†

Kelly drifted in and out, never quite asleep enough to become unaware of the cold. In some dreams she was running again, pursued, about to be caught. In other dreams, she was naked and Jeri was about to hold her, to gather her into arms that would drive away the cold and the night. Each time she woke, she found herself shivering beneath a dazzling array of stars until, inevitably, they began to dim and then vanish in a slowly paling sky. She couldn't force herself to sleep any longer, so she stood and started walking in long circles that were out of view of the heights until, just as the sun rose, she heard the sound of an engine.

Kelly cautiously worked her way toward where the road began its switchback route up from the plain. She found a vantage point where she could remain hidden among the rocks. As luck would have it, the rising sun shone on her directly, its increasing warmth like a welcoming embrace. Kelly had almost fallen asleep by the time she heard the truck approaching. Peering around the edge of her hiding place, she saw the vehicle with its soldiers in back. The night's revelry had taken its toll. For their sakes, Kelly hoped no wars were imminent, because this group looked like they could be beaten by a troop of Brownie Scouts. She waited until they had driven out of sight, and then she climbed the path up to the ruins.

Louise Bolingbrook must have crawled to their packs during the night because when Kelly found her, she was wrapped in her sleeping bag, still sleeping. As Kelly stared, the Englishwoman opened her eyes.

"Good morning, Louise. Would you like your tea here, or up on the terrace?"

†

Louise Bolingbrook hoped she had her apprehension under control as she watched the riders approach. She had anticipated the meeting with Detsen Phurba for weeks, perhaps even longer than that if she counted all of the occasions when she remembered him as her first real love, and wondered where he was and how he was. She had rehearsed so many things to say—angry words, querulous words, forgiving words. She had wondered how best to present herself, and now the time was here. She watched him ride up the switchback trail, coming ever closer until he was near enough to dismount and turn toward her.

She felt herself become shy and go all English reserved. She certainly recognized the boy in the man, but time's alchemy had transformed the golden bloom of youth into the more tempered and measured hues of age. She wanted to go to him, but she felt stiff, encased in formality. Perhaps he had forgotten all about her. He was a monk, after all. Perhaps she had never been that important to him.

The monk handed the reins of his horse to his companion and then looked directly at her. Detsen's smile performed a magic of its own. With each step he took toward her, years fled away like seeds blown from a dandelion.

"Louise," he said, "dear Louise." And he spread his arms to gather her into a most unmonklike hug.

Her reserve disappeared; the shyness was gone. This was the man she remembered. "Oh, Detsen, it's been so long. I've missed you."

"Come talk with me. But what's happened to your leg? Is it bad? My companion has skill in healing. Shall I call him?"

"No, no. Not right now. Besides, it looks as if Tashi and Geraldine need his attention more than I do. Whatever happened?"

"It seems they met the Chinese army, and if Tashi is to be believed, the army was no match for your young friend."

Louise and Detsen gazed at Jeri and Kelly for several moments. Jeri was sitting on a section of broken wall, her face tipped up to the sun, while Kelly knelt beside her applying a salve. The bruising scrape along Jeri's cheek had swollen so that one eye was only a slit.

"Do they know how obvious it is that they love each other?" Detsen asked.

Louise smiled, remembering another time. "I think that, like most young lovers, they are only aware of each other."

Detsen laughed quietly.

"She's not quite a friend, Detsen. Her people are from

Londonderry."

"I see. And does this affect the two of you?"

Louise sighed. "Yes. And no. I admire her, and I have relied on her to get me here, but she's dangerous. I can't reasonably approve. She accepts no law but her own."

"Sometime you must read about the Hindu goddess, Durga, who rides a tiger and has a weapon in each of her ten hands."

"I can see how that might apply to Geraldine, but what of her companion?" Louise told Detsen of the night before, how Kelly had risked herself when Louise hurt her leg. "I wish she was going back to her own life."

"But I think this is her life. Look at them, as if they were separate aspects of the same Bodhisattva."

Louise watched as no matter how carefully Kelly administered salve, Jeri winced from the pain. For an instant the air seemed to waver. Louise had the sudden impression that she was seeing through several layers of time, as if this were a scene repeated like the diminishing vibrations of a note struck on a bronze cymbal and echoing down the ages. Louise watched until the ghost images coalesced back into the present.

Detsen waited to see if she had more to say, and when it was clear she didn't, he spoke again. "Tell me about you, Louise. What are you doing now? Specifically. Talk to me as if we've met after only a few weeks."

"Oh, Detsen, I... The UN. I work for the UN. With refugees. My work, it's like fighting a fire in a high wind—just when you think the fires are out, some spark flares up again. We're going to set up some new centers for refugees from Afghanistan. The Russian withdrawal has left the country at the mercy of warlords, some of whom are quite vicious."

"Afghanistan." Detsen shook his head. "I traveled through there when I came back from England. It is so full of a sweet beauty, appearing even more delicate because it sits side by side with harsh terrain. That was several years before the United States lured the Russians into invading."

"Yes. That advisor to former President Carter, Brzezinski, still boasts of this. I've heard him."

"I fear for the world more than ever," Detsen said sadly. "There will be an unavoidable and very bitter harvesting from the proxy wars that the KGB and CIA have so thoughtlessly seeded. But even here, in our poor imprisoned land, we have heard of the compassion of Louise

Bolingbrook."

"Oh, Detsen, I do nothing. I've so often longed to talk to you. I can only channel aid, not stop the flow of injustice."

"Does that seem small to you? The future lives in the smallest acts of kindness. We can't predict the consequences of our actions, we can only believe in our need to act."

For an instant, Louise remembered the sweetness of an overripe banana that was all she ate one day in a Japanese prison camp, and how such seemingly small sacrifices had saved her own life, had fed her conscience and launched her toward a life of service. Another memory made her smile, and the monk looked at her quizzically.

"You said practically the same thing to me all those years ago, Detsen. Have you learned nothing more?"

Again he shook his head, but then he brightened. "You're here now. Unbelievable. You are so often in my mind. I confess that when I was in prison and should have been gaining proficiency in meditating, I more often escaped in memory to England and our time together."

He was giving her what he could, and Louise understood that she would remember this gift, feel the shifting shape of it in time to come. "You have never been far from my memory, Detsen. Often, after some complicated, wearying day, when I thought I couldn't face the next morning, I would think: 'Detsen would approve of this day.' Even when I was angry with you for not coming back, I could never think ill of you."

The monk closed his eyes for a moment, and then, opening them, smiled as if they had merely been commenting on the weather. "It seems we cannot ignore what goes on around us. I hear you have questions for me."

"One in particular. How can we best help Tibet?"

"I fear there is little hope for Tibet, but there may be ways to ease the suffering of Tibetans. Come, I have more pages for you. Proof of how Peking is undermining our autonomy little by little. My own monastery is becoming window dressing for the occupiers. Soon we will be little more than a destination for tourists, a kind of Disney Tibetland. We need help maintaining true traditions, help protecting the people, if possible."

Kelly peered warily at the clay pot of salve that Nuru had given her. "Is this really yak butter?"

"Sure. What else would it be? Medicine, tea… it's always yak butter up in the Himalaya." Jeri tried to put humor in her words, but the attempt

315

was feeble.

"Jeri, what else is wrong? Tell me."

Jeri looked away, sick at heart. She wanted to hide the words far away, but so much depended on not hiding from Kelly.

"The fight. I loved it. If Tashi hadn't stopped me, I would have killed one of those soldiers. I wanted to. Kell, I thought I'd accepted that there's danger for you if you stay with me, but I think it's worse. These aren't the best words, but they're all I can come up with—it's your heart that will be corrupted. You'll lose what's whole and good that I love about you, and it will be my fault."

Kelly sat back on her heels, staring up at Jeri. She thought she understood.

"Maybe we should go back to Cleveland, and I could get on for the summer semester. I think I could even get you on my insurance. I can teach, and you can keep busy around the house until you find something suitable."

Jeri's look of horror was so spontaneous that Kelly almost laughed. She set the pot of salve aside and took the plum-sized crystal from her pocket. Tiny rainbows danced inside the clear quartz talisman. Kelly remembered very well that Jeri had promised never again to ask her to leave, but this moment required more than invoking that promise.

"Look at me, Jeri."

Jeri was reluctant to meet Kelly's eyes, but Kelly waited until she had Jeri's full attention. "When you found me on that mountain road, I had just left the most corrupt life you can imagine. I had been living in a place where every day, every hour, people were dying and almost no one was there to help. Imagine the story of Sleeping Beauty turned inside out. She's awake and everyone else is sleeping, and she can't wake anyone to the horror that's happening. She's screaming while everyone else sleeps and dreams. That's AIDS, Jeri, that's AIDS where I've been, where they dream they're all good people in a land without racism or homophobia or a history steeped in injustice."

Kelly stopped. Sermonizing was just a distraction. She took a deep breath and continued.

"I can never go back to sleep again. I won't. I want to be with you. No one gets to have a safe life. No one gets to have clean hands. Believing that illusion, making that kind of innocence the goal, ignoring anything that challenges the illusion, that's where corruption grows. The best we can hope for is to stay awake. You're awake. I want to be with you because with you is where I belong."

You can't know that, Jeri thought, and she would have said it, but then it was as though she heard Kelly for the first time. As if finally she was able to get her own damn self out of the way and hear what was being said.

Kelly did know. Like Arkadia had known. Jeri's strength was considerable, but so was Kelly's. Jeri had thought she was the wiser one because she knew how vicious and careless the world could be, but Kelly knew more than that. Kelly would keep her sane; Kelly would keep her moving toward what her heart and her life needed.

She reached for Kelly's hand. "Yes. You do."

Requiem for Vukovar
Book 3
Refraction Series

Angela Koenig

Affinity
Rainbow Publications

2017

Angela Koenig

Acknowledgments

I have read too many sources over the years to list them all for their invaluable contributions to my understanding of the breakup of Yugoslavia, but I do wish to cite one in particular: *Yugoslavia: Death of a Nation*, Laura Silber and Allan Little, Penguin Books USA Inc., 1995.

I want to thank Sharon Karp and Nicole Ferentz for their continual encouragement and support. None of my books would have been possible without them.

I offer my abiding gratitude to my dear friends in ILS whose keen and passionate minds, lively humor, and generous hearts have inspired and sustained me for two decades. Nor do I forget how well they create the lucky in potluck.

Special thanks to the women of Affinity E-Book Press who believed in me enough to bring this book to press.

And finally, I wish acknowledge the brave people of Vukovar. This novel will quickly fade, but their courage belongs to history.

The cover image is a rendering of the Vukovar Water Tower which was damaged in the siege and is now a memorial of the war.

Dedication
To the Vukovar Medical Center

The story of the Vukovar Medical Center and its satellite clinics is a story of rare courage, of fidelity to duty and principle. Professionals and volunteers treated the sick and wounded of all ethnic and religious affiliations for months under desperately dangerous conditions. Despite inadequate food and water, lacking electricity for light or heat, babies were born, surgeries were performed, and patients were kept clean, fed, and nursed under a never-ending storm of bombs. In a city of heroes, the staff of the Vukovar Medical Center set the highest standard for dignified and selfless devotion to patients and to the principles of the healer's vocation. If the human spirit is a work in continual effort, then none have ever added more to our honor.

Angela Koenig

Author's Note

"Only part of us is sane: only part of us loves pleasure and the longer day of happiness, wants to live to our nineties and die in peace, in a house that we built, that shall shelter those who come after us. The other half of us is nearly mad. It prefers the disagreeable to the agreeable, loves pain and its darker night despair, and wants to die in a catastrophe that will set back life to its beginnings and leave nothing of our house save its blackened foundations."

Rebecca West, Black Lamb and Grey Falcon

Chapter One

Through the taverna's open door, Kelly Corcoran could see fishing boats bobbing alongside the wooden pier, a view drawn in extremes of light and shadow by the Adriatic sun. A steady breeze that Jeri called a *maestral*, welcome on this hot June afternoon, drifted into the long, narrow room, carrying a pungent sea smell along with the odor of things cooking in olive oil and garlic. Kelly lifted a thimble-sized cup of dark liquid to her lips, took a cautious sip, then closed her eyes to better savor the bitter taste of the sweet, thick, almost chewable coffee.

Kelly was the only customer in the taverna. Three men were drinking at a rear table, but one was the owner and the other two were his friends. Kelly assumed they were friends because the intense argument they were engaged in would bring anyone else to blows. Not that she understood Yugoslavian, but people speaking loudly and interrupting one another were usually arguing.

Not Yugoslavian. Jeri said the language was Serbo-Croatian.

Jeri had promised to be gone about an hour, but the hour was up. Not long enough to worry, perhaps. Jeri still had not explained why they were in the Yugoslavian city of Dubrovnik, but Kelly hoped they might stay a while. That morning she had jogged from their hotel near the docks to a road that took her past a fish market into hills overlooking the city. The view of the sea and city below had been as refreshing as the exercise.

After the florid confusions of India, Kelly was finding the familiarity of Europe as comfortable as a well-worn flannel shirt. She had been plotting a route from Delhi to the Taj Mahal when Jeri announced they were going to Dubrovnik at the request of her friend and occasional colleague, Rafi Gregoric.

"Is that a country, state, or city?"

"City. On the Adriatic Sea. That's the one between Italy and

Yugoslavia. Dubrovnik is in Yugoslavia."

Between India and Yugoslavia, Kelly's usually keen sense of distance and direction had been completely confounded by a combination of old trains, buses, boats, and far too many hot, jolting, canvas-covered trucks. Still, whatever the transportation lacked in comfort, it made up for in its ability to avoid officialdom. Not once during the entire journey from India had they been asked for their fake passports.

After the last boat dropped them off at a small port, Jeri had acquired a battered yellow Yugo, probably from the same source that provided messages and fake passports. The small car felt downright airy after the boat where they had been kept below decks with a load of wooden crates. Unfamiliar place names continued to accumulate as they drove. Jeri explained that they were north of Dubrovnik, in Dalmatia, the seacoast of Croatia that was a republic in Yugoslavia. Hearing only Dalmatia, Kelly started looking for spotted dogs.

As the sun rose over the mountains, the road south along the Dalmatian coast revealed an unending panorama of blue seascapes and green inland ranges. The narrow highway led through several small villages but Kelly saw not one spotted dog.

"There!" Kelly pointed to a fruit vendor at the side of the road.

"What?" Jeri was startled into braking the car, narrowly missing the first truck in a military convoy going in the opposite direction.

"That's the hundred and first Dalmatian I've seen!"

Kelly really didn't understand why Jeri was upset. She was sure her count of the population was accurate. Maybe Jeri had been away from the U.S. for so long that she had never heard of the movie. Kelly tried to explain but Jeri didn't seem to care.

Late in the day, Jeri steered the Yugo off the road and onto a hilltop overlook. At first, all Kelly saw was a gilded sea that looked as if the sun had set it ablaze. Then she noticed the city below and, even exhausted past the point of giddiness, she gasped aloud.

"Dubrovnik." Jeri sounded as satisfied as if she were a magician who had pulled the city from a hat.

Red-tiled roofs clustered along the shoreline and a growing number of lights flickered in the deepening twilight. A circular section, called Old City, lay out in the water surrounded by pale marble walls glowing creamy rose in the fading day.

"Dubrovnik used to be called Ragosa, and she once rivaled Venice as a center of trade and power in the Mediterranean. Venice is farther up the coast we just drove down," Jeri said.

She took Kelly's hand and they watched the timeless drama of sunset until the sea became a strip of darkness dividing the stars from the city lights.

The argument in the rear of the taverna jolted Kelly back to the present. Someone had hit the table hard enough to make bottles rattle. Jeri had introduced Kelly to the owner when they arrived, but Kelly couldn't remember his name. Even if a night of decent sleep in a hotel bed had done wonders for her mental state, the man's name was not something easy to remember, like Luke or John.

Not-Luke-or-John saw her looking toward him and he started to rise but Kelly shook her head. She still had half a thimble of coffee. The owner turned back to his companions. Kelly had been hearing anxious and angry voices since arriving in Dubrovnik. From these men, hotel clerks, some people near the newspaper kiosk where she'd searched for an English headline after her morning run.

"What's going on here?" Kelly had asked Jeri when she returned to the hotel that morning.

"I'm not sure yet. It's complicated."

Well, yeah, complicated, of course. Kelly had heard of the Balkans. She couldn't name all the countries that referred to, but she knew that Yugoslavia was definitely one. The Balkans were a historical rumor with a bad reputation, less a location than an adjective for things fragmenting with unpleasant consequences. Somehow, they had even caused World War One. Complicated indeed.

†

The Peace and Brotherhood Bookstore was just inside the walls of Old City and catered to tourists. Jeri O'Donnell worked her way around a table of recent publications with titles in several languages as she scanned other customers. A stout bald man was perusing periodicals near the front of the store, while a young couple, local by their appearance, browsed in the paperback section. Only these three, and they had been inside when Jeri entered.

Troubled times were affecting the tourist trade. The situation in Croatia was much more disturbing than Jeri had anticipated. The military convoy she and Kelly had passed on the coast road was just one example of reports of deteriorating relations among Yugoslavia's several republics. One of the republics, Slovenia, was going to make a break for independence any day now, and then Croatia would be dragged along. Not kicking and screaming with reluctance but nowhere near as well prepared for independence as Slovenia. That would be the end of peace and brotherhood.

Jeri looked about for someone in charge. She was uncomfortable with leaving Kelly alone for long. When she asked Zlatko, the taverna owner who had sent her to the bookstore, he had claimed the situation in Croatia was stable.

"Nothing will happen. It's all just a bunch of loud people who want to hear themselves talk," he'd said. His tone had belied his words.

Jeri looked at the table in front of her. Some of the titles were English. Maybe Kelly would like a book called *Jurassic Park*. Or the one more amusingly titled *Hitchhiker's Guide to the Galaxy*.

Jeri looked about again. There was just herself, the other three browsers and still no sign of a clerk in the store. If Rafi's message was so damned important, then he should have picked some more reliable messengers. It wasn't like him to leave so much to chance.

Jeri willed herself to composure. Rafi had asked a favor and she owed him anything he wanted. She owed him her life.

The jangling bell over the door announced the entry of two young women who looked very much like tourists. Both were in their early twenties, blonde and tanned, wearing khaki shorts. One of them had a maple leaf sewn on her backpack, but Jeri thought it could easily have been a rainbow flag. She carefully avoided eye contact and any possible recognition of sisterhood as they passed her on the way to the paperback section. Jeri had dressed in tan slacks with a white blouse in order to appear nothing more than a stylish local woman.

The bell finally brought a clerk from the rear of the shop, a gray-haired woman on the farther edge of middle age. Jeri walked over to the counter.

"Do you have a history of Romany?" she asked in Croatian.

"No. We have nothing like that." The woman's gaze sharpened and her features fell into an expression of distaste as she very obviously considered that Jeri herself might be Gypsy.

"Oh? Borisav called and said that such a book had arrived. I shall return when he is here." Anger churned below the surface, but Jeri gave away nothing of her feelings. So good to be back in Europe where everybody hated somebody.

"Wait, please. Borisav is here." The mention of her employer's name bent the woman's attitude toward courtesy.

While she waited, Jeri looked around. To the right of the counter was a section of used books. She leaned close to read the faded letters of a title that was almost like encountering an old friend. Perfect. This was the book for Kelly.

"May I help you?" Borisav seemed the same age as his clerk but with a decidedly more gracious manner.

"Yes. I was hoping to find a book on the history of Romany. I believe you called."

"Of course. Come with me." He led her through a heavy curtain to a back room containing the clutter and machinery of any office.

"You are—?"

"Estellija." Jeri filled in the blank in the question.

"Good. Yes." He moved behind his desk and lowered his voice. "Unfortunately, our friend is unable to be in the country just now. He asks that you to go to Vukovar and escort Alenka, his sister, to Sarajevo where she will be safer."

"Safer? How dangerous is the situation?"

"No, no, no danger." Borisav shook his head but it sounded like his automatic response to any tourist. He paused and then amended his answer. "I think he only wants his sister farther from Serbia. Vukovar is just across the Danube from Serbia."

Borisav rummaged around on his desk and found a large envelope. "Here. German marks for expenses and an address in Zagreb."

"How much for this?" She held out the used book she had found.

"Please. It is yours with my compliments. Now, Marta will be assured that I really did have business with such an attractive young woman."

"Thank you." Jeri turned to go.

"Estellija. Wait. I also have an address here in Dubrovnik where you are to pick up another car. We think that you have may have been followed, so a change will be good sense. Please, be cautious."

†

Another fist hit the table where the argument in the taverna continued. Kelly might not know the reason for the journey to Dubrovnik, but she was beginning to think that the summer of nineteen ninety one was not the best of times to visit.

Kelly vaguely recalled Yugoslavia figuring in the news before she left Ohio. That was when she and Billy would watch the nightly news on successive channels, a ritual to take them from one day to the next. Not long before he died, Billy began watching game shows instead, as if he wanted no more tales of the world he had to leave. Kelly tried, but couldn't recall any of the stories about Yugoslavia, only her dismay at seeing tanks rolling through a town that looked very much like the one where she had grown up.

She had been thinking of Billy at the kiosk that morning where she had looked for a newspaper. Even the papers that used an alphabet she recognized were in another language, and she found only postcards in English. One of them read: "The famous walls of Dubrovnik's Old City with a view of Mt. Srd in the distance." The postcard view of red-tiled roofs caught much of what she had seen while jogging. In that instant, she wanted so very much to be able to send the card to Billy. He would have loved this city. He had a tourist's eagerness for foreign lands and it had been his stories that sent her to Nepal after his funeral. Where she'd met Jeri. Kelly had bought the postcard.

Jeri had raised an eyebrow when Kelly showed her, but she'd said nothing.

Now, waiting for Jeri, Kelly turned the postcard over, wishing again that she could mail it home to Ohio. A sudden sensation of vertigo threatened to overwhelm her as she became aware of the impossible distance between this ancient city on the Adriatic and her family's farm in Ohio. Dizziness, along with a rapid heart rate, was so strong that Kelly gripped the edge of the table. The panic attacks didn't occur often, not anymore, but when they came they were sudden and severe.

Kelly reached into a pocket for the plum-sized quartz crystal from Nepal. Almost oval, with an inner brightness as clear as the high Himalayan air, each of the crystal's six sides gave a view of the interior where tiny rainbows played hide and seek. The stone had a name, a secret name: Keeper. She kept it and it kept her. Holding the crystal was like holding an anchor. Her heart began to slow and she took a deep breath.

Kaju, the young Sherpa she had met in Nepal, who intended to become a monk, had seen her with the crystal and how she often took it out to hold it. He had explained the meaning of *terma*, a tradition in Tibetan Buddhism that meant "hidden treasure." Such treasures were said to be concealed messages waiting to be found. Kaju assured Kelly that even if she was not the one for whom the message was intended, just its physical presence would transmit grace and comfort.

You took life as you found it. Her brother, George, had never anticipated the existence of AIDS, but he never denied the life that took him to that illness. Kelly could only hope for equal courage to accept her own path as bravely and steadily as George, his lover Russell, and their friend Billy had managed to walk theirs.

You took life as it found you. If you were on leave from teaching college literature and composition in Ohio, and you met your life's love on a mountainside in the high Himalayas and you wanted to stay with her forever, no matter her past, so be it.

Kelly's panic finally ebbed. She was homesick, that was all. The European familiarity of Dubrovnik was making her homesick for the even more familiar land of childhood.

But Ohio wasn't home anymore. From now on, home was wherever Jeri was.

A shadow broke the sunlit doorway and, as if responding to her thought, Jeri appeared, long dark hair wound in braids around her head, suggesting she might be older than the cusp of thirty. Kelly's reason for being in this unlikely region stood framed by light and darkness as Jeri paused to let her eyes adjust to the interior. Kelly's joy at seeing her was like the tolling of a bell that dismissed all doubts about where she wanted to be.

Chapter Two

Habit and caution directed Jeri's eyes as they adjusted to the relative darkness of the taverna. She received a slight nod from Zlatko, the owner, as he continued his animated conversation with his companions. Her gaze returned to the room's only customer, the woman in her mid-twenties with short, sandy brown hair who was gazing at Jeri with obvious adoration. Unlikely and undeserved, Kelly was a gift from a world that should have sent punishment Jeri's way, and there were moments when she felt punishment might be easier to bear. Loving gave fortune a hostage and Jeri was well acquainted with the fickle nature of fortune.

Jeri remembered her first sight of the lost woman standing in mountain mists on a roadside in Nepal. Jeri was there retrieving her life, strand by strand, from the meaning to which others had twisted her. Jeri had felt an immediate attraction to the stranger whose strength had also been visible despite the apparent sorrow. The arrival of Kelly had only deepened Jeri's resolve to control her life, but where she could risk herself without a qualm, she had learned a new kind of fear. The mere thought of harm to Kelly made her shudder.

Jeri allowed herself a moment of full awareness of her feelings and then she lowered the register to an ordinary range. She put on a smirk, and playing to Kelly's stare, she sauntered toward the table.

"Whyn't you just take a picture?" she asked, combining impudence with the South Boston accent of her adolescence.

"Oh, I will. Want to hear what else I'll do?" The grinning face tilted up and olive green eyes boldly returned her gaze.

Jeri would have bet money that she was beyond blushing. She would have lost. The cramped quarters of their recent traveling arrangements had led to some interesting pastimes. Memory and desire combined to be Jeri's undoing and a surge of heat rushed to her face.

"Did you find what you were looking for?" Kelly's grin grew wider and she crinkled her nose, enjoying Jeri's embarrassment.

"Yeah. A bookstore. Here. I think you might like this." Jeri took a very thick book from the worn canvas haversack she carried. The old pack was not exactly an accessory that went with the rest of her stylish clothes, but it was as much a touchstone as Kelly's crystal.

Watching Kelly's delight as she took the volume in both hands, Jeri decided discovering the old book had indeed been fortunate.

The English major in Kelly was so hungry that she wanted to lunge for the cloth-bound book. She had left all her vacation reading in a hotel room in Nepal, abandoning everything except for a guidebook to the Himalayas and a worn paperback translation of *Dante's Inferno*. Kelly would read milk cartons and cereal boxes if there was nothing else available, and while occasional English language newspapers had filled some of the lack, she and Jeri had more often been where local alphabets made even milk cartons inaccessible. When there were milk cartons.

"I've never heard of this." The ink of the print had long ago worn off the dark red cover and Kelly reverently traced the title words with a finger. "*Black Lamb and Grey Falcon*," Kelly read aloud, "by Rebecca West. I have heard of West."

"It's on any respectable list of the most important books of the twentieth century. West still sets the standard for understanding the Balkans."

"It was written before World War Two." Kelly had made it past the cover and onto the first pages.

"True, but she was a woman who knew how to see connections, say, between the railroad she was riding on and the old Roman Empire road it was built alongside. Anyone who wants to know Yugoslavia still reads this. West was English, so she knew what Americans don't understand about how long memories can be in other parts of the world, how much the past feeds the present." Jeri paused. "Or how it devours the present."

Kelly, sensitive to Jeri's shift in tone, stopped paging through the book.

"Jeri, what is happening here? And what does it have to do with us?"

"That's two questions. I want a drink first. Ready for a beer?"

Kelly nodded. A beer would be good after the thick coffee.

Jeri called in Croatian to the men at the back table as she went behind the bar. She returned with two bottles. She settled, tilted the bottle for a long drink, and then began.

"You know I owe Rafi."

"Of course. He saved your life in Chechnya."

"He should have left me. I was as good as dead and we could both have been killed. God, he took such a chance, not only with the people hunting me but with our commanders."

"That's when Rafi started to call you Stella, right?"

"That's right."

"And it was Rafi who helped you make a life after you left the IRA and the English were still hunting you, because to them you're a terrorist."

Jeri nodded.

That would have been before the Berlin Wall came down. When there was still an iron curtain. Kelly had a sudden vision of a murky international underworld where terrorists merged with revolutionaries and criminals. Nepal had been easy compared to the possibilities that could emerge in Europe. In Nepal, Jeri's history had not mattered to her on a gut level, but the European familiarity that she was finding so comfortable, also brought her back into contact with her conventional understanding of right and wrong. Her sympathies had always been vaguely on the left end of liberal, along with some more radical ideas that had never led to action. Jeri had crossed the line between thinking and acting. Kelly wondered just how much of Jeri's history she was about to encounter. She hoped her unease didn't show.

"What does he want us to do, Jeri?"

Jeri smiled, acknowledging the "us" that Kelly had used to show her involvement.

"Rafi's father died last winter. I think his mother died years ago. I learned today that he wants me to get his sister from his hometown. From a place called Vukovar, and then take her to Sarajevo. He thinks she'll be safer once she's out of Croatia, or at least farther from the border with Serbia. He always talked about her as if she was a child but I think she must be a teen-ager by now."

The mental breath that Kelly released felt like one she had been holding ever since Jeri had told her they were on their way to Yugoslavia. The place names were meaningless to her, well, not Sarajevo, that's where World War One started and where the Winter Olympics had been a few years before, but this request sounded so ordinary. Just take someone to another city. Prison breakout, assassination, bombing, Kelly hadn't known what to expect. Jeri said she owed her life to making up for the violence she had once been part of in Northern Ireland, but Kelly knew life was rarely that neat. She still wasn't entirely put at ease. Rafi's request was almost too simple for all the cloak and dagger shenanigans they had gone through to get to Dubrovnik.

"Where's Vuk–Vuko–whatever? I've never heard of it."

"Vukovar. It's a pretty city on the Danube, north and east of here. I've never been there but Rafi sometimes talked about growing up in Vukovar. Not much. We kept a lot of our personal stories to ourselves. Not lack of trust, you understand, but you never knew when you might be forced to give answers and the less you knew the better. For everyone."

"Do you know why he needs this? And can't go himself?"

"The people I talked to don't know where Rafi is, but obviously he thinks Alenka might be in danger."

"And you? Do you think so?"

"Not Alenka personally, but the city may be at risk. The Danube is the border between Croatia and Serbia, and that makes Vukovar a target for trouble between the two."

The high-pitched screaming of gulls fighting over something carried into the taverna.

"Rafi was never what you'd call an alarmist, but maybe he's worried because their parents were a mixed marriage."

"What does that mean?" Kelly was caught off guard. Just when she thought she was getting some understanding, she tripped over a new twist in the culture. "I grew up thinking that meant two people from different religions who get married."

"It can mean that here, but it means just a little more. Religion and ethnicity are all tangled in Yugoslavia, but Rafi and Alenka's mother was Roma. That's another word for Gypsy and all Europeans have a lot of prejudice against Gypsies. Getting back to religion, most Croatian Yugoslavs are Roman Catholic and most Serbian Yugoslavs are Eastern Orthodox. Or one of Rafi's parents could be Muslim. I don't know. We never talked much about religion."

"Muslim? Here? I thought Yugoslavia was a communist country where everybody was an atheist." Kelly turned a suspicious eye to the Rebecca West book. Apparently, there was a good reason it was so thick.

Before Jeri could answer, a raucous group of dockworkers burst through the door, instantly filling the taverna with noise and commotion. It took all of two or three seconds for the newcomers to notice the presence of women, and several of them headed toward Jeri and Kelly like bees to a flowerbed. One introduced himself in Croatian, and Jeri answered him in that language, but then she shifted to accented English.

"This is my cousin, Laura. She is from America." Jeri used the name on Kelly's passport.

"You are American! I am Nino. I have some English, too." Nino was delighted. He was a burly youth with dark hair, and he wore a t-shirt bearing a large red and white checkerboard inside a shield, a symbol that Kelly had seen in several variations since arriving in Dubrovnik.

"This is my friend, Dushko. We work together. I have a cousin in Toronto. That is like America, yes?"

Friend Dushko handed Nino a beer. Roughly the same age as Nino, Dushko had a shock of curly brown hair and a shy smile.

"We shall all drink to Croatia, yes? To Croatia." Nino raised his bottle and swallowed most of it.

Jeri smiled and drank. Kelly took her cue from Jeri and joined in. She was still off balance from the quiet taverna's sudden transformation into a boisterous bar.

Dushko's English was even more accented than Nino's. "You are very brave to stay when American embassy is saying all Americans to leave Croatia."

Kelly toppled her beer but caught it before it spilled. She hoped the distraction was enough to cover her initial surprise at the news.

Jeri's eyes narrowed but her shrug was exaggerated. "Why should she worry? She is with her cousin."

"Of course! There is nothing to worry about." Nino was offended. "Americans are listening to stupid Europeans. There is no reason to leave. Europeans think we are a country of primitive people but Croatia and Serbia will not fight. Do stupid Europeans think Dushko and I will fight? We are civilized people." Nino slapped his friend on the back.

Dushko smiled gamely at Nino's assurances. "I will get more beer." He pushed off toward the bar.

"He is not like most Serbs," Nino informed Jeri in a lower voice, one Croatian to another. "We have worked together on docks for two years. He says nothing good about Chetniks."

Dushko reappeared with four beers, but Jeri shook her head. "We have to go now. I am from Zagreb but we have cousins here who are expecting us." She glanced toward the owner who was now working behind the bar and caught his eye. He nodded.

Nino managed to look momentarily sad before the extra beer from

Dushko consoled him. Kelly slid the Rebecca West book into her small daypack. As the two women left the taverna, a song broke out behind them, one that started with one or two voices but quickly swelled to a rousing chorus.

"What's that?" Kelly asked. They had paused outside the door to let their eyes adjust to the light. The day was slipping into early evening but the sun was still strong.

"The song? Something about Croatia *uber alles*. Unfortunately, for having such a bad beat, far too many people want to dance to it." Jeri shook her head. "Come on, I have a place I want to show you."

"Jeri, why are Americans supposed to leave?"

"The papers say that Croatia is going to declare its independence from Yugoslavia any day now and I suppose the US State Department thinks there'll be fighting if that happens. A lot of people here are going to wake up some morning soon and find out that the person living or working next to them has just become a foreigner and probably an enemy."

"Like Nino and Dushko?"

"Let's hope not. Come on. I want you to see Old City."

Jeri began to point out interesting places as they walked, as if she really was a native Croatian showing off her famous city to an American cousin. There was a lot to point out in a city that was more than thirteen hundred years old.

"Before Columbus discovered America and made the Atlantic more important for trade than the Mediterranean, Dubrovnik was on a direct line from Rome to Constantinople and trade with the East. That's the Pile Gate up ahead and we can take it into Old City."

As Jeri talked, Kelly began to fit the region into the more familiar narratives of European history that she knew. The problem was that she was woefully foggy on the Ottoman Empire, but she did like hearing Jeri talk. She could almost see Jeri drawing her thoughts from a deep well of feeling and knowledge, combining fact and commentary. Jeri liked lecturing, enjoyed sharing what she knew. It was times like this that Kelly could glimpse the Rhodes Scholar that Jeri had been until the troubles of Northern Ireland sucked her in and spit her out into an Ulster prison.

They walked through the Pile Gate into narrow streets where only foot traffic was permitted, and Jeri led the way to steps made from marble, polished by centuries of passing feet. The top of the wall was wider than the cobbled streets below and the view, either inland toward the hills or outward to the Adriatic, was stunning. Kelly reached for Jeri's hand instinctively.

"What do you think, Kell?"

Kelly thought she would like to pluck this moment out of the flow of time and wrap it for a keepsake. The marble-paved squares, the narrow cobbled streets from which motor traffic was banned, the jumble of ancient buildings, even the cats that seemed to watch from every shadow and corner, all combined like some marvelous legend come to life.

Once upon a time, two happy lovers came to a fabled city....

And Jeri had just called her "Kell." She had never told Jeri how much she loved to hear that name. George had always called her that and she'd thought of it as her secret name, never to be heard again after he died.

"I think I love you past bearing," Kelly said.

†

Jeri squeezed Kelly's hand, understanding that all deep feelings rise from within a single source. "Well, if you get too choked up, that church over there belongs to St. Blaise. He's the patron saint of the city."

She waited for Kelly to get the joke, and got a swat on the arm when she did. "Serves you right for the hundred and one Dalmatians," Jeri said with a grin.

Any kid with a Catholic background would recognize the saint who could protect you from ailments of the throat, particularly if you choked on a fishbone. If Jeri remembered right, February third was the feast of St. Blaise and the day you got your throat blessed with candles. She could remember her mother taking her and the other kids to the front of the church, up to the communion railing where the priest placed chilly beeswax candles to either side of her neck while he chanted a prayer that echoed in the cavernous space. It was a wonder the things that got into your memory and never left.

Jeri and Kelly walked slowly seaward along the wall until they came to a place where they could sit and watch the sun set over the Adriatic. They could also see anyone who was approaching. Gulls wheeled and screamed overhead. An elderly husband and wife walked slowly by, arm in arm. Two young suntanned women in khaki shorts consulted a guidebook as they passed. Jeri recognized them from earlier in the bookstore. A young man and his girlfriend strolled along hand in hand. It was a thin trickle of people for an ancient city whose continued existence depended on tourists.

Jeri leaned back on the bench, scanning everyone who passed.

"Maybe they'll quit looking for you." Kelly's comment was wistful.

Jeri knew that Kelly still hoped Louise Bolingbroke, the UN official and British citizen they had helped in Nepal, might derail the official pursuit of Geraldine O'Donnell, formerly of the IRA, or at least slow it down.

"They can't. Too much reputation rides on getting me. And revenge. The British SAS think I killed one of them." Jeri kept her voice empty of emotion. "Now they'll be looking for you, too, Kell. Don't ever forget that."

A family group of at least three generations walked slowly by—an older woman dressed in black, a married couple, and three children, two of them barely school age. They all looked so somber that they appeared out of place among sightseers. Even the small children looked downcast.

"Dubrovnik is already getting refugees from the border areas." Jeri sighed.

"I still don't understand what's going on."

Jeri searched for a way to simplify Yugoslavian politics.

"It's as if New York's governor was running the United States. Serbia is a state but its president is running the whole country of Yugoslavia right now. He also controls the army. Croatia wants to be independent, just like Ohio would if New York was dictating everything. The fact that Croatians and Serbians are different religions and ethnic groups only complicates political matters. Another complication is that there are other republics in Yugoslavia besides Serbia and Croatia but those two are the big problem at the moment."

"Why can't the Croatians just leave if they want?"

"Good question, but the borders don't make clear ethnic nations. For example, there's a place called the Krajina that's not far from here. It's Croatian land territory but it has a large Serbian population. The Serbians want to be part of Serbia if Croatia secedes. Croatia won't let that happen because, obviously, it wants to keep its own land, and because none of the ethnic Croatians who live there want to be part of Serbia."

"Sounds like Northern Ireland all over again. Two populations with different ideas about whose country it is."

"Sounds like a lot of places. Especially now that the Soviet Union is about done for, more ethnic groups and once-upon-a-time countries that the world never heard of will want to run their own lives again." Jeri paused. She knew she was lecturing.

"Sorry. I do go on. I don't know if there'll be a war, but you do remember the boxes in the boat that brought us into Croatia?" Jeri paused and saw a smile gather on Kelly's face as she not only remembered the boxes but also some of the activity that took place on them. Jeri hurried on before she, too, got sidetracked by memory.

"The boxes all carried guns. The European community has put an embargo on arms to Croatia, so they need to be smuggled in. The fact that Croatia is arming, is part of why the US Embassy thinks there may be fighting."

A bank of clouds lay low on the horizon, edged in crimson and gold, as if some dramatic painting by Titian or Raphael. Below the clouds, the sea blazed in shimmering red and purple. Gulls wheeled in a painted sky, the distant sound of a motorboat rose and then faded. The evening smells of things cooking in olive oil and garlic accompanied by laughter and radio music drifted up the wall. Everything radiated a timeless peace.

Chapter Three

Kelly was seeing more troubling signs as she and Jeri walked toward their hotel outside Old City. Groups of tired people looked more like baffled refugees than genial tourists. Several cars went by, their horns blaring, full of shouting young men leaning out the windows and waving red and white checkerboard flags.

"That's the symbol for Croat nationalism," Jeri said when the first car passed them.

Kelly started seeing the checkerboard symbol everywhere, on flags in store windows, on T-shirts. At the kiosk near their hotel, the red and white checkerboard shield was posted above the counter.

"Jeri, look! Did something happen?"

Several papers carried pictures showing numerous dead bodies. Jeri peered closely at one.

"Don't worry. Those are pictures from World War Two. The Croatians are dredging up all the old atrocities they say Serbs committed then."

"You don't sound very sympathetic."

Jeri sighed and looked around, lowering her voice. "Croatia was no slouch in the atrocity department. They allied with Nazi Germany and the story goes that even the Nazis were horrified by how viciously they went after Serb partisans. I guess I'm surprised anyone wants to bring up old atrocities at all."

"Why are you so upset?" Kelly took her cue from Jeri and lowered her own voice.

"Because this could be a new kind of country, a real new beginning, but it's promoting the same old diseased nationalism. The cliché is to say that hatred in the Balkans is centuries old and will never go away, but the hatred is only as old as the latest politician fanning it for his own gain. Like President Tudjman here in Croatia and like President Milosevic in

Serbia. Two peas in a fucking pod."

Jeri stopped herself from going on.

"Sorry. I do get aggravated." She managed a weak smile. "I'm probably just hungry. Let's go to that restaurant we saw this morning. The one by our hotel that looks like it should be in a Renaissance fair."

They walked on and by the time they reached the restaurant, they were hungry. The menu promised a variety of fresh seafood, and with the shortage of tourists, they were guaranteed great service.

"Bass was about the only fish I ate growing up. It never tasted like this." Kelly had ordered *brudet*, a dish suggested by the waiter, with several kinds of sea fish cooked slowly together in tomato sauce.

"You might think I had lots of seafood in Boston, but actually I remember that everything we ate tasted like boiled potatoes. This is wonderful. Remind me to always vacation where you get to stand in for a hundred tourists."

Jeri had ordered *pašticada*, a plate of Dalmatian beef that the waiter had described in such detail that Kelly thought she would faint from hunger before the food ever came. When Jeri gave her a slice with the thick sauce of dried plums, onions, and carrots in red wine spiced by rosemary, sage and nutmeg, Kelly thought she just might die. Happily.

"Tell me a story about Ohio farm life, Kell. I like hearing those."

"Do you know *Fern Hill* by Dylan Thomas? I love that poem. When I was little, I used to fancy myself as Prince of the Apple Towns. Did I ever tell you that the next farm over had a tree that everyone said was planted by Johnny Appleseed himself?"

"About a dozen times. I always heard Johnny Appleseed was a bit of a pervert."

"No!" Kelly was surprised at her own sharp protest. "Maybe. I can't say for sure, but I think that was just vicious gossip."

"I had no idea you felt that way about Johnny Appleseed."

"Now, you know, so speak kindly of him. He was something of a mystic actually, a Swedenborgian. I went over to the tree once. It was down by the creek and was in bad shape, old with a lot of suckers. I tried one of the apples. It tasted terrible. Sour. I don't suppose he planted the tree because apple trees don't live that long, but I did try to learn more about him."

"What's a Swedenborgian? Swedenborgianism?"

"It's a kind of nature philosophy. They say it influenced Helen Keller and Robert Frost." Kelly rarely ran into gaps in what Jeri knew, and she found it enjoyable to explain the religion and philosophy that had once been popular.

Kelly had learned how to savor ordinary moments stolen, despite the lidless gaze of disaster. The last two years had been lived in company with her brother George, and his lover Russell, and then their friend Billy, as the relentless diseases of AIDS took all three. Kelly had learned to accept the good times, learned not to let the grim specter of tomorrow take away the hour's grace. It was a skill to be used again as the murky currents of danger in Croatia generated dangerous shadows in which Jeri's past also hunted them.

"Another carafe?" Kelly shared out the last of the wine.

†

Jeri took the opportunity to gaze at Kelly. In the ambient restaurant lighting that relied on both real and electric candles, Kelly's walnut hair took on ginger highlights. Her face appeared open and charmingly eager on first glance, but looking deeper Jeri could see the strength of character in the firm mouth, the shadowed reserve in hazel olive eyes that hinted of her recent collisions with loss.

A certain innocence formed Kelly's strength. Jeri could see it clearly, since her own had been lost long ago. A clutch of love and sadness gripped her. *If only we'd met before,* Jeri found herself thinking.

Before what? The astringent voice of her irony asked. *Before you became a murderer?* Contentment fled. The ease of the evening drained away, replaced by awareness of her own moral predicament.

"No. No more wine."

†

Kelly caught the end of her lover's silent drama as she turned back, and could only guess at the reason for Jeri's averted gaze. "Do you want to go back to the hotel?" she asked quietly.

Jeri moved her hand to cover Kelly's on the tabletop. "I do, but I can't right now. I have to go out again. Do you want me to walk you back?"

Disappointed, Kelly kept her voice light. "No. We're just across the square. Go ahead. Will you be late?"

"Probably. I'm getting another car and papers for us. I'll try not to be too late."

"Another car? Do you just order them up like sodas?"

341

"Yup. I don't like the color we have now. Besides, I need to talk to someone about the best way to get to where we're going. I know it seems like I know about the situation here, but there's considerably more that I don't."

"Okay. Jeri? Take care. I love you."

Jeri squeezed her hand.

Kelly watched Jeri rise and wind her way among the tables. She paused in the doorway, looked back, smiled and waved. A small farewell gesture. Just a local woman who had dined with a friend from school days, or a foreign cousin, on her way home. Jeri created a whole narrative in a few gestures.

†

Jeri recognized the two women sitting at a table near the door as she exited the restaurant but she carefully ignored them. The odds were still that they were just tourists. The hotels in the area catered to vacationers, so it would be strange not to run into someone several times who was staying nearby and visiting the same sights. She chalked it up as her own peculiar situation of part outlaw and part fugitive that made her sensitive to a simple, predictable coincidence.

Several cabs were cruising the area, so finding a ride outside the restaurant was easy enough. Jeri gave the driver an address that took her to a residential hillside section of Dubrovnik. Very little traffic passed as she stood and watched the lights of the taxi disappear. She waited a bit longer and when the street was empty, she began walking.

Traffic increased as she proceeded downhill. She passed horn-honking joy riders still celebrating Croatia's status, whatever that currently was, as well as the occasional taxi or delivery van. Close to an hour after leaving the restaurant, and certain that she had not been followed during her twisting route, Jeri finally approached the address she had been given by the bookseller.

Sedna Jukic, daughter of Zlatko the taverna owner, lived with her two children above the little shop she owned. Sedna had been waiting for Jeri and opened the door immediately.

"You're late. Did you have trouble?" Sedna was standing on a step and glanced at the street over Jeri's shoulder.

"No, there's a lot of traffic for this time of night and I wanted to be careful."

"Good. We think you're being followed, but we don't know why or by whom." Sedna turned and led the way upstairs to a small kitchen. "Slivovitz? Wine? Coffee?"

"Thanks. Just water. Wait." Jeri had thought of something. "Do you have a thermos?"

"Of course." Sedna disappeared downstairs to her shop for a few moments and then returned with a medium-sized thermos.

"Have you heard from our friend?"

"No." Sedna's tone suggested that Rafi's continued absence was becoming worrying. She brought Jeri a glass of water.

"Does anyone know what's happened to him?"

"Not that I've heard. There's been no fail-safe signal, so he's probably okay. The last I knew he was in Belarus looking at shipment of chairs."

"Chairs?" As an enterprising entrepreneur taking advantage of the complications of the Soviet breakup, Rafi had brokered some strange items, but chairs?

Sedna lifted an eyebrow. "Chairs. Last month it was orchestra instruments from Ukraine. Next month it will be tanks. Still, something's not quite right or he would do this thing himself."

She gave Jeri the empty thermos along with a set of keys and several maps.

"The car is two streets down. Turn right at the corner. And be sure to park it far away from the one you have now. Just leave those keys with your concierge and tell him Zlatko will come for them."

"It's probably the Brits who are following me."

"Maybe. They don't act like the British, but there are more and more freelancers these days." She shook her head in disgust at the thought of amateurs.

"Any change in Croatia's situation?"

The discussion of the latest twists in politics claimed the women's attention for several more minutes and then Jeri left.

†

Kelly finished her wine slowly but the heart had gone out of the evening. At least she had Rebecca West to read. Looking around the restaurant, Kelly recognized the two Canadian women she had seen on the city wall. They looked just like tourists, but then so did she. Jeri had taught her to be suspicious of coincidence. As Kelly stared at them, one turned and caught her eye, then winked and favored her with a wide smile. The stranger might as well have shouted over the dinner noise that she assumed they all belonged to the same sisterhood.

Kelly gathered her things, but as she walked by the two women, they smiled.

"Have a glass of wine with us, mate?"

Kelly recognized an Australian accent. Not both Canadian, then, even though both had similarly healthy faces and deep tans. Maybe they just used the maple leaf to signal they weren't Americans and didn't support the recent war in Iraq. A lot of people had resisted going to war with Iraq for Kuwait.

Kelly was tempted by their invitation. It would be nice just to sit and share an hour's conversation. Check if they really were gay. Enjoy the company.

Before she could make an excuse, one of them had pushed out a chair. "C'mon, mate, have a seat. I'm Carol, Carol Willis."

Fear of being rude overcame her reluctance and Kelly sat. An attentive waiter hurried over with a glass for her. The table already had an almost full carafe.

"Are you from Australia?" The words were out before Kelly thought. A where-are-you-from conversation was the last one she wanted to take part in.

"I'm the Aussie. Liz is a Canuck. We met in Marseilles about a month ago. Great luck, eh? So who was that good-looking babe?" Carol made the question cheeky but charming.

"Connie? She's my cousin," Kelly answered. She and Jeri had decided that *cousin* could cover a multitude of close or distant consanguinities.

Liz raised a disbelieving eyebrow, but Carol laughed. "Not too far removed, I hope."

Everyone laughed. Kelly's first impression of the two women had been that they were almost twins, but up close they were quite different. Carol appeared chatty and gregarious, but what she meant for eager interest felt more like something greedy as she leaned toward Kelly. Dark roots gave away the actual color of her hair and her dark brown eyes were small above cheeks that were tending toward fleshy. Liz, on the other hand, leaned back and her pale blue eyes traveled slowly over Kelly, appraising her.

"We've been pen pals since we were kids," Kelly said. "Connie lives in Zagreb and we just met in person finally. Not the greatest time to be here, is it?"

"But you hit it off, right?" Carol was not to be deflected.

"Oh, yes." Kelly was becoming distinctly uncomfortable.

"I didn't get your name?" Liz was definitely the cool one. She didn't even bother to smile.

"Laura," Kelly answered.

Carol started to pour wine into Kelly's glass, but Kelly put her hand over it.

"No, thanks. I really am tired. We did a lot of walking today. And I've got some heavy reading to do." She slipped the book from her bag and hefted the copy of *Black Lamb and Grey Falcon*, exaggerating the weight.

As she left, Kelly went over the short visit. She'd only made up a bit of a story but she hoped it wouldn't come back to haunt her. She still felt uncomfortable. Maybe Liz had been jealous. If they just met a month before, maybe Liz thought Carol was more flirty than friendly with strangers.

The hotel clerk was the same one from the early morning, a young man in a crisp white shirt, reading a newspaper. He nodded to Kelly as she entered and climbed the tiled stairs to the second floor.

The single room was meant for the frugal traveler, but it was the most comfortable place she and Jeri had been for a very long while. Comfortable and private. Kelly had regarded the wide bed and its clean sheets with interest when she first saw it. She and Jeri had managed some interesting activity while traveling, but making love was difficult for Jeri at the best of times. It didn't take a degree in psychology to figure out why. She'd killed people and she was haunted by regret so she'd arranged her own punishment with an emotional logic that defied reason. Then again, maybe the logic was reasonable.

Kelly had not been surprised the night before when Jeri had snuggled close and then fallen asleep. More than tired, they were both exhausted, but Kelly had hoped tonight would be different, especially if they were leaving soon. No question that she sometimes found the situation frustrating but it was far from impossible. She could not imagine any circumstance that would make being apart from Jeri better than being with her.

But it would be nice to put this bed to more use than just sleeping.

Kelly showered, enjoying the luxury of warm water, and then propped the pillows for reading before slipping into bed. She opened *Black Lamb and Grey Falcon* and found the section on Dalmatia. She wished she had a map. She liked maps and her imagination was longing for a visual structure for her new information. Dalmatia was once called Illyria, which probably put it north of Greece, and had been the home of Olympias, the mother of Alexander the Great. Another Illyrian woman, Queen Teuta, had been accused of piracy by Rome. A pirate queen. Kelly wished West had added more about her. Kelly decided she might as well go back and start at the beginning.

The beginning was several pages of fascinating but befuddling history of emperors and archdukes and archduchesses and assassinations. Kelly also found an extraordinary comment by West, claiming she knew almost nothing about Yugoslavia but concluded: "That is to say I know nothing of my own destiny." Kelly suddenly had a strong foreboding that her own destiny might be located here.

She was drifting into sleep when she remembered a line from the opening scene from Shakespeare's *Twelfth Night*. After being shipwrecked, Viola asks: *What shall I do in Illyria?* Now that was a good question.

"Hey, bookworm. Let me take that."

Kelly barely woke as she felt the book lifted off her chin, followed by the sensation of a familiar body sliding in beside her.

"Hi, baby. Did you get your people met?"

"Yeah. Go on back to sleep."

"Mmm." Soft lips feathered over her forehead. Kelly tucked herself into welcoming arms and then slid back into uneasy dreams of assassinations and betrayals.

Chapter Four

Kelly woke early. Easing herself carefully from the bed, she found her running shorts and T-shirt where she had arranged them on a chair the night before. She debated whether to wake Jeri with a kiss before leaving, but then decided to take a moment just to enjoy looking at her in the dim dawn light. Jeri was as close to relaxed as Kelly ever saw her. Covered by a single sheet that was tucked around her in toga-like folds, she rested on her side, her dark hair loose and long. Kelly was tempted to slide back into bed but she didn't want to lose the stamina and strength she had gained while hiking through the Himalayan Mountains.

Jeri's eyes opened. Immediately alert, she took in Kelly and the room.

"Running?"

"Oh, yes. I'm just ready to go." Kelly stepped forward and kissed Jeri lightly. "Go back to sleep."

Their room was on the second floor and Kelly took the stairs down to the small lobby. Two young men behind the counter paused in their conversation as she crossed a tiled floor that contained a mosaic of an octopus surrounded by several dolphins. The clerk was the same young man as the day before. Perhaps he had a room of his own at the hotel with a supply of crisply ironed white shirts. His companion was younger and was wearing a polo shirt. He had also been there the previous day.

"Good morning, miss."

Both men smiled as they greeted her. It took so little for a traveler to lock onto a relationship. Two encounters and a stranger felt like an old friend.

Outside in the parking area, Kelly went through her pre-run stretches. The air had a heady odor that was as rich as orchestral music. Composed in part of hosed down sidewalks, harbor sea drift, and a number of things that might be better left unnamed, the overall effect was to create a smell that would probably forever recall dawn in Dubrovnik.

"Morning, mate. Mind if I run with you?"

Here was the down side of meeting strangers while traveling. Kelly recognized the voice of Carol Willis even before she turned to see a woman in green shorts, yellow tank top, and white sneakers.

"No. Nice to have the company."

"Which way are you going?"

"I thought I'd head to the road along the sea cliff. It goes up about a mile from here and then has a great view."

"Sounds like a good choice. Liz thinks I'm crazy to use prime sleeping time for running, but I like being out this time of day. Besides, she's so naturally thin she has nothing to worry about."

Carol continued to jog in place and Kelly noted that while she was a bit shorter she was quite muscular. Her thighs were those of a serious runner.

†

Jeri lay awake listening to Kelly walk down the hall to the stairway. Listening to events take place outside her vision was a skill that she'd honed in an Irish prison. She stretched and tried to go back to sleep but found that her mind was already awake.

They needed to leave Dubrovnik soon. Sedna had agreed that the political crisis in Yugoslavia was deteriorating much faster than anyone had expected. Rumor had it that Slovenia was declaring itself independent that very evening which meant Croatia needed to move quickly. And some incident had occurred near Vukovar at a place called Borovo Selo in May. That incident was probably what caused Rafi's concern for his sister. The Serbian villagers of Borovo Selo had engaged in a pitched battle with Croatian policemen and a number of police had been killed. Maybe. Rumors about what had happened were still generating media discussion, much of it contradictory as to who started what and caused how many casualties.

Jeri thought that everything had really gone to hell with no way back during March when Milosevic had orchestrated his power grab in Belgrade. She and Rafi had talked about it then. Rafi thought the fate of Yugoslavia was foreordained several years before in nineteen eighty seven, when Milosevic had been just another not-so-pretty face in the Belgrade bureaucracy. The minor politico had turned up at a rally in the province of Kosovo and told a crowd of Serbs that no one should dare to beat them.

"That was the day, Stella. That was the day he realized he'd found the key to power. That was the day he picked up the flag that better men refused because they knew that raising the ethnic flag in Yugoslavia will destroy the country. But Slobo dared. Now Slobo Milosevic is the darling of the Serbs." Rafi had been disgusted as well as unhappy. He claimed to have been committed to international socialism, but his attachment to his own country was apparent. Now he claimed he had been converted to international capitalism.

Back in late winter, Jeri had been too taken up with planning the escape of an extended family of Kurds from Iraq to pay much attention to Yugoslavia. There had been rioting then in Belgrade but there had also been an unrelated war going on in Kuwait and Iraq.

Croatia didn't want to declare independence so soon because its national guard was weaker than the federal army, and the federal army was controlled by Slobo's people in Serbia. Slovenia was ready to go now and had no reason to wait. It was tucked up north, far away from Serbia, and itching to take its thriving economy off into modern Europe. But if Croatia got left behind, while Slovenia declared independence, then Croatia would be at the mercy of Serbia and the army.

Jeri didn't have much sympathy for Croatia. Kelly had guessed right about that. Tudjman and his party had put it in their constitution that Croatia was the state of the Croatian nation, a short little phrase that meant nobody but an ethnic Croatian could ever be a true citizen. How could any other group ever feel safe when they were constitutionally defined as second class? It was a situation that made Croatian Serbs understandably and realistically nervous.

Truth be told, Jeri rather preferred Serbia. It was a scrappy nation, a lot like Ireland, that had fought for centuries to maintain its identity while ruled by foreigners. Rafi disagreed with her. He thought Serbs were far too prone to be violent while claiming to be victims, but then Rafi himself was Croatian even if he had become an exile much like Jeri.

Christ! If she was awake enough to start taking sides in an area as complicated as the Balkans, Jeri decided she might as well get up.

It didn't matter who was who here. What mattered was that she and Kelly needed to get to Vukovar and find Rafi's sister, Alenka. And it was high time to leave Dubrovnik. Sedna had mentioned rumors of fighting in the Krajina, the border region through which Jeri wanted to drive. Add to that those two blonde women in the restaurant. That coincidence had been bothering her, and Jeri hadn't stayed alive and free by believing in innocent coincidences.

Jeri felt an increased level of consciousness as she got up and found a map that would show her the best route from Dubrovnik to Zagreb and from there to Vukovar. She felt her mind gearing up, her instincts on alert. Truth was, she enjoyed that edge.

†

Kelly and Carol jogged away from the hotel along a cobbled street that made running tricky. Where it turned toward the harbor, the road became tarmac and much smoother. They ran past the fish market already bustling with activity. Fishermen, who had been out long before dawn, offered their catch to restaurant owners and householders while boats rocked gently in the nearby harbor.

Kelly found her stride and let the rhythm take her. She'd been an occasional jogger in college but after she began caring for George and Russell, she took to running more seriously. Some physical outlet had been necessary and running became her metaphor. Sometimes she was training, like Rocky Balboa for the big fight. Sometimes she was running away, fleeing from death. But ever since Nepal, she was always running toward Jeri.

The Australian woman ran alongside, actually ahead. Kelly noticed that, imperceptibly, Carol Willis had increased the pace for both of them. Not that it was a hard stride to match. Kelly could manage the increase with no difficulty. They ran past the last buildings and then out onto a gravel road that began with a slight incline and then became steeper, taking them toward a low ridge behind the city. As they reached the level ground of the ridge, they were rewarded by a view of mountains inland and swelling waves seaward. The sun was above the horizon, already strong and hot, but a dawn wind provided relief.

Illyria had been the name of this coast in past times. Kelly remembered reading this in Rebecca West's book. Before the Romans controlled the world, Greek ships had sailed along these shores. Kelly wondered if she'd run here before, along this sea, breathing this same salt-scented air. Something she knew seemed to hover just ahead, just past awareness, as if what she could see was only a thin veil trembling between her and a deeper knowing. She ran toward knowing but it fled even as she approached. A longing she couldn't name took her near to tears.

"Let's head back," she said to Carol.

They changed direction and saw Dubrovnik below, wavering in the light and shadowed mist of early morning. They had come farther than Kelly thought. The coast road that angled up on the way out was now a downward slope, and with the runners' speed increasing, the gravel road was tricky. The sea, visible over the edge of the road, was a classic blue, a Michelangelo painting blue. Kelly slowed deliberately, savoring the view. Running fast was rarely her preference, though on the few occasions that she had run with Jeri she'd sometimes let the former track star nudge her into a race. She had not done too shabbily either.

Carol Willis slowed her pace to match Kelly's, but before long, she had them both gaining speed again.

Later she claimed it was a loose rock. Kelly hadn't noticed it, but the road was inarguably covered with gravel. Carol gave a short cry that was the only warning before Kelly saw her falling, and she instinctively stepped aside to avoid stepping on Carol. Even so, Kelly felt some part of the woman tripping her, arm or shoulder, and then she was falling sideways, toward the edge of the road.

Only there was no edge, not here where the road curved, not with a drainage culvert that was shortened to send rainwater to the sea below.

Kelly had a sickening view of rocks jutting up through the shallow water of low tide. She either had to fall now or try leaping across the culvert despite the fact that her momentum was sideways, not forward. If she missed she was dead.

She chose to fall. She stiffened her leg and tried to make a sideways move that could brake into a full turn, but she felt the gravel sliding under her feet. Desperately she managed to push back with her other foot, but she could gain no traction.

Kelly threw herself down in a last desperate attempt to stop. She was on the ground and sliding and knew that she'd lost her gamble—she was going over the edge. She grabbed at the ground, her nails tearing on the loose stones. Then, suddenly, one foot caught on a rocky outcrop just over the edge and she slowed, slowed. Stopped. Kelly lay a moment with her cheek against the hot gravel, flooded with the relief of being alive. Pain swiftly dissolved the relief. Carefully, she inched to a safer distance from the edge and managed to stand.

Both her palms were scraped and one was bloody from a deep cut. Both stung. Some of her nails had shredded when she'd scrabbled for a hold. One shoulder felt sore, and likely to get worse, but she could move it, as well as her arm. And her thigh and knee on that side, too, her right side, had wide scrapes with blood beginning to ooze.

Carol Willis had her own scrapes and bruises. She was brushing gravel from her shorts and limping toward Kelly.

"Laura, I'm sorry, I'm so sorry." Tears welled in Carol's eyes as she apologized.

Beneath her pain, Kelly felt anger stirring. They'd been running too fast. She'd been pushed to run fast. And the fall had taken place at the one spot along the road where the danger could have been lethal, not just painful.

A van came toward them, going uphill, then slowed and pulled to the side of the road. A taxi going the other way, into the city, honked angrily at the van. Kelly waved to the taxi and the driver waved back and stopped. Carol seemed torn, she had been closer to the van and had started toward it but then she followed Kelly to the taxi.

Maybe Kelly was just mad. Hurt and mad and she probably wanted to blame the Australian woman more than she deserved. It was natural to want to make someone responsible for any accident. Kelly hid her feelings, not wanting an argument, just wanting to be rid of the woman. When they arrived at the hotel, she shook her head as Carol offered to accompany her.

"Can we get together for dinner tonight?" Carol asked. "Please. On me, mate. I owe you one, really."

"Don't worry about it. Accidents happen. If Connie doesn't have plans, I'll stop by later and see how you are. Get some rest."

Kelly watched as the taxi drove up the street and then stopped at another hotel on the square, not all that far away. She supposed Carol could really have come out of her own hotel and seen her getting ready to jog. Maybe she had picked up too much paranoia from Jeri. She nodded to the hotel clerk and carefully climbed the stairs. As she entered the room, Kelly felt her anger drain and fear flood in. She began shaking uncontrollably.

†

Jeri had a map laid out on the table and looked up with a welcoming smile.

Kelly was leaning against the doorway, eyes closed.

"Honey, what's wrong?"

"I fell."

Jeri hurried to her side and then led Kelly to a chair by the sink.

"Jesus, Kell, it looks horrible. Is anything broken?"

"No. I'm just bruised and scraped. Carol got hurt, too, but it could have been a lot worse."

"Carol? Who's Carol?"

"An Aussie. From the restaurant last night. She was going jogging, too."

"You'd better start at the beginning."

"Did you see those two women tourists at the restaurant last night? The ones who looked gay and Scandinavian?"

Kelly skimmed over the meeting at the restaurant and then described the accident, as Jeri managed, ever so gently, to wash gravel and dirt from the scrapes. A cold fury was replacing her worry so Jeri kept her head bent as she listened. She knew that if she looked up there would be no hiding the fury that had her heart beating wildly

She was a fool, a complete fool. She had seen the women and she had let Kelly go out on her own this morning. And she had been congratulating herself on her edge. If anything had happened to Kelly— Jeri felt a wave of nausea.

"You think she might have pushed you deliberately?"

"I don't know. Maybe. But she had some bad bruises herself. And she seemed really sorry. Then I saw a taxi and that was a piece of luck, because I don't think I could have walked too far. I suppose the van could have brought us back."

"Van? What van?"

"One that had just been coming up the hill. It was driving uphill from the city but it pulled over across the road."

"Did you see anyone inside?"

"No. The taxi was coming the other way and honked because it had to slow down for the van, that's all I saw. I was so glad to see it I didn't pay any more attention to the van. I don't know if it was just an accident. I think it probably was."

"It doesn't matter, not really." Jeri had her anger under control now.

"If you ever have doubts, any doubts at all, you act on them. Always. Doubts don't come from nowhere, they come from your instinct, and your instinct comes from that smart place that aims to keep you alive." She had turned over one of Kelly's hands and tenderly kissed the wrist above the scraped palm.

"I saw them last night, too, those two women. On the city wall and then at the restaurant. Even before that, they were at the shop where I got the book. That's just way too many damned coincidences. I'm so sorry. I should have been paying attention and never left you alone."

"It's okay, really, but what are we going to do when we run into them again?"

"We won't." *If we did I'd kill them.* "We're leaving as soon as I finish getting us ready. I have the new car. Well, not new. It's another Yugo, but a different year and color. There. How do you feel now?"

"I'm fine, now." Kelly took a deep breath and sighed.

✝

To test her leg, Kelly got up and walked over to the small balcony to the open doors. Her knee hurt but not like it was serious. Despite everything, she was going to miss this city. A slice of sunlight was moving into the shadowed square below and Kelly inhaled deeply of the sea-scented morning air. Pigeons pecked their way over the stones and gulls cried stridently as they wheeled overhead. A toddler, boy or girl was impossible to make out from this angle, ran laughing across the cobbles while the mother followed leisurely. The scene really begged for a video camera. Kelly would have liked to be an ordinary tourist for just one more day, with nothing to decide but which museum to see, and where to have lunch, and whether to look at old churches or explore narrow alleys.

Kelly felt a hand on her shoulder drawing her away from the balcony, and then Jeri's arms were around her and Jeri was kissing the nape of her neck. Kelly leaned back, relaxing into the embrace, enjoying the soft warm breath on her skin that was summoning the first signs of desire. She started to reach for Jeri but a twinge of pain from her sore shoulder made her wince. She laughed.

"Am I doing something funny?"

"Not at all," Kelly felt lips on an earlobe, fluttering like butterfly wings. "Don't stop. It's me. I think I'm impotent."

"Impotent?" Jeri did stop. "What do you mean?"

"What would you call a dyke with no hands?" Kelly held up her scraped palms.

There was a bit of a pause as Jeri managed a complicated maneuver that both turned Kelly around and drew her close. Then Jeri was sitting on the bed while Kelly was standing only a breath away.

"Easy," Jeri murmured, the words muffled because she was now nuzzling Kelly's belly while her hands slid upward and slipped both T-shirt and running bra over Kelly's head in one move. "I'd call her real easy."

"I guess it's true what they say." Kelly felt Jeri's mouth on her breast. "Kissing does make it better."

"Yeah? How about this, does this make it better?"

"Oh, yes, that's better, too." Kelly's running shorts joined her other clothes on the floor and she stood naked, open to Jeri. "Please, take off your shirt. I want to feel you against me."

"Like this?" Jeri eased out of her T-shirt, leaned back on the bed and, careful of scrapes and bruising, pulled Kelly down on top of her. "Is this better?"

Kelly tried to answer but she was becoming incapable of words. It was such luxury to be made love to in the daytime, on a bed, in the morning twilight of the hotel room. After the close quarters of boat holds, after the canvas covered backs of trucks where privacy was more imaginary than real, after kisses stolen during night-time bus rides, a hotel room with just the two of them and a bed was like being in Eden.

Jeri was taking her time, leisurely kissing her way from breast to belly while she moved in and around and out of Kelly in a slow rhythm. Kelly managed to use her wrists and move Jeri's head up to her own until they were mouth to mouth.

"I love you," Kelly whispered.

And in that instant, leisure fled and desire rose to claim them both. Kelly could feel Jeri's urgent need to hold her, keep her, take her. And even in that surge of fierce passion, she could feel that Jeri was struggling to maintain control of her rhythm, to follow Kelly's response.

"It's okay, love, let go. I want whatever you want."

And Jeri did let go. Suddenly, as if a wave of darkness descended, Kelly was swept into the swelling intensity of Jeri's desire and her own. She had no idea whose was whose. She only knew colors, dense and vibrant, and time wasn't time, and for an instant, she was back on the road above the sea and looking out over a wilderness of storm merging wind and wave and she and Jeri were there together and they were the sky and the sea and the land holding against the storm's wild assault. Then she was back in her body as she came in a series of implosions that flooded through her, leaving her limp and exhausted.

They lay together, ragged breathing becoming slower. Kelly opened her eyes to see Jeri's head resting on her. A wisp of hair curled damply along the back of Jeri's neck. Idly, Kelly traced the length of it with her lips.

Making love with Jeri always took patience and attention because the woman carried too many memories to allow pleasure to be simple. Slowly at first, Jeri began to respond, and then Kelly's awareness of

Jeri's growing desire rekindled her own. It wasn't only that her hands were sore, Kelly was hungry for Jeri. She wanted to be filled with this woman who had arrived in answer to every hope she'd ever cherished, every dream of love she had ever nurtured but hidden away, fearing that such desires for meaning, for caring, for utter trust, were impossible outside of dreams. Love and desire, the beat and counter beat of her heart, swept her on, and when, predictably, she felt Jeri begin to draw away, Kelly would have none of it. She insisted, tenderly and patiently, but she still insisted, and after a while she felt Jeri give way to her, felt resistance melt and slowly transform.

Kelly opened to the fear and need. Jeri was so afraid for Kelly, afraid of her own intensity, afraid of the turbulent emotions that were being invoked. And truth to tell, Kelly was hard put to ride out the rise and fall of anger followed by pain, by rage that was succeeded by remorse, by despair that trembled toward hope. The terrible thing was how quickly each of these extremes claimed Jeri and then swung her on to the next. But Kelly stayed focused, steady, until she heard her own name called over and over, and in a long, sobbing shudder, Jeri came to her.

Once again they lay together, tangled and damp.

"You're so beautiful." Jeri sounded uncharacteristically shy. She raised herself on an elbow and her hair fell around both of them as she kissed Kelly's brow. "I love you so much."

Chapter Five

"Kell? I've been thinking." Jeri didn't take her eyes off the road.

Kelly felt like a lazy cat that has finished off a bowl of thick cream. Her thoughts were drifting among the puffy white clouds over the mountain country that looked as if Julie Andrews might soon appear and begin singing how alive the hills were. Kelly slowly took her eyes away from the scenery to look quizzically at Jeri, who stayed focused on driving. The road was level for the moment, but during the past hour it had twisted sharply through a series of sharp curves, forcing Jeri to keep a slow speed.

"You have? Good, because you're going to have to think for both of us for a while, love. I won't be able to think for at least another day or two, maybe not even until next week." She was well into a sensual yawn and stretch when a twinge made her gasp.

"What's wrong?" Jeri was shifting gears as they came to yet another incline and curve.

"Nothing. I'm okay. I'm just getting stiff from the fall."

"What hurts?"

Kelly checked. "My wrists. My right shoulder. My leg, probably, though I can't tell just sitting here. It's not bad. I'm sure I can walk off most of it."

"That's what I want to talk to you about, Kell. As long as we're here, in Europe I mean, I want to go to this place I know. After we take Alenka to Sarajevo. It's a kind of training school. You're good, really you are, one of the best quick studies I've ever seen, but you need training and you need to sharpen your instincts. This place can give you the basics in hand-to-hand stuff."

Kelly's stomach went sideways, taking her contentment with it. To cover a reaction that she didn't quite understand, she joked. "You mean a boot camp for outlaws?" But her mind was saying *for terrorists.*

"You could call it that." Jeri took her eyes off the road. "You look scared."

"I guess I am." Kelly hesitated. It was one thing to bind her life to Jeri's and another altogether to know the people Jeri knew, to begin moving in their circles.

"Talk to me, Kell. This is one of those times that silence could be a very bad thing."

Kelly nodded. Jeri was right. This was important and if she kept her thoughts to herself, they could be the tip of a wedge coming between them. She wasn't that clear about what she feared except that more than anything she feared discovering a thought that would create the separation. Surely a blanket denial would be better. Despite her bone-deep confidence in the love that bound them, she was not so foolish as to think that the bond could not be damaged.

Once, in Nepal, Kelly had responded to a surprise revelation from Jeri in a way that almost separated them. Despite how strong Jeri might appear, she still had surprising areas of vulnerability. Jeri had made reference to her time in prison, an experience that Kelly had been unaware of until that moment. The prison had been at Armagh in Northern Ireland. Kelly hadn't recoiled in horror, but even her mild reaction was enough to trigger Jeri's sensitivity about class. Even being a Rhodes Scholar had not undone growing up in Boston's Southie neighborhood, a background that telegraphed all manner of suspicion and tainted character to potential friends, employers, or lovers.

Kelly struggled to resist the inconsistency and irrationality that informed many of her attitudes, but she carried a load of middle class conventionalism that would never disappear. It was not morality, far from it, since it allowed for any amount of wrongdoing as long as appearances were kept up. It could scarcely even be considered judgmental since it made none, preferring instead to transport transgressors into a huge silent void. Kelly remembered that her mother never disapproved of anyone, rather she felt sorry for them but never actually explained why. Asking for explanations was also a breach of convention.

So, once again, it would appear that making a life with Jeri meant more than simply following her anywhere. It meant undoing the habits of a lifetime. Kelly took a deep breath.

"Okay, here goes, and bear with me, because I'm not sure what I have to say. I am scared. I grew up hearing echoes of the counterculture, but it was never really part of my life. I used to think that being gay inoculated me from the worst isms. That was naïve, I know, but I didn't have any other reason for why George and I were different from other people where we grew up. I still think the gay part of me is the source for all the true things I believe."

Kelly was at least making some sense to herself, thinking out her ideas as she spoke.

"All you and I had to do in Tibet, all I had to do, was keep going and not get caught. I didn't really have to decide anything about what we were doing or who was against us. I mean what could be wrong with helping a UN official learn about the persecution of children? So I didn't have to think about what was right or wrong, or how right or how wrong. It seemed that just being with you was the beginning and end of what was right."

Kelly looked at Jeri who was staring ahead at the road, and she willed her next words to be true, willed herself to be in that place of understanding. "It still is."

"And Bolingbrook was there," Jeri added as she nodded.

"That's true. I hadn't thought about that before. She had all the authority of the UN behind her, plus her own reputation, so she brought along an assumption that what we were doing was okay. She was kind of like a mother, giving permission just by her presence."

"I'm sure she wouldn't mind hearing you say that, Miss Corcoran, but I'm confident that the last thing Louise Bolingbrook would want is for me to think of her as my mother." Jeri caught the British inflections perfectly. Jeri's humor diminished much of the tension that had entered the car.

More at ease, Kelly continued. "It's different here. I know you had reasons for what you did in Ireland."

"Don't confuse reasons for doing something with making it right."

"What I mean is that all the attitudes I was raised with are trying to take over again. This stuff about training…who would train me, and to do what?"

Suddenly, Jeri was standing on the brake and fighting to control the spinning car. She managed to miss a tree that had fallen across the road but Kelly heard branches scrape against her door. Kelly braced herself against the dash, causing her scraped palms to sting mercilessly while her shoulder sent out wave after wave of pain. The Yugo spun around another half turn before sliding to a halt.

At first the dust kicked up by the slide obscured Kelly's view, but as it settled she saw what had made Jeri stop. Two large trees blocked the road. The little car faced toward a tangle of branches and behind the trees Kelly saw a number of men in army camouflage uniforms with rifles. There were over a dozen, maybe half again. The soldiers stared at them with their guns pointed upward.

Three of the soldiers detached themselves from the group and began walking toward the car, two of them carrying their rifles loosely but pointing at the Yugo. Kelly remembered that she strongly disliked the sound of bullets anywhere near her. The third man, with only a holstered pistol, appeared to be the leader.

Jeri spoke low and fast, barely moving her lips. "They're Yugoslav Federal Army, not Croatian. Remember what we rehearsed. We're on our way to Belgrade. Whatever you do, keep your hands clearly in sight."

Kelly felt more than a little confused. The particulars of the Yugoslavian political situation were still beyond her. Why it was important that they were going to Belgrade, the capital of Serbia, rather than Zagreb, the capital of Croatia, was puzzling. As far as she knew, they were in Croatia but Jeri had decided that being Croatian carried some risk.

†

Jeri leaned out the window, following her own counsel by keeping both hands on the steering wheel, and smiled at the man in charge. As he neared the car, he lifted one hand, holding the first two fingers against his thumb. Jeri nodded and returned the same gesture.

Jeri's face was calm but her heart was thudding. It was impossible not to remember another time she had been stopped at a roadblock on a road in Armagh, with her cousin, Fiona, and her cousin's boyfriend. Within minutes, Jeri was no longer a Rhodes Scholar at Oxford but a prisoner of the English Crown, and Fiona and Devlin were dead. Her cousin and the boyfriend had turned Jeri's rental car into a smuggler's vehicle. They thought her American ignorance of the political situation would be protection, and instead it got them killed.

The Yugoslavian officer's attitude relaxed when Jeri offered him a mildly flirtatious greeting. The officer adjusted his stance so that he could see into the car for a better look at Kelly. He favored her with a smile that was quite charming.

"Good day," he said in passable English. "Your cousin says you are here from America."

"This man is a captain. He says the war has started. Croatia declared independence today. I can't believe it. I can't believe they're being such idiots!" Jeri spoke in a tone of disbelief but she added a wink that only Kelly could see.

"But that's terrible!"

"Do not worry, miss. I am telling your cousin the safest way to get home. I hope you enjoyed the sea." He stepped back, gesturing as he spoke.

The captain gave his instructions and information in Croatian, and then he favored Jeri with a smart salute. He leaned down again and added in English for Kelly, "Good-bye, miss. I hope you enjoy your visit."

He gestured to the two soldiers who had accompanied him and they began pulling the smaller tree aside so the Yugo could pass.

Jeri kept her smile broad as she watched the men work.

†

Kelly was surprised to discover that she'd been hoping a way might be found for the country to avoid the impending crisis, as if it truly mattered to her. She wanted life to continue the way it had felt in the dockside taverna, on the evening walk on the walls of Dubrovnik, the way she had imagined a timeless lapping of blue waves against marble. She waited for the captain to move out of hearing range before she spoke.

"Who are these men?"

"He's JNA. That means Yugoslav Federal Army. Everyone is uniform is JNA. I'm not sure about the others. Some of them may be volunteers."

The captain returned to the squad behind the tree. The two soldiers who had accompanied him to the car stayed behind, still watching the women closely but too far away to hear anything they said.

"Do you notice anything about these men?"

"Not really. Except that I don't like them."

"Don't let that make you quit looking. They say they're federal troops and that the war just started, but they didn't just get here. The stumps where the trees grew, the wood is dark. It was cut down quite a while before yesterday. And the leaves on the branches have shriveled. I'd add the way the uniforms look, like they've been out of barracks for several days, but that could be from maneuvers. Still, it's a sure bet that this roadblock has been here longer than just one day. It was set up before any declaration of independence."

They had to drive through the group of soldiers. As the Yugo slowly passed, the captain saluted them again. He had been speaking to someone wearing a different uniform, a very odd uniform. The man was styled so self-consciously, from tight jodhpur fatigue pants to mirror sunglasses to shoulder length hair, that he looked like a James Bond villain. The man contributed a comment that made the men around him laugh uproariously. It was aggressive laughter that any woman hearing it from a group of men would recognize. Kelly knew that a comment of sexual intent had been made about Jeri and herself. It had been a long while since she'd heard men laugh like that, and along with anger, the laughter also aroused an old familiar fear.

"Don't let it get to you, Kell," Jeri said, reading her thoughts. "Remember it's a weakness. Now you know something about them and they don't know much of anything about you. It gives you an edge. You can always use information and anger."

The Yugoslavian captain waved for them to keep driving forward, guiding Jeri through with large and humorous gestures while the James Bond villain posed in an attitude of arrogance, his long, dark hair riffling in a breeze that Kelly thought he must have ordered along with his outfit. Once Jeri reached the road on the far side of the fallen tree, the captain called good-bye. The long-haired soldier next to the captain said something, obviously another obscenity from his tone and leer, but the captain hissed him to silence.

"That was odd." Jeri frowned as they drove slowly away.

"Which part? The beginning, middle or end?"

"The captain said to be sure not to stop until we get to the next town. Then the other one said that it was too bad we weren't Croatian and the captain made him shut up. I wouldn't have thought anything about it if the captain had just let the comment go."

"Why are they here? Aren't we still in Croatia?"

"I'm sure we are but this route got us closer to the Krajina region than I wanted to be. Damn. It's too dangerous to be on this road. If there's trouble, we're going to be right in the middle of it. The next opportunity, we're heading back for the coast. It will take longer to get to Zagreb that way, but there's no point in taking chances. Damn!"

They drove on in silence but the roadblock had diminished any sense that they were simply driving through pretty country. Kelly reconsidered Jeri's suggestion that she get some training in self-defense. It was about more than her sensibilities. The encounter with the soldiers had shown how dependent she was on Jeri. Knowing how to take care of herself would also take some of the responsibility for her safety from Jeri's shoulders. She needed to know a lot more about how to read situations.

"What was that gesture you used with the captain?"

"What do you mean?"

Kelly held up her hand with the first two fingers against her thumb.

"Oh, that! That's how Orthodox Serbs make the sign of the cross. Croat Catholics only use their fingers, no thumb. And of course the Muslims don't make the sign of the cross."

"That's it?" Kelly asked incredulously, staring at her own hand. "Like some secret sorority sign? You can only tell one kind of person from another by how one person holds their hand to start praying?"

"Not just that. One goes from right shoulder to left and the other goes left shoulder to right. And some words sound different. When I practice Serbo-Croatian with Rafi, he always points out the differences. Then there are the alphabets. Croatians use the same one we do and the Serbians use the Cyrillic which looks like Russian."

"And the Muslims use Arabic?"

"No. They use the Croatian mostly. "

"Oh, that helps! Jeri, I don't understand at all."

"Don't worry. I just have a few more facts than you do and I don't understand either."

The road continued on relatively level ground for a kilometer or two and then began winding through hills that were covered with more grass and brush than trees.

"Jeri, tell me again what the Krajina is? I'll look it up later in West's book, but tell me now."

"It just means border. In the last century, this used to be the borderland between the Austro-Hungarian Empire and the Ottoman Empire. Refugee Serbians who were fleeing from the Turks were given land here so they would have a stake in keeping the Turks from coming any farther. Ironic, huh? The folks you invited in to fix the problem have now become the problem. Now, Serbia wants it because, according to Milosevic, wherever there's a Serb, that place becomes part of Serbia."

"Anywhere?"

"Well, he probably won't send the JNA to Chicago."

The road inclined into a steep grade and Jeri slowed in order to downshift. Even so they almost drove by a woman who was sitting close to the road. She was as still as any rock outcropping from the hill itself, but she was dressed in black and the solid color stood out from the mottled background. Her bent head hid a view of her face. What truly caught their attention was somebody trying to pull the woman away who then gave up as their car drew close, someone who scuttled away to disappear into nearby brush.

"Something's wrong with that woman," Kelly said. "She looks sick."

Jeri had already stopped. She set the hand break and got out of the car. When she called out, she got no reply.

"I'm going to take her some water." Jeri reached into the back seat of the Yugo for their plastic water jug.

Kelly opened her door and climbed out slowly. She truly had stiffened up since the morning, and the sudden stop at the roadblock hadn't helped her shoulder at all. She moved it around gingerly and then followed Jeri off the road, climbing toward the woman who still had not moved.

Only a few meters upslope from the road, slumped over a bundle on the ground in front of her, the woman gave the impression of being quite old. She wore a black dress with a black scarf tied country style under her chin. As Kelly came closer she could see strands of gray hair escaping from the scarf, and then she saw that along one cheek what she had taken for part of the scarf was a huge bruise from jaw to forehead, a swollen darkness with dried blood along the edges. One hand rested on the bundle in front of her. The old woman gave no response to Jeri's greeting. Indeed, she seemed not even to hear it.

Jeri stopped abruptly, as if she had slammed into an invisible wall. Kelly heard her gasp, and when she turned, it took several tries for her mouth to make words. Something was wrong, terribly wrong.

"Kelly, wait. Oh, God, don't—"

Don't what? Don't look? Don't come farther? Don't see?

It wasn't a bundle lying in front of the woman. It was a child, a boy probably. Somehow you always see gender and his hair was short. Maybe ten or twelve.

Try to see anything other than all the dried blood on the face and short hair. Still, one's eyes kept going back to the white bone exposed where the throat had been cut, where black flies crawled. One kept looking away, only to be drawn back again to the horror of that wound. Even on the farm where she grew up, Kelly's family had taken animals to market, they never slaughtered anything themselves. Chickens. They chopped off chickens' heads. Then there was always a lot of blood.

Kelly thought she had seen enough when George and Russell, and then Billy, one after another, had suffered through the hydra-headed opportunistic diseases of AIDS, the pneumonias, the wasting, the cancers. But Kelly had never seen anything like this.

So, there were worse ways to die than among friends in a bed with clean sheets.

Kelly sank to her knees, unable to move. Her mind, desperately skittering about searching for any form of escape, registered that they all must look like some modern religious tableau—the woman seated with her son, she kneeling, Jeri standing. Kelly wasn't sure if they were viewing the baby Jesus just born or the dead Jesus, taken down from the cross.

Jeri spoke again to the woman but she got no answer. Kelly looked up from the boy, glad of a reason to turn away from the sight before her, and saw someone else coming toward them. It was another woman, no, younger, a girl really, not much older than the dead boy. Her short blond hair held twigs and crushed leaves. She was dressed in jeans, a loose shirt, both of which were covered in dirt. Her age was difficult to determine because her face was also very bruised, swollen, and scratched.

"Do you know these people?" Jeri asked, translating her own questions as well as the girl's answers for Kelly.

The girl nodded but stood a short way away. "My mother. Franjo, my brother."

"What happened?" Jeri's voice was low, kind.

"Chetniks." A halting answer, unable to manage many words.

"When?" Jeri asked.

"Yesterday."

Jeri handed the jug of water to the girl. She reached eagerly for it, but then only sipped. She tried to hand the water to her mother but was ignored.

"Is there anyone we can get to help you?" Jeri asked.

The girl shook her head. "Do you have some food for her? We have been out here all night and she will not leave Franjo."

The older woman seemed as fixed as if she had grown roots.

"We have some bread and cheese but you can't stay here."

"We have nowhere to go. They burned our home."

The girl looked away, started to talk, stopped, and then finally managed. "She won't talk to me. She knows that I will have a Chetnik baby."

"A what?"

"They said that after they shamed me. 'Now we have put a Chetnik in you.' They made her watch when they put it in me and now she will not speak to me. They made Franjo watch before they killed him."

Only flies droned in a silence that stretched on and on.

"Kelly!"

Kelly felt Jeri's hand on her shoulder, rousing her from shock.

"Go check the Yugo. There may be a jack or something we can use for a shovel. And bring back my canvas pack. There's bread and cheese in it."

Kelly stood up and went down to the car. She supposed that only throwing up once on the way was the sign of some kind of strength. Underneath their packs in the trunk, she found a folded trenching tool along with a hammer, two wrenches and a screwdriver. Whoever had given Jeri the car certainly had foresight, although Kelly hoped that grave digging didn't come up all that often.

Another wave of nausea caught her. Not for an instant did she doubt that the soldiers they had just passed had done this, or knew who had. Men who could rape a daughter and slit the throat of a son and make the mother watch both. Kelly gripped the trenching tool and used the pain from her scraped palms to help her gain control.

Jeri nodded with grim satisfaction on seeing the small shovel. "We can start digging over there," Jeri said, pointing toward a pine tree. "I told the mother what's going to happen, and at least I saw her eyes move. Here, I'll dig. I forgot about your hands, Kell. Can you find rocks, the bigger the better? The grave won't be that deep and rocks will help to cover the boy. There are still wild animals in these mountains." If there was any irony in the last statement, Jeri didn't seem to intend it.

"How are you?"

"I'm okay, Jeri. It was those men from back at the roadblock, wasn't it?"

"Yeah. As sure as if we'd seen them. See if you can get the woman to eat something."

Kelly nodded, but when she offered food, the old woman shook her head. At least there had been some reaction. It was the first real sign that she was in the same world as they were. Without waiting for any agreement, Kelly tipped the bottle to the woman's lips and was rewarded by seeing her swallow.

Gathering rocks was a good task. The hillside provided many about the size of a bread loaf and Kelly carried them to where Jeri worked beneath the pine tree. The ground was dry and hard and although Jeri bent to the work with a will, the grave deepened very slowly.

"Jeri? What will these women do after we finish?"

Jeri rested and wiped sweat from her forehead. It was hot even high above sea level. She looked toward where the two women still sat, the girl a short distance from her mother.

"Vojna, that's the daughter, says that all the rest of their neighbors, their Croat neighbors, have already gone. She says her father was away and they waited for him to come home, but he never did. Then the Chetniks came and burned the houses. The village was just over that hill. Vojna and her brother and mother tried to run, that's why they're here. The Chetniks caught them. We'll take them with us. We can't leave them."

"What are Chetniks?"

"It's a name left over from World War Two. It used to mean resistance fighters against the Nazis. Now it means Serbians, paramilitary, a kind of volunteer militia. The ass with the sunglasses back at the roadblock was absolutely a Chetnik."

"Which way will we go? We can't go back." Kelly felt her thoughts were like rubber balls that kept bouncing about wildly, unable to stay on a single idea.

"There's a map in the car. Maybe we can keep on this road for a way, but now we really must get out of the Krajina as soon as possible."

"You said those were Yugoslavian soldiers, not Serbian."

"Serbia's running Yugoslavia now, so the two are pretty much the same thing, at least here in the Krajina. I expected the regular army to be more civilized than the paramilitaries. I didn't think this sort of thing would happen, or not so soon. The people I talked to in Dubrovnik kept saying nothing would happen."

It was early evening when they buried the boy. The mother went where she was directed, as easy to move as a puppet. She did not respond to words but she took direction from Kelly. Kelly guided her over to the pine tree. Vojna followed, crying silently. When the child reached for her mother's hand the woman pulled it away. Angry, Kelly went over to the girl and placed an arm around her. Vojna leaned toward her, finding comfort in Kelly's closeness.

Kelly had seen such coldness before. At Russell's funeral, his family had been as distant from George as it was possible to be while standing

367

around a grave. Even in death they wouldn't forgive their son for being gay, much less acknowledge his gay lover. After everyone else had left, George had sat down beside the grave, his head bowed, spectral thin. He had barely spoken above a whisper but Kelly had heard him.

"Wait for me, Russ, my friend, my brother, my love. Once I was afraid to go, now I want to go. I'll be with you soon."

Yet in spite of her anger at the old woman's hardness, Kelly's heart went out to her. The many lines on her face had been drained of meaning, as if they no longer bore any relation to the joys or sorrows that had created them. No one should endure what she had been made to witness.

Jeri lifted the dead boy and carried him to the shallow grave. She laid him tenderly in the ground and covered his face with his torn and blood-stained jacket. For a moment she seemed at a loss, unsure what to do. It was a look and manner so unfamiliar to Jeri that Kelly came forward to help. She looked at Vojna and her mother, but neither woman had anything to offer. Kelly took a handful of dirt, and let it fall, then another. Jeri took the shovel and gradually filled the shallow grave.

Once the dirt had been replaced, Jeri and Kelly laid stones carefully on the grave. They could only hope the low mound of rocks would discourage animals. Then there was nothing left to do, and the four women just stood in silence.

Words came to Kelly of their own accord, part of what she had been thinking as she gathered stones. She knelt near the head of the grave, and sat back, resting rather than taking an attitude of prayer, and put a hand on one of the stones.

"Go in peace, Franjo, son of this land," she said solemnly. "May the god of your fathers guide you home."

Jeri translated the words.

In the lingering dusk, Jeri shepherded them all back to the Yugo. The old woman went easily enough. At the car, she climbed into the back seat and Vojna joined her. In such a small car they were still able to sit without touching. Again, Kelly offered the woman some bread and this time it was accepted.

"Do you know where we are?" Kelly asked. Jeri was using a small flashlight to see the map.

"Yeah. I think there's a road off this one a few kilometers ahead. We can take it back to the coast." She folded the map and took the water bottle.

"What are you doing?"

Jeri had walked to the front of the car. She found a short stick, poured out some of the water onto the ground, and then stirred, making as much mud as possible. She smeared the mud over the headlights.

"This will give us a little light to drive by, but it should give us a chance to see other lights before they see us. We're lucky it's dark. If we passed by soldiers now with Vojna and her mother, we'd all be in trouble."

Jeri started the engine. "Did you mean that about a god?"

"Not really. But it felt right."

†

Jeri drove very slowly and not only because the light from the headlights was so dim. She did not want to come up on a house or a village by surprise. Vojna had said there were no villages until past the turnoff but Jeri was taking no chances. With no exact idea of their danger, she intended to act as if everything was perilous. She glanced over at Kelly, who was staring straight ahead. Jeri reached out and found her own hand gathered in by both of Kelly's. Love, reassurance, acceptance of where they were, so much more than any words might ever manage, was in the way Kelly took her hand.

Jeri had not anticipated in any way the turn that events had taken. Rafi's request had been so simple. Drive to Vukovar and then drive to Sarajevo. She certainly had not anticipated getting caught in a civil war.

Jeri felt so proud of the woman beside her that she shook her head in wonder. She knew Kelly had a core of enormous strength, but it took a very brave heart to go through a day like this and not fold. Kelly had nearly been killed in the morning, and then in the afternoon had witnessed the horrible death of a child. She had borne everything, dealt with each shock as it came.

"Kelly?"

"What, love?"

Their voices were barely above a whisper. Jeri looked in the rearview mirror. She could see the open eyes of the passengers in the back seat.

"Earlier, when we were talking about you going through a training course, remember?"

"Yeah. That seems so long ago now."

"I just wanted to make you safer. I promise you, I'll never ask you to do anything that you'd regret doing. That you didn't think was right."

"I know. I want to do it though. I want to know more."

They rounded an easy curve and the road took a gentle downhill slope. Jeri saw a faint glow ahead. She stopped, then reversed back around the curve before pulling the car off the road. She rolled down the window and listened to the silence for several minutes. After a while she could make out the faint sound of far off voices.

"I'm just going to look. You'll be okay?"

"Sure. Be careful."

Jeri reached under the front seat and found the release where she expected it to be. When she brought her hand back up, it was holding a large handgun. She searched again and found a piece of equipment that extended the barrel. She looked over at Kelly and got a grim nod of approval. A quick glance in the back seat showed two pair eyes watching her intently.

"It might be better if all of you wait for me outside the car."

Kelly helped Vojna and her mother out of the Yugo and over to a shelter of sorts by some trees while Jeri changed out of her white blouse and into a dark T-shirt and jacket. Kelly was shrugging stiffly into her own jacket when Jeri came to help. Jeri adjusted the shoulders unnecessarily and then pulled Kelly close in a hug.

"If you have to leave for any reason, go that way. I'll find you."

Jeri pointed in a direction that Kelly took to be west. Toward the sea.

"Just hurry back. We'll be here."

Jeri could hear the men long before she reached them. She left the road and made her way through the trees at a cautious pace, slowly placing each foot so that no leaf, twig or rock gave her away. Flickering firelight guided her while loud laughter and raucous talk covered any sound of her approach. They were drinking, most likely slivovic, the strong, homemade plum liquor that was a favorite throughout the country.

The closer she got, the trees became sparser and Jeri went to ground, crawling in order to get even nearer. Several men, maybe ten or twelve, stood or lounged around a metal barrel from which bright flames shot skyward. None wore a real uniform, but most had longish hair and beards and all wore an olive wool cap associated with Serbian irregulars.

They looked like just a bunch of village louts until you took into account the weapons that each one carried. Jeri swore to herself as she recognized up-to-date Kalashnikovs. These men were very well armed for irregulars, evidence of powerful friends in the Yugoslav Federal Army.

Vojna's face, the dead Franjo—Jeri wanted to use her own gun, step out into the open and spray bullets like cleansing water through the arrogant, drunken revelry. She struggled to control her quicksilver temper. She might have been inclined to more sympathy for Serbs than Croatians that very morning, but her sympathies were changing fast. She still believed the fight was more about land grabbing than about the past or some principle of nationhood. These thugs were not only letting themselves be used by the head thug in Belgrade, they were quite willing to be used. In fact, Jeri bet, they were probably having the time of their lives now that someone had called off all the rules.

Jeri eased her grip on the SIG. She could have done it, she'd wanted to shoot someone since the morning when she realized how close she'd come to losing Kelly. Through her own complacency. She was the one who said you have to see the hunters before they get close and she had seen the hunters and ignored them. It was one thing to toss your fate, win or lose, on a roll of the warrior's dice, and another to be stupid. She had been stupid by not paying immediate attention to the Aussies or Canadians or whoever they were.

If Jeri stepped into the clearing with surprise for an ally, she knew she could kill more than one before slipping away. But that would put her back on the road she'd left in Ulster. She didn't think she would be able to meet Kelly's eyes again if she let loose the reins on her temper

Jeri remembered Kelly's eyes and how they had changed as she stared at the dead boy. Disbelief, horror, all the feelings of a stunned soul had played over Kelly's blood-drained features as she confronted the evidence that men could slit the throat of a boy. In that instant, Jeri had wanted more than anything to step between Kelly and knowledge of, let alone the sight of, such an act.

One man by the fire called out to a group standing a bit farther off. Jeri looked in that direction and gave closer attention to two men she had first overlooked. They were replicas of the Hollywood type who had been at the roadblock. The same tight camouflage fatigues, same gym-sculpted physiques, same dark, stylishly long hair.

The coin dropped. She knew who they were—Arkan's Tigers.

Of course she'd heard of them. The Tigers were a Belgrade gang who strutted around like armed roosters, preening and posing, and the combination of arrogance, vanity, cruelty, and guns made them genuinely dangerous. They fancied themselves to be a military unit but their real business was smuggling, providing anything for a price—guns, drugs, women—anything someone was willing to pay for. Arkan, not the leader's real name, had the run of Yugoslav army headquarters in Belgrade, but he was also known throughout the rat holes of Europe's murky criminal underworld.

The Tigers were a type Jeri knew from Southie, her old Boston Irish neighborhood. She'd grown up among guys who were too smart to ever do anything straight. An angle, there always had to be an angle. Her older brother had been like that and he was dead now. Michael Joseph O'Donnell had been as short as Jeri was tall, and he'd learned young to slip in and out of tight spots. He turned this minor talent into cash by running deliveries for the neighborhood drug dealer and hiding guns when cops came around.

When one of the dealer's ripped-off clients came looking for his money back, it was Mickey O'Donnell he shot. Dead or damaged before twenty was a common story on the streets of Southie, and very few home folks had been surprised to learn that Mickey O'Donnell's little sister Jeri had ended up in prison. It was just another Southie story.

Jeri liked to remember Mickey showing up on a sweltering summer day with a bag full of popsicles for his brothers and sisters. She also remembered that the owner of the corner shop never charged Mickey because he was afraid of trouble.

A branch snapped to her right, dispelling her memories, and heavy footsteps shuffled in her direction. Jeri froze. Damn. The person approaching was close enough that any move on her part could alert him to her presence. She leaned deeper into the shadows, so slowly she felt like she was melting.

The footsteps stopped. Suddenly, she heard the unmistakable sound of someone pissing. Luckily, Jeri was out of the man's aim. Her situation was ludicrous, but if there was any humor, Jeri was immune to it. She felt only relief that she was unlikely to be discovered. When the man finished and returned to his companions, Jeri carefully withdrew into the darkness and headed back to where she had left Kelly and the Croatian women.

†

Kelly sat cross-legged on the rocky ground, staring into the dark. She was trying to find a shape to the day's bewildering changes and it was eluding her. Yesterday, she would have said she had encountered death already, would have thought that she had a vantage from which to understand life. As of the end of this day, she realized she knew nothing, nothing at all. She had seen sanitized, hospital death, clean and combed, even leisurely death. She had never known that it was a gift to die in bed, with your affairs put in order, with someone who loved you by your side.

Unbidden, unwelcome, the memory of the night she had been questioned by the British agents in Nepal returned to Kelly's mind. They were looking for an IRA fugitive, Geraldine O'Donnell. *We can show you pictures,* they'd said. And they had. They had set before her pictures of the victims who had died from an IRA bomb. She had told Kelly that it went off prematurely, that it was meant to be called in to the local authorities, but it was still a bomb that Jeri accepted responsibility for setting.

No! Kelly's heart cried out. *No, that's different.*

How different? Was the bomb different? The way the unsuspecting victims had died different? She loved Jeri, that's what was different. But surely there was something more, some absolute difference, not just a difference contingent on her own position in the matter.

George, her heart wailed for her brother. *George, I don't understand.*

Hold on to love, Kell, that's all we can know. Don't ever let go of love.

Kelly could hear the words in her brother's voice, in his tones. It was what he would say. Among other things, love was about forgiveness, the refracting element in which change can become possible. Her hand went to her hidden crystal and she clutched it against the darkness.

Kelly heard a rustling, then a quiet series of thumps from someone tapping on the Yugo.

"Up here," she said and soon she felt Jeri settle beside her. "What did you find?"

"Guys with guns, playing soldier. Drunk. Probably the meanest combination in the world. We're going to have to leave the car and walk if we want to make it back to the coast."

"You really know how to show a girl a good time don't you?"

Jeri's arm went round her and hugged her very tightly.

That night the ground was too hard to make it possible to sustain anything but a light doze. Kelly was wakened countless times, either by her bruises or to brush away insects, and each time she would wonder how sleeping outdoors had acquired such a reputation for being romantic. Then, as she shifted in search of a comfortable position, she would feel Jeri's arm about her tighten and she would meld into the presence of this woman who, even here at the edge of chaos, could bring such immeasurable comfort to her bruised heart.

Chapter Six

Dawn was still a debatable idea when Kelly woke from a fitful dream and decided not to bother trying for more sleep. Jeri was already down the hill at the car, rummaging in the trunk of the Yugo. Jeri's old green canvas knapsack lay on the ground beside Kelly's newer camouflage- patterned pack. Kelly felt hungry but what she really wanted was a cup of that thick Mediterranean coffee from Dubrovnik. She drew a deep breath and let it go. The trip from India had taught her a lot about travel as endurance, Compared to that series of stuffy, dark and cramped spaces, being outside was genuinely comfortable and the lack of coffee only a minor regret.

Less than that, when she considered the company and the situation.

Vojna and her mother were still sleeping under a tree not far from Kelly. Sophija Susik, that was the woman's name, although Kelly would no more call her by her Christian name than she would her own mother. Kelly rose quietly, walked a short distance away so she wouldn't disturb Mrs. Susik and her daughter, and proceeded to go through a series of stretches. She leaned gingerly against a tree trunk and extended, feeling the stretch through her back and along her calves. Her hands were scabbed and tender where they'd been scraped, not completely usable but healing. Her wrists and shoulders were still quite sore.

Kelly walked toward the car and was greeted by a smile as Jeri looked up from her work.

Gods, please don't ever let me get so used to seeing her, that I forget how utterly beautiful she is, and how a smile on her face can pale the dawn.

"How's your leg? We're going to do a lot of walking."

374

"Better than I expected. I scraped it more than I hurt the muscle."

"Good. There won't be much to carry." Jeri gestured toward the things on the ground. "I think we should take any tools, but that's all we'll have that's heavy. We had more in Nepal. I am assuming you're willing to carry that great, heavy book I found for you." This last was delivered with teasing irony and just the hint of an Irish accent.

"Oh, yeah." Kelly knelt beside Jeri to rest her head a moment against the other woman's shoulder. "And I'll count myself lucky if that's all the heavier the history of this country weighs on me."

"Jesus, Kell, that's a big thought for so early. Here, try this." From somewhere in front of her, with the flourish of a magician, Jeri produced a thermos. She twisted open the cap and the heavy aroma of coffee drifted out.

"You're kidding! How did you do this? When?" Kelly's mouth gaped momentarily and then she grabbed the shiny metal container.

"I have many talents."

"Anything else I should know about?"

"Well, I can look at a bingo card and remember all the numbers."

"You're kidding."

"Nope. Used to drive my sister crazy. She'd lose track of her card and I'd call a bingo for her before she could."

"I don't think that's going to be that useful here." Kelly considered as she savored the coffee.

"You never know. Croatia is a Catholic country."

"Okay, maybe. I'll keep my eye out for a church bingo night. Just don't ever lose this talent." Kelly felt the dark brew coursing along her veins, waking up cells as it went.

"Sorry I don't have bacon and eggs."

"This is plenty enough good for me," Kelly said. This was a phrase first used by Kaju, the Nepali Sherpa youth, and it had become a kind of talisman for the two women, a reminder of their history and affection.

When Vojna and Mrs. Susik joined them, Jeri produced bread and cheese and all four women ate sparingly. Jeri explained to Vojna her plans for the day and, although Mrs. Susik took no part in the conversation, Kelly thought that she was listening. The old woman still looked as if she might simply lose air and become no more than a heap of dark clothing.

Jeri drove the Yugo in among a stand of trees before they left. "Insurance," she said. "I have no idea what might be made of the car when it's found. Likely nothing. There are bound to be abandoned vehicles and homes all through the Krajina, but it costs nothing to hide it."

Jeri kept the keys and then rejoined the group, slipping them into the old knapsack.

"Nice hat," Kelly said, looking at the soft-brimmed, green cotton hat that she had suggested Jeri buy in Dubrovnik. Her own hat was a similar style but in one of the new miracle materials for the well-outfitted outdoorswoman.

"Where's the gun?" Now that was something hiking outfits were short on—places to hide guns, stylish holsters, and bullet belts.

"I can get to it if I have to."

†

They walked west through the morning, watchful, careful to keep out of open areas. Jeri went first, followed by Vojna and then Mrs. Susik. Kelly walked last. The events of the day before receded for Kelly and the beauty of the hill country claimed her. A breeze countered the increasing heat, but the green land, full of wildflowers and birdsong, admitted to no wars or rumors of war.

The small group walked under cover of trees most of the time, keeping a wary watch for other travelers. Kelly and Jeri were still in shape from walking through the highlands of Nepal, and Vojna and her mother were countrywomen, used to the outdoors and to hard work. A formation of jets screamed past, flying low from the east and surprising them, but Kelly dismissed any notion that the planes had anything to do with them. After several hours of walking, they came to a clear stream, filled their water bottles and rested. Jeri took the opportunity to talk with Vojna. The girl seemed in better spirits than the day before and her dark bruises, still ugly, had begun to fade to yellow. Even Mrs. Susik seemed to be improving. When they rose to go on after their rest, she spoke for the first time.

"I'm ready," the Croatian woman said.

Kelly glanced at Vojna and caught a look of relief and affection on the girl's face, a look that showed clearly the child's need for her mother. The look disappeared quickly when Mrs. Susik turned away without looking at her.

"I can't believe Mrs. Susik really holds what happened to Vojna against her. Is there anything we can do?" The group had stopped for a longer rest around mid-afternoon and Kelly was feeling heartsick at the way Mrs. Susik ignored her daughter, as if the child did not exist.

"Not yet. Maybe never. It's up to them to get through this. We'll just have to settle for getting them to safety."

They ate most of the bread and cheese. But there hadn't really been enough to make up for the energy spent in walking all day and it would probably be quite a while before they found anywhere to get more food.

The night was another calm, clear night. If the ground was no softer, at least the sky was full of familiar stars. In the morning, they finished the last of the coffee and the food. They walked more slowly now, aware of hunger.

†

Late in the afternoon, the travelers crossed a tree-covered ridge only to be greeted by the acrid smell of burning wood. Jeri led the way as they proceeded cautiously into a shallow valley, using trees for cover. When they reached the edge of the trees, they could see across a wide meadow to the far side where a group of charred buildings still smoldered. Jeri motioned for the others to wait while she went ahead.

The buildings were part of what had recently been a prosperous farm—a house, a barn, several smaller outbuildings, all grouped around an open space. Jeri wondered if Kelly might find the scene reminiscent of her Ohio home, but she was glad that Kelly had stayed behind. As she came closer to the buildings, she could discern other odors mixed with the smell of wood smoke. She hoped that it was only animals left in the barn when it was set on fire. In the open ground between the barn and the house, Jeri saw a burned out car and the bodies of two dogs that had been shot. One of them was a spotted Dalmatian. By the time she reached the house, Jeri had steeled herself against whatever she might find.

She peered through the battered door of what was probably the oldest part of the house. In an earlier century, these stone walls had been the original cottage and the rest of the house had been built out from it. The newer part of the structure had been wood, and the fire had taken that portion of the building entirely. Smoke still rose here and there from fallen beams. Jeri stepped cautiously into the old building into what had been a kitchen. Things were strewn all over and what wasn't broken was severely bent. Holes along the plaster on the upper walls looked as if they came from automatic weapons. The air was so thick that everything appeared to loom and blur through twilight gray.

There seemed little reason to linger, but Jeri took some steps into the room. At the far end, she saw a doorway.

She did not want to go down. The smell was unmistakable. She recognized it from funeral fires in India and Nepal. There was almost no chance anyone could still be alive in the cellar. But there might be. Jeri reminded herself that whatever she found, they could only be people, and surely they deserved one sympathetic witness to their fate. She set her jaw and walked down the sooty stairs.

She was right. No one was left alive.

A noise from the kitchen above drew her back from the underworld. A part of her mind was reading it like that, as an underworld where grim and desperate specters were found. For long seconds her stomach threatened to convulse but she gained control. She did not look back as she stepped into the kitchen. The room now seemed full of light compared to where she had just been but it still took her a few seconds to recognize Mrs. Susik. The older woman saw her and her look was a question.

Jeri shook her head.

"Don't go down. There's no reason."

The older woman nodded.

Jeri found Kelly and Vojna outside in the yard. They were standing near the outside entrance to the cellar where Jeri had just been, where it looked as if a large plank had fallen across the door. Or it had been placed there in order to bar an exit.

"What happened?"

"The people who lived here were burned out." Jeri looked up toward the tree-covered hills above the farm. They needed to leave soon if they were to put distance between this place and wherever they would spend the night.

What kind of people did such things to their own neighbors?

Wrong question. She'd come from Ulster, for Christ's sake, where neighbors made the best of enemies. And before that, Jeri remembered her mother taking her and the younger kids out to shout at the cops and the black kids the cops had been protecting in Boston's busing wars. Her mother and her mother's friends, they never killed anyone, but Jeri would be the last to say they weren't capable of it, weren't capable of throwing stones as easily as words. *But that was different,* said a portion of her mind. *Isn't it always,* answered another. People did such things. Better to ask how you became immune to such hate. Better to ask what ways there might be to make it stop.

"Jeri!"

Kelly was looking at her, eyes full of concern. Jeri knew she had to snap out of it, but she was still struggling to leave behind the horror of the cellar.

"Jeri, what's wrong?"

"Nothing." She got the word out, felt it becoming distantly true. "I'll be okay."

Jeri saw Kelly staring toward the body of the spotted dog. The ability to think of something clever and then to even say it was impossible.

"Let's get out of here. This is no place to be."

Mrs. Susik emerged from the soot-blackened doorway, a burlap sack in her hands. Jeri took one last look around the farm, the farm that once had been the home of a prosperous and, maybe, happy family. She turned away and began walking toward the hills.

Kelly walked beside her in silence for a while. "Jeri, what did you see back there?"

Jeri stopped walking. She must have set quite a pace because Vojna and Mrs. Susik were far behind. She began to shake her head and then didn't. Not talking to Kelly, that was not a practice to start. For the sake of connection, she had to try.

"The family I suppose. I'm not sure how many. They must have gone down to the basement for refuge when the fire started. When the attackers started the fire."

"And they were caught down there?"

"Some were shot. By whoever threw torches in and then blocked the cellar door."

"Oh, dear God, no!"

"Kelly, please, don't ask me anymore."

Kelly started to extend a hand but then didn't.

When Mrs. Susik and Vojna caught up, they walked on. It was Mrs. Susik who called a halt for the day.

"We should cook now, before it gets dark and our fire can be seen." The Croatian woman directed her words to Jeri.

It was the sight of the mother and daughter working together, albeit wordlessly, that helped Jeri get through the evening. Mrs. Susik had salvaged food in her bag, as well as a pan to cook in. Jeri and Kelly collected firewood while Vojna and Mrs. Susik prepared a meal. At first, Jeri was sure she could eat nothing that had come from that house, but as she watched the older woman, whose face looked as if it had been carved from stone into an attitude of eternal endurance, Jeri wrestled with her own mind.

This was not the first time that atrocity had stalked this countryside, not in a land with thousands of years of history as a crossroads between empires and civilizations. Slavs and Illyrians, Rome and Constantinople, Turk and Christian, these were only a few of the groups that had struggled to dominate this area, and none of these had bloodless hands. But history, so vital to an understanding of the region, was in the end irrelevant when it came to understanding how to live. In the end, you aimed to stay alive and to keep those close to you alive. It was a lesson you learned from women. While Jeri was paralyzed by the horror, Mrs. Susik had wakened to the needs of life and she had known what to look for in the burned out house, not evidence of atrocity but food for her own.

The older woman and her daughter worked with the habits ingrained during a life together. But they did not speak. Now and then Vojna let her gaze linger as her mother turned away, a gaze composed of tenderness and pity and horror.

Jeri ate what she was given. She had a task and that was to use whatever skills she could muster to get them all back to the coast.

"Mrs. Susik is a quite a cook." Jeri forced herself to mean her smile. She repeated her compliment to the Croatian woman.

Mrs. Susik nodded. "We did this when I was a girl. We ran from the Chetniks then, too."

"That would be World War Two," Jeri added when she translated for Kelly.

Nature seemed determined to make up for the human horror of the day. The night sky was full of summer stars. Kelly pointed out the constellations she knew as she and Jeri lay side by side.

"George taught me some of the constellations. We'd take our blankets and go to a hill near the creek behind the barn. Our folks let us sleep out there sometimes in summer, as long as we got back in the morning in time for chores. Did you have a place where you could go like that?"

"Yeah, the fire escape." Jeri heard her own bitterness and struggled against it. "The roof sometimes. Mom let us go up to the roof on really hot nights. You had to take a ladder to get up there. It was never really dark. There was always a haze over the city. I don't think I saw real stars until I went to England, but they came as such a surprise that I kept remembering them when I was in prison."

"I forget about that sometimes, that you were in prison."

Jeri smiled wryly in the darkness. "So do I. In that crazy way you forget about something that you never forget. I hated it, of course. I'm a hothead by nature and taking orders goes against everything I understood as a kid. But as a place to learn discipline, you can't beat prison. It was easy to like the Provos there. Nobody else was serious."

"Serious? I'd have thought that prison was one of the most serious places you could be."

"Not really. Most everyone was ridiculous, fighting for lovers, or for status, or for no good reason at all. Most of the women had a single drama that was the only world they lived in. They wanted to be rich, or they were being persecuted. The political women always had a sense of themselves, a sense of purpose. Well, maybe one or two others, but they were surviving on their own."

"You're thinking of someone in particular."

"You're good, you know that? You're really good. You got my mind to switch gears." Despite the day, Jeri smiled in the darkness. "You remember, I've talked about Arkadia O'Malley before."

"She was one of the serious people?"

"Oh, yes. It was as if she wasn't even in prison, but had chosen it like some Irish monks used to choose to be walled into a beehive-shaped rock cell as their spiritual path. Have you ever heard of an *anam cara*?"

"No."

"It's Irish for *soul friend*. It's the term for someone who becomes a spiritual adviser and it's an old term in Irish. So old that I think it may be one more thing that comes from the Druids rather than from Rome and Patrick. Arkadia was *anam cara* to me. Without her, I think I would have lost myself forever."

†

The next morning, Kelly had resigned herself to no coffee or perhaps a possible sniff of the interior of the thermos when the smell of fresh coffee drifted past her closed eyes. Mrs. Susik was up and cooking. Kelly's eyes snapped open and she saw that two small bubbling pots sat at the edge of the fire. Mrs. Susik had mashed coffee beans with rocks and then thrown them into the boiling water. The other pot held something thick and gray that smelled a lot like oatmeal.

Kelly thought of her mother and decided that the Susiks and Corcorans probably had a lot in common as farm families. She was reminded of the stories of European immigrants who populated Willa

Cather's America. Reminders of rural life were even stronger when Mrs. Susik handed her a greasy biscuit kind of thing to eat with the oatmeal. People who worked outside for their livelihood never worried much about cholesterol or calories. Kelly ate what she was given despite the unappetizing appearance. A day of walking would need all the calories she could manage. When she finished, Kelly helped Vojna clean and gather their few belongings.

"Here, I can put that pan with my pack."

Vojna understood the intent if not the words, and nodded shyly. The child seemed a bit easier this morning, as if sleep was helping her gain distance from pain, but her face was still bruised and her eyes were swollen. Kelly had heard the child whimpering during the night.

Kelly pointed out a few wildflowers growing among the raised roots of a tree but after Vojna looked and smiled, she turned away and her face returned to its reflection of sorrow. Mrs. Susik was still not speaking or looking at her daughter.

The group kept to higher ground when possible, now and then finding paths to follow. Once, they saw a line of what was probably a squad of soldiers walking a path lower down and across a valley. The women stopped, hidden by distance, until the soldiers crossed over a ridge, but after that they proceeded even more cautiously. Jeri was particularly watchful, walking point, constantly scanning the land. Now and then, Kelly would take a moment to simply look at Jeri as she strode ahead, and let the sight of the woman fill her with a confidence and affection.

Late the next morning, the travelers began to encounter other refugees. As the four women trudged around the crown of a low hill, they found several people resting in the dusty shade of an apple orchard. The group appeared to be an extended family, perhaps a dozen or so women plus a number of children. The newcomers were watched with no particular interest, and received only a nod here and there. Even Kelly and Jeri attracted little curiosity, although their clothing set them apart from the country folk.

At first, Kelly saw only the group, as if she had stumbled into a very peculiar bus stop, but then her eyes began to register signs of trauma. Faces stared into vistas of private misery. One woman wore house slippers instead of shoes, slippers that were already nearly worn to pieces. Another woman was wrapped in a ragged shawl over a slip. People had left their homes in a terrible hurry, grabbing whatever they could or escaping only in what they had been wearing. A number of faces

Refraction Series

bore signs of bruising. Even the children were oddly quiet.

"Kell, tell me what you think." Jeri had taken out the map and was studying it.

She pointed to a place that Kelly found meaningless except that the sea seemed not too far away. The map lacked features, designed for drivers, not hikers or refugees. "I'm not sure. I think we must be about here."

"You're probably right. We've been on a general down slope despite all the hills. You can tell by how much hotter it is." Kelly compared what she remembered of the past days with the minimal features of the map.

Jeri refolded the map.

Vojna plucked Kelly's sleeve and gestured for her to follow. Kelly nodded to Jeri and went after the girl. Vojna ran ahead, and then stopped beneath a smallish tree.

"*Alica*," she said, pointing upward.

Vojna had brought her to a cherry tree. To Kelly's eye the bright red fruit didn't look ripe, but gingerly, at Vojna's urging, Kelly sampled a cherry. A little dry, but the taste was sweet and flavorful. Vojna gestured for Kelly to take off her hat and they both picked until it was full of cherries.

Jeri was waiting near Mrs. Susik when they returned with the fruit. Kelly held out her hat. "*Try some of my purple berries.*" The color might be off, but the line from "Wooden Ships" seemed appropriate. "*Probably keep us all alive.*" Odd to think that a song, about an apocalypse, had become appropriate.

Mrs. Susik took some, murmuring words that probably meant thank you.

"Is *alica* the word for cherry?" Kelly asked.

Before Jeri could answer, Mrs. Susik broke into what was, for her, a long discussion. Hearing her say more than a few words was so unusual that both Americans waited until they were sure she was finished before Jeri translated for Kelly.

"She says that the frost was heavy this year and ruined most of the cherry crop. She says at home they have many cherry trees and make *rakija,* a kind of brandy, but this year they have only this kind, the alica cherry, which is okay but not to her mind the best."

Kelly nodded, pleased by the ordinariness of Mrs. Susik's small discourse on cherries. So it had begun for her, the process of memory healing grief, a process that was like someone entering a destroyed home and retrieving items of value, items to be kept and cherished. Perhaps

383

soon, she could find a way to retrieve her daughter again.

†

"Excuse me." The words were in heavily accented but passable English.

Jeri turned to see a woman wearing a black dress and a headscarf. She was not young but her age was obscured by the dark purple bruising that blurred her features. She looked no different from the other refugee women. Then she removed the scarf and her pale blond hair with streaks of gray was so short that it contradicted the rest of her traditional appearance.

"I'm Dr. Djindjivik." The woman repeated her name slowly. "Jin-ji-vik." She attempted a smile, but her lips were swollen and split. "I heard you speaking. Are you Americans?"

Jeri nodded.

Dr. Djindjivik held out her hand. "I went to medical school in Massachusetts. I used to be a good non-aligned citizen, you know, alert to any hint of neo-colonialism, but I would like nothing more than to see an American tank coming over that hill. Intervention begins to sound like a sweet word. You didn't, by any chance, just come from the Mother of all battles in Iraq, bringing with you some of George Bush's tanks?"

"Sorry, it's just us. But I am starting to be tempted to change my own attitude about intervention."

"So why are you here without any tanks?"

"We were taking the short way to Vukovar." Jeri liked the wry doctor immediately. She went on to give a brief description of how they had found the Susiks.

"Since we are all going the same way, I look forward to a long talk with you this evening." Dr. Djindjivik nodded to Jeri and Kelly and greeted Mrs. Susik. Then the doctor went to Vojna and spoke a few moments before rejoining her own group.

When the other refugees rose to leave, Vojna and Mrs. Susik, then Jeri and Kelly followed. Kelly amended her previous image. The orchard wasn't a bus stop, it was the land squeezing out drops of misery that were joining to become a trickle flowing toward the sea.

The group walked through the afternoon, becoming larger by ones and twos. Jeri worried that they were also becoming a larger target but she was unwilling to look for a separate way. These people went slowly but there was no hesitation regarding direction. They knew where they were going. Toward evening, the refugees took shelter on a rocky hillside. A number of small cook fires were hastily lit, but as the light slipped out of the day, the fires were extinguished. This was a group that had grown wise to the needs of survival.

True to her word, Dr. Djindjivik came to visit as the twilight lengthened. She spoke a long time with Vojna before joining Jeri and Kelly. The child only nodded while looking down at first, but then she spoke a few words and let the doctor touch her in an easily read gesture of reassurance.

"Rape has become as much a Chetnik weapon as a rifle." The Croatian doctor seated herself near the two Americans. "You probably wonder why an educated woman is dressed like this. My nurse gave it to me when we realized the Chetniks had come and were shooting all the educated people in our town. They came to my clinic and I would be dead if my nurse hadn't thought to find an old dress that a woman left behind when she'd been taken to hospital some months before. She should have taken it herself. They cut her throat after they beat my husband to death. Did you know that there's a Serbian word for beating with a rifle butt? *Kundaciti*. This from a people who never tire of telling you how they are so civilized, that they had the first forks in Europe. Who would know such a word would be necessary? Me, I was only raped."

The compulsive length at which she spoke belied the doctor's intended irony. Jeri judged that perhaps she and Kelly were the first people who appeared to the doctor as witnesses to her plight, more than as fellow sufferers.

Dr. Djindjivik apologized. "Please, forgive me. I talk too much. What are you doing here?"

"We just got caught behind the lines, so to speak. Please go on talking. It's so hard to understand what's happening here. Jeri knows your language but I'm afraid I only have English."

Dr. Djindjivik nodded. She acknowledged Kelly's lifeline even as she took it.

"Understand what's happening here? I wish I did. I used to be so proud to be a Yugoslavian. I felt like Tito, at last, made us a country. Brotherhood and unity, the old communist partisan slogan of World War Two. And he made us free of both the West and the Russians. He was harsh, a dictator, but I'm a doctor and I can appreciate harsh measures in the service of health. Even after he died, it seemed everything might still work. Until Slobodan Milosevic went to Kosovo."

"Yes. I have a friend who told me about that." Jeri explained Rafi's theory briefly.

"Many causes make an event possible, but if one man bears the most responsibility, it is Slobodan Milosevic of Serbia. It is Milosevic who keeps telling the Serbs that they are in danger, even as he keeps giving them a bigger and bigger stick with which to beat everyone else. That's what he said to the Serbs in Kosovo at a rally that day—'no one should dare to beat you'—and that was the end of Yugoslavia. After that, there were Serbs and Croats again, Kosovars and Slovenes and Bosnians. Milosevic was only a party hack until that day, but then he rode all the way to the top by making the Serbs think he was the one who would speak for them. We could have all been Yugoslavians, but instead, he wishes to make Serboslavians and so the rest of us have to be driven out."

Dr. Djindjivik's version of recent history supported Rafi's, but Jeri suspected the woman was focusing on history to see past her own part in the tragedy.

"Who was it that murdered people in your town?"

Dr. Djindjivik's face twisted in remembered pain. "Chetniks. The leaders were mostly hoodlums, longhaired hoodlums. Young, cold, vicious."

"Arkan's Tigers."

"So. You know this man, this Arkan?" Dr. Djindjivik's voice came out in a hiss.

"Yes. He has a reputation. I almost met him several years ago when he was just another thug in Belgrade."

Dr. Djindjivik raised an eyebrow, but Jeri shook her head with a grim smile.

"Another life, Doctor. Please continue."

"These men started it, but the Yugoslav army was there and didn't stop them. They stood by and watched. And the Serb people of the town, they disappeared. Some of the Chetniks were from the next town. I know because I was the doctor to their wives and children. It wasn't hoodlums from Belgrade who raped me, but men from the next town. I must remember that I am lucky they were drunk and no one recognized me."

The women were silent. They could hear the murmur of other voices in the darkness. Someone not far away was weeping and trying to do it quietly. Jeri was surprised at how unsurprising the sound of weeping in the night had become.

"Let me tell you a story. It is a story I keep telling myself. My father was Croatian, but he was no Ustasha, no ally of the Nazis. He fought with the partisans."

Didn't they all? Jeri thought sourly, but she kept the thought to herself.

"When he came home to our village, which is by the Bosnian border, the people assumed he had been a German ally and they beat him up and arrested him. My mother was Muslim and she got word to my father's old commander, a friend of Tito himself, and the commander came in person to our town and made them release my father."

Jeri amended her thought. Probably, the doctor's father had fought with Tito. She shouldn't be so quick to judge the people of this country.

"So that was our town, a mix of Serbs and Croatians and Muslims. During the war someone had destroyed the mosque. They just blew it up. After the war, the government had no favorites, they suppressed all the religions. But we wanted our mosque, and so, stone by stone, the people started building it again. Everyone helped. Croatians carried stones, Serbs left money in a little box at the entrance. And on the weekends, everyone came and helped with the building. When it was done, the entire village had a celebration, and everyone got drunk, although the Muslims didn't drink in public, but went off to the edge of the village with their friends. This is where I come from. This was the country I had."

From below and far off came the sound of thuds. A startling sound.

Guns, Jeri thought, *large guns*.

"But if the people were so close, what happened? How can they start killing one another?" Kelly asked the question but Jeri had been thinking it.

"If you find out, be sure to let me know. All I know is that when it happens, it happens quickly. Like a divorce. Everything comes apart very fast and all the love disappears."

They talked a while longer and then Dr. Djindjivik bid them a good night and went to rejoin her own group.

"Jeri, what did Dr. Djindjivik mean about the forks?"

"Oh, there's this story the Serbians like to tell about how some king came to Belgrade, from Italy I think, and was given golden forks as a gift but didn't know how to use them. It's meant to show that Serbia was civilized long before the rest of Europe. Being civilized, that's a big concern here."

†

"Plenty enough good for you?" Kelly looked up from Mrs. Susik's morning biscuit to see Jeri's wry smile.

Kelly appreciated the attempt at humor, but found it hard to do more than nod. She had not slept well, troubled by dreams too disjointed to remember, other than that they were full of conflict. She wiped her hands on the grass. The biscuit lacked much flavor but even the ground bits of bean in the coffee felt like nourishment. Kelly looked around to find Mrs. Susik talking to another refugee woman. The two seemed to be discussing something about cooking. Yet another step toward rejoining the world.

"Good morning." Dr. Djindjivik greeted them all and then spoke briefly to Vojna. The doctor took the girl a short way and then introduced her to another girl her age. The two nodded shyly. As the group began to move, the girls walked along side by side.

In the afternoon, the refugees reached a dirt road and joined a straggle of others who were heading west. There were some men in this group, most of them elderly. A creaking, two-wheeled cart, pulled by a weary donkey and driven by a grim-faced teen-aged boy, held an old woman and a child. Behind it came a modern tractor. A century or two had been wrenched indiscriminately out of the countryside and tossed onto the road to the sea.

Jeri left to talk to the new people and came back to tell Kelly what she'd learned.

"We're on the road to Split. It seems that we're probably out of the fighting area now. The Krajina Serbs aren't interested in trying to take this area, or at least that's what the guy I was talking to thinks. He could be wrong."

A surprising wash of relief flooded over Kelly. It was a measure of just how frightened she'd become since they first found Mrs. Susik and her daughter. Her conscious mind might cling to the illusion that she was an American and somehow immune, not really part of what was happening around her, but another part knew that if the people who were committing the atrocities found them, she wouldn't be asked for her passport. She took a deep, deep breath.

"How far are we from Split?" she asked.

Jeri didn't answer. Her head was to the side, listening. It was as if someone had frozen the scene. Other people had stopped moving and, like Jeri, were listening.

Then Kelly heard it, too, first the whine and then the sound of people suddenly aware of the danger. Then cries of panic drowned in the rising rumble of approaching planes. Images from old movies, of World War Two planes strafing running people, leapt out of Kelly's memory. Now, she could see several jets as the rumble became the scream of a dive.

Kelly started to run but Jeri grabbed her and pulled her down onto the gravel at the side of the road.

The planes didn't fire, but terror flashed through the refugees as the jets thundered by, passing overhead so closely that someone might have reached up and touched them if everyone wasn't already lying flat, trying to melt into the hot dust of the road.

One after another, again and again, the jets dived, whipped low over the column, creating a roar and a concussive whump of air before rising to circle and dive again. It wasn't clear that the planes were simply diving and not firing. Kelly lay flat on the dirt. Her hands over her ears did nothing to keep out a noise that surrounded her like the air itself. She was barely aware of Jeri's protective arm thrown over her. Then through the noise and the fear came another sound, the occasional, deeper thud.

"Vojna! No!" Jeri's cry disappeared into the roar of the planes.

Kelly heard it and raised her head. The noise of the passing jets seemed to shake the very air as Kelly saw Vojna running away from the road and into the field with several other refugees. She saw it, but it simply made no sense, as if some connection between her eyes and her brain had broken. It made even less sense as Kelly saw Vojna float up into the air just before she heard another of the odd thumps.

Then it became so quiet that all one could hear was one's own heart shuddering. The fading whine of the jets was Kelly's only indication that she had not gone deaf. Vojna lay out in the field, and so did two others who had run from the road.

At first, the crying child sounded so normal that it seemed a signal that the episode was over, until it became evident that the child was near one of the silent figures lying in the field.

"Land mines. Stay here, Kell. Keep Mrs. Susik here."

†

Jeri took several quick steps off the road and then paused to assess her next moves. She could see where some of the runners had stepped, marks that promised more or less safety if she just walked the same route. Not entirely. They might have simply stepped over a firing mechanism that was now waiting patiently for something else to trip it, a mechanism that could wait patiently for minutes or years.

Jeri forced herself to focus down, to ignore the need to run to the crying child. She lowered herself to her hands and knees. There. She saw the green tripping mechanism of a mine as it protruded an inch or so above the ground. She looked around and selected a stone, and then ripped the sleeve from her shirt. Again she ripped until she had a strip of pale cloth to tie onto the stone. She knelt down and placed the stone with its flag. Not much of a marker, but maybe enough to warn off the next person. As she crept along on hands and knees, Jeri saw an old branch, dry and brittle, and she took it with her. She could tie pieces of her sleeve to small sticks from the branch.

She swore aloud as she passed the first person killed by an exploding mine. Christ almighty, the kid had been hit by the kind that flew up and radiated shrapnel, a mine meant to kill, not just maim. To judge from the last trip mechanism she'd marked, the field was planted with a variety of mines, from anti-personnel to anti-tank. Maybe some bloody-minded officer had said, *Get me mines,* and the ordnance sergeant had replied, *Try these, sir, and see which you prefer.*

As she passed Vojna, Jeri wanted to just sit back and cry.

What had it all been for? She and Kelly might as well have just kept driving that day for all the good they'd done. She hadn't protected Vojna at all. What had been the point? So she could see again what it looked like when a person she knew died? Christ, she'd never expected the bomb to go off as the bus full of people passed the car. They always called in warnings. No one was supposed to have been killed by the bomb. Is that what the soldier thought who planted the land mines? They're not meant to hurt anyone, just to scare people

Maybe if she just got up and started walking, this whole cycle of agony would end. It would be fitting to go in an explosion. Just stand up and walk. It would be all over, and it would be finished for her. She'd get what she deserved. Kelly could go home and have a normal life. The world could get on with its perverse and bloody absurdities, and she could quit having to know about it.

Don't be ridiculous, said a voice in her head. *This isn't about you, it's about that child out there.* The voice was familiar. Kelly had evoked the woman with the grim mouth and the sharp eyes that day at the burned out farm. In truth, she was never far from Jeri's conscious mind, but she seemed particularly present these days in the midst of this morally complicated chaos.

Don't be ridiculous. Arkadia O'Malley would never have said that to Jeri, but more than anything, Jeri never wanted that woman to think she was ridiculous.

Jeri sighted along the ground. She saw another tripping mechanism and she marked it carefully, moved on.

"It's a terrible error of the age," Arkadia O'Malley had once said. "A terrible error to think that we're each separate and single. Individualism denies the links we have to one another, the connections of our souls and the needs of our hearts. We belong to one another, so don't ever be so absurd as to think that what you do is nobody else's business."

Jeri heard the words in accented Irish English. A prisoner who had learned how to be truly free, the woman with steel gray hair and the piercing eyes of a hawk had awakened Jeri to remembering that she had a soul.

A bird chirped, a piece of life returning to the broken landscape. Jeri's hand, moving lightly at ground level, encountered a tripping mechanism that was almost completely covered by dirt. Jesus, she could have missed that one so easily.

She marked it and moved on. She owed Rafi. She had made promises to Kelly. She knew now for certain that Rafi's sister Alenka would need her. If she died here due to carelessness, it would be an act of despair, surrender, and she would not surrender yet.

Jeri reached the child, a girl of two or three. Her mother lay crumpled a few feet away. The child seemed to be in shock, her sobs monotonous and repetitive, but there was no sign of any wounds. Carefully, Jeri sat back and drew the youngster into her lap, soothing her with nonsense sounds and gentle petting. The sobs didn't cease, but they grew a little quieter. Most likely, the explosion had terrified the child, maybe even temporarily deafened her. Jeri sighted her route back and then stood. She'd marked safe steps with shallow indentations as she crawled out. Now she walked back, carrying the child, following her own marked path.

It was if everyone on the road released a collective sigh when Jeri reached safety. Without thinking about it, Jeri handed the child to Mrs. Susik. Then she turned to Kelly and received an embrace so strong she thought she might have bruised ribs before it was over.

"Oh, Jeri. Oh, baby. I was so scared. Oh, thank you for coming back. I couldn't bear losing you. Not now. Not ever."

"The child seems to be well enough. Are any of the people out there still alive?" It was Dr. Djindjivik.

"No. I'm quite sure."

"You are a very brave woman."

Jeri looked at the doctor. She saw a face marked by fatigue, concern, and the bruises that were fading toward yellow. "I think that bravery has become more common than bread these days." She took the woman's outstretched hand and held it for a long moment.

Most of the refugees moved on, but a small group stayed behind to recover the bodies and bury them. There was an old priest among those who remained, so this time Mrs. Susik had the comfort of religion when her child was placed in the ground. This time the woman wept, long and loud, and although Kelly stayed beside her, she could not help wishing that Mrs. Susik had been able to show some of this feeling to Vojna while her daughter was alive. But undoubtedly that was part of the woman's grief. Undoubtedly she understood that with her two children dead, she could no longer show any of the love that she would never stop feeling.

After the three young Croatians were buried, and those who had stayed behind prepared to move on, Kelly saw Mrs. Susik begin to move back to her own people. The woman still looked to her and to Jeri but there was a motion, as sure as gravity, back to the folk who knew her needs, understood her feelings, shared her rhythms. The doctor had also left the child in Mrs. Susik's care while others searched for relatives of the youngster.

A tractor, pulling a flatbed, rolled by. Its pace was scarcely faster than a walk, but when the driver indicated that they should ride, Kelly helped Jeri get Mrs. Susik aboard and then climbed on gratefully as the people already riding made room.

Chapter Seven

"If I tell you who owns this apartment, I'll have to kill you."

It wasn't much of a joke, but Kelly smiled anyway. She was willing to just enjoy the small Zagreb flat without giving too much thought to the real owner.

"I suppose you're off to get a Yugo. You should just get a six pack."

"Tomorrow. Don't worry. You may not believe this but the CIA's been paying for the Yugos." Jeri was lounging in a worn, thickly upholstered chair.

"You're kidding! How? Wait, don't tell me, I'll be safer that way."

"Back when the country was happily communist and the world was nicely divided between democracy and the evil empire, some folks here were a kind of loose-knit opposition. Actually, they were coffee-drinking, I'll-speak-my-mind-because-I'm-really-a-poet student types, but some smart noodle in Washington thought they'd look good on paper and sound good at meetings as 'our resistance group in Zagreb.' One thing led to another and the folks here got on the CIA cash roll and nobody has ever thought to take them off. Hence, one consequence is that we get very cheap Yugos."

Kelly glanced around the small room. She really was nervous. She mimed being listened to by some bug, but Jeri just laughed.

"I honestly doubt it. Not with everything else that's going on these days. Besides, the CIA gets Yugos cheap because Lawrence Eagleburger used to be on the board or something before he went to the State Department as an expert on this region. Hell, he might still be on the Yugo board for all I know."

"What are you talking about? Who has a name like that?"

"Eagleburger? He's just a big guy at work in your old-fashioned military-industrial complex. It gets even cuter when you remember that Yugo manufactures arms, too. They now mostly manufacture arms for

Serbia. Eagleburger's real pro-Serbia."

"I can't remember it because I never knew it. You're the spook expert." Kelly thought a moment, trying to arrange all the information, and then gave up. "I don't even want to know about it. Don't tell me about any more conspiracies until after I get a really good bath. Actually a really good shower, with really cold water."

"You take your bath and I'll see if I can call Alenka." Jeri stretched and slid even lower into the comfort of the chair. She looked as if she might forget about moving for days.

Kelly stared at Jeri. The possibility of using a telephone had never occurred to her. Parts of the past hundred years seemed to have dropped out of her awareness, leaving her with a sense of reality, like a puzzle with missing pieces. Of course there were still telephones. She looked around the room and, for the first time, the television set registered in her awareness as a piece of technology, a household appliance, something more than furniture with a doily and a china vase on top. Gingerly, as if she were from another age, one that might consider such things the work of demons or gods, she approached the set and touched, but did not turn, the dial. She glanced back to see Jeri watching her with a fond and amused smile.

"Yes, Virginia, this is still the age of television."

"I think I'll wait until after my shower. Unless you want to go first?"

Jeri shook her head.

It was a real shower with cool water, and the soap bar had an old fashioned lavender smell. As Kelly worked to get a thick bubbly lather, she noted that she had few bruises left to remind her of the near fatal fall in Dubrovnik. The whole episode seemed so long ago, diminished by the events that had followed in the Krajina.

Kelly stood beneath the rushing water, her eyes closed, wishing the moment could last forever. They had left Mrs. Susik in a coastal town, with other refugees, with her own people. The older woman had taken on the care of the child. Kelly had feared Mrs. Susik would fall back into the shock that had gripped her when she and Jeri first saw her on the hillside, but instead, Mrs. Susik had struggled to be a comfort to the youngster who was as alone as the old woman among the other refugees, every one of them with a heart-wrenching tale of loss.

Maybe they would adopt one another. Kelly recognized the thought for the pretty thing it was, a wispy hope that she and Jeri had accomplished something of lasting value, that their entry into Mrs.

Susik's life had brought some good. The events of the past few days suggested the notion was simply self-delusion. If you waited for time to give value to actions, you were likely to be gravely disappointed. Today could rip the heart out of every last one of yesterday's hopes. She and Jeri had only arrived to witness one station in Mrs. Susik's journey of suffering and then accompany her to the next.

Maybe that was about all you ever got to do.

†

Jeri was thinking that not everyone lived in a war zone. Much of her own mind was a war zone. The rushing water from the shower sounded as soothing as peace. Kelly's mind wasn't like hers. Not yet. But it would be if she continued to accompany Jeri along roads taking them through the shadowed valleys of history. Jeri had to think of a way out, find a place where they might live in some degree of safety, where maybe even Jeri could find a bit of peace.

Rafi would help. He'd know something she might do that would keep Kelly out of danger. He wouldn't be able to stop the SAS, the British Special Air Service. They would be relentless in hunting her and they wouldn't put too fine a point on not harming Kelly. Rafi thought the Brits had lost track of her in Nepal, and wouldn't think of looking in Yugoslavia, but he hadn't realized just how close to war his homeland had drifted. She and Rafi had both lost sight of how this was a part of the world where misery always waited in the wings, waited to take center stage and savage people's hopes and dreams.

Jeri looked at the telephone. She would call Alenka. She and Kelly would go to Vukovar and then take Alenka to Sarajevo. It was a beautiful city in a beautiful land. Maybe in Bosnia, Jeri and Kelly could find somewhere calm, someplace safe.

†

Later, long enough to have washed away at least the dust of Dalmatia if not the memories, Kelly emerged from the bathroom in a borrowed robe with tan stripes. She found Jeri staring bemused into some space in the middle of the room.

"She called me Auntie Stella. Alenka called me Auntie Stella, and said she'd been expecting me to call. She doesn't want to leave home. She has a boyfriend. I told her we'd discuss it when we get there."

395

Kelly stared at Jeri a moment. She was almost used to the yo-yo ride between the bizarre and the banal that characterized life in Croatia. Fully aware of all the irony and incongruity involved, she drawled, "Honey, I don't feel like going out. How about we just stay in and watch TV tonight?"

"Plenty enough good for me."

There wasn't much to watch. One channel showed a line of women with candles and rosaries marching for peace around the Yugoslavian Federal Army headquarters somewhere in Zagreb. Another ran a music video showing soldiers running in slow motion, like a stylish modern dance, to the Dire Straits' song, "Brothers in Arms." They settled on an episode of *Bonanza* that neither remembered having seen.

†

The sweet scent of lilacs and linden trees was fading like the grace of heaven from the streets of Zagreb to be replaced by a humid heat the next morning. Jeri drove into the heart of the city, along impressive boulevards punctuated by green parks. Dubrovnik had been a gem, cut and polished, but Zagreb was old stone, hewn and dressed, a working city. The heavy baroque buildings were Central European echoes of Old Vienna and the Austro-Hungarian Empire.

They parked near the university and discovered that Zagreb was also a city preparing for war. Sandbags had been heaped in front of shop windows to protect them from aerial bombing. Helicopters buzzed ominously overhead like angry wasps from a disturbed nest while, on the ground, people hurried about their business wearing a range of disbelieving expressions.

The television had informed them that, in accord with some pressure from the European Community, Croatia and Slovenia were going to wait before going ahead with their plans for independence. This was supposed to stop any further conflict, but even those people who hadn't spent the last few days hiking through the Krajina, where war was no longer a rumor, believed the accord was no more than just words.

Jeri was too preoccupied to play the tour guide, but she managed a comment here and there.

"They used to say that Belgrade was the heart of Yugoslavia, and Zagreb was its brain, but don't let that fool you. It's a working city, even if it does have a great university. And did you know the two capitals are connected by the Highway of Brotherhood and Unity."

"Does the irony ever end here?"

"Honey, you ain't seen nothing yet. I've got a big surprise for you."

The two women emerged from a side street into a large open market. War and rumors of war hadn't stopped the country folk from bringing in their fruits and vegetables to the city. Vendors had the sharp expressions inspired everywhere by the exercise of commerce, and once again Kelly was reminded of Ohio. The faces around her looked like any she might have seen gathering for early Mass on Sunday mornings. A helicopter whined overhead and Kelly looked up to see it disappear behind the massive spires of a cathedral.

"St. Stepan's." Jeri followed the direction of Kelly's gaze.

"Think they have a bingo night there? You could make us some spare change."

"Are you making fun of my special skills?"

They wound their way among tables of tomatoes and cherries, but Kelly began to wonder if Jeri's circular route might be about more than shopping.

"Are you worried someone's following us?" Jeri had stopped at a stall with a collection of sunglasses.

"A little. I had an odd feeling when I picked up the apartment keys yesterday, but I was careful driving back." Jeri tried on a pair and tilted her head, turned from side to side.

"I just want to make sure. What do you think?"

"I think these look better. But to be honest, I haven't seen anything yet that didn't look great on you."

"You wouldn't be just a little biased?"

"Now, you're fishing. You know you're stunning." Kelly's face crinkled into a broad grin.

"Thanks. You're not half bad yourself."

"That's all I get? 'Not half bad'?"

Jeri bought the glasses that Kelly had suggested and they moved on through the market to the accompaniment of more banter. Jeri appeared to drift, but their steps were bringing them closer and closer to the edge of the market. At a stall featuring melons, Jeri took hold of Kelly's arm and guided her quickly between two tables. In seconds they were out of the crowded square. Jeri led the way through a twisting series of alleyways and emerged into another large square in front of a massive building.

"The presidential palace." Jeri indicated the impressive structure on the far side. "It's not an unusual place for people to gather—you're about to see why—and I want to check out a couple things. If I give the word, we're going to leave by that alley to your right."

Kelly glanced toward the alley and saw a gray cat idly licking a paw until it seemed to feel her gaze. Forgetting that it still had its tongue hanging out, a look that would be ridiculous on any lesser animal, the cat stared back at Kelly.

"Watch this," Jeri said as she nudged Kelly and nodded toward the large building. "It's the changing of the presidential guard, dreamed up by some lunatic choreographer at the national theater."

A squad of drums and trumpets suddenly emerged, tootling and thumping and looking dignified only by contrast to the tin soldiers who followed. It was all so absurd, so utterly disconnected with the events of the Krajina, with the helicopters buzzing overhead, that Kelly stared, gape-mouthed. This was a cartoon version of martial behavior. The musicians were followed by a troop of guards in black pants and red tunics with gold frogging, complete with white gloves. They stomped and wheeled, directed by officers in cream tunics with black capes.

Billy would have been delighted. Kelly could almost hear his queenly quips delivered in the studied disdain that was always at odds with the young-boy look he so cultivated. She hadn't really appreciated his ability to read the world's absurdity until he came to help her care for George. Then she understood that what she had taken for lack of seriousness, was how he could stay engaged with a world that had become appalling. He would have so loved this march of the tin soldiers. For a few seconds, Kelly imagined that she was sharing the scene with Billy, George and Russell.

"See their neckties?" Jeri asked.

"The cravats?" They were one more piece of sartorial flourish begging for an Oscar Wilde comment.

"Exactly. *Cravat* because Croats invented it."

The Guard wheeled about and lined up to present their old-fashioned rifles, although from what Jeri said about the state of Croatian armaments, these guns might be about as good as it got. Jeri's attention was on the small crowd.

"Do you see anyone?"

"No. But you can be sure there are reporters, covert and overt spies, violence junkies and all the other scavengers who smell blood on the wind. Come on, Kell, let's get out of here."

"Is something wrong? Did you see someone?" Kelly asked as they slipped down the alley. The cat had disappeared.

"No. Sorry. It just didn't seem funny anymore."

"Sure, but not everything can be as good as watching *Bonanza* in Serbo-Croatian."

They wound their way through a series of narrow streets and alleys until they came to a small cafe with a handful of tables outside.

Kelly picked a table but when Jeri didn't sit, she sighed. "You're going to leave me here again, aren't you? Oh, well, if you get another Yugo, I wouldn't mind a green one this time."

Kelly watched Jeri walk away and then thanked the waiter who brought a cup of coffee on a saucer along with a small pitcher of cream. Real cream. Even in the shade it was desperately hot. She sipped the coffee and looked around. Nearby an elderly gentleman was reading a paper and, at another table, a group of young people who looked like students were carrying on a heated discussion that could only be political.

Kelly opened her pack and took out Black Lamb Grey Falcon, looking for a section about Zagreb. She found one. Zagreb, she read, was full of those vast toast-colored buildings, barracks and law courts and municipal offices, which are an invariable sign of past occupancy by the Austro-Hungarian Empire.

That was West, the reporter. She read on and came to West the poet.

Zagreb makes from its featureless handsomeness something that pleases like a Schubert song, a delight that begins quietly and never definitely ends.

Kelly found a description of the market where she and Jeri had just been.

"Lady."

Kelly emerged from Rebecca West's memories to see a tow-headed youngster, somewhere between ten and twelve, standing near the table.

"Lady, tall lady say you come."

Kelly frowned. She looked around. A few people were walking along the street. The elderly gentleman and his paper were gone, but the students were still arguing. No one appeared to be paying her any attention.

"Tall lady say you come."

"Where?"

The child shook his head. He didn't seem to understand her or have anything more to say. The phrase might be his only English.

Kelly didn't believe him. Jeri would have sent a different message, she was sure. She looked over at the table full of young people but no one was looking her way. She glanced toward the cafe entrance, but the waiter was nowhere to be seen.

"No. I don't understand."

"Tall lady say you come."

"I don't understand."

He didn't seem that disappointed. He stared a few more seconds and then trotted off up the street. Kelly watched him, but his direction gave her no information. The street was empty of pedestrians. Kelly's mind was working furiously. Somebody had sent the boy. Somebody was watching her. She slipped the book into her backpack. She thought she knew the way back to the apartment, but that seemed like the last place she should go.

Clutching her backpack, she walked decisively toward the table with the student types.

"Excuse me, do any of you speak English?"

Several faces turned toward her, one or two with welcoming, if quizzical, smiles.

Someone fell into her, knocking her off balance and then grabbing her to keep her from falling. Kelly felt hands like iron vises gripping both arms just above her elbows even as she heard the apology in English that was completely at odds with how she was being held. She let her backpack fall into the lap nearest her.

"Sorry. Steady there. Are you okay?" The words were reassuring and friendly but just above a whisper Kelly heard the hiss of the real message. "Make any kind of a fuss and you're a dead woman, right here and right now."

†

Jeri drove past the café, looking for Kelly. She drove around a corner, parked, and then, warily, proceeded back on foot. She saw nothing out of the ordinary, just a middle-aged couple at one table and a young man at another. The street was clear in either direction. There was nothing at the table where she had left Kelly to indicate anyone had ever been there, not even an empty coffee cup.

Kelly would not have just left. She knew Jeri was coming back and that her absence would be alarming.

Jeri gazed around the café again and stopped at the table with the young man. Her stomach lurched. On the table in front of him was Kelly's camouflage-patterned daypack, the one where she kept her books. Jeri would recognize it anywhere.

Clever boy. He'd set it there for a signal. Jeri sauntered past the youth, a dark-haired, narrow-faced boy. He saw her. She kept going and he followed, carrying the pack. A short way up the street, Jeri waited for him.

"I saw you together earlier. You left and your friend stayed." He handed her Kelly's pack.

"What happened?"

"She asked us if anyone spoke English and just then a tall man bumped into her. Tall, but also big. She dropped the pack into my lap. I was going to give it back but she shook her head and then I saw another man, not as tall, grab hold of her. I was sure she dropped it on purpose. This used to happen sometimes when I was young, not a lot but we knew not to interfere. They took her to a big, blue Jeep, which is not all that common here in Zagreb. I'm sorry I couldn't help."

Jeri swore. In Serbo-Croatian. The youth looked alarmed and impressed.

"You did okay. You might have both got hurt. At least now I know what happened. I can't thank you enough for waiting for me."

Jeri meant to be reassuring but she was frantic. *Not half-bad. Oh, Kelly, I'm sorry.*

Ten minutes later she was making a phone call. "Jovan? Shamrock. Who could do a body grab in daylight, using a Yankee Jeep? Jesus! Do you know where they'd go? Well, then, do you know if they'd leave the country? At least that's good news. Look, here's what I need—find out who's the head spook on the ground here, for the Brits."

†

Kelly was finding breathing difficult. A heavy cloth hood had been slipped over her head and she could feel perspiration getting salt in her eyes. Being forced to lie on her stomach between the front and rear seats with a heavy foot on her back while the vehicle bounced and swerved added to her discomfort. She was unable to concentrate on much more than breathing, but she tried to keep track of direction, to gain some sort of idea of where they were going. Once or twice there was a shift in gravity and in gears to indicate going up a hill and then down but that was all. After a while, Kelly wasn't too sure that she might not have passed out.

The vehicle finally stopped. With the minimum of fuss, she was pushed and pulled from the car, but the hood was left on. She bent her head forward so she could see down. Not much. A bit of cobblestone. Air though. Breathing was easier. The sweet scent from a linden tree? No sounds. A shift in the ground from cobblestones to flagstones. The sound of a door, a heavy door, scraping a floor. Inside it was cool, not air-conditioned cool but large-roomed old-building cool. Pushed down a corridor of dark, much-scuffed wood, then down steps with someone holding an arm so she didn't fall. She did stumble. Through another door. Someone put a metal handcuff on one wrist and attached it to her other behind her back. Then she heard the door slam and lock.

Assholes. They'd left the hood on for spite. They knew she could get out of it, but they'd just left it on. She managed to shake it off. Maybe that was a good sign. They didn't want her to recognize them because then they'd have to kill her. The thought was far from reassuring.

Even without the hood, there wasn't much light. What little there was filtered through a narrow, boarded up window about five feet long and situated ten feet above a grimy concrete floor. The room was about fifteen by twenty feet, and it had the unmistakably musty smell of a basement. Plaster walls, crumbling here and there. Cobwebby corners. A pillar about two feet square with the same crumbly plaster stood dead center in the gloomy space, and just beside it was a wooden chair, the only other thing besides her in the room.

Kelly paced the room, trying to keep her anger as a way to keep her courage. She took the chair over to the outer wall, but even standing on it she would be unable to reach the window. She didn't try. The prospect of falling while handcuffed was a deterrent.

Only the dim light seeping through the boards had made it possible to tell time and after a while that disappeared. Perhaps it was two, possibly three, hours later before anyone came to the room. Kelly heard a key. When the door opened, she was blinded by a very bright, hand-held light aimed directly at her.

"Put the chair back where you found it. Sit in the chair. From now on, whenever you hear someone at the door, make sure you're sitting in that chair. If you're asleep, you get up and go to the chair." A woman's voice. Angry, stern.

Rules. They were the boss. They were going to make the rules.

Kelly stayed where she was.

Two of them still. One held the light, blinding her while the other one went to the chair that was still along the wall. He did not try to avoid being seen as he took it back to where it had been. Then he came for

Kelly. She realized it would be useless to fight him so she let him take her to the chair and sit her down. Then he put the hood back on. They took her from the room and down a hall. They were deliberately rough, shoving her off balance and then grabbing the cuffs before she fell. Into another room and then directed to another chair. The cuffs were opened only to be relocked in front of her. Small favors. The hood was removed.

She was sitting in a normally lit room, a room with featureless white walls. About five feet in front of her, at a desk, was a large, middle-aged man with peppery, steel-gray hair, tending toward overweight. She twisted around on her chair. The people who had brought her had withdrawn to the back of the room to either side of the door. One was the man who had bumped into her at the cafe. He was tall, brawny as a football player. She recognized the woman. Liz. The Aussie or Canadian who had not gone running with her. *Liz thinks I'm crazy to waste good sleeping time,* Carol Willis had said.

The stony face Liz presented gave no sign of recognizing her. Kelly turned back to the man behind the desk.

He seemed an ill-tempered person, someone who was missing a meal and quite ready to blame her. He stared at her, a little disgusted, like an interviewer who's quite sure the person he's seeing is not qualified for the job his firm is offering but who will have to waste his time anyway.

"I wish we could put these preliminaries behind us, Miss Corcoran. You're going to deny that's who you are, I am going to insist you are who you are, we're going to go round in circles and it's all going to be a waste of my time." His accent was vaguely British. Everything was so much about him, an accent seemed one more thing he could scarcely bear to trouble himself with.

"I have no idea what you're talking about. Please, let me go. This is all some bizarre kind of mistake." Kelly bet herself that he'd yawn.

He didn't. Instead he sighed. "Take her back to the room. I have real work to do."

Kelly tried not to be dismayed at the prospect of being returned to the basement room.

"Liz, you remember me, don't you? What's going on? Just tell me what's going on."

But the woman might have been a robot. She put the hood back on Kelly. She took turns with Ernie pushing her down the hall. Kelly wasn't sure why she wanted to call the brawny man Ernie. It just seemed to fit. Liz and Ernie.

When they reached the room, Kelly's hood was removed.

"Go sit in your chair," Liz said.

As she did so, Kelly saw that a pail had been placed beside the chair. They left her hands cuffed in front. When they closed the door, there was no light at all. Kelly tried to twist so that she could get the Himalayan crystal from her pocket, and she might have reached it, but she was suddenly afraid that she might lose it, or her action be seen and the talisman taken from her.

†

Alfred Toland was a gray man. Wisps of gray hair stuck out every which way from a round head with saggy cheeks, faintly gray with unshaved stubble. He wore rumpled gray slacks and trudged along the narrow walk, past sandbagged windows. An utterly nondescript person. Jeri followed on foot. If this was Britain's senior spy in Croatia, it made a kind of backward sense. He would be a spy because he didn't look like one. Her contact had sworn that the several days, long days in which Jeri had fought from rage to panic and back again, the days it had taken to find out about Toland, meant that he was very sure of his information.

†

"I'm sick to death of this stupidity, Miss Corcoran."

The interrogator spat the words with such venom that even Kelly's name emerged like a slap in the face. She had little defense against his attacks. She felt filthy from using the pail for a toilet with her hands cuffed, grimy from sleeping on the hard, gritty, cement floor. Her sense of time was completely gone, thrown off by the haphazard episodes of waking and sleeping that her captors allowed. She was tired, terribly tired. Sleepiness was a sickness. Sometimes they brought her to the interrogation room and she'd sit for an hour or so staring at an empty desk. Other times, the man would be there and speak to her in a reasonable, almost friendly tone, only to suddenly fly into a rage, berating and belittling her.

"Why are you here? Where did you take the guns? Where is O'Donnell? This woman you insist on defending is a murderer. Is this how you were brought up, to consort with terrorists? With people who have no regard for their own or anyone else's life? You're making your family suffer, you know. They have no idea what happened to you or where you are. You could be dead for all they know. What kind of ungrateful daughter are you? Think of how they feel, wondering if you're dead or alive. Of course you don't care, any more than your murdering girlfriend cared about all the people she killed and maimed when she bombed innocent human beings."

Kelly had to keep her eyes open. They kicked the chair from under her if she closed her eyes. She couldn't close her eyes but she tried to shut out the words. She tried to remember Jeri inching across the minefield, risking her life for the child stranded amid lethal explosives. Jeri saved people, she didn't kill them.

Kelly tried to stop thinking. Even if she said nothing out loud, she was engaging in an argument with the man by remembering, by trying to counter what he said. That was a mistake. Trying to point out the wrong parts made her more susceptible to possibly correct parts. Before this, she'd never thought about how words worked, how maybe people were hardwired to believe what they heard, and how it took an act of will to derail that process of accepting meaning. Maybe that's why lying was counted as a sin, because words could be arranged to say anything, sense or nonsense, and then the hearing mind would try to make them mean properly.

But if she shut them out completely—or as completely as possible—she would start to fall asleep again and then find herself falling to the floor.

They took her back to the basement room. They made her sit in the chair until they left. It had to be some part of daytime because there was a dim gray light that let her see where they'd put her food and water: by the pail that no one emptied.

It had to do with guns. That was all Kelly could figure out. They were interested in guns.

She felt sick and lost with her fear. She didn't really know what to do, how to think about what was happening.

Oh, Jeri. Come get me. Please find me.

What would Jeri do? She wouldn't have been caught in the first place. Kelly imagined Jeri twisting free of the iron grip of her captor at the cafe. That was a good thought. So was imagining Jeri twisting free, turning and kicking the man's shin while driving her fist into his neck. Only they wouldn't have come after Jeri in the same way. They would be afraid of Jeri.

The light was gone from the window. Kelly stared into the darkness, and misery overwhelmed her. Deliberately she set about recalling Jeri, remembering her face, hearing her voice. Through love and memory she called her to come into this place of terror and torment.

Kelly remembered Jeri when she would stand listening, attentive, letting the spirits of a place flow into her. She remembered seeing Jeri stride through the hills in the Krajina and how following her there had seemed right, appropriate, just as it had seemed right to follow her through the high, thin air of Nepal and Tibet. Jeri had been so much in her element that the white-hot core of her was visible. She was a warrior, with a warrior's soul.

The word itself was stirring and substantial. Sure, war was part of it, but so was guardian, the one who warded off danger. To be a warrior was a calling, a vocation. Jeri had the fierce soul and courageous heart of a warrior in a time that was uncertain how to value or use warriors. She was born to be a guardian at the service of those who needed protection from harm. This was an age that had forgotten how once there were those few who were all who could stand between a people and annihilation. Once, when people huddled in the dark, when they'd been one of the smaller prey on the great savannahs, it was the warrior who stood between them and the beasts of the plains, the warrior who learned the skills that would make a ring of safety in the night and hold through to dawn.

Once, Kelly had believed in a perfectible world. Not perfect, but perfectible. You kept a vision of what was better, if not best, and you kept trying to get closer to that vision. But she'd lost her faith when George died. Then Jeri brought a new kind of faith, one more muted, a sense that faith isn't given to a vision but to another person. This had all been so clear in Tibet where spirit had felt closer, as if the thin mountain air made a more permeable barrier between worlds.

If Jeri was a warrior, who was she?

Then, suddenly the answer came. She was the one through whom balance was renewed, the way of beauty restored. All the elder peoples had understood that violence, even when necessary, damaged balance, and a ceremony of restoration, of reconciliation was required. Love was the ceremony. This was why they needed one another, why together they could achieve unity and wholeness. For an instant Kelly understood completely. She was flooded with understanding, and meaning was not something within the mind, but saturated everything she was. She understood so well that she did not even try to hold on as it seeped away, like sand through her fingers, like sand through time's hourglass. It was sufficient to keep the memory that she had understood.

†

The man called Albert Toland exited from the nondescript stone building to join other Zagreb citizens on the boulevard hurrying home for the evening. He even wore the same expression of most Croatians, apprehensive that some new episode would soon push them closer to war with their former sister republic of Serbia. Jeri kept him in sight from the café table where she had been waiting for him to emerge. She let him get half a block ahead before following and then kept him in sight until she was fairly certain of his direction. At the next intersection she turned and began walking briskly, almost running. She wasn't too worried at setting an odd, even noticeable pace. If she had guessed right and explored these streets well enough, she did not expect to be back again.

Jeri turned left and, almost loping, hurried along a street that was parallel to the one Toland had been on. After three blocks, she turned left again. Now she assumed a normal pace because she wanted her breathing to slow back to that of an ordinary pedestrian. If her timing was right, she would arrive at the intersection before Toland. She reached the corner. There he was, fifty feet away, coming toward her. She walked toward him. As they passed, she pivoted and took hold of his arm.

"Albert Toland? Please do exactly as I say. I have a gun aimed at you, and there's very little reason not to shoot you, because I can deal with your replacement just as easily. Walk slowly up the street and turn right. Good man."

If grabbing people was the name of the game, Jeri could play too.

†

"Pay attention! Why won't you listen to me? I'm only trying to show you what's good for you. You queers think you're so special, but all you care about is yourself—if it feels good, do it, right? Self-centered and self-indulgent, that's the lot of you. What do you think is important to a kid who will never see his father, because your girlfriend and the other Republican scum, cowards, every last one of them, ambushed those poor innocents, killed them before they could defend themselves? Do you think that kid or his mother cares if your girlfriend shoves her hand between your legs?"

He began describing Jeri and Kelly together. Pornographic, ugly words combined into lewd phrases, images evoking whole scenes in repetitive details, spoken in a voice dripping with disgust. It was quite

407

possibly worse than rape, because he was taking her memories and twisting them, giving them back to her in a muddied and fouled form. He took what she loved and made it grotesque, as if he had slipped into her mind with a sledgehammer and was bent on smashing all she held dear. Like a hypnotist, he repeated himself, using a rhythm that let her drift toward sleep, knowing that he was directing the images formed by her raddled mind. Then he would scream for her to wake up and the words would start again.

"You might as well tell me what I want to know. You think somehow you're going to get away from here but even if you do, you'll never be able to be with her again without hearing my voice. It's over, Miss Corcoran. Finished."

Kelly felt the tears well up and slide down her face. She was so tired. So very, very tired. You could be so miserable without sleep that it made you sick to your stomach.

"I don't know what you're talking about," she said.

They took her back to the room and shoved her through the door. A tin plate of beans with a square of cut bread, along with a tin cup of water, had been placed on her chair. The pail had been emptied while she was out, but Kelly went to the farthest corner. Her hands hurt and she was too tired to eat. It had been hard, so hard to get through these hours—days?—but always she had felt there would surely be a way out, an end. For the first time the probability that Jeri would never find her, maybe they might never be together again, slithered into her thoughts. Warriors and visions of meaning were simply elaborate webs of self-deception. She couldn't find Jeri in her mind.

†

"I want you to tell me where you take the people you kidnap, Mr. Toland."

"I have no idea what you're talking about. I can't imagine who on earth we'd want in Zagreb."

Jeri described the two people who'd taken Kelly and saw Toland's eyes shift. He knew the men.

"I have something to trade. Remember the mission that got lost on the way to Chechnya in '88? I know how that happened. I know who told the Russians your guys were coming."

His eyes narrowed. "I'm more impressed that you even know there might have been a mission. Tell me what you know and I might throw in the fact that whatever happened here is a freelance job. We're not running anything like this in Croatia."

Bit by bit, Jeri began trading the information that the Americans had a Russian mole in their midst. Not the name, she didn't have the name. But she could prove he existed and that was currency London could use with Washington. Rafi had given her this currency that she'd been saving and she considered it well spent.

†

Kelly quit trying to recall Jeri or George. Their comfort made her weaker, more vulnerable than she already was to the man who was scrambling her mind. He would use them, had used them, was using them, distorting the reality of them that she cherished. She tried to go somewhere else. Like considering prepositions. She had a fondness for prepositions. They were underrated compared to nouns and verbs. Prepositions made relationships. Sister Aloysius Gonzaga had made her class memorize a list of prepositions. *About, among, around,* it had begun.

Lists were good. Kelly imagined a map of the United States and began naming the fifty states, even though she kept losing count. Curiously, it was usually Michigan or Minnesota that she forgot. She tried, but she never had been good with the state capitals. Poetry was also good. Once she had fallen in love with the images in Stephen Spender's "Seascape," and she felt she had always known "Fern Hill" or "Lady of Shalott," but after a while, the pain in lines like *I'm half sick of shadows* or *wake to the farm forever fled* outweighed their comfort.

"Just confirm your name, Miss Corcoran, and you can go back and sleep until morning. Just your name, that's all."

"Laura. Laura Wimmel. Please, let me go."

Kelly took walks around the Ohio farm. She'd start from the front gate, the white wood gate and fence that kept the chickens out of the yard and protected her mother's flowers. Sometimes she'd go to the barn, past the tool shed and the chicken coop. Sometimes she'd take the path through the shade trees on the north to the alfalfa field and then walk down the fence line to the creek. Most times it was a lazy little creek lined by old trees, but some years when there was a lot of rain, it got considerably deeper. Not a river, but too deep to wade.

†

"Wake up. Go to your chair." The voice of Ernie, the football player, was behind the light.

Kelly lifted herself off the floor and stumbled over to the chair. So what if it was compliance, the creation of habit. She was too tired to resist.

She fell asleep. She slumped, woke, and realized the bright light was gone. It was a game and they'd just won another round.

†

"Get up. Go to your chair."

Kelly got up. This time they had really come for her, Liz and Ernie. They pushed her and shoved her down the hall toward the interrogation room.

"How did you get into the country, Miss Corcoran? How did you get to Yugoslavia?"

"That's not my name," Kelly mumbled.

"What? Speak up!"

There was some slight commotion behind her but Kelly had grown profoundly disinterested in the events of this room. Then she saw the surprised look on the man's face. He started to stand up.

"Sit down or give me half a reason to shoot you. I don't care which."

Kelly recognized the voice but she already knew who was there from the interrogator's startled look. She knew she ought to feel glad, but instead she felt embarrassed.

"Sit on the floor. There beside Mr. Big Shot." The menacing voice delivering the orders shook with fury.

Liz and Ernie came forward and eased themselves to the floor. Kelly watched with some curiosity. There had been so little variety lately. Jeri had the gun that she'd carried through the Krajina in one hand. The other hand was holding one of the guns that had just belonged to Kelly's captors, while the second guard's gun was firmly tucked into the waistband of her jeans.

"Who has the key to the cuffs?"

No one moved or spoke. The interrogator was staring at her as if she were some annoying interruption who must soon disappear.

"Oh, good. I was so hoping for this. Do you know Serbo-Croatian?" No response. "They have a word, *kundaciti*."

With no other warning, Jeri walked to the side of the desk and slammed the butt of a gun into the interrogator's jaw and the result was a horrid mix of outcry, cracking bone and splitting flesh.

"It means to bludgeon with a rifle butt, isn't that a good word? Sorry I don't have a rifle. Want to hear the word again? Now where's the fucking key because I really, really, want to hit you some more."

The man mumbled.

"What?" Jeri drew back her hand just as the man spat out blood and the word, "key," at the same time Kelly said, "Connie, don't!"

Jeri stared at Kelly with a look Kelly was sure she'd remember until she died. "Oh, God," she breathed, barely a whisper. "Baby, it wasn't necessary."

Jeri turned back toward the football player who was reaching into a pocket. There was such murder in her look that he needed no warning. Slowly, carefully, he brought out the handcuff key. He started to toss it to Jeri.

"No, you. Unlock the cuffs. Move slow, but I'd really like it if you made me shoot you."

When Kelly's hands were free, Jeri spoke slowly, quietly. "Go on ahead. The stairs are to your right. Go up one floor of stairs, turn left, and take the hall to the big door. It's easy. Can you do it? Good. When you're outside, turn right on the street and you'll see our car. It's the only one. Go on. It's safe. I won't kill anyone, I promise, though by God, I want to. I do want to."

Kelly nodded and left. The building was old and it was like walking through an empty school at night. The hall seemed longer than Kelly remembered. The door was heavy and she was afraid she might not have the strength to open it. Then she pushed through.

It was evening. The air smelled so clean.

There was only one car on the street, a Yugo. Kelly stood at the door of the Yugo and waited until she saw Jeri approaching. The tall woman walked with more determination than hurry. Kelly couldn't think what to say to her so she just got in the car. Jeri got in the other side. She gave Kelly an anxious look before starting the engine.

"I must smell really bad." Kelly stared straight ahead through the window.

"We can fix that."

"It was necessary."

"Why?"

"They wanted our souls and they couldn't get them as long as I didn't say our names."

"Then you did good, baby, you did real good. Now you go to sleep and I'll take care of everything form a while."

Chapter Eight

Jeri steered the Yugo through narrow, twisting streets and then onto a wider road that took them out of the city and away from Zagreb. Kelly stared through the windshield into the darkness. She could not be said to be thinking and after a while she dozed.

Kelly woke when she felt the car slowing and saw that the sky ahead had grown pale. Jeri slowed almost to a stop before turning off the highway onto a narrow lane that sloped upward. After a bumpy kilometer, a gateway blocked the road. Jeri stopped and put the hand brake on but kept the motor running while she got out, opened the wrought iron gate, and then drove the Yugo into a cobbled courtyard. She parked close to the wall of the courtyard and then came around and opened the car door on Kelly's side.

Kelly shrank back from the extended hand. "Oh, God. I'm sorry. I don't know what's wrong with me."

"Nothing that can't be fixed." Jeri stepped back from the car door. "There isn't a thing wrong with you, Kell. I'd be more worried if you were acting like nothing awful happened."

Kelly got out of the car and then stood waiting.

"Kelly, listen to me. There's no one here but us. Come in and rest. I have all your things with me. If you want a shower, I'll show you where it is and I'll wait right outside the door for you. Then there's a room with a clean bed where you can sleep for as long as you want. I'm going to be right outside that door, too. That's all there is to think about right now."

That sounded okay. Kelly thought maybe that might be okay.

Kelly thought she was managing. Her hands had swollen and there were marks where the cuffs had chafed, but she could make her fingers work just fine. The bathroom had blue-patterned tiles. Kelly started to close the door but then left it open. When she came out of the shower, she found a stack of folded clothes on a chair by the door. Jeri was

413

waiting in the hall. She smiled at Kelly and then led her a few steps to a room with a large bed on which was a turned back comforter showing pale blue sheets. Floor-to-ceiling curtains covered sliding glass doors. Two upholstered lounging chairs were spaced alongside the wall opposite the bed. The floor was tile patterned in soft earth tones. Kelly noted remotely that this all seemed a bit expensive.

Kelly started for the bed, and then suddenly felt how large the room was. "Maybe you could sit inside the room while I sleep? At least until I fall asleep? And keep a small light on?"

"Done."

†

Only after she was sure that Kelly was asleep did Jeri let the rage she felt shape the contours of her face. She regretted deeply that she had kept her promise to Kelly and killed no one. But if she ever saw one of those people again, they were dead. Toland hadn't seemed to think it would matter. He said they had a loose government connection, and he had been vague about which government, but they were private and mostly they were about guns. That's where you made your money in a war, guns, and the new country of Croatia needed guns badly.

As far as Jeri could figure, she and Kelly had become a blip on someone's radar when they entered the country with an arms shipment. If she'd known more about the crisis looming over Yugoslavia, Jeri might have considered another way to get to Dubrovnik. Of course, it was still likely that Toland was covering for something. You just never knew for sure when you dealt with governments.

Jeri stared at Kelly, seeing little more than a form curled beneath the thick comforter, watching the rhythm of her breathing. She was so relieved to have Kelly back, alive and not damaged physically, that she found her presence infinitely soothing. As for Kelly's mental state, that was another matter. Jeri had seen the effects of prison before, of interrogation, and isolation.

Kelly hadn't been held that long. She might only need rest, real sleep. On the other hand, the interrogators had been experts and their methods had obviously been intense. Plus, Kelly was still fragile from the deaths of her brother and her friends. Jeri saw how she struggled with that daily, trying to find a context, a way to accept death and keep love. Then factor in the events they had been part of in the Krajina and there had been some extreme shocks recently.

But Kelly was strong. Hadn't she just walked out of a war zone? And take the fact that she hadn't ever let go of their cover story. Hell, she could have told them. They did know. But Kelly wasn't about to give anything away. *Don't ever give anything away,* she'd said to Kelly more than once, referring to anyone who might be following them. *Make them work for what they don't know.* She'd never meant for Kelly to die trying to defend just their identity. But what if Kelly had told them sooner, would they have kept her at the same location or would they have moved her? Say to somewhere that Toland wouldn't have known about. Or would they have even left her alive? God. Jesus, maybe Kelly had called it right.

But she shouldn't be here at all, said a voice that Jeri didn't want to hear. She tried to silence the thoughts, but they persisted. You need to send her home. This is your life because you blew it, but she hasn't. She can still go home. She hasn't done anything that anyone will need to make her account for. All she's guilty of is consorting with a known criminal, and there are a few strings that you could pull to make that disappear. You need to let her go, make her go.

Then she remembered what she'd said. *"I'll never ask you to leave me again."* Maybe Kelly would want to leave when she woke.

Tá tú an coimeádaí mo chroí. You are the keeper of my heart. Jeri whispered the phrase in Gaelic and English.

†

Kelly woke to the sound of birds. A length of sunlight fell between curtains. She saw a figure standing by the window, gazing out to the day, a tall woman. She wondered for an instant why Jeri wasn't beside her and then she remembered everything and a wave of misery swept over her. She shut her eyes to keep it out and sleep took her away again.

†

After the initial exhaustion was relieved, Kelly's sleep grew fretful and restless. She tossed and turned and the noises she made were almost words. Jeri ached to go to her. Maybe that would be the right thing to do, maybe she could slip in beside her and just hold her. But then Jeri thought not. She felt instinctively that Kelly was caught in a process that she needed to get through on her own. To interrupt that work would leave it unfinished.

415

†

The next time Kelly woke, the only light in the room was from the small lamp that was always on. Jeri was again sitting in the chair across the room and Kelly almost felt like she could have imagined her previous waking. Almost.

"Will I ever get synched up to day and night again?"

"Sure. Are you hungry?"

Kelly considered. "Yeah, I am."

"Good. Don't go anywhere."

Jeri left the room and returned with sandwiches so quickly that Kelly knew they must have been made and waiting. She got out of bed and put the plate on the tiled floor in front of her. The bread was thick Croatian bread that was a meal in itself, and the cheese was also thick, with a lot of flavor. Kelly ate several bites, then stopped, as if the food had stuck in her throat.

"I'm not sick. They didn't hurt me. I don't need to be treated like an invalid."

Jeri said nothing.

"I don't even know what they wanted. Something about guns. Like they think you know who's shipping guns into the country. Where did you get this place? It's like a rich person's home."

"I called in a favor. It is a rich person's home."

"I thought the IRA was poor. I thought Irish Catholics were oppressed poor people." Christ, where was this coming from? Kelly couldn't believe her own words. She was trying to pick a fight.

"Some are. This place doesn't belong to a Provo."

"What the hell is a Provo? Why don't you just say IRA like everyone else? Why are you so fucking perfect?" Kelly picked up her plate and threw it across the room. The dish hit the wall and fell to the tile floor, shattering. She stared at the wall. Silence filled the room like water in a fish bowl. Then Kelly stood up, crossed the room, and carefully began picking up pieces of bread, cheese, and broken plate.

"I thought I'd never see you again. And then—then—I thought that was probably for the best, because you could never trust me again. Not after what they were doing."

The storm that had been building finally broke. With pieces of food and broken plate in both hands, Kelly sat on the cool tile and began to weep. Jeri was beside her instantly. Gently, she took the pieces of jagged

416

plate from Kelly's hands.

The theory was that you were supposed to cry and the feelings would move through you and then it would be over. Only Kelly couldn't stop. She lost track of what and whom she was crying for. George, of course. Always George. And Vojna. She had really liked Vojna. She'd had thoughts of how the young girl was going to make a new life in one of the pretty seaside towns of Dalmatia. And for herself. Kelly cried for herself, lost in the dark, caught and kept in the dark while they tried to steal her mind, her heart.

"They never came close," Jeri whispered, as if reading her mind. "They never came close to finding your heart. I have it. I'll always keep it for you."

So Kelly told her all that had happened. She remembered a lot more than she wanted to.

"I should have killed the bastard. Jesus, I should have killed him when I had the chance."

Jeri thought that Kelly had started sobbing again, and it took her several seconds to realize that Kelly was laughing. Only a little out of control.

"You should have seen him. I knew it was you, before I saw you, before I heard your voice, because I saw his face. He was so scared. After all those days of being the head bastard in charge of everything right and good, suddenly you were there and he was scared to his toes."

"Really? I was just making sure he didn't try anything to make me have to kill him."

"Oh, he was scared. After all those hours when I had to keep my eyes on him and guess his mood and think who and what he was, he couldn't keep me from seeing how you scared the shit right out of him. God, I liked seeing you hit him."

"Really? Why did you make me stop?"

Kelly quit laughing. "I guess I liked it too much. I wanted you to kill him, I really did, and then I remembered where we are and how that gets done here. How easy people die here."

"You mean it. It's not just words, you would have killed him." Kelly paused and stared at Jeri.

Jeri couldn't hold Kelly's eyes. "Yes," softly, and then louder. "Yes. And I'd be sorry now. You pay and pay dearly if you have any humanity at all."

"That's how it was in Ireland? In Ulster?"

"Oh, Kell, that was different. I didn't think I had a real choice back then. History, my life, they put me where I had so few choices if I was going to live in the world. And I thought it was my home, my true home. You have to protect your home. And you want to keep faith with those you love. I loved Fiona and Millicent, and I'm not sure they would like how I've just left them behind."

Kelly nodded. She felt the tears begin again and leaned into Jeri. When the arms went around her, Kelly remembered just how much she had missed being held.

†

"Kell?"

"What?"

"Do you remember the day I promised I'd never ask you to leave me? But if you wanted to go, I would truly understand."

Jeri felt Kelly grow very still in her arms, felt the muscles stiffen, felt the almost imperceptible withdrawal.

"Do you want me to go?"

"Oh, baby, I just want you to be safe. To have a good life."

"That isn't what I asked." Kelly had pulled herself away from Jeri and was staring at her with amber-flecked green eyes whose fierceness was undiminished by the redness from crying. "Do you want me to go?"

"No. Never." Maybe she ought to have lied, but she couldn't. Not to Kelly. She stood, helped Kelly to her feet and then led her to the bed.

"Stay with me? Just hold me?" Kelly asked, as if Jeri might refuse.

Jeri lay down beside Kelly and gathered her close. Slowly, slowly, ever so gentle and full of care, it became more than just holding. The head bastard in charge of everything right and good had been dead wrong. Kelly didn't think of him at all.

†

Kelly started jogging again. Jeri watched her leave and it took a fierce effort of will not to go running after her, but it was necessary for Kelly to go alone. She took the road away from the highway, farther into the hills and Jeri watched as she topped a ridge and disappeared from sight. Then Jeri went back inside to call Alenka and let her know that she and Kelly would be delayed again. Alenka said not to worry, that everything was fine.

†

418

The villa had several books but none were in English. Kelly found an atlas and she understood the maps without needing translation. For the first time she started to fix Yugoslavia and its various districts such as Kosovo, Montenegro, Bosnia, Slovenia, and Serbia into her mental geography. At times Kelly would be struck by the reality of where she was, and how different this was from anything she had ever known, and it would feel like some form of reincarnation. This life was so loosely connected to the way she had lived before meeting Jeri. At other times, Kelly felt she had stumbled into her inevitable destiny, that everything before had been on a trajectory aiming her toward Croatia, that this had always been her fate. Then, and usually in response to either notion, she would think that it just was what it was, that the reality of now was somehow fixed, and essentially unknowable. She could remember the feeling of profound understanding that had occurred while she was a captive, and remembering would steady her emotionally, but she could not recall the details in any rationally meaningful way.

†

"Jeri, were those people part of the English specials? Like in Nepal?"

"No, honey. Those were SAS in Nepal. These were something different, and probably not even Brits."

"Who are they?"

"They're freelance. They're not with any government, they hire themselves out to governments."

"Like, have magnifying glass, will spy for food? I don't get it."

"Yeah, about like that. They're calling it outsourcing. Rafi says it's becoming more common by the day. Welcome to the brave new world where anything can become a business if someone wants to pay for it. Maybe just, meet the new boss, same as the old boss. Most of these mercenary types are usually aligned with a government. Governments say it's cheaper but I think it's about less responsibility. Maybe..." Jeri stopped, aware that Kelly wasn't listening. That happened a lot. One minute she was there and the next she was gone.

"Come on, Kell, let's go for a walk."

Opposite the road where Kelly went running and behind the villa, the land rose in a series of steep, wooded ridges. The two women climbed steadily in companionable silence, pausing now and then whenever a clearing allowed them to look back onto a view of summer green.

"This would be a good area for making a contour map," Kelly said at one such pause.

"Maybe you like squiggly lines, eh? Commas or contours?" Jeri was aware that, once upon a time, Kelly had wanted to be a professional cartographer.

"It is funny isn't it? You start one place and end up somewhere quite different."

"That must be a mapmaker thought."

They walked on until they reached the summit of the highest ridge. The woods ended and the farther side the land fell in a gently sloping series of fields. The near fields looked to be grazing land, too rocky for planting, but below these were cornfields with leaves long enough to be swaying in the afternoon breeze.

"Wait!"

Kelly had started to walk forward for a better view but Jeri wanted them both to stay among the trees where they would be less visible.

Kelly quickly stepped back, but despite Jeri's caution they had been seen. A single man was coming toward them from about a hundred yards away. He must have been in the trees. He was dressed in worn denim pants and a loose shirt but he was carrying a Kalashnikov. Jeri's eyes swept the area behind him without moving her head. Though she could see no one else, she was fairly certain he wasn't alone. She felt the SIG in the small of her back, held by the waistband of her jeans and hidden by her shirt. She kept her hands in sight at her sides.

"Just look natural."

"Tell me you didn't just say that!" Kelly swung toward her with a look of total disbelief.

"Exactly what I meant." Jeri smiled and moved close to Kelly's side. She kept the smile on her face as they waited.

The man coming toward them carried his Kalashnikov easily, familiar with it. A sturdy man tending toward weight, somewhere between thirty and fifty, he would look like a farmer under most circumstances.

"Who are you?" He stopped a few yards away.

"We're Americans. We work for a newspaper." Jeri spoke in Serbo-Croatian but gave the words an awkward accent. She had no idea whether he was Serbian or Croatian yet. She had already discussed with Kelly the cover they would be using from now until they reached

Vukovar.

The man continued to eye them suspiciously. "What are you doing here? There is no reason for newspaper people to be here."

Jeri considered her answer carefully. It could be perilous if she guessed wrong about his nationality. "We drove down from Vienna. A friend of a friend has a place on the other side of these hills, and we were very tired so we are stopping for a while."

"You came through Slovenia and Croatia?" He addressed Kelly, not Jeri, and he asked in English.

"Are those places between here and Austria?" Kelly looked confused but she had heard the word Vienna.

"English! You speak English!" Jeri interjected. "Oh, wonderful. I've been hoping to get some idea of what's going on and my Yugoslavian just isn't that good. My name is Connie."

"I am Rade. I could understand you, but the language is Serbian, not Yugoslavian."

That answered the question of nationality. A Croatian would have said they were speaking Croatian.

"Are you from around here, Rade?" Jeri asked.

"Yes, my home is over there." He nodded toward the cornfields down the slope. "I learned to speak English in Australia. My father worked there when I was a boy."

"Is there trouble here?" Jeri pointed to the Kalashnikov.

"Trouble? We live surrounded by Croats. What else can there be, but trouble? We must prepare. Milosevic sent these guns to us."

Rade nodded, and as he did so, several more armed men emerged from the tree line. Jeri's heart thudded as she saw the hostile faces. She looked behind her and was relieved to see no one there. She counted eight men that she could see, although she was sure there must be more.

"We patrol. Even before Borovo Selo we were patrolling.

"But isn't everyone here neighbors?"

"No more. Maybe once, but soon this will not even be our country. The new constitution says Croatia is for Croatians. We know what that means. Serbians will be a minority. We won't be safe unless we protect ourselves. Have they heard of Borovo Selo in Austria?"

"A little, but it was very confusing."

"It's not at all confusing. Tudjman sent in thirty mercenaries from Albania. They're even more bloodthirsty than Croats, but we were able to fight them off."

"You were there?"

"No, no. We, the Serbs."

"Albanians? Why were they there?"

"Belgrade got rid of the Albanians in the Kosovo police force because they could not be trusted. Then Tudjman hired them because he knows what kind of people they are."

Kelly didn't have to pretend now to be confused, it was apparent as she looked to Jeri for explanation.

"I'll explain it later." Jeri did not want to take her attention off the man with the Kalashnikov.

"There is nothing to explain. It will soon be just like before, during World War Two. Do you know about Jasenovac?" Rade was hostile as well as insistent.

Jeri knew. She took a deep breath and turned to Kelly. "Jasenovac. That name here is the same as saying Auschwitz. Thousands of Serbs were murdered—"

"Hundreds of thousands! Me, everyone you see here, we all had family at Jasenovac. We all know how cunning and cruel the Croats are."

"Nazis and their Croatian allies, the Ustasha, killed Serbians, Jews, Gypsies. Croats, too. Communists, anyone who was antifascist." Jeri continued as if Rade had not spoken.

"Tell her about the *srbosjek*," Rade interrupted again.

Jeri stared at Rade. He was glaring at her, challenging. His companions were stepping closer. They had heard and it was as if Rade had uttered some secret password that could set them all in motion.

"No," Jeri said. "No. We have to go back now."

She should come up with a story that explained why they had to leave, but all she could do was imagine history hovering over them like a curse clawing its way into reality. Atrocity begetting never-ending atrocity. She should say something that would assure Rade that she and Kelly were sympathetic if not wholly on his side, but she couldn't. She just couldn't be part of this conversation any more.

"Wait. Tell me why America won't help us? We were allies with America in the war. Why haven't you come to help us?"

Jeri just shook her head as she and Kelly walked away. She felt profoundly tired. Kelly walked ahead of her and Jeri could feel the presence of Rade and his countrymen like an itch crawling on her spine.

"What's a sur-boss-yek, Jeri?" They were near the villa before Kelly asked.

"It's sickle meant for cutting grain by hand. It's attached to a kind of glove so that it's easier to use. It got its name, though, at Jasenovac.

Serb-stabber. It was good for cutting throats. One Ustasha guard boasted that he had cut over a thousand."

Kelly moved to Jeri's side and took her hand. "It's nice here, but we should probably go soon."

"Are you really ready?"

Kelly nodded.

"We can go in the morning."

†

When they returned to the villa, they packed their few belongings, and then took their supper and a bottle of wine to the patio at the back of the villa. A slight breeze fluttered about the late summer night, cooling and keeping away bugs.

"Do you know what happened at Borovo Selo?"

"Not really. I'm really not clear. Something about the wrong flag being put up and then policemen being killed. Everything seems to escalate into more violence and more rumor. But the people I talk to think it's because of Borovo Selo that Rafi wants us to get Alenka and get her away from the border region. He's sure the fighting will get a lot worse."

"Do you get it, Jeri? Do you get it at all?"

Jeri stared into the darkness. She thought she understood what Kelly was asking. Something about right and wrong, about guilty and innocent, something fundamental about human beings.

"There's a Polish poet, Czeslaw Milosz. He was trying to explain what it meant to have lived through occupations by Stalin and then Hitler and then Stalin again, how if a person just managed to survive that inevitably meant something had been broken. He said he couldn't take an American seriously, couldn't take any Westerner seriously. That we didn't have the imagination to understand what can happen inside a soul that sees death become as common as road kill for years on end. I don't get it, Kell, not really. And I don't know if that's a strength, or a weakness."

"Was it like that in Northern Ireland?"

The quiet stretched for minutes. The question was almost forgotten and then, very faintly and very far off but still unmistakable, they heard a smattering of gunfire.

Chapter Nine

"Even Kansas can't be this flat." Kelly was staring at the countryside as it slid past the Yugo windows.

"That's Slavonia out there. They say if you stand on a pumpkin here, you can see the whole region."

"Are there Slavonians like there are Croats and Serbs?"

"I don't think so. I think there are just Croats and Serbs living in Slavonia."

Perhaps it was the prospect of traveling that put Jeri and Kelly in a lighthearted mood. They returned the villa to the tidy state in which they'd found it, but the easy work allowed for those small absurdities often indulged in by people in love. Kelly was reminded of half-grown kittens as they played an impromptu game of catch with a pillow. When Jeri finally locked and closed the gate to the secluded villa that had been their refuge, Kelly felt as if they were exiting a dark valley.

The sense of ease persisted as Jeri drove the narrow country highway.

"Cornfields! Are you sure we're not in Kansas anymore?" Kelly laughed. The tall green stalks stood like sentinels on either side of the road, obscuring everything but a blue sky with long trailers of high, white, feathery clouds.

Without prelude, Jeri burst into song. "Oz never did give nothing to the Tin Man, that he didn't already have."

To Kelly's delight, Jeri sang the song all the way through. She liked the song and she liked listening to Jeri sing. Kelly could scarcely believe that she'd been given back her life. She resolved to pay close attention to moments like these, bright moments of joy.

Jeri slowed the Yugo and Kelly saw that several cars in front of them had stopped.

"Checkpoint. Alenka said even short trips are taking hours longer these days."

As they drew closer, they could see uniformed soldiers checking the cars.

"JNA. Yugoslav People's Army. Probably just another name for Serbian soldiers but at least they're regular army."

They were close enough now that Kelly could see soldiers who looked more bored that zealous.

"Just act natural, honey." Kelly grinned at being able to use the phrase on Jeri.

"This is natural." Jeri scowled.

They were ready with their story of being from an American newspaper, a story that permitted them to speak English. Both Serbia and Croatia were aware that they were being watched closely from beyond Yugoslavia's borders. The general rumors were that Tudjman was counting on good international press to make up for Croatia's lack of arms. If he publicly followed the arms embargo and didn't try to circumvent it too obviously, then other Europeans and the Americans would protect the new country. Perhaps he was hoping that the world just might think of Croatia as it had thought of Kuwait and come to its rescue. Jeri said Tudjman was whistling in the dark but, in the meantime, she was ready to take advantage of the desire for good press relations.

Serbs, not Croats, however, were manning this roadblock, and they weren't as eager to please reporters as Croatians were. Two soldiers approached the Yugo, but they were polite enough. Still, they argued with the reporter's choice of destination.

"Why do you want to go to Vukovar? You should go across the Danube to Novi Sad, which is a very beautiful city. You'll get nothing but lies in Vukovar. Croats have no regard for the truth. They lie worse than Gypsies and they have no loyalty to anything. Even Hitler's generals were surprised by how they—"

"My editor asked me to go to Vukovar particularly. How can I argue with a man who won't even give me money to rent a decent car?"

"What about your friend? Why is she going to Vukovar?" The speaker was someone who might be a good-natured fellow if he was at home and out of uniform.

"Same editor. He's trying to save money. She's going to do a piece about Croatian cuisine." Jeri shrugged elaborately.

"What Croatian cuisine? They have terrible food. Whatever seems like a good food, they have stolen from Serbians, who were eating with forks while Europe was still ripping meat apart with their hands."

Jeri smiled her most pleasant and conspiratorial of smiles as she opened the trunk for the soldiers and showed them a space containing only her backpack and Kelly's.

"But of course there are guns in this car. Just think how many I can smuggle through in this ridiculous vehicle."

The soldier tried to maintain his serious demeanor but he and his comrade both smiled as they looked over the dented Yugo. It certainly didn't even appear capable of concealing a fork.

"So was that one of them?" Kelly asked as the soldier waved to them to drive forward.

"Yeah. That was one of Arkan's men. I think I'd rather see buzzards." Jeri knew who Kelly was referring to. She'd seen him too, lurking behind the regular army soldiers, wearing black, but the dark glasses and long hair and attitude were unmistakable.

"So where did you hide the gun?"

"Never you mind. And that's guns."

"Gun - zz? With an s? With that little phoneme that indicates plural? How many zz's?"

"We're not gun runners, Kelly. Jesus, you're always like this after we go through a roadblock. I can't take you anywhere."

"How many?"

"Just two. I kept one from your friends, Liz and Ernie. You should see them, Kelly. Ernie had a decent Beretta but Liz, the ole bulldyke wannabe, had a SIG Sauer. It is some hunk of—what? Why are you looking at me like that? You can have the other one, if you want."

About six kilometers past the Serbian roadblock, they had to go through a Croatian stop, the nationality made clear by the small red and white checked shields the men had sewn onto their shirts. The Yugo was practically waved through by these youngsters who looked like they should be in school, not at a roadblock. But a youngster with a gun, Jeri remembered, was the most dangerous animal on the planet.

The road snaked over the level land, occasionally taking them through small towns. There was little traffic and the towns appeared sparsely populated. It seemed that people were avoiding strangers.

The proximity of Vukovar was signaled by an increase of trees and buildings alongside the road. There was one more roadblock on the outskirts of the city, this one manned by uniformed men, but the red and white checked shield had been sewn onto the shirts. The little Yugo was waved through with only a cursory inspection.

Inside Vukovar's city limits, Jeri stopped and waved to a woman who was riding by on a bicycle. The woman slowed and came to the open window. Jeri asked something in Croatian and the woman gave an elaborate answer accompanied by gestures.

"Did you just ask for directions?" Kelly asked as the woman bicycled away.

"Yeah. Why? I figured she'd know where Pijacu Street was. Pee-yat-soo means market."

"You mean you don't have a detailed map of all Europe etched into your brain? Along with most of the other continents, of course."

"You can't think I know everything."

"But you do. That's what I really like about you."

"My mind. You like my mind."

"Maybe one or two other things."

"Yeah, well, you're not half—" Jeri stopped abruptly, hearing the echo of the last time she had told Kelly she wasn't half bad.

"Kell...I..." Jeri gripped the steering wheel and her knuckles were dead white. They were still parked and Jeri bent her head to the wheel. Her voice was muffled. "I nearly went crazy when they took you. I kept hearing myself say that—that you're not half bad—and I thought of all the things I really wanted to say to you, things I don't have words enough for. I swore that if I ever got you back I'd never say anything again but how much I love you."

Jeri raised her head and looked at Kelly with a tight, almost twisted expression, looking like someone who was waiting to hear the word that activates the firing squad.

"Jeri, I swear, love, that's all I've heard you say in every word since you found me."

After turning a corner at a small manicured park, Jeri drove a short way up the street and parked. Twelve Pijacu Street was a two-story olive-hued building on a street with other similar structures. The houses were dun or pink or blue, hues too flat-toned to qualify as pastel, with windows and doors outlined by large gray stones. Jeri walked to the door, but even before she could decide to knock or look for a doorbell, she heard a window open overhead and two heads appeared, one of them a dark-haired young woman and the other a large-eared dog.

"Auntie Stella!" The cry of delight was accompanied by excited barking.

The speaker disappeared and in less than a minute Jeri found herself inside one of the most enthusiastic hugs she had ever experienced.

Jeri saw Kelly laughing as she was captured in the enthusiastic embrace of a young woman whose dark brown hair was cut in a short pageboy. Alenka wore a light-weight pastel plaid smock over knee-length khaki shorts. Her round face held a wide smile as she turned toward Kelly.

"Auntie Laura!"

Kelly was circled by the arms that had just released Jeri.

"Come in, come in. Oh, my manners are terrible. You must be Auntie Laura, Auntie Stella's very dear friend."

Alenka was a pretty eighteen. She would never be called thin no matter what she weighed, but to the appreciative eye she looked as sweet as ripening fruit.

"You're just what I expected! Oh, I'm so glad you're finally here. I thought you would be here soon. Ever since you called, I have been watching for you every day. You look just like Rafi said you would. He said you were tall and magnificent, like a queen on a chess board." She spoke accented English, but she was quite at ease using it, neither did her assurance and infectious openness need any translation.

Jeri shared an alarmed look with Kelly as they followed Alenka up the stairs. Alenka had been friendly on the phone but never as effusive as this. She, of course, bounded up the stairs with more energy than seemed possible. At the open door to the apartment stood a large dog of uncertain parentage who eyed them carefully but whose tail moved in such a whole-hearted wag that it moved most of his body. Perhaps Alenka and the dog had merged personalities.

"This is Srijeda." Alenka bent to wrap her arms around the dog whose tail managed to increase its wagging. She laid her head against the dove-colored gray and creamy gold side of the handsome animal.

With just enough hesitation to assure Srijeda that the decision to be friends was up to him, Kelly moved forward to fondle the great head that looked much like that of a St. Bernard though his fur was far less thick. He leaned against her, indicating that her attention was quite welcome.

"Srijeda, this is your Auntie Laura and that's your Auntie Stella. He likes you, Auntie Laura, especially that thing you're doing with his ears. Srijeda means Wednesday. In our family, Papa always said 'maybe next Wednesday' whenever he didn't want to do something. He always thought that getting a dog was like that, a thing for next Wednesday. Then one day we were at the market and there was this box of puppies and this one was so beautiful. Papa said, 'I suppose this must be Wednesday,' and that's how he got his name. I think Papa was very surprised, though, that Srijeda never quit growing. Now he is just the biggest baby in the whole world."

Jeri decided there was no point to being the only person not sitting on the floor and joined the group, although she was less inclined to join in the adoration of Srijeda. He looked her in the eye for a second, one conspirator to another, it seemed, as if to agree that, yes, he was the best ice-breaker in Vukovar, and then he closed them to better enjoy his rightfully due attention.

"I think Papa let me get a puppy because we were both also sad at knowing that Rafi was gone and we might never see him again. That made Papa so unhappy. He came home once when Papa first got sick, but now I have only heard him on the phone and I have no idea where he is. Do you know, Auntie Stella? Is he in jail?"

"I don't think so. He's somewhere in eastern Russia, but he wasn't more specific. That's all I know."

"He was a fool, a fool to leave us." The statement was so unlike what they had already come to expect from Alenka that both women simply stared at her. Bitterness and sorrow marked her words and she seemed far older than she had just moments before.

"Only a fool would leave his family like he did. Papa never got over missing him but he never said a bad word. Me, though, for me there is very much anger that he is not here now. With me. With Vukovar. He should have been at his father's funeral. He should have sung the requiem and carried the coffin."

†

The hand that Kelly had been using to pet Srijeda moved over to Alenka's arm. "I'm sorry," she said. "This must be awful for you, going through this all alone."

With no warning at all, Alenka threw herself into Kelly's arms and started to sob. Kelly soothed her until Alenka's storm of feelings passed. She wiped her eyes and smiled, and soon enough was as irrepressibly talkative as ever, although now Kelly could recognize the occasional shadows in her sunniness.

"Stepan, that's my boyfriend, you will just love him, Papa did. He will be here tomorrow. Since yesterday he has been in the suburbs on guard duty. He says if the Chetniks realized how few bullets he and the other national guard have, the war would be over today but I tell him he worries too much. Maybe Rafi was more political than me because Mama was still alive when he was growing up and I know she had troubles. I was only six when she died. She was Roma, you know, and I think from some things that Papa said, Rafi took on her troubles. People say horrible things about Roma without even thinking. Rafi looks more like her and I look like Papa who was Serbian but he was also Croatian on his mother's side so no one ever made much about it. We were all just Yugoslavian. Oh, things are all mixed up here, but I'm not going to leave. This is my country and it needs us all now to stand against those people who are so primitive. Most of us are as modern and civilized as Europeans are supposed to be. Come, I will show you the rest of the house."

The apartment was the entire second floor and quite old-fashioned. High ceilings had ornate plaster scrollwork around the edges, and one sitting room had wallpaper with colorful flowers and vines on a dark gray background. The dining room was paneled in dark wood on all the walls. A number of heavy wooden cupboards, armoires, sideboards, and desks were scattered throughout the rooms. The effect was too dark for Jeri's taste, but Kelly was charmed. She thought Rebecca West would surely have had some arch comment to make about the apartment's relationship to the Austro-Hungarians.

"Auntie Stella, this is your room and across the hall is one for Auntie Laura."

Kelly looked at Jeri who nodded.

"Thank you, Alenka, but we only need one room."

"You must each have a room for yourself. Please, it is no trouble and I want you to be comfortable."

"One will do fine, Alenka. That is what will make us most comfortable."

Jeri's meaning slowly occurred to Alenka.

The young woman's mouth dropped open, a hand flew up to cover it, and then she started to giggle.

"How modern!" She was delighted. "Oh, that is so wonderful." Just what was so wonderful, or what was so modern, was unclear, but it was obvious that Jeri and Kelly's relationship was giving Alenka some kind of reflected sophistication. She looked from one to the other, beaming like an aunt at a wedding.

A knock on the door interrupted the lesson in modernity and Alenka flew to open it. Kelly wondered if she ever just walked. Srijeda was already at the door, wagging his tail.

"Mama Marija! Come in. These are my new American aunties. Auntie Stella, Auntie Laura, this is my neighbor, Mama Marija."

Marija Antoljak appeared as reserved as Alenka was bubbly. She stood stolidly in the doorway, making no secret of the fact that she was judging these visitors to her neighbor, her building, her world. Stern, frowning, not tall but very stout, with gray hair in a braid that circled her head like a crown, Marija nodded to the two women.

"It is good that someone comes to visit our Lenka," she said. Jeri translated.

Marija entered the apartment and made her way to the kitchen. She carried a large dish of something that filled the room with a mouth-watering aroma, something to wake any appetite.

"You do not seem to be the type of women who cook," she pronounced, "and I know my Lenka thinks the oven is only for storing empty pans. I will bring some more."

As good as her word, Marija left only to return in minutes with a tray full of such things as bread and coffee. She was accompanied by her husband, Ivo, who made no pretense of being there for any reason but to meet the two women from America.

"There, now you may give your guests a proper meal." Marija ushered Ivo out the door.

While they ate, Alenka explained Marija's presence. Marija and Ivo Antoljak had taken her under their wings ever since her father died. Kelly guessed that Marija had taken care of the motherless youngster long before that. Perhaps the bird analogy was not precisely appropriate, Kelly decided, thinking of Marija's husband. They were more like two elk, large and attentive, dignified, careful not to overstep their boundaries, but adding a formidable presence to the young woman's life. They had three children of their own, a son in Budapest, a daughter gone to Canada, and a married daughter who lived in Osijek, a town north of Vukovar.

The meal was more than proper. Kelly tried to remember when she'd last had home cooking that consisted of potatoes and meat with thick gravy. She watched with satisfaction as Jeri, who liked food well enough when it was put in front of her but who normally ate with all the interest of a furnace being given coal, actually reached for a generous second helping.

Srijeda positioned himself near the center of the linoleum kitchen floor, on his side, perhaps auditioning for some kindergarten cutout of the profile of A Dog. Alenka chatted.

After a while—and despite Alenka's more or less ritual protestations—Kelly began washing the dishes. Although she would never describe herself as domestic, it felt reassuringly homelike to have her hands in warm and soapy water. Usually when she began a project of scrubbing and dusting and sorting and straightening, it was an inconsistent affair with little or no follow-up. George had been much better, and Billy had been able to walk through a room while things flowed into place behind him, and spotlessly, of course. Tonight, as the evening light faded from the day and the kitchen became a haven, a harbor in a strange land, Kelly found nothing further to wish for as she put one sparkling plate after another into the dish rack on the old-fashioned sink, listening as Alenka chattered and Jeri slid in an occasional question.

Alenka was going to university. She thought she would probably do something with computers but it was still all very new and she hadn't begun to make up her mind but—and this always came as a surprise to people if she did say so herself—she was very smart with science and numbers. Alenka and Rafi's grandparents on her mother's side had disappeared during Hitler's war when the Gypsies were taken away along with the Jews. The Roma word for the Holocaust was the Devouring. Alenka's mother was just a baby then and she had escaped the fate of her relatives by being left with a Croatian family who raised her as their own daughter. That was how she escaped most of the terrible way that Gypsies were treated, but there had been one time—this was a family story—when she and Rafi had gone somewhere on the train, to Hungary maybe, and the people had been very rude and worse. Things like that didn't happen anymore. Wasn't her best friend at university, Branka, a Serb, and wasn't their whole group of friends so mixed up in heritage that they were like a small Yugoslavia—Slovenian and Croatian and Bosnian and Montenegrin?

Srijeda lifted his head, and then rose clumsily to all four feet and cocked his head. The three women in the kitchen looked at him. He barked. Just then, they heard a series of thumps, not too far away, but not yet close.

"What was that?" Kelly asked although she knew.

"Nothing. It is nothing." But Alenka's words were more like a prayer than information. She sighed. "It is mortars from the Yugoslavian navy. They are shelling parts of the city, but not always. They have not done this for several nights now."

Jeri swore.

Kelly stared at her hands that still had soapsuds from the dishwater, listening to the distant shells.

"It is nothing," Alenka said again.

Chapter Ten

The smell of coffee and the murmur of voices woke Jeri and Kelly the next morning. Kelly focused on the coffee. The strong aroma flowed past her like a siren song, promising a day of delight if only she hurried. Kelly wasn't sure if there were Rhinemaidens in the Danube, but an image of sirens with stiff sprayed hair brewing coffee while singing something Wagnerian from their river rocks threatened to convulse Kelly in a wave of giddy laughter as she followed Jeri into the kitchen. Caffeine deprivation clearly unhinged her.

They expected to find Marija and Alenka but, instead of Marija, a young man in rumpled camouflage fatigues was sitting at the table. A loose strand of chestnut hair hung over a narrow face drawn with exhaustion.

"Auntie Stella, Auntie Laura, this is Stepan. Stepan Sipek. We have known one another all our lives."

Manners won over weariness and Stepan rose from his chair to acknowledge the introduction.

Kelly took a thick mug of coffee from Alenka and held it close to her nose, savoring the rich scent. The aroma alone was a potent caffeine delivery system. Stepan resumed his seat when Jeri sat, but Kelly remained standing, leaning against the sink.

"Have you come to take Alenka away from Vukovar?"

Stepan gazed steadily at Jeri but before she could answer, Alenka broke in.

"No. No one is taking me from Vukovar. They will not ask and I will not go. I do not want to hear any more of this."

"You should go. My own parents have gone."

"So? You are still here. This is Vukovar."

"Rafi thinks you should go to Sarajevo," Jeri said.

"Oh? And where is Rafi? My brother should be here, with his

434

family, with his people in his own country."

"More and more people are coming for shelter from the farms and smaller villages with terrible stories," Stepan said.

"Oh, stories!" Alenka muttered as if her tone alone could substitute for an argument.

Stepan smiled at her and the smile suggested that Alenka often resorted to attitude in arguments between them. He turned his attention again to Jeri. "I am part of the national guard. You know of this?"

"Alenka told us. The guard is the Croatian defense force. Were you in the federal army? The JNA?"

"I was. So were some of the others in my unit. When Croatia declared independence, we came home. It took some time because we were stationed in Kosovo, of course."

Kelly remembered that Jeri had told her the army had been shifting people around for at least a year.

"They think we are so stupid that we don't notice. To the Krajina, they send officers and men who are born Serbs, like Ratko Mladic. To Bosnia-Herzegovina, they send Bosnian-born Serbs. But Croatians and Bosnian Muslims, they send us to Kosovo and Macedonia, as far from home as possible. This from people who say that Croats make tricks. This Milosevic, he is the trickiest of all. He has been planning this war for a long time."

Stepan looked down at the table. Then he looked at Jeri again but it was Alenka to whom he was speaking. "Last night there were two trucks that came through our station that were full of wounded people. They say that there is much fighting now at Osijek and Vincovci."

Kelly looked at Jeri. "Didn't we drive past Vincovci on the way here?"

Jeri nodded, her mouth a thin, grim line.

"Why are they doing this?" Alenka asked the rhetorical question with such distress it was as if she thought someone in the kitchen might have an answer. The question also revealed there were cracks in the reassurance she tried hard to project. "With Slovenia, there was a little fighting only, and then honor was satisfied and then the Yugoslav army goes away. Why not here, too? Why won't the army go away?"

"You know. They say this is Serbian land because Serbs live here, and in Slovenia there were no Serbs." Stepan paused. "They bring wounded through in trucks now because ambulances are being shelled. I saw an ambulance yesterday, clearly marked with a red cross on white. It was like a saltshaker with all of the bullet holes. But most holes were in the cross. It had been used for target practice."

Alenka started to respond but Stepan held up a hand to keep Alenka from interrupting. "And I have heard from more than one place that there are groups who are under the control of Zeljko Raznatovic—"

"Arkan." Jeri all but hissed the name.

Stepan nodded and continued. "—who are going through the villages and making the worst of terrible crimes. They use knives and axes to kill."

"Oh, Arkan! He is this scarecrow everyone uses to scare everyone. I am not leaving Vukovar. This is my home." Alenka lapsed into her own language and Jeri stood up, motioning for Kelly to follow.

"This is between them," she said when they were out of the kitchen. "It sounds like an argument that they've been having for a while."

They walked down the hallway to the large room at the front of the apartment. Heavy curtains covered the windows on one side while a large bookcase took up most of the adjacent wall. A black grand piano was the central feature of the room while an overstuffed sofa, chairs and small tables were arranged around the edges.

It wasn't long before Alenka joined them. "I am sorry. We say these things to one another often these days. Stepan is tired. He is going to his mother's house to sleep, but he will give me a ride to university first. Is there anything you need before I go? Auntie Stella, you have a key. And even if you go out and forget, you can always ring the bell for Marija or Ivo and they will let you in. Marija is always here."

They were quiet after Alenka left with Stepan.

"Maybe she's right." Jeri broke the silence. "Or wrong. But we can't decide for her. She's not a child, no matter how Rafi thinks of her, and she can make her own decisions. Obviously she has been making them for a while now. But I can't just go away and leave her either."

The sight of Jeri unsure of her next move was novel to Kelly.

"Let's give it a few days. I like staying here." And then she spoke to change the subject. "Is that a picture of Rafi?"

"Where?"

Kelly pointed to a picture on a small round table at one end of the sofa. It was a family portrait in muted colors. The woman was dark-haired, an older version of the Alenka they now knew, zaftig and beautiful and holding a toddler on her lap. The little girl gazed up at her mother, reaching for her face with one chubby hand, while the older woman gazed at the camera with a sad expression. Behind her, gazing at the camera, was a sandy-haired man, a thin man whose glasses gave him a bookish air, wearing what was probably his Sunday suit. Beside him stood a boy of twelve, maybe more, and the man had one hand on the boy's shoulder. The group, other than the baby, all wore what Kelly thought of as camera expressions.

"Yes, that's Rafi."

Kelly picked up the picture and stared intently at the figure of the young Rafi, looking for the man who figured so importantly in Jeri's life and now in her own. She wondered when or if she would ever meet him. The boy had dark hair and dark eyes, his mother's coloring and his father's spare frame. There was mischief in his look, but also an aspect that was very serious, as if even at this age something troubled his mind, something he was determined to face. The boy stood with his shoulders back, staring straight into the camera but he leaned ever so slightly toward his mother as if he might step in front of her.

"I see it," Kelly said. "I see why you would be friends. You're both willing to put yourselves forward, to draw fire, so to speak." She handed the picture to Jeri.

"Jeri—Auntie Stella, I mean. Should we keep with the passport names?" Kelly kept her voice low.

Jeri thought for a moment. "It's awkward, I know, but I think we should. Mostly for Alenka's sake." She couldn't think of a situation where knowing the real names of her guests might become a problem for Rafi's sister, but old habits are strong and Jeri meant to keep shared information to a minimum.

Kelly nodded and Jeri continued to look at the picture, caught in her own web of memories.

Kelly drifted over to the piano and ran her fingers lovingly over the smooth dark wood. She shuffled through the stack of music books and found several that were familiar despite being written in Croatian. She sat down and tested her skill and the piano's tuning. The true notes that she heard indicated that the instrument was for more than show, but her fingers were stiff, strangers to an exercise that once had been a daily routine.

"I didn't know you could play."

"I do have one or two skills that life out of a backpack doesn't give much opportunity for using." She smiled as she remembered a particularly tricky run of notes. "But it's been years since I've had a chance to play. Not since I went away to college, really."

She skipped further exercise and opened a music book. Tentatively, she began Beethoven's "Fur Elise". The piece might be a bit of a cliché, but despite that, the gentle loveliness, haunting and delicate, carried her to a plane where the yearning for love was timelessly woven into the memory of love. Kelly revised her thought. Perhaps the player might be a cliché, but the song was eternal.

Srijeda thumped his tail against the floor.

†

Alenka came home late. She gamely attempted to be hostess to her guests, but after the basic forms were satisfied, all three women turned in for the night. No shelling disturbed the city that night.

Early the next morning, heedless of any conventions regarding privacy, or of any worries that the sophisticated customs of modernity might be in progress, Alenka gave only the most perfunctory knock before entering her aunties' bedroom.

"Wake up, you old sleepyheads," she cried. She bounced onto the foot of the bed, giving Jeri scant seconds to avoid having her legs sat on. "I have a big day planned for us, and already we are late."

Kelly thought that was very likely an exaggeration but she had no objective way of telling. Heavy curtains covered the room's single window and the only light entering the room was the electric light from the hall. She sniffed and noted that the lovely coffee of the day before was in evidence. She peered over the edge of the down comforter to see Alenka beaming like a Buddha. The young woman's extraordinarily infectious good spirits were once more in evidence and impossible to resist.

"I have asked Marija and she says that we may use their bicycles. I am taking you to see Vu-Ko-Var!" She sang out the name of the city, accenting all three syllables like a magician producing a bouquet of flowers.

"Come on, you old sleepyhead." Kelly joined in, pulling away the pillow that Jeri was trying to keep over her head. "We are going to see Vu-Ko-Var!"

Alenka took them first to the back of the apartment building where Marija waited with three large bicycles that appeared to be ancestors of the modern kind of light metal and narrow tires that Kelly was more used to seeing. Marija also had a covered basket that she fastened securely to the bicycle that Jeri chose.

"It is just a little in case you become hungry," said the solid woman. She made it sound as though becoming hungry was some fault that

438

foreigners had brought among the good people of Vukovar. And if this were indeed the case, then she would muster a most heroic effort and rise to the occasion.

Kelly had been in Croatia too long already to think that the day was anything but a dream snatched from the jaws of a crouching nightmare, a fact that made it wonderfully memorable. Alenka led the way through a city only just beginning to wake up. The unmistakable odor of a river, strong and rich, surrounded them. Morning river mist made the streets somewhat slick, but the late summer sun was quickly asserting its presence, dispelling the mists and drying the streets even as the three women pedaled along.

They rode past small parks landscaped to exquisite perfection, with flowers tended so lovingly that they looked like the product of a master painter. They rode through a modern business district and past department store windows full of dummies, elegantly dressed in silk and gowns and black tuxedos, portraying the postures of moneyed leisure, past cafes with people reading the newspapers before their workday started. They rode past solid baroque buildings that echoed the streets of Vienna, signaling the once-upon-a-time presence of the Austro-Hungarian Empire.

"Vukovar is the door to Slavonia," Alenka called back from her lead position. She made the guidebook phrase sound almost new as she spoke it with pride. "Slavonia has fed Europe for centuries."

The sun had driven away the last of the mist and a deep blue sky lent vibrancy to all the other colors as Alenka led the three women to the front of the Eltz Castle. It looked more like a manor house than a castle to Kelly, but she liked the balanced charm of it along with the ochre coloring so common in the city. Then she turned and saw, at the farther edge of the castle grounds, the fabled Danube flowing past in magnificent indolence.

First there is the River. . . . The words seemed to flow into her mind.

If, as T.S. Eliot says, the river is a strong, brown god, then the Danube sits among the elder gods of the planet, with her sister the Rhine beside the Nile and the Amazon, the Indus and the Ganges, the Yangtze, the Tigris and Euphrates. The Danube begins in Germany's Black Forest and flows east over 1,700 miles before spilling into the Black Sea, and along the way it unites peoples and divides countries. Like all the great rivers, the Danube sang a song that long ago lured the human race out of the forests and off the plains and down from the mountain caves.

The vision of the Danube mesmerized Kelly. No matter what

flourished or diminished along its banks, this great being would continue.

"It is called the Dove of Vucedol." Alenka was pointing proudly to a poster of an oddly shaped bird. Kelly had seen the poster in so many places along the bike route that Alenka might well have called it the Dove of Vukovar. In this particular incarnation, the poster was spread on a board in front of the Eltz Castle.

"It is from the—oh, how do you say—" she muttered something in Croatian.

"The Neolithic," Jeri translated. "The New Stone Age."

"Really?" Surprised, Kelly gave the figure deeper attention. She had dismissed the dove as some recent piece of graphic design, clever but not particularly noteworthy. Now, aware of the figure's age, she remembered more. She remembered reading about the little known cultures of ancient Eastern Europe. The Dove of Vucedol was an artifact from this era as well as this area, both of which lay outside the traditional timelines for charting the course of civilization's rise. She wished she could remember more now that she was here. A scholar named Marija Gimbutas had collected and published a mass of evidence that suggested there might be birthplaces of civilization other than just along the Tigris and Euphrates Rivers, but Kelly couldn't recall the theory with any exactitude. She'd skimmed the books and marveled at the pictures and then committed impressions rather than facts to memory.

Alenka, the happy tour guide, was still explaining.

"Vucedol is a place near the city where the archaeologists have found many old things and our dove is the most famous. If it were not for this stupid war, we could ride there so quickly. It is a place with a beautiful view. But we will stay here for this morning. Maybe another time we can go. Look, for our picnic I have brought wine from Vukovar's wineries. Our wine is quite famous. We are still a most civilized city."

It did seem most civilized to stroll down to the paths along the Danube. Even the presence of armed Croatian guardsmen did not diminish the pleasure of viewing the great river. The young men warned them to stay on the lookout for Serbian gunboats, but they shared Alenka's pride in their city and were unwilling to forbid access to the visitors.

"The Vuko River bends near here. That is where the name comes from. Vukovar, city on the Vuko River. In the medieval age, it was a fortress city but that was nearly destroyed when the Ottoman Turks left and there was a great battle, so that is why most of the old buildings are from the time when we were ruled from Vienna."

Kelly gazed east across the wide river. She sensed Jeri behind her and then felt Jeri's hands on her shoulders. Kelly leaned back and let Jeri rest her chin on top of her head. The slow dignity of the great river was entrancing.

"I think that the river is a strong brown god." Kelly quoted T.S. Eliot softly.

She thought Jeri might not have heard but then Jeri replied with a few lines farther into the poem. "The brown god is almost forgotten by the dwellers in cities—ever however implacable, keeping his seasons and rages, destroyer, reminder of what men choose to forget."

"Wow. I didn't remember that part."

"I wish I didn't. We're learning too much about what men choose to forget."

Never far from Kelly's awareness was how a short a time ago she had despaired of ever seeing Jeri again. She reached into her pocket and squeezed the plum-sized crystal from Nepal.

"I think we should go back for Marija's food. I am so hungry." Alenka drew them back to the present.

They strolled back to the castle and unpacked the basket in the shade of several oaks. The conversation shifted from regional history to the more personal. Alenka had taken several vacations to Slovenia and the Alps that ranged the border between Slovenia and Austria and Italy, but she had never been to Dubrovnik. Kelly and Jeri took turns describing the famous city on the Adriatic Sea, however, they said nothing of the journey from Dubrovnik to Zagreb.

Marija had packed baked chicken along with homemade bread and a cucumber salad.

Kelly took another piece of chicken and laughed. "I wish I was a food writer. I'd make Marija famous throughout the world."

"We told the soldiers at the Serbian road block on the way into the city that we were newspaper writers." Jeri answered Alenka's questioning look. "It didn't seem likely that a paper would send in two news reporters, so we made Laura a food writer."

"Yes? But you cannot write the full truth until you have tasted the dessert." Alenka took a carefully wrapped box from the basket. When the cloth was removed, she presented an entire cake with thick, dark chocolate frosting.

"All right. Marija gets the Nobel Prize for cooking."

"There is such a thing? Oh, of course not, but you are right, there should be."

They must have all drifted off in a lazy haze of rich food, wine and mid-day warmth. The next thing Kelly was aware of was the thump of what she now recognized as shelling. The sounds were distant, like the thunder of a storm that might approach or might pass by. Jeri was sitting up and gazing into some middle distance, listening, evaluating. Alenka was staring at the remnants of the picnic, her mouth set tight, her nostrils flared, a study of anger and sorrow.

The thumping stopped.

"I'm going to go ask the guard if they know where that was," Jeri said.

Alenka nodded and handed the box to Jeri. "Take this with you. Marija will be glad to know that they had some of her cake."

Jeri took the box and walked toward the river, her stride quick and long.

"She is quite beautiful," Alenka said.

"Oh, yes. She is."

"Not just the way she looks, which is so very dramatic and strong, but—oh, my English is not good enough for this—it is how she intends, as if she were an arrow or a spear."

"Or a sword, in honorable hands." Kelly's voice was almost a whisper.

"I am so glad you are both here." Alenka was still looking after Jeri. "I feel how you are with one another and it is a good thing to be close to. Have you met my brother?"

Kelly shook her head. "Not yet, but I hope to soon."

"I was sure he would have said if you had. He spoke so much of his great comrade Stella the last time I saw him, but that was more than three years ago. I was very young then. I am often so lonely for Rafi. He does seem closer with Auntie Stella here. When he was still at home, he was sometimes like an uncle, and too grown up for a little sister, but then at other times, he was a comrade and it would be just the two of us. He changed though, after Mama died, and all the fun went out of him."

"I know how you feel," Kelly said. "I miss my brother, George. He was older, too, but he was always my best friend."

"Why do you miss your brother?"

"He died last year. He had AIDS."

They were quiet together. After a while, Alenka blew her nose. "I have a friend from many years. Andrija. I was the first person he told that he was gay. He says he is okay and takes the proper care, but I worry for him."

Jeri was coming back across the neatly trimmed green grass.

"Perhaps we should leave," she said when she reached her two companions. "The guard says the fighting is near an area called Baranja, but they've also had word by radio that gunboats have been sighted on the Danube."

On the ride back to Pijacu Street, Alenka led the trio to a busy sidewalk café where her university friends congregated. A number of them were present. As Alenka introduced her American aunties, Kelly felt her stomach clench. For a few seconds she was back in Zagreb, back in the noisy café from which she had been abducted. Jeri must have been remembering too, because she placed a hand on Kelly's arm.

"Do you want to leave?" she asked in a lowered voice that only Kelly could hear.

"No. It's okay. It will be okay. Just give me a minute. But, stay close?"

Kelly's breathing eased as she sat and glanced around at all the youthful faces. Slowly she felt herself transported from memory of Zagreb and terror, and back to the Ohio student union where she had taught until George became ill. This group was not unlike her own students had been, sweet of face and intense of discussion. They struggled to speak English in deference to Alenka's aunties, but Kelly noticed that, although she only had the rhythm and a very small vocabulary, she was beginning to break down the jumble of sounds into separate words. She was picking up Croatian. Serbo-Croatian.

"Auntie Laura, this is my friend, Andrija."

He was a pleasant-looking youth, sandy brown hair and dark brown eyes, a bit shy as he stood and took her hand and then Jeri's. The slight pressure of his grip and extra warmth of his smile suggested that Alenka had probably told him how modern she and Jeri were. Alenka seemed anxious after she introduced aunties and friends but then relaxed as the conversation, awkward at first in the presence of strangers, resumed.

They spoke of the war, of course.

"Where is George Bush?" asked a beefy young man, as if Jeri and Kelly might be able to produce the American president. "Didn't anyone tell him that Croatia is on the way back to the United States from Iraq? We will make him president for life if he will come here with his army."

"Somebody told him that there is no oil in Croatia," answered an earnest young woman with dark hair.

"Why should America care when even Europe won't help us?" A

young man with thick glasses shook his head. "Half of Europe thinks we are still Ustasha, worse than the Nazis, so we deserve whatever happens, and the other half thinks that we are just being the primitive Balkans, doomed to act out ethnic hatreds for all eternity."

"You are too bitter, Petar," said Andrija. "No one would think you were Ustasha, your family was Chetnik. Besides, Europe won't let this go on much longer. When they find out what is happening, they will force Milosevic to stop."

"I used to be proud we were Chetniks and fought the Nazis, but not anymore. Now the name means only Serbs who fight for Serbia. I am Croatian. And when will Europe come to help? Before or after Vukovar is turned into rubble?"

"Petar! Don't be ridiculous. They're only trying to scare us. Who would want to damage a city as beautiful as this?"

"If any of you had any sense, you would leave while it was still possible," Petar grumbled.

"We will leave when you do, Petar." Alenka put on a jolly voice. "We will be right behind you as you leave the city."

"You know I have to stay. I am in the guard like Stepan."

"You use that for an excuse so no one will know your secret—you love Vukovar just like the rest of us."

Petar grumbled something more, but a small smile played at the edge of his exasperation.

The conversation drifted on, never straying far from the war. After a while, only Petar and Andrija were left. Petar had said little after his earlier outburst. Kelly had had been watching him, seeing how he stared at the table while his sensitive features fought against revealing anguish. He had taken off his glasses to massage the bridge of his nose and a shock of hair fell across his forehead. Kelly caught Andrija staring at Petar while trying not to let his interest show. Andrija looked away as Petar raised his head, but it was to Alenka that Petar spoke, and with a fierce intensity.

"Please, Alenka. Think about going. I know you argue with Stepan, but I listen to my cousins and uncles and their friends. You have no idea how fast civilization can disappear and leave behind the old hatreds."

Kelly would have smiled if the situation had been less serious. Alenka, Stepan, Andrija, Petar. War might rumble about the stage but the drama of who loved whom was still being played. Kelly actually felt like an older aunt.

†

The day had woven the three women into a comfortable cohesion. That evening, when Kelly went to the front room and played the piano, Jeri found a book on the history of the Ottoman Empire and settled into one of the comfortable chairs. For a while she focused on reading, but then she gave herself over to the music and just drifted until the aroma of fresh coffee drew her toward the kitchen. Alenka had spread her books over the kitchen table and she was concentrating so hard, she didn't hear Jeri enter. Srijeda was under the table, his head propped on the rung of a chair, and he barely bothered to lift an eyelid at Jeri's appearance. Jeri helped herself to a cup of coffee, thought a moment and then poured another for Kelly. Alenka smiled and nodded to her but was instantly reabsorbed into her work.

Jeri walked back to the front room, bemused by the aura of domesticity. Kelly contributed by looking grateful for the coffee but did not pause in her piano playing.

The turning of a key in the lock brought Srijeda padding down the hall and by the time the door opened and Stepan entered, his tail was wagging furiously. Stepan was dressed again in his guard uniform, but someone had washed them. The young man nodded to Jeri and stood a few minutes listening to the music before joining Alenka in the kitchen.

Jeri was becoming aware of some contradictory feelings and tried to sort through them. On the one hand, she was almost comfortable with the homey scene, though she knew she was not like Alenka and Kelly who swam in it as easily as fish in a pond. Thinking that, Jeri found a knot on the thread she was following—resentment. To her surprise, Jeri recognized that she resented Kelly and Alenka for their familiarity with this kind of life. If Kelly were asked, she'd probably say that she hadn't felt this way since such-and-such time, while if Jeri were asked, she'd have to admit that she'd never felt this way.

Certainly not in South Boston. Her family hadn't been at the bottom, not by a long shot, but Jeri didn't recall that ease or peace was ever a resident of her household. Somebody was always yelling, inside or outside, in the apartment halls or in the streets. Some of her first memories that didn't involve cockroaches were of being surrounded by angry people when her mother took her into the streets to demonstrate in Boston's busing wars. On the wrong side, of course.

Eamon O'Donnell wasn't precisely an alcoholic, and there was always enough money for food, but no one would ever call him a slouch in the drinking department. He called it being Irish. He had a heavy hand with discipline, all his children learned that, but he took no pleasure in it, and he never lifted a hand against his wife. If he had, Jeri was sure that her mother would have belted him all the way to County Down. That was a favorite phrase for Kate O'Donnell. "Watch yourself or I'll belt you all the way to County Down."

Jeri could hear her mother's Boston accent echo in memory. Eamon had come from Ireland, but Kate was third generation American Irish. And she was more likely to join Eamon at the neighborhood pub than to try and talk him home. They got along well enough when they were out. It was when they came home that their faces grew tight and their voices angry.

"You could always set a dinner plate for anger at our table," Jeri had once told Arkadia O'Malley, the woman who had been her saving at Armagh Prison.

"From the comfortable way that frown sits on your face, I'm not in the least surprised," the older woman had answered.

Jeri had clung to her own anger, a grinding emotion that honed away extraneous attitudes or interests. It was how she kept her focus, kept her guard on streets where a moment's inattention could cost a life or limb. It wasn't until she took track in high school that she found a way to outdistance her anger. She exchanged the cigarettes that had been part of her streetwise persona for the sense of well-being that accompanied a body trained and exercised.

In Armagh prison, curiously enough, there had been moments of near-contentment. To be so completely ruled by others had a sort of peace to it, but Jeri had resisted that peace with all her will. She kept her anger, muzzled and hidden, but she kept it. She trained. Focused. Learned whatever was available from whatever the donated books might teach. West Indian history, the Gaelic language, Pakistani geography. When she was with Arkadia O'Malley, she learned to be almost content. Jeri loved the woman and wanted to be her lover, but Arkadia told her they had other things to be for one another. Jeri never got to say good-bye. The authorities turned her loose abruptly, and it was a condition of her release that she never contact any of her prison acquaintances. So it was that, after three years and no trial, one morning she woke up a prisoner and by noon she was eating lunch as a free woman. And by nightfall she had taken the first steps to becoming the IRA volunteer in fact, that they had imprisoned her for, in error.

The music Kelly was playing sounded familiar, but Jeri knew little about the classics of music. Kelly had told her that if she was able to play something then it was likely to be one of the better-known pieces. This one had a light sound, not light as in trivial or frivolous but light as in the sun slipping through leaves and dancing in a shaded glade. An odd thought, not her usual way of thinking, more like Kelly's way. Jeri looked over to see if Kelly was somehow sending thoughts along with the music, but she seemed to be completely engrossed in playing. Even so, Jeri sometimes suspected that the woman could follow her into her memories.

A wave of contentment reached her and Jeri leaned back in the chair, pleased to recognize the feeling and no longer resentful of the evening's domesticity. The light in the room from two lamps was soft, glowing. Kelly glanced over and smiled and then was instantly absorbed back into the music. She peered at the open book, concentrating. Jeri could tell she was trying for something more than just getting the notes right, trying to find the meaning in the combination of sounds, find the magic, reaching for the moment when the separate sounds flowed into a unity of form and feeling.

This was one of the moments a lover treasured: to see the beloved unaware, to see while being oneself unseen. Like being granted a moment of natural grace when the spirit of the other is revealed whole and timeless. Kelly had closed her eyes, the better to hear the music. Jeri felt it flow to her, and she accepted the cascade of sound as a gift. She drank in the look on Kelly's face, a look she usually saw from much closer, intent concentration, lips parted in the shallow breathing of passion.

Kelly opened her eyes and looked directly at Jeri. A smile played at the corners of her mouth.

Damn, but the woman was something else! Could she really read Jeri's mind?

Kelly winked.

Jeri shook her head in admiration as Kelly began the series of notes that signaled an ending and finished with a flourish. The music disappeared into the silence.

"Would you like to stay here for a while?" Jeri asked.

Kelly considered and then nodded. "For a while."

"This isn't the safest place."

Kelly nodded again. "I know, but I bet nobody follows us here."

Chapter Eleven

The rumble of autumn thunder woke Kelly. She and Jeri were still tangled in the last embraces that had preceded their falling asleep. Kelly shifted but it was impossible to get any closer so she settled for kissing the arm near her face. She felt a slight answering pressure that indicated Jeri was also awake.

Alarmed barking by Srijeda accompanied another rumble.

Not thunder. Kelly remembered that the nighttime rumbling had not been thunder for a long time, and now it was closer.

Jeri was out of bed and slipping into a sweatshirt and jeans and tossing clothes to Kelly before the next crash.

"Shoes! Get them on quick."

The noise separated into the sounds of airplane engines punctuated by more explosions.

Please, God, Kelly prayed to any deity that might be listening. *Please, not yet.*

Now.

The rumble was overhead, was everywhere, the explosions deafening and endless. The building shuddered while noise made thought impossible. Things were breaking, shattering. One was simply a small mammal waiting for the huge rolling dice to cease and then one would know if life or death had won.

Arms lifted her, moved her, then she felt herself on the floor, covered by Jeri. Kelly tended to forget the woman was so strong.

The noise lessened. Jeri rose, her weight, her presence, the safety of her gone.

"Come on. Let's find Alenka and Stepan."

There was still a house outside the bedroom. No broken roof or wall was apparent, although the feel of things beneath Kelly's feet explained why Jeri had insisted on shoes. Against all odds, the light switch worked.

448

Chips of plaster, glass, and other broken things lay scattered over the floor. Kelly saw Stepan emerge into the hallway, wearing pants and an unbuttoned shirt. Alenka followed him, in a robe.

"Kelly, help Alenka get dressed. Stepan can check on the Antoljaks. I'll go make sure the gas is off."

The explosions were less but Jeri still had to yell to be heard.

Alenka's hands shook as she buttoned on a shirt. "For the first time I am glad that Papa is not alive." She paused. "He loved this building. It was from his grandfather. And Papa loved Vukovar. He would be in misery at what is happening. I think maybe he is lucky."

Kelly took over the task of fitting buttons to buttonholes for Alenka. There was comfort in comforting.

As the noise of explosions receded, other sounds drifted in through the windows, sounds of voices calling from the street. Alenka pulled aside a curtain and Kelly saw that the windows were shattered. That was where all the glass had come from.

"My God! The Lackavic house across the street is broken. We must go." Alenka stared into the dark outside.

"We should bring blankets," Kelly said, thinking of shock.

"And water." Jeri had returned. "Water to drink."

"Ivo and Marija are not hurt." Stepan had also returned. "They are going out to help. I have brought flashlights for us."

The smell of smoke was strong on Pijacu Street, smoke and the acrid tang of explosives. Up and down the street, people were emerging from their homes. A block away, the glow of fire outlined a building. The apartment across from 12 Pijacu, also a two-story structure, was crushed on one side, beams and inner walls visible and jutting at odd angles, pieces of plaster dangling from wires, pipes leaning toward nowhere, but so far no smoke was apparent. A woman with disheveled hair, barefoot and wearing only a dirty nightgown, stood staring up at the ruin.

Kelly shook open one of her blankets and approached the woman, meaning to wrap her against the chill air. As Kelly came closer, she saw that it was blood, not dirt, that was darkening the woman's nightgown, blood from a wound on the side of her head.

"Madame . . . madame." Kelly tried to get her attention but the woman seemed not to hear. As the blanket was wrapped around her, the woman turned her eyes from the damaged building but she didn't seem able to focus. Kelly gently directed her off the street and toward Alenka. She was relieved to see Marija hurrying toward them, bringing more blankets. Marija spoke rapidly to the wounded woman, who was

449

gradually regaining focus.

"She is saying that she is fallen into the street." Alenka's English was becoming something of a casualty. "The noise that breaks the house throws her to the street."

†

Ivo emerged from his house carrying a crowbar and on his way, as most neighbors were, to the next street to fight the fire. Jeri stopped him.

"Ivo, do you know how many people live there?" Jeri pointed to the nearly demolished building.

Ivo thought there were three families in the Lackavic house. In normal times there were only two, but relatives of the people on the first floor had recently arrived. Fleeing from the fighting in the countryside that had grown increasingly vicious, they had come to what they thought would be the safety of the city. Altogether, probably ten to fifteen adults and children had been living across the street. Ivo thought that he had seen some of the residents among the neighbors on the street, but he wasn't sure.

There was still a front door blocking access to the building but it was wedged in place. Faint voices could be heard from the other side.

Stepan ran to see if anyone could be spared from the fire.

Together Ivo and Jeri forced the thick old door to move. The planes were gone and it had grown quiet enough that the screech of cracking wood was loud against a background of distant cries and sirens.

Inside the building, flashlights revealed thick, murky air that Jeri judged was more dust than smoke. The hall was crisscrossed with fallen wood and piping, but she and Ivo made their way slowly, careful to avoid hanging wires that might still carry live electricity. They came to a stairway and Ivo called out. There was no answer from below, but from above, they heard cries that increased. Testing each step before trusting it with any weight, they crept up. At the top, they emerged into another hallway, but the destruction here was much worse than below. In one direction, the hall was completely blocked by debris, in another, they could see outside because the wall was gone. Now, they could hear moaning as well as cries for help coming through the debris.

Jeri swore in several languages, one of them Croatian, using terms that surprised Ivo, and then she got her temper back under control. "Swine and bastard children of swine. If the JNA is half as good as they claim, they have to know this is a residential area."

450

"They know." Ivo was grim. "Radio Vukovar has been saying that the Yugoslav Federal Army is targeting places that have no military value. Like Eltz Castle, the Medical Center, the Franciscan Monastery, homes of ordinary people."

Any place that had cultural, or communal, value. Anywhere that would discourage or destroy the spirit of the people of the city.

"Hall-o-o-o. Can anyone hear me? It's Ivo, your neighbor."

"Ivo." The voice was faint, coming from behind the wreckage, and a fit of coughing followed the name. The moaning continued.

"Hold on, Josip. We're coming for you." Ivo leaned toward the jumbled wood and called out. "Josip, can you get to a window? We could get a ladder."

"Won't work, Ivo. We're caught here in the hallway. I've got the kids, but I don't where Marta is. I can hear her and she sounds pretty bad."

The crash of a mortar falling and exploding somewhere not far away made the trapped children cry out. Apparently the attack was not yet over for the night.

Jeri tied her flashlight to a standing board with some loose wire, and aimed the light along the hallway. "Let's work with just mine for now," she suggested. "No sense to using up batteries we may need later."

Ivo nodded. "Good, but I have more if we need them. I have been preparing for something like this."

It was slow, perilous work. They had to test every large piece of wood or wallboard before removing it. It would be very dangerous to bring down more of the building by mistake. Slow work, but Jeri and Ivo got one another's rhythm. At some point, Stepan and two more people arrived.

"Everyone from downstairs is safe," Stepan said, "but they think the whole Lackavic family is trapped in here."

Jeri remembered Alenka saying the family was ethnic Serbian. Not surprising, since about a third of Vukovar was ethnic Serbian, but it was ironic since the JNA claimed they were bombing to protect the Croatian Serbs.

Clearing the hallway went faster after Stepan and the other two men joined the work, and now they also had two saws and a hand axe along with the crowbar. Pale light, visible through the space that had once been a roof, showed that dawn was approaching. Jeri could see Ivo's face now, and she thought her own was probably as streaked with soot and dust as his. The older man's hair, usually a thick shock of white, was peppered gray with the grime that kept sifting from the ceiling with each new shudder of the building. He seemed to feel Jeri looking at him and he paused to clasp her shoulder, his blue eyes soft in a wordless smile.

Along with the slowly increasing light came still more shelling. The last week had seen an increase in mortars fired from across the Danube and from the suburbs, and this day after the aerial bombing was apparently going to be no different.

Kelly brought hot tea and bread to the workers and Jeri took a few minutes to rest.

"What's happening outside?" Jeri wiped her damp forehead with the back of her hand, leaving a streak of grime behind.

"They took Mrs. Babic to the medical site at the Tesla school. They have a clinic set up there. Mrs. Babic is the woman whose head was hurt. I couldn't tell how she was. She never seemed to come out of shock." Kelly used her shirt cuff to wipe away some of the sooty smear from Jeri's brow. She went on talking.

"Marija and some of the other women organized a way to check the block and no one else besides the Lackavics seems to be hurt or missing. We're moving into the basement. Marija's directing the project. She and Alenka are arranging living areas. It seems most of Vukovar is moving to a basement."

"Sounds like a good idea."

"Jeri? A bunch of rubble fell on the Yugo. I think it's destroyed."

"Damn! We won't be able to get another one here."

"And the bad news is?"

Jeri grinned. "Are you sure you didn't drop some rubble on it yourself? I know you think Yugos grow on trees, but—" She turned as a boy of about ten tapped her arm to get her attention. She nodded to him.

"Miss Estellija? I think I can crawl through the hall and get to where Mr. Lackavic is. Maybe not all the way, but I think I can get some water to him."

The boy spoke Croatian and Kelly didn't understand, but seeing that Jeri's attention was once again completely engaged in the work, she withdrew.

A nearby explosion shook the building, perhaps from leaking gas, and more dust sifted down in a cloud, causing everyone to cough. It also caused a wave of misery in the people trapped behind the debris. The children cried out, more afraid than hurt, but the moans coming from Mrs. Lackavic, which had quit for more than an hour, began again.

†

Kelly found a way to fit into the work by joining a line that was passing debris from the work area out of the building. It took two more hours until they came to where Marta Lackavic was trapped. A beam had fallen across her upper legs and hips, pinning her to the floor. She had lost consciousness again when the rescuers reached her, and that was probably a blessing considering how badly she appeared to be hurt.

"How is she?" Josip called. He and his children were still trapped, but they were very close to being freed. They had been quiet since the young volunteer had been able to bring them water. He had not been able to get all the way, or they might have been able to bring out the children, but the water had been more than welcome.

Ivo frowned. He was exhausted and his half-century-plus age was evident. He wanted to tell his neighbor the truth but he hesitated because of the children. He settled on a partial truth.

"She needs to go to hospital, Josip. She is unconscious now."

"Get her out," Josip called. "We are not hurt here."

Marta Lackavic moaned when she was picked up and carefully placed on blanket-covered boards. Her eyes opened but she was not really conscious. Kelly held a pad made from a towel to reduce bleeding that had started again when they moved the woman. Ivo and Jeri followed the injured woman outside to the street.

"Yakov has a truck." Ivo pointed to one of the other rescue workers. Yakov was a small, wiry man. "Would you and Laura go to the hospital with her? Take her to the hospital, not to the Tesla Center. We can finish here."

Marta was carefully placed in the truck bed and then surrounded with more blankets. Jeri and Kelly rode with Marta in the back, keeping the blankets in place that protected the injured woman from being bounced and jostled as much as possible.

The streets of Vukovar were pocked with holes and strewn with rubble. Neither Jeri nor Kelly had ventured far from Pijacu Street recently and the look of the city came as a shock. On every block, there were damaged houses, some totally destroyed. The aerial bombing was new but the mortar fire was also destructive.

As they drove through a deserted commercial area, Kelly recognized the department store she had seen the day she and Jeri and Alenka had gone by on bicycles on their way to a picnic by the Danube. In a bizarre twist of circumstance, the elegantly dressed dummies were still standing in the bored postures of moneyed leisure, but the roof was gone from their section of store and the jagged fragments of plate glass that survived in place were spider-webbed with cracks.

Through the missing back window of the pickup, Kelly could hear their driver praying. He kept repeating a phrase as he backed up or sped around piles of rubble. As they neared the hospital and the mortar shelling grew heavier, Yakov's praying got louder. Suddenly, Kelly recognized the words.

"Head eem oop, head eem oot – Raw - hi-i-i-de! Head eem oop, head eem oot – Raw - hi-i-i-de!" The nearer they came to the hospital, the louder Yakov shouted.

If the damage in the streets of the city was a shock, the sight of the hospital was even worse. The Vukovar Medical Center, which ought to have been a haven, had been instead the target of intensive shelling. Debris littered the grounds. Shell holes, surrounded by petal-shaped burn marks, blossomed on the walls like grim flowers from hell, gifts from demon suitors. It was contrary to sanity, to humanity, to all the rules of civilization.

Yakov, daring fate, drove them as close as possible to a doorway blocked with heaps of rubble and kept the motor running while Jeri and Kelly scrambled to remove the wounded woman. Broken glass crunched beneath their feet and Kelly heard the stuttering thump of automatic gunfire as she and Jeri lifted the makeshift stretcher. Someone from inside the building ran out to help them carry Mrs. Lackavic. As Kelly struggled to hold the stretcher and keep from slipping on the broken cement and cinders, she heard Yakov speeding away, still yelling. "Rawhi-i-i-de!" Someone held the door open and as they rushed inside, Kelly felt a spray of grit as bullets hit a wall above her.

Inside, despite the superficial chaos, the hospital was a haven. Jeri and Kelly were directed toward a hallway that was being used for triage. Hospital workers moved among the wounded, speaking quietly, working efficiently. Marta was semiconscious and moaning again.

Kelly glanced around the room and then dared not look again. If this collection of the burned and the bloodied were among those considered least damaged, her mind quailed to think of those who might be even more hurt. A medical worker made a quick check of several new patients, including Marta Lackavic. Then she left.

Kelly caressed Marta's forehead, murmuring soothing nonsense. The middle-aged woman was younger than her graying hair indicated. Not that long ago, when such evenings were still possible, Jeri and Kelly would take Srijeda out and down to the little park on Pijacu Street. They had encountered Marta Lackavic several times, presumably on her way home from work. At first, she had greeted Srijeda, knowing him for a neighbor, but soon she had begun to greet Jeri and Kelly, too, with a nod and bright smile as she bent to fuss over the large dog. Then the shelling had increased and leisurely evening walks slipped into the past.

The medical worker reappeared with some anti-bacterial salve and a damp cloth. She had noticed that Jeri's hands were scraped and blistered from hours of work without gloves. Kelly took the cloth and medicine from the aide.

Kelly's jaw clenched as she applied the salve. "I don't understand. How can they get away with this? We're only hours away from Vienna or Rome or Paris. Doesn't anyone care that the people of this town are being slaughtered?"

"The rest of Croatia cares." Jeri grimaced as Kelly worked a particularly sore area. "Vukovar is giving everyone in Croatia courage. And holding up the JNA. You've heard Sinisa Glavasevic on the radio, praising the courage of everyone here. And Serbia cares. They thought the Yugoslav Federal Army could just walk across the Danube into Croatia and on to Zagreb, but they can't. Vukovar is like Stalingrad where the Nazi drive into Russia was stopped. The JNA could have bypassed the city but they chose to stop and fight. It's a decision that's costing them in real military terms as well as well as in world opinion."

"Yeah," Kelly muttered. "And like the Alamo where everyone died. Why doesn't the rest of the world do something?"

"As long as no other country recognizes Croatia, it's a civil war, an internal matter."

"On what level does that make sense, Jeri? Where in the name of anything holy does that mean something sane?"

Yakov entered the hospital and joined them as they waited. There were no chairs, so Yakov found a place on the floor with everyone else and leaned back against a wall, closing his eyes. Kelly had not noticed before that he was wearing a flannel pajama top tucked into his loose jeans, a flannel with pictures of little pine trees sheltering smiling rabbits.

A woman whose gray hair was caught in a tidy bun came through the waiting room, stopping here and there to speak to patients or to the people accompanying them. Kelly thought the woman was another aid worker until she reached Marta. She removed the blanket that covered the unconscious woman and her eyes narrowed. Gently replacing the blanket, she called out in a voice that wasn't particularly loud but still cut through the noise with sharp authority. In a matter of minutes, medical aides came to take Marta Lackavic.

"Can you say how long before we can know something?" Jeri asked the woman. "Her family was still trapped in their home when we left, and they'll be anxious to know how she is."

"Go home," the woman said. "She has serious damage to her upper legs and maybe her hips, but you already knew that. Have someone come tomorrow and ask for me. I'm Dr. Bosanac."

Yakov watched her leave. "We must be sure to tell Josip that Marta is being seen by Dr. Vesna Bosanac herself. That will comfort him."

"Why is that?" Kelly asked after Jeri had translated for her. She was reassured but not entirely surprised that the doctor had a wider reputation. There was something about the woman.

"Dr. Bosanac is the director." Jeri translated Yakov's answer. "Everyone knows how she manages things here so that in spite of the hospital being a target, anyone who comes can still get treated. The city safety committee stored a large supply of medicines early in preparation for this siege. It was her idea to set up satellite clinics, like at Tesla, once the shelling made it difficult to get here."

Yakov pointed out through the doorway. "We are down that way about two blocks." Without a further word, he was out the doorway and running. The sound of "Head eem oop" drifted back.

Jeri glanced at Kelly. "Head eem oop?"

"Head eem oot," Kelly answered.

The two women sprinted after Yakov.

†

Alenka and Marija had made a very comfortable living area in the basement of 12 Pijacu. At one end, a kind of kitchen had been arranged with a large table, a little wood stove for cooking as well as warmth, and shelving turned into a pantry. Both Ivo and Marija could remember the circumstances of World War Two when they were children, and the experience had given them the foresight to collect and stock items from potatoes and candles to batteries. At the far end of the basement, boxes had been situated to create separate sleeping areas and blankets had been hung to create some privacy.

Supper was a thick potato soup, seasoned with Marija's magic, but eaten in near silence as everyone considered the changes since the night before. After a while Stepan cleared his throat to get everyone's attention.

"There is still a path out of Vukovar through a cornfield. It's not entirely safe, but I want you to know." He glanced around the table, ending fondly with Alenka.

She looked at him and they could all see that her eyes were swollen. It had been a difficult day for everyone, but particularly heartrending for Alenka. "I cannot, Stepan, you know I cannot. You've heard Sinisa Glavasevic. '*Because who will remain if we renounce ourselves and flee into our fears. Who will inherit the city? Who will watch it for me, when I am gone... ? Who will watch my city, my friends, who will carry Vukovar from the dark?* '"

The words of the eloquent young radio announcer hung in the room for a few seconds and then Alenka burst into tears. Stepan hurried to her.

"It's all right," he soothed her. "I knew what you would say."

Quietly, the others left the table.

Jeri joined Kelly in their little alcove. A mattress took up most of the space, and a candle on an overturned box provided light.

"I've been talking to Stepan," Jeri began. "That path out of the city, what do you think?"

"Sounds like a trick question to me." Kelly sighed. "What about Ivo and Marija? Or Alenka?"

Jeri waited.

"I'm scared, don't get me wrong," Kelly continued. "I'm scared most of the time, but it's not like when I was kidnapped. Everyone else here is scared, too, but we give one another courage. If we leave now, just leave them behind, I don't think I could do that. I don't want to do that, Jeri. These people are so brave, they just want to live their lives. It's not like they did anything to make this happen. I feel like it's important to be here." She took Jeri's hand. "The medical center at the Tesla school, Alenka and I were talking about going there to work."

Kelly took the Himalayan crystal from her pocket with her free hand and noted how the candlelight played in the interior of the stone. Like firelight from a campfire, but the mountains of the Himalaya seemed very long ago and far away.

"Come with me." Jeri rose and Kelly followed her upstairs. The constant shelling remained at a distance for the moment. Inside Alenka's apartment, Jeri turned to Kelly.

"I want you to learn how to use this." The gun she held out was the one that she had taken from Ernie. "I can show you how it works without actually shooting it."

Kelly stared at the gun in Jeri's hand. Simply the sight of it seemed to impede her breathing.

"Talk to me, Kell. Tell me what you're thinking."

"That I don't want to do this. That I do. That the gun is really cool. Did you know that I can remember the first time I went into the dime store at home—it wasn't a dime store anymore, of course but everyone still called it that—the first time I didn't go to the cap gun section? Other girls were dating before I was ready to quit playing with toy guns. George had a Red Ryder BB gun that I was pretty good with. Farm kids, you know. I always wanted one of my own, I always wanted to be a cowboy, with a pair of six shooters, and then I grew up and I joined the other side, the one that says handguns are a really big problem. And they are. You regulate cars and drivers."

Kelly was aware that the words were just rattling out of her. "I suppose I still think that, but it doesn't mean anything here. Handguns are hardly a problem in the middle of a war. But if I take it, that means that I'm agreeing to kill a person, doesn't it? I'm crossing a line by doing this."

"You don't decide ahead of time. This is practice, just in case. Like a fire escape outside a window, you want it there if you ever need it." Jeri took a deep breath. "You don't have to carry it around, but it would be good if you knew where it was and how it worked. It's better to have the option than not to have it. If the time comes when you need it, you'll know."

"You mean there's more to using this than just point and click?" Kelly took the gun and held it in her hands, staring at it. Just the heft of it was serious. She didn't look up when she spoke. "You're leaving, aren't you?"

†

Jeri looked away from Kelly. This was the moment of decision and Jeri felt her resolve begin to weaken. "I've been talking to Stepan. They can use me. There are things I know how to do, things that I was taught, that will help. Things I'm good at, Kell. I know how to do street fighting, I know how to make engines not run and things explode. I know ways to stop tanks and armored vehicles and the JNA is bringing in a lot of those. And there are other women fighting at the front."

"I know," Kelly whispered. "Look at me, baby, it's okay. I've been waiting for this. I know who you are. There. You better show me how to use this silly thing."

They worked into the evening. Jeri was under no illusion that she could teach Kelly how to shoot well in one lesson, or teach her how to cross the line that would make her kill another person, but if it came to a time when Kelly needed to make a choice, she need not be distracted by being a complete stranger to the weapon. There weren't any extra bullets to practice with, there was only the one clip to be found in this city under siege, but Jeri taught Kelly everything else she could think of aside from actual firing. Her goal was to make the feel of the handgun, the size and weight and working of it as familiar as possible.

"Should I go with you? We could be together."

She answered so quickly that Kelly knew she had been thinking about it.

"If you want, but to be honest Kell, I don't think it's the best idea."

"Why? Because you'll worry about me too much?"

The shelling had come nearer and a particularly loud, close blast, made them both smile at the irony of Kelly's question.

"Right. I won't worry at all about you here. If you had any training or if you had the language, it would be different."

When they went back to the basement, they found that the others had accommodated to their new quarters, melding into a family of sorts. A single lamp hung over the large round table, and the electricity, always erratic these days, was working for the moment. Ivo was talking quietly with Stepan while Alenka studied. A small set was tuned to Radio Vukovar, and although Kelly didn't understand the language, she recognized the voice of Sinisa Glavasevic, the young man whose voice was becoming the voice of the city to the outside world and a source of courage and comfort to his fellow townspeople. Jeri went to Marija and spoke quietly. The older woman nodded and then she directed Jeri to bring a chair close to the light.

Marija found a towel and placed it around Jeri's shoulders, a large towel of gold and blue that almost looked like a cape. Kelly felt her heart wince as she realized that Marija was about to cut Jeri's long dark hair. It was necessary; she understood that. Where Jeri was going, short hair would be needed for all sorts of reasons. Marija made the first cut and a dark strand slid to the floor. Kelly had to stop herself from rushing to grab it. Ivo, Stepan and Alenka stopped what they were doing and watched, as mesmerized as Kelly. Jeri stared straight ahead. Only Marija seemed immune to the sense of import, although even her stern features softened.

The length was gone now. Marija began to trim, to shorten more, until Jeri's hair looked much like Stepan's. It was a ceremony. Jeri was being reborn in some way, although Kelly had no idea what was being left behind, or what new thing gained. The light from the single hanging lamp made odd shadows as Marija moved, not distorting, so much as moving, the scene into the realm of myth. Jeri changed, looking more resolute, the angles and planes of her face grew stronger, more pronounced.

"You are ready, Estellija." Marija stepped back.

"What do you think?" Jeri asked.

Alenka handed her a mirror. "Oh, Auntie Stella. You are elegant. But I think you could shave your head and still be beautiful. Isn't it so, Stepan?"

Stepan muttered something, his youth suddenly revealed in his boyish awkwardness. Only the low lighting protected him from being seen to blush.

Jeri and Alenka both looked expectantly toward Kelly. She wasn't sure of her voice. Jeri appeared ready to dismiss the cutting of her hair as meaningless and yet there was something unusually vulnerable in her eyes, something straining not to show.

"I think you are more Estellija now."

Jeri's eyes narrowed and she caught her lower lip between her teeth.

Kelly laughed deliberately to break the oddness of the moment, and she reached out to run her hand over Jeri's head. "Nice. Really nice. You're just as always, of course, and Alenka is right, you'd look great if you were bald."

But Kelly was thinking how Stella or Estellija meant star in various languages. She felt as if Jeri had stepped into another dimension. For an instant Kelly was back on a broken wall of rock in Nepal and time was shifting in front of her like a slideshow. *Who are you?* she had asked, knowing deeper than the words that the woman next to her was already part of her life although they had just met. And she had known and not known the answer then as now.

Kelly wasn't sure why she and Jeri had decided to keep the passport names of Constance and Laura. Perhaps a reluctance to admit they had hidden their identity from the very beginning, a sense that these names might be important later, several motives merged together. They had made no great effort to keep up the camouflage, and more than once they had slipped and used Jeri and Kelly in front of Alenka, but Alenka preferred aunties Stella and Laura, as if those names made them belong to her. And now, *Estellija* had become a name all its own.

†

Later, Jeri and Kelly made love with particular fervor—fervor and caution considering the basement room arrangements. The shelling continued like a thunderstorm from hell, but the house above remained free from a direct hit. Weary as they were from the long day, they were reluctant to sleep, to lose their awareness of one another.

"Kelly, if—"

"Don't. Don't say it. You're coming back, that's the end of it."

"But—"

"No! Say it. Say you'll be back."

For a few seconds Jeri resisted, and then Kelly felt the tenseness leave Jeri. "I'll be back, baby. I will."

Kelly was as relieved as if some arrangement had been made with fate. She took Jeri's head in her hands, meaning to kiss her but then the novel feel of the short hair distracted her. "I like how it feels," she said.

"Stop that, you make me feel like Srijeda."

"You do feel like a puppy."

"I haven't had short hair. I haven't cut it, since I got out of prison."

Kelly grew still. "Have you been thinking about prison?" Jeri rarely spoke of that time.

"I've been thinking about Arkadia O'Malley. I've been wondering if she would approve of this choice." She paused. "I've made a lot of choices that would disappoint her, but I don't think this is one."

Kelly thought about what she knew of the woman who had been so important to Jeri in the women's prison in Armagh in Northern Ireland. Arkadia O'Malley was somewhat of a mystery as none of the other inmates knew why she was there. She was older than most prisoners and kept to herself, but she took care of the library, such as it was, and there was a strong sense of the academic about her. O'Malley had taken to Jeri, becoming her savior as well as her mentor, and her conscience, if truth be told. It was nearly certain that without the stern but clear eyes of the Irish woman, the young American would have given in to the bitterness of her incarceration for something she had not done. Arkadia O'Malley had tried to steer Jeri away from taking up the gun in the fight for a republican Ulster, but other circumstances had weighed heavier in Jeri's decision. Not the least of which had been a sense she owed it to her dead cousin, Fiona, to continue the fight for her cousin's cause.

461

Jeri's past was assuredly complicated.

†

Jeri was remembering something O'Malley had said to her.

I'm not trying to take away your choices, Geraldine. But I do hope that you'll be able to make them from solid ground. If you let that great heart of yours serve you, if you find a place to use your courage and keep your fine integrity, too, I'll have nothing to say against it. But I want you to have a free mind partnering that heart.

"I never cut my hair after they let me loose from prison," she said to Kelly. "It had something to do with remembering her. I lost her path but I kept my hair so I could find my way back. Something like that. I hardly thought of it until tonight. It doesn't make a lot of sense."

"Sure it does. Sense goes sideways as well as in straight lines. Arkadia O'Malley. I like saying her name. I hope I get to meet her." And that too, felt like an arrangement made with fate.

It was still dark when Stepan woke them to take Jeri to the war.

Chapter Twelve

Jeri's eyes were night adjusted but the squat, dark shape of a tank, about twenty feet away on the other side of a broken concrete wall, revealed few details aside from its outline. Tanks always reminded her of toads and this one looked like a particularly bloated toad. She and Petar lay side by side on an inclined heap of rubble, by a broken wall that let them look down toward the armored vehicle. No one had been more surprised than Petar himself to discover that the bitter young graduate student had a talent for sneaking around in the night. After he had volunteered to accompany Jeri once, he had become her usual companion. Earlier reconnaissance, hours before when there had still been light, had shown that there was another tank parked about a car's length behind the first. Two toads.

The tank crews were inside a nearby abandoned house that had more or less escaped the shelling. Not many buildings in the city could make the same claim. On this street leading directly into the city of Vukovar, most of the buildings had become jagged shells. The roadway itself wasn't particularly narrow, but debris from the ravaged houses had clogged the street so that passage presented a challenge to something the size of a tank.

Vukovar as a home for living residents existed underground now. The shelling broke all the rules developed to protect noncombatants, and it continued to devastate government buildings, historical sites, religious centers—even the Orthodox Church of St. Nicholas, where Vukovar's Serbs worshipped, had not escaped. Above ground, Vukovar was a city for the dead. It was no longer possible to bury those who died and the air was a constant reminder of the fact.

Still Vukovar held out. Against the JNA that had been touted as the third largest standing army in Europe, the vastly outnumbered, poorly equipped defenders of the surrounded city hung on, day after day. On paper, the Yugoslav army developed by Marshall Tito had impressed both Eastern and Western blocs. Now in Vukovar, Croatian guardsmen and volunteers had only scant small arms and armor-piercing weapons to hold off tanks and warplanes, but they also had their wits and their courage. So they stood, and held the Yugoslav army from advancing, and gave heart to all of Croatia.

A scraping sound and a sudden burst of light distracted Jeri from the plan that she was rehearsing in her mind. Partly off its hinges, the door of the building where the tank crew was sheltering had been pushed open. A JNA soldier in uniform emerged, stopping momentarily to get his bearings. Jeri felt a tap on her shoulder and she turned her head to Petar who was only inches away. He pointed, not to the soldier, but toward the lead tank.

Jeri cursed silently. Darkness had hidden the sentry now moving to greet his comrade. In a few more minutes Jeri would have started her approach to the tank. Seeing him now was luck but not the kind of luck you should ever count on or you'd be long dead.

"Hey, Milos, I brought you a bottle."

"Great. Just what a sentry needs."

"Lighten up, brother. It's just a war. Drink and forget it."

"It doesn't bother you? Shelling ordinary people all day?" Sentry duty was apparently leaving this man too much time to think. "Yesterday they were our countrymen."

"All day all night, who cares? Sorry to interrupt your good mood. Do what you're told and drink when you can. Do you want the bottle or not?"

"Yeah. Thanks."

The sentry watched his comrade rejoin the men in the house. The door was left ajar, allowing a bit of light to escape. For a while there was only the whump and whistle of distant shelling and then the sentry raised the bottle in the direction of the city.

"Here's to you, city of courage." He took a long drink. "I'm going home."

Jeri and Petar watched with fascination as he walked off, away from the city.

"And here's to you, brother." Petar kept his voice low. "That sounded like a Montenegrin accent. He probably is going home."

Jeri hoped the allotted luck for the day had not yet run out. Briefly, she explained her plan to Petar and then slid into her battered old backpack. Momentarily, a flood of memories from Ulster threatened to overwhelm her. The pack was all she had brought out of Ireland besides memories. She'd had it with her the day that she left a car bomb that destroyed a bus on the streets of Belfast. Kelly had asked her once why she kept such an old-fashioned thing and Jeri had told her the story. "Guess you're the only person I know who has actual luggage for baggage," had been Kelly's rueful comment.

Thoughts of Kelly brought Jeri back to the present but she set them aside. Careful not to dislodge any bits of rubble, she made her way over the wall and down to where she could cross to the tank. Once there, she slid through the gap between the first and second wheel pairs. She knew the T-55. She'd studied it years before when she trained for urban fighting in Romania. The T-55 was the workhorse of the world's tanks, tough but so simple to operate, that crews needed very little training. The JNA had brought a large part of its tank force to Vukovar, thinking to overwhelm the weapons-poor defenders, only to discover that the T-55s were vulnerable to anti-tank weapons.

Jeri's knapsack carried several anti-tank shells.

There was another vulnerability she was hoping to exploit. The tank's internal ammunition supply lacked good shielding. Jeri closed her eyes to better visualize the interior of the tank and then took several of the shells she was carrying and began prying a space for them with the long bladed knife she carried.

Jeri froze, startled by the sound of stones dislodged nearby. For long seconds, all was silent. Whatever had caused the noise was also motionless, listening. Then she heard the skittering of small feet. Rat, dog, cat, it could be anything. She needed to hurry before something more dangerous happened by. She finished placing the shells and moved to the next tank.

"Did we have enough for both?" Petar asked when she rejoined him behind the wall.

"I hope so," Jeri answered. She explained briefly about the internal ammunition supply. "Shall we see if it works? Here, you do the honors."

Petar wasn't familiar with the phrase, but he was boy enough to want to do the blowing up, especially as this particular instance would involve no killing. The primary explosions tore open the dark and Petar lifted his head to look. Jeri pulled him back to the cover of the wall just as the secondary explosions ripped through the night. Metal and rock became shrapnel and then Jeri allowed herself to look before urging Petar to leave quickly, before any of the tank crew got themselves together enough to come hunting for them.

She saw enough to know that no more tanks or any other motor vehicle would use this way into Vukovar, not for a long while to come. They had blocked the street to anything but foot traffic. As she and Petar began making their way back to their lines, the energy gained from a successful mission drained away, leaving her nearly exhausted.

†

Kelly took one end of the soggy gray sheet and passed the other end to Alenka. They twisted, wringing water into a large metal washtub. Then they shook the sheet and hung it over a wire that was strung along the hallway of the Tesla School basement. They returned for another sheet and repeated the process. Washing for the medical center was a task at which they had become quite adept. They were using rainwater. The fire truck that usually delivered water had been absent for several days, and there was a rumor from the central Vukovar Medical Center that a sniper had killed the driver.

After the last damp sheet was placed over a line, Alenka slid wearily to the floor. Kelly joined her. Despite the smell of bleach hanging heavily in the corridor, the hall smelled better than the crowded gymnasium. Originally designed to be a bomb shelter in a nuclear war, the huge space was thick with cigarette smoke that did nothing to cover the odor of unwashed humans. Since the city was no longer safe above ground, the makeshift treatment center had become home to hundreds of people.

"I want to go home, Auntie Laura."

Kelly looked at her hands. They were red and she could smell the bleach that they had absorbed. She was Auntie Laura now, even to people at the shelter besides Alenka. Like Aunt Jemima or Mama Cass, she was Auntie Laura. Or Lord Byron. Titles had a curious way of becoming a name. Lady Godiva. She was awfully tired. Lack of food was sapping her mental as well as her physical energy.

"I want to go home," Alenka repeated.

"So do I," Kelly answered, thinking of low hills with trees splendid in their autumn colors, of harvested cornfields stretching in long rows of stalk stubble, of rolled hay bundles waiting to be stacked. Late autumn in Ohio. Pictures of turkeys and pilgrims getting everyone in the mood for Thanksgiving. For huge tables laden with food.

"Auntie, I'm sorry. I forget sometimes that this isn't even your home."

A series of shells exploded above them. The school basement was a

466

satellite medical center as well as a shelter for people who had sought refuge after being bombed out of their own homes, so of course it was a target of the Serbs—or the Yugoslav army—or the Chetniks. Kelly had lost track of which name was the more correct term to use for the people who were shelling unarmed civilians along with sick and wounded human beings.

"It is now, Alenka."

"No." Alenka shook her head sadly. "You are not ashamed. If this was your home, you would feel shame. "

"What are you talking about?" Roused from her listlessness, Kelly looked sharply at the young woman beside her. No one was immune to the depression of days spent without enough food, without sunlight, without peace from the incessant shelling, but Alenka had never spoken like this before.

Alenka had changed very much in the days underground. At first, she had shared her spirit and attitude with the children of the center. She could make them laugh, she could get them to sing songs like "Beautiful Vukovar", and she made up games that caused even the adults to smile. But at last, the dread and hunger sapped even Alenka's reserves, her soft roundness had narrowed, and shadows had gathered around her eyes.

"I thought we were modern, that we were part of Europe at last and there was so much to be done. We could move into history and become healthier and wiser and kinder and smarter, we would be part of what makes the world better, but look—we are primitive savages. Just as everyone has said about us. Nothing but savages. No wonder Europe doesn't want us. No wonder they will not come to help us."

Kelly put her arm around Alenka, remembering how awful it had felt to live inside a plague, while the rest of the country simply ignored the existence of AIDS. She would hear George talking on the phone, then he would hang up, stand staring into space, and Kelly knew he had learned one more name to add to the list of his condemned friends. There were so many. The startled stare that was becoming his permanent expression, and a marker of how far his illness had progressed, also seemed a reflection of his wonder at how long this could go. How long until the dominos stopped falling. Then Kelly would go to the drug store, the grocery store, the college, and all around her she would see people oblivious to the plight of the plague victims in their midst.

Sometimes the Tesla center reminded Kelly of the AIDS ward where the wasted figures of the dying were tended to by people scarcely less damaged, people who loved them. In another life, Kelly had given the quote from Edmond Burke as a theme to one of her composition classes: *The only thing necessary for the triumph of evil is for good men to do nothing.* Her students hadn't done too well with it, but then neither had the rest of the human race.

But evil was not triumphing. Kelly thought of places where people were buying some new flavor at Starbuck's, where they were driving in aggravating traffic jams, where they were walking to the office copy machine, or driving on one of the lovely autumn roads. They were completely ignorant that, in a remote corner of Europe, a handful of simple and ordinary men and women were proving once more that the most human thing of all was to be brave and resourceful, to survive and struggle to help others survive, to risk, to lay down your life for people you might not even know.

She couldn't deny the presence of the worst of humanity: butchers and rapists, snipers who shot hapless children. Two days before, a mother had come to the shelter carrying her six-year-old daughter. The two of them had been making their way to the school after their neighborhood was about to be overrun by JNA soldiers. A sniper bullet had torn the child's leg and by the time the mother and daughter reached the school, it was too late to get anesthetics from the Vukovar hospital. The child screamed throughout the amputation, throughout the auditorium where the residents huddled, not one person daring to look at another.

The best and the worst were in Vukovar, striving in a hideous contest to define the limits of the human soul.

"Vukovar is a light," Kelly said, to herself as well as Alenka. She gripped the crystal in her pocket with one hand and with her other arm, she hugged Alenka. "What's done here is important. The truth of it will live on and you're part of it."

Kelly felt Alenka's head nod against her. The young woman was no longer crying. Even tears took energy.

"I still want to go home. Do you think we can try to go to Pijacu? I miss Marija and Ivo. And I want to see Srijeda."

†

Jeri followed Petar away from the smoking ruins of the tanks they had destroyed. She wanted to see Kelly. She very much wanted to see Kelly. She wanted to leave Vukovar. She could not remember any of the reasons she once had for staying. The noise and stench of a city under siege was growing unbearable. She kept going only by immersing herself in doing the next thing to be done, the next task of sabotaging equipment, stealing ammunition, setting tank traps, fouling water supplies—anything that disrupted order and morale behind JNA lines. She recognized that she was tired and getting careless, like tonight when she had missed the presence of the sentry.

So far she had avoided combat. Wrecking roads and tanks made good tactics and was much more effective than getting into firefights, but every so often an accident would happen and trading gunfire with the regular army would take place. She knew that many of the JNA soldiers were reluctant fighters like the tank sentry had been, but it was because of what happened to her that made her avoid direct engagement. Something inside Jeri awakened like a slumbering demon, quickened and amplified and sang in her blood like a drug when she joined battle at close quarters. Discipline for Jeri was to grasp her battle skill as one would hold a sword and not let its bright exhilaration overcome and take hold of her. Better for her soul to stick to sabotage.

How absurd was it to worry about the state of your soul when you were fighting a war? God, she needed to see Kelly, to be reminded that living was more than just one thing after another, that days weren't just a line of falling dominoes but something full of tone and depth, shading and echoes. That love too, sang in the blood. It had been more than a week since she had been to Pijacu Street and getting there was ever more dangerous as it meant dodging snipers while finding a way through a landscape that changed utterly from one hour to the next.

"Petar."

The boy stopped, alert, crouching. Jeri could almost see his features in the faint predawn light.

"Petar, you go back. It's not far. I'm going to Pijacu for a few hours. I'll be back by tomorrow night."

"Do you want to go alone?"

"I'll be okay. You let Stepan know."

Petar started to turn away when an improbable noise stopped both of them. They stood staring at one another and then heard it again—the long, low, distressed moan of a cow. It stopped as a shell exploded nearby, and then the sound started again. And something else, something higher, thinner, but also distressed. Human.

Without really thinking, Jeri started toward the sound. It led her through what might once have been a garden or a courtyard and then past demolished concrete and shattered wood. She saw the cow first. It appeared to be tethered outside a high stone enclosure that somewhere else would be a fence but here was actually what was left of a building. A tile roof partially covered one corner. Jeri could see the inside in detail by the light of a flickering lantern but she rather wished she couldn't.

The cow had stopped lowing for the moment but the woman was still moaning. She was naked and lying across some broken, splintered, former piece of furniture that kept her in place for the three men who were currently engaged in some discussion near a heap of articles in the far corner of the room. Dirt or bruises covered her back and buttocks and what was probably blood streaked one leg. The men, dressed in the camouflage fatigues favored by Arkan's Tigers, were uninterested in the woman at the moment. What Jeri could see of the items they were checking looked like loot, candlesticks and silverware, wooden boxes of cloth, even a broken vase. One of the men looked toward the moaning woman with annoyance and muttered something. His companion, who was closer, took a step and knocked the woman to the ground with a fist and then kicked her into silence.

Petar had followed Jeri. She put a hand on his arm. "I've got this. Make sure none of their friends comes along."

No war is known for promoting good behavior, but the disintegration of Yugoslavia was reaching for a new low. Rape was becoming more than a random atrocity, more than incidental collateral damage. The Chetniks were raping as a deliberate weapon of terror and with enthusiastic ferocity.

Jeri had one of the handguns she had brought from Zagreb. She took a deep breath to get her rage under control and fixed the layout of the area. She walked through the doorless entry to a place between the men and where they'd stacked their rifles against a wall. Then she shot the man nearest to her, the one who had kicked the woman. Jeri aimed for a second man but the gun jammed.

Useless piece of shit. It wasn't the first time the bullets had fouled. Whoever had sold Zagreb these cartridge magazines needed to be pistol-whipped.

The advantage of surprise was gone. Jeri reassessed her moves. The remaining two Chetniks didn't have their rifles but one of them had found an axe and the other had grabbed a long-handled rake with short curved prongs. Jeri tossed the gun aside, crouched, and took her knife from its sheath. The man with the rake grinned and poked it at her like a lion tamer. He was tall and thin with a long reach in addition to the rake's handle. Maybe this building had once been a shed for the cow, or a tool shed at any rate. Jeri saw a three-legged stool a few feet away and edged toward it, keeping her eyes fixed on the two men. The one with the axe was older, not quite past his prime, but he was sturdy and had a pistol in a holster at his waist. He seemed to think the axe was enough.

The older man muttered something that Jeri didn't quite hear and the men began to separate, one to each side of her. She was close enough now to bend and pick up the stool with her free hand. It gave her a sense of balance as well as a shield. She backed away, keeping the men from circling her.

"You're going to pay for this. I'm going to make you eat your own balls." The speaker was the Chetnik with the rake, and he was swinging it back and forth in short but vicious arcs. He was confident enough to be enjoying himself.

Jeri could smell the two men. They reeked of sweat and garlic and brandy. Hand-to-hand fighting was personal. They hadn't figured out yet that she was a woman. Everyone in the trenches looked pretty much the same, especially now that the fall rains had turned the dirt to mud. Her jeans were loose and filthy, but she'd picked up a camouflage jacket and a cap that the Croatian guard wore. Still, she saw the speaker frown as she grinned back at him. Something was nagging him about her. She could see him trying to figure her out in the bottom of whatever thick, twisted muscle that passed for his brain.

He suddenly stepped closer and swung the rake hard, like a baseball bat. He didn't really think about it, he just decided that he needed to swing. Jeri leaned back and felt the rush of air as the steel prongs swept past. The man with the axe moved more to her left. He, at least, was thinking. Jeri needed to even the odds quickly.

Keeping her eyes on the axe man, she moved toward the rake man. He accepted the invitation with a huge roundhouse swing. Jeri's plan worked perfectly. Before he could recover his balance, she stepped forward.

"Eat your own balls," she said. Her knife might have nicked a rib but then it slid between. She kept it sharp.

Jeri turned to face the last Chetnik. He was worried now and thinking about his pistol but he didn't want to loosen his grip on the axe. He pulled it back and held it with both hands and then feinted toward her left. She read him, parried with the stool anyway, and shifted as he spun the axe the other way and swung it toward her right. She let it come close. They might have been moving in slow motion, she felt she had so much time. It was like reading a chess game a dozen moves ahead. Just as he got a grin on his face, she spoke again.

"That your best shot, Slobo?"

Her voice let him know she was a woman, something she intended. First, he'd think he had to be better than she was and that would make him more likely to do something stupid, and less likely to try for his pistol. Second, she wanted him to know that a woman was beating him. The first happened right away. He was furious. His face went red and he swung the axe at her with all the finesse of a charging bull. She laughed as she stepped out of the way. This was going to be much too easy. He swung again using less muscle and more accuracy.

Jeri caught the axe head in the legs of the stool and pulled. The idiot thought it was a tug of war. He should have let go of the handle and grabbed for her or for his gun, but instead he pulled, determined not to lose his axe, while all she wanted was to use it for a kind of fulcrum and swing toward his side. And when she let go of the stool, he lost his balance and fell backward. It wasn't a great cut, but she didn't want the knife to get deflected by a rib, so she slid it into his belly and then twisted the blade up.

He knew he was dead. He dropped the axe and then just sat down holding his stomach together. Jeri picked up her gun and put in a new magazine. Then she walked over to the man sitting on the floor and shot him in the head. She could have used half a dozen reasons, starting with the way the woman on the floor looked, but the truth was that she liked seeing his arrogance turn to fear. She held off the shot just one instant too long.

That's what would give her nightmares. That instant when she had to accept that she was very like the man she had just killed.

Did you think you were different? If the woman is your sister, the dead men are your brothers. Even in the horror that was Vukovar, her conscience sounded like Arkadia O'Malley.

The adrenalin vanished. She wanted to vomit. Petar had found a coat from the pile of loot and was covering the woman. Jeri went to help. She'd have to put off going to Kelly.

†

Kelly felt a clutch of fear at the thought of going to Pijacu Street, but it passed. They could try when it got dark. Snipers couldn't see in the dark. The attempt would be one more thing to take her mind off how much she missed Jeri. Maybe Ivo and Marija had news from her or from Stepan.

As if to thwart Alenka and Kelly personally, the incessant rain of mortars increased as soon as it became dark, and sometime around midnight planes flew over and dropped bombs that shook the ground. Night was no time for dreams in Vukovar. Some hours after midnight, the shelling lessened and its focus shifted closer to the Danube.

"Do you still want to go, Auntie Laura?"

Kelly did.

So they slipped out into darkness where the lurid light of distant explosions vied with the smell of unburied corpses as to which effect was the closest approximation of hell. Kelly let Alenka lead. She had no idea how to find her way through the rubble and simply stayed close to the younger woman. Kelly could imagine no way being safer than another. It was fate now that would keep the two of them alive, or some deity, or some unraveling of circumstance and sequence far too complicated to try to influence. It occurred to Kelly, as they inched along, that if she died here it wouldn't matter whether anyone knew her as Auntie Laura or as Kelly, she would become just another dead body.

She missed Jeri. They had been apart too long. Kelly didn't believe anything had happened to Jeri. She would know. Her heart would know. But they had been too long apart. Travel through Vukovar was desperate at the best of times. On his last visit, Stepan had said that Jeri had gone on patrol and had missed the chance to accompany him. Kelly thought he was leaving something out so she waited to see if Stepan might explain, but when he didn't, Kelly let the matter rest.

Far too long apart, my love, far too long apart: The refrain repeated like an old folk song.

Several rounds of mortars came in their direction but they knew the missiles would fall short. People in Vukovar had learned to read the sounds.

"Wait," Alenka whispered, and pushed Kelly back against a wall. Footsteps. Heavy, like boots. Someone was coming along the street ahead. Impossible to know if it was friend or foe. Ever so cautiously, Kelly and Alenka eased through a doorway, or rather half a doorway since the top of the building was gone. They pressed themselves against the section of wall between them and the street and waited for whoever was on the other side to pass.

Shelling drowned any sounds, but Kelly was sure the passerby had stopped. Her heart thudded in her chest. She was sure someone had paused just on the other side of the stone wall, and she was afraid that Alenka was going to take a chance and move, giving them both away.

473

She reached for Alenka's hand in the darkness, found it and squeezed. A return pressure reassured her.

The smell of cigarette smoke drifted over the wall.

They waited. Hours seemed to go by. Maybe it was only minutes or maybe the person had fallen asleep. At last they heard the crunch of boots on rubble, walking away. They would never know if hiding had been necessary but they were still alive.

Once more Alenka led the way. Walking was easier now because the world was gray as dawn was approaching. Hell gained another dimension with the torn and shattered shapes that became visible around the two women. Alenka stopped. Kelly could see the young woman's confusion.

"Where are we, Auntie Laura? I do not know where we are." Alenka's hands covered her mouth, her eyes wide and horrified. "The trees are gone. All the beautiful trees."

Kelly looked around. When she and Alenka had gone to the center, the buildings on and around Pijacu Street had been marked by war but, for the most part, they had still existed. All around them now was a desolation of heaped stone, odd portions of standing walls, doorways that led nowhere, a paneless window frame on a pile of stone, still with its patterned curtain.

"We have to get inside somewhere soon," Kelly whispered. Snipers came out in daylight.

Alenka nodded, her hands clasped tight against her mouth in an attitude of prayer. "This way, I think. This way."

Twelve Pijacu Street was gone. A corner of it remained, a forlorn corner standing above the litter, the rubbish, the heap of life turned into junk. Kelly had no idea what Alenka was seeing, what she might be mourning, but for herself, she thought her heart might break as she saw the wreckage of the piano. She stepped toward the ruined keyboard and stopped. Lying just beneath the black and white keys, Kelly saw the family photo. The frame was broken and the glass cracked, but the picture was still intact. Kelly picked it up for Alenka.

Alenka had found the doorway to the basement. Kelly followed her.

It was empty. It smelled empty, damp and musty, a basement but nothing worse. Alenka found matches and lit a candle. The flame flared, and Alenka lit another candle.

Ivo and Marija and Srijeda were gone. The basement bore signs of the shelling that had destroyed the building above, a toppled cabinet, fallen plaster, but there was no sign of the people Kelly and Alenka had left here. Nothing suggested where they might have gone or why. It was possible that Ivo and Marija were among the unburied, that Srijeda had become one of the animals that now prowled the devastation of Vukovar. Kelly quietly went to explore the back of the shelter and leave Alenka alone for a moment.

The sound of the door scraping open preceded the fall of daylight down the stairway and for a moment Kelly's heart lifted, sure that she was about to see Jeri. She even took a step toward the stairs before caution stopped her. Alenka was closer to the stairs and it was the look on Alenka's face as she stared at the intruder that made Kelly step back, deeper into the dark.

Alenka still spoke English to her, but Kelly had picked up more Croatian as she worked at the school. She didn't understand all that the stranger was asking, but she heard a word here and there, and the fact that he had his rifle pointed at Alenka needed no translation.

"I am alone," Alenka said, in Croatian, quite clearly, and Kelly understood that she meant for Kelly to hear. To hear and stay hidden. Then she added something like, "but my husband will be here."

The man laughed. His accent was too strange for Kelly, she couldn't translate anything, but it wasn't necessary. He was Chetnik. Chetniks raped Croatian women. Then they killed them. Or not.

The gun was nearby, in the alcove that had been a bedroom. The gun that Jeri had given her. Kelly knew where she had left it, along with the book by Rebecca West. She had been debating with herself whether or not to bring both back to the school. The gun was in her pack on the other side of the basement. The man was at the foot of the stairway, his rifle still pointed at Alenka. The rifle had a scope mounted on it and Kelly took that to mean he was a sniper.

The stranger took another step toward Alenka, enjoying her fear, taking his time. He was talking the whole while. Kelly stepped backward and sideways, making sure of each step, keeping inside the shadows. His back was turned to her now and she let herself move farther. She was under the stairs, where Marija had created a pantry of sorts. Kelly avoided boxes, a pail with a mop beside it. She was terrified she would kick something, make a noise that would reveal her presence.

Kelly had maneuvered herself past the stairway. She could see the sniper's back. She didn't think Alenka could see her, but the Chetnik seemed to have said something to make the younger woman react because Kelly heard Alenka say something that she recognized as a string of obscenities. You didn't spend a lot of time in a bomb shelter with several hundred refugees and not learn to recognize when people were cursing.

Again Kelly heard the sniper's feral laughter.

Kelly slipped through the blankets where Marija and Ivo had curtained off their bed, and then through the area that had been Alenka's room. She slid her feet quietly, pausing at anything that felt like an obstruction.

"Why? Why are you doing this?" Alenka's wail was high with unfeigned fear.

Kelly reached the alcove she had shared with Jeri and slid behind the sheet that surrounded the area. She was hidden here but it was considerably darker. She had a general idea where she had left her pack. The mattress was on the floor. She knelt down on the mattress and felt around in the dark. She found the crate that they had used for a table. The pack should be just to the right of it.

A noise made her blood freeze. She heard the Chetnik hit Alenka and she heard Alenka cry out. She bit her lip to silence herself. It was almost impossible not to rush out to Alenka's defense. You needed to be schooled in this, Kelly realized. A person had fight or flight instincts and you had to be schooled to do things like methodically feel about in the darkness for a backpack that might or might not be there. She heard Alenka cry out again and she swallowed her own stifled cry.

Damn. Where was it? Where had she left it? Had Marija decided to move things around? Had she decided to rearrange the living areas? Where in the fucking hell was the backpack?

There! She felt the unmistakable shape of the book first. She needed to be careful, quiet. It wouldn't do Alenka any good if she fucked up now. Kelly lifted the pack, brought it to her. Everything was taking too long, it was like in a dream, like every move was an effort through thickened air—but the zipper didn't stick and there was the gun and it felt just the way it had the dozens of times Jeri had made her break it down and load it that day. Kelly's hands were remembering even if her mind was flipping about like a frantic rabbit.

Kelly's mind quit. It just shut down and the phrase *fucking shit* took over like a tape loop. She stood up and stepped outside the sheet. She saw how Alenka had been knocked to the floor, how the Chetnik was bending over her, setting his rifle onto the table with one hand while his other hand fumbled with his pants.

"Aim for the body," Jeri had said. "Give yourself a big target."

"Fucking shit!" Kelly screamed aloud and when the man turned, she aimed for the chest.

The first shot hit, spun him back, but the noise and kick of it was a surprise even though Kelly had tried to anticipate both. Her second shot went wide and high and the ricochet sound of it was another thing to fear. He was up on one knee now, looking at her, screaming at her. It wasn't his voice that bothered Kelly, it was that he was looking at her and he knew she had hurt him. She had the urge to apologize, to excuse herself, even as she took aim, steadied both hands and shot again. And again.

Then there was one more dead body in Vukovar.

Kelly knelt beside Alenka and set the gun on the table beside the Chetnik rifle. He had used the rifle butt but Kelly couldn't remember the particular word. *Kundaciti*? Whatever the word, Alenka was bleeding from a great gash above her ear. Kelly glanced around and saw a dishtowel. Water. There was a little left in the pantry beneath the stairs where Ivo had stored several containers. And alcohol. The pantry also contained a half bottle of vodka. Kelly came back to Alenka and cradled the girl's head in her lap. She dampened a corner of the towel with water and vodka and wiped the edge of the wound.

A shadow fell into the basement and a figure stood framed in the open doorway. Kelly's stomach clenched but she managed to reach for the gun.

†

Halfway down the steps, Jeri paused, giving her eyes a chance to adjust to the dark. When she could see, the sight was startling. A man lay to one side of the communal table, face down and presumably dead. Alenka, blood streaking her face, was lying with her head in Kelly's lap while Kelly pointed a gun directly at Jeri.

"Steady, babe, it's me."

Jeri waited until she was sure that Kelly understood before continuing down the steps.

It was while she searched for Marija's sewing basket that Jeri found the note from the older couple. They were sorry; they had one last chance to attempt to escape using the path through the cornfield, the last route out of the besieged city, and go to their daughter in Osijek. They were sorry to leave. They were taking Srijeda. Pray for them, please, as they would pray constantly that soon they could all be together again.

Jeri read the note to Alenka while Kelly cut away the hair from around the wound. It wasn't deep but it bled heavily like all head wounds.

"Do you think that they got away?" Alenka asked.

Jeri nodded slowly. "It is possible. Very possible. We can't be sure when this was written, but I think that some have come in or left through the cornfield even a few days ago. It's closed now, but I think Ivo and Marija could have got out."

"And Srijeda," Alenka added.

"Drink this." Jeri handed Alenka a small glass of vodka. "We're going to sew that hole in your head closed. We don't want all your thoughts leaking out."

"Don't be silly, Auntie Stella, I haven't had a thought for weeks."

Alenka took Jeri's hand while Kelly made stitches with the needle and thread that had been soaked in the vodka. The young woman winced and her grip tightened against the pain, but she didn't cry out. Kelly worked quickly. She had watched the doctors at the school shelter sew wounds many times.

"Your head looks fine," Jeri said when Kelly finished. "I came to tell you that Stepan has been taken to the medical center. It's not horrible. It's his leg and it's a wound that will heal. He should be okay soon. He wanted me to tell you he would be fine."

"He would say that if both his legs were gone."

"I know. But I saw him and he should be okay."

The sober look that Alenka gave to Jeri contained her understanding of all the things that were definitely not okay. "Can I go the hospital?"

Jeri considered. "After dark we can try. And the good news is that I brought some food. Beefsteak."

"Auntie Stella, can you get him out of here? I do not want him in my father's house if you can get him out." She nodded toward the corpse that they had all been ignoring.

Jeri glanced toward Kelly who had closed her eyes. Kelly opened them. "Yes, let's get him out. It will be worth the risk."

†

Kelly still felt nothing. Removing the Chetnik was simply a problem to be solved. The hard part was getting him up the stairs. The sunlight had disappeared and a fall drizzle had taken its place. Jeri and Kelly carried the dead man to the edge of the street and across, removing him not only from the basement but also from the house that no longer existed. Mortars continued to fall, but the two women seemed to have avoided the notice of snipers. Perhaps Kelly had killed the one assigned to this area. They hurried back inside and Jeri fixed a board across the door for a bar.

"Jeri?"

"Yes, love?"

"I'm okay, really, but I don't think I can cook meat. I know we need it, but—"

"I'm on it. Go talk to Alenka."

Kelly thought the young woman might have fallen asleep, but instead she found her in the area she had shared with Stepan, weeping silently. Kelly sat down on the mattress beside her and put an arm around her. Alenka continued to weep and Kelly waited.

When the sobs slowed, Kelly spoke. "Thank you for being so brave. You probably saved our lives by pretending to be alone. I wish I could have kept you from getting hurt."

"I miss Srijeda."

"I know. Me too."

"I don't think I love him."

"Srijeda?"

"No, silly. Stepan. He is so good and we have been friends for so long, but I don't think I have the right feelings for him. It is this war. I think we both need to take care of one another, but I don't think it's love. And now he's hurt, and I wish I did love him. Love like I see with you and Auntie Stella.

Chapter Thirteen

Jeri, Kelly, and Alenka made their way toward the Vukovar Medical Center on a November night when the usual drizzle turned into a full-scale storm. Mortars still fell from Serbian positions along the Danube, but the wind and heavy rain slowed the shelling so that the discomfort of the storm was balanced by the relative safety it provided to the three women. Alenka said she was fine, but it was obvious from the way she moved that her head hurt, and they stopped often to let her rest.

As they neared the center, the amount of shelling increased, as if the hospital was a light in the darkness attracting a ghastly new kind of exploding insect.

Jeri stopped them one last time. "We have to run from here. Snipers. Can you do that?"

Alenka nodded and started off immediately, Kelly following. Alenka almost made it to the doorway, before she stumbled. Both Kelly and Jeri caught her as she started to fall, not sure if she was hurt by a sniper's bullet or her head wound. Together they pulled and carried her into the hospital where a medical worker quickly conducted the dripping and shivering women to the shelter of a lower floor.

"What have we here?" A woman with a stethoscope cast a practiced eye over the bedraggled group.

Not waiting for an answer, she took Alenka's hand and led her to an area of stronger light. Kelly recognized Dr. Vesna Bosanac from her first visit to the hospital. Although she looked a bit rumpled and showed signs of weariness in the dark circles beneath her eyes, her voice was alert and calm. She nodded thoughtfully as she removed the makeshift dressing fashioned from a dishtowel. It was soaked with rainwater, but there appeared to have been little blood seepage.

"Good work," Dr. Bosanac commented as she removed the last of the dressing. "Who did the stitching?"

"She did." Jeri nodded toward Kelly and translated.

Dr. Bosanac glanced at Jeri in her Croatian guard jacket with more interest. "You are not from here?"

Jeri smiled grimly. "We are now."

"These are my aunties, Dr. Bosanac." Alenka smiled wanly at the gray-haired woman. "Auntie Laura and Auntie Stella. We have come to see my Stepan who was brought here from the front. Stepan Sipek."

Auntie Laura and Auntie Stella might not be the strangest sights Dr. Bosanac had encountered in the last several months, but one eyebrow rose as she looked at the two American women.

"We hear rumors of a fighter, a foreign woman named Estellija, who appears like a demon behind the JNA lines. They say she sows considerable fear and confusion." Dr. Bosanac did not appear unpleased by what she had heard.

Jeri shrugged. "Rumors in war are always exaggerated."

Dr. Bosanac stared at Jeri a few more seconds and then turned her attention back to Alenka. She cleaned and redressed the wound herself. "Your wound is not bad, rest should heal it. I see no signs of a concussion. I think I know where we will find your Stepan. Come with me and I'll take you to the soldiers."

Progress through the underground corridors was difficult because beds had been set into every open space available. Patients were sleeping two to a bed in many cases. The arrangement, one of necessity, had the advantage of at least increasing body heat since the hospital's generator was damaged again and the air was quite chill.

Stepan was dozing when they reached him in the bed he shared with another Croatian guardsman, but he opened his eyes at the sound of approaching footsteps. Jeri was used to the drawn and weary faces of the frontline soldiers, but to Alenka and Kelly, Stepan was almost unrecognizable. His pleasure at seeing them almost erased the signs of pain, hunger, and fatigue that had aged his youthful features.

"Alenka! And the aunties." He managed a smile and lifted a hand so he could clasp Alenka's. His bedmate turned toward the wall in a gesture toward privacy.

Alenka pulled the young man's hand to her and kissed it fervently before bending forward, careful not to hurt him, and gave him a more cautious kiss on his mouth. "How are you? I have been so worried."

"They tell me there is no need to worry. They say that you and I will be dancing again before long."

"Again! Stepan, you and I have never been dancing. You are always

481

too much dignified." Alenka spoke with some of her former spirit.

"I know, but I didn't want to tell them that. It made them happy to say such a thing. But what happened to you?"

Alenka hesitated. Then she started the story. She and Stepan were now speaking in Croatian and Kelly drifted on the rhythms of the speech, a habit she had acquired at the Tesla School. She leaned against Jeri and a welcoming arm went round her shoulders. The day, which had begun with killing a man and ended with crossing the ruined city in the dark and rain, had been desperately perilous and exhausting.

Dr. Bosanac had left but she returned with a stool for Alenka so she could sit beside Stepan's bed. She gestured for Jeri and Kelly to follow her.

"Come with me. I think you both need some rest. Our accommodations are a little crowded, but I have some floor space available for a few hours." She spoke with a certain grim humor.

†

In her dream, Kelly knew it was the Danube, this wide river where the several councils always gathered. The boat was waiting to take her to the island where she was to conduct the ceremony and she was not ready. She held the baked-clay dove that marked her office, but something was not right, had not been right for a long time, and she hesitated. Shallow water lapped at her feet. She glanced at the boatman, her brother, who stood with the long pole, holding the low-sided craft steady here in the mist among the tall grasses. He smiled at her and she was unaccountably pleased to see him. Drums sounded from the river island, calling, reminding her that it was time to make the crossing. She glanced back at the beloved face of the Keeper who stood, as always, attendant to her needs. She turned again to the boatman, and saw with horror that he was angry with her, screaming and bloody-faced. She held the gun straight in front of her but nothing happened, it was useless, and the man she had killed was coming for her and there was nothing she could do to stop him.

†

"Kelly, Kell…baby, wake up. It's only a dream, you're safe."

Holding Kelly was the only comfortable piece of where she was. She was cold, her clothes were still damp, and she ached from the hard floor.

"Tell me the dream, love."

Kelly recounted the dream. After finishing with the appearance of the Chetnik, she attempted a joke. "How will we ever get any sleep if we both keep having nightmares?"

"I'm so sorry. I suppose dreams come from our souls to remind us that killing is wrong. But there isn't always a choice, at least if we want to live."

Jeri wanted to tell Kelly what had happened with her recently, but in all honesty, at least when she was awake, the death of the cow bothered her more than that of the three Chetniks.

"I want to go to that school you were telling me about."

For a moment Jeri thought Kelly was referring to the Tesla School, but then she remembered the day they had driven so carelessly out of Dubrovnik and into the unfortunate heart of Croatia. "Kell—"

"When we get out of here, I want to learn. If you hadn't taught me what to do with the gun, Alenka and I would both be dead by now. I'll think about what it all means later, but I know I want to learn how to be strong when I need to be."

†

Kelly crossed and recrossed the border with sleep. The dream images still retained the texture and substance of reality. Even though she suspected that the woman who had lived along the Danube—might still be living on the far side of a misty curtain for all Kelly knew about the way time worked—even though that woman would not approve, Kelly was who and where she was. *Different lives have different needs*, she thought to the other woman, with whom she likely shared a soul. She let her mind drift to the image of George's face and took comfort in seeing him. When the nightmare face threatened to return, Kelly brought herself back to the present and Jeri's arms.

Jeri fell asleep. Kelly was sitting with her back against the wall and Jeri laid her head in Kelly's lap and was asleep. Several other people were sleeping or attempting to in the little room. Privacy had become a mental rather than a spatial matter in Vukovar. It was so unusual to see Jeri give up her vigilance that Kelly could not even guess at her weariness. She scarcely dared to breathe for fear of waking the sleeping woman.

Jeri's hair had grown into a confusion of thick dark curls, reminding

Kelly of pale marble statues of Alexander the Great. One strand outlined the edge of an ear. Kelly didn't remember taking time to examine Jeri's ears before. Not with her eyes, at any rate. It wasn't an unusual ear, but it had a certain delicacy, like the G-clef sign on a music staff. The lobe was pierced but Jeri had never worn earrings in the time she and Kelly had known one another. Kelly wondered when Jeri's ears had been pierced. High school? Earlier? She must remember to ask.

An emotion, a series of emotions chased one another across Jeri's sleeping face but she didn't wake. Kelly had to restrain herself from attempting to wipe away a streak of grime that grayed a portion of Jeri's jaw line. Kelly wondered what dreams came visiting to trouble Jeri's sleep, but she declined to speculate too far along that path. It wasn't as if Kelly was eagerly confronting all the other conditions of her own life and simply ignoring the one small aspect of having deliberately killed another human being.

She had been living in a siege for more than two months. The experience of Vukovar was more like being trapped in some medieval castle than like living in the modern world. Kelly had seen sights and heard sounds and smelled smells that she wanted desperately to forget, and killing a man was just one more horror to add to the list. Like Alenka, Kelly wondered where Europe was, where the UN was, where America was, that the massacre of Vukovar was allowed to go on and on.

Jeri opened her eyes, instantly present. A small smile curved the corners of her mouth, affection softening her features. She lifted one hand and placed it along Kelly's cheek.

"I knew you were here," she said. "The whole time, I knew you were here."

†

Alenka had slept by Stepan's bed, but the whole corridor was awake when Jeri and Kelly arrived.

"This is Anton." Stepan introduced the other soldier who shared the bed.

"He was here another time, when the bomb fell." Alenka greeted the Aunties. "That was the first time he was wounded. Stepan, tell them the story."

"The bomb?" Jeri lifted an ironic eyebrow, wondering what would make one different from the many. Even now the rumble of explosions continued like the ticking of a monstrous clock.

"This was a big one," Anton said. "Two hundred and fifty kilos. Two bombs, actually."

Jeri was impressed. She translated for Kelly. "That's big. Each bomb would be almost as tall as a man."

"It happened one day when the planes came to destroy this medical nest of military activity," Stepan added.

"Oh, yes," Anton couldn't refrain from interrupting. "We are bedridden patients by day, but at night we pick up our infusion bottles and swarm all over the Chetniks." Everyone laughed. "The first bomb, it blew up the second floor and shook the building like an earthquake. The whole surgical wing was blown apart. But the second...." he started to chuckle, unable to go on.

"The second came through six floors." Stepan shook his head. "This guy with an arm wound—this guy was sleeping and he wakes up to find a bomb in his bed. Can you believe this? He wasn't hurt at all, but you can bet he was surprised."

A series of jokes went round all the patients, jokes on the theme of bombs in bed. They weren't particularly original or even humorous, but they did entertain the wounded guardsmen, and the more obscene the better.

"Why didn't it explode?" Kelly asked.

Jeri translated her question and this set off another round of ribaldry. It was Stepan who finally managed to answer. "They say the detonator was missing, Auntie Laura, but I think the guy in the bed maybe thinks that God is Croatian."

"God may be Croatian, but He and Zagreb both seem to have left Vukovar." Anton's comment stirred a round of less humorous laughter.

Jeri had heard the charge before, that Tudjman was leaving Vukovar to be demolished in order to sway world opinion through sympathy. If this was true, world opinion appeared less than cooperative.

"Now when did Vukovar ever need Zagreb?" No one had seen or heard Dr. Bosanac approaching. "We are not forgotten here. We are all very important. There was no Croatian army before but there is now. And because of Vukovar, everyone knows that the Chetniks will not be able to beat an army when they cannot even beat one small city. Imagine, our Vukovar has stopped the entire Yugoslavian army that once made all of Europe afraid. So no more about how we are forgotten. We will be remembered. Tell me, how are all of my patients today?"

Dr. Vesna Bosanac moved among the beds, stopping to talk, to examine bandages. Strands of gray hair escaped the bun that held her hair from her face and she brushed them aside unconsciously. She was not a tall woman and, so many months into the siege, she should have appeared worn and exhausted, but instead, she seemed to radiate energy. Dr. Bosanac had been the subject of admiring gossip at the front, and Jeri remembered hearing that she had been a pediatrician before she became the medical director. It was her practical foresight in the spring and summer that had prepared Vukovar Hospital and its satellites for the agony of siege. Indeed, one mark of her success as a health worker and a director was the extent to which the Serbian news media was vilifying her.

As Dr. Bosanac moved among the guardsmen, it was easy to think of her as a pediatrician. She radiated the kind of calm that can soothe anxious children and she spoke to each man as if he might be her son. And so he might. Jeri knew that Dr. Bosanac's own son was with the guard at the front.

Dr. Bosanac reached the bed holding Stepan and Anton. "Hello, Anton." She smiled at Stepan. "Anton thinks we do such a good job here that he couldn't stay away. Your visitors seem to be doing well, Stepan. I hope they aren't wearing you out." This last was spoken with a certain humor since any distraction from the reality that shook the medical center even as they spoke was a welcome distraction.

Dr. Bosanac examined Alenka's head wound and once more pronounced Kelly's stitches well done.

"Perhaps you should take up a medical career? No? Ah, well. I would like a few words with you." She nodded to Jeri.

The two women made their way through the crowded halls. Jeri drew a few stares, but most of the people they encountered were more interested in a nod or a word from Dr. Bosanac than they were with the tall Croatian guardsman in camouflage clothing who accompanied her.

They came to a small room that was full of files and lit by an oil lantern. A bald man was sitting at a long table, writing in a small script. Even in a place such as Vukovar, paperwork had to be maintained. At a nod from Dr. Bosanac, the man excused himself. For a moment, the medical director seemed about to be overcome by fatigue but she steadied herself and looked at Jeri with a direct gaze.

"I have received word that Vukovar must surrender soon. You will need to be somewhere else when that happens. You have gained enough notoriety that I doubt you would survive surrender. If you were Croatian, maybe. I think you will be safest if you go back to the units."

The news was not unexpected. In so many ways, Vukovar barely continued to exist. Even so, Jeri's heart lurched and she had to blink. "What about Laura and Alenka? Should they stay?"

"Yes, of course." Dr. Bosanac sighed. "The hospital will be as safe as any place. Perhaps more. There will be international observers here to see that all is done correctly. But you will not be safe anywhere there are Chetniks in charge."

"And you?" Jeri asked, thinking of the reports on Belgrade television that had called her a Nazi, a female Dr. Mengele who experimented on Serbian prisoners.

"Nothing to worry." She made a gesture brushing aside concern and shrugged. "Maybe it is time for us to quit. I have cases of gangrene. In a modern hospital in the nineties, I have cases of gangrene? That's criminal. We have bought time for Croatia, but now we have no more. And you? Why are you here?"

"I was here and I knew how to help. I'm not the only volunteer fighting for Vukovar."

"No. No, you are not, and I am personally very grateful. Now I would like it very much if you would go and stay alive."

"It was a privilege to meet you, Dr. Bosanac. An honor. Please do what you can for Alenka and Laura."

Jeri walked back toward the soldiers' area through the chilly, crowded basement. As she turned the corner of the corridor, Jeri saw Kelly and Alenka and Stepan, her family, such as it was, together. She made sure of her smile before going to them.

"What did Dr. Bosanac want?" Alenka asked. Kelly and Stepan waited for Jeri to answer, trying to keep their apprehension from showing.

"She had a message for me to take back to the Commander. Which I must do now. Can I get a comradely hug before I go, Stepan?"

Stepan grinned and held out his arms.

"Oh, Auntie Stella. I thought you could stay longer." The hug that Alenka gave Jeri was like a child's hug as she wrapped her arms tightly around the tall woman and laid her head against her.

Then it was time to say good-bye to Kelly. Jeri held out a hand. "Walk with me."

They walked along the underground corridor, but it wasn't until they were near the stairway that they found a space where only a few people were nearby. Jeri drew Kelly into the shadows. The noise of falling shells made a kind of privacy.

"Vukovar is going to surrender," Jeri said. "Very soon. Dr. Bosanac says you and Alenka can stay here at the hospital. There will be international observers here."

"Oh, no, Jeri, no." Which of the many possible things Kelly was protesting was unclear. Maybe all of them. She put her arms around Jeri and held her. "And you?" Jeri could scarcely hear the words with Kelly's head pressed against her, but she could still hear the misery. "Where will you be?"

"I have to go. It seems I have a certain reputation with the Chetniks and Dr. Bosanac thinks I'll have a better chance of escape with the guard. Listen. Go to Zagreb. You'll be civilians, you and Alenka. Stay with her. Go to Zagreb and call this number." Jeri said the number and then repeated it. "Ask for Shamrock."

"Shamrock? That's your spy name?"

"Jesus, Kell, what did you expect? Something from James Joyce? Spies aren't all that creative, just sneaky."

And then they were making love, standing up, in the shadows. It was too fumbling and frantic to be satisfying, but then it wasn't about being erotic, it wasn't even about comfort, it was about clinging desperately to life, to one another. Their minds and hearts had agreed to necessity, but their bodies were as frightened as children, helpless, resisting separation, demanding an impossible immersion of each into the other. By now, the siege had made them far too wise regarding the probability of survival, and each moment together was wretched with the knowledge of imminent separation. Jeri and Kelly both strove to quiet the hysteria that mounted with each kiss, with each graceless and demanding touch. At last, they simply held one another, trying not to surrender hope, the darkness hiding their tears.

"Come back to me," Kelly pleaded. Her voice was sick with the understanding that these could very well be their last moments together. "Please, come back to me."

"Yes. Know that as long as we're apart, that's all I'll be doing. Every step I'll be coming back to you. I'll find a way, baby, I promise I'll find a way."

†

Kelly found more than enough work to keep her busy in the days that followed. The kitchen was in a constant struggle to provide food, not just to patients and staff but to people from nearby shelters who no longer had food. The hospital had plenty of Izosan and chlorine tablets to treat water and make it safe to drink, but with only a liter a day for drinking and washing for each person, it was impossible to maintain proper hygiene. The water supply for the medical center was limited at best after the city water system was destroyed, and on the worst days, getting it could cost a life. Three firemen had already died bringing water in cistern trucks. One day when the kitchen had received no water because the shelling had people too terrified to venture out, it was Dr. Bosanac herself who went.

Kelly did dishes. The work absorbed all her energy and left her too tired to think. She preferred it that way. The trance of exhaustion was better than the terror that paced at its edge. She worked every day until Anica, the kitchen manager, insisted that she quit.

"You have to eat, Auntie Laura. Take this." Anica spoke in English. "We'll make a proper peasant of you yet."

Kelly took the square of bread, spread with a little lard and sprinkled with dry pepper. She managed a wry smile. "I was born a peasant, you know. Mom used to keep a can of bacon grease on the back of the stove for frying eggs or chicken."

"Yes? There, you have a pretty smile when you use it, now, go visit your friends. But come back here to sleep, at least it's a little warmer."

Kelly didn't need language to read the anxiety on the faces of people that she passed on the way to Alenka and Stepan. She had said nothing, but the pending surrender of Vukovar was now a rumor that everyone avoided saying aloud. The wounded soldiers' corridor was unusually quiet as Kelly made her way toward the young couple. They had a smile of welcome for her but she could see that pain and worry were bothering both of them. Nor did fear and hunger make the best of conditions for healing wounds.

"Auntie Laura, sit here." Stepan adjusted himself so there was room for her at the foot of the bed. This required that Anton also move, but the other guardsman appeared to welcome her arrival only a little less than Stepan and Alenka.

Kelly greeted her little family with kisses and sat.

"We were talking about when we were young," Alenka said.

"You're still young."

"Of course that's what an old lady like you would say, but when we were children, we would take our bicycles and go down to the river. Stepan's parents and mine both forbid such a thing. They said it was too dangerous."

Everyone paused for a smile over what had passed for dangerous in happier times.

"It was dangerous, you know." Stepan was remembering the children they had been from the vantage of his current wiser age. "Especially when we took that boat. If the current had caught us, we might have ended up in Belgrade."

"I know." Alenka giggled, once again a mischievous child. "Remember how angry Rafi was when he found us?"

"Oh, yes!" The memory brought an expression of alarm. "He promised not to tell, but I believed him when he said he would beat me if we ever did such a thing again."

†

Darkness made it impossible to see the men gathered on either side of her, but Jeri knew they all felt the same feverish anticipation that had her wound to a nearly impossible pitch. She felt as taut and quivering as a drawn bowstring. A hand suddenly clasped her own and she gripped it back. Petar had been extraordinarily pleased when she returned, and now he kept closer than her own shadow.

Jeri steadied her breathing. They were about to attempt their break out, attempt to find a way through JNA lines and gain the relative safety of Vincovci. Anything could happen. Anything was about to happen. The defenders of Vukovar might survive to see another day, or they might all be massacred in the field they were preparing to cross.

The signal came down the line and Jeri heard movement on either side. She stepped out with her squad, placing her feet carefully, looking for a good balance between speed and stealth. This was not the same as slipping alone behind enemy lines. Unless the whole universe had gone to sleep, someone was going to make a misstep soon that would alert the enemy and then they'd all be in the soup. It was inevitable.

Impossible to know what started it. One second the noise was behind them, as the usual shelling sought their lines, the next they were surrounded by explosions and the clatter of automatic weapons. No need for caution now. Jeri started running. She yelled for Petar and heard him scream back her name. The air seemed to have taken on substance. It shook and rippled and running through it was like a dream in which one's feet would hardly move. Jeri wanted to throw herself down and huddle against the ground, but instead she put Kelly's face in front of her and tried to remember that the only way to see Kelly again was to keep moving, to somehow keep moving. To her left, she saw a bright blossom of flame and several figures floated away from it like dolls tossed into a wind. To the right was darkness and Jeri went toward it instinctively.

Stuttering, rattling flashes broke out of the night ahead, ripping what was left of the fabric of the air and this time Jeri did hurl herself to the ground and continued forward by crawling. She thought she saw a blackness unpunctuated by the stuttering flashes. She yelled for Petar to follow her but she had no idea if he could hear, indeed if he was even still nearby. She felt a hand on her foot, knew it for Petar, and she began scuttling, as low to the ground as a lizard.

†

Kelly woke to the clanging of metal pots. She had stolen a few minutes break near the cooking stove and fallen asleep in the aura of warmth. A peculiar atmosphere pervaded the kitchen, a kind of cheerful despair.

"Anica, has something happened?"

"The soldiers have escaped." Tears and smiles marked the woman's broad face. The siege had taken weight from her, but she still maintained a roundness of feature and form that expressed so well her kindly soul. "The soldiers have escaped. I just now see Dr. Bosanac and she says that her son is in Zagreb. Never before have I seen her weep, but today she has tears. Three times he was wounded, but now he is safe in Zagreb."

Wounded three times! Kelly pressed her hands to her mouth, unsure whether to weep or laugh. It must have been horrible, but some had made it.

Oh, please be safe, she thought, wishing she had the comfort of prayer, or knew a direction toward which to aim the hopes of her heart. *Oh, Jeri, love, be safe.*

"We must prepare now for the Chetniks," Anica added and the happiness fled from her. "Vukovar has surrendered. I think soon you should go to your friends. No one knows what will happen next."

It was the silence that was odd. The scuff and squeak of shoes on a tile floor, the creak of a bed as someone shifted position, the sound of a door closing around the corner, the wheels of a rolling cart, the sniff of someone with a cold. Tiny sounds that had been concealed for months returned like jittery sparrows. Everyone whispered or spoke in the lowest of tones, which only increased the nervous anxiety of waiting for the arrival of their conquerors.

The conquerors were quite correct when they arrived. There were the officers who came, presented unreadable faces and left. There were the soldiers, youngsters who kept their curiosity checked behind a formal bearing that also hid what just might, in some cases, be embarrassment. More officers arrived and strode past impatiently, shiny boots colliding sharply with the floor, obviously intent on getting to the next important place. The soldiers stood at corners, reducing the movement of the hospital staff, like sheep dogs monitoring a flock.

"We have to leave," Alenka said to Kelly.

An officer had come and issued a series of instructions to the people in the corridor ward. Alenka and Kelly were not the only friends or family who were with the wounded soldiers. The impatient officer barked several commands that were in no need of translation. "Hurry up, quickly!" sounds the same in any language.

"Stepan." Kelly hugged him tightly. She had grown very fond of this young man.

"Auntie Laura." He grinned. "You will take care of Alenka, yes? Take her to my parents in Zagreb?"

"I'll take care of her," Kelly said. "We'll see you in Zagreb." Then she stepped back to give Alenka a chance to say good-bye.

Kelly found it hard to believe that the young woman who walked toward her from Stepan's bed with such dignity was the same child who had flown down the steps to greet her and Jeri in the late summer. But as soon as they turned a corner of the corridor, Alenka sagged against the wall, sobbing.

"Why did I ever say I didn't love him? You must think I am a horrible person."

"I think nothing like that. Now isn't the time for sorting out such things. Besides, I can see how you do love him."

The correct young JNA soldiers directed them to a room on the first floor, one that was still somewhat intact, where many of the hospital's civilians had been taken. The last time Kelly had been here was the day that she and Jeri had ridden to the hospital with Yakov and Mrs. Lackavic. She and Alenka waited for instructions.

And waited. At one point an officer of some high rank came and talked at length. From the stony looks on the faces of the people around her and the way that Alenka occasionally squeezed her hand, to restrain herself from speaking, Kelly was glad that she didn't understand. Alenka might have been able to stay quiet but a few people closer to the officer finally interrupted, at which point he gave them all a haughty glare and stalked out. The room broke into a buzz of murmurs.

"It was a political talk," Alenka said to Kelly. "The colonel says we can stay now that they have liberated Vukovar. He says Dr. Bosanac has been arrested. He says they will protect all Serbs and Serbian property. They will be sending a staff from Belgrade to run the hospital. Those who want to leave may go to the Croatian border. Someone asked him why there were Chetniks in the hospital when he had promised that only JNA would enter."

"I still don't understand how you can tell the difference."

"Oh, Auntie Laura." Alenka attempted a flash of her old humor. "They have different uniforms."

"Oh."

"Yes. The Chetnik paramilitaries have a Serbian flag and four S's like the Cyrillic Cross on their uniform."

"Oh."

"You must learn to pay attention to these things. You probably also forgot to notice that we have been liberated."

Still, it wasn't until the next morning that people from the medical center who chose to go to Croatia were allowed to leave. Kelly and Alenka were put on a bus along with hospital personnel and a few civilian patients. Others, who wanted to leave, were distributed among the vehicles of a JNA convoy.

"Where is Stepan? I don't see any of the soldiers?" Alenka opened the bus window and leaned out, but a JNA soldier sternly told her to close it.

A woman sitting a few seats away spoke and when she was finished, Alenka nodded and turned to Kelly. "She says she asked earlier and they say the military men have been taken ahead. That is why we have had to wait. That is good, I suppose." She turned to stare out the window.

Seeing the hospital from the outside in daylight was a shock. The medical center was pocked and pitted by the months of savage shelling. Sections of the wall had gaping holes and much of the roof was missing. But horrible as that was, the passage of the convoy through the devastation of Vukovar was worse. For some it was their first time outside the hospital in weeks. For everyone, it was the first view they had had of the city without fear of being hit by a grenade or mortar or bullet in months. A gasp could be heard now and then, a sob, but otherwise all that was heard was the low-gear sound of engines as the convoy wound through the ruin and destruction, negotiating roads that barely existed due to all the holes.

Here and there soldiers could be seen collecting people from basements, marching small groups toward some unknown destination. Or the sight of men carrying every imaginable manner of looted items

Alenka leaned back and closed her eyes.

"Are you all right?" Kelly asked, fearful that the head wound was hurting again.

"I don't want to look anymore. That's all."

Kelly leaned back and thought of Jeri.

If Vukovar was terrible in its devastation, it was almost worse when the convoy reached Negoslavci, worse for its lack of any marks at all. The small village lay to the south of Vukovar and no sign of war had touched it. Despite their loss of leaves to November cold, the trees looked like sentinels guarding a road to sanity. The houses, all without a broken window or a lost tile, tucked behind hedges or gardens, appeared like dwellings in the landscape of an alternate reality. But if the road was the way to sanity, then the people on the bus were inmates from an asylum. People along the road stared at the convoy, and Kelly took from their expressions a notion of how she and Alenka and the others must look, dirty, gaunt, haggard, alien.

The convoy stopped and it soon became clear why this village had been spared. Townspeople gathered and began shouting and throwing things. "Ustasha!" Kelly heard, the only word she really recognized, but the rest must have been terrible because Alenka threw her head into Kelly's lap and covered her ears. A rock struck the window and Kelly ducked, but the bus was a military vehicle and the glass held. Kelly wanted to look away. She had never felt the intensity of directed hatred before. The faces she saw screaming at her were ugly with rage.

Someone from the crowd broke and ran for the door. A JNA soldier jumped in the way and forced the man back. For a moment the crowd quieted, but it wasn't long before the shouting resumed its furious pitch.

Again someone from the crowd rushed the bus and this time the door was forced open. A man in a paramilitary uniform, waving an automatic pistol, pushed his way through and into the aisle. He shouted while the crowd outside roared in approval. Kelly could feel Alenka's body shaking and she held the young girl down, protecting her as best she could. The Chetnik was drunk. Even in another language, Kelly could distinguish the slurred words and ranting tone. He was several rows away, and everyone was terrified. A burst of gunfire erupted, ripping a hole through the top of the bus, but a JNA soldier came aboard and shouted at the paramilitary. The interruption only momentarily stopped the wild ranting, but it gave time for two more soldiers to arrive and use force to remove the Chetnik.

Then the convoy began to move again.

"It's okay, Alenka, we're moving again. We're safe now."

"No, we're not." Alenka's reply was muffled. "This is like a dream where you try to escape and it just goes on and on."

Kelly thought Alenka must have the gift of prophecy when the convoy returned to Vukovar before nightfall.

†

Stepan wished he wasn't so afraid. It would be easier if he wasn't afraid.

"What is the name of this place? Where are we?" he had asked when he and the other wounded Croatian guardsmen, about two hundred, were taken off their buses and brought into a large warehouse that smelled of machinery grease and oil.

"What do you care? Does it matter where you're going to die?" The drunken Chetnik had laughed and then beat him. All the guardsmen were beaten.

Stepan believed he was going to die here and, yes, he would still like to know the name of the place. He hurt where he had been hit but that wasn't as bad as being afraid. There shouldn't be anything to be afraid of. He'd seen so many people die that it wasn't as if he hadn't known all along that it could happen to him. He was Catholic, not all that good, but he had never done anything that God couldn't forgive. He was worried about his parents, about Alenka. She would go see them in Zagreb, he was sure of it, but he wondered how long it would be before anyone knew what had happened. He hoped they would know soon. It would be terrible for them to wait for him for months, or years even. Better they should know.

He loved them all so much. Better to feel love than anger or fear. He heard shooting from near the door. Anton was trying not to cry too loudly. Stepan wished he could take Anton's hand, but he thought that might make it harder for both of them. He wished he could have told Alenka that Sinisa Glavasevic was here, too. That he had seen her favorite radio reporter on the bus with the guardsmen. They had beat Glavasevic, too.

"Remember the day Alenka and I took the boat?" He didn't say it loudly, but Anton heard. Anton always liked this story. "The sun was very bright. It was a perfect summer morning in Vukovar."

495

Alenka had run ahead and she called to him from the bank that she had found a boat. She was so beautiful. That was the day he'd first known he loved her, that he wasn't a child anymore.

"Ovchara," said the Chetnik who had just shot Anton and was now standing over Stepan. "The name of this place is Ovchara."

But Stepan didn't hear. He was sending his boat out onto the sun-flecked ripples of the Danube. He meant to catch the current and ride it as far as he could.

†

Just maybe the convoy was going to make it through this time. Kelly and Alenka had both been overcome by the lassitude that accompanies helpless misery. They'd been allowed off the bus once in the morning to go to a bathroom but other than that they were kept in the same seats as the day before. And once again the convoy had left Vukovar, proceeded, stopped for no apparent reason, gone on for no apparent reason, stopped again.

Kelly was worried about Alenka. She had lost interest in anything outside the bus, and dozed intermittently while leaning against Kelly. Kelly couldn't see any sign of infection around the wound but the young woman's forehead did feel hot to the touch.

One of the other bus passengers plucked the sleeve of Kelly's jacket, said something. Alenka looked up.

"She says we have to change buses here." Alenka's voice was dull, uncaring.

Kelly picked up her stained nylon book bag. She still had *The Inferno* and *Black Lamb Grey Falcon*. Alenka carried nothing. Outside an overcast sky dimmed the sunlight, but it was bright enough to make the bus passengers squint. Kelly put an arm around Alenka's shoulders wondering where to go next. She peered down the length of the convoy, seeing other refugees standing, waiting for direction.

There seemed to be no one in charge, no one directing them. Automatically, Kelly checked her pocket for the presence of her crystal talisman from Nepal. It was there. She was tired, but she kept repeating meaningless words to Alenka, reassurances that comforted neither of them. And then she stopped.

She saw Jeri. Who had already seen her and was striding toward her. The bus must have crossed the border into Croatia. Until that instant, Kelly hadn't realized how little she had dared to hope, hope that Jeri was still alive, hope that they would be together again. So now she simply stood and watched the tall, dark-haired woman walk toward her, savoring the pure joy of the moment, seeing her own radiant heart take shape in Jeri's smile.

Alenka recognized some change in Kelly and followed her gaze. "Auntie Stella," she breathed, disbelieving. Then her hands flew to her mouth and something seemed to catch in her throat.

Jeri paused and allowed a man who had been behind her to move forward. He was a dark-haired man, perhaps in his late twenties. Kelly thought he looked familiar. He came a few steps closer, his face twisted and his lips a thin line.

"Alenka?" Almost a whisper. He held out his arms.

Kelly turned to Jeri, who had reached her side. "Rafi?"

"Yes." Jeri's arms folded around Kelly.

"How did you find him?"

"It's a long story. And we have time, baby. Now, we have time again."

Angela Koenig

End Notes

Siniša Glavašević [1960 – 1991] From *Voiceseducation.org*, "A story about a City":

"Who will take care of my city, my friends, who will lead Vukovar out of the darkness?

No back is sturdier than mine and yours, and so, if it is not too much of a burden, if you still have some youthful murmur left in you, join us. Someone has been touching my parks, the benches on which your names are still carved, the shady places where you gave and received your first kisses—somebody has simply stolen it all away, as how else does one explain that not even a Shadow remains? No shop windows where you marvelled at your own happiness, no more cinema where you watched the saddest of films, your past has simply been destroyed and now you have nothing left. You have to build anew. First, your past, by seeking out your roots, then your present, and then, if you have the strength left, invest it into your future. And do not be alone in the future. And you need not worry about the city, the city was always within you. Only hidden. So that the executioner cannot find it. The City—you are the City."

About the Author
Angela Koenig

Angela Koenig was born in California, raised in Nebraska, and now resides in Illinois. She has worked at a number of occupations including janitor, teacher, house painter, proofreader, and telephone operator. A practicing autodidact, some of her interests are recent and ancient history, literature, Gaelic, and geology, yet when all is said and done, it's reading that's the point. She always wanted to write, and there's an unfinished novel about an orphan puppy started when she was in fifth grade. She believes that story is serious stuff, that through fiction we can see further and feel more deeply, and she hopes that her stories contribute to this goal.

Other Books from Affinity eBook Press

Faith in Rayne by Dannie Marsden
Welcome back Rayne and Lisbet from *Rayne Comes to Town* and *Rayne's New Beginnings*. Their life has flourished since meeting. Rayne ventures to Telluride, Colorado, where both adventure and trouble land at her feet. Lisbet heads to Telluride to reunite with Rayne, her head filled with dreams of their future only to have her dreams come crashing down. Can she find the strength to fight for Rayne, allowing her faith to guide them back to their love?

Fortunes by Alane Hotchkin
Despite the curves life has thrown Remmy Garrick, her life is going along pretty good except mysterious things keep happening at her job sites. State Investigator Kira Kirpatrick is assigned the case, and everything about Remmy draws Kira to her. Circumstances beyond their control throw their lives into a frenzy. Does Kira have the courage to step up and accept the love Remmy is offering, or will she continue to hide behind her secrets and let them control her?

Captivated by Annette Mori
Juliet Lewis has one too many quirks for her own well-being. Snooping was bound to get her in trouble. Sexy police officer Tanner Sullivan gets Juliet's attention and she wants to know more. Will Tanner turn out to be her jailor or savior? Sparks fly when the obsessive-compulsive Juliet and the paranoid Tanner cross paths in this quirky thriller with a new twist around every corner.

Pausing by Renee MacKenzie
Jordy Chapman is the Emergency Service Coordinator at Cypress Haven mental health facility in Naples, FL. Keira Yeager's family owns an upscale furniture store in Naples and orchestrates a generous donation of furniture to Cypress Haven. When the two meet, they hit it off immediately. Will a Yeager family's anguish and misunderstanding

threaten their new relationship?

Breaking the Silence by JM Dragon
Still grieving five years after the death of her father, Dilana Sterling is a
shadow of the woman she once was…a successful author with a string of
best sellers, and a longer string of women. Rachael Alderman, a teacher
at the local orphanage, lives a quiet, yet satisfying life. When Dilana and
Rachael meet, they develop a friendship that leads them on personal
journeys of self-discovery. Will their memories of the past prevent them
from moving toward each other, or will they find a path that leads to each
other so they can experience life together?

The Termination by Annette Mori
Codee is having a bad day and it's only going to get worse. Sawyer, a
compassionate young woman, is resigned to her fate. Her only question
is what fate is that? After slipping on ice, Codee wonders if she is
hallucinating and fallen into an Alice type rabbit hole. The only thing she
knows is that she needs to save Sawyer. Enjoy this satirical romance,
with all of its twists and turns, that just might make you go hmm...

The Next Time by Erin O'Reilly
What if you had the chance to make history stop repeating itself? Would
you sacrifice today for a chance at a better tomorrow. There is a moment
in everyone's life that defines their future. For Jac and Carol, that time is
now. Jump ahead twenty-five years and meet Carol's granddaughter
Livvy. She is ready for a challenge and is fleeing the nest and getting on
with her life. Read this wonderful love story that spans several lifetimes.

Secret of Stone Creek by Natalie London
Jennifer Cameron arrives in Stone Creek, Wisconsin to sell her
grandparents' large Victorian home. While there she is intrigued by a
twenty-four-year-old never solved murder. Her attraction to the lovely
and mysterious librarian, Diana vies for her attention. Follow this
suspenseful whodunit to its conclusion.

The Promise by JM Dragon
An accidental meeting with Melissa Grant, leads to an unexpected offer

for Kris Lake—refurbishing a beach cottage, with the help of Melissa's granddaughter Claire. Do outer imperfections prevent them from reaching the beauty that lives inside and the chance of a happy new life? Find out in this lovely romance that will fill you with heart-warming sensations throughout the story.

Christmas at Winterbourne by Jen Silver
The Christmas festivities for the guests booked into Winterbourne House has all the goings-on of a traditional holiday. The only difference is that this guesthouse is run by lesbians, for lesbians. Join the guests and staff at Winterbourne for a Christmas you'll not soon forget.

The Review by Annette Mori
Silver Lining, a successful lesbian romance writer, has the crazy idea to sponsor a contest where the first reader who posts a review wins a home-cooked meal with an offer to fly the winner to Washington State. Jasmine, the winner, has engaged in subtle flirtations with Silver. Bizarre messages from the unknown fan has Silver questioning the wisdom of a relationship with Jasmine.

South of Heaven by Ali Spooner
Kendra Drake has taken over as Captain of her father's shrimp boat. As a favor to her father, Kendra has agreed to give fellow shrimper, Lindsey Bowen, a chance to work on the boat but first must prove herself to Kendra and her crew. Lindsey finds a way into Kendra's heart. Will it only last for the summer?

Catch to Release by Lacey Schmidt
On the verge of success, lesbian folk-rock star, Shay Greenaura, finds herself caught up in more than just her music. Threats have her manager hiring a security firm for protection. Addison Weller, a former Diplomatic Security Services agent is called in to assess the threats against Shay. Their undeniable attraction, brewing silently between them, could prove to be a fatal distraction. Follow this fast-paced adventure to its surprising romantic conclusion.

Affinity
Rainbow Publications

eBooks, Print, Free eBooks

Visit our website for more publications available online.

www.affinityrainbowpublications.com

Published by Affinity Rainbow Publications
A Division of Affinity eBook Press NZ LTD
Canterbury, New Zealand

Registered Company 2517228

www.ingramcontent.com/pod-product-compliance
Lightning Source LLC
Chambersburg PA
CBHW051935020726
47501CB00001B/127